C000001251

THE LANCE BRODY SERIES

BOOKS 1 AND 2, PLUS PREQUEL NOVELLA

MICHAEL ROBERTSON, JR.

ISBN: 9781976974595

DARK BEGINNINGS

(Lance Brody Series, Book 0, Prequel Novella)

AUTHOR'S NOTE

DARK BEGINNINGS is a 100-page prequel novella and the true beginning of the Lance Brody series. I hope you enjoy joining Lance on all his adventures.

-Michael Robertson Jr

Dark Beginnings

1993

PAMELA BRODY WAS A LOT OF THINGS.

Pretty? Absolutely, in that girl-next-door sort of way.

Funny? Hell, she was downright knee-slap hysterical when she got going. Witty and quick as lightning.

Smart? Name a book and she'd probably read it. She had the start of a small library piled in stacks around her home. Everything from Freud to Stephen King to a biography of Benjamin Franklin.

Odd? Well, yes, that word did get tossed around in conversations in which her name would come up. Not so much in a negative light, but in a *we can't really figure her out* way. The fact that no serious boyfriends had managed to stick around longer than a month or two only fueled the small town's gossip fires further in this regard. Who was she, really?

The list of adjectives was immense and varied.

But the adjective that would best describe twenty-four-year-old Pamela Brody on the night of April 13, 1993, was *aroused*.

Which *was* odd. Since on that night, at just a few minutes past eleven o'clock, Pamela Brody was scaling the fence of the

Great Hillston Cemetery. Yes, that was actually its name, as if there were anything great about death.

Pamela swung one leg over the top of the wrought-iron rails, then the other, her flowered cotton sundress catching momentarily on one of the rods before she pulled it clear and let herself fall the five or six feet to the ground. Her dress puffed out around her like in that scene from the *Alice in Wonderland* cartoon, and then her bare feet hit the grass and she bent her knees and rolled once before popping back up quickly and saying, "See? Easiest thing in the world."

From the other side of the fence, staring at her and clearly trying to figure out what he'd gotten himself into, the young man in the tweed jacket who'd stopped in town yesterday for a week's worth of business said, "I never said it wasn't easy. I suggested it wasn't the best idea. We're trespassing, and ... well..." He shrugged, nodding toward the scene behind Pamela. "You have to admit it's a bit creepy."

She smiled at him coyly, turned her head just slightly and said, "I didn't take you for the type to be afraid of ghosts."

They'd met last night at the local sports bar. He'd stopped in because it was the first place he'd found to get something to eat that was close to his motel, and she'd been there to watch the Chicago Bulls match-up against their Eastern Conference rival, Detroit. He'd noticed her right away; the way she sat alone, seemingly oblivious to the crowds around her, the simple way she was dressed—in a sundress similar to the one she wore tonight, only the slightest hint of makeup on her face. She appeared completely and at ease with herself and her surroundings. She appeared so *neutral*. A few folks stopped and spoke to her, each one greeted with a smile and some polite conversation, but her attention always turned quickly back to the game, especially when MJ had the ball.

"I'm not afraid of ghosts." Even as he said the words, he didn't believe them himself. And honestly, one didn't often question oneself about the existence of ghosts. It wasn't something most people held serious debates about on a whim—or on a *date*. But it was amazing how quickly the plausibility of the spirit world came into view when one stood mere feet away from one of the oldest and largest cemeteries in the state, and with the hour quickly approaching midnight. He looked up to the sky, just as a strong gust of wind blew through, rattling the iron fencing and whistling through tree limbs. A black cloud rolled across the moon, a cancerous spot growing across the surface. The man ran a hand through his blond hair, sighed. "I think it might storm."

Pamela turned and walked away, toward the tombstones and mausoleums. Another breeze blew and kicked her dress up around her thighs. She made no effort at modesty, just shouted back over her shoulder, "So now you're afraid of getting wet, too?"

At halftime he'd gone over and sat on the stool next to her, offered to buy her another drink. She turned and looked at him and when her eyes met his, he was filled with something he could only describe as being dunked into a perfectly warm bath. She smiled, and his world lit up, his head reeling with the strange mixture of love and sensuality and desire this girl seemed to put out ... radiate. She accepted the drink—an iced tea, which he found cutely conservative—and they introduced themselves and they talked about the game and what he did for work and what there was to do in such a small town, and with two minutes left in the game he asked if he could take her to dinner tomorrow night. She had smiled, accepted, and then kissed him on the cheek before standing and leaving the bar.

Leaving him alone on the stool and wondering who this girl was he'd just met.

After the flash of Pamela's bare thighs, the man cursed under his breath and then heaved himself up and over the fence. His loafers slipped on the railing, but, tall as he was—a good bit over six feet—the effort needed was minimal. He landed softly on the other side and found that he'd started to sweat despite the cool spring night. He took off his jacket, folded it over his arm and hurried off after Pamela.

She was walking through the rows of headstones, periodically stopping and kneeling down to examine the names and dates and epitaphs. Sometimes she would reach out and rest her hand on the marker, a gentle gesture of sympathy. Sometimes she would shake her head slowly, as if digesting terrible news. Sometimes she would grin and stand and act like she'd just heard a dirty joke.

The man watched her silently for a while, then came up behind her and said, "Do you do this often?"

She turned and took his hand and led him away with her, deeper among the graves. "People are always so sad about death," she said, running her fingers across the top of another stone. "They bring so much negative energy into these places. I wish more of them would stop and appreciate the beauty around them."

"Beauty?" he asked.

She stopped and let go of his hand, holding her palms up and gesturing at all around her. "Look around. Look at all these tributes to lives lived, all these markers of memories. Entire generations of people lie here. Histories." She raised a hand to her ear. "Listen," she said.

Another gust of wind blew through the trees, screamed through gaps in mausoleum walls. Then silence.

The man shivered. "What am I hearing?"

She looked up at him and smiled. "Peace," she said. "The voices of the resting."

A light sprinkle of rain began to fall, tiny droplets of water peppering Pamela's forehead, as if she glistened with sweat.

The man grew irritated as the cold rain increased and his shirt stuck to him, his hair matting to his head.

Only the sight of Pamela's nipples stiffening beneath her dress kept him in place, made him ask, "Pam, why are we here? Why did you bring me here?"

She went up onto her tiptoes and kissed him on the mouth, rainwater dripping down both their faces. When she pulled away: "Because I like you. And this is one of my favorite places. I wanted to share it with you."

A crack of thunder shouted in the distance. Not on top of them, but closer than the man would have liked. He glanced back the way they'd come, back up the pathway between the headstones. Through the fencing he could still barely make out the darkened shadow that was his car, parked along the back-road they'd taken. So close, yet it seemed so far. Something urged him to go back, to get in that car and drive away. Away from Pamela and away from Hillston. Work be damned.

He shivered, wiped water from his eyes, and then turned back to Pamela. When he saw her, when he met her eyes, that warm-bath feeling hit him again. He let his gaze soak her in, his eyes slowly rolling down her body, admiring the way the wet fabric clung to her and showed off her slender figure. He felt a stirring down below, and just as quickly as the thought had occurred to him, the idea of the car and running away fled from memory.

Pamela said nothing. She took his hand and pulled him deeper into the cemetery. He allowed her to lead him, following a twisting path of gravel around a small bend. When they made it around the corner, Pamela pulled him left, into the grass. His

11

loafers squished and squashed through the soggy ground, and if he'd not been overcome by the allure of the woman before him, he would have cursed at the thought of having to purchase a new pair.

Another crack of thunder boomed, this time much closer. Too close. The rain kicked up another notch, and soon the sound of the falling droplets drowned out all other sound. The clouds rolled in heavier, completely engulfing the moon. Darkness seeped in. He could only see a few feet in front of him now, enough to make out Pamela's slim shoulders.

A few yards ahead a large oak tree, one that looked as though it had begun its life well before the first person was laid to rest in the Great Hillston Cemetery, sprawled up and out of the earth. It towered toward the sky, its limbs forming a near-perfect umbrella from the rain. Pamela pulled him under the cover, and then the two of them stood there together, hands still intertwined, and watched and listened to the onslaught of weather.

Then a bolt of lightning sliced through the sky and the man was again hit with the urge to run. He turned to protest their misadventure, but Pamela had pulled away and was peeling off her dress. Even in the near-darkness he could make out the fine curves of her body, his eyes lingering at her chest, small but firm and perfect. Her wet hair fell around her face, dripped onto her shoulders. Her intentions were clear.

The man tossed his jacket onto the ground under their canopy of branches and fervently undressed. She smiled as he struggled with his pants, hopping from foot to foot like a clumsy fool.

But then he was with her, laying her down atop his jacket—another new purchase that would need to be made—and feeling the surprising warmth of her skin. They kissed, hungrily, and any concern the man had had before vanished as quickly as

Pamela's dress had. She guided him inside her, the warmth of her nearly melting him, his arms and shoulders shuddering. For the next few minutes, the entire rest of the world evaporated, and the man marveled at how he could ever have been so stupid to want to turn away from what would end up being the most erotic moment of his life. He knew he wouldn't be able to continue much longer; he was getting close.

And then the lightning streaked the sky and crashed to the ground what felt like mere feet from where Pamela and the man were lying. And when it did, two things happened.

First, the man let out a small groan of pleasure as he finished, spilling himself inside her and nearly falling forward on arms of jelly.

Second, when the lightning crashed down, electrifying the air around them and seemingly rattling their bones, the darkness had lit up in a brilliant flash of white and gold, a single pulse from a great strobe light. A freeze frame in the night.

And the man had screamed.

Not because he was startled by the noise and the light, but because when the great spotlight had flashed on them, the man had seen the faces of what had to be at least a hundred people all around them, a close circle of spectators all huddled together and watching with great interest.

Just a blip, a quick snapshot that would be forever etched in his memory. But he knew exactly who they were, as well as he knew his own name.

The spirits of the Great Hillston Cemetery had come out for a show that night.

And they'd been smiling.

After he'd screamed, the man struggled to untangle himself from Pamela, slipping on the wet earth and scrambling after his clothes. He didn't offer any parting words, no explanation. Fear had seized him, a puppet master, and he the puppet. He shoved himself into his pants, putting them on backward, grabbed his shirt and left his shoes and jacket behind. And then he was running, back down the path, back to his car.

Pamela Brody watched him go, never once even calling out after him. Simply stunned at what had just unfolded before her. After a while, she laid her head back and closed her eyes, listening to the sounds of the storm around her, feeling surprisingly at peace.

She would never see the man again.

The list of adjectives was immense and varied. But after that night in the Great Hillston Cemetery, you could add one more word to the list.

Pregnant.

Nine months later, she gave birth to a healthy baby boy. She named him Lancelot.

Lance, for short.

1995

PAMELA BRODY HAD NEVER KNOWN HER PARENTS. SHE'D been put up for adoption at birth and had been unlucky enough to draw the short straw in regard to her new adoptive guardians. An alcoholic "father" and neglectful "mother" had managed to keep her alive for the first four years of her life, but, as the social services worker had put it in Pamela's case file, it was nothing short of a miracle the girl had survived.

Malnourished, dirty, and living in a suburban façade of a home that was nothing but despair on the inside, Pamela had been rescued a month after her fourth birthday after a neighbor had peered over a backyard fence one afternoon and saw the girl walking around naked, unsupervised, and eating a stick of butter.

"She was singing," the neighbor had said when asked if there was anything else he'd like to add. "She was singing that song from *The Wizard of Oz*. The one about the rainbow. But she only kept repeating the first part."

After being saved from the nightmare of a home she'd started in, Pamela had bounced from foster home to foster home, before finally ending up in the Home for Girls. It wasn't that she misbehaved or was disrespectful. All the foster parents simply shrugged their shoulders and confessed it was as if Pamela had no interest in being a child, or letting them be parents. She was withdrawn and acted as if other people weren't there. She sat at the dinner table for meals and said her pleases and thank-yous, but conversation was brief and forced.

Everyone agreed the only time Pamela looked truly happy was when she had a book in her hands.

She lived at the Home for Girls and attended school and made decent grades. The Home for Girls wasn't some run-down *Oliver Twist* disaster full of beatings and rationed food, but instead a dull, quiet place. State employees who cared just enough to keep the job—because it certainly wasn't the pay keeping them from jumping ship—and enough tax money and donations throughout the year to keep the home hospitable and comfortable enough for those few young women who had nowhere else to go.

Pamela made some friends at school but didn't socialize as often as most teachers would have liked. She wasn't odd and wasn't made fun of—no more than your average high schooler, that is—but most agreed she was simply uninterested in most of the things that a regular fifteen- or sixteen-year-old woman might be. She seemed happy enough and was pleasant enough to talk with—quite funny at times, actually—but it was as if her head was always in the clouds. She dated some, but it never amounted to anything serious . Living at the Home for Girls made having boyfriends difficult, if not impossible at times.

At age eighteen, the very next day after her high school graduation, Pamela Brody packed a small bag and walked out of the Home for Girls and never looked back.

The first time she looked into the face of her newborn baby boy, the memories from her early childhood—memories a therapist might be surprised she could remember, given how young she'd been—resurfaced for the first time in years, and she quickly shoved them away and promised herself, promised her son, that she'd be the best mother she could possibly be. She promised she would do anything to keep him safe.

She swore Lance smiled back at her as she had the thought.

And for these first two years, as she watched Lance sit in his high chair and smear the chocolate frosting from his birthday cupcake across his face, occasionally sticking his fingers in his mouth and sucking at the sweetness, Pamela Brody felt she'd been upholding her promise fairly well.

Lance always had clean clothes and a clean diaper. He never went hungry. He had toys—mostly secondhand items from thrift stores or gifts from friends—and had already developed a fascination with books, albeit big bright ones made of cardboard and full of pictures.

Pamela managed to balance her work schedule and coordinated with friends to make sure Lance was cared for at all times. She refused to take him to a daycare—it was too much like a group home in her mind. Sometimes this meant having to drop shifts and have a few less pennies in the paycheck come payday, but they always managed to make do. Money and material possessions had never mattered much to Pamela Brody. Life mattered. Happiness mattered. Her son mattered.

And Lance was a what you'd call a dream child. Even in his early days, he cried very little. He didn't throw tantrums or fits, didn't wail incessantly for hours for no reason. He usually sat quietly in his playpen or his swing or his high chair and simply looked content.

Most people would also agree that Lance's eyes seemed to be the eyes not of a child, but of a person much older, much wiser. If you really looked at the boy long enough, you almost felt that he was looking right back at you, and then deeper. As if he was connecting with you on a level you really couldn't understand or believe.

Pamela Brody had told one of her closer friends—Lizzie, who worked with her at the town's library—that sometimes she was certain she could actually communicate with Lance by looking into his eyes. She said sometimes, when she was feeding him and he refused whatever she was offering, turning his head and pursing his lips or spitting it out once tasted, she'd stop and look at him and simply concentrate on the question "What is it you'd like to eat then?" And if she thought hard enough about it and could keep her concentration, suddenly, like a clown springing out of a jack-in-the-box, the image of carrots, or applesauce, or sweet potatoes would pop into her head as clear as day. And Lance would eat it. Every time. "See?" she'd told Lizzie one day during their lunch break. "He can *tell* me what he wants to eat."

Lizzie, though polite, had nodded and changed the subject.

But though Lance was well behaved and intellectually advanced—as far as Pamela Brody was concerned—she also couldn't deny that there was something else going on with her son, almost as if he had managed to learn a secret he was holding on to, unable (or unwilling) to tell her.

Sometimes, while the two of them played or read together, Lance's attention would snap away from whatever they were involved in, his eyes darting to some unoccupied space in their living room or kitchen and locking on to something intently. Pamela would follow his gaze and see nothing—a chair or a lamp or the stove, everyday items Lance ignored ninety-nine out of a hundred times. He would stare for long moments, Pamela's voice or her actions unable to snap him out of whatever trance he'd fallen into. Sometimes Lance would smile, giggle even, as he looked into nothing. This bothered Pamela for reasons she couldn't quite put her finger on.

But not as much as it bothered her when her son's eyes would suddenly go wide with fear. Those moments sent chills down her spine, causing her to scoop Lance up in her arms and rush him into a different room or leave whatever building they'd been visiting or shopping in.

But the worst moment for Pamela Brody, the moment that solidified her ever-growing suspicion her son was legitimately seeing things that she could not, came in the middle of the night when Lance was eighteen months old.

She was awakened by the sound of Lance crying, loud sobs that made her own throat feel raw. She jumped from bed, threw on her robe and crossed the hallway to Lance's small bedroom. The small nightlight plugged into the wall socket was still there —she could see its faint outline by the light of the moon coming through the slats of the window blinds—but it was not glowing. Just a darkened, empty plastic shell.

Lance's cries tapered off as soon as Pamela entered the room, growing quieter and quickly becoming just soft moaning and whimpers. She rushed across the carpet to his crib, ready to reach down and scoop him up.

Her arms and hands froze mid-scoop.

Lance was standing in his crib, his tiny hands gripping the bars and peering out.

He was facing away from her, his back turned to her and his gaze fixed on the corner of the room where the old wooden rocking chair sat. This was where Pamela would rock him to sleep at night or sometimes sit to read books as he napped, occasionally peering through the bars as he slept and letting her heart fill with joy at the sight of him.

As Pamela's eyes adjusted further to the dim light, she took one more step closer to the corner of the room, ready to reach out for Lance and ask him—though she knew he could not answer, as least not with words—what he was looking at.

She stopped again. Felt ice in her veins.

The rocking chair was just beginning to settle, slowly creaking back and forth, back and forth.

As if somebody had just left, quietly sneaking away.

While the event with the rocking chair had caused an uneasy feeling that would not dissipate until the sun came up, Pamela Brody was much more curious than concerned.

After only a few minutes of rocking Lance in the very chair in question, she laid her son back to sleep in his crib and slipped out of the bedroom. But she did not sleep. She went to the kitchen and made herself a cup of tea and sliced a small sliver of the pie she'd made yesterday. Then she sat at the kitchen table and lifted the mug to her lips and felt the steam rise across her face. She sat like that for a long time, slowly sipping, and thinking about everything that had seemed different about Lance from the day he'd been born.

She knew that people with special cognitive abilities were abundant on earth—those with greater senses of perception or memory or awareness than others. And she would have no problem admitting that Lance might very well be one of those people. But she felt he was also *more* than that. The intense stares that could seemingly communicate thoughts and ideas across brainwaves were a prime example of this. That bordered more on telepathy than simple awareness and perception.

And then, of course, there were the distant stares, when he would fixate on things that simply were not there for such lengths of time. Pamela considered the rocking chair again, the way it had impossibly rocked in the still room. Then she very quickly, right there in her small kitchen with a plate full of pie crumbs and a mug with the cold leftovers of her tea, accepted that Lance wasn't staring at *nothing*. He was simply staring at things the rest of the world couldn't see.

Pamela felt a chill wash over her at this realization, and she quickly turned around in her chair and stared back into the living room through the kitchen entryway, as if she'd suddenly noticed that she wasn't alone in her own home in the middle of the night.

There was nothing in the living room. No shapes or shadows scurrying out of sight. The battered recliner was still upright and unmoving. The afghan was still draped across the rear of the couch where she'd left it.

She carried the empty plate and mug to the sink and washed them both, then headed down the short hallway to her bedroom, carrying with her not a sense of fear, but what she could only describe as some unusual sense of pride.

Pamela Brody did not believe in coincidences. Lance was hers for a reason.

My boy is special, she thought as she laid her head against the pillow, hoping to squeeze out a few hours of sleep before starting her morning routine. *And I need to be ready for him.*

After Pamela Brody's early childhood and uninspired adolescence, Lance, and whatever abilities he surely possessed, felt like a peace offering from the universe.

1999

Lance continued to be a healthy child, and as his body grew, so did his abilities.

Pamela often relied on him to find missing items around the house—keys, purse, sunglasses—and while most folks would admit Lance seemed to be able to locate missing household items quickly, often they would not admit it was because he was using some sort of extra sense, a mind-tic that guided him to the correct location. Not that Pamela often inquired about other peoples' opinions of her son. She had made a decision the night of the rocking chair incident, just before she'd fallen to sleep, that whatever made Lance different—*special*—it was probably best to keep the information to herself. If people became scared or worried or maybe a bit too curious, it could mean bad things for Lance. For Pamela. Images from a number of science fiction movies had popped into her head, sad and frightening pictures of children with wires and electrodes and sensors strapped all over their head, locked away in cleanrooms with men in white coats all looking on stone-faced and waiting for results, pens hovering over clipboards.

Her son was a human being. Not an experiment.

Aside from being a mental bloodhound and helping Pamela locate lost items, Lance's telepathic link with his mother also seemed to be getting stronger. Pamela would occasionally test this by thinking of simple questions and concentrating on her son.

Are you finished eating? she would think, sitting across from Lance at the kitchen table, watching him fork the last bits of food into this mouth.

"Yes, ma'am," he would say, acting as though nothing unusual at all had just taken place.

Eventually, Pamela graduated the testing to things a little more strenuous. She would stand in the kitchen while Lance was in his bedroom reading and ask him, *I'm about to make a pie. Do you want to help?*

And sure enough, a few moments later, she'd hear the bedroom door open, followed by Lance's footsteps coming down the hall.

It was exhilarating.

It was terrifying—but in the best of ways.

Pamela Brody was not one to fear the unknown. She embraced all walks of life and all things philosophical and all ideologies. She worshipped life and all its mysteries. How lucky was she that her son was perhaps one of the greatest mysteries of all?

And he only kept surprising her with more gifts...

On one Saturday afternoon three days before Thanksgiving, and roughly a month before Lance would turn five, the doorbell of their small home rang—a tired-sounding chime barely audible over the sound of a teakettle that had just begun to scream. Pamela moved the kettle to a different burner and headed toward the door, wondering who could be visiting. Lance had been in the living room, coloring on the floor, and when she entered the room, he didn't look up to her, but simply said, "Bad man out there, Mama."

Pamela Brody froze on the carpeted floor, watching Lance use a red crayon to color in Spider-Man's suit. Meticulous. Well within the lines.

The doorbell's chime gave it another go, and Pamela stayed put.

Only when she heard a mumble from the other side of the door, and heavy footsteps walking down the wooden porch steps, did she venture toward the door and peek out from a window. A man in a sport coat and blue jeans was just past their mailbox and headed down the street.

The next day, a Hillston sheriff's deputy had stopped by and asked Pamela if she'd seen a man walking around the neighborhood yesterday. Apparently the man was going door-to-door claiming to be accepting cash donations for the local soup kitchen to help provide for the needy on Thanksgiving. He did not, in fact, work for the soup kitchen or any other charitable organization and had managed to disappear with roughly five hundred dollars in stolen cash.

Bad man out there, Mama.

As Lance had grown out of the infancy and then toddler stages of his life, his shifts in focus, those times when his eyes would lock on to things unseen by others, the sporadic flashes of fear and concern across his face, dwindled away. By the time Lance was five, although Pamela Brody had certainly not forgotten those moments from Lance's life and would *never* forget the night of the rocking chair incident, she could now go days, sometimes weeks, without having the thought cross her mind.

All that changed on the first official day of summer in 1999.

School had been out for a couple weeks, but Pamela and Lance had done their lessons earlier that morning—Pamela having decided to homeschool Lance herself, at least until grade school. She wanted to develop a better understanding of her son's abilities and intellect and personality before subjecting him to the harsh reality of the public school system. But mostly, she wanted to protect him as long as she could.

It was a beautiful day, the sun out and the weather warm but not sweltering. An occasional breeze blew in their faces as they walked hand-in-hand down the street, headed toward the park. Lance had a junior-sized basketball under one arm, while Pamela carried a basket with a light lunch, a blanket, and a paperback novel she would try to finish while Lance played.

Though today she wouldn't be able to help herself from keeping an extra eye on her son. Not after what had happened a week ago.

Last week, on the local six o'clock news, the pretty blonde behind the anchor desk had put on her serious face and alerted everyone that three-year-old Alex Kennedy had gone missing. He had last been seen playing in his sandbox in the Kennedys' backyard, which was no more than three-quarters of a mile from the Brodys' house, as the crow flies. Mr. Kennedy had run inside to answer the telephone and returned ten minutes later to find his son nowhere in sight.

Proclamations of child abduction ran rampant. Doors and windows were double-checked at night by parents across the entire town. Peaceful Hillston had been shocked awake.

There had been constant reminders on the news each night. The sheriff's office had held a press conference with Mr. and Mrs. Kennedy onstage, looking pale and exhausted and hardly aware of their surroundings. Mr. Kennedy looked particularly ill. Pamela could not imagine his guilt. If Alex Kennedy was never found, the man's ten-minute mistake would haunt him for the rest of his life.

So far, no leads had surfaced.

But Pamela tried not to let the event deter her good mood. Lance had done very well with his lessons today, and the look of excitement on his face as he carried his basketball toward the park was enough to make her smile big and warm her heart. She hoped to be able to save up enough money by Christmas to be able to buy a cheap hoop for the driveway.

Birds sang overhead.

Today was a good day.

They entered the park and followed the jogging trail north, which would give them a nice walk past the baseball fields, wrap them around the pond, and then deliver them to the basketball courts. There were two covered picnic pavilions near the courts, but Pamela always preferred to spread her blanket out under one of the nearby trees.

There was a softball game being played on the first field, cheering parents absorbed in the action.

Joggers ran by, folks with dogs tugging on leashes, snouts sniffing and tongues hanging.

On the playground, squeals of delight echoed, swing set chains squeaking, and footfalls on the wooden bridges spanning the play area.

They walked, shoes crunching on the trail's crushed gravel. Lance had pulled away from her and walked ahead, tossing his ball in the air as he went, looking back occasionally to make sure Pamela was still close by.

As they rounded a bend and began to pass the pond, Lance stopped.

Pamela stopped too, waited. Sometimes—though rarely—Lance liked to watch the ducks splash in the water. But this interest had waned as he'd gotten older.

Pamela looked toward the water. She saw only a single other person nearby, a man on the opposite side of the pond, fishing pole cast and cooler at his side. The ducks—only three today—were near him, perhaps hoping for some tossed bread.

Lance was looking right, toward the other side of the pond, where there was nothing but grass and a small wooden dock that served hardly any purpose. He began to walk.

"Lance," Pamela called, her voice barely above a whisper.

She could feel it. She couldn't understand or articulate it, but she could sense something off in her son at that moment.

Rocking chair.

She followed Lance as he made his way toward the dock, doing her best to stay close, but also not interfere. She was curious, and a small part of her scolded her for risking her son's safety to satiate her own curiosity. But she knew Lance, knew he was smart enough and well behaved enough not to do something to jeopardize his life.

Though there was now another part of her that was going to make absolutely sure and sign him up for swimming lessons at the local YMCA as soon as she got the chance.

Lance continued toward the dock, then slowed, veering slightly left and walking toward the water's edge.

Then he did something that made Pamela Brody's heart stop.

The water rippled as a strong gust of wind blew across its surface, and Lance raised his hand and waved.

Waved at nobody.

Waved at nothing but the empty pond.

Then he stood still for a full minute, the basketball once again tucked under his arm, his eyes locked on to the water.

And Pamela knew. She knew before he spoke a single word. Maybe it was her direct connection to her son's mind; maybe it was a sudden full realization of what

Lance's abilities truly were. But she knew. All the same, she knew.

Lance turned and looked at her, his face pure innocence. "Mama," he said. "That boy from TV is in the water. I think he needs help getting out."

Alex Kennedy's drowned body was pulled from the pond later that day.

Later that evening, a sheriff's deputy who was only a few weeks on the job was sent to the Brodys' house to ask questions.

His name was Marcus Johnston. He'd gone to high school with Pamela, and they talked for hours that night. Marcus left with much more information than he'd expected. Information he would likely take to his grave. Secrets he would keep for a girl he hardly knew.

Because for some reason Marcus Johnston couldn't quite nail down, it only seemed to be what was right. And in a world so full of wrong, a little more right seemed like an okay thing to provide.

"I'M TELLING YOU, LANCE, IT'S MY BLOODSUCKING EX-wife! Is the alimony not enough? She's got to come steal from the store, too?" Nick Silverthorne's face was the color of a tomato, and he pulled at the thinning hair atop his head. "I mean, I knew she was lowlife ... *trailer trash*. But I can't believe she'd have the goddam balls to come in here and steal from me. Like she didn't get enough in the divorce? Bloody hell, Lance, never get married."

Lance Brody leaned back in the musty chair in his boss's office. Nick Silverthorne had owned the Hillston Sporting Authority for nearly twenty years, with two additional stores in surrounding counties. He'd done well for himself. A smart man who could always swing a deal and always turn a profit. He'd just happened to get caught up with the wrong woman early in life and then have said woman consistently increase his blood pressure while decreasing his bank account.

Lance's mother had said she hadn't been surprised to learn of Nick Silverthorne's affair. "I imagine a man can only take so much of a particular blend of crazy."

This was about as much of an insult as Pamela Brody offered toward anybody. Lance had smirked when she'd said it.

"Sir," Lance said, "with all due respect, why haven't you installed any security cameras in the store yet?"

The Hillston Sporting Authority's security system consisted of deadbolts on the front and back doors, an in-floor safe in the back office where Lance and Nick Silverthorne were currently sitting, and the super complex password of Password456 on the store's computer.

"Do you have any idea how much those damn things cost?" Nick asked. "I put a few in the new stores, you know, since I can't always be there to keep an eye on things, and I about fainted when I got the bill. No, sir. We've never needed those things in Hillston, and we don't need them now."

"Sir," Lance said, "we're getting robbed. So—and again, I say this with all due respect—don't you think we ... well ... sorta do need them now?"

Lance had worked for Nick Silverthorne since his freshman year of high school, and after three years of learning his boss's nuances and tics and mood swings, he felt comfortable enough saying such things. Being on the Hillston High School varsity basketball team as a freshman had made Lance a bit of a local celebrity, and Nick loved bragging that Lance spent a lot of his off-season and after-school hours in the store, helping guests and keeping things running smoothly. Still, Lance felt the air change in the room slightly, and he uncrossed his long legs, bumping his size fifteen shoes on the front of Nick's desk. He stood, stretching his back. At six foot six, he had a hard time with a lot of chairs, could never quite get comfortable.

Nick Silverthorne stared down at his desk and thought about Lance's comment. He shook his head. "She's not even taking that much," he said. "It's like she's just doing it to annoy me."

"Didn't you get her key back? When you all ... you know?"

"Of course I got her key back! Doesn't mean the bitch didn't make more before she returned it."

"And you didn't change the combo on the safe?"

Nick Silverthorne glared at Lance. "Why would I change the combo if I didn't think she could get in the store?"

Lance glanced at the clock on the wall. He had to get going. He was helping set up for the girls' volleyball game. All members of the basketball team had to volunteer to help at other sporting events, and tonight was his night to work. Not that he minded. There were worse sports to watch than girls' volleyball.

Lance shrugged. "You're right, sir. Of course. Have you called the police?"

Nick shook his head. "Not yet. But if she thinks she can just keep getting away with this..." He sighed. "I know, you've got to go." He stood from behind the desk. "See you tomorrow?"

Lance nodded. "Yes, sir. I've got the morning shift."

Nick was about say something but stopped, then said, "Thanks for letting me vent about the ex. I know it's not your problem. Just nice to scream for a bit sometimes, you know?"

Lance thought about the many conversations he'd had with his mother over the years. Conversations he could have *only* with her. "Yes, sir. I do."

Nick nodded. Smiled. "Okay, get out of here." Then he held out his balled fist toward Lance, expecting Lance to bump it. It was a gesture that Nick Silverthorne appeared to be about a decade too old for, but Lance always obliged.

Only this time, when Lance and Nick's knuckles met, Lance was hit with an instant flash of events, some deep-down and locked-away memory from the depths of Nick Silverthorne's mind. Something the man obviously had no ability to bring forth into his current state of consciousness.

Otherwise, he would know everything. Just like Lance did now.

Lance had to suppress a chuckle as he left the office and headed off toward the high school.

Lance had no idea why making contact with some people caused those instant-download moments. And often it was not a one hundred percent occurrence with the same person. Take Nick Silverthorne, for example. Lance had bumped knuckles, shaken hands, punched shoulders, and slapped high fives with Nick a thousand times over the past three years, and never once had he been gifted one of Nick's memories or gotten a vision of some snapshot from Nick's life.

It was unexplainable. Just like all Lance's other gifts and abilities. The confusion and frustration that surrounded Lance's talents sometimes caused him so much anguish he would sit awake for hours at night, asking questions to the darkness and always circling back to the heaviest of questions: *Why me?*

There was no answer. Not from his mother and not from the universe.

Lance supposed he could have asked his father if the man had any inclination as to why Lance was the way he was. But Pamela Brody had never even so much as told Lance his father's name. She'd been honest enough about the situation—blunt, in fact—telling Lance his father was a one-night stand and that the man had literally run away after the deed was done. She always told the story with a laugh, but Lance was always left feeling empty. Not because he didn't love Pamela and appreciate her ability to raise him as a single mother and make sure he had everything he ever needed in life, but because he still had questions. He always had questions.

He was left with nothing but simply accepting who he was. No further explanation needed. It was the only way to cope and survive.

Every night, though, he went to bed longing to be normal.

He'd seen things nobody should never have to see. He knew things that most people were never supposed to know.

Sure, his gifts came in handy, and sometimes even allowed him to have some fun, but there was a dark current running beneath all the light. Always there, always lurking.

The darkness was what scared him.

———

The following morning when Nick Silverthorne arrived at the Hillston Sporting Authority, he found the front deadbolt unlocked and the music already playing from the overhead speakers. Lance was behind the counter, sitting on a stool and staring down at a laptop Nick had never seen before. He had a bemused look on his face.

"Morning, sir," Lance said, waving.

Nick walked to the counter. "You're here early," he said. "Your shift's not for another hour."

Lance shrugged, grin still on his face. "I wanted to show you something."

Nick searched Lance's face for an explanation. "Okay."

"One of the girls on the volleyball team is in the A/V club. They help record all the school events and produce our truly terrible morning announcement pseudo-news show. She let me borrow this." He pulled a clunky video camera from beneath the counter and set it down. "And this." He pointed to the laptop.

"Okay," Nick Silverthorne said again.

"I'm know I'm only supposed to unlock the store when I'm

first one here in the morning, or if there's an emergency," Lance said, "but I thought I would try and help you figure out what's been happening to the cash from the safe." Lance looked sheepish, almost coy, as if there was something he wasn't quite letting on about.

Nick's eyes narrowed to slits. "So you came back here last night and what? Camped out?"

Lance smiled. "Sort of."

"Why the hell do you have that stupid grin on your face?" Nick said.

Lance spun the laptop around so the screen faced his boss. "Press the space bar."

Nick looked at the screen and saw a full-screen video already loaded. He hit the space bar and watched, slackjawed, as the on-screen version of himself strolled through the front door of the Hillston Sporting Authority wearing pajama bottoms, brown slippers, and a ragged Hillston High School t-shirt. He walked across the floor, moving in slow, almost exaggerated movements, shuffling his feet and teetering from side to side, almost as if he were drunk.

The on-screen Nick approached the door to the store's office and the camera followed, keeping a good distance behind. After a minute, the camera got closer and peeked inside the door frame. On-screen Nick was hunched down by the in-floor safe, mumbling over and over to himself as he spun the dial. *"Gotta pay the bitch, gotta pay the bitch, gotta pay the bitch."*

The Nick Silverthorne of the present widened his eyes as the on-screen Nick lifted the lid to the safe, reached in and retrieved one of the bank bags. He unzipped it and rifled through it, pulling out a handful of twenties and sticking the rest back in the bag before replacing it and the top of the safe. He spun the dial and stood up.

On-screen Nick retreated the way he'd come, exiting through the front door of the store and locking it.

Nick Silverthorne's eyes looked slowly from the screen, met Lance's. "What in the hell?"

Lance couldn't help himself. He laughed at his boss's disbelief. "You're sleepwalking, sir. You're stealing from yourself!"

Nick Silverthorne was quiet for a full minute, glancing from Lance and back down to the screen where the video sat frozen, finished. He blinked a few times, as if clearing his thoughts, and then started to laugh louder than Lance had ever heard the man laugh before.

"Why in the hell didn't you wake me up, you asshole!"

Lance clutched his stomach, laughing so hard it started to hurt. "I ... I think I heard somewhere you're never supposed to wake somebody sleepwalking. It can screw with their head or something."

Nick pointed at the screen. "How much more screwed up can I get?"

The two of them laughed some more, and when the raucous noise finally died off, Nick thanked Lance for solving the mystery before he went and called the police on his batshit crazy ex-wife.

"I coulda sworn it was her," Nick said. Then he scratched his head. "Shit!"

"What?" Lance said.

"I know who the thief is, but I have no idea where I'm putting the money!"

The laughter broke out again.

Later that day, as Lance was finishing his shift, Nick called him back into the office. On top of the desk was a hiking backpack that sold for almost as much money as Lance made in a single paycheck. Nick pointed to it. "New models should be coming in in the next couple weeks. We need to dump the existing inventory, have a markdown sale."

"Sure," Lance said. "How much?"

Nick shrugged. "I'll figure it out. But you take that one."

Lance was genuinely surprised. "Seriously?"

Nick picked up the bag and tossed it to Lance. "Yes. Payment for keeping me from looking like a fool."

Lance caught the bag and examined it, grateful. "Thank you, sir. I mean it."

Nick nodded. "I know you do, son. I know. Now get out of here and go have some fun with the rest of your Saturday."

2015 (I)

A FEW WEEKS INTO THE FALL OF 2015, THE TEMPERATURES had finally subsided from blistering ninety-degree days to a more acceptable seventy-five. When the sun began to set in the evenings, things cooled off even further, dropping to mid- to low sixties, creating that much-loved fall chill. The kind of chill that made you think of pumpkin spice everything and flannel shirts and brightly colored leaves. The kind of chill that made you snuggle up to your loved ones on the Hillston High School bleachers for Friday night's football game and sit inside for your Saturday morning breakfast out at the cafés, instead of on streetside patios or courtyards.

An unmistakable change came when summer ended and fall began. Along with the change in weather came a change in lifestyle. People began preparing for the upcoming holidays—first a choice of Halloween costumes, then what size turkey to buy, and finally whose house would be hosting Christmas dinner and which church service would best fit a family's schedule on Christmas Eve. The pools closed. Men who could usually be found on the golf courses or out fishing on the weekends were suddenly self-sequestered indoors, huddled around television sets and devouring as much college and pro football and potato chips as their wives would allow. Women were rarely spotted in the wild outdoors without a cardboard-cupped latte or hot chocolate.

All these things happened almost instantly, an unspoken, natural transition. All these things were welcomed, especially after such a brutal summer of heat and dryness.

But in Hillston, Virginia, there was another big event to signify the beginning of fall: Centerfest.

Centerfest was a large celebration held in the downtown streets one day a year. The festivities were always held on the exact date Hillston had been founded. This year, it would be a Wednesday. A nuisance to some, but tradition was tradition.

Both local and out-of-town vendors set up tents and booths to sell every imaginable art or craft. Food trucks smoked and steamed and fried and grilled all variety of mouthwatering items, filling downtown with a mixed aroma of charbroiled sweetness that would cause even the fullest of stomachs to grumble for more. Carnival-like games were set up—the basketball hoops with overinflated balls, the impossible-to-knock-over cans, basket and ring tosses, balloon darts—all the expected entertainment displaying rows of large stuffed animals as prizes, which few people were ever spotted actually carrying away from one of the booths.

There was live music and face painting, and the local fire department put on safety demonstrations. There was a makeshift petting zoo sufficient for only the smallest of children.

Centerfest was Hillston's biggest event of the year, and people always looked forward to it. Not because of the five-dollar sand art their kids could build or the three-dollar funnel cakes, but because the air was always cool and crisp, and the company was always good.

For Lance and Pamela Brody, this year's Centerfest would be the day that would forever change their lives.

2015 (II)
(THE REVEREND AND THE APOSTLE SURFER)

Three days before Centerfest was when Lance saw the Reverend for the first time.

The Hillston Sporting Authority had been very busy for a Sunday afternoon, but Lance hadn't been surprised. The last few days before the official start of the PeeWee and Rec League football and soccer seasons were always a madhouse in the store as procrastinating parents rushed in on their lunch breaks and piled through the door after work to quickly buy all the supplies their son or daughter needed for the first game or first practice. Nick Silverthorne always loved it. "A rushed shopper is a shopper who doesn't care about the price," he always said.

Lance had seen the evidence to support this claim.

But as Lance had left the store at just past six thirty on that Sunday evening, leaving Nick alone to finish out the day and lock up, he'd seen something else. *Someone* else. Someone he'd never seen in Hillston before.

A block east of the Hillston Sporting Authority was a small café that did big business. Lance knew the owner—Mary Jennings—and had graduated with her daughter, Kate. Mary had started Downtown Joe ten years ago with a menu that consisted of coffee and croissants. Now she ran an operation that employed a dozen people, had a full-service breakfast and lunch menu and cozy indoor or outdoor seating. It was *the* only spot most Hillston residents thought about when they wanted to go out to grab a cup of coffee. Being as close as it was to the store, Lance had spent much of his own money at Downtown Joe, and every time he said hi to Mary, he told her to tell Kate hello.

Kate was away at college, just like most of the other kids Lance had grown up with, and probably had a hard time even remembering Lance's face when—if—Mary ever actually delivered his greetings.

Lance wondered what his life might be like right now if he'd left Hillston. What would he be doing right this moment if he'd accepted one of those basketball scholarship offers? Would he be at the gym, working on his game? Would he be at the dining hall with friends—new friends—devouring plate after plate? Or maybe he'd be at the library with the cute girl from his History of Western Civilization class, supposed to be going over notes for the next day's big quiz but both really just flirting and waiting for the other one to suggest they hang out again sometime, somewhere other than a library with open notebooks in front of them.

But he hadn't gone.

Couldn't.

It was too unpredictable. His gifts, his curse, they'd developed over the years, and while he might never fully understand them, at least in Hillston he'd grown to learn what to expect from them. And in Hillston—sleepy, tiny Hillston, Virginia—things had already been bad enough.

Lance had grown up seeing the lingering spirits of the dead —some nice and well dressed and seemingly at peace, despite their continued presence among mortals, but others ... others appeared in a form resembling the moments of their deaths, or worse. Car crash victims with dented faces and necks that hung at unnatural angles, arms and legs twisted and snapped with bones popping through skin. Murder victims with knife wounds gaping open between shredded bits of clothing, or bullet holes—small and black and sometimes so innocuous-looking it was hard to believe it was enough to end a life—peppering their torsos or marking their temples. Cancer patients who'd finally succumbed to that deadly disease, their bodies emaciated and always heartbreaking.

Lance had seen more than just the human spirit. He'd also seen the evil beyond the veil. He'd seen things from a world that was not ours, a place where suffering and pain were the fuel on which entities thrived. Call it Hell, call it Purgatory, call it Walmart on Black Friday—the things that came from this other place were things that no person should ever have to see.

He'd seen all these things—*endured* all these things—and he'd never even gone any further from home than away games with the basketball team and a few short day trips with friends.

Friends that were gone now. Friends that had moved on to real lives that stretched beyond the Hillston county lines and had infinite possibilities.

And then there was his mother....

How could he ever leave her?

It wasn't that she was incapable of taking care of herself—far from it! She was one of the most capable and strong women Lance had ever met in his life. Yet ... there seemed to be some bond between them that was deeper than just your normal mother/son variety. It was as if on some deep-down level, some place that existed far beyond anything our human minds were meant to comprehend, Lance and Pamela Brody coexisted. They survived because of each other.

Or maybe it was because she wasn't just Lance's mother, she

was his best friend. A best friend who knew everything that he was.

A friend who would never leave him.

The Reverend derailed Lance's regretful thoughts of what-could-have-beens.

He sat alone at one of the wrought-iron patio tables outside of Downtown Joe. He was tall and thin and sat ramrod straight in his chair, a black dress shirt tucked neatly into black dress pants. Dress shoes, scuffed and worn, flat on the ground, his knees bumping the underside of the table. Lance could see the white collar insert peeking from beneath the shirt's fabric as he came upon the man from the rear, and as he passed by and turned to look at the man's face, he saw the single white flash on the man's otherwise completely black outfit, right there at his throat.

He's a priest, Lance thought. *Some sort of minister ... or reverend.*

His face was clean-shaven and smooth. Pale, as if he hadn't seen the sun in a year's time. Despite the man's thinness, loose skin drooped around his neckline, and wrinkles dissected his forehead and grew from the corners of his eyes. His nose was large and curved, like a crescent moon. He could be forty, he could seventy. It was hard to tell with the thick crop of gray hair he wore parted on the side.

The Reverend was taking a delicate sip of coffee, steam rising from the cup, visible in the cooling evening air. His other hand was placed flat atop a small leather-bound black book that rested on the table, as if he were about to swear an oath.

Lance kept walking and then turned the corner at the end of the block, taking one last peek at the man before he disappeared from view. The Reverend placed his coffee cup back on the table and reached for the little black book, flipping to a specific page and starting to read.

See you soon, Lance.

The words invaded Lance's mind and disrupted his thoughts like an alarm waking him from a drowsy morning sleep, a sudden burst of awareness that snapped awake the brain in an instant state of confusion. Lance came to a stop on the sidewalk, his sneakers nearly skidding on the concrete. He stood silently and looked all around, checking for anybody, looking for any possibility that the voice he'd just heard had not originated inside his own head.

But he knew it had.

There was no question. Lance knew better than to try and explain the unexplainable. Some things were just better left accepted and unquestioned. His entire life, for example.

Somebody had just sent him a message—*See you soon, Lance*—and there was no mistaking the voice's tone.

It had been a threat.

And then, there on the sidewalk, a slow trickle of dread grew and spread through Lance's body. He breathed in deeply, gathering his resolve, then turned and walked back toward the street he'd turned from. He rounded the corner and stared back down the block toward Downtown Joe. The patio table was empty. Just a white ceramic coffee cup with a couple dollar bills pinned beneath it, loose ends flapping in the breeze.

Lance stood there on the corner of the block for a full minute, watching the faded green bills do their dance in the wind, and then he heard the motor—a slow, whining purr of an engine making its way slowly closer, echoing along the walls of the buildings near the other end of the block.

And then it emerged, slowly revealing itself bit by bit as it appeared from behind Downtown Joe, crossing the street perpendicular to Lance. An antique Volkswagen bus—something Lance had only seen in movies and TV shows. It brought to mind grainy film and faded colors and waves and sand and shirtless guys who said *dude* and *totally* and had long hair and didn't own a pair of shoes. Something from the seventies, maybe sixties.

The bus was two-toned, the majority of its body a Creamsicle orange, with white accents along the windows and top. And sure enough, as if the universe was playing some sort of cosmic joke with Lance's thoughts, in the driver's seat was a man with blond hair down to his shoulders. The skin on his arms, protruding from his sleeveless t-shirt, was the deep reddish-brown color reserved for only a select few groups of people—lifeguards and construction workers among them.

Also surfers and your general variety of beach bum.

The van disappeared after crossing the street, swallowed by the downtown buildings. Its low-whining engine faded away into nothing.

Lance stood still long after the bus was gone.

See you soon, Lance.

The Reverend had been riding shotgun.

Dread followed Lance home.

He walked the streets and sidewalks he'd walked hundreds of times in his life, a path home he could practically follow blindfolded, but he wasn't alone this time. This trip home was different. This trip home—in a way Lance could only recognize as the part of his brain tuned into the things unseen, unspoken— seemed to carry some extra weight to it, as if it were somehow important ... or maybe final.

But the dread was there, for sure. Lance felt it there, growing in his chest as his sneakers beat the concrete and asphalt. Felt its coldness spread through him along with the soft breezes rustling the treetops as he approached his neighborhood.

Things had changed.

Changed in a way Lance knew could mean nothing good.

See you soon, Lance.

The voice, the tone, the underlying threat. All three of these things would be worrisome enough, but they weren't what bothered Lance, weren't what had him swiveling his head back and forth with each step, eyes scanning for the Creamsicle Volkswagen bus.

Lance had read many peoples' thoughts throughout his life, caught glimpses of their memories and secrets and current state of mind. Often, it was accidental. Even more often, it was as if the universe, or whatever power controlled the universe, granted him these access key cards into peoples' minds when it was needed the most. Lance didn't know why—just another item on the unexplainable list that was his life—but figured it was that a full-time pass into the minds of others would perhaps be too great a power—too great a temptation—for even the strongest-willed human to handle.

Lance had always been the fisherman in these thought-retrieval episodes. Casting his telepathic reel and seeing what he could hook.

Today was the first time in his life somebody had ever found their way into *his* head—other than his mother. With his mother, he'd always assumed it was the mother/son bond that sometimes allowed them to communicate with each other. And even in those instances, which had become fewer over the years, it still seemed to Lance more like his mother simply sent him an invitation to read her mind, a mental text message that Lance could retrieve and read if he desired.

Today with the Reverend had been different. Today, it felt as if his mind had been invaded, as if the man outside of Downtown Joe had sliced open Lance's brain as easy as a hot knife through butter, had pried open a gap and shouted his message. No resistance, and no waiting for approval. He'd kicked in the door and stomped into Lance's mental house.

And he'd done it from nearly a block away.

All of this brought Lance to two terrifying conclusions.

First, the Reverend was extremely powerful. Lance didn't know how far the man's gifts reached, but his ability to deliver his message into Lance's mind spoke volumes.

Second, the message itself, with its tone and the manner in which it was delivered, along with its implications, meant that the Reverend—and possibly the Surfer—knew what Lance was. Maybe not completely, but enough.

And they were coming for him.

Lance walked up his porch steps and opened the front door. Stepped into the living room.

His mother was in the kitchen, singing softly, her voice meshing with the occasional clang of a pan, or the whipping of a spatula. The smell of apples and cinnamon and sugar wafted throughout the house. The windows were open, and the house was almost chilly, the curtains flowing in the breeze. A row of candles were lit on the mantel above the fireplace, autumn scents like pumpkin and leaves.

God, Lance loved his home.

Loved his mother.

Which is why, when he walked into the kitchen and said hello, finding her folding a crust atop a pie they would likely share together later tonight, along with coffee and tea, and she asked him how his day was, he lied.

"It was fine. Busy day at the store, but nothing unusual."

It was the first time he had ever lied to her.

It would also be the last.

Lance and his mother had each had two slices of pie as they read together in the living room, and Lance had washed his down with two cups of coffee.

But it wasn't the caffeine that was keeping him awake now. It wasn't the fear of the Reverend, either—at least not completely.

It was guilt.

Lance had lied to his mother for her own protection. That was how he was looking at it. That was the only way he could somewhat justify his actions in his mind. Yet his dishonesty sat uneasily on his heart, churned in his stomach. His mother had always been there, a helping hand held out and a voice of reason waiting to speak, throughout all the dilemmas and discoveries and outright bouts of confusion and anger Lance had displayed throughout his life. And he would be eternally grateful to her. At times even felt he was undeserving of her patience and perseverance with him.

So why lie? Why now?

He didn't want to upset her, that was one reason. No child ever wants to send their parents into a panic. Parents are extremely protective beings, ready to fight and claw and scrap and find solutions. Lance simply didn't want his mother to begin to dread and worry about his situation until he perhaps understood it in greater detail. Maybe Lance was overestimating the magnitude of what had happened on the street outside of Downtown Joe. Maybe the Reverend was in Hillston to *help* Lance. Maybe he knew of others with Lance's gifts and was ready to lead Lance to the support group he'd desperately desired his entire life.

Unlikely.

But there was one thing of which Lance was certain—

mostly certain, that is. Whether the Reverend was out for blood or out for peace, his interest was in Lance. Not Lance's mother. If things did get bad, if things did turn toward the darkness that Lance knew all too well roamed the earth, it was better that he be the one it came after, not Pamela. He wouldn't be able to live with himself if something happened to her because of him.

It's not her fight, Lance thought as he finally slipped off to sleep. *It's mine.*

Lance did not sleep well, his slumber disrupted by a nightmare of him running through a dense crowd. A street, downtown Hillston, packed tightly with people who were all smiling and laughing and not even noticing him as he plowed through them. He could smell fried foods and sugar in the night air, could hear a band somewhere close by, speakers blasting electric guitars and the *thump thump* of the drummer's bass. The hair on the back of Lance's neck was prickling, electricity running through his veins. He ran through the masses, no idea where he was going, a strange, terrible emptiness filling his chest as he went.

He woke up sweating, his sheets twisted and his pillow half off the bed. The sun was up, slipping through the blinds, and Lance smelled bacon cooking and coffee brewing.

He smiled. His mother always brewed him coffee, even though she never touched the stuff.

This small token of his mother's love sent a fresh wave of guilt through him as he stood and dressed and went out to the kitchen.

He'd taken three steps into the living room when he froze. He heard it first, the familiar whining purr of an engine. A noise he would never forget in a million years, though he'd only heard it once before. And once the sound reached his ears, his head jerked toward the front windows, which his mother had open, the chilly morning air enough to make him shiver. He caught just the tail end of a vehicle turning at the end of the street, headed back toward town.

A bus.

Creamsicle orange.

"Lance? Everything all right?"

He turned at the sound of his mother's voice. She stood in the entryway to the kitchen, a fluffy white robe wrapped tightly around her, those ridiculous toe socks on her feet. Rainbow-colored. "You look like you've seen something."

Most folks would have said, "You look like you've seen a ghost," but not Pamela Brody. She knew better. With Lance, the answer could very well be "I did."

Lance did his best to smile. "I'm fine," he said, walking toward her. "But I can definitely use some coffee."

Lance did not leave the house all day. Instead he stayed in and tried to read and tried to watch TV and tried to take a nap. But he was only half-committed to any of these tasks. His mind was always on lookout, always checking out the windows, waiting to see Creamsicle orange. Waiting for the Reverend.

See you soon, Lance.

Aside from the Volkswagen sighting early Monday morning, nothing else had happened to set Lance on alert. His day had been a miserable mesh of paranoid hours, his mind racing, searching, trying to dissect and make some sense of what he'd seen, what he'd been told. He'd been incredibly unsuccessful, and after the uneventful day, by Tuesday morning he was ready to go out, determined to try and get some answers, find some clues.

His shift at the store started at nine thirty, but after saying goodbye to his mother, he was walking through the door of Downtown Joe at just past eight fifteen. By then, the before-work coffee grabbers should be gone, and he was hoping to have a chat with Mary Jennings without a lot of eavesdropping ears.

The bell above the door chimed as Lance stepped through, and he held the door open for Mrs. Vargas, who was in her sixties but looked as though she could be forty. A cougar if there ever was one, she was dressed in yoga pants and a hoodie, expensive running shoes on her feet. Cardboard cup of coffee—nonfat, no whip, no sugar, for sure—in one hand.

"Thanks, handsome," she said as she passed by, touching Lance's arm with her free hand. Lance was hit with a sudden image of Mrs. Vargas lying in her bed, naked, with Will Sanders fumbling in front of her, struggling to pull off his pants and join her.

Lance let the door close and laughed under his breath.

Will Sanders was only a year older than Lance and had been the basketball team's second-best player. He was currently attending Virginia Tech. Lance had seen him in town last summer when he was home visiting. He wondered if that was when ol' Will had decided to test the whole "with age comes experience" theory.

Cougar indeed, Lance thought, then wondered if the universe had shown him that image just to put a smile on his face. Boy did he wish he understood how any of this stuff worked. He needed a manual.

Downtown Joe smelled like heaven, if your idea of heaven was full of coffee grounds and pastries. The tabletops were clean, the floor had been freshly mopped, and the display cases full of freshly baked goods were so crystal-clear and smudge-free they were practically invisible. They whole interior had been outfitted for fall: scarecrows and pumpkins and wreaths made of orange and yellow leaves. The chalkboard menu's largest item was the Pumpkin Spice Latte. "Better than Starbucks!" the sign proclaimed. Lance believed it.

Mary Jennings was behind the counter, reaching into one of the display cases with a gloved hand and pulling out a slice of banana bread, placing it in a small bag and handing it to the man at the register. "You know you're making me fat, Mary," the man said, taking the bag and handing over some cash.

Mary smiled. "And you know I take that as a compliment."

The two shared a quick laugh together and the man took his banana bread and left, leaving Lance and Mary alone in the café, the music playing softly from the overhead speakers—country today—and a coffeemaker humming and buzzing as it brewed into a fancy new pot.

Mary saw Lance and smiled. "Morning, Lance. Be right with you, I need to grab a pan out of the oven. Back in a jiffy." She twirled, the apron she wore puffing out around her waist, and then disappeared through a door that led back to the kitchen.

Lance stood, listening to Kenny Chesney strum a guitar and sing about summer love, and heard some clanging noises from the back as Mary did her work. Now that he was here, Lance was uncertain exactly how to proceed. He'd come seeking answers, but what was he going to ask? He wanted to know more about the Reverend. Anything. What his name was, where he was from, when he'd gotten into town, heck, what kind of coffee he'd had. Right now, the Reverend was a complete mystery, a stranger with at least one shared gift with Lance—the ability to get into other people's minds. Though admittedly, the Reverend appeared to be more powerful than Lance in this regard.

Mary might suddenly think him crazy, coming into her store and asking after a customer from two days ago. But certainly she'd remember the man, right? He wasn't a resident, that was a fact—small-town benefit, you know almost everybody—and his look had been quite distinctive. As Mary reemerged from the back, Lance tossed his self-consciousness aside. He knew he had to get whatever information he could out of her, even if she thought him rude or prying or strange.

"In a little early today, Lance. How's Pamela?"

Lance smiled and stepped closer to the counter. "She's great, thanks for asking."

"Wonderful. I keep meaning to swing by the library and see what books she's got to recommend for me—she's so *good* at figuring out what I like to read—but it's hard to get away from this place. You know?"

"Sure," Lance said. "People love it here. You should be very proud."

Mary's face reddened. "Thank you for saying that, Lance. You're always such a sweet young man. Now what can I get you today? The usual?"

"Yes, please. That would be great."

Mary nodded and grabbed the fancy coffeepot, filling the largest cup Downtown Joe offered. She popped a lid on it and slid it across the counter to Lance. "On the house today, sweetie."

Lance started to protest, but she cut him off. "Don't even try, mister. You're one of my best customers. Loyalty should be rewarded, right?"

This sounded very much like something Lance's mother would say. He stopped his attempts to pay and simply said, "Thank you. I appreciate it."

When he didn't turn to leave, Mary eyed him with a curious look. "Is there something else, Lance?"

Lance stood, feeling the warmth from the coffee cup in his

hand and trying to find the right words to ask his questions. Mary's look went from curious to concerned, and just before Lance could speak, the speakers overhead let off a sudden burst of static—a quick second of digital fuzz—before the music came back into focus.

Only it was no longer country. Kenny Chesney had been silenced.

Now the song playing was "Surfin' U.S.A." by the Beach Boys.

Mary's brow crinkled, and she looked up to the speakers in the ceiling. "Well, that's odd."

The realization of what the song was sent ice washing through Lance's veins just as the bell above the door to Downtown Joe chimed and Lance heard footsteps fall in line behind him. And not normal footsteps you'd expect to hear in the fall weather—not sneakers or boots, but the sticky slap of rubber against skin. Flip-flops.

Mary Jennings's face lit up with a smile. "Well, hello again! I didn't think you'd still be in town."

"Can't say I did either, babe," a voice that sounded as if its owner had just finished smoking the world's largest joint said from behind Lance. "But it seems we've got a bit of gnarly situation on our hands. The boss man is pretty sure we'll get it taken care of soon, though, so no worries, right? We'll be catching a wave out of here in no time."

Lance turned around and stood face-to-face with the Surfer. The man who'd been driving the Creamsicle bus. He looked at Lance with eyes that were as blue as a pristine ocean. "How's it goin', bro?"

Lance took a step back. He was a good six inches taller than the Surfer but felt entirely too close, suddenly revolted by the man's presence. A feeling as though the man were literally covered in some sort of slime, a sickly substance that radiated off him and affected anybody too close. There was something wrong with the Surfer. Something bad.

The man wore bright blue board shorts and a sleeveless yellow t-shirt, his hair now pulled back into a small ponytail. The flip-flops on his feet were grimy with dirt. He stared at Lance with a sort of dumb grin, waiting.

"I'm well," Lance said.

The Surfer nodded. "Righteous." Then he turned and asked for an iced latte.

Lance thanked Mary again for the coffee and left Downtown Joe. He made his way to work, locking the door behind him and keeping it that way until the very second the store was supposed to open.

Lance spent the following hours distracted. Customers came and went, each chime from the bell above the door caused Lance's head to dart that direction, poised and ready to see the Reverend or the Surfer coming to fulfill their promise.

See you soon, Lance.

But each new arrival to the store proved to be no threat, just another regular Hillston visitor looking for new hiking boots or a new softball bat or a jockstrap. Lance mindlessly performed his duties, easily managing to smile and act like himself as the customers carried out their transactions. All the while, his thoughts were focused on what had happened with the Surfer this morning in Downtown Joe.

The music, for starters. There was no way that was a coincidence, the odds of the station that had been playing glitching like that, only to land on a channel that just happened to be playing an oldie about surfing just as the Surfer had walked through the door. No way.

His mother's words echoed in his head. "The universe is too smart, too calculated for us to accept the concept of a coincidence, Lance. Do you, a person with your gifts, honestly believe things could be so random?"

No, he couldn't. His mother might have some quirky ideals and thoughts, but this one was a bit Lance tended to agree with.

And who *was* the Surfer, really? The darkness and pain and evil that had seemed to radiate off the man had been enough to cause Lance to stagger back, doing all he could not to run in revulsion. The Surfer was somebody bad. Someone who had done terrible things. And that trick with the music? He certainly had some sort of special ability. If there had been any doubt in Lance's mind that the Reverend wasn't here to pay him a friendly social visit, the Surfer had completely erased those doubts.

But why don't they just come? Why are they slowly revealing themselves to me?

And that's when two scenarios occurred to Lance. One, the Reverend and his Apostle Surfer were testing him, trying to see if Lance was really who they believed him to be. They were giving him clues, dropping breadcrumbs to lead him to their intentions, and when Lance confronted them, they'd be waiting.

Or two ... and this scenario slammed into Lance's gut with such a force his head felt dizzy and light with fear ... they were misleading him. Distracting him.

Maybe the message didn't imply they would arrive for him. Maybe he would come to them. And the only way Lance could think of that he would willingly go somewhere the Reverend and Surfer were waiting for him would be....

His mother.

Lance quickly recalled his mother's work schedule. She didn't work today and wasn't scheduled to volunteer at the YMCA either. She'd be at home. Alone. And because of Lance's dishonesty, she was completely unprepared for anything or anyone bad to show up. Completely unaware there was a new evil in town, and it was coming after the Brodys.

They'd played him. They'd set him up and gotten him so worried about himself, he'd forgotten all about the people around him.

Lance bolted from behind the counter, calling out, "Is anybody still here?" When nobody answered, he rushed to the door, flipping the hanging sign from OPEN to CLOSED and rushing out onto the sidewalk, barely remembering to lock the door behind him.

He ran with everything he had, crossing streets without looking and ignoring the few blaring horns from the sparse morning traffic. His legs were still strong, but his lungs burned, his stamina not what it used to be during his playing days. His heart was pounding in his ears as he turned down the street into his neighborhood and kicked into another gear he wasn't sure he still had. His head swiveled all around, eyes peeled for the Creamsicle orange.

He was close now, one more block. He could see his front yard, and at the sight of it, he had a very strange, yet very normal thought. *I'll need to cut the grass one more time this year.* And then he almost laughed at having such a trivial thought during what could be such a pivotal moment in his life.

He ran through the grass and bounded up the porch steps, slowing just enough not to knock the front door off its hinges. He threw open the door and stopped.

His mother sat on their living room sofa, a mug of tea in one hand—Lance could smell the lavender and honey—and an open book on her lap. She saw his face and instantly asked, "Lance, what is it? What's wrong?"

Lance scanned the room, saw no one but his mother. Felt a soothing relief.

"Lance?" she asked again. "Tell me."

So he did.

They'd gone into the kitchen and Pamela had sliced Lance a piece of pie, pie he hadn't thought he wanted yet somehow had managed to eat half of before he'd even begun to tell his mother what he'd been keeping from her. There was still coffee in the stainless-steel pot, and she poured him a cup and reheated it in the microwave, setting it beside the pie plate. He took a sip without thinking. It was too hot and had gone bitter, but he drank it all the same.

Finally, Pamela sat down at the table across from him, a fresh mug of tea cupped in her hands. "When you came home two days ago, I could tell something was wrong. You know me, Lance. I've never pushed you to tell me things you didn't feel the need to, and I won't change now. You're the smartest boy I know, and I trust your judgment."

Guilt.

The heaviest of guilt plowing through his gut.

He began with an apology—which his mother quickly and almost sternly dismissed—and then filled her in on the Reverend and the Surfer. All that had happened.

"Funny song to pick as entrance music, isn't it? The Beach Boys? How old is this man?"

"That's the part that bothers you?" Lance asked. "I picked up one of the worst vibes ever from this guy and you're concerned about his taste in music?"

"It's just peculiar, that's all."

Lance finished his pie. "That's the whole story," he said. "I don't know when, and I don't know why, but I know they're going to come for me. They know what I am, and they want me."

"For what, do you suppose?"

"Does it matter? Clearly nothing good. Otherwise, wouldn't they have, I don't know, just introduced themselves to me instead of quasi-stalking me around town and sending me telepathic messages with severe threatening undertones?"

Pamela nodded. "Fair point."

Lance waited for her to say more. He was not rewarded. Finally, he asked, "So what should we do?"

His mother looked at him and smiled. "Nothing."

"*Nothing?*"

Pamela stood from the table and placed her empty mug in the sink, then turned to face him, leaning against the counter. "Lance, what do *you* suggest we do? Run? Flee our home, our lives?"

"Mom, I *know* they're dangerous. Trust me."

She nodded. "Maybe so, Lance. But that doesn't change my question. Yes, they're dangerous. Well, guess what, some might call you dangerous, too, given your gifts." She held up a hand before he could protest. "Yes, I know, not a fair comparison. What I'm trying to tell you is you seem so sure this is a battle you're going to lose. Why is that?"

"I ... I don't know."

"A feeling? Your instinct?"

Lance closed his eyes and searched for that feeling he'd carried with him as he'd run home from work. Remembered the disgust he'd felt at the aura of evil that had oozed from the Surfer. Remembered the way the Reverend's message had slammed into his head with zero resistance.

"It won't end well," he said finally. "I can't explain it—"

"You never can."

She smiled at him, but he couldn't bring himself to return the favor. "I can't explain it, but this is different, Mom."

"How so? We've been through some whoppers over the years, Lance."

"That's the worst part. I honestly can't tell. It's like the picture is fuzzy, and all the pieces are scrambled. I just can't help feeling—and this is the part that scares me the most—like this is the end of something."

Pamela Brody had a heck of poker face. She only stared and nodded, her face unflinching at her son's news.

"But also," Lance said, "it might be just the beginning."

They were quiet for a long time then, both trying to wrap their minds around everything they'd discussed. Finally, Pamela walked over and placed her hand on Lance's shoulder, leaned down and kissed the top of his head. "Maybe it's both, Lance. Maybe it's both. Either way, this is all part of it."

"Part of what?"

She smiled at him. "Whatever it is you are. This is the way it's supposed to be."

"Even if they kill me?" He was starting to become irritated with her apparent ignorance to the true danger of the situation. Her reliance on fate or destiny or whatever master plan she believed his life was following.

"You're not the only one with an instinct, Lance," she said, walking back into the living room. "You've got something they don't fully understand yet."

Lance and his mother spent the rest of Tuesday evening inside. Pamela made a chicken pot pie for dinner—one of Lance and his mother's favorite diner-type foods—served with fresh rolls, and Lance couldn't tell if she was simply trying to appear as though everything was normal between the two of them, of if she honestly, deep down, had no concern in regard to what Lance had revealed to her earlier over the tea and coffee and pie.

As he helped her clean up after dinner, he came within half a breath of telling her he thought they should leave. Not forever, but just for a few days. He had some cash saved up—not much, but enough—and they could go on a mini-vacation. Someplace a few hours away, where they could find things to do to take their minds off the Reverend and the Surfer, and maybe avoid whatever altercation was sure to be headed Lance's way. He'd call the bus station and see what was available for the next day.

But would that work, really? They'd found him once, couldn't they find him again? Could the Reverend track Lance with his mind, the way Lance sometimes found himself tracking down lost items, or walking in a certain direction without really meaning to, only to find himself exactly where he needed to be? If Lance had that kind of power, it was quite possible the Reverend had it at exponentially greater levels.

Lance just didn't know. So he'd stayed quiet. Finished with the dishes and then excusing himself to his bedroom. Feeling sick and lost.

His mother called out after him, "Are you excited for Centerfest tomorrow?"

They went together every year. Lance, of course, once he'd gotten to be about eleven or twelve, would always arrive with his mother but then drift off to walk around with his friends, trying to show off at the games to win pretty girls prizes, but he'd always find his way back to her. It was essentially a tradition.

"Sure," Lance said. "I could sure go for a funnel cake right now."

He closed his bedroom door.

Lance awakened just after seven on Wednesday morning, and the moment he opened his eyes, he felt it. The feeling, the instinct, the verification. It was going to happen today.

They would come for him. He was certain.

The Hillston Sporting Authority was always closed on the day Centerfest was held. "No point," Nick Silverthorne always said. "Half the people who come in off the street just want to use the bathroom, and the other half just want to get out of the sun for a bit. Nobody comes to buy anything. Might as well keep the doors locked and enjoy the day. I do love a good fried Twinkie."

Lance hadn't disagreed.

He dressed and found his mother in the kitchen, much like he did most mornings, and when she turned to look at him, he felt another wave of grief, an unexpected sadness.

Pamela handed him a mug of coffee. "Today?"

Lance nodded.

"But you don't know what?"

Lance shook his head.

Pamela smiled. "Well, we won't let that ruin the day, now will we?"

And that's when Lance felt something different: a fresh, warm blanket of happiness and love. He looked at his mother and marveled at her resilience and optimism. Her faith in him—his abilities—was absolute. Her belief that he was walking a predetermined path was unwavering. Whatever happened today was supposed to happen, and it would not be Lance's last challenge. That was the way she saw it, and nothing was going to change her mind.

Lance sat at the table. *I'll fight. I'll give everything I have because I can't let this woman down.*

The hours ticked by slowly, and Lance spent most of them in his room, trying to shake the oddest of feelings, an annoying drip at the base of his brain that was telling him to take a good look around, because he'd never see this place again.

He'd prove the drip wrong. He'd prove it all wrong.

But when his mother told him she wanted to leave in a half hour's time, Lance couldn't help but feel like a death-row inmate who'd just been told he'd be taking his last walk very soon. No matter how hard he told himself otherwise.

I'll be back here tonight, he told himself. *Whatever happens, it'll be okay.*

But it never hurt to be prepared.

Before he left his bedroom and met his mother at the front door, he did two things.

One, he called Marcus Johnston—now the mayor—whose number he'd had memorized since he was ten years old, and told him to expect a call tonight, because Lance might need help. The mayor pressed for more, but Lance gave him nothing else. Because honestly, what he could he say?

And two, he grabbed his backpack from the floor by his closet, tossed in a few items, and slung it over his shoulder.

Then he met his mother in the living room, and they both headed out the door for the last time.

They walked together down their street, already able to hear the low murmur of noises coming from town. A cacophony of far-off voices. An indeterminable genre of music being played through powerful speakers.

The air was cool as the sun began to set behind the horizon. Breezy. Lance felt goose pimples along his arms and watched his mother pull the sleeves of her sweater down over her hands. She didn't question his backpack. Didn't say a word until they got closer to the actual event. They continued on, silently, and as Lance looked around at his surroundings, seeing houses and landmarks and trees he'd observed his entire life, the silence between him and his mother seemed to say it all. "This has been our life together," it said. "And it's been wonderful."

But tonight, it might very well come to an end.

These heavy thoughts weighed Lance down as they walked. The burden he'd carried with him since he'd been born suddenly seemed to take on more heft than ever. Lance didn't subscribe to any particular organized religion, but he'd read the Bible. As they walked and Lance contemplated the events which might be about to come, he thought about the story of Jesus in the garden of Gethsemane the night of his capture. What must it have been like, knowing, waiting? Ripe with the knowledge that only you could perform what needed to be done, whatever that may be.

After Jesus, he thought of Aslan, the great lion in Narnia, who'd so willingly and confidently strolled through the White Witch's mocking crowd, head held high as he arrived to sacrifice himself.

Am I that brave? Lance asked himself. *Am I at all worthy of these gifts?*

The voices and the music got suddenly louder and Lance came back from his thoughts and found that they were standing at the end of Church Street. The block or two of Church that was dedicated to Centerfest was full of people. They milled about from craft tent to craft tent, from booth to booth. Ahead, Lance could just make out a glimpse of Main Street, running perpendicular to Church. Main Street was the main artery of Hillston, and thus Centerfest. Plumes of smoke and steam rose over the roofs of the buildings, and his stomach, despite the situation, grumbled with hunger.

There was no way his mother could have heard his stomach,

but as if on cue, she reached out and touched his arm, saying, "Before anything else, let's get you that funnel cake."

She smiled at him, and Lance was again hit with an overwhelming urge to convince her to leave with him for a while, to leave whatever was about to happen in Hillston for somebody else to deal with.

But of course, there was nobody else. And Pamela was already making her way through the crowd, headed for Main Street. Lance followed her, his head well above most of the other patrons out this evening, following the top of his mother's head as she made her way forward. The air continued to grow cooler, almost rapidly, as the sun finally disappeared completely and the streetlights and shop lights became all that lit downtown Hillston. His mother spilled out onto Main Street, and Lance turned left to follow her toward the rows and rows of food vendors. Brightly painted food trucks with compressors and propane tanks hissing and growling on their rears, torso-sized menu boards plastered on the street side, advertising anything and everything you could ever hope for from a carnival environment. Lance watched a group of small children run by, all holding half-eaten and dripping snow cones, their mouths stained every color of the rainbow. He heard fryers frying and smelled grills grilling. He saw a man wearing a clown suit spinning cotton candy onto a paper stick for an elderly couple standing hand-in-hand, anxiously awaiting their treat with grins on their faces. Lance passed by people he knew, waved and nodded hello. A few looked as though they wanted to stop and talk, but Lance would not stop following his mother. He hated the possibility of appearing rude, but he wasn't letting her out of his sight tonight. Not for anything.

Finally, Pamela stopped in front of one of the food trucks and got in line. Lance came up beside her, looking at the menu board. Aside from funnel cakes, this truck offered fried Oreos, fried Twinkies, fried pickles, fried ice cream, and, seemingly out of place, bottles of water.

"What are you going to have?" Lance asked.

His mother had been studying the board as well. "How do you fry ice cream? That seems inconceivable, don't you think?"

"Cleary some sort of witchcraft, I suspect. Maybe we should go to another truck. I don't want to turn into a toad or have my head shrink after eating whatever they give me."

His mother made a show of thinking about what he'd said. "There'd be less laundry if you were a toad."

Lance grinned. "And less, well, you know, me."

She nodded. "There is that. I do enjoy having you around."

Lance was about to make a witty retort, but found he couldn't. There was a sudden lump in his throat that needed swallowing.

"I'll just have a pinch or two of yours, if that's all right," Pamela said as they stepped up to order.

"Or course."

Lance paid for the funnel cake and they walked further down Main Street, eating their sweet and heading toward the First Bank & Trust parking lot. From the parking lot came a swirling glow of neon lighting mixed with the popping of air rifles and balloons, the clinking of plastic rings against glass bottles and the all-too-familiar echo of basketballs being bounced. The parking lot was home to the game booths.

"I'm finished," Pamela said, brushing powdered sugar from her hands. "The rest is yours."

Lance picked up what remained of the funnel cake, folded it in half, and demolished it in two bites.

His mother watched him. "I'd say I'm impressed—or disgusted—but by now I'm just used to it."

Lance laughed and tossed the empty paper plate into a nearby trash can. "Come on, let's go see if I can get one of these overinflated basketballs into one of these too-small hoops. I love seeing the disappointed faces of the workers when I win."

"Lancelot Brody, that's awful. I thought I raised you better than to revel in somebody else's misfortune."

"Mom, they're ripping people off. You're not meant to win. It's basically rigged."

Pamela considered this. "Really?"

Lance nodded.

"Okay, then, go win yourself a cheap stuffed Spongehead."

"It's SpongeBob."

She waved him off. "Just go win."

Lance did win. He paid two dollars to the man behind the counter at the basketball shoot and then bounced the ball a few times on the ground, getting a feel for it. He tossed it in the air twice, feeling its weight. As expected, it was way overinflated and probably would have landed on the bank's roof if Lance had bounced it hard enough off the ground. Instead, Lance took two steps backward, positioning himself further away from the goal than most of the other participants, and then shot and swished two shots in a row. He didn't even take off his backpack. He did indeed win a stuffed SpongeBob, which he quickly gave to a young boy who had been watching. The boy's parents thanked Lance, and the game attendant gave Lance a sly smile that seemed to say "Congratulations, but now get out of here."

Lance wished basketball was his only special talent. A normal talent that could take him places and that people understood. He'd never forget the confused voices that had come from the other end of phone calls with college coaches when Lance called to politely decline the scholarships they'd offered him. "So where *did* you decide to go?" they always asked. Lance wasn't sure many of them believed him when he said he wasn't planning on going to college. "I'm staying home," he'd say. And then they'd usually hang up.

Lance and his mother stopped to watch a few of the other games but did not play. Lance knew what his mother was patiently waiting for, one of the biggest reasons she came out to Centerfest every year. The music.

Pamela Brody loved live music. She loved the energy from the bands, loved the pounding of the speakers, loved the crowds. She loved how people transformed in front of live music, how their problems and inhibitions seemed to melt when the right song came on and the tune and the beat and the melody carried them to a different place they usually kept locked away, deep down.

She loved to dance.

She'd stand by herself, or she'd join a crowd of other free spirits, and she'd sway and twirl and step along with the music. Her eyes would close sometimes, like a Southern Baptist churchgoer during their favorite hymn, and as Lance would watch her in her long skirts or woven sweaters, with her hair done in braids or sometimes just loose and falling halfway down her back, he would flash to the images he'd seen of Woodstock and smile. She would have fit right in.

He loved seeing her as happy as she was in those moments. Mostly because it made him forget about himself for a while. Lance wasn't stupid. His gifts were a curse not only upon himself, but also his mother. She'd had to deal with things just as much as Lance had. Lance always longed for a normal life, and he couldn't help but wonder—and feel guilty—about whether his mother desperately wished she'd been given a normal child. She'd never indicated such a thing, but then, Pamela Brody wasn't the type of person who would.

He shook himself out of these thoughts and said, "Come on, let's go find the band."

Pamela watched a young girl of about three try to toss her red plastic rings atop the scattering of glass bottles at the ring toss tent, then followed Lance as he led the way out of the bank's parking lot.

They didn't have to search very hard to find the band, because the bandstand was set up in exactly the same place it'd been set up every year since Lance could remember—with the exception of that one time when Lance was about fifteen and some poor sap had mistakenly scheduled the Hillston Farmers Market parking lot to be repaved and lined a day before Centerfest. But tonight, as usual, Lance and his mother walked another two blocks down Main Street and then turned onto Bedford Avenue to be greeted by what seemed like a thousand people packed under the pavilion-like shelters that stretched north for roughly a quarter mile, perpendicular to the street. The city had set up folding chairs under the wooden structures for people to sit and enjoy the show, and while the majority of the seats looked to be filled, there was a massive mosh pit scene spilling out into the parking lot on the other side of the pavilions.

This was where people ended up who just wanted a quick taste of the music before moving on, or those who were young enough and full of enough energy to stand and enjoy the tunes. This was also where people danced. This was where Lance and his mother were headed, he knew.

At the far end of the Farmers Market parking lot, the stage was raised high, a good three or four feet above the heads of the patrons. Speakers as black as night and as loud as jet engines stood like sentinels on either side of the platform, pushing unhealthy volumes of sound out into the night air, permeating downtown Hillston. The band onstage was a local favorite, a young rock group whose sound resembled eighties megastars more than anything more modern, which was ironic since the lead guitarist and singer had graduated a year ahead of Lance. This kid—because he was, after all, a kid in Lance's mind—who now stood onstage singing a Phil Collins cover, to the crowd's delight, was the same kid who'd electrified Hillston High School basketball crowds with electric covers of the day's most popular hip-hop offerings during pregame warmups. He was talented. Lance suspected his band would be playing in venues a lot larger than the Hillston Farmers Market very soon.

His mother took the lead and headed out onto the black asphalt of the parking lot, weaving between clusters of people who stood by, swaying along with the tune or nodding their heads to the beat. She found a small gap in the crowd, a hole that had appeared almost out of nowhere, as if it'd been waiting just for her. Lance followed, trailing just a few feet, and when Pamela stopped in the clearing, which was a little to the left of dead center of the crowd, Lance stopped behind her. She pulled up the sleeves of her sweater now, the crowd and all the walking causing her to grow warmer, and after a few seconds—that was all it really took—Lance could practically see his mother morph into that other person she became in front of the music.

Lance, who was six-six and as graceful as a gazelle on the basketball court, had all the rhythm of a garbage truck. Opting to join the head nodders, he stood back and smiled as he watched his mother get carried away into her special place. During the second song, Martin Hensinger—the local dentist and an avid reader who frequented the library—found his way to Pamela, and the two of them exchanged some small talk and laughed and half-performed a brief awkward dance together before Martin bade her farewell.

Lance had never seen his mother go on a single date his entire life, and again the guilt of her burden pummeled him. How different—how much better—would her life have been?

"Get away from me, creep! Get *away!*"

A young woman's voice struck a chord in Lance's mind, rattled in his head the way the bass from the speakers onstage were rattling his stomach. His vision blurred for a moment, as if he'd been struck. When it cleared, it was as if the music and noises from the crowd had diminished, as if some great hand had turned down the master volume knob on the whole event.

"Help!"

The voice again, coming from his left. Lance turned his head and looked into the sea of people surrounding him. Most were facing the stage, taking in the music. A few leaned toward each other in half-screaming attempts at conversation. They clutched plastic cups of soda or cardboard cups of coffee and hot chocolate (Courtesy of Downtown Joe!). They bit into candy apples and funnel cakes and steak-and-cheese sandwiches. They all looked happy and relaxed. Nobody seemed distressed.

"Somebody help me! *Please!*"

Lance started in the direction of the voice, stretching up on his toes, occasionally jumping up as he pushed through the crowd, scanning the horizon over the flood of heads.

And then he saw her. Just a fleeting glimpse of a thin teenaged girl dressed in jeans and a Hillston High School hoodie, blond hair splayed out behind her as she struggled. Somebody was pulling her into the alley that ran between the rows of buildings on Main Street and Woodson Avenue. She swung her free arm in an off-balance attempt to attack her assailant, then struggled to turn and get in one last view of the crowd that was seemingly ignoring her cries for help. She opened her mouth, as if to expel one last scream, one last plea, but before she could make a sound, she was violently jerked into the blackness of the alley's mouth.

Lance was moving again now, looking all around him, stunned that nobody had heard this girl cry out. Nobody else was heading toward where she'd been taken. They weren't even looking that direction.

They can't hear her, he thought. *The music is too loud!*

He ran.

But how come I can?

The answer was obvious.

Because of his gifts.

Because of his burden.

Lance Brody was meant to hear the screams because that was his life. He was a light in the darkness. An unassuming protector. Forever obligated, indebted to the world.

Because what was the alternative? Stand by idly and let the world burn? Let the evil win without batting an eye?

What honest human being could do such a thing?

He ran toward the alley between Main and Woodson, not even slowing as he reached the dark slit between the buildings. He bounded in, heart pounding and ready to fight one, maybe two pieces of scum who thought it was funny to violate a helpless young girl. His eyes adjusted to the low light, his footfalls echoing off the encasing walls, and when he saw the scene in front of him clearly, he skidded to a stop so hard the rubber on his sneakers literally squealed against the asphalt, and he had one devastating thought: *I've lost. Just like that.*

Standing fifteen feet away in the shadows of the alley was not a young girl fighting for her dignity and safety, nor was it one or two pieces of scum looking to have some fun by roughing up some innocent bystander.

Standing fifteen feet away in the shadows of the alley, looking as comfortable as ever in his board shorts and sleeveless t-shirt and flip-flops, was the Surfer.

Confusion washed over Lance. He was smart enough to understand that he'd been tricked, baited into a trap like a rabbit in the woods, but he didn't understand how. Who was the girl? *Where* was the girl?

The Surfer smiled at Lance in the darkness, as if reading his thoughts, and that was when Lance was hit with an even deeper

realization of the powers he was up against. The Surfer, somehow, had been the girl, or ... had created her ... or ...

What is *he?*

Lance didn't have time to contemplate the mysterious man
before him, because just as his mind finally allowed in the
instinctive thought to turn and run away, get the heck out of the
alley before something terrible, something *final* could happen,
he heard the steady rumble of tires over asphalt echoing into the
space behind him. He turned halfway, keeping one eye trained
on the Surfer, and saw the Creamsicle Volkswagen bus slide
into view, completely blocking the mouth of the alley,
completely blocking Lance's way out.

The Reverend was in the driver's seat, his white collar
seeming to twinkle in the alley's darkness as he stared out the
window toward Lance. Past the Reverend, through the van and
out the passenger window's glass, Lance could see a blurred and
congested image of the crowd in the parking lot, their focus still
locked onto the stage, the music. His mother was among them,
and Lance wondered if she'd noticed that he'd gone. How long
had he been gone? Time had seemed to slow now that he was
here, trapped between two foes, but in reality, he'd probably
only been gone from the crowd for a minute, maybe less.

Hi, Lance. Ready to go?

The Reverend's voice slid into Lance's thoughts, as smooth
as sliding into silk sheets. No hesitation, no resistance.

Just hop on in and we'll go for a ride.

Lance stared back, turning fully toward the bus, his gaze
focused solely on the Reverend's eyes. He concentrated and
shot back a message of his own, curious to see if it'd be received.

Who are you? Lance asked. *What do you want?*

Lance heard movement behind him and spun around
quickly, the Surfer having taken what looked like two steps
closer. His hands were at his sides, and he didn't seem to be

carrying any sort of weapon, but when Lance remembered the whole damsel-in-distress trick the man had somehow conjured, he wasn't sure any physical weapon would be necessary.

Just make it easy, Lance. The Reverend whispered in his head. *We don't want to hurt you. You're too valuable to us.*

Lance ignored the voice, let his eyes fall over his surroundings, searching for some sort of escape. He clearly couldn't exit the way he'd come in, because of the bus, but he might be able to get past the Surfer and exit out the other side toward Church Street. But still, the thing with the girl, the overwhelming sense of slime and evil he'd felt coming off the man in Downtown Joe ... he was more dangerous than he looked on the surface. Lance didn't want to get close to him—*feared* getting close to him. It was potential suicide.

He saw the handful of metal doors set flush into the wall, service and delivery entrances for the stores and shops, a place for employees to take the trash to the Dumpsters. Each door had a single keyhole and no knob. A small button to ring the bell next to each. They could only be opened from the inside, for security.

Get in the bus, Lance. We have great plans for you.

The music from the stage continued to play, the speakers pumping and the bass thundering. Lance felt his heart pound-pound-pound louder and faster in his head, thought about his mother, out there alone, wondering what had happened to her son, searching for him in the crowd, crying out his name.

Another noise behind him, the Surfer gaining another step.

You're brave, Lance, the Reverend said, and then louder: *But you're ours now.*

Lance's mind spun wildly, desperate for a solution.

And don't worry, we'll take care of your mother.

And just like when a lit fuse finally reaches its end, Lance's temper ignited in a spark of rage and fury that tinted his vision red. His hands balled into fists and his muscles tightened and he poised himself to run straight at the Reverend and jump clear over the Volkswagen if need be. He sucked in one deep breath of air, heard the Surfer begin to move rapidly behind him and....

One of the metal service doors swung open on rusty hinges with a screech that echoed loudly through the darkness. A short man, stocky and balding, stepped out into the alley, freezing when he saw Lance and the Surfer standing outside the door.

"Oh!" he said. "Wasn't expecting anyone out here." The man looked as though he sensed he'd walked into some sort of trouble and started to retreat back inside the building, the metal door swinging slowly closed behind him. Lance sprang into action, the quickness that had been so beneficial on the basketball court now helping to save his life. His arm darted out and caught the door and flung it open, hard and wide, the metal slamming into the Surfer's body as he reacted a second too slowly to Lance's movements. There was a dull *thud* as the metal met flesh and bone, and Lance jumped over the door's threshold and quickly spun around, grabbing the door's push bar and quickly jerking the door closed.

"Hey! You can't be in here!" the balding man protested fearfully. "We're closed!"

Lance didn't even look at the guy, just turned and ran for the front of the store, for an exit. The building was dark, all the lights off save a few emergency overheads that glowed dimly in the gloomy space. These buildings were all old, smelled of must and failed businesses. Lance scanned his surroundings and saw large pieces of wooden furniture in various states of assembly—sawhorses and cans of stain and electric sanders. He pushed through a gray swinging door, emerging into the storefront. He saw an elegantly staged dining room set on his left, a king-sized four-poster bed on his right, wooden tables and chairs and barstools and rolltop desks scattered everywhere. He knew where he was—Hillston Furniture Co.

Hillston Furniture Co. closed at five o'clock every day. Closed on Sundays. Five o'clock had long since passed, and with Centerfest happening, the store had likely been empty for hours. There was absolutely no reason the stocky balding man should have been here, no reason that alley door should have opened.

His mother's words: "Do you, a person with your gifts, honestly believe things could be so random?"

He certainly could not. Especially not tonight.

He thanked the universe for the assist and ran to the front door. The deadbolt was locked, but a quick turn of the thumb latch and Lance was in the street, bounding out into the chaos of Centerfest once again. The noise and the smells and the unknowing people. Unknowing that right now something major was happening, something that could forever change Lance's life—*and who knows what else?*—was going down right under their noses. They were just too busy with their games and food and arts and crafts to notice.

And maybe that was okay.

Lance turned left and ran down the sidewalk behind the food trucks, rounding the corner of Main and Bedford. He saw two things at once: his mother emerging from the Farmers Market pavilions, her eyes locked onto his with a clear understanding spread across them—*It's happening, isn't it?*—and the Creamsicle bus with its reverse lights on, attempting to do a three-point turn to head toward a small exit ramp, the place where every other Saturday morning, the local vendors and farmers would drive their pickups off Woodson Avenue and back them up to the pavilions to unload and set up shop. It was the only way out with the bus. The rest of the roads were closed off, packed with people and tents. Lance watched it for just a moment, long enough to see the Surfer back in the driver's seat and the Reverend riding shotgun.

Disappointing, Lance. Shouldn't have run. Now it's worse. You'll see.

The Reverend's voice creeped into Lance's head again, and Lance cast out a mental middle finger, raised high. He hoped the Reverend could see it. He hoped it jammed him in the eye.

Pamela was not running, but she walked quickly across the street and joined Lance on the sidewalk. She didn't speak, only looked to him. Lance took her by the arm and hurried up the block, back to the intersection with Main Street. They spilled into the street, people parting around them like a stream around a pile of rocks.

"I saw the bus," Pamela said, her eyes still trying to lock onto Lance's.

Lance was using his height and scanning the crowd, searching for any sign of the Surfer or the Reverend. Though now—a terrifying thought—he wasn't sure he'd actually be able to spot the Surfer outright. The trick with the girl in the alley had changed Lance's entire perspective of what he was up against. "I'm glad you didn't go running toward it like some crazed mother bear protecting her cub."

Pamela gave a slight nod. Somebody bumped into her as they made their way past, and a bit of apple cider spilled from a large plastic cup, just missing their shoes. The person apologized over their shoulder and moved on.

"Something told me not to," Pamela said. "I knew you wouldn't be there if I went."

"Something? Or someone?" Lance asked, finally meeting his mother's eyes.

Pamela only shrugged.

Lance Brody wasn't one to question premonitions or unexplained hunches. Instead, he used his lifetime in Hillston to pull up a mental map of downtown and the surrounding streets, calculated the roads that were still passable and not shut down for the night's events, trying to list all the possible routes the Creamsicle bus could be headed.

They're not done, Lance knew. *They're going to keep coming.*

He mapped out a route back to their house, using a few offshoots down some side streets and one gravel path that ran parallel behind their neighborhood. If he could get back there quick enough, his mother would have some time to grab a few things, and then they could head to the bus station.

Do they think I'll leave town? he wondered. And then, with some disappointment in himself, *Do they think I'm that much of a coward, not to stay and fight?*

But this wasn't running. This was surviving. For both Lance and his mother.

"Let's go," Lance said, pulling his backpack off one shoulder and digging for his cell phone. He flipped open the pay-as-you-go flip phone his mother had given him years ago and dialed Marcus Johnston's personal cell number by memory. He put the phone to his ear and once again took his mother's arm and led her back down Main Street, back the way they'd come what suddenly felt like ages ago. Back toward home. For what might be the last time in a good long while.

Pamela came along after him, but Lance could sense her resistance. He had halfway turned to look back at her, when on the third ring, there was a "Hello?" in his ear.

"It's happening," Lance said. "There's people after me and my mom, bad people. I need you to tell the police to stop an orange-and-white Volkswagen bus if they see one. Just stop the bus and don't let the driver or passenger out of their sight. No questions, okay? I just need enough time to get us out of here."

"Out of here?" the mayor asked.

"Yes."

"Lance?"

"Yes."

"Where are you going?"

There was a tugging on Lance's arm, gentle at first and then more prominent. "Lance," his mother said.

"Home first," Lance said. "Then, I'm not sure where we're—"

"*Lance!*" His mother's voice echoed loudly, causing Lance to stop talking. He glanced around, but none of the other patrons seemed to have noticed or cared. Too much going on. He turned and looked to his mother. She tugged his arm and nodded toward the street stretching out to their left—Avenel Avenue. There were only a few tents set up on Avenel, a couple of jewelry vendors and a man selling pencil sketches of local landmarks. After the first half a block, the street was empty except for the lines of cars parked along the curb on either side, stretching far back into the darkening street. A few streetlights glowed from the distance, and the occasional headlights flipped on as cars pulled out of spaces, headed home. A good stream of people walked in either direction, both toward and away from Main Street—the newcomers, and those who'd had their fill. But the scene was nothing like the packed madhouse of Main Street.

Avenel was where Pamela was pulling him. Lance resisted, planting his weight. "Where are you going?"

"Trust me," she said.

Lance thought out more routes in his head and didn't see how going down Avenel helped them at all, except to get them out of this sea of people. Which Lance actually sort of liked at the moment, as it helped them blend in.

But then he thought back to what Pamela had said to him after he'd escaped from the alley—"Something told me not to. I knew you wouldn't be there if I went"—and crossed his fingers that whatever had intervened with his mother's intentions was taking the wheel now as well. And besides, Hillston wasn't that big. They could get back to the house from anywhere.

And at the end of the day, yes, he did trust her. More than anybody on earth. More than himself.

"Lance?" It was Marcus Johnston in his ear. "Lance, where are you going?"

Lance took one last reassuring glance at his mother and said, "East on Avenel."

"Toward the cemetery?"

Lance felt his heart do something funny, a cold trickle of fear pouring over his head as he realized that if they continued half a mile up the road on Avenel, past the downtown businesses and the few abandoned buildings, yes, they would eventually run into the intersection with White Birch Lane, which led directly to the main entrance of the Great Hillston Cemetery.

"Yes," he said. "I guess so. Just tell them to stop the bus if they see it, okay?" Then Lance ended the call and ran with his mother up the street, toward where—unbeknownst to Lance, and Pamela, too, really—he had been made what he was.

This time, they did run. Both of them together, Lance leading the way with his fingers intertwined with his mother's, trying to keep himself from going so fast that he would end up dragging her. The eyes of the people walking along Avenel stared at them, mouths slightly ajar, curious as to what they were witnessing. Folks looked around, heads darting left and right and up and down the street, thinking maybe something bad was happening—a crazy person with a gun or a knife, or maybe somebody had yelled bomb!—but they saw nothing. Only Lance and his mother running away from Hillston's biggest and best event of the year.

"Maybe she's sick," Lance heard a man say to his wife as they ran by. "Maybe she's going to spew her fried pickles."

Lance had no concern with what people thought. He knew —somehow, he knew—that whatever he and his mother were suddenly caught up in had repercussions larger than any of the folks gawking could possibly imagine.

Lance only wished he knew what those repercussions where. Wished, now more than ever in his life, that he knew what his purpose was, or if he even had one.

The cars continued to line the street three blocks down Avenel, and the people continued to meander and stare as Lance and his mother ran. At the intersection with Vine Street, there were two sheriff's deputies in bright orange vests, one of them holding one of those plastic orange cones used to direct traffic. They were leaning against one of their police cruisers and chatting and watching the people and did no more than glance in Lance's direction when he ran by with his mother in tow. For the briefest of moments, Lance slowed, thinking this was why his mother had wanted to come this way, because she knew there'd be help here. They'd be able to jump in the rear of the police cruiser and have two of Hillston's finest escort them to safety.

But two things happened all at once that caused Lance to forget all that and run even faster, pleading with his mother to keep up.

First, just like when he'd been younger and his mother had mentally asked him to help her find the house keys or sent him the message that dinner was ready while she was in the kitchen and he was playing in his room, Lance sensed her mind knocking on his consciousness's door. He answered and she said: *Don't stop. Not here. They can't help us.*

Second, as Lance slowed to possibly request the assistance of the two sheriff's deputies, he saw a vehicle spit out of the darkness further down Vine Street, tires squealing as it took the right turn too quickly, and its headlights were suddenly pointed directly at Lance, barreling toward him at much higher speeds than the posted twenty-five-mile-per-hour limit.

The deputies turned in unison, jumping at the noise.

The vehicle had appeared quickly, and though the headlights were now blinding, obscuring any clear view of it, Lance had seen enough as it had made the turn.

The Creamsicle bus.

Coming for him.

Fast.

They ran, letting go of each other's hands and sprinting up the street. The deputies were shouting something at the oncoming bus, an incoherent mixture of commands and warnings. People had stopped walking now, half of them staring at the deputies, heads cocked sideways in curious inquisitiveness, half of them watching Lance and Pamela run.

Another block up Avenel, the cars were still lining the streets, but the lot on the right side of the sidewalk was vacant, just an expanse of grass and weeds where Lance had heard McGuire's Pool Hall had once stood in the midseventies before closing and eventually being torn down by the city. Lance pulled his mother in this direction, their feet leaving the hard asphalt and falling softly onto the grass and dirt. They cut the corner of Avenel and White Birch Lane, making a diagonal across the empty lot. To his left, Lance saw more parked cars along the sidewalk of White Birch, which would eventually end as the city street stopped and a rural road began. Ahead and slightly to his right, Lance could make out the looming wrought-iron fence surrounding the Great Hillston Cemetery, a sliver of moon hanging in the night sky above like a winking eye.

Lance risked a glance behind him and saw the tiny silhouettes of the two deputies jump out of the way as the pair of headlights rounded the corner with another squelch of tires and made their way up Avenel.

They've seen us, Lance thought. *We've got to hide. We'll never outrun them.*

They were reaching the edge of the vacant lot now, Lance impressed with how well his mother had kept up, her lean body and long legs striding across the grass with an elegance he'd had no idea she possessed. *Guess I know where I get my athleticism from.* At the far corner, at the edge of White Birch Lane and Route 411, which led toward the county line, was a crushed gravel parking lot tucked away by the side of the entrance to the cemetery. A place for visitors to park and funeral processions to gather on the days of burial. Tonight, it was an overflow lot for Centerfest, and the lot was nearly full, cars parked two rows deep along the edges.

And then he heard the screaming.

He stopped and looked back, watching in horror as the Creamsicle bus sped up Avenel, people jumping and diving out of the way as the headlights tore up the street. The bus was swerving, dodging in half-hearted attempts to avoid pedestrians, but clearly not overly concerned if there was collateral damage.

All because of me, Lance thought. *This is all my fault.*

The bus was three-quarters of the way up the street, making its way toward White Birch Lane. Pedestrians fled in every direction, some jumping on top of cars, some diving back into their cars, others filing into the vacant lot in which Lance and his mother stood. High-pitched shrieks filled the night air, men shouted curses that echoed off the old buildings. The two deputies ran far behind, their arms out, pistols raised in the direction of the bus. But of course they would not shoot. No way. Not with all the people around.

And then Lance was hit with the brilliant idea to turn around and run back the way they'd come and then cut down

Avenel and across Main and head back toward home. They'd be going against the grain, so to speak, but the Creamsicle bus would have to do the same. And with the roads closed off, the Surfer and the Reverend would essentially have to make an entire loop around the outskirts of downtown to get back toward Lance's home.

It would buy him and his mother enough time to get to the bus station, maybe. But, sadly, Lance realized they wouldn't be able to stop at home first. It would be too risky.

He turned to grab his mother's hand and lead her back toward Avenel, but his jaw dropped when he saw that she'd already run further across the lot, headed for the crushed gravel parking lot and the cemetery. She turned and called over her shoulder, "Come on!" Lance said a bad word under his breath but was left with no choice but to follow her.

Lance's backpack bumped and jostled against his back. He reached for the straps and pulled them down in one swift jerk, tightening the bag against him. His mother was only a few feet ahead of him, but Lance felt she was much further. She had an agenda, some deeper understanding of the events unfolding around them than Lance had. She veered right just before they reached the crushed gravel parking lot, and Lance heard the strumming of an acoustic guitar and a male voice singing pleasantly. He looked over the parked cars and saw a man standing in the middle of the parking lot, guitar case flipped open at his feet, standing and smiling and singing to a good-sized crowd who'd gathered around him to watch and listen before heading toward downtown and the main activities. The sounds of the chaos taking place a few blocks away had not yet reached them, drowned out by the man's music and singing, blocked by their turned backs. A young boy maybe five years old ran up to the man and tossed some loose change into the opened guitar case and then ran back giggling to his mother's side.

Lance turned and saw his own mother running along the line of parked cars, headed toward the wrought-iron fence encircling the cemetery, stretching on into the darkness further than Lance could even see. He looked back toward the man playing the guitar and was shocked to see the singer looking directly at him. Still singing, the man winked at Lance, then turned back to his crowd. Startled and confused, Lance turned and ran after his mother. Found her to be impossibly far ahead of him. How long had he stopped and listened? It felt like only seconds, but now his mother had reached the fence and was....

What is she doing? Is she ... trying to climb it?

But no, that wasn't quite right. She was at the fence, facing it, and her hands were gripping the iron rods, poised as if ready to begin to hoist herself up and over. But she stood motionless, her head bowed down, almost as if in silent prayer.

Lance ran to her, his feet suddenly very heavy, his legs feeling as if he were trying to sprint through wet cement. He trudged along, fighting his fatigue. Only a few short yards to go before he'd reach his mother.

And then he stopped, gasped.

The rest of the world seemed to fade away. The music from the parking lot and the sounds from the street and, further away still, the occasional thump of the bass coming from the speakers from the Farmers Market bandstand all vanished. The air grew still and Lance's ears felt as if they needed to pop. It was if he'd stepped inside a giant bubble, one that was shielding out everything except him and his mother ... and the spirits lining the interior of the Great Hillston Cemetery's wrought-iron fence.

There might have been a hundred of them, maybe more. The spirits of so many of Hillston's past residents huddled packed together in a semicircle that stretched deep into the cemetery, deeper than the light allowed Lance to see. But he saw them, lost souls dressed in suits and dresses and outfits spanning decades, centuries. Men and women, young and old, children, and even two dogs who sat quietly at one man's side, as if waiting patiently for their dinner. Every single one of these ghosts had their gaze fixed on Lance's mother.

And every single one of their mouths moved rapidly, as if muttering some repeated incantation or chant, over and over and over.

Lance took a small, tentative step closer, watching his mother as she kept her head bowed, her hands tightly gripping the fence. The mouths of the spirits continued to mumble, mutter, and as Lance stepped closer, he heard indecipherable bits and pieces of their words. It was as if his head were a weak antenna, struggling to tune in to a far-off station that would not come in clearly. He stepped closer still, the spirits' gazes never looking his direction, only locked on his mother. Lance tried to concentrate, tried to home in on the staticky signal of the dead, but found he couldn't. It was as if ... as if he were being blocked, and he understood with a fresh wave of fear that frightened him to his core that he wasn't meant to hear what was being said. The spirits' message was a secret, meant only for his mother.

The squeal of tires on asphalt suddenly burst through the bubble that Lance had seemingly stepped into, and he turned around quickly, his eyes landing on the Creamsicle bus that jumped the curb at the corner of Avenel and White Birch before bounding back over the sidewalk, narrowly missing the front bumper of a parked pickup truck and turning sharply right, headed up White Birch. Heading for the crushed gravel lot.

We've got to get out of here!

Lance turned, ready to rip his mother free from the fence, even prepared to be violent about it if he needed to, but he only froze. Stopped and stood still at what he saw.

His mother stood directly in front of him, a few feet away

from the fence. Tears streamed down her face, falling harder and faster than Lance had ever seen. His mother did not cry, not that Lance could ever remember. He looked quickly over her shoulder and saw that the inside of the fence was empty, just the trees and headstones casting shadows in the soft moonlight. He looked back to his mother, opened his mouth to speak and found he couldn't.

"My boy," his mother said, her voice quivering against her tears, but also filled with ... was it happiness? "My sweet boy. Oh, what great things you'll do."

Lance stood, perplexed. "Mom, what—?"

"I am so proud of you. Always remember that," she said. Then: "Tonight is not the end." Then she smiled, reached up and kissed him on the cheek, her tears warm against Lance's skin. Their eyes met then as she pulled away, and Lance saw some final decision being made behind his mother's gaze. "I love you," she said.

And then she ran.

She bolted like a horse out of the gate, taking off away from Lance, leaving him standing alone in the grass by the fence. She ran hard and fast toward the crushed gravel lot and then kept going, back down White Birch. Lance looked on in stupefied awe and shock and disarming fear as he saw the Creamsicle bus plow forward, sprinting, eating up the short distance to the parking lot at a rapid speed, forty, maybe fifty miles an hour. And Lance knew what would happen next. The bus would reach the lot and jump the curb and spill out onto the grass, silhouetting Lance against the fence behind him. He'd stopped for too long, been too caught up in the moment. There was no way he'd outrun them now. They'd run him down in the grass, or they'd trap him against the fence, or ... whatever happened, he knew he was caught.

Then he looked back to his mother and was dismayed to see

her suddenly jerk to her right, darting out between the row of parked cars along the sidewalk and stepping out into the street.

"No!" Lance yelled with a voice he could barely find. A strangled cry that didn't even travel far enough for the people in the parking lot to hear.

Pamela Brody had timed it just right. She'd run down the street, keeping herself hidden behind the rows of cars, listening for the noise of the engine, watching the flash flash flash of the headlights filling the spaces between the cars. And then she'd made her move, jumping out in front of the Creamsicle bus as it barreled its way forward.

The Surfer hadn't even had time to hit the brakes. There was no squeal of tires—not until after. There was no blare from the horn, no sudden jerk of the steering wheel in a desperate attempt to avoid an accident.

The front end of the bus smashed into Pamela Brody's body with a noise that Lance would never forget, a crunching of metal and a smashing of glass and the sickening thud of a human body being thrown twenty feet through the air and landing in a crumpled heap on the asphalt.

Now the bus did stop, the tires screeching and the smell of burning rubber filling the air.

People all around, people who'd been diving out of the way and standing wide-eyed on the sidewalk and fleeing for their own safety, began to react. Lots of them screamed, male and female shouts echoing all around. Some fled, desperate not to get involved in whatever tragedy had happened. But others, most, reacted in a way that would later make Lance smile, would help him to remember the good in people at a time when he thought he would never see the good in anything again. They started to run *toward* the Creamsicle bus, which had come to a stop a few feet from Pamela's body, one headlight busted out, the engine purring softly as the vehicle sat motionless.

And that's when the realization of everything came crashing into Lance and he was jump-started again, spurred from his crippling disbelief at everything he'd just witnessed.

"Mom!" His voice was hot now and full with panic ... sadness. "Mom!"

He ran with everything he had toward his mother's body. Already people gathered around her, many of them on cell phones, all placing frantic 911 calls. An angry mob had formed around the bus, knocking on the windows and pulling angrily on the door handles, tugging and jerking and trying to get to whoever was inside and was responsible. The Reverend and the Surfer were now targets. Villains to the residents of Hillston.

And when Lance was within twenty yards of the scene, he saw the reverse lights switch on from the rear of the bus and watched with primal rage as the bus backed up, slowly at first, as a warning to all who might be standing in the way, and then with a quick burst of acceleration that sent people jumping and diving and scattering away. Lance watched in horror as one man had his foot run over. Another's shoulder was hit so hard by the bus's sideview mirror that he spun around like a top before collapsing to the ground in a cry of pain.

The two sheriff's deputies were both on their radios, shouting at whoever was listening on the other side of the connection, and as the bus began to execute another three-point turn and speed off down Route 411, they pulled up their pistols and fired off three or four shots in quick succession, aiming for tires.

They missed.

The bus drove off in a blur of speed, vanishing into the night.

And then Lance was at his mother's side, pushing people out of the way and collapsing on the street next to her.

"Mom," he said, emotions so strong and heavy in his heart he could literally find nothing else to say. "Mom..."

She was flat on her back, one arm bent awkwardly at the elbow. One of her legs twisted grotesquely out sideways. There was blood pouring from her forehead, dripping down her closed eyelids. It ran from her nostrils and spilled from her lips. She looked horrific.

But to Lance, she was still the most beautiful woman on earth. "Mom," he said again.

Pamela Brody's eyes flitted open, bloodshot and unfocused. But she saw him ... deep down, Lance knew she saw him. She coughed, blood bubbling in her throat, and offered a small smile. "Just enough time, Lance. You have just enough now."

There was shouting behind him and then a strong hand fell on Lance's shoulder, gripping it tightly. Lance jerked his head back, turned to find Mayor Marcus Johnston standing there, a look of sheer dismay spread across his face. The sheriff's deputies were on the group now, yelling at people to step back, to get away from the scene of the accident so paramedics could arrive and take over. There were protests, shouts, but Lance heard none of this. His turned back to his mother, found her eyes opened only to slits. She tried to speak, but the noise was barely a whisper. Lance leaned closer, cupping the back of her head with his hand and leaning so close he could still smell the scent of her shampoo and the sweet sugar from the funnel cake over the metallic stench of the blood.

And something his mother had said the day before, a mystery he could not let go unresolved, seemed all at once crucial. "Mom," he said, doing his best to stay strong. "What is it I have? What is it you said I have that they don't fully understand?"

Pamela Brody, despite her pain, despite her life fading from her, smiled. "You have me."

She coughed again, and Lance felt as if his heart had split in two.

"Go, Lance. It's only what's right," she said. Then, with one last breath, "I love you."

And she was gone.

An hour later, after the sheriff's deputies and the paramedics had controlled the crowd, and Marcus Johnston had helped Lance slip away unquestioned—after first tearing the young man away from his mother's lifeless body—Lance was sitting on the seat of a rattling charter bus, his backpack on the seat beside him, leaving his hometown behind.

Pamela Brody had sacrificed herself for Lance for reasons he did not—and perhaps would not—ever fully understand. But there were two things of which he was certain.

One, his mother had learned something from the spirits of the Great Hillston Cemetery. Something that had moved her enough to feel as though she needed to end her own life in order to prolong Lance's. "My sweet boy. Oh, what great things you'll do."

And two, the Reverend and the Surfer were not finished. Lance might have won this battle, but he was acutely aware that this was a war that had just gotten started.

Lancelot Brody, exhausted, drained, confused, devastated, empty, leaned his head back onto the headrest and found himself with no answer to anything other than to try and succumb to sleep. Succumb to the blackness, where hopefully nothing would chase him, and maybe, if he was lucky, he'd see his mother's smiling face again.

DARK GAME

(Lance Brody Series, Book 1)

[1]

His mother had always told him that a fresh slice of pie and a hot cup of tea were all any good soul needed to temporarily forget their problems. The type of pie and the flavor of tea were of no consequence. Fresh and hot, that was all that mattered.

For the first twenty-two years of his life, Lance Brody had shared many an evening in his family home's kitchen, crowded around the small table with his mother, eating her fresh pies and discussing the way of things. He'd never acquired the taste for tea, however, and preferred coffee for their long discussions. Black. His mother hated coffee, but his substitution of another hot beverage in place of the tea—instead of something from a bottle—seemed to satisfy her.

Alcohol was strictly forbidden in the house. If there was a familial reason for this, Pamela Brody had never told Lance. Nor was religion to blame; the only time Lance's mother ever prayed was when the Bulls were in a tight one with whichever NBA opponent they were competing against, and those prayers were directed at unseen basketball gods who inevitably cared little about an individual's libations. She had no affiliation with the team, nor the city of Chicago. When Lance had finally asked her why she had chosen the Bulls as her team, she'd simply replied that she liked their mascot. He was funny. Her love of basketball in general was a mystery to Lance, as she'd never played the sport herself, but it was the only organized activity she'd ever encouraged him to participate in throughout his entire upbringing. But the alcohol—she said it poisoned the mind and the body, and Lance could see no argument against that. He'd never tasted a drop of the stuff.

Not even on the night she'd died, when no pie seemed big enough and no coffee black enough to alleviate the pain.

He hadn't cried, not then, and not for most of his life. Crying was something his mother had been strangely against. Strange because of how much she'd stressed being at peace with oneself and understanding and trusting your feelings. She hadn't said this the way a condescending therapist might to an uncooperative husband, but in a way that suggested self-strength and confidence. It was what *you* felt inside, who *you* were that mattered in life. "Embrace yourself, Lance. Only then can you fully embrace others." He might have been eight when she'd first offered up this token of wisdom. A typical conversation to have with a second-grader. Typical was something his mother had never come close to achieving. She had been extraordinary. Not in the same ways Lance was extraordinary—wouldn't *that* have been helpful?—but in a way that allowed him the trust and confidence in her to share his world with her and have her love him and help him and stand by his side as he grew and developed in every way you could imagine, and in ways you couldn't.

But now she was dead and Lance was completely alone, stepping off a bus two hundred and thirty-seven miles away from home with the previous night's horrific events still burning fresh in his tired mind.

He had no plan. Hadn't had time for a plan. The bus was the first one headed out of his town, and he didn't care much where it was going. He'd had to leave, been forced to run.

Now he was here.

He was hungry.

Food was as good of a start to a plan as he could think of.

He didn't need to wait for the bus driver to haul his luggage from one of the holding bins along the bottom of the bus. Everything he'd been able to take with him from home was stuffed into his backpack—an expensive thing gifted to him by the owner of a local sporting goods store years ago, when Lance had helped him with a problem—and the backpack had remained in the seat next to him for the bus's entire trip. He adjusted the straps over his shoulders, turned and thanked the bus driver for getting them all to their destination safely—an act that was met with a confused expression and a mumbled reply that might have been "You're welcome"—and then headed across the street, through a large and mostly empty parking lot, and stopped briefly on the sidewalk.

He breathed in deeply and closed his eyes. Exhaled and opened them. Turned right and started walking, the soles of his basketball sneakers making gentle scraping sounds against the concrete. A warm breeze blew into his face, and a warmer sun was just rising above the horizon at his back. He walked with the traffic, the occasional vehicle slowly passing by on his left. The drivers all looked bored. Looked like they'd rather be anywhere else. It was Thursday morning, so Lance imagined that might surely be the case if they were all headed to a nine-to-five so they could pay the mortgage. *Well, that's* one *thing I don't have to worry about.*

He kept walking.

A mile later, after passing a small strip-mall and a McDonald's, he found what he'd been looking for. The momentary flit of happiness the sight caused him was so brief it might not have happened at all, just a teasing scent carried off by the wind before it could even be enjoyed.

Lance felt something pushing it away.

The diner was called Annabelle's Apron and looked like it might have been built before Nixon resigned. A rough shoebox of a place with a shiny aluminum front and lots of windows. The roofline looked to be sagging a bit, and there was no telling whether the bright neon signage atop it actually still had any juice left, but there were a few faces on the other side of the glass windows, and all of them were forking food or sipping coffee. Lance stepped off the curb, allowed a pickup truck to back out of a parking space, and then crossed the lot and pulled open the door.

The interior of Annabelle's Apron looked, sounded, and—most importantly—smelled exactly as Lance had hoped. Directly ahead was the long counter with a matching row of stools. A few folks seated there, elbows resting atop the counter as they read the morning paper while they ate. The windows were lined from end to end with booths, the upholstery a bright blue—robin's egg, that's what his mother would have called it—and the tabletops showed their age, full of cracks and streaks and blemishes. The battle scars of thousands of meals, tens of thousands of cups of coffee and tea and glasses of orange juice and soda pop. The air hummed and chimed with the noise of the kitchen crew working hard, glimpsed sporadically through the open window behind the counter. Two waitresses went to and fro from table to kitchen to table. Smiles plastered on and only a faint sheen of sweat on their brows so far. Hushed conversation and soft-playing country music from a lone over-head speaker were occasionally punctuated by the yelling of a young child in the rearmost booth—a location surely chosen as a strategy by its not-our-first-rodeo parents.

And all of this was accompanied by the smells of bacon and eggs and butter and coffee and biscuits.

Lance had been standing at the door for too long, and the woman behind the counter called out as she refilled a patron's coffee, "Sit anywhere you'd like, sweetie. Be right witcha."

He looked over his shoulder, back to the parking lot and the everything beyond it. Scanned the horizon. The sun was higher now, almost full-form. Then his stomach grumbled and he took a seat at the counter, setting his backpack at his feet and taking the laminated menu from the woman who'd told him to sit. The menu was smudged with grease and dried grape jelly, but the text was readable. Lance ordered four scrambled eggs, bacon, hash browns, and a large stack of pancakes. The woman behind the counter—early sixties, Lance guessed, and with a look of no-nonsense experience creased into her aged brow—looked him up and down one time before asking, "And to drink, sweetie?"

"Coffee, please," Lance said.

She nodded and tore the order ticket from the pad in her hand and turned to post it on the wheel in the window. She spun the ticket into the kitchen, where it was quickly snatched by a fleeting glimpse of a cook's hand, and then she returned with a black plastic coffee mug and poured from a full pot. "Just brewed this one, sweetie. You're its first." She winked and asked if he needed cream or sugar.

"No, thank you," Lance said, doing his best to smile.

"Margie, I'll take some of that," a gentleman—a regular, apparently—called from the end of the counter. The woman— now Margie—put a hand on her hip and said, "You've been tryin' to get some of this for twenty-three years, Hank Peterson. Today's not gonna be no different!" This got a chuckle out of Hank and the two other waitresses, and Margie went off to fill Hank's coffee.

Lance sat in silence, looking down at the counter and

listening to the sounds around him and sipping his coffee as he waited for his food. His mother had always said that diners were some of the greatest places on earth because everything was real —the food and the people. Honest Americans cooking good ol' American comfort food. The potential of diners always excited her, like each one was an individual mystery just waiting to be unraveled.

Margie refilled Lance's coffee.

His food arrived shortly after.

The bars on the stool were a little too high for him to comfortably rest his long legs—at six foot six, this was the type of problem he'd grown accustomed to—and he had to adjust himself repeatedly to keep his legs from falling asleep. But the coffee was strong and the food was delicious, and the general ambiance of the diner did its best to revive his spirits.

Margie cleared his plates when he'd finished. "I wasn't sure you'd be able to eat it all, t'be honest. Large stack usually fills up most folks."

Lance wasn't most folks.

"I don't suppose you'll be wantin' nothin' else?"

Lance was about to say no, but then paused. Said, "Do you serve pie?"

Margie laughed. "You kiddin'?"

"No, ma'am." Lance shrugged and smiled. "I have a high metabolism, I guess."

"We don't set it out till lunch, but I can get you a slice from the back. Apple okay?"

"Is it fresh?" Lance asked, feeling a twinge in his heart.

Margie smiled. "I bake 'em fresh every morning." Then she disappeared into the kitchen and came back a minute later with a large slice of apple pie on a tiny saucer. "That's bigger than a normal serving," she said. "Figured you could handle it."

Lance felt the warmth of the woman's kindness and smiled and nodded. "Yes, ma'am. Thank you very much."

He was halfway through his pie—it was fresh, as promised—when he noticed the woman sitting on the stool next to him. He wasn't sure when she'd arrived, but she was there now and looking directly at him.

"I used to put more cinnamon in it," she said. "I don't know why they cut back on it. It was much better that way if you ask me. I think it's too sweet now."

The woman looked much older than Margie, eighty at best but more likely closer to ninety. She wore a plain brown cotton dress and brown leather shoes, stockings visible on the bit of ankle that showed at the hem. Her hair was gray, but still thick, done up in a tight bun atop her head. Her face was so deeply wrinkled it was as if her skin were modeling clay, and somebody had dragged the tines of a fork up and down its entire surface.

"I don't think it's too sweet," Lance said, then turned to see if Margie was in earshot. "But I do think less sugar and more cinnamon would be an improvement."

The woman nodded once. "Of course it would." Then she was quiet for a while, staring ahead toward the kitchen window. Lance stared ahead with her, waiting. She spoke again, this time a little quieter, sadness creeping into her voice. "I don't know why the thing with the pie bothers me so much. They've kept things pretty much the same around here all these years, but the pie ... I was darn near famous for that pie. People used to come from two counties over for *my* pie, and then one day these floozies decide to up and change the recipe. Who do they think they are?"

Lance considered this, took his last bite. "Well," he said, "the folks that remember *your* pie, they're going to know that *this* pie isn't your fault. In fact, if it was as good as you say, those folks are probably just as disappointed as you."

She looked at him and smiled. Her teeth were yellowed, but mostly intact. "I suppose you're right, son. I suppose you're right. Guess I never thought of it like that." She pointed an arthritis-gnarled finger at him. "You'd have liked my pie. I know it."

"Yes, ma'am. I believe I would have."

Then they were quiet again. Margie cleared Lance's plate away and he declined more coffee. Hank Peterson paid his tab and left his newspaper when he was finished. The man two stools down took it and flipped to the sports section. The family with the loud child had left and been replaced by two high school–aged boys who looked sleepy, and Lance wondered why they weren't in class. Through the kitchen window, he could see one of the two waitresses counting her tips and joking with one of the unseen cooks.

"So," Lance said, turning to look at the woman on the stool next to him, "how bad is it here?"

The woman closed her eyes, almost as if she were fighting back tears. When she opened them, she suddenly looked very tired. "Bad," she said.

Lance nodded. "Yeah ... that's what I was afraid of."

"Are you going to help?"

"I don't know if I can."

"You don't believe that."

Lance placed a twenty on the counter, stood and grabbed his backpack. "No," he said. "But sometimes I wish I did."

He waved goodbye and thanked Margie and then headed for the door. He stopped. On the wall to the left of the door was a photograph in a rough wooden frame, yellowed with age. It was a picture of the woman who'd sat next to him, only in the photograph, she was behind the counter, holding a whole pie in her hands and putting on a small grin for the camera. Beneath the photograph was written:

Annabelle Winters
1905-1990

Lance turned and looked at the barstool where she'd been sitting, now empty. Then he took one last glance at the photo and pushed through the door, out into the world.

[2]

LANCE DIDN'T ALWAYS SEE THE DEAD. HIS WORLD WASN'T A
nightmare where he walked around all day amongst restless
souls and lingering spirits with unfinished business. He didn't
check out at the grocery store staring into the faces of demons.

But demons *were* real.

And he did see the dead. Not every day, but frequently.
Most were friendly, though often troubled. Others were not so
friendly. Annabelle Winters had been of the former variety,
despite her pie grievances, and her visit had had a clear meaning
that was nothing to do with pastries.

Lance continued west on the sidewalk. The traffic on the
road to his left diminished to only single vehicles passing by
with large spots of silence in between. He'd apparently left the
outskirts of town—where the strip malls and diner had been—
and made his way into what passed as downtown. It was a quiet,
tranquil setting—old-school, a place where you could imagine
Andy Griffith as sheriff, or Hallmark coming to town to film a
Christmas special. The street was lined with rows of brick
buildings with dull-colored awnings. Above the awnings, large
hand-painted sections of the brick exteriors—badly faded by the

sun and years of rain—advertised businesses and stores whose proprietors (and revenue) had surely died long ago. He glanced into a few of the windows on his right as he walked, saw a bakery, a small hardware store, a used bookstore, a lawyer's and a CPA's office side by side. A few faces stared back, eyes locked onto him as he passed. He couldn't blame them. He knew that in a town like this, newcomers would be easily spotted. Especially ones as large as he. He tried to smile, hoped he'd succeeded.

He kept walking. Passed more businesses and crossed side streets before downtown finally spat him out onto an intersection of two rural routes that stretched off into land beginning to show signs of residential development and larger industrial buildings. He crossed the main road and headed south. The sidewalk wasn't as well maintained here, and his sneakers kicked up stray rocks and chunks of concrete as he went. Weeds grew through cracks. The sun was getting hot, and his t-shirt began to stick to the small of his back. A half mile later, he stopped. Ahead he could see where the sidewalk finally died and bled into grass, and a memory flashed in his head of his mother reading to him from Shel Silverstein's *Where the Sidewalk Ends*. He enjoyed the image briefly before storing it away.

He stepped off the sidewalk and walked into a crumbling parking lot with only a handful of cars that could be called clunkers at best. He'd found what he'd been looking for.

Another telltale sign of a small town is that a lot of things are named after their owners. Annabelle's Apron was the first example, and now Lance stood in front of Bob's Place. An L-shaped one-story museum of a building whose sign—medium-sized and, again, hand-painted—advertised simply: ROOMS. BAR. The office was at the far end of the longer segment of the L, and the rest of the structure was punctuated with eleven blue doors that had once likely been deep and royal, but now more resembled the light (robin's egg) blue of the diner's tables. A Coke machine hummed at the L's intersection, an ice machine with the words *Out of Order* written across its door standing silently at its side. Window A/C units drooped from next to each room's door, only one of which was buzzing and rattling in the window frame as it worked. Two modern satellite dishes were mounted on the roof above the door to the office.

Lance checked the license plates on the few cars parked in the lot as he headed toward the office. Found all but one to be in-state. The lone exception was from Alaska. Alaskan plates always seemed very foreign, Lance found, considering you had to drive through a whole other country to get from Alaska to the forty-eight.

Large trees loomed from behind the building, the perimeter of what appeared to be deep forest. He grabbed the handle of the office's glass door and pushed. A small bell mounted above the door frame jingled loudly as he did so, and he was instantly overwhelmed with the smell of lemon—some sort of cleaning product that had been applied so heavily he felt like he'd stepped into a bottle of Pine-Sol. He coughed once and his eyes began to water, blurring his vision.

"Oh my goodness, I'm so sorry! I wasn't expecting anyone so early!" a female voice, high and pleasant and young, called from somewhere ahead. Lance used the sleeve of his t-shirt and wiped his eyes, then breathed in heavily through his mouth. When his throat stopped burning and his vision began to clear, he was genuinely surprised at what he saw.

The outside of the building suggested that the office's interior would be run-down at best. At worst, it might have had hourly rates posted on a sign beside a pane of bulletproof glass, which the desk attendant would sit behind and take wads of cash through a sliding metal drawer and immediately forget any faces seen coming or going.

In actuality, the office was immaculate. The floor was a freshly polished (maybe it *was* Pine-Sol) wood whose color matched an elegant front desk that ran along the short left wall. Centered on the right-hand wall, a large television was mounted above an entertainment center with a satellite receiver sitting on top, along with a large tray full of various neatly arranged liquor bottles. Six small glasses and a small ice bucket with tongs filled the rest of surface, nearly sparkling in the overhead lighting. An old but inviting leather couch provided seating. Lance looked at the liquor for moment (*It poisons the mind and the body*) and then over to the front desk, behind which stood a girl whose beauty was as elegant as the office itself. "Is that the bar?" he asked, pointing to the entertainment center.

The girl smiled, a grin that suggested she wanted to laugh, but her professionalism kept it inside. "It is."

Lance made a show of looking around the office—heck, you could go ahead and call it a lobby—and then shrugged. "Not what I imagined."

The girl's smile was still there, but now it was her turn to shrug and say, "I could say the same thing."

"About the bar?"

"About you."

Lance left the door and made his way to the desk. His left sneaker squeaked and nearly slipped out from under him on his first step. He caught his balance before going down, and the girl behind the desk said, "Careful! Again, sorry. I would have put out the wet floor sign, but like I said, I wasn't expecting anybody at this time of morning."

Lance carefully stepped across the floor and then rested his hands on the desk, a gesture he hoped would show that he meant her no harm, wasn't about to pull a gun or blade and demand whatever it was she could offer. Now that he was closer, he could see the girl was his age at the most, maybe a bit younger.

"But I thought you said you were imagining me."

"I'm sorry?"

"A second ago. You said I wasn't what you'd imagined. Why were you imagining me if you weren't expecting me?" *And why are you flirting, Lance?*

Because I've had a really terrible and really long couple of days and it feels good to have a normal conversation with a pretty girl.

He finished justifying himself to himself just in time to hear the girl give off a soft laugh, and watched as her stiff and professional façade crumbled and she visibly relaxed. "I wasn't expecting exactly you, exactly today. I just meant you aren't exactly the type of guest we usually get."

"And what type of guest do you think I am ... exactly?"

She shrugged. "Normal."

Well, that's exactly *where you're wrong, my dear.* "How so?" he asked.

She rolled her eyes. "Look around. Do we look like the type of place nice wholesome folks stop for the night? Families on vacation? Businessmen en route to a conference? No. The folks I give keys to are usually weathered and beaten. Down on their luck and satisfied with the first roof they can find over their head for the night before they wake up and head off to wherever else life plans on shitting on them. They drink, they do drugs—sometimes they deal drugs, and trust me when I say I'm not afraid to call the police if I suspect that's going down. I've got a shotgun under the counter and Daddy taught me how to use it when I was ten."

Lance held her eyes as she spoke. He was entranced by her confidence and honesty.

"Now you," she said, "you've got baggage, I know that.

Otherwise you'd have hitched a ride another twenty miles down Route 19 like everyone else and got a room at the Holiday Inn Express or the Motel 6. But whatever your baggage is, you carry it well. You're clean, you're handsome, and your clothes aren't tattered and falling apart. That logo on your backpack means it cost more than most people who stay here probably make in two weeks' time, so you've either got, or had, a steady job. Or somebody gave it to you—because I don't think you'd steal it. You just don't have the look. And if somebody gave it to you, it means you've got friends. And trust me, the last thing somebody who stays here has is a single friend in the world."

When she finished speaking, she reached back and tightened the hair tie holding her blond ponytail in place and then adjusted the collar of her black dress shirt. She wore matching black dress pants that were sleek and formfitting. Her makeup was light and simple. Blue eyes that pierced. Lance was impressed with her powers of observation. She wasn't completely right about him—and honestly, nobody would ever be. Unless there were others like him, which he deep down believed there had to be, the Surfer and the Reverend having all but proven this—but she'd come close.

Instead of confirming or denying any of her analysis of him, he turned and spread his hands out, gesturing at the immaculate and upscale look of the office. "Then why all this, if your guests are of the class you say they are?"

She responded instantly, and almost defensively. As if she'd been asked this question before and was tired of some underlying accusation. "Because if I have the chance to be a bright spot in their otherwise dark days, it's my responsibility as a respectable human being to be just that. I can make them feel comfortable. I can let them enjoy some nicer things, even if just for an evening. Most of these folks, despite everything I just said about them, at their core, they're still nice people. The rest of the world has just stopped giving them a chance."

Lance was floored at the size of this girl's heart but worried about her potential ignorance to the evil in the world. "And if they're really not nice at their core?" he asked.

She shrugged. "The shotgun, remember?"

Lance said he did remember, and suddenly he felt very tired. The night-long bus ride—which he'd stayed awake for, staring out the window at nothing but passing cars and expanses of field and trees—was finally catching up to him, and the burst of energy the food from the diner had provided was wearing off. Lance explained this to the girl, not wanting to appear rude and bored with talking to her, and he asked if he could have a room. She said it was twenty dollars a night and gave him the key to room one, which was right next door to the office. He gave her a twenty and thanked her. He turned to leave and then stopped.

This girl was extremely honest and seemed to have an adept ability to read people—and maybe situations. "Hey, listen," he said, knowing his question was going to sound weird, but also knowing this was his best chance of making his job a little easier. "You live here? In town, I mean."

She looked at him for a moment, eyes searching for a meaning to his question, before she finally nodded once.

Lance took a breath and said, "Do you think there's anything bad going on? Like ... I don't know," (*Don't say it, Lance. Don't say it.*) "Evil?" Then quickly, "I mean, you know, like ... anything out of the ordinary been happening lately?"

She didn't move, just stared at him for what felt like an hour. Then she finally reached behind the desk and (*Oh God, she's going to pull the shotgun on me*) brought out a newspaper. She held it out to him. "I almost forgot, all guests receive a complimentary paper at check-in." Lance stepped forward and reached for it, and when his hand touched it, she leaned forward and whispered, "Come back here tonight at eight. Daddy works graveyard, so he won't make a surprise visit. We can talk then." Then she stood, straightened her shirt and said, "I hope you enjoy your stay."

Lance took the paper and was still processing the girl's words as he made his way to the door. He turned back. "Hey, what's your name?"

"Leah," she said.

"I'm Lance," he said, then walked through the door and out onto the sidewalk.

He'd taken two steps when he stopped dead and sucked in a quick, deep breath. He staggered back a step. He closed his eyes and concentrated hard as the cold feeling tried to bury itself in his chest. It didn't last long, but the gloomy feeling that accompanied the moment lingered in the air. Lance opened his eyes and looked around at the parking lot, then out to the road. Turned his head up and looked to the sky, still bright and clear.

It knew he was in town. It knew what he was.

[3]

THE ELEGANCE AND UPKEEP FROM THE MOTEL'S OFFICE didn't make its way to the guest rooms, but it was still better than Lance was expecting. Not that he really would have cared either way, but still, being comfortable never hurt.

The room was small, and dark because of the heavy curtain drawn across the window. Some sunlight shining in would have helped to erase the gloomy feel, but Lance planned on sleeping some if he could, and he definitely didn't want any peering eyes looking in on him. A double bed was centered on the left wall, its headboard plain and chipped. The bed was neatly made, and the comforter, though worn and faded and thin, appeared clean enough. The carpet had been vacuumed recently, because the tracks were still visible, and either the small nightstand and TV table had been wiped down in the past few days, or the room was oddly devoid of dust. The television was a small, unimpressive flat-screen—something off the clearance rack at a discount electronics store, or a Black Friday special used to reduce some dead inventory—and beneath it was a basic satellite receiver, an ominous blue circle glowing from its center. The devices looked like something brought back from the future compared to the rest of the room's décor.

Lance gently set his backpack on the bed and checked the bathroom, switching on the light from outside the door and peeking in. The fixtures were old and chipped and had stopped shining years ago, but he could smell disinfectant and bleach and didn't see any visible signs of soap scum or mildew or, well ... urine or feces. It was always good not to see urine or feces. They could dampen a mood really quick.

He used the toilet and then washed his hands, unwrapping the mini bar of soap next to the hot water knob and finding that it had nearly no smell at all. But it would clean—that was soap's job, after all. Smelling nice was just a bonus. He avoided looking at himself in the mirror, not ready to face how terrible he might look after the past couple days.

Hey, Leah said you were handsome.

Yeah, but she also thought I was normal.

He went back to the bedroom and double-checked that the door was locked and then secured the chain. He stole a quick glance out the window, finding only the same parking lot with the same cars, and then pulled the curtain shut tight and lay down on the bed. The pillow was soft and smelled like detergent—something off-brand, bought in bulk for cheap, but better than nothing. He closed his eyes, took two big, heavy breaths, and tried to drift off to sleep.

He couldn't.

How could he?

His past few days had been a whirlwind that had resulted in him having to flee the town where he'd been born and raised, the town he'd loved his whole life. And his mother ... *tragedy* seemed too weak a word. He tried to push out the images of their last few moments together, but it was impossible. With the realization she was gone surfacing once again, and the sadness filling him from the inside out—his own sadness this time, not the looming threat of an outside presence—Lance clasped his hands behind his head and looked around the tiny dark motel room, feeling more alone than he'd ever imagined was possible. Alone and carrying a burden that even now he still didn't fully understand.

He missed her. Loved her.

But still, he did not cry.

He closed his eyes again and tried to focus. Tried to concentrate on the one thing he could right now that would keep his mind busy and dispel—if only temporarily—his sorrow.

The dead didn't show themselves to him for friendly social visits. He'd yet to have one appear and invite him to a barbecue or tell him that his hair looked nice. They came with a purpose. Lance suspected that showing themselves to him required a great deal of energy—whatever great unseen force somehow governed their celestial world—and they would not go to such efforts without sufficient cause. They usually came for two reasons: to warn him, or to ask for help. Though Lance supposed the two usually went hand in hand, as the warnings in turn required him to take action.

Annabelle Winters's appearance was no different.

He'd felt it when he'd gotten off the bus. After he'd crossed the terminal's parking lot and stood on the sidewalk trying to figure out which way he wanted to go, he'd felt that ping of evil. There was no other way to explain it. Evil could not remain undetected by those attuned to the frequencies along which it traveled, and Lance, despite his best wishes, was more attuned than most. There was something bad lurking in this town, something that had taken root and would continue to blacken what it touched until there was no more to feed on, or until somebody stopped it.

Lance sighed heavily on the bed, adjusted the pillow

beneath his head. Most of his friends from high school had gone off to college, graduated, and were in the beginning stages of starting a family. Nice jobs in big cities. Friday nights on the town with new friends. Golfing and running 5Ks and spending lazy mornings on the couch with girlfriends and fiancées on the weekends. And here he was, by himself in a dingy motel in a forgotten sleepy town, getting ready to try and "crack the case," as they say, battle the forces of evil, and probably end up getting himself killed in the process.

And nobody would ever know or care.

He sighed again and rolled over onto his side, stared at the locked door and wondered what was outside, what was waiting for him. He longed for golfing and 5Ks. Longed for a taste of normalcy.

Instead, he feared a fresh, unknown evil. Was terrified to look out the window and find a Volkswagen bus the color of a Creamsicle waiting for him.

He glanced at the newspaper he'd set on the nightstand, was about to reach for it and stopped. Through the paper-thin wall behind him came a soft singing. A slow tune that sounded both beautiful and sad, soothing.

Leah, he thought. *She thinks I'm handsome.*

She continued on with the song, this girl who thought he was normal, her voice imperfect but sweet. Lance didn't know how long she went on, because he finally drifted off to sleep.

[4]

GO, LANCE. IT'S ONLY WHAT'S RIGHT. I LOVE YOU.

Lance gasped and jumped up from the bed, his mother's last words to him still echoing faintly in his mind as the dream faded and the room took shape before him. He'd dreamed of that night, the one so fresh it was still cooling, the one where he'd lost his mother and had fled. The night that had ultimately brought him here. Bob's Place.

Leah.

He listened, trying to pick up any signs of her. The singing that had lulled him to sleep was gone, as were all other noises from the other side of the wall. The motel room was darker, the sun having shifted across and beyond his window, leaving only a dim strip of gray light to come through the crack between curtain and wall.

Come back here tonight at eight, Leah had told him. *Daddy works graveyard.*

The fact there was still light outside at all told Lance he'd not missed his deadline, but he had no idea how long he'd slept. He unzipped the side pocket of his backpack and retrieved the pay-as-you-go cell phone he'd had for years. A black plastic flip phone, the device had been a gift from his mother. She'd purchased one for herself as well, a matching one that they often had gotten mixed up, and her number was one of only a handful Lance had programmed into his phone's memory. As he flipped open the screen, he suddenly had two very conflicting thoughts collide in terms of what he should do with her stored number. Part of him, the first part to show its face, said to delete it. It was of no use to him anymore and would only be a painful reminder of her absence every time he scrolled past it. The second part, the one a split second slower to reach him but carrying a seemingly more powerful suggestion, told Lance to call the number. Let it ring the four rings that would go unanswered before switching to voicemail and letting Lance hear his mother's voice again.

(Hi! *It seems our paths weren't meant to cross right now. I can't wait to talk to you soon!*)

Lance's mother hadn't asked people to leave a message. She had always been of the mindset that information reached her when it was meant to reach her, and that if she'd missed somebody's phone call, the conversation—and thus the information—could wait. Lance had told her this was ridiculous—as he'd said of a lot of the things she'd suggested over the years—but the tenet had never seemed to cause any trouble for her or him, so ... what did Lance know?

(*I can't wait to talk to you soon!*)

Lance would never talk to her again.

Conflicted, and with the wound still open, he did nothing with his mother's number and simply checked the time. It was almost seven o'clock. He knew that he'd been tired—the long sleepless night catching up with him—but he was surprised he'd managed to sleep the whole day. The way he was feeling, he wouldn't have been surprised to discover he'd never get a full night's rest again.

He was hungry, but with only an hour to spare, he decided to investigate the (what he guessed to be) one clue Leah had so subtly given him. He'd been nearly out of the motel's office when he'd questioned her thoughts on any bad happenings in town, and her response had been to hand him a newspaper. She had told him to come back to the office at eight, but she could have done that without the newspaper. Lance glanced at it, sitting neatly on the nightstand next to him. *There's something in there*, he thought. *There's something in there that'll help me.*

He revisited the bathroom, washed his hands, and then turned on the small lamp on the nightstand. The bulb gave off a quick, loud buzz and then died. Lance sighed. He didn't want to switch on the main overhead light. Call it paranoia, but a light that bright would be more visible from the outside. Say, to somebody across the street looking for signs of life in one of Bob's Place's rented rooms. And though he had nothing to go on except that feeling he'd been hit with upon first exiting the motel's office hours ago, Lance was almost positive somebody would, eventually, start looking for him. *Join the club*, he thought.

Lance walked across the room, the outside light fading quickly, and unscrewed one of the three bare bulbs installed in the light fixture above the bathroom sink. He used it to replace the fried bulb in the lamp, then pulled the pillowcase off one of the bed's two pillows and draped it over the lampshade to further dampen the light. Satisfied, he sat with his back against the cheap headboard and picked up the paper. The first thing he noticed was the date. It was from last week. He started reading the first headline.

Forty-five minutes later, he'd finished the paper. He'd read the whole thing, front to back, then neatly refolded each section and reassembled the paper to the extent that it looked as if it'd never been read at all. He stared down at the front page again, his eyes darting all over the headlines and the smaller text beneath each, picking out words and phrases and desperately searching for something he might have missed.

He'd read the entire paper, ads and all, and had seen nothing—felt nothing—about any of the articles that appeared to be cause for alarm. Of course, he knew that the workings of evil would often go undetected. It wasn't as if he'd expected a headline to scream out BAD PERSON DOES BAD THING! PLEASE HELP US, LANCE! But he figured he had a better eye (and a better gut feeling) than most when it came to reading between the lines about these sorts of things. Plus, Leah had given him the paper for a reason. He knew that as well as he knew his name was Lancelot Brody, so the fact that this girl had seen something he hadn't bothered him. Somewhere in these thousands of words on these sheets of paper was a starting point for him, and he was blind to it.

"Oh well," he said out loud to the room, choosing not to dwell on the issue. Because he had another way to get his answer, you see. Lance was gifted, but he wasn't too proud to admit needing help. "I'll just ask her." His voice was groggy and sounded weird bouncing off the motel's walls. He cleared his throat and stood, stretching and giving off a big yawn. He ran his tongue across his teeth and the roof of his mouth, wished he could brush his teeth. He'd have to go shopping soon. He had nothing but what was in his pockets and his backpack, which didn't amount to much in terms of daily living. He didn't even have deodorant or a clean pair of boxer shorts.

He checked the time on his phone. Ten minutes till eight. He went to the bathroom, which was now thirty-three percent gloomier thanks to his lightbulb excavation, and ran the cold water from the tap. He splashed his face and then dried it with the small hand towel. He finally braved a look in the mirror and saw that he wasn't too bad off. He could use a shave, and he had bedhead—both from the bus's seat and the bed's pillow—but otherwise he looked okay. He searched the countertop for a mini bottle of mouthwash but was disappointed. There was only the bar of soap and the hand towel. He supposed Leah and her father (*Daddy works graveyard*) could only stretch the budget but so far.

The two remaining bulbs above the sink flickered, once, twice, then remained fully lit. Lance stopped moving and looked ahead into the mirror, listened. He heard nothing but the weak hum of the bulbs and saw nothing but his own reflection staring back at him.

It's nothing.

He switched off the bathroom light and went back to the bedroom, grabbing his backpack in one hand and the newspaper in the other. He swung the pack's strap over one shoulder and made his way to the door, unlocked the handle and unlatched the chain. He pulled the door open a crack and peered out.

The sun had mostly set, and only the faintest traces of dusk still remained, the night air looking pallid and the deepest of grays. Single bulbs inside cracked plastic domes were mounted above the doorway of each of the motel's rooms, but the light they offered was laughable. Lance could see the glow of light from the office's door falling from his right and it cast long shadows on the sidewalk outside his door and into the parking lot. The lot itself was almost entirely deserted. The car from Alaska had moved on, and only two other vehicles remained, a battered green Ford pickup with a rusted-out bumper and a faded blue Jeep Cherokee with expired tags and a stuffed Garfield the cat clinging to its passenger-side window.

Lance looked through the crack and across the street, where a lone streetlight stood high like a sentinel, its branch-thin pole arching over the road and casting a dome of orange-yellow light.

There was no traffic. Not a single car going either direction, nor any to be heard approaching.

Small town, Lance thought. *Some good, some bad. Just like people.*

He opened the door the remainder of the way and stepped outside. The air had cooled considerably, and he shivered once as his body adjusted to the temperature change. He pulled the door securely shut behind him and patted his pocket to verify he had the key. He turned right, about to take the two steps—two for Lance, three or four for average folks—needed to reach the motel's office and get his question answered.

The streetlight across the road flickered.

The single bulb above his room's door went out entirely with a loud *crack!*

And then a long gust of wind, strong and unexpected and unexplained, *whooshed* across the parking lot like a tidal wave, rocking the two cars on their axles before slamming into Lance. His body was flung backward like he weighed nearly nothing, and his head snapped back, smashing into his room's door with the sound of a heavy knock. Stars peppered his vision before fading, fading along with everything else as the gray evening sky began to allow the blackness to creep in from the sides and swallow everything in sight.

Lance slid down the door and landed hard on his rear, toppled over onto his side.

The newspaper fell from his hand, its pages scattering like buckshot across the parking lot and out into the street and the field beyond.

Then the wind stopped completely and the night was as still as before. Not even a gentle breeze to rustle the leaves remained.

[5]

HE WAS BACK AT ANNABELLE'S APRON. HE SAT ALONE AT THE counter, no other stools occupied and none of the tables either. The music that'd played from the single speaker was no longer humming a tune, and the smell of bacon had been replaced with something rancid, spoiled. Something like rotting meat. The lights were dim, the air was still. He turned in his stool and tried to look out the windows but found nothing except a solid pane of static, like a television channel that refused to tune in correctly. He turned back around, and when his arms slid across the countertop, he saw that he'd smeared a thick layer of dust, creating one arm of an incomplete snow angel. It was if the diner had been deserted for years.

"Don't let a little bump on the head scare you off."

Lance spun back around and found Annabelle Winters sitting in one of the booths by the windows of static. She looked out, as if seeing everything Lance couldn't, and then turned to face him. "It would only come after you if it thought you were a threat."

"What is it?" Lance tried to say, but he was interrupted by a voice coming over the speaker above.

122

(Lance!)

He looked up, saw a black sky in place of the diner's ceiling tiles.

(Lance!)

He looked back to the booth were Annabelle had been sitting and saw—

Leah grabbed him by the shoulders and did her best to sit him up. "Lance, can you hear me? Are you okay?"

He felt her fingers dig into the meat of his upper arms as she used all her strength to push him forward. His head swam at the change of direction, the parking lot going in and out of focus and the cars doing a little jitterbug on the asphalt. He closed his eyes and took two deep breaths. Opened them. The cars had stopped dancing and his vision was mostly back to normal. But the back of his head was throbbing and he had a headache that produced a sharp stab of pain at the base of his skull with each beat of his heart.

He looked to his right and painfully tilted his head up. Leah, same outfit from earlier, only now he noticed she was wearing black Nike sneakers. Maybe she'd been wearing them all day—a touch Lance liked—or maybe she'd changed out of dressier shoes once she knew peak hours were past and she was ready to slow things down for the day. Lance mentally scolded himself for so easily getting sidetracked. Leah's choice of shoes was officially the least of his concerns at the moment.

"I assume you can hear me?" she said, hands now on her hips.

Lance nodded. "Yes."

"So are you going to answer me? Are you okay, or do I need to call an ambulance?"

Lance took another deep breath and then slowly pushed himself off the sidewalk outside his room and stood. His surroundings did another half jitter but then remained focused.

With him standing at his full six-six height, Leah looked very small so close to him. He took a step back so as to not intimidate her. "Yes. I'm okay." He rolled his head on his shoulders, his neck making one sharp cracking sound. "I've got a headache, but otherwise I think I'm fine."

Leah's stature relaxed a little, and she blew a wisp of loose hair out of her face. "Thank God. I really didn't want to have to bring an ambulance out here. We get a bad enough rap as it is." She leaned to the side and looked at the back of his head. "Yeah, nice goose egg back there. What happened, anyway?"

Lance reached a hand up and gingerly touched the back of his head, felt the lump that'd formed, and then looked across the street. The streetlight was glowing strong. A small coupe drove along the road and then was out of sight. Lance nodded toward the office. "Let's go inside. Then we can talk."

Leah glanced across the street. Something like fear flickered in her eyes and then it was gone. "Okay." She turned and pulled open the door to the office. When they were both inside, she drew the blinds down across the glass and locked the deadbolt.

"What if somebody needs to check in?" Lance asked.

Leah walked to the window next to the door and flicked a switch attached to a small neon sign that advertised NO VACANCY. It burned a dull red behind the set of blinds she then pulled down over it.

"That's false advertising," Lance said. He tried to grin, but found the motion caused more pain in his head.

"Daddy'd be pissed to hell and back if he found out I did that," Leah said. "But what he doesn't know won't hurt him. So long as I get it switched off by morning."

"What if he gets sick on the job, decides to go home early and stops by here to check on things?"

Leah thought about it a moment, then continued, "Daddy

hasn't taken a sick day as long as I can remember. I don't expect him to start now."

Lance shrugged.

"Do you need some ice?" Leah was already moving toward the entertainment center with the wet bar on top. She looked around at what she had to work with, shook her head, and then said, "Be right back," and disappeared through the door at the rear of the room. She was back a minute later with a dish towel. She pulled three ice cubes from the stainless-steel bucket beneath the television and wrapped them in the towel. Motioned for Lance to sit. He walked over to the leather couch and slowly eased himself onto it. This time everything in his sight stayed where it was supposed to. *I guess that means no permanent damage done.*

Leah stood in front of him and held out the homemade ice pack. "Might get a little wet, but it's all I've got."

Lance took it. "Thanks." He leaned back into the couch's leather and used his right hand to hold the ice against the back of his head. It was cold—too cold—but felt good all the same. Leah was still standing in front of him, watching his every move. They remained that way, looking at each other in silence for a full minute before she finally said, "Well?"

Lance glanced down to her sneakers. "I like your shoes," he said.

"You wha...?" Leah looked down to her feet, then glanced at Lance's basketball shoes, as if maybe he was making fun of her.

"I like it when girls wear nice-looking sneakers," Lance said, reassuring her. "Makes them seem more laid-back, in my opinion."

She looked at him for another moment, and Lance could see her trying to conjure up some sort of response. She finally settled on, "You were going to tell me what happened?"

Lance shifted in his seat. "Oh, yeah, sure. Can you sit down, please? You're hovering over me and it's making me nervous."

"*I'm* making *you* nervous? I'm a small young girl all by myself with a big stranger of a man."

Lance respected her caution but didn't completely buy it. "If you thought I was dangerous, I wouldn't be here right now. And"—he pulled the ice pack from his head and showed it to her, melting ice dripping onto his cargo shorts—"I wouldn't have this."

Leah didn't move.

"Face it," Lance said, "you've got a special intuition about people. You know I'm one of the good guys. Just like I know that I can trust you."

Then she smiled, and Lance was taken aback by how cute she really was. "How do you know you can trust me?"

Lance wanted to tell her that he could practically feel the good energy that came off her, touch the honesty she had in her heart. "When I asked if you thought anything bad was going on around here, you invited me back, and you gave me that newspaper. Which, I regret to inform you, I lost when I had my accident outside."

Leah didn't respond to his explanation of trust, but she did move and sit on the other end of the couch, leaning against the arm and pulling her knees up to her chin so she could face him. Apparently Bob's Place wasn't strict about no shoes on the furniture. "Which you still haven't told me about. What happened to you out there? All the lights in here dimmed, and then I heard a bulb explode outside. When I looked out, you were on the ground and down for the count."

Lance continued to hold the ice pack to the back of his head, water dripping down the back of his neck and down his shirt. He shivered as the icy droplets snaked down his spine. He tried to figure out how much of the truth he wanted to tell Leah. In his brief time with her, she seemed more levelheaded than most folks, but Lance's hard-to-explain abilities were more than even the most open-minded and trusting types of people could usually accept. In fact, it was those who were, in society's eyes, less deserving of respect and trust that usually found Lance's gifts to be a matter of fact instead of fiction. Few people had ever learned the truth about him, but that small group had been diverse enough for him to be able to form this clear divide of understanding.

Which group did Leah fall into?

If she believed him—either completely, or partially—she could prove to be a valuable asset. He would never expect, nor want her to get involved if things had the potential to be dangerous—which, after the violent gust of wind, he was pretty sure things would be—but she could be helpful in other ways. She was a local, and a local would have the type of knowledge he might need, and would know where to go to find other answers. If she trusted him and they worked together, he might be able to cleanse—*Cleanse? Who are you, that little woman from* Poltergeist?—this town of whatever evil had found its way here more quickly than if he were at it alone, and then he could get back to—

Get back to what, Lance? What exactly are you going to do? Where are you going to go?

—figuring out what his next move would be. Figuring out the rest of his life. His life alone.

If Leah chose not to believe him, she would think he was just a kook. She would remove him from the safe harbor category of "normal" guests she'd so quickly placed him in and drop him right down into the pit of the "typical" guests Bob's Place was accustomed to. She would understand why he was drifting. She would understand why he'd chosen to stay at Bob's Place instead of making his way another twenty miles to the Holiday

Inn. She'd think him a loser. Just another crazy person passing through who'd never amount to anything and should have an eye kept on them at all times. She'd might ask him to leave. Throw him out. And then he'd be all—

Where will I go?

—alone again with just his expensive backpack and his troubled mind and his dead mother's voicemail greeting to keep him company.

She won't do that. She's more like you than not. She's one of the good ones.

The ice was almost completely melted now, the dish towel just a soppy mess with a few small ice chips left over. Lance stood, his vision solid but his headache no better, and placed the wet towel inside one of the small glasses atop the entertainment center. Leah's eyes never left him as he moved. He sat back down and turned to lean against the other arm of the couch, so that the two of them were able to face each other comfortably. He got situated, took a long, heavy breath, and said, "You can ask all the questions you want, but it might be easier if you just let me finish first before you do. Is that okay?"

Leah's brow crinkled, apparently confused at the depths to which the conversation appeared to be diving. But there was no apprehension in her voice when she quickly answered, "Okay. I can do that. Promise."

So he told her.

He told her the condensed version of why he was different. Told her a couple stories from the past—the less dangerous type of stories—showing her how his talents had been used to help people, and some humorous tales of how he'd used them to help himself. She'd laughed at these, but he could see the gears turning behind her eyes, could see her brain scrambling frantically, trying to decipher what exactly it was she was hearing, probably wondering if this was all a dream.

He did not tell her that he occasionally saw ghosts, or spirits, or worse. That part was always the kicker, always the part where even the ones who'd begun to trust him finally held up their hands and said they'd heard enough. If the time came, and it was needed, then he'd tell her.

He also did not tell her two mysterious and powerful men (*Are they really men?*) were after him. Hunting him.

He finished talking, and Leah was quiet for a moment. She looked absently around the office, eyes darting from place to place as she thought. Finally, her eyes found his again and she said, "So ... you're like a psychic?"

"A little."

"Or maybe ... clairvoyant?"

"Sort of."

"You've got, like, a sixth sense?"

"Maybe more than six. I'm a lot of things, honestly. I don't fully understand it myself."

"How do you sleep at night?"

"In a bed, usually." He knew the joke was dumb, and sure enough, it fell flat. Leah looked at him for a moment, not realizing at first he was attempting to be funny, lighten the mood a bit after his speech. Finally, a small grin twitched her lips, and she reiterated, "No, seriously, how do you sleep with all that going on?"

He nodded. "It's not always easy ... but ... think of me like a radio, okay? I can sort of ... switch on and off, or not tune into certain channels unless I want to. Sometimes things tune in *for* me, but that's not an everyday thing."

Leah nodded, trying desperately to understand.

"But," Lance continued, "things can also tune into me. I guess ... I guess I sort of broadcast my own signal all the time, and other ... things can pick up on it. And that's not always good."

And a realization lit up Leah's face. "And that's what happened outside?"

Smart girl. Smart, smart girl.

"Yes. That's what happened outside." Lance told her about the strong sense of dread he'd been picking up since he arrived in town, then added the bit about feeling as though whatever evil was present had noticed him (picked up his signal) and was concerned. "It knows I'm here, and it knows I can feel it. It's worried I'll intervene with whatever it's got its teeth into around here." He told her about the flickering lights, and then the gust of wind that'd knocked him out.

"It can control the weather?" Leah had asked, eyes wide.

Lance thought about it. "Yeah, maybe."

Leah was quiet for another moment, deep in thought. When she came back to the present, she said, "So, you're kind of trapped in between, aren't you? You're here, with all the rest of us, but it's like you've also got one foot on the other side—wherever that is—right?"

Lance thought about the analogy. "I don't know if I have a whole foot on the other side, maybe just a toe or two, but yes. I'd say that's accurate."

Leah's expression had turned to one of pure excitement and fascination now. "Do you have any idea how you got to be this way?"

"My mother had a theory," he said. "But forget about that for now. I've done a lot of talking. Tell me what you think is wrong in this town."

So she did.

[6]

"You lost the newspaper I gave you?" Leah asked, mocking heartbreak.

Lance grinned, and a streak of pain bolted through the back of his head. "Sadly, yes. I would have gone after it, but, well ... I was unconscious."

"I suppose you think that's an excuse." Leah got up from the couch and walked back to the check-in counter.

"My mother never allowed excuses," Lance said. "So it's merely a fact. Conscious awareness or not, the paper is gone and I was the last to have it in my possession. Hold it against me if you want."

Leah crouched behind the counter, disappearing from view. Lance could hear her rummaging through whatever lay behind the wooden panels. "Daddy doesn't particularly care for excuses either," she said, "though I doubt he and your mom had similar parenting styles." She popped back up and triumphantly held a newspaper above her head, like she'd just won a trophy. She came back to the couch and tossed it into Lance's lap.

"It's not the same paper," he said, noticing different head-lines and pictures.

"You're right," Leah said. "You are gifted."

Lance said nothing, just looked at her.

"It's from two weeks ago," she said.

Lance looked back down at the black-and-white pages. "So there was a story about what's wrong in this paper too?"

She smiled a little, and Lance knew she was playing some sort of game with him. "There's a story about it every week. At least for a few months out of the year."

Lance scanned the headlines again. Quickly skimmed an article about a farmer out on Route 19 having to rescue two of his cows after they got stuck in a ravine. Not exactly worthy of print, in Lance's mind.

Leah sighed. "I'm sorry. I was just ... I guess I wanted to see if you could, you know..."

"Read your mind?"

She grinned.

"I don't work that way," Lance said. "I don't ... I told you, I don't understand how I work. Things just happen sometimes, and sometimes they don't."

Leah shrugged. "Worth a shot. You're the first psychic I've ever met."

"I'm not a—"

Sports! There would be an article about sports teams every week!

Lance was a quiet for a moment, his mouth frozen midsentence as Leah's clues clicked together. Then he looked down and opened the paper, finding the sports section. When Leah saw where he'd ended up, she whispered, "*Not psychic, my ass.*"

He shook his head and said. "No, really. It just suddenly made sense. The weekly article. Small town like this, it was a logical conclusion."

"Uh-huh, sure."

Lance looked down at the front page of sports and said, "Okay, I made it this far. Help me out."

Leah scooted across the couch, so close now he could smell her shampoo and a whiff of what remained of the perfume she'd probably administered early this morning before coming into work. Lance was suddenly very conscious of his lack of deodorant and toothpaste. He'd need to get to a store as soon as possible, especially if girls were going to be sidling up to him on couches.

Not what should be concerning you right now, Lance.

Whatever...

Leah leaned over further and tapped her index finger, the nail clean but unpainted, on the top story, the headline in large bold font.

MCGUIRE LEADS WESTHAVEN TO 3–0 START

Lance recalled the sports page from the newspaper he'd lost. "They're four and oh now. They beat a team from"—he paused to think—"Newberry, last week. They scored a touchdown and a field goal in the fourth to seal the win."

Leah nodded. "Nice memory."

"Like you said, I am gifted." Lance looked at the black-and-white snapshot chosen for the article's picture. A Westhaven High School player was walking off the field toward the sideline, helmet off and dangling from one hand while he used his other to high-five a man who Lance assumed must be the coach. The photo's caption read: WESTHAVEN QUARTERBACK ANTHONY MILLS AND HEAD COACH KENNY MCGUIRE CELEBRATE VICTORY OVER NON-DISTRICT FOE.

Coach McGuire was somewhat atypical for a football head coach. He was a small man, short and very thin, and he wore small rimless glasses that sat low on his nose, a look that seemed more fitting for somebody closer to sixty than the early forties

McGuire appeared to be. He wore a Westhaven High ball cap on his head, and a pair of large earphones with built-in microphone were draped around his neck. An iPad was clutched in his non-high-fiving hand. Lance smirked; the man almost seemed to be a biology teacher playing dress-up as a football coach.

Leah was quiet as Lance read the full article detailing a Westhaven blowout. He finished, considered his location, and then said, "Small town like this, I'm guessing high school football is a big deal, right?"

Leah threw back her head and laughed. "A big deal? Go ask for a tire rotation and oil change down at Clarence's Tire and Lube on the morning after a Westhaven loss and see for yourself. Service with a smile? Forget it."

Lance understood. His hometown had been enthusiastic about high school sports as well. The time junior year he'd missed a ten-foot jumper to win a close one midseason had haunted him for weeks. People had still smiled at him in the streets, but he had known deep down they blamed him for the loss. Fortunately, Lance knew better than most that sports didn't exactly rank high on life's important bullet points.

Leah leaned back against the couch cushion, kicked off her sneakers and pulled her feet under her. Her socks were so white they could blind you. Lance remembered the overwhelming smell of disinfectant from his entrance earlier and thought: *She keeps everything so clean, and I look and smell like a stowaway.*

"Would you like to guess how many AA state championships Westhaven has won in the last three years?"

Lance hedged his bet and guessed two.

"All three," Leah said. "Three years, three titles."

"Wow," Lance said. "That seems ... improbable."

"You think?"

"No competition? Weak district? Region?"

Leah shook her head and passed on the question. "You know how many games they won the season before their first title?"

Lance knew she was playing to some sort of buildup. Shrugged and said, "Six?"

"One. They beat one stinking team. I remember because it was my sophomore year, and my date to the homecoming dance, a safety who was terrible, just like the rest of the team, sprained his ankle on the second play of the game."

"So no dancing?"

"*That's* your question?"

"No, I have others. I just ... my mind's funny, remember?"

She smiled. "Try and focus here, okay?"

"Yes, ma'am. So the local high school team went from being the Bad News Bears to winning three titles in a row?"

"Correct."

"Doesn't seem like the sort of thing that happens overnight. Or in one off-season, in this case."

"Exactly."

"So what changed?"

Leah looked up to the ceiling, in contemplation of her answer. Lance looked up too, and another sharp crack of pain shot through his skull. He'd really hit that door hard, and was about to ask Leah if she had any ibuprofen when she said, "Everything changed. Everything except the players."

"I'm not a football expert, but I've played enough basketball in my life to know that it's going to take at least *one* new player for a team to improve from a nearly winless record to winning a state title."

"Well, there was *one*, but he was just a placekicker." Leah closed her eyes and thought. "Okay, yeah, sure there were a few seniors from the losing team that graduated, and then some JV kids moved up, but the core team was still there, and none of the rising players were what you might call game-changers."

"So ... the change?"

"The coach, for starters. Coach McGuire's first year at Westhaven was the first year they won state."

"Did he have a winning record where he coached before?"

Leah's face went blank for a moment, then she looked at him and said, "You know, I've never even thought about that. I've only focused on him since he's been at Westhaven. All I know is he and his wife came from Georgia. They were both schoolteachers. She worked at the library part-time the first year they were here, then she took over as vice principal at the high school a year later. That was my senior year."

"Big jump from putting books back on the shelf at the library to being vice principal of a high school. Small town or no small town."

"Mr. Barnes, the vice principal she replaced, retired and moved to Florida with his wife, who'd just been diagnosed with dementia. Apparently they had a son there."

Lance thought about this, somewhat surprised that no internal candidates, no longtime high school staff, might have gotten the job. But he moved on. "So the team got a new coach. What else?"

"The paper mill sold to new owners."

This seemingly unrelated bit of information made zero sense to Lance. So he nodded his head and said, "Elementary, my dear Watson."

"What?"

"Sherlock Holmes. Well ... it's a misquote. He never said that exactly, but people get the idea."

"Uh, okay."

Another fallen-flat joke. He was on a roll. "I don't understand why a paper mill selling to somebody new affects the football team."

"Ah, right." Leah readjusted her legs under her. "It wouldn't normally, I guess. But in this case, it did, in a big way. When the paper mill sold to the new owner, some big business out of Atlanta, they moved in a new general operations manager. Glenn Strang. Glenn's son, Bobby, was the placekicker I mentioned."

Lance's brain was trying to figure out how any of this had anything to do with the team's miraculous turnaround. "Unless Westhaven's offensive strategy was to kick fifteen field goals a game, I fail to see why this changes much. And you've already suggested that the new kicker wasn't a big deal."

Leah shrugged. "Well, he wasn't, in terms of being an on-the-field contribution. But ... his daddy quickly became the piggy bank for a school football program that'd been having the players wash their own uniforms at home. Before Strang, it would be generous to say the Westhaven athletic department was on a shoestring budget. It was more like a stray thread of a budget. But Glenn Strang is apparently a huge sports fan, played D-1 football somewhere out west and then had a somewhat lucrative stint as a pro. Now that he's got more money than he knows what to do with, he's living vicariously through Westhaven players by making sure they've got the shiniest, most sophisticated everything. Uniforms, training equipment, you name it. He contributes to the other sports programs as well, but I think it's just so he doesn't appear biased. Everybody knows football is his baby."

Lance thought about this. Could understand the situation fully. He knew some people could never let go of a game they loved, and he also knew from his one and only season of officiating peewee basketball that parents were just about always borderline insane and dangerous fans of their kids. He supposed dumping a ton of money into a program was a good enough way to support that habit.

"But, a new placekicker and fancy new equipment still doesn't take them from zeros to heroes. You can't buy a game."

Well...

"Wait, are we talking about bribery? Payoffs? Kickbacks?"

Leah closed her eyes and took a deep breath, shook her head. "No. Well, I don't know, maybe. There ... there's something else, too. Something worse. The thing that came to mind when you asked me earlier if I thought something bad was going on around here."

"Enlighten me."

A dull, thunderous sound was suddenly heard in the distance. Faint, but noticeable. Leah's eyes widened and her face went pale. She jumped up from the couch and quickly pulled on her sneakers, hopping from one foot to the other as she did so. Her eyes darted around the office, checking everything and nothing at the same time. "You've got to go!"

The booming noise was closer now, very close. "That's Daddy's truck! He'll kill you if he finds you with me!"

Lance jumped up from the couch, the threat of death always a motivation to move quickly if needed. "I thought you said he was working. Never takes a sick day. Employee of the year. Master of—"

"*He doesn't!*" Leah spun around on her heels, her eyes darting over every inch of the office. Lance headed for the door and she yelled, "No! He'll see you!"

The booming of what Lance now realized was a truck's exhaust muffler was nearly shaking the windows in their panes. He stopped halfway to the office door, almost turned back, and then continued. He heard Leah begin to protest again, but then he quickly flipped the NO VACANCY sign off and unlocked the office's door. He turned around and Leah was disappearing into the black mouth of the now-open door at the rear of the office. She was half-hidden in shadows as she waved frantically for him to follow her.

Lance ran across the freshly polished office floor, one continuing thought in his head.

It knows I'm here, and it definitely doesn't like it.

[7]

Leah had pulled Lance into the doorway and then told him to hide. She'd given him one hard shove, pushing him out of the way of the door she was closing behind her, and then she was gone, leaving Lance alone in a dark, unknown space, hiding from a man he'd never met, for a reason he didn't fully understand. He chalked it up to an overprotective father, remembered the supposed shotgun behind the check-in counter, and quickly decided any man who'd give his young daughter a shotgun to use at will on any human being who might pose a threat was a man whom Lance would like to try and remain on proper terms with. Lance also remembered the panic he'd seen in Leah's eyes when she'd first recognized the sound of her daddy's truck. It was a true panic, one which alluded to fierce repercussions should she be caught.

Lance did as instructed and tried to find a place to hide. Because apparently being behind a closed door in the near pitch black wasn't good enough.

Lance turned around and closed his eyes for a moment, then reopened them, trying to let them adjust. The thundering from the truck muffler was now right on top of them, Leah's daddy having clearly arrived in the parking lot. It rumbled on for another ten or fifteen seconds and then stopped completely. The newfound silence was almost as deafening as the noise had been. *Need to move fast now. He's here.*

As things came slowly into focus, Lance was surprised at what he had found. He'd seen the door at the rear of the office from the first moment he'd stepped inside Bob's Place earlier that day and had noticed it again as Leah had helped to nurse his injuries after the Great Ghost Gust and their subsequent conversation. But the entire time, he'd assumed it was some sort of utility closet, laundry room, or storage area. A place where you'd find the mop buckets and the bottles of bleach and boxes of mini-soaps. A room with a musty smell and a hard concrete floor with edges lined with mousetraps, a small grubby window perched high that was so covered in grime you couldn't see out. As the room's objects became clearer, what he found instead was a bedroom.

The space was small, but well furnished. To his immediate left, flush against two walls, was a twin-sized bed, made neatly and with a small stuffed animal of some sort propped between two pillows. A wooden nightstand sat next to the bed with a small lamp atop it and a paperback novel with a bookmark sticking out the top of the pages. On the opposite wall, a tiny square desk with an office chair hugged the corner. From atop the desk, the dull green glow of a power cord plugged into a laptop provided just about the room's only light. To the right of the desk was a wide dresser, a mirror mounted to the back that showed Lance a dull reflection of himself in front of the door. A small TV cart was in the corner opposite the desk, and the flat-screen resting there was no more than fifteen inches. A spark of light from his right caught Lance's eye, and he finished his scan of the room by noticing another door. It was open just a crack, and a small amber glow was beckoning him.

Outside the room, a door opened and heavy footsteps fell on the hardwood.

"*Daddy?*" Lance heard Leah say, her voice traveling from the direction of the check-in counter. "I thought you had to work tonight."

There was no answer, and Lance imagined Leah's daddy—who was surely a large lumberjack of a man who could grab Lance by the shoulders and rip him in half—standing in the center of the office, furrowed eyebrows above eyes trained directly onto the door Lance was still standing behind. Waiting —no, *hoping* to hear a tiny sound, any excuse to kick the door open and destroy whoever was behind it, whoever was dumb enough to try and spend the evening with his daughter.

This day is going a lot worse than I was expecting it to. And that's saying something.

"Boss told me to go home." A new voice, deep with bass and fitting Lance's imagery perfectly, sounded no more than two feet from the door Lance was still standing motionless behind. "Told me he'd made a scheduling error. Didn't need me tonight."

Leah, closer than she'd been before: "Why didn't he call you? Did you have your cell phone off again? I keep telling you—"

"I had it on." A quick, powerful retort. Leah stopped talking. "Boss said he'd forgotten until right when I showed up. He'd been in a meeting with Mr. Strang and some other folks, something about a fundraiser, he told me, and he forgot all about the scheduling error until he saw me at my post."

There was a moment of silence before Leah ventured, "But..."

"I don't ask questions, Leah! I do what I'm told."

Lance heard footsteps across the hardwood, heading his direction. He held his breath and the amber light caught his eye again. He turned toward the partially opened door and walked as softly as he could across the floor toward it. Grabbed the handle and pulled gently, begging for the hinges not to whine. They didn't, and Lance slid into the new room and closed the door softly behind him.

"So why'd you come back here, Daddy? Why aren't you home, or out with your buddies."

There was more silence again, and Lance didn't like it. Leah's daddy was thinking about something, contemplating some move he wanted to make. Lance could nearly sense it. Somehow, in some fashion, Leah's daddy knew Lance was here.

Maybe.

"On my way out to the parking lot, Strang himself found me and asked if you were minding the shop tonight. I said you were, and he'd mentioned that he'd heard on the police scanner earlier that there'd been reports of a suspicious-looking man heading down Route 19, toward the motel."

Though they were slightly muffled, Lance could still hear the words, and his heart stopped in his chest for a moment. *He knows. He knows I'm here and he's going to kill me. Okay, maybe he won't kill me, but I doubt he wants to sit down and talk about things.*

The paranormal and supernatural and whatever else you wanted to call the things Lance had dealt with his entire life didn't scare him half as badly as a pissed-off human being with easy access to a loaded weapon. Especially one with an attractive daughter to protect.

"Daddy, you worry too much. Been business as usual here. And besides, I've got Bonnie behind the counter if I need her."

Bonnie?

Lance hadn't met Bonnie.

A loud sigh, clear as day, was followed by, "If I'd known you were going to pick something so girly, I'd never have told you about people naming their guns."

Oh. Bonnie.

"It's not girly! It's because of Bonnie and Clyde! She was a badass!"

Silence again, and Lance looked around the room, waiting for the bedroom door to be flung open any second now and the search to commence.

He was in a bathroom. One larger than he'd expected, based on the size of the bedroom. There was a porcelain bathtub to his left with a showerhead sticking out of a crudely tiled wall like a weed. The shower curtain ran along a circular rod, half-open, swirling with a pattern of flowers and vines. A toilet to Lance's right, and between tub and pot was a wooden vanity with a single sink. A medicine cabinet with a mirror front mounted above the sink, and Lance again looked straight into his own reflection. There was a neatly organized arrangement of products on the countertop, and a toothbrush holder held a single brush. *No boyfriend, then, I guess.* And Lance wondered why this information mattered to him.

The source of the amber light that had caught Lance's eyes was a plug-in nightlight glowing beneath a plastic cover next to the sink. Lance's other senses kicked in and he inhaled the sweet smells of shampoos and lotions and perfume, briefly imagined Leah standing in front of this mirror and—

"Seriously, Daddy, everything's fine here. I was just going to read a little bit until I was ready to go to bed, then I'd lock up and go watch some TV."

Another long, pregnant pause. Lance found himself just wishing the man out there *would* kick the door down, try and come find him. At least then he'd know what the heck was going on out there.

Expecting some sort of demand for an explanation, or at

least words of warning uttered in a threatening tone, Lance was surprised when all Leah's daddy said was, "Leah, you'd tell me if there was something I needed to know about, right? You know I only want what's best for you. Always have."

Leah laughed. "Yessss, Daddy, of course I would. But you got to believe me. Things are just as boring here as they've ever been. You're being paranoid."

"I'd rather be paranoid than regretful."

Lance had to agree with the man. And he noted how good of a liar Leah was turning out to be.

And then nobody spoke for what seemed like an eternity. Lance pressed his ear against the closed door and heard nothing. He contemplated opening the door a crack but feared the noise it might make. Finally, he heard Leah giggle and say, "Okaaaay, Daddy, now go get out of here and enjoy your night off."

The heavy footsteps started to retreat, the bell above the door gave its jingle, and soon after that, the booming muffler was once again rattling Lance's eardrums. It idled for a minute or two, and then the noise dissipated as Leah's daddy, thankfully, drove away.

Still, Lance did not move. He would stay right where he was until Leah came to get him.

He turned away from the door and moved to sit on the toilet and wait, but he froze midstep. Twirled back around and faced the door, his heartbeat drumming in his ears. He saw nothing but the closed wooden door. He looked back over his shoulder, into the mirror, and saw only his reflection.

A second ago, there'd been somebody else with him in the darkened bathroom. Somebody else's reflection looking straight at him. It'd all happened so fast that Lance hadn't had a chance to make out much, but he was certain of two things.

The young man looking back at Lance had skin as white as milk and blackish-gray eyes like a shark that seemed to pierce

Lance's skin. Dark lips that looked swollen. The person who'd stared back from the mirror was dead, Lance was certain of that.

The second thing Lance was certain of was that the boy had been wearing a t-shirt with some sort of graphic and writing on the front. Lance closed his eyes and forced himself to think, to rebuild in his mind what he'd only briefly seen—or hadn't seen.

He stood still in the bathroom, eyes closed tightly and his mind closed off to everything else. The graphic came to him first. It'd been a single letter, printed large in the middle of the shirt in a fancy script, words printed above and below.

The letter was a W.

And then, just like that, the words fell into their places.

WESTHAVEN FOOTBALL

[8]

THIRTY MINUTES HAD PASSED AND LANCE HAD TO PEE, which was an ironic task to be avoiding because he was sitting on a toilet. But he didn't dare use it. Not until he was absolutely sure he was in the clear from whatever potential there might still be of Leah's daddy giving him a face-to-face introduction to Bonnie.

So Lance sat alone in the darkened bathroom, amber glow from the nightlight letting him see just enough to notice whether any more dead football players were hanging out with him, waiting their turn to use the john.

Lance could only assume the young man he'd briefly seen in the mirror was a Westhaven player. There was the t-shirt, sure, but the boy had also seemed to be built like a person who'd spent more than a few afternoons in the school's weight room, throwing around dumbbells and downing protein shakes like water. He'd been big, broad shoulders filling out the neckline of the Westhaven Football t-shirt's fabric. But all those muscles couldn't stop whatever had ended the young man's life. And that was the part Lance was curious about.

Not just the cause of the boy's death, but also why his ghost had been present. Unlike the spirit of Annabelle Winters, which had been what Lance could assume was an accurate representation of Ms. Winters at the time of her death—old, but pleasant enough and without physical wounds or oddities—the football player's spirit had been more like a corpse. Something long dead and rotting and full of blackness. The image reminded Lance of a drowning victim, one whose body had been submerged for far too long.

The eyes... the eyes were the worst part.

Was the football player's ghost supposed to frighten Lance? Its presence supposed to cause him to flee back to the bus station and get the heck out of Dodge? Or was it possible this young man's ghost had been some sort of spy, doing the bidding of whatever dark and malevolent forces were obviously at play.

Neither option seemed appealing to Lance. But, neither much bothered him either, at least not in the sense his assumed-antagonist was surely hoping for. He would not flee, because where would he go? Plus, he'd done nothing of any significance worth spying on, other than sit on a closed toilet lid for half an hour after listening to his new friend's father come within what seemed like inches of making things much worse than they needed to be.

He was rolling all these thoughts around in his head like a handful of marbles when Leah nudged open the bathroom door, stuck her head in, and said, "You are extremely patient."

Lance looked up to her, startled. He'd been so deep in thought he'd not even heard the bedroom door open. He'd seen two ghosts in one day, which was something that had happened only one other time. Back when...

"It didn't seem like you wanted me to meet your father, and from what I gathered, he didn't seem too keen to meet me either. It was in the interest of both parties for me to stay put until called for. I figured he might be the type to stake the place out, peek through the windows and wait to see if you'd lied to him."

"Well, you're right. If he'd have seen you... well, I'm not sure what would have happened, but it wouldn't have been good." A pause. "For either of us. But he does trust me. He's been long gone."

Lance stood from his sitting position and stretched his lower back. "So why'd you keep me waiting?"

Leah shrugged. "Just being cautious, I guess. And maybe I was curious just how long you'd wait." She gave him a grin, and Lance returned the favor by telling her he needed to pee.

"But you've been in a bathroom all this time!"

He shrugged. "Just being cautious, I guess."

Leah left and closed the door, and Lance relieved himself with the level of self-consciousness reserved for every guy the first time or two he urinates with a new female companion within earshot. He was certain he sounded like a firehose open full-strength into a swimming pool. He flushed, washed his hands and dried them on his shorts. Then he opened the bathroom door and found Leah sitting on the edge of the bed. She'd turned the bedside lamp on and was staring at him intently.

"You're the first guy I've ever had in my room. You should feel very privileged."

Lance stood in the open doorway connecting the bathroom and bedroom. "It is an honor I will receive with respect and gratitude."

"Do you always talk so weird?"

"I didn't know I talked weird. So, yes. Probably."

"You're just different, that's all."

No kidding. "Different than what?"

"Most people I talk to."

"Well, if you spend most of your time here, I can certainly believe that."

The words were out of his mouth before he realized how rude they must have sounded. He blushed, his face warm with regret, and quickly stammered, "I mean ... it's just ... you said the folks who come through here usually aren't the... what I meant to say—"

She giggled, cutting him off. "Ah, so you are human. It's good to know you can get flustered. You struck me as kind of robotic earlier."

Lance recomposed himself, leaned against the door frame. "It doesn't happen often. So now *you* should feel privileged."

"Noted."

The silence sat in the air before them like the last slice of pizza, waiting for somebody to make a grab for it. Lance reached first, tackling what he figured to be the elephant in the room. "So, you live here, at the motel?" He gestured to the room, the bathroom.

Leah sighed. "Yes, and it's just as glamorous as it seems."

Lance recalled his home (*It's not your home anymore, Lance. You'll never go back there again. At least not for a very long time*), the small two-bedroom house he'd shared with his mother his whole life. The unkempt look of the place, the flea market furniture and garage sale knickknacks. Glamorous was a word Lance knew wasn't necessary to make someplace a good home.

He recalled the conversation he'd overheard earlier, when Leah had been fibbing to her daddy. "But your father doesn't live here?"

"You think we'd be sitting here if he did?" And that was all she had to say on the topic.

Lance shrugged. "Doesn't look so bad to me."

"Yeah. It'll do for now. One day I'll get a better place. One day I'll leave this whole town. At least, that's what I keep telling myself."

Lance wanted to tell her he'd just done exactly what she

was longing for, left his hometown behind in a cloud of bus fumes, but that wasn't something he was ready to talk about. It was something he might *never* be able to talk about. So, he moved on. "Before you sequestered me in your bedroom, you were about to tell me what else was bothering you about the football team. You said there was more to it?"

"See, that's what I'm talking about! Who says 'sequestered'?"

Lance thought for a second. "People who know its definition and can intelligently use it in a sentence, like they do with most words?"

Leah looked at him for a long moment, as if unsure if he was kidding or being mean. *Way to go, Lance. You're a real winner with these one-liners.*

"Are you hungry?" Leah asked.

The change of conversation was drastic, but by no means unwelcome. "Famished."

Leah jumped from the bed and headed back into the motel's office. "I'll order a pizza. I'll tell you what I know once it gets here."

Lance watched as Leah picked up the desk phone at the check-in counter and placed an order, not bothering to ask him what his preferred pizza toppings were. She ordered a single large with grilled chicken, green peppers, and mushrooms. Lance was impressed with the selection, though he might have added some pineapple. Leah hung up the phone and looked at him as he made his way back to the couch. "That okay with you?" she asked.

"Sounds great. I'm not too picky with my pizza."

Leah nodded. "I figured as much."

"What's that mean?"

"Guy as big as you, and as lean ... I didn't figure you'd find much to complain about with pizza toppings. Or any food, for that matter."

Lance remembered his breakfast. Remembered Margie's laugh after he'd ordered his slice of pie to wash down the rest of his meal. The thought of pie caused the image of his mother's face to jump to the front of his mind, half-hidden behind her mug of tea, steam curling around the edges of her brow as she listened intently to anything he'd ever had to say to her at the kitchen table.

"Hey, you okay?" Leah's voice snapped him back to the present.

He shook his head to clear it, the dull pain at the back of his head having throttled down to only a minor ache. His vision readjusted to the girl before him, this nice young woman who'd been able to sense in him some sort of genuineness—the way he'd been able to sense it in her—and allow this near-instant friendship to mature so rapidly. And, allowing himself one last glance back to the memory of his mother's face, Lance thought to himself, *Mom would like her.*

"Yeah, sorry. I just...."

"You spaced out on me. Am I boring you already?"

Lance smiled. "No. No, you're not."

They sat on the couch together while they waited for the pizza, Lance constantly glancing in the direction of the windows and straining his ears to pick up the noise of a rumbling muffler headed back their direction. Leah turned on the television and they watched a rerun of *The Big Bang Theory*, both of them happy to have the show's laugh track fill the silence of the room. Lance knew they were both growing more comfortable around each other, but the white noise definitely helped to make things a little less awkward.

The sound of a small, whining engine in the parking lot was quickly followed by three quick knocks on the office door.

Lance jumped in his seat at the noise, still on edge with the threat of Leah's father's wrath, but Leah calmly stood from her curled position on the couch and said, "It's just Brian with the pizza."

Lance stood anyway, ready to make a run for it, or at least be able to defend himself, if Leah was mistaken. But when she opened the door, Lance only saw the face of a young man dressed in baggy jeans and a pizza shop polo standing on the sidewalk. Leah greeted him and they exchanged common pleasantries, handed him some cash she'd pulled from her pocket, took the pizza, said goodnight, and then closed the door. "I went to school with him. He was a year older, but we had some of the same friends."

"Didn't seem too talkative," Lance said.

"You probably made him nervous."

Leah sat back down on the couch and set the pizza box on the cushion between them. She opened it and took a slice for herself and began watching TV again. Lance devoured four slices in the time she'd eaten two and declined any more when she asked. She closed the box and then went behind the check-in counter, bending down and reappearing with two bottles of water. "All I keep in the mini-fridge is water, so I hope you're not a soda addict."

Lance took the bottle she'd extended to him and quickly downed half of it. "I hate soda," he said after gulping. "Nothing but sugar and poison."

Leah nodded as she watched the television show's final scene. When it was over and the credits began to play, she used the remote to mute the volume and then turned to face him, her demeanor serious.

Lance picked up on her sudden mood shift, could practically feel the sudden burst of sorrow and fear that had flooded her system, as if she'd done well most of the evening in blocking out whatever troubling thoughts haunted her, but was now ready to let them break the dam.

"So what's the *real* problem?" Lance asked, as gently as he could.

Leah took a sip of water, glanced once at the TV and then back at Lance. "Westhaven football has won three straight state titles. Each year, one player from the team has gone missing. None of them have ever been found."

9

THREE YEARS.

Three football state titles.

And now, with a sinking feeling in his gut that threatened to dislodge his recently ingested pizza, Lance feared there were three dead high school students to round out the statistics. One of them for sure was dead, because Lance now had a good idea who the young man was he'd seen in Leah's bathroom mirror. He hoped he was wrong, suddenly wanted to be wrong about this more than anything in his life. But he recalled that feeling of dread he'd experienced since arriving in town, the attack in the parking lot, and even Leah's daddy's somewhat inexplicable night off from work, and could not shake the feeling that they were the result of nothing but true evil. And true evil didn't play games. True evil went for the kill.

An entire country, forty-eight contiguous states, and this is what I end up in the middle of on my first stop from home. Talk about luck.

"You already knew, didn't you?"

Lance looked up from the floor, where he'd been staring as he'd processed what Leah had told him. She was looking at him longingly, expectantly, as if she desperately wanted him to say yes, he did already know, and he had the answer to fix it all. Maybe he'd made a mistake in telling her about his abilities. Maybe he'd inadvertently made himself out to be something bigger in her eyes than he truly was. The girl looking back at him from the opposite side of the couch was a girl looking for the truth she figured only he could provide.

But Lance wasn't ready to tell her the whole truth. He would not tell her about what he could see. What he *had* seen. Not yet. It was still too early, and he was still afraid he'd come off as some sort of lunatic and she'd feel foolish and embarrassed and disappointed in herself for even considering trusting him. Leah was smart and headstrong, but she was still young and carried a lingering bit of innocence. Lance did not want to accidentally take that away from her.

But there was something else, a new feeling Lance could feel coming from her. Mixed with the look in her eyes—that *longing* look—that seemed to be more than just simply pleading for his help, but begging, Lance could feel her sorrow washing over him like a fine mist, cold and sticky and making his skin prickle. Again he got the impression that she'd been keeping something buried, something more important than she'd been letting on, and now she was tired of the masquerade and had removed the mask.

There was something very familiar about the pain coming from her. Lance quickly recognized it as a weaker version of what he himself was currently—

Oh. Oh no.

Lance ignored Leah's question and asked one of his own. One he was terrified he already knew the answer to. "One of those boys ... one of them was your brother, wasn't he?"

At the mention of her secret, of the truth Lance had somehow managed to excavate from her inner thoughts, Leah closed her eyes and a single tear spilled from each, slowly trailing down her cheeks until they fell to the couch with audible *plops*. Lance sat still, unsure of what he should do. Part of him wanted to reach out a comforting hand, be a reassuring shoulder to cry on. But another part, a part that carried the echoes of his mother's voice, told him that Leah was strong enough not to need those things right now; she'd been down this road before, often, and the best thing to do was to let his new friend move at her own pace. Lance was there to help, and a big part of that was going to be to listen.

So he remained where he was on the couch, slouched into the corner with one leg pulled under him, his other size fifteen sneaker flat on the floor. He never took his eyes off Leah, and when she was finally able to regain the composure she'd been so effortlessly displaying, she looked up at him with wet eyes and smiled. Lance smiled back.

Leah wiped her eyes with the back of her hand and sniffled. Lance wished he had a tissue to offer. "He was the first," Leah said. "The first casualty of Westhaven High School's historic football run." Leah smiled again and gave off a small laugh. "God, he wasn't very good, but he tried so hard. Loved the stupid game. I think he'd have been happy just being the water boy, just to be around it, you know?"

Lance nodded. He did know. He'd known plenty of guys like that in high school. Ones who would shoot baskets and run full-court with anybody all day, every day because they loved to play. But they didn't quite have the skillset to back up the passion. They'd gladly volunteer to be equipment managers, statisticians, videographers, anything to be at every game and have an inside connection to the team. To be a part of the basketball family.

"It's ironic, isn't it?" Leah asked.

"What?"

"The thing he loved is the thing that ended up killing him."

Lance bit his tongue, citing compassion as the reason he asked, "What makes you sure he's dead? You said none of the players had been found."

Leah looked at him, and instantly Lance had known his bluff had been called. "Don't patronize me, Lance. Don't act like everybody else and pretend that bad things haven't happened and that there's still hope and all that other bullshit people always say to a victim's face before going home and closing their doors and then shaking their heads and saying things like 'Oh, that poor thing. Bless her heart. Such a tragedy. Blah blah blah.' You know the truth, and I didn't have you pegged as the type of person who would shy away from it."

Lance sat, stunned. *This girl is ... wow. Just ... wow.*

His level of guilt at hiding the true nature of his abilities was growing stronger by the minute, but still he refrained. It wasn't the time. He needed more information about what he was up against. "Okay," he offered. "Your brother—oh, what was his name?"

Lance quickly regretted the use of past tense, but the damage was done.

"Samuel," Leah said.

"Okay, so Sam was the—"

"No. Never Sam. He always liked to be called Samuel." She smiled another sad smile. "He said it was more distinguished. No wonder he wasn't a superstar athlete, huh? Concerned about things like that."

Lance waited a beat before continuing, letting Leah finish off her memory. "So Samuel was the first of the three players to disappear, correct?"

"Yes."

"Okay, then that's where I need to start. Tell me exactly

what happened, as best you can. Maybe we can put some pieces together."

Leah looked at him for a long moment, and Lance wondered if she'd suddenly decided this was all a bad idea. Maybe she'd finally realized she was talking about something she normally kept locked away down deep to a man who was practically a stranger. But then, softly, she said, "You know, I've been over the details of Samuel's disappearance a million times—with the police, with Daddy, with friends—and another ten million times in my own head. It's never done a single bit of good. Nothing I saw and nothing I know has ever helped anybody come any closer to helping me get any sort of closure. My brother is dead, I know that." She paused. "And I can't explain it, honestly I can't, but you're the first person I've ever met who I think for some reason might be able to finally help me figure out why."

And then, in a move that both melted Lance's heart, and also made his skin come alive with electricity, Leah reached across the cushion that separated them and squeezed his hand.

With that simple touch, Lance's own demons and problems dissolved for an instant, and all that remained was a will to help this young girl find out what had happened to her brother.

Him and two other boys who had obviously suffered at the hand of whatever force was after Lance as well.

For the next fifteen minutes, Lance sat in his corner of the couch, eyes fixed on Leah as she did her best to summarize her story.

Leah and Samuel's mother had "gotten sick" a year and a half before Samuel had disappeared. Leah didn't say what exactly had been wrong with the woman, but sadly, she'd passed on just a few quick months after falling ill. From there,

Leah's family home had become a disaster zone. Her father, who'd been an overly aggressive social drinker to use the politest of terms, had let go of whatever small part of the wagon he'd been holding on to. He was rarely seen at home without a bottle in his hand and rarely seen in town unless it was on a barstool. "He always went to work, though," Leah said. "He never missed a single day at the mill. Even the days he could barely stand. Daddy's got flaws—bad ones—but he's loyal."

Lance chewed on this information for a moment before asking, "And how was his relationship with you and Samuel, after your mother passed?"

Leah's face fell, and Lance had a good idea what she was about to admit. "Not the best," she said. "He loves us, don't get me wrong, but he just ... after Momma, and the drinking ... he ... I don't think he ever meant to...."

"He hit you," Lance said. It happened every day in this country, but that didn't make the sting any duller as he looked at this sweet girl's face and imagined a burly fist connecting with one of her eye sockets.

Leah offered a sad, small grin and shrugged. "Only once with me. Nothing so bad. Just a hard slap across the face one day when I talked back. I knew he felt terrible about it as soon as it happened."

"And Samuel?"

Leah closed her eyes, and Lance didn't want to know what she was seeing behind her closed eyelids.

"Yes, it was worse for Samuel. I don't know why. He never did anything wrong. But he just always seemed to be in Daddy's way when the time came for an outburst. After all this time, part of me can't help but wonder if he was doing it on purpose. Trying to protect me."

"Sounds like a good brother."

Leah's face lit up. "He was the best." Then she continued on.

When football practice had started and the new coach—Coach McGuire—had the team doing two-a-days in what could only be an attempt to figure out why these young men had only won a single game the previous season, Leah had started spending more and more time helping out at the motel.

"Daddy's daddy owned this place until he died," Leah said. "Daddy inherited it, and since it was all paid for and, like I said, Daddy's loyal, we've always kept it. At that time, we had more hired help here, but I was sixteen and looking for a good reason to get out of the house and out of Daddy's way. So I asked Daddy—one day when he was surprisingly sober—if I could work part-time. I said I wanted my own spending cash so I could go out with friends. I think he knew the real reason I was asking, but he was too ashamed to admit it."

"And now you basically run the place?" Lance asked.

"Basically."

"Impressive."

"I don't have much else to do. It keeps me busy, and I like helping people."

"That's a nice way to look at it."

The two-a-days seemed to have helped, because Westhaven had won their first game of the season. And their second, and their third. The parents were happy, the fans were happy, the sports boosters were happy, but more importantly, the players were happy. The morale and camaraderie of Westhaven's football team were high, and the intense schedule of grueling practices that Coach McGuire had created suddenly seemed more than worth it. Leah said that Samuel looked forward to practices and pre-game meals and film sessions even more than he usually did, and from what she gathered, the rest of the team felt the same way.

After the fourth victory in a row, Coach McGuire invited the entire team over to his house for a barbecue. Parents were invited as well, and even though Leah and Samuel's daddy was unable to attend, Glenn Strang, father of Westhaven's new placekicker and largest new donor to Westhaven's athletic programs, was in attendance. He'd announced to everybody there that if Westhaven could win their fifth game in a row, they'd all be invited to a pool party at his home.

"He stood on top of Coach McGuire's lawn mower to make sure he could be seen and heard," Leah said. "Samuel said he looked like an expensively dressed meerkat, the way he suddenly popped up over the crowd."

Westhaven won the next game, and Strang kept his word. After the first pool party, the Strang home became somewhat of a regular hangout for Westhaven players. Glenn Strang told the team that his door was always open if any of the boys needed a place to study, clear their head, stay the night, or anything.

"It was pretty weird, if you ask me," Leah said. "It was like he was running some sort of shelter for the football team. I mean, his house is practically a mansion by this town's standards, and Mrs. Strang was always home to help the boys with schoolwork, or fix them a good meal, and everybody seemed to genuinely like Bobby—that's the Strangs' son. But some parents started grumbling that their sons were spending too much time away from home. More specifically, too much time at casa de Strang."

Lance had had similar team barbecues and parties hosted by parents of players or the coaches, and even the high school principal. But none of these people had essentially given him a key to their home and asked him to come by anytime for any reason. It wasn't exactly a red flag, but it certainly was an oddity.

"But the trouble really started when word got out that a lot of *female* students were making their way to the Strang house along with the players."

"Uh-oh," Lance said. "So the place went from shelter to brothel?"

"Brothel is a little harsh. Some of those girls are my friends, thank you very much. But basically it didn't take long for a group of horny high school boys to realize that if their parents wouldn't let them take a girl to their bedroom and close the door, maybe they could find someplace to be alone with a girl at their home away from home. A place as big as the Strangs' house, and with limited adult supervision, it was worth a shot. And it paid off for quite a few."

"Interesting."

Leah leaned forward, as if about to divulge some secret bit of evidence. "What's always bugged me about the whole situation is, I don't know if the Strangs knew about and were encouraging what was happening at their home, or they were simply naïve and ignorant. I mean, they obviously cared about the players and Bobby's friends, but I've always wondered how involved they actually were in everything. How hands-on. Does that make any sense?"

Lance nodded. "I think so. Basically you want to know if the Strangs were the problem. Point-blank."

Leah thought for a moment. "Yeah, basically. I just think their whole open-home policy was bizarre. And there's no denying the link between the timing of their showing up and entering the players' lives, and the team beginning to win, and ... and my brother's disappearance."

"Did Samuel spend a lot of time at the Strangs' house?"

Leah nodded. "Oh yeah. I used this place as my escape"— she gestured to the room around them—"and Samuel jumped all over the Strangs' freestanding invitation to use as his. He was constantly there. He and Bobby Strang got to be very close."

"What did your father think of that?"

Leah shrugged. "Daddy was still drinking a lot, and I think, just like with me and the motel, he knew Samuel was protecting himself. Daddy's not dumb, he was just ... broken for a while."

"He's better now?"

"He's getting there."

Lance left things at that. "So when did Samuel disappear?"

"Three days before the state championship game."

"And that's all? He was just here, playing football, spending a lot of time at his friend's house, and then one day he was gone?"

"Yes."

"And you didn't notice him acting different at all, like something was wrong? Who was the last person to see him?"

"No, he seemed completely normal. Funny enough, it was Bobby Strang who saw him last. They had been in town, getting some burgers for lunch, and Samuel told Bobby he had to go, that he was going to see his girlfriend."

"He had a girlfriend?" Lance asked.

Leah's face grew somber again, and she took a deep breath. "This is the other part that kills me, the part I can't understand. Samuel and I were always close, being only a year apart. It's just the way we grew up together. We had no secrets. He still came by the motel as often as he could to say hi, or bring me some takeout for dinner, and we always talked about what was going on in our lives."

"Okay."

"And not once in all those visits, all that time together, even two days before he vanished, did he ever mention a single word to me about having a girlfriend."

Lance had no brothers or sisters of his own and briefly let his mind wander to explore what it might be like to have somebody who shared his blood and was that close to him, somebody he could always trust and count on and speak freely to without fear of judgment. Somebody he could share his world with.

He quickly realized this person had been his mother, and his heart thumped a beat of anguish. God, how he missed her.

"So who was this girlfriend?" he asked.

Leah threw her hands up in frustration. "That's the worst part of the whole thing. Nobody I've spoken to, not the other players, not other students, and not even Bobby Strang, even knew Samuel *had* a girlfriend. She's a phantom. Nobody has the slightest clue who she was."

"But she could very well have been the last person to have seen your brother alive."

"Exactly."

"Well, then, we have to find her."

10

LANCE OPENED HIS EYES AND WONDERED WHEN HIS bedroom ceiling had become so dirty. He didn't remember ever seeing it so filthy, with blackish-gray smears of dust and cobwebs dancing in the corners with unseen swirls of air. It was an odd thing. His mother had always kept things very...

The memories flooded him, and he sat up, remembering everything that had happened. His eyes focused on the dull surroundings of his motel room, and he remembered where he was.

He remembered last night.

After Leah's revelation about her brother's mysterious girlfriend, she'd quickly gone on to explain that Samuel had been the first, and one Westhaven football player had followed in her brother's disappearing footsteps in each of the past two years. Two years in which Westhaven had won state titles.

Three years.

Three championships.

Three missing

(*Dead?*)

boys.

Lance had had more questions, and Leah had seemed to have more information, but at that point it had gotten to be a few minutes after midnight and Lance's headache was starting to kick up again. Plus, his afternoon nap was wearing off, his body once again beginning to feel weary, and he knew he needed sleep.

"Let's meet for breakfast in the morning, then we can get to work," Leah had said as he'd thanked her for the pizza and made his way to the office's door.

"Get to work?"

Leah had cocked her head to side. "Well, yeah. You know … solving the case."

Lance had been tired and had hated to admit that Leah's enthusiasm to begin chasing down what he knew to be something neither of them were likely capable of dealing with was beginning to irritate him. A normal person might have been quick to vocalize such annoyances, but Lance had better sense. He knew Leah was hurting and had been for some time now. Whatever small flame of hope she'd been holding on to had been doused in gasoline and had exploded the moment Lance had told her what he was and shown an interest.

"I'm not a detective," he'd said.

"No," she'd said. "You're better than a detective. You actually care."

It was the truth. "You know Annabelle's Apron?"

She'd rolled her eyes. "Hello, I've lived here my whole life, and there aren't a lot of options. Daddy says Ms. Winters used to make the best pies in the state."

Lance had nodded. "She told—" He'd caught himself. "That's what I've heard. Meet there at eight?"

Leah had shaken her head. "Nine. That way the kids will be in school and the adults at work. You heard Daddy earlier. Folks have already reported you as *suspicious*. The fewer people who see us together, the better."

Lance agreed but knew that no matter how careful they were in their appearances, there was something worse than peeping human eyes keeping tabs on him. Something that would not be easily deterred. He had said goodnight and taken the few short steps to his motel room, his sneakers crunching the shattered plastic from the overhead light that had exploded earlier. He had shuffled a few of the broken shards around on the concrete and looked up at the now-blackened hole where the bulb and globe had been, looked across the parking lot to the road, the single streetlamp still casting its dull glow.

The air had been still and cool, but Lance knew better than to think it innocent.

After a quick check of his small room, which included looking into the mirror for surprise guests and pulling back the shower curtain to examine the empty tub, Lance had kicked off his shoes and fallen asleep almost instantly when his head had touched the pillow.

And now he was awake, a stranger in a town that held secrets that did not want to be revealed. *But how far will it go to stop me?*

The motel room's window was traced by an outline of gold as the early-morning sunlight squirted through the cracks. Lance stood and stretched, felt the lump on the back of his head and was pleased to find that it'd gotten much smaller than the night before. After rubbing his eyes, he found his vision to be fine and his headache to be gone. All that remained was the tender area of skin around the knot at the base of his skull. In time, that would heal.

He checked his flip phone and saw it was a quarter to seven. No missed calls or voicemails had been logged, which didn't surprise him in the slightest. He'd gotten few phone calls before, and he imagined, with his mother gone, he'd get even fewer now. He sighed, found his phone charger in his backpack and plugged it into the wall behind the nightstand. Once his phone was sucking down juice, Lance went into the bathroom and took a shower, extremely thankful for the motel-provided mini bar of soap, even if it did look as if he were scrubbing himself with an oversized Tic-Tac.

Finished with the shower and having dried himself, he looked at the pile of clothes he'd discarded on the floor and was slightly repulsed at the fact he would have to wear the whole outfit again. Socks, boxers, everything. He needed to go shopping, as soon as possible. He looked suspicious enough as it was, so wearing the same outfit every day to go along with eternal morning breath and his pits likely reeking of BO did not seem like the best option.

He shook out his clothing, a half-hearted attempt to de-wrinkle them, and then dressed. He unplugged his cell phone and slid it into his pocket, then repacked the charger. After a thorough check of the room to be sure he'd not left behind any personal items, he slid his backpack onto his shoulders, peeked through the blinds and scanned the parking lot for any movement. He went outside.

His hand went immediately to his face, shielding his eyes from the sun. He squinted and looked down to the asphalt, letting his eyes adjust. When they finally did, he looked to his right, toward the motel's office door, and found himself wanting to go in that direction. To pop his head inside and offer Leah a quick "good morning" and tell her he was looking forward to their breakfast

(*It's not a date*)

together. But then he was stepping off the sidewalk and making his way across the parking lot. *Stop being silly, Lance. That's not why you're here.*

The pickup truck was gone, but the Jeep with the stuffed Garfield suctioned to the window was still in the same place. Lance met the cat's plastic eyes as he walked past the car and wondered who it was that owned the vehicle, what kind of person he or she was, where they were headed.

His sneakers found Route 19, and before he turned to walk back toward town, he noticed the plume of smoke rising high above the trees in the distance. It had to be miles away, but still it was impossible to miss, a great gray pillar growing toward the sky. "That's got to be the paper mill," he said to the road, and he wondered if he'd make his way there, if whatever mystery he was attempting to solve would draw him toward that black smoke.

He walked along the sidewalk, back into town. A few cars passed him by, one going so far as to drive in the other lane as it passed, making sure to give Lance all the room he needed. *Well, at least I know not everybody's out for blood around here.*

Back in the heart of Westhaven's downtown, Lance turned off the main drag and walked two blocks down a side street. He found a small CVS on the corner and went inside, an elderly gentleman greeting him with a large smile and a loud "G'morning!" Lance returned the greeting with a smile and a nod and grabbed one of the plastic baskets from a stack near the door. Ten minutes later he'd made his purchases: toothbrush, toothpaste, deodorant, shampoo, soap, shaving cream, disposable razor, a small travel first-aid kit, a three-pack of white athletic socks, a three-pack of boxer shorts, and a pack of spearmint gum. "Is there someplace close where I could buy some clothes?" Lance had asked the man at the counter as he paid.

"Depends what sort of clothes you're looking for, son."

Lance looked down at his t-shirt and cargo shorts, his scuffed sneakers.

"I see," the man said. Then he pointed over his shoulder, as if this was a display of precision direction giving. "Sportsman's is a block over, but Harry doesn't open until nine."

Darn. Looks like I'm wearing the same thing for breakfast as dinner.

"Thank you very much," Lance said, and then asked, "Restroom?"

Lance followed another of the man's pointing fingers and carried his shopping bag to the back right corner of the store, where he found the men's room. Inside one of the stalls, he changed his boxers and put on a fresh pair of socks. Then he brushed his teeth and applied a thick layer of deodorant. He stuffed everything into his backpack and then headed toward the front of the store to leave. The elderly gentleman behind the counter was reading the day's newspaper, and as Lance was about to exit the store, he had an idea. "Excuse me, sir?"

The man peered at Lance from atop the paper. "Yes, son? Something else I can do for you?"

Lance hesitated for a moment, realizing this could be a bad idea, but he wanted to get a feel for things. He knew he had to ask. "I'm just passing through, on a way to visit a friend of mine a little further north. I told him I was coming through here, and he mentioned to me that he thought he heard that a bunch of high school boys have disappeared around here over the years. Is that true, or was he just pulling my leg? Trying to spook me, or something?"

It was like the air had suddenly been sucked out of the room. The man's smile faltered and the newspaper went all the way down to the counter. Then the man looked Lance dead in the eyes and said, "What are you, a reporter? Somebody looking for a scandal, to stir up trouble?"

"No, sir. It just sounded to me like you already had trouble. You know anything about it?"

The man stared at Lance for another hard second and then

picked up his newspaper. "Move along, son. Your friend is waiting for you."

Lance left the store and stood on the sidewalk outside the automatic doors. When he looked over his shoulder, he saw the man behind the counter looking at him through the window, his face partially hidden by a large advertisement promising Buy One, Get One Free for any bottled beverage. Lance waved and smiled. The man's face disappeared.

Lance sighed. *Well, that didn't go well.*

He checked his phone and saw it was nearly 8:30. Time for breakfast.

As he walked to Annabelle's Apron, he wondered if the man from CVS was already on the phone, letting everybody know that a *suspicious* man had stopped by this morning ... and he was asking questions.

[11]

HE WALKED THROUGH THE DINER'S DOOR AT TEN BEFORE nine and found Leah seated at the counter on one of the stools. She had one hand curled around a coffee mug, the other wrapped around her iPhone, her thumb aimlessly scrolling the screen. Her hair was down this morning. It looked clean and was shining in the sunlight pouring through the diner's windows. Gone was the black business suit, in its place a pair of green khaki shorts and a red t-shirt, a pair of white-and-red Converse sneakers on her feet.

Lance loved the girl's sense of style. He felt even more conscious about his lack of different clothes. He'd never been one to care much about his own appearance, but he didn't want to come off as a bum, and he hated feeling dirty.

As usual, because of his size, many of Annabelle's Apron's guests' eyes followed Lance as he made his way toward the counter. He smiled at a few that were close enough to notice, and they offered quick grins before turning their attention back toward their plates and newspapers. He had barely reached the counter when Margie came through the kitchen door and saw him, her stern face noticeably softening for a moment as she said, "Well, good morning! The man with the bottomless pit for a stomach returns. I told the afternoon staff all about you yesterday. They thought I was making it up. Said nobody could eat all of that and still walk out the door of their own accord." The woman laughed, and Lance noticed that her smile was very nice. He hoped that she got the chance to use it more often.

He waved back and sat himself on a stool, leaving a one-stool gap between himself and Leah. "Sounds like folks around here need to eat more," Lance said to Margie as she slid a coffee mug in front of him. "I used to put away twice that on game days back when I played ball."

Margie filled his mug. "Football?" she asked, her eyes lighting up.

Lance shook his head. "No. Too skinny for football. Basketball."

"Oh," Margie said, seemingly disappointed.

"Margie, sweetie, I'll take some of that coffee over here, and some of your sugar to go with it." Hank Peterson was in his same spot at the end of the counter, coffee mug held out like a street beggar.

Margie rolled her eyes. "Your wife's sugar not good enough, Hank?" Then she winked at Lance and went to fill Hank's coffee.

"Well," Leah said, speaking to him for the first time, "you've certainly made a reputation for yourself. Never known Margie to take to a stranger so quickly. She's usually, well, sort of a bitch. You know, in that Great American Diner sort of way."

"I think she just likes me because my bill is high. Plus, well, I'm downright charming."

Leah had no comment on Lance's level of charming. Instead, she stood from the counter, grabbed her coffee mug and said, "Come on, let's go get a booth so we can talk without everybody listening."

Lance stood, and when Margie saw him and gave him a questioning look, Lance raised his eyebrows and shrugged his shoulders, as if to say, *What am I going to do?*

He followed Leah through the smattering of tables, only a few of which had actual diners seated at them, and ended up sitting in the same rear corner booth where the family with the young child had been yesterday morning. Lance sat with his back to the side of the building, facing the front. Leah had her back to everything except him and the window behind him.

Remembering Margie's look, Lance said, "It's not going to be a secret very long that we're here together."

Leah shrugged. "I know. I thought it'd be better coming in later like this, but I wasn't even thinking about the people working here. Oh well. It's not like we're making out and causing a scene. For all anybody knows, you could be my cousin, or something."

Lance's brain had stopped listening at the words "making out" and he had to push away the images they conjured in order to bring his focus back to the present. "Okay," he said.

"Okay, what?"

A waitress brought them menus just in time to save him. Leah held up her hands and said, "I'll just have some wheat toast and jelly, Sarah."

Lance handed his menu back as well and ordered his same breakfast from yesterday.

"You know her?" he asked once the waitress was out of earshot.

Leah nodded and took a sip of her coffee. "Few years older than me. She used to be a cheerleader for Westhaven. Was supposed to go to college on a scholarship."

"What happened?"

"She got pregnant by the high school math teacher."

Lance swallowed a steaming-hot sip of coffee faster than he

wanted to. He coughed and said, "Whoa. That's pretty scandalous."

Leah raised her mug in a toast. "Welcome to Small Town, USA."

They were quiet for a bit, both sipping coffee and waiting for their food. "Who's watching the motel?" Lance asked.

"Renee. It's her normal shift, but I told her today I might need her to work some extra hours. I told her I had some things I needed to take care of. She doesn't mind. She needs the money."

"How many people do you have working for you?"

"Technically, they work for Daddy, but ..." She looked up, mentally tallying. "Five, if you count Martin. He's a handyman that Daddy pays a fee each month to be on standby. In case something needs fixing."

"A handyman on retainer," Lance said. "Not a bad gig."

Leah nodded. "And he's the sweetest guy in the world."

Their food came, and as Leah spread jelly on her toast and Lance poured syrup on his pancakes, Lance asked a question that had been nagging at him from the early moments of Leah telling him the town's troubled past. "So, what exactly do the police have to say about everything?"

Leah took a bite and wiped her mouth with a paper napkin. "Not much."

"Come on. Three kids gone missing. They've said *something*." Lance forked eggs into his mouth and washed it down with a bite of pancake.

Leah sighed. "You're right. Sort of. They honestly did seem to make a decent effort when Samuel disappeared. At first, anyway. But when the leads—which were essentially zero—led to dead ends, they started looking a little closer at the home life."

Lance swallowed another bite of food, knowing all at once where this was going. "They think he ran away." It wasn't a question. It was fact.

Leah nodded. "Again ... small town. Sheriff's office all knew about Momma passing and knew Daddy was drinking a lot." Then, embarrassed, "He's spent more than one night in the drunk tank after having a few too many and getting started on the wrong topic of conversation. Daddy's got a short fuse."

And the alcohol makes it shorter, Lance thought, feeling a twinge of anger at the memory of Leah's confession that her father had struck her and her brother.

She continued, "Everybody knew things weren't the best at our house. They knew I'd been working extra hours at the motel, and then ... well, when they found out Daddy'd hit us a few times, that was the final nail in the coffin. They immediately assumed Samuel had had enough."

Lance shook his head. "And just like that, case closed?"

"More or less. I mean, technically the case is still open—cold now—but nobody's following up with it. The last time any member of the sheriff's office came to see me was after the second boy disappeared. After the third, the state police got involved, or at least pretended to, but that fizzled out almost as quick as it started."

Because he was trying his best to give Leah his undivided attention, Lance was eating slower than normal, but still he was almost finished with his meal. Leah had only eaten half a piece of toast. "They can't possibly think they're *all* runaways. That's asinine."

Leah took another bite, her toast surely cold by now. "Do you read a lot?"

"What?"

"Asinine. That's what I was talking about last night. Who says that in daily conversation?"

Lance finished his coffee, thought about the shelves and shelves of books he'd left behind at his and his mother's home. The tattered paperbacks from yard sales, the hardbacks from library sales and used bookstores. He'd been making his way through all the titles, even going so far as to make a list in a notebook he kept in his nightstand. His mother *had* read them all. She was the most well read person he'd ever known. His stomach tightened at the thought that he'd never get to finish his list. "Does my vocabulary really bother you that much?"

She smiled. Shook her head. "No. I just think it's fun to give you a hard time about it. Honestly, I kinda love it."

The tightness in Lance's stomach was replaced by a warmth and fluttering.

"Anyway," Leah continued, "yes, the other two boys were also assumed to be runaways. Actually, that's the only thing that seems to make sense out of any of this."

"How so?"

"All the boys, Samuel included, had reasons enough to make the sheriff's office believe that their wanting to fly the coop was acceptable. On top of that, they were all eighteen. No longer juveniles."

Sarah stopped by the table to refill their cups, and Lance ordered a slice of pie. He asked her to make sure Margie knew he was ordering it, and to tell her that it was the best pie he'd had since his mother's. He figured a little damage control couldn't hurt. Maybe if he was polite enough and sucked up enough, Margie wouldn't label him suspicious as most other folks seemed eager to do.

"You know Samuel's story," Leah said. "Chuck Goodman's family had owned the hardware store for like a billion years, but the new Walmart fifteen miles up Route 19 finally put them out of business. Chuck's father took it pretty hard, and there were rumors they were going to move during Christmas break to be closer to Chuck's mother's family."

"And the police thought Chuck was unhappy with the arrangement and lashing out by running away?"

"Pretty much." Leah finished her last piece of toast. "Martin Brownlee's brother was in the Marines, got killed overseas somewhere. His father shot himself a month after they got the news. Martin's mother seemed to be handling things as well as she could, but when Martin vanished, nobody asked a lot of questions about him. Why would he want to stick around in that sort of situation, a lot of people asked."

"To take care of his mother?"

Leah shrugged. "I'm just telling you what people were saying."

Sarah brought Lance his pie, and he started to eat. Then he asked, "So what does the town think? What do they think happened to those boys?"

Leah's face was calm, but her words carried a tremor of anger that was only barely being suppressed. "You grew up in a small town?" she asked.

"Not as small as this, but yeah, pretty much."

"Well, around here, football is the only goddam thing that matters to these stupid people. It's like ... like ... like they've got nothing else to live for, like there isn't a whole vast world out there with other things to see and explore and people to meet. Football. And now that we've been winning, it's only gotten worse." She took a sip of coffee, as if trying to let herself settle down. "People around here accept the idea of those boys being runaways because that's the easy way out. It means that nothing's wrong except those boys' heads, and as long as Westhaven keeps winning games, people can keep on smiling and everything will be all right."

Lance was quiet, thinking about all Leah had told him. He finished his pie, and when he looked up, she was staring out the window. He thought he saw a tear in her eye, but it might have just been a glare. "And you think it's going to happen again?" he asked.

She turned her head and looked at him. "Don't you?"

Lance closed his eyes and took in a deep breath, letting his mind reach out through the town, sending out the sensors that he didn't understand how he could sometimes control. It was out there, that permeating sense of dread that seemed to hang throughout Westhaven like invisible fog. He'd felt it when he'd gotten off the bus, and he felt it now. And it could feel him. "Yes. I do."

Leah's face looked thankful. "So what do we do now?"

Lance pulled out his flip phone. "I don't want to sound too forward here, but may I please have your phone number?"

Leah looked at his phone as though it were something recovered from a time capsule. "As long as you promise not to wait three days before calling."

Lance opened his phone and went through the laborious process of typing out Leah's name to add a new contact. "Does your thumb get cramps working that thing?" she asked.

Lance smiled, keeping his eyes on the screen. "Number, please?"

Leah laughed and recited the digits, adding, "Man, I just got a wicked chill. Must be a draft somewhere."

Lance's thumb froze over the keypad, one last digit stored away in his memory that needed to be typed. He pressed the button slowly, the cold chill Leah had brought to his attention enveloping him, the booth, everything around him. He hit the SAVE button and then shut his phone.

"You going to give me yours now?" Leah asked.

Lance lifted his eyes from the scratched tabletop. Used all his willpower not to show how startled he was.

The young man standing directly next to their booth had been burned badly. He was muscular and well built, just as the boy in Leah's mirror had been. Only that boy's swollen face and blackened eyes were nothing compared to the charred and disfigured body Lance was looking at now.

The boy was naked, every inch of his skin marred and melted, a hideous orange and red and black swirl of blood and blisters and bone showing through splotches of missing skin. The boy's eye sockets were empty, traces of white and yellow and green fluids caked and dried to the remaining caverns where eyeballs should have been. Half the boy's left cheek was gone, slightly yellowed teeth winking out at Lance from a blackened and drooping gum line.

Lance felt his food shift in his stomach.

"Hey," Leah said. "You holding out on me?"

Lance's vision blurred for a moment. He shook his head and looked at Leah, the dark figure next to their booth still looming in his peripheral vision. "I'm sorry, what?" he asked, doing his best to sound cheerful.

"That antique phone you have—it does receive incoming calls, yes?"

There was a slow movement out of the corner of Lance's right eye.

"Oh, yeah, sorry. Let me know when you're ready."

The boy was reaching his right arm toward Leah, skeleton-like fingers, more bone than skin and tendons, outstretched in a menacing claw.

Leah held up her iPhone. "Been ready."

Lance recited the beginning of his number. *It can't hurt her. It can't hurt her. It can't—*

"Okay. Next."

He finished rattling off the remaining digits just as the tip of one of the blackened fingers touched a few wisps of Leah's golden hair. Lance wanted to jump up, wanted to grab her and pull her away and get the heck out of there. But that would mean he'd have to tell her the truth. All of it.

"Hey." She was looking at him, concerned. "You okay over there?" She laughed. "Did you eat too much?"

The door to the diner exploded open, slamming against the wall and rattling the windows. All eyes in Annabelle's Apron locked onto the source of the noise.

A short man, maybe five-five but built like a refrigerator, his width nearly filling the entire doorway, stormed into the diner and looked around, eyes wild. "Leah!" he called out.

Uh-oh.

"Daddy?"

Lance looked to his right. The burned boy was gone.

[12]

ANNABELLE'S APRON WAS OVERCOME WITH A HUSH. IT WAS like a scene from an old-time Western, the eyes of spectators flicking back and forth between two opposing foes and waiting to see what would play out before them. Waiting to see who would make the first move.

Leah's daddy's eyes locked onto his daughter, and he quickly made his way down the walkway between the rows of booths and tables, his girth causing him to bump a few chairs along the way. Some of those chairs had people sitting in them, but nobody seemed to mind. Especially not Leah's daddy.

And then he was there, standing in the exact spot the burned boy had been just seconds ago.

Lance preferred the burned boy.

Up close, Leah's daddy was even wider. His forearms and biceps looked ready to rip phone books in half, and his chest and shoulders stretched the white undershirt the man was wearing to the point that it seemed ready to explode off his body. The legs of his blue jeans looked more likely to be covering tree trunks than human thighs. The heavy, steel-toed work boots seemed primed and ready to kick a man's teeth in or stomp a rib cage until the bones inside rattled around like castanets.

And the man was completely bald. Not a single hair on his egg-shaped head. Whether this was by choice or by genetics, Lance didn't have time to ponder, nor ask. The man's bloodshot eyes squinted, the blood vessels road mapping his nose squished together as his face grew into a snarl. "Who the hell are you?"

Lance wished he had been standing. At least then he'd have a significant height advantage. And could run away. But there was no running now. If he tried to make a move out of the booth, the walking cinder block of a man before him would surely snatch him up and slam him down. Lance liked his clavicle in one piece. So, he did the only thing he knew to do. He played dumb, and he hoped he was as charming as he thought he was.

Lance stuck out his hand. "I'm Lance, sir. Pleasure to meet you. Would you like to join us?"

Leah's daddy's snarl intensified. "Don't give a fuck what your name is. I asked who you were."

"*Daddy!*" Leah said. "What's gotten into you. We're just—"

"Shut your mouth. Now!"

Leah's face reddened, and Lance felt his anger begin to rise. But he had to keep it cool, otherwise this definitely wasn't going to end well.

"I'm sorry, sir," he said. "I don't know how else to answer you. You asked who I am, and my name is Lance. If you want to know more, I'm afraid you're going to have to be more specific. Otherwise, I fear we may be here awhile, and well... I've already eaten."

Leah couldn't stifle her laugh, a noise that seemed to catch everybody off guard. Her daddy shot her a look that could have knocked over bowling pins. Then he turned back to Lance, the muscles in his arms practically twitching, the veins pulsing.

"You want specifics? Here they are. Why in the fuck are you in this booth with my daughter?"

A number of answers filled Lance's mind, the truth being one that he thought would get the biggest reaction out of the man, but might also cause the most damage. Leah, fortunately, had the golden answer.

"*Daddy!* If you'd shut *your* mouth for a minute, you'd know that I'm interviewing him for a job."

Lance and Daddy both looked at her and said, "What?"

"Yes," she said. "Travis is going to start taking classes at the community college at night, and he's looking for another job to work in the daytime. So Lance here is interested in taking his spot at the motel. He stayed with us last night and asked if I knew of any place that was hiring, so I mentioned he could maybe work for us."

Lance marveled at Leah's quick thinking. "That's correct, sir. I've always had a bit of an interest in the hospitality industry, and your establishment seems like just the right type of environment to—"

Leah's daddy held up a scarred and calloused hand. Lance stopped talking. The man's features softened, his stance shifting to one less intimidating. He eyed Lance for a hard fifteen seconds, and Lance felt an absurd urge to smile big, as if for the school picture. Then the man's gaze switched to Leah. He took a breath and said, "That's really all this is? You're tellin' your daddy the truth?"

"*Yes*, Daddy. I know the rules."

The rest of the diner patrons slowly began to turn their attention back to their own tables, the sound of forks on plates and coffee mugs refilled by waitresses helped to bring the place back alive. The idle chitchat began to start up again.

Leah's daddy took one more glance at Lance before saying

to his daughter, "Come by the house sometime soon. I'll make dinner. It's been a while."

Leah smiled, but Lance already knew it to be artificial. "Yeah, sure. That sounds nice."

Her daddy nodded once, then turned and went to the counter, saying, "Margie, I'd love some coffee."

Lance watched as the woman gave the man a mug and filled it, then she leaned over and the two of them started talking quietly, Margie's eyes flicking in Lance's direction every so often.

"Don't take it personally," Leah said. "Gossip is gossip is gossip."

"I guess," Lance said. "But word sure did travel fast."

Leah turned and looked across the diner, scanned the few remaining customers. "And the worst part? It could have been any one of them."

Lance stared at the wide back of Leah's daddy, imagined all the hours spent at the paper mill, building those muscles to the shape they now were. "What's his name?" Lance asked.

"Who? Daddy?"

"Yes."

Leah glanced toward her father. "Samuel. My brother was a junior."

And in that moment, after feeling as though he'd narrowly averted a beatdown of the greatest magnitude, Lance felt pity for the man at the counter. He'd lost his wife, and then he'd lost his son. The only thing that mattered at all anymore was currently seated directly across from Lance. Lance's mother had told him that alcohol poisoned the mind and the body. But it sure as heck didn't dampen a father's urge to protect his only daughter.

"That was some quick thinking," Lance said.

Leah shrugged. "Thank God it worked. But now I have to

tell Travis he has to lie to Daddy if the topic ever comes up. Shouldn't be that big a deal, though. Daddy doesn't come around that often. He leaves most things up to me."

Lance nodded, took a sip of coffee that had begun to grow cold, bitter.

"So what do we do now?" Leah asked. "What's the first step?"

Lance had considered this during his walk from the motel to the CVS, and after listening to Leah tell him the stories of the rest of the boys who'd gone missing, he was certain of one question he wanted asked. "I want you to go do your best and see if any of the other two boys had girlfriends at the time they disappeared. Ask around, talk to people. You'll know much better than I would who to go see."

Leah nodded, but Lance could tell something was disappointing her. "And what are you going to do?"

Lance looked out the window to the mostly empty parking lot. "I'm not sure yet. But I'll figure it out. Times like this, I usually do."

"You know that makes, like, no sense at all."

Lance nodded. "Yeah, I know." He pulled some cash from his pocket and tossed it on the table. "I'm going to get out of here. That should cover yours too, so now we're even from the pizza." He stood from the booth. "Call me if you find out anything, and I'll do the same."

He made a show of waving to Margie as he left. "The pie was delicious!" he called to her. And then he wondered if Annabelle Winters had heard him, and was shaking her head.

If she was there, he wondered if she'd seen the burned boy.

[13]

LANCE WALKED BACK TO THE CVS AND THEN NAVIGATED A few more blocks until he found Sportsman's, a large storefront nestled between a dry cleaner and a martial arts studio that was advertising free first lessons to kids ages six to twelve. Lance looked through the glass front of the dry cleaner and saw a small woman with gray hair perched on a stool behind the counter, the eraser of her pencil bouncing against her bottom lip as she studied the crossword puzzle book she held. The rack behind her held only a few garments waiting to be picked up.

Lance pulled open the door to Sportsman's and was greeted by modern pop music playing through overhead speakers—something by one of those trendy new boy bands who liked to wear skinny jeans and slick their hair up and sing about love and sex at the ripe old age of seventeen. Lance didn't care for the music, but the décor was refreshing, like finally finding a person who speaks your native tongue after traveling abroad. The store was large and separated by category: hunting and fishing, camping, baseball and softball, basketball, football, golf, you name it. The entire back wall displayed athletic shoes of every make and model. Large cutouts and posters of the likes of Kevin Durant and Cam Newton and Rickie Fowler were bright and flashy and surely convinced folks they *needed* the same shoes these insanely gifted athletes wore.

The air smelled of leather and rubber and new shoes and competition.

There didn't appear to be any other shoppers in the store. Lance figured this was because it was still early. A store like this wasn't going to survive long in this town without some revenue. And if Leah's words were true, which Lance figured them to be, athletics really did appear to be more and more the lifeblood of Westhaven.

Lance's eyes gravitated to the basketball goal on display in the corner, an expensive model gleaming and beautiful, and he was hit with the urge to find a ball and go dunk it as hard as he could. Just to feel normal for a bit, to relax. But there was no time for that. He wasn't here to have fun.

A man wearing chinos and a Sportsman's embroidered collared shirt stepped out from behind one of the aisles. He held an old-fashioned clipboard in his hand and a pencil tucked behind his ear. "Hi there, welcome to Sportsman's. Can I help you find something?"

Yes, I'm looking for something that's been killing off your town's football players. Something from the supernatural line, probably. Not very flashy, but gets the job done.

Lance smiled and nodded toward the racks of clothes near the wall of shoes. "Need some new outfits. I think I see where I need to look."

"Be sure and let us know if you need any help." The man flashed a quick smile and then disappeared back into his aisle.

Lance found a clearance rack of t-shirts and managed to find three in his size. Then he did the same with basketball shorts. In the hunting and fishing section, he found a pair of brown-and-green camo shorts.

At the checkout counter, the man in the chinos rang up Lance's purchases and the total exceeded the amount of cash Lance was carrying. He slid his debit card from his wallet, wondering for the first time just how far his money would stretch. He'd saved up a decent amount from part-time work back home, odd jobs here and there. But he'd never held a full-time position anywhere, and sooner or later, he was going to run out of money. He'd have to find work. Or play the lotto.

His mother would scowl at him for that joke. The lotto was for the unambitious.

The transaction was approved, and Lance asked the man if he'd mind terribly if he used one of the fitting rooms to change. The man gave him a quick glance up and down, as if his question had suddenly provoked concern, but then smiled and nodded and said that was no problem at all. As Lance thanked him and began walking toward the fitting rooms the man called out, "Did you buy that backpack from us?"

Lance turned and smiled. "No, sir. It was a gift from a friend."

The man nodded. "I didn't think I'd seen you in here before. You new in town?"

"Just passing through," Lance said, then wondered just how true of a statement that was. His thoughts of the future were too overwhelming to dwell on. He had to focus on the task at hand.

Lance changed his clothes, pushing his two-day-old t-shirt and cargo shorts into the bottom of his backpack and pulling on one of the new shirts and pair of basketball shorts. He instantly felt better, almost reenergized, and as he was walking back down the center aisle of the store to make his exit, he caught himself whistling along with the tune playing overhead.

Then he saw the pictures and stopped.

To his left, the wall next to the exit door was a collage of photographs of local sports teams and athletes and newspaper clippings of exciting headlines, some framed, some not. The wall was meant to look causal, haphazard, abstract, but Lance knew that somebody in the store had taken great pains to make it only appear this way. This was somebody's baby, a side project that was fueled with passion.

Here was a shot of a basketball player shooting a three, a defender's outstretched arm desperately trying to prevent the shot.

There was a team photo of the Westhaven 2011 women's tennis team. A small group of young girls wearing white skirts and matching red sleeveless tops, their rackets all held sideways across their bodies like they were posing with a trophy.

Below this was a framed front page of the *Westhaven Journal*'s sports section, the headline screaming: WEST-HAVEN WINS FIRST EVER STATE TITLE!

And next to this, large and framed and clearly meant to stand out, was a team photograph of the Westhaven football team. They were in celebration in the end zone of the field they'd just played on, organized but excited and jubilant in their victory. There were three rows, the rearmost row standing while the middle row knelt and the front row sat on the ground. Some boys held their helmets high in the air, cheers frozen on their faces. Others had tossed their helmets to the ground, dotting the green of the field with their discarded armor and making it look like a ravaged battlefield. There was a large—insanely large—trophy on the ground between the middle boys in the front row. It towered up and gleamed in the sunlight, a lens flare popping from one side. The boys' faces were sweaty and dirty and tired, but they were clearly living in one of the best moments of their lives.

The frame was a dark polished wood without a speck of dust, and there was a large gold placard in the center of the bottom panel. The engraving read:

WESTHAVEN HIGH SCHOOL FOOTBALL TEAM
2012 VIRGINIA STATE AA CHAMPIONS
FINAL SCORE: 28–7

Below the header in a much smaller script were the names of the players and coaches. Lance scanned the names, recognized Coach McGuire and Chuck Goodman and Martin Brownlee. He didn't see Leah's brother Samuel's name. This would have been Samuel's team, the year he'd disappeared. The lack of even an honorable mention or in memoriam side note was more unsettling than Lance cared to admit.

He looked at the photo, with no way of knowing which boy was which, as the names on the placard were simply alphabetical. Then he moved on to the two smaller framed shots to the right of this large one, each one inching folks closer to the door. They were the team pictures for each of the following two state titles Westhaven had won. Chuck Goodman was not listed on the second picture. And on the third and final photograph, showing last year's team once again celebrating with another large trophy and more large smiles, Martin Brownlee's name was nowhere to be found.

Something else caught Lance's attention, and he went back down the row of photographs to take a second look. The rear row of boys in each picture was bookended by coaches and staff, clearly recognizable by the headsets and ball caps and khaki pants and shirts and playbooks and Gatorade-soaked shirts. Kenny McGuire, Lance knew because of the picture he had seen in the newspaper Leah had shown him, but the other men's faces were anonymous to him.

But it wasn't the coaches who caught Lance's eye. In each picture, starting with Westhaven's first state title, there was another man with the group. He was tall and broad-shouldered and clearly built like a player past his prime. His hair was peppered with gray, but his face appeared younger than the rest of him. In the first picture he was standing by the coaches, a small gap between himself and coach McGuire. He wore a dark blue sweater and crisply pressed jeans with loafers. The second and third picture, he was kneeling on the grass with the middle row, beaming just as big and bright as the players. And in the last picture, the man was again adorned in a sweater and loafers, only he'd decided to casual it up some with a Westhaven ball cap. This time, he was seated on the grass next to the front row, his arm draped around the player to his left.

There was a clear resemblance between the man and the boy, and before Lance's mind fully made the connection, a voice next to him said, "Never seen anything like it in all my years."

Lance, startled, turned and found the man with the chinos and clipboard next to him. "What haven't you seen?" Lance asked.

"That team." The man pointed to the picture of the first title team. "They were about the sorriest group of ball players I've ever had the misfortune to witness. And then"—he snapped his fingers—"state title the very next year, and every year since." He shook his head. "If I was a betting man, I'd have lost big-time. Hell, the whole town would have lost. Don't get me wrong, we'd support those boys and cheer and holler 'til our throats went raw, but we knew they stunk up the place."

Lance nodded and asked the same question he had asked Leah last night. "What changed?"

The man shrugged. "Got to be the coach. McGuire doesn't look like much, but he's whipped those kids into shape. Can't deny it, right?"

Lance didn't answer. He wasn't so sure. Instead, he pointed to the man in the picture, the outlier. "Who's that? He doesn't look like a coach."

Chino man leaned forward for a better look, then his eyes brightened and he smiled like he'd just found twenty bucks in his pocket. "Oh, that's another blessing our poor team received. Glenn Strang has given those kids every advantage he possibly can. Don't know what we'd do without him"—then, in a whisper —"or his money." Chino man laughed, and Lance went along with it. The connection his brain had started before was finalized. The boy Glenn Strang had his arm around in the last picture was his son, Bobby.

"Yeah," Chino man said, "McGuire and Strang—those guys really turned it all around. Thank God they showed up when they did."

Lance thanked the man and left the store, wondering just what else had shown up in town the day Kenny McGuire or Glenn Strang had ridden in.

[14]

LANCE WALKED AWAY FROM DOWNTOWN, INTENT ON dropping his purchases off at his motel room—now that he was clearly staying another day, at the least—and then deciding where he should go. If Leah had done as he'd asked, then hopefully she'd be well on her way to trying to dig up any info she could about whether either of the other two missing boys had had girlfriends at the time they'd disappeared.

Ordinarily, a high school boy having a girlfriend wouldn't be enough to set off the alarm bells in Lance's head. But it was the fact that Samuel had hidden his relationship from Leah that made Lance suspicious. He knew she wasn't the type of person who would exaggerate the closeness she shared with her brother. If she said they were thick as thieves, Lance believed her. Plus, in a town this small, Lance had a hard time understanding just how a member of the football team, an active member of the town social circle, could even manage to keep something as significant as a girlfriend a secret. It seemed fairly impossible for Samuel and his girl to go out to dinner, a movie, a walk in the park, *anything*, without eyeballs noticing and word of mouth traveling.

There was, of course, the possibility that Bobby Strang was not being honest. Leah hadn't mentioned whether Bobby's statement about Samuel needing to go see his girlfriend had been given to her straight from the horse's mouth, or passed on via the police during the investigation. Either way, if Bobby Strang had made the girlfriend thing up, that meant he was either covering for Samuel, or for somebody else. Maybe even himself?

By the time Lance made it back to the motel, he'd all but decided he'd like to have a chat with Bobby Strang, and he hoped he didn't have Leah out chasing a red herring. But there was nothing wrong with leaving no stone unturned. Her brother had been missing for years now. His case wasn't going to be solved instantly, no matter if Lance was helping or not. His gifts helped with things like this, sure. But life wasn't an episode of *Murder, She Wrote*. Jessica Fletcher, he was not.

The Jeep with Garfield as a passenger was gone from the lot, as were all other cars except a dirty early-model Honda Civic with an Obama bumper sticker from his first campaign. There was a long scratch along the passenger-side door, and as he walked past, Lance saw a tattered copy of *The God Delusion* by Richard Dawkins lying on the floorboard and thought the car seemed entirely too Democratic for a town like Westhaven. The car was parked directly outside the door to the office, and Lance figured it must belong to Renee, the woman Leah had watching over things. He contemplated poking his head inside to say hello but thought better of it. Enough folks around Westhaven had already pegged him as a suspicious weirdo. No sense adding to the list. He'd keep his attempts at making friends to a rule of necessity.

He approached his door and saw that somebody—Leah, more than likely—had swept up the broken bits of plastic and glass. He looked up and found that she'd replaced the lightbulb as well.

Who needs Martin the handyman?

Lance slid his key into the lock and opened the door.

He stopped.

His bed had been made, and fresh tracks on the carpet showed that it'd been vacuumed since he'd left. *Leah?* he wondered. *Or was it Renee, or somebody else—a housekeeper? Does a place like this even have housekeepers?*

Even though he'd had zero personal belongings in the room at the time it'd been straightened up, his stomach still did an uneasy twirl at the thought of Leah poking around in here while he was gone. Not that he didn't trust the girl, and not that he possessed anything physical that would unravel his secrets, but it was the age-old tale of guy-meets-girl self-consciousness that even Lance himself was not immune to.

He liked Leah. Even at this disastrous, tragic, and earth-shattering moment of sadness and confusion in his life, human nature and biology and a human's desire to find love and companionship refused to take a backseat.

He pushed the thoughts away. He couldn't ignore what he was feeling, but nothing said he had to accept it.

He wasn't ready. It was too soon.

He didn't even have all the details of exactly what had happened after he had left town, after the night when—

His cell phone buzzed in his pocket, a hard vibration that caused his heart to lurch and snapped him back from his thoughts. He dropped his backpack onto the bed and fumbled with his phone, flipping it open. He'd received a text from Leah: *Working on more, but Chuck Goodman's sister is meeting me for lunch. 1 @ Frank's Pizza. Can you come?*

Lance studied the message, first impressed with how quickly Leah had managed to drum up a potential lead for information, but also concerned that his presence would make Chuck Goodman's sister uncomfortable, especially when dealing with what was already sure to be an uncomfortable subject. But again, he was going to trust his new friend. He convinced himself that Leah would not have invited him if she felt Chuck's sister would not be okay with it.

He began thumbing his worn and faded keys and texted back: *See you there.*

He had no idea where Frank's Pizza was located, but he usually had a way of finding things.

He went to the restroom and relieved himself and washed his hands. There was a freshly wrapped bar of soap at the sink, and clean towels hung from the rack next to the shower. He glanced back at the toilet bowl to make sure he hadn't dribbled or dripped any on the visible surface. He'd probably die if he ever knew Leah had wiped up his dried urine.

Back by the bed, he unzipped his backpack and separated his dirty clothes from his new purchases. He stuffed all the dirty items into one of the Sportsman's bags and then placed his new items in the other bag. He left his toiletries in the CVS bag and walked to set it and the bag of dirties in the bathroom. Back in the bedroom, he checked his phone once more for new messages, found none, and then left.

Outside, the sun was at its peak, and Lance was glad it was fall and not summer. Otherwise he'd bake to a crisp having to walk everywhere. He kicked himself for not buying a cheap pair of sunglasses at CVS. He didn't particularly care for sunglasses, or the way he looked in them, but they sure would help right about now. He squinted his eyes against the brightness and headed across the parking lot, a soft breeze helping to push him along and making the air feel crisper than it looked.

He had about forty-five minutes before he had to find Frank's Pizza and meet Leah and Chuck Goodman's sister, so he figured he had enough time to see Westhaven High School.

He couldn't say exactly why, and he didn't know exactly

what it was he planned on learning during the middle of a school day. With times the way they were, you couldn't hang around near a school for long without somebody calling the police. Whether you were wielding a candy cane or an AK-47, somebody would notice, and the repercussions would be just as swift either way.

Still, he walked.

He headed back toward town, but at an intersection he usually continued straight through, he stopped, closed his eyes for a moment, and then turned left, heading down another rural route that seemed nearly as desolate as the previous. The sidewalk vanished, and he was forced to walk on a grassy shoulder, the blades growing high enough in some spots to reach above his sneakers and tease his shins. Far off to his left he could still see the black plume of smoke rising above an expanding tree line, only now he could begin to make out the top of the smoke stack that spewed it. There was no doubt it was the paper mill.

The Strang family was another oddity in Lance's mind. On the surface, they seemed harmless, maybe even the good guys. Glenn Strang was an ex-player who still loved the game, loved his son, and used his fortunate financial means to help provide for an underfunded athletic program at a small-town high school. Admirable. Bobby Strang, from what Lance had heard from Leah, was probably the placekicker because he didn't have the skill or talent to play other positions. This could have been a point of discontent for Glenn Strang, but the man seemed to be taking it all in stride, being just as enthusiastic about his son and the team's accomplishments as he would if Bobby had been the quarterback. Aside from this, all Lance knew was that Bobby and Samuel had become close friends. And if Samuel was anything like Leah, that meant that Bobby couldn't be too bad a character. Lance still wanted to talk to him.

It was Mrs. Strang that Lance knew nothing about. Leah

had told him that she stayed at home and cooked meals for the boys and probably played team mom more than other actual mothers liked, but she hadn't factored into the story much at this point.

Before Lance could think about her any further, Westhaven High School began to grow out of the weeds ahead on the right like a desert mirage.

The school had a larger campus than Lance had expected, with three one-story buildings separated by covered sidewalks, giving the appearance of an eagle spreading its wings. The architecture was dated—fifties or sixties most likely—with weathered brick walls and peeling white paint on the overhangs covering the sidewalks. In front of the center building, which Lance assumed to be the office, a wide traffic lane looped across the buildings and connected on each end to the main road. There was a single bus parked here, along with several cars that probably belonged to office staff. A larger parking lot flooded out from the side of the right-most building, and it looked like a used-car lot where the dealings were in cash only and *warranty* was a foreign word. There were more pickup trucks and mud-splattered SUVs than Lance could count.

The door to the office building swung open, and a blond-haired woman wearing a simple skirt and light sweater stepped out and held the door wide. A single student walked out of the office with a yellow slip of paper in his hand and headed toward the left building. He was staring down at the sidewalk as he went, downtrodden and slow-moving. *That's a boy who just got in trouble*, Lance thought, then realized that if a bell rang then, the students would come flowing out of the buildings like a school of fish and he didn't want to be standing out here all alone, sticking out and being noticed. Lance's eyes followed the boy until he disappeared inside the other building. He looked back to the office just in time to see the door swing shut.

But he needed to see more. He was looking for something else.

Lance walked a little further, taking a few steps up the cracked asphalt leading toward the school's lot. There was a flagpole in a small section of grass outside the bus loop, the Stars and Stripes flying proudly alongside the deep blue of the Virginia state flag and the black and white of the DARE program's own banner. Lance's own high school's flagpole had looked exactly like this, and he again felt that twinge of longing for home.

Keeping in the grass, he continued up the entrance just enough to try and get a look behind the buildings. Halfway to the parking lot, he was able to see a fourth building behind the middle one, a large domed roof rising up over what was clearly the school's gymnasium. He thought back to his four years on the basketball team and tried to remember if he'd ever played against the Westhaven team. It would have had to have been in the state tournament, which he had only been privileged to go to his junior and senior year—no titles, unfortunately. He didn't think they'd ever played each other.

He wanted to see the football field. It was probably behind the gym, Westhaven's pride and joy stuck in the middle of what otherwise looked like a cornfield. But Lance didn't dare venture further. He was probably trespassing as it were, and he didn't want to push his luck.

He looked back toward the flagpole and studied the small brick marquee beside it. Beneath the WESTHAVEN HIGH SCHOOL insignia, a white message board with black plastic letters advertised upcoming school events. Lance read through the list, stopped, pulled out his phone to verify the date, and then smiled. He'd picked a good day to show up in Westhaven.

The football team had their next game that night. It was a home game, and he wished he'd thought to ask Leah about when the next game was sooner. It would have saved him a trip out here.

Thinking of Leah, he remembered lunch, and as he turned to head back to the road and start back into town, he heard the crunching of loose bits of asphalt and gravel under tires as a car slowly pulled into the drive behind him.

Without even looking, Lance immediately knew he would see a police cruiser when he turned around. Cops, for some reason, were easy to sense. The good ones ... and the bad ones. The problem was it was difficult to tell at first.

You took too long, Lance. He scolded himself. *This was a bad idea.*

Or ... or something knew you were here.

The sound from the tires stopped, and Lance heard the gentle hum of a car window being lowered. "Help you?" a voice dripping with Southern accent asked.

Lance, slowly, turned around and offered his best smile to the man behind the wheel of the sheriff's department car. "Afternoon, Officer." He waved. "No, sir. Just on my way into town to have lunch with a friend."

And then the thing Lance had hoped would not happen, did happen. The man behind the wheel rolled up the window, unfastened his seat belt, opened the door, and stepped out.

15

Lance had seen enough national news television footage ("*Such a sad place our world is,*" his mother often said as they watched. "*So much hate. So little love*") and he knew that being a stranger in town was recipe enough for a potential disaster, so he stayed perfectly still and didn't say a word as the sheriff's deputy stepped out of the car and stood with his hands on his hips, one palm resting on the butt of his holstered pistol.

It had been unwise for Lance to come here, but it was too late for regrets. He knew from Samuel Senior that he'd already been on the police radar since yesterday, and now he was only fueling the fire of the town's suspicions of him. He'd been caught loitering around a freaking school, of all places.

Lance stood. Waited. The deputy took another step closer and his eyes met Lance's, and all at once Lance let himself relax a little. The man had kind eyes, not the eyes of a power-abusing ruffian dressed as an officer of the law. He took another step forward and—Lance could hardly believe this—stuck out his hand. "Deputy Miller," the man said, and boy was that accent heavy. "What brings you to Westhaven, young man?"

Deputy Miller was almost as tall as Lance, but even thinner, an Ichabod Crane physique with spaghetti limbs and an Adam's apple that looked as if the man had swallowed an arrowhead. His uniform was loose-fitting, and he'd adjusted his hat twice since stepping out of the car. Lance shook the man's hand and

(*Single-story house in the nice section of town, green lawn, likes to garden, wife named Jen with red hair, pregnant with baby number two, first son's name is Ben, they joke because it rhymes with Jen, there go Ben and Jen, Jen says he works too much, but he says they need the money and Jen says they aren't that bad off, church every Sunday, third pew, plays on the softball team and always brings his famous triple-chocolate brownies to the potlucks*)

had to stifle his surprise as Deputy Miller's life flooded through his veins and into Lance's mind. He pulled his grip away fast, unintentionally rude. Deputy Miller's eyes scrunched in confusion.

I hate it when that happens. So weird.

Invasive was the word he used when he really thought about these occurrences, which took place at random in his life. He'd tried to make sense of whose touch prompted such visions, but the demographics were so varied and inconsistent it was hopeless to try.

Lance offered another big smile, hoping they could move on from the awkward handshake. "Nice to meet you, Deputy."

"Likewise, son." Deputy Miller looked right, down the road and toward town. "Meeting a friend for lunch, huh?" The question wasn't exactly accusatory, but Lance knew the man was trying to make sense of Lance's tale, trying to assess any potential threats to himself or his town he'd sworn to protect.

"Yes, sir," Lance said, speaking as casually and confidently as he could. "I'm on my way a little further north to visit some family, but I got off the bus here yesterday to say hi to a friend of mine I haven't seen in a couple years. Catch up a little before I headed on." Then Lance relied on good ol' small-town cama-raderie. "You probably know her, actually. Leah, over at Bob's Place?"

Deputy Miller's face lit up, and Lance knew he was off the hook. "Sam's little girl? Sure, I know her. Heck, I've known her since she was this big!" He held his hand out, just below waist-high. "Good girl, she is. Good girl."

Lance knew he had to try, for Leah, and for the town. He'd take any info he could get. "Yeah," he agreed. "She is. Her brother was a good guy, too. Always makes me sad, what happened to him."

Deputy Miller's smile didn't falter, but his energy took a hit. He stood still for a moment, as if Lance's most recent words were taking longer to process than the rest. He looked directly at Lance, but it was like he momentarily lost focus, thinking back to something long ago.

But then he was back, snapping his fingers and saying, "Is that who you're going to meet for lunch? Little Leah?"

Lance nodded. "Yes, sir." He was becoming increasingly amazed at how folks in Westhaven said absolutely zero about the missing boys. Not even the vaguest of acknowledgments.

Deputy Miller turned and motioned for Lance to follow, and he opened one of the back doors to the cruiser. "Hop on in, I'll give you a lift. I'm headed into town myself."

Lance didn't move at first, looking into the rear of the open cruiser and calculating his options.

"I know, it's a little weird," Deputy Miller said with an almost-embarrassed smile. "But I can't let you ride up front." He shrugged. "Against the rules."

Lance took another glance toward Westhaven High School, read the marquee again to verify there was a football game tonight, and then sighed. What choice did he have? He could refuse the officer's ride, but that might make him seem more suspicious. It might cause more questions to be asked. He replayed the flashes of Deputy Miller's life in his mind, like the memory of a movie he'd seen long ago and could only remember the good parts. *He's a decent guy. He believes me. And Leah's smart. She'll quickly catch on and verify everything I've said if asked.*

Lance smiled and started toward the cruiser. "Hey, yeah, that would be great! Thanks so much. I really appreciate it. That's the problem with taking the bus into town. It's hard to get around afterward."

Lance folded himself into the rear seat of the cruiser, sliding his backpack off his shoulders and setting it in the seat next to him. "Yeah," Deputy Miller said, "we had a couple folks try to be Uber drivers for a while, but Uber's a little too sophisticated for a town like us."

Lance looked down to his shorts pocket, where his flip phone lived. "Yeah," he agreed. "I could see that."

Then Deputy Miller said, "Everything in?" Lance said it was, and the back door to the cruiser was closed and Lance was locked in.

The bell rang, an old-fashioned physical bell from the sound of it, not the new digital tones that got played over speakers at more modern and up-to-date schools, and like racehorses out the gate, a sea of students began to pour from every exterior door of Westhaven High School and scatter in every direction. Lance watched them through the window of the cruiser. Even at this distance he could see them smiling and laughing and joking. He could see the popular girls and the jocks and the FFA leaders and the chess club members. He saw them all and, as he'd done so many times in his life, he wondered what it must feel like to be normal. To be able to be a student and an athlete and only those things, instead of living with his gift, living with one foot firmly planted in a dimension of the world that nobody else could see.

The front door of the cruiser opened and the noise from the kids intensified as Deputy Miller folded his own long and lanky frame into the driver's seat and closed the door. He took off his hat and tossed it onto the passenger seat, and through the partition, Lance could see the man was losing his hair on top, a beanie of baldness starting at the center of his skull and working its way outward.

"Let me guess," Deputy Miller said, "You're going to... hmm ... Frank's Pizza?"

Lance smiles. "You got it. How'd you know?"

Deputy Miller shrugged. "Not a lot of choices around here, and Frank's is always popular with the younger crowd. Figured it was there or the diner."

Lance nodded. "I've been there. I liked it. Margie seems nice. Seems like she runs a tight ship." And then Lance wondered why he felt compelled to offer up this information to Deputy Miller, why he was telling more of his story than necessary. Not that there was anything wrong with him visiting Annabelle's Apron, but when you were sitting in the back of a cop car, you couldn't help but feel like you were under interrogation, no matter how casual the conversation.

Deputy Miller sat still in the driver's seat and watched as the last of the students disappeared back inside the school's buildings. Two boys wearing black t-shirts and baggy jeans were left alone outside the building closest to the parking lot, huddled around a large orange trash can. One boy produced something small and white and rectangular from his pocket, shook it, and as the other boy reached out, Lance realized it was a pack of cigarettes. Deputy Miller reached forward and flipped a switch on and off, creating a quick *bleep-bloop!* from the car, and the boys' eyes darted up, saw the cruiser. And then they dashed off around the rear of the building.

Deputy Miller shook his head and sighed. "There's always those kind."

Lance knew what he meant. Those kind were everywhere. Always.

Deputy Miller put the car into drive and made a three-point turn, then drove along the front of the school, following the same path the buses would drive in a few hours' time. At the stop sign, he waited for a pickup truck to pass by, and then a Jeep, and then a small sedan.

Then there was no more traffic, nothing coming or going in either of the two lanes. The car's engine idled and that was the only sound Lance could hear. They do not move. The gearshift was still in drive and Deputy Miller's hands were still on the wheel and the road was clear and they did not move an inch. Lance let a full minute pass, his pulse beginning to drum in his ears, and he was about to ask Deputy Miller if everything was all right when the deputy's arm reached up and flicked the turn signal up, signaling a right turn.

Lance felt his stomach tighten, and the drumming in his head grew louder.

The town, and Frank's Pizza, and Leah, these things were to the left, back the way Lance had walked.

The car began to move, slowly at first, and then with a sudden burst of speed, as if Deputy Miller had accidentally stomped on the gas instead of the brake. The car fishtailed out of the school's driveway and the tires squealed on the rough black-top. Lance's backpack slid across the rear of the cruiser and Lance followed it, both bag and boy slamming into the door of the car. Deputy Miller's hands seemed clumsy on the wheel as Lance watched the man overcorrect, whipping the wheel back in an unpracticed motion and rocking the car back and forth as it tried to straighten out. Lance reached up and braced his palms against the roof of the car to gain some balance, and as he sat up and the cruiser finally straightened out, he looked into the rearview mirror and instantly knew he had made a mistake.

Deputy Miller's eyes were nothing but solid whites, rolled up into his head like a man convulsing. His mouth hung open, slack, his tongue poking out and a bit of drool dripping down to the breast of his uniform. Lance sat up straighter and saw the speedometer needle pass seventy, and it felt like a hundred from the backseat. The car was straddling the center line, and all it was going to take was one car coming the other direction, cresting a hill or turning from a side road into their path, and they'd be dead. There was no question about it.

And Lance took another look at Deputy Miller's face that wasn't his face and knew that this had been the plan all along. He'd been found, and he'd been tricked. It was no accident that when he'd shaken the deputy's hand, he'd gotten a glimpse into the man's life. It had shown the life of a simple and good family man in order to disarm him, to have his guard lowered. Whatever force was here in Westhaven knew more about Lance than he'd imagined. It knew the specifics of his gifts, it seemed, and now it was exploiting them. He'd been baited and lured into the back of the cruiser, into a rolling cage from which he could not escape and in which he would now likely die.

He'd failed.

He'd failed the town, and he'd failed those boys and—worst of all—he'd failed Leah. She'd put so much faith in him, and he'd seen the hope he'd inadvertently inspired in her.

And now he was going to die and nobody would ever see him again. Just like Samuel.

His anger and his frustration and his fear overcame him. He pounded on the partition and began to shout. "Hey! You're never going to win, you know that, right? It won't go on forever!

If I don't stop you, there will be somebody else! I'm not the only one!" And then as he fell back into the seat, he thought, *I can't be the only one. Just can't be.*

Deputy Miller's head snapped to the right, so hard and so fast Lance heard something crack. The whites of his eyes were still all that was visible, and his throat muscles shifted and his tongue slid back and forth and his lips twitched as a series of deep gurgles and grunts spilled from his mouth. They were audible, but indecipherable, like the sounds of an animal or an invalid.

Lance was not afraid, only angered even more that this *thing* inside Deputy Miller thought Lance could understand it. Lance slapped his hand against the partition, and Deputy Miller snarled and bared his teeth and barked in response, spittle flying against the Plexiglas. Lance jumped back, and that was when he saw the semi in the distance.

The road was flat, and the truck was still a good distance off —a half mile maybe—but at the speed they were traveling, that would be eaten up in no time. Lance heard the air horn screaming through the air, imagined the driver wondering what in the world this policeman was doing. The driver would be braking, doing his best to avoid an accident, but unfortunately for Lance, the truck could be completely stopped and it would likely make no difference. If they hit it going this fast, the cruiser would crumple like a soda can and Lance would quickly be a lot thinner.

He smacked the partition again, Deputy Miller's white eyes still staring vacantly at him. Lance's mind raced, spun and spun and—*This is really it. I'm going to die. Less than forty-eight hours after my mother and I'm going—*

BEN AND JEN. BEN AND JEN.

The thought smacked him so hard he could barely register its meaning. Then he saw the face of the innocent man caught in a terrible darkness he deserved no part of, and Lance screamed, "Ben and Jen, Ben and Jen, Ben and Jen! You love them so much and they love you and you have a new baby on the way and you are so happy and so lucky and blessed and you don't want to leave them! If you can hear me, Miller, fight! Fight! Ben and Jen, Ben and Jen!"

The truck ahead was stopped, but the cruiser was not.

Lance pounded the partition, his hands stinging with each blow. "Ben and Jen, Ben and Jen, Ben and Jen!"

The eyeballs flickered, a small sign of life. Then the hands on the wheel shifted—marginally, but they shifted!

Lance's heart was about to burst from his chest, the truck getting impossibly closer with each millisecond. He sucked in a deep breath and yelled, *"BenAndJenBenAndJenBenAndJenBenAndJenBen!"*

Deputy Miller's body shook, like he'd gotten the most violent of chills. His eyes rolled forward, bloodshot now and watering. He saw the road, saw the truck. He screamed. Lance screamed. The brakes were slammed, the wheel was jerked. The police cruiser missed the truck...

But it flipped over and rolled off the road and rolled through a field and came to rest upside down fifty yards away. Lance heard crashing metal and cracking glass and the sound of Deputy Miller's screams. And then he heard nothing.

16

LANCE SLOWLY OPENED HIS EYES, SAW A CEILING FAN *wobbling back and forth as it spun lazily above his head. The ceiling was cracked in a few places, but clean. He tilted his head and saw the rest of the room: warped wooden floor, antique dresser and full-length mirror, a nightstand with a glass of water and a Monday-through-Friday pill container beside a pair of thick reading glasses. Warm light spilling from a small lamp. He lay on his back atop a small bed, a hand-sewn blanket covering him up to his waist. The room smelled of apples and cinnamon, warm cider ... or maybe pie.*

"You need to be more careful."

His head darted left and found Annabelle Winters gently rocking back and forth in a rocker in the corner. There was an open book on her lap and Lance saw it was the Bible.

"You have the gifts, and you have the strength, but that's nothing if you're careless."

"Where am I?" *he tried to ask, but his voice didn't work. His vocal cords pinched.*

"You were lucky this time. Miller was always one of the good ones. If it'd chosen someone else—well..." She trailed off, and Lance knew exactly what she meant.

He tried to sit up further and

There was an explosion of light and pain. His head throbbed and there was something warm trickling down the right side of his face. His right arm tingled, and when he squeezed his hand into a fist, he cried out. Something in his arm was on fire, burning beneath the skin with every twitch of his fingers.

He opened his eyes and the small room was gone, replaced by the sideways view of the rear interior of Deputy Miller's cruiser.

Lance lay on his side, his head pressed against what felt like a bed of needles. He sat up, slowly, and when the cruiser began to spin in his mind he vomited onto the floor. He closed his eyes and took deep breaths, willing his racing heart to steady a bit. He looked down to where his head had been and saw the bits of broken glass, touched the side of his face and felt a few loose shards stuck to his cheek. He pulled one out with a sting and dropped it, watching it fall into his pile of puke. He took another deep breath, closed his eyes again and mentally examined his body. Aside from the head injury and whatever was wrong with his arm, he appeared to be okay. If Deputy Miller hadn't—

Deputy Miller.

Lance looked through the partition and saw the lifeless body. Miller's torso had been nearly impaled by the steering column, his body slumped and askew and his neck hanging at an angle that told Lance all he needed to know.

Ben and Jen, he thought, and he was filled with a great sorrow in knowing the happy family would never be the same. They had suffered a tragic loss, and they didn't even know it yet.

And it's my fault. It's all my fault.

(*You need to be more careful.*)

He should have never gone to the school alone, a stranger walking down the road, looking like trouble. He knew better. He could have waited, asked Leah to drive him and show him what he needed to see. But he'd been careless. And now a man was dead.

He heard a voice, close but faint. He looked up and turned around, and through the rear glass he saw a man wearing faded jeans and a solid red t-shirt talking animatedly into his cell phone. In the distance, the semi was still parked in the middle of the road, its door hanging wide open.

The truck driver. He's calling for help. I've got to go.

He wasn't sure why the last part of that thought occurred, but it did. The man who'd been driving the truck was surely on the phone with 911 or whichever emergency services line he'd called, and the people who arrived would definitely be able to treat his wounds and make sure he was okay and handle the situation with professional training and skill sets.

But eventually, the questions would start. Questions Lance would likely not be able to answer truthfully.

And to make matters worse, if whatever plagued this town could possess one cop (*one of the good ones*), it could surely possess somebody else. Lance didn't have time to take chances right now. He'd gambled once today, thinking he'd made the right choice, and it had nearly killed him.

He glanced at the shattered glass next to him, then followed the trail of shards to the window. The pane of glass was half-missing, a diagonal section with jagged edges all that remained. Lance raised one his large sneakers up, his head pounding with the motion as he leaned back and his right wrist screaming, and then carefully kicked at the remaining glass. It was splintered and full of spiderweb cracks already, and it only took three soft kicks from Lance's size fifteen foot to finish the job. The rest of the window shattered outward and fell to the ground.

Lance took another glance toward the truck driver, heard the words, "I think they're both dead, you've got to come quick!"

He had to move quickly. He winced as he sat back up and pulled himself forward. He gripped the edges of door where the window had been, a few splintery remains digging into his fingers, and then he used his legs to push off and threw himself over the edge and forward, falling to the grass. He felt the urge to vomit again but closed his eyes and counted to ten and willed himself to keep it down. When he opened his eyes, the truck driver was staring directly at him, phone pressed to his ear, mouth hanging open like a man who'd just seen a magic trick.

Lance stood, slowly, and reached inside the busted window. He pulled his backpack from the wreckage, slung it over his shoulder. Just as the man came out of his startled state and started to say, "Hey! One of them is alive!" Lance turned and ran as fast as he could toward the trees, which were only a hundred yards away but in his current state felt more like a mile.

There was shouting behind him, screams to stop and wait and that help was on the way. When Lance didn't stop, the yelling became angrier, profanity interlaced with accusations of Lance being crazy and stupid and obviously up to no good.

Lance did not stop to turn and look. His head felt ready to burst and his arm hurt with every movement, but Lance was still in decent shape and his lungs didn't complain much. He reached the tree line and entered the woods and did not stop for another fifty yards. Only then did he bring himself to slow down and turn to see if the truck driver was following him.

He saw nobody.

He held his breath to listen and heard nothing but the rustling of the branches and leaves around him. The truck driver was not coming.

He had to move. He had to get away.

But he had no idea where he was.

Leah.

He slapped at his shorts pocket with his right hand and groaned at the pain. His cell phone was still there. He reached in and pulled it out and scrolled through his contacts. Found Leah's name and pressed SEND.

She answered almost immediately, and to her credit, she didn't interrupt or ask too many questions as he quickly explained he'd been in an accident and needed help. He told her he'd been at the high school, told her what direction they'd been heading, and told her he was currently a woodland creature.

She told him to keep walking, that he'd come out on the other side right along Route 19. She'd be waiting.

Lance ended the call, double-checked to make sure the truck driver wasn't following, and then started to walk.

[17]

LANCE HIKED HIS WAY THROUGH THE WOODS, AND eventually he heard the distant sounds of sirens, emergency crews coming to handle the wreck he'd just escaped. He wondered if they'd search the woods for him and quickened his pace. He covered what he guessed to be roughly half a mile before the tree line reappeared and he stepped out into the sunlight. Just as Leah had said, maybe twenty-five yards ahead, the faded blacktop of Route 19 stretched to his left and right, seemingly heading nowhere in both directions. He looked around at the empty fields and tried to get his bearings. He figured the motel was to his left, though he couldn't be sure how far. To his right, if he kept walking twenty miles, he guessed he'd hit the town with the Holiday Inn and other bigger-town amenities Leah had alluded to.

He was ashamed that for the briefest of moments, just a fleeting flash of an idea that popped into view and then vanished before it could be fully absorbed and comprehended, he wanted to walk right. Wanted to trudge the twenty miles on foot and maybe hope for a kind person to stop and offer him a ride and leave Westhaven and all its evil behind.

He'd left his home—been forced to leave was more accurate —to move on from his painful past and avoid the unpleasant drama that was sure to follow. It had taken every ounce of will he'd had to step onto that bus and leave behind the only world he had known. He'd picked the destination seemingly at random, the first ride out of town, never imagining that where he ended up would be just as problematic as where he'd left. In the brief time he'd spent in Westhaven, he'd been looped into a terrible secret, a secret he understood better than anyone else in town, and had now been attacked twice. This last time, it had nearly been fatal. How many more chances would he get? Despite his insatiable longing to see his mother's face again, he was fully aware that he was not ready to join her in whatever form of afterlife perhaps existed.

Lance wanted to live.

Between the choice of uncertainty and death, he chose uncertainty.

And was it really a coincidence he'd ended up in Westhaven? Was it really just happenstance he'd decided to stay at Bob's Place and had met Leah and learned of this town's horrible history? He almost rolled his eyes at his mother's words.

The universe is too smart, too calculated for us to accept the concept of a coincidence, Lance. Do you, a person with your gifts, honestly believe things could be so random?

They'd had a similar conversation on more than one occasion, especially as Lance had gotten older, but this particular speech had stuck with him for years, like a favorite scene from a movie. She'd said it after they'd watched an episode of *The X-Files* on Netflix one night. Something from the show's plot had provoked it, and Lance remembered that the only answer he'd offered was a half-hearted *I don't know*. He hadn't been in the mood for philosophical discussions that evening. He'd loved his mother more than anything on earth, but at times she could be exhausting.

And now, another of her tidbits of wisdom floated down to him, and he knew there was no way he was going to head right and find that Holiday Inn.

I know you didn't ask for this, Lance, but you have it. And whatever higher power decided you were meant for this, you are indebted. You have an obligation. Don't you see, Lance? You are a bright spot in a dark world. You are meant to help people. And that's not something you can turn your back on.

The sound of a car engine caused Lance to stiffen, and he briefly considered turning and diving back into the trees. But it was too late for that. The car was only fifty yards away and had definitely spotted him. He stayed in place and tried to look innocent—as innocent as one could look with a blood-streaked face— and watched as a black Toyota 4Runner slowed down and pulled off the road, parking directly in front of him.

The passenger window rolled down and Leah's face brightened his mood. "You look like crap," she said. "Get in the back."

Lance didn't comment or question. He got in.

The 4Runner was a newer model and its owner had kept it clean. As Lance squeezed into the rear seat, having to twist his feet sideways to fit behind the front passenger seat, he noticed the floorboards looked freshly vacuumed and the air smelled of pine and Armor All. The seats were black leather and the trim was tan. This was a nice car. He looked at the driver and saw a tall, heavyset woman wearing black yoga pants and a long-sleeved Westhaven High School t-shirt. Her black hair was short and spiked with gel, her mascara was heavy and her eyeliner was thick. She looked as if she could be about to step onstage with a punk rock group and smash a few guitars.

As Lance took in the woman's features in the rearview mirror, he suddenly realized she'd been staring right back at him. This silent staring contest had lasted nearly thirty seconds before Lance realized nobody had spoken since he'd gotten into the car. Embarrassed for being caught gawking, he said the first thing that came to mind.

"I'm sorry if I get blood on your seats."

The woman looked at him for another second or two, then turned to Leah, eyebrows raised.

Leah giggled. "I told you. He's not like anyone you've ever met." Then, quickly turning to Lance, "But ... you know ... in a good way!"

Lance's head felt woozy and he was still breathing hard from the run through the woods. His heart was beginning to settle, though, and it felt more reassuring than he'd expected to be back with a friend.

"Don't worry about the seats, honey," Miss Mascara said. "But I am worried about the blood. Let's get you somewhere we can take a closer look." Her voice was throaty and sultry. Based on her appearance, Lance would have guessed her to be close to Leah's age, probably a little older. But based on her voice? She could be forty-five and a chain smoker.

None of this mattered now. Lance felt the urge to vomit coming back, and he groaned a bit and started to lay down across the seats. "Need to go," he said, barely a whisper. "They might try ... and find me."

"Who?" Leah asked.

But Lance's eyes were closing as he felt the car begin to move.

Who? That was the question of the hour.

"The motel," Leah said. "Let's get him there and you can do your thing. Then we can talk."

Lance felt the car accelerate and then the woman craned her neck back to him and said, "Try and stay awake, honey. You might have a concussion."

Thankfully, the ride was short and Lance managed to let the girls help him out of the car and into his motel room. He sat on the bed and Leah ran to get him a bottle of water from the lobby, and the woman in yoga pants came in a minute later holding a large red first-aid kit.

"Lance, this is Chuck Goodman's sister, Susan," Leah said. "She's a paramedic. Lucky for us, right?"

(*Do you, a person with your gifts, honestly believe things could be so random?*)

Lance, despite the headache and the dull fire in his arm, could only offer a small laugh at this revelation.

Miss Mascara—Susan—gave Leah another questioning look. "I think he might be delirious."

Lance laughed again, harder this time, and then held up his hands. "No, no, it's just ..." *I miss my mother.* "You reminded me of a joke somebody told me one time. I'm fine. Mentally, anyway."

Susan set the first-aid kit on the bed next to him—it was huge, the real deal, not some tiny thing you'd buy at Walmart for your family fishing trip—and unzipped it, flipping it open and donning a pair of surgical gloves.

"Okay," she said. "Let's take a look."

Soon after Susan started her work, the sound of a police siren came fast and then faded as it traveled past on Route 19.

SUSAN GOODMAN ASKED LANCE TO LIE BACK ON THE BED and he did so, his eyes focused on her makeup-heavy face as she asked him questions and probed at his head and body. She popped a few pills into his mouth and he swallowed them down with a gulp from the bottle of water, not concerned about what he was ingesting. He trusted this woman. He could feel her warmth the same way he could feel Leah's.

A short time later, and after nearly falling asleep twice in the process, Lance listened as Susan told him he had a small laceration on his scalp, but nothing a little glue and a small bandage couldn't fix. His wrist, however, was definitely sprained, and maybe had a small fracture.

"I'm leaning toward it being sprained," Susan said as she slowly helped him sit up, "because I think the pain would be a lot worse if it was broken." She poked and prodded at his wrist a little more, and only when she attempted to bend it down did Lance grimace in pain. "See?" she said. "I can wrap it now to stabilize it, but a proper brace would probably do you well."

Leah had brought a wet washcloth, and Susan cleaned Lance's face of the dried blood. Then she wrapped his wrist thick with gauze and clipped it tight. She stood back. "How do you feel?"

Lance stood, slowly, and was happy that the room didn't spin or wobble in the process. He took stock of himself, searching his nervous system for anything in disarray. Aside from a dull ache from his head wound and the pressure in his wrist, he felt fine.

"I think I'm okay," he said. Then, without thinking, he took a step forward and hugged Susan, the top of her head coming in just below his chin. "Thank you. This was very kind of you."

Susan laughed and stepped out of the embrace. "That might just be the drugs I gave you talking."

Leah laughed.

Lance shrugged. Drugs or no drugs, he was grateful for Susan's help. Her appearance was definitely out of the ordinary for a young Southern woman, but there was no denying her kindness and her skill.

"So," Susan said, "Leah here tells me you think you can tell us what happened to our brothers. I asked her what you could do that the police couldn't, but she wouldn't really tell me."

Lance looked at Leah. She gave him a *What was I supposed to say?* look.

"But," Susan continued, "frankly, I don't care what you know or do, or ... whatever. All I care about now is answers."

The room stayed silent.

"So is it true?" Susan asked, leaning against the wall and crossing her arms beneath her broad chest.

"What?" Lance asked.

"Can you help us?"

Lance chose the honest answer. "I can try."

Susan, whose face had been hard and unreadable most of the time Lance had known her, offered a grin and nodded her head. "At this point, that's all I want. Somebody to keep trying."

Lance got the feeling that suddenly the woman's hard exterior was softening, and the resurfacing of her brother's disappearance was weighing heavily on her.

"It's been so long," Susan said, and now Lance was certain her eyes were forming tears. "But I've never given up hope."

Lance had been down similar roads before and hoped his face did not betray his knowledge that he was almost certain all these boys were dead—Chuck Goodman included. His mission was to find out why, and to save future victims. The answers would give families closure, but it would not bring their brothers and sons back. God, how Lance wished he could change the past.

Susan took a deep breath and composed herself, wiping under her eyes with her index fingers and offering a small chuckle. "Sorry," she said. "I'm not usually one to blubber all over the place."

Lance asked Leah, "Should we talk here, or go somewhere else?"

"Wait," she said. "You haven't told us what happened to you yet. How'd you end up in a police car, and how did it wreck?"

Lance shook his head. "No time right now, but trust me when I tell you it's bad news, and people—the police, for starters—are probably looking for me. So is it safe to stay here, or not?"

Leah considered this. "Let's go to my room behind the office. That way if somebody does show up looking for you, I can show them your room and they can see you're not here. Maybe they'll think you ran off, skipped town, whatever."

Lance nodded. "Fine." He grabbed his backpack and followed the two girls out the door, hoping there wouldn't be a Westhaven police cruiser sitting in the parking lot, waiting like a snake ready to strike.

The sky had grown cloudy, and the air had cooled. A strong breeze rattled through the motel's overhang, and Lance shivered at the memory of the wind that had knocked him back last night. But the parking lot was empty except for Susan's 4Runner and the Honda Civic he had assumed was Renee's. As they walked the short distance to the office, Lance glanced to his left and saw the paper mill's smoke curling up to meet the incoming gray clouds.

Inside the office, a middle-aged woman with long black hair graying at the roots was behind the counter. She looked up from a paperback she'd been reading and, upon seeing Leah, straightened up. "Hey, Leah, I didn't think you'd be back till later." The woman's face reddened softly, as if she'd been caught breaking the rules. She added, "I finished all the items on your list. Didn't take long." She laughed nervously. "Been a slow morning."

The woman's eyes were tired, and Lance wondered when the last time she'd gotten a full night's sleep had been. The dark circles said it had been a while. Her fingernails were painted red, but it was a sloppy job, and the black zip-up hoodie she was wearing had a few obvious stains on the arms and chest. She looked like a woman hanging on for dear life.

Leah smiled, and instantly the woman's face relaxed. Lance, special as he was, knew it didn't take his gifts to be affected by the warmth Leah exuded. "Thanks, Renee. I appreciate it. But, hey, why don't you go ahead and go home for the day? I can handle it from here. I've got some things to work on."

Renee's face fell, and it looked as though she was searching for something to say. Leah beat her to the punch. "Don't worry. I'll pay you for the whole shift. My treat—for all the hard work you do around here."

Renee smiled, and though her teeth were coffee-stained and an upper molar was missing, there was no denying the appreciation it carried.

"Go on, get out of here. Go spend some time with your kids. Get some rest." Leah nodded toward the door, and Renee thanked her again and again and then was gone without so much as a simple introduction to Lance and Susan.

When the office door closed behind Renee and the Civic's engine rustled to life, Leah said, "Daddy would kill me if he knew I'd just let her do that."

"It was nice of you," Lance said.

Leah nodded. "I feel so bad for her. Sweet woman, but she's made some bad choices. Great worker, though. Can always count on her. Amazing, when you consider she's got three jobs. I wish I could pay her more."

And that was the end of that. Leah took a look around the office, tidied some things up behind the check-in counter, and then headed to her bedroom. Lance and Susan followed.

The small television was on, but the screen held nothing but static. The volume was turned down completely. "Ugh, I hate it when this happens," Leah said, walking over to the set. "Thing turns on by itself sometimes and always just hits an empty channel like this." She reached to hit the power button.

"Wait," Lance said, his voice dry, his pulse quickening.

Leah froze, her hand an inch from the power button.

Lance stared into the black-and-white static of the television screen and watched as the gray outline of a figure revealed itself, popping in and out of focus in a strobe-like fashion. Just a gray mass at first, and then edges shifted and aligned and became more defined, falling into their correct place.

It was the dead boy from the bathroom mirror, staring back at Lance with those intense black eyes. Only now ... now, Lance would swear the face looked... sad. Pleading, almost. Lance wanted to reach out and touch the screen, wanted to talk to this ghost in the machine. But just as the thought hit him, the figure vanished, replaced by more blurred static.

"Okay," Lance said. "You can turn it off now."

Leah turned the television off and stared at Lance. Susan shifted her weight from one foot to the other, unsure what to do.

Lance thought about the boy's face, about the new sense of sorrow he seemed to pick up on. Then it hit him. He looked to Leah. "Do you have a picture of Samuel?"

[19]

Lance had asked Leah if she had a picture of her brother before he'd fully realized what he'd done. He was now desperate to see what Samuel looked like, but he knew that seeing the picture and then possibly being forced to explain his request in front of Susan Goodman was not something he should do right now. With Leah, in private, maybe. But not with Susan. Nice as she was, and regardless of how trustworthy Lance assessed her to be, there was no way he was going to share his biggest secret with two people in one day. It was too risky. Plus, he and Leah had bonded, formed more than just a hey-can-you-do-me-a-favor relationship. Lance was certain of this, and he figured Leah could feel it as well.

"Yeah, of course I do," Leah said, taking two steps toward her dresser.

Lance spoke quickly, trying not to sound panicked. "Okay, cool. Show me later, okay? I want to talk to Susan."

Leah stopped and met his eyes and—boom—just like that, she got it. "Yeah, you're right. Susan's already done more than she thought she'd do today. Right?" Leah gave the woman a

228

playful swat on the arm and sat down on her bed, motioning for Susan to join her.

Susan's eyes shifted between Lance and Leah, clearly understanding that there was something more going on than she realized, but either she didn't want to understand or she just respected whatever the two of them were up to. *God bless her*, Lance thought.

Susan laughed, though it sounded forced. She sat on the bed, her weight sinking down into the old mattress. "No biggie. I have to work the game tonight anyway."

There was silence then. Outside the wind picked up again, and the building shook and rattled with a particularly strong gust. Lance's mind again floated to his attack the night before, and that jump-started his train of thought.

Lance's size had always intimidated people. Whether on the basketball court, or just in everyday life, when you were six-six, people noticed, and with this size came an unwarranted air of power and authority. Lance didn't really understand it, but he accepted it. He'd be lying if he said he hadn't used this to his advantage on an occasion or five. But this wasn't one of those times when he wanted to intimidate. Susan Goodman was a good woman who, like Leah, had suffered a great loss, and she might have some information that could help Lance keep others from having to experience the same thing. He needed Susan relaxed. He needed her to open up to him.

Lance closed the door to the bathroom and then sat down on the floor and leaned against the door, his long legs stretched out in front of him like he was just hanging out with some buds, about to shoot the breeze for a while.

Susan Goodman stared at his basketball shoes.

"Size fifteen," Lance said, grinning. "And, yes, they're real."

Susan looked up, looked back to Lance's shoes, and then up again. Then she busted out with a laugh so loud and infectious the three of them were in near-tears in a matter of seconds. When the laughter died down, Susan wiped the tears from her face and all at once grew very solemn. She took a deep breath and said, "Chuckie wore a size fourteen. I always joked he could be a clown if football didn't work out."

Lance gave her a minute to relish her own memory of her brother, then he softly asked, "Tell me about him. What was your brother like?"

Susan became a burst pipe, spewing anything and everything about the late (presumed) Chuck Goodman.

Chuck and Susan didn't seem to have had the same relationship that Leah and Samuel had enjoyed. Susan admitted to using her power as the older sister to torment Chuck—Chuckie —when he was a young child, and she'd continued the job well into their adolescence. As Chuck had gotten older, he'd started to tease and torment back. But at the end of the day, the harassment between siblings had been mostly of the playful nature, and the two had genuinely loved and respected each other.

"He punched a guy once," Susan said, looking past Lance and seeming to stare at the wall as she spoke. "For me, I mean. We were in the high school parking lot, and some guy said my ass was—how did he put it? 'Too big for my britches.'" She laughed. "Chuckie walked right up to the guy—some sophomore who thought he was hot shit because he dipped on school grounds and drove a pickup truck that clearly compensated for a tiny dick—"

Boy, she remembers this very clearly, Lance thought.

"And then Chuckie said, 'That's my sister,' and socked the guy in the gut. Poor kid hit the ground and gasped for air for what felt like five minutes."

"Did he get in trouble? Your brother?"

Susan and Leah both laughed then. "You kidding me?" Susan said. "Football players at Westhaven are like the celebrities out in LA that get arrested for DUIs and picking up hookers. It brushes right off."

Lance nodded. He understood. He'd been granted such privileges as a basketball player in high school. Not that he'd used it to get away with being a troublemaker, but there were definite perks to being a well-respected high school athlete. Just ask one.

Lance asked, "Was Chuck good at football? Like, could he play in college, even if just Division 3?"

Susan thought about this for a moment, looking up to the ceiling and closing her eyes.

When she finally looked down and opened her eyes, Lance watched as the tears began to stream down her face and his heart melted. "We always called him superstar, my family did," Susan said. "We built him up, acted like if he kept working hard and stayed passionate, he could make something of himself with football. We all encouraged him because he just loved it so damn much." She paused. "But honestly, no, he wasn't great. He was just ... big. I mean, look at me. My parents are big, and they made two big children. Not fat, mind you—though I could afford to lose a few pounds—but just ... wide. Stocky. Large frames. Chuck lifted weights to put on muscle, but he was big without it. But he wasn't quick. His footwork was always sloppy, and his reflexes were nothing to write home about. His size is what served him well on the team. If he got in your way, he was hard to move. But I don't think that would have cut it at the next level."

Lance said nothing, just nodded.

"But he always tried hard," Susan sniffled. "Every day he did his best."

Lance hated to continue the questioning. It made him feel like a detective. But, in a sense, that was what he was. "No other trouble at school, or at home? Leah told me about your family's store, about it having to close."

Susan nodded. "Yeah, that was a tough time. I had already graduated and was taking classes at the community college, so I wasn't too concerned about Daddy saying the family was going to move. I had means to survive around here on my own. But yeah, Chuck was pissed. He didn't want to leave his friends, and he certainly didn't want to leave the football team. I think even then he knew that whichever new high school he ended up at, he might not make the team. Chuck wasn't stupid. He knew his own limitations, even if we tried to give him a big head."

Lance waited to see if there was more, but when Susan didn't say anything else, he asked, "But was he upset enough to run away?"

Susan looked at Lance like he was stupid. "Didn't you hear what I just said? The last thing on earth Chuckie wanted to do was leave his friends and team behind. My brother did *not* run away. I don't give a shit what the fucking police said. These small-town Podunk bastards don't even know which end of the gun to point out."

Again, Lance nodded. Then he went for the million-dollar question. "What about a girlfriend?"

"Yeah, sure, he had a couple."

Lance and Leah both perked up at this, and Susan sensed their sudden interest, offering a concerned, "*Why?*"

Leah turned sideways on the bed and pulled one of her legs underneath her. Facing Susan, she asked, "Was he dating anybody when he went missing?"

Susan looked at Lance, then at Leah, and then she shook her head. "No ... no, he wasn't. He'd broken up with that Yates girl during the summer, right before football started up. He told me it was just a fling, anyway, and that he needed his head straight for Coach." She laughed, a sad, weary laugh. "See what I mean? He loved that damn sport."

Lance felt let down, and he could clearly see Leah did as well. They'd wanted the answer to be yes. They'd wanted a name, a person to lay blame on and interrogate further. And then, as if their disappointment had sparked a rush of memory, Susan sat up straighter and said, "Although ..."

She looked down at the floor, her brow furrowed in thought. Lance stayed quiet, letting her work out whatever it was she was unraveling. When she finally looked up at him, she said, "He never said he was dating anybody, but there was the perfume."

"Perfume?" Leah asked, getting excited.

Lance stayed calm. It was nothing, until it was something. "What do you mean?" he asked.

"I used to stay up late, doing my homework at our kitchen table. Chuckie didn't have a curfew—town this small, good kid like he is—it just wasn't needed. Mom and Dad trusted him. In the last month or so before Chuckie disappeared, I can distinctly remember him coming home late—I'm talking one or two in the morning—looking half-stoned, and when he came through the front door and walked by me in the kitchen—I remember, God I remember like it was yesterday—I smelled a woman's perfume on him."

Leah's eyes darted to Lance, and he could see the fire in them, the flash of excitement that they might be on to something. Lance stayed realistic. "You ask him about it?"

Susan shook her head and sighed. "No. I never did. I mean, I didn't like to pry into Chuckie's life. Tease him, sure, but I respected his privacy. He did the same for me."

"So it's possible the perfume belonged to a friend, some girl who hung out in his social circle?"

Susan made a face. "I ... I guess so."

"But?"

She looked at Lance. "How much do you know about perfume?"

"Let's say zero, less."

"Right, okay." Susan thought for a moment. "I guess the best way to explain is that the scent I smelled on Chuckie didn't seem like something a high school girl would wear. It wasn't all sweet and sugary and fun like a lot of the Bath & Body Works lotions and sprays. It was, I guess, more mature. It smelled more like something a *woman* would wear. Not a girl. Stronger, more floral." When Lance said nothing, Susan said, "It smelled like something my mom would wear. That's the last thing I can think to say."

On the one hand, Lance was deflated. They hadn't really gained any new insight into what might be happening to the Westhaven boys. On the other hand, there was this one small connection: Samuel's last words had been about going to see a girlfriend nobody knew about, and Chuck Goodman had come home smelling of perfume when his closest family had believed he wasn't involved with anyone, having just gone through a breakup. Statistically, assuming Bobby Strang was truthful about Samuel's parting words, two-thirds of the boys who'd vanished had a mysterious female presence linked to their disappearances.

Lance, Leah, and Susan chatted a bit longer, and then Susan said she had to go. Lance gave her another hug and thanked her again for helping him with his injuries, and also for talking to them about her brother. At the door to the office, Susan stopped and said, "I don't see how it's possible, after all this time, but you'll let me know if you find out anything, won't you?"

"Of course," Leah said. "You'll be the first to know."

Susan gave Leah a pained smile and then cast one final appraising glance at Lance before leaving. When her 4Runner was out of the motel's parking lot, Leah turned to Lance. "What do you think?"

Lance studied the clouds through the closed office door for a moment. "I think I'm ready to see that picture of your brother."

She nodded and took his hand and led him back to her bedroom.

[20]

THE LAST TIME A GIRL HAD TAKEN LANCE BY THE HAND and led him to her bedroom, they'd done a lot more than just look at pictures.

But Lance was always careful. His mother's words, which had followed him when she was alive and now haunted him in her death, always echoed in his head during those certain "moments of indiscretion." There'd been no talk of birds and bees; thankfully his mother had allowed him to grasp those concepts on his own, along with the help of the public education system's health classes. But there had been a warning, one spoken with grave seriousness.

A child will only make you vulnerable, Lance. You carry enough of a burden as it is. Don't add to that load, not until you're good and ready and fully understand what you are.

Lance was unsure he'd ever fully understand what he was, so children seemed like a far-off dream he might one day catch up with. But ... he was a human male, after all. He had urges just like everyone else. He could never be too careful.

Leah left the bedroom door open and pointed to her bed. Lance sat, holding back a joke about not even getting dinner first. Leah pulled one of the dresser's bottom drawers open and took out a small stack of books—all of them were Westhaven High School yearbooks. She spread them out on the floor, checking the years on the front covers, and then selected one and joined Lance on the bed. He got another whiff of her shampoo and tried not to be obvious that he was inhaling deeply, enjoying the scent. Leah flipped through the yearbook's pages, the faces and smiles and scattered collages of hundreds of students flashing by, and then stopped, smoothing the pages open and holding it out for Lance to see more clearly.

"Here," she said, pointing at one of the small squares on the page. "That's Samuel." She laughed softly. "What a dork."

Lance watched Leah's face as the smile grew large and held, her eyes locked onto the eyes of her brother's picture. He wondered what memories she was visiting in her head, which of the best moments of her and Samuel's childhood was replaying and causing that grin on her face.

Lance looked down at the picture. Leaned in closer just to be sure.

Samuel was well built, broad shoulders and chest. His grin was forced, like somebody who didn't like to smile on cue. On his head was a mop of sandy-blond hair. The resemblance between the boy and his father was there, as well a small resemblance to Leah.

But one thing was for sure. Samuel was the dead boy Lance had seen in Leah's bathroom mirror, and again in the fuzzy television screen.

Lance tried not to let it show that he'd discovered this disturbing fact, so he quickly blurted, "Chuck Goodman in this yearbook, too?"

Leah thought for a moment. "Um, yeah, should be." She flipped through some pages, going to a different class. Her finger traced the list of names and then followed a row of pictures. "Yep, here he is. God, I'd forgotten how big he was."

Lance looked down at the picture. Leah was right. Chuck Goodman was a large boy, nearly filling in the entire square allotted for his picture, and Lance understood what Susan had meant about her brother being "hard to move." But the real reason Lance had asked to see Chuck Goodman's picture was to see if he'd been the burnt boy who'd appeared at the diner earlier that morning. He wasn't. It didn't mean Chuck wasn't dead—Lance now assumed all the boys were deceased. It just meant he'd yet to show himself.

Lance had just started to consider the differences between Samuel's appearance in the mirror and television screen, and the burnt boy in the diner, when Leah asked, "Why'd you want to see their pictures?"

Lance tried to be quick. Shrugged. "Just wanted faces for the names." He left it at that.

Leah wasn't buying it. "Bullshit."

Lance stayed quiet. Kept his eyes on Chuck Goodman's faded yearbook picture.

"You know something," Leah said. Then her eyes drifted toward to the corner where the TV sat on its cart. "When we first came in here and the TV was on, you made me wait before turning it off. You were just staring at it ... like you were ..." She trailed off. "Lance ... what did you see?"

He couldn't tell her. Couldn't bring himself to expose his secret just yet, couldn't break this girl's heart with the finality of her brother's death. Whether she'd already accepted the idea or not, Lance didn't yet want to deliver the final blow.

"Nothing," he said, and he couldn't meet her eyes.

"You're lying. Aren't you?"

Lance said nothing. Hated himself on the inside.

Leah nodded. "I'll take that as a yes." She stood up and

tossed the book into Lance's lap. He caught it, and as she stormed out of the bedroom, he called after her and she ignored him. He threw the yearbook onto the bed and followed her into the office. Leah was already behind the check-in counter, absentmindedly sorting papers and checking things on a laptop. She didn't so much as raise an eyebrow in Lance's direction.

Lance leaned against the counter and waited to see if she'd acknowledge him. After a couple minutes of cold-shoulder action, he finally said, "Look, I'm sorry."

"Great," she said.

"No, really."

"Really. Great."

Lance sighed. "Would you just—"

"Do you have any idea how much I'm risking for you?" Her words shot like darts from her mouth.

Lance stepped back. "For *me*?"

"Yes, you!" Leah pushed a strand of hair out of her eye. "Since you've walked into my life, I've lied to Daddy, twice. If he takes this job away from me, I don't know what my next step is, Lance. I've been here my whole life. This is all I know. I've got a high school diploma from the middle of nowhere and I've managed a roach motel. And now—now!—I'm harboring somebody the police are probably out looking for right now. I could be arrested, Lance. I'm not positive about that, but even the possibility scares me." She was on the verge of tears now. "Look … I don't have a lot, and I don't mean much to hardly anybody, and even though you say we're doing all this to try and find out what happened to my brother—and, yes, I know I sort of pushed your hand to help—I think we all know Samuel and the rest of the boys are already dead and nothing we do is going to change that and … and…"

The tears came now, spilling down her cheeks, and Lance did the only thing in the entire world he could think to do—the only thing in the entire world he wanted to do. He leaned his tall frame over the counter, grabbed the front of Leah's shirt and pulled her forward, kissing her hard on the mouth.

His heart pounded.

There was the smallest moment of resistance.

And then she kissed him back.

He tasted her tears, salty and wonderful, and drowned in her scent. The kiss flooded him with a warmth, melted the tension he'd built up, and he felt the same process occurring in Leah, watched her body relax and loosen.

When they finally pulled apart, staring at each other with faces more full of surprise than any sort of regret, Lance spoke first. "I'll tell you everything," he said. "But you just have to follow blindly a little longer. Just until I get a better understanding of what I think I know."

She stared at him, breathing hard after the kiss. Her tears had stopped, dried streaks on her cheeks.

"Neither of us can solve this alone," Lance said. "I need you. And I need you to trust me."

Leah was quiet for a long time, and Lance started to think she wasn't going to go along with it. Whatever damage had been done, the kiss, the new naked truth between them, couldn't repair it.

Finally, she said, "What do we do next?"

Lance felt the relief wash over him. "There's a football game tonight. Will you be my date?"

[21]

WHATEVER DRUGS SUSAN GOODMAN HAD GIVEN LANCE, they were starting to wear off. For nearly an hour after the kiss, he'd sat on the couch in the office while Leah did some work behind the counter. She would occasionally run outside to this room or that and return a short time later, always first glancing at him on the couch, as if she were concerned he might have run off.

His head was starting to throb behind his cut, and the pain in his wrist, while not unbearable, was irritating. He stood up, stretched, and told Leah he was going to go lie down to try and take a nap. And really, what else was there for him to do? He wasn't going to go risk walking into town again by his lonesome. He'd learned enough to know he wasn't going to learn much else today. The town's citizens answered his questions vaguely at best, and usually acted like he was off his rocker for even bringing the topic of the missing boys up at all.

But he was looking forward to the football game. Not because of the competition, but because of who all might be in attendance.

Leah told him she'd wake him if he wasn't back by the time

they had to leave. "As long as you don't mind me slipping into your room," she said with a grin. "But in all fairness, you've spent a lot of time in mine already."

Lance thought about covering the short distance between the couch and check-in counter and kissing her, but he restrained himself. *Keep it organic*, he thought. Then, *And by the way, you know this is a bad idea. What's your plan with her?*

He told his subconscious to shut up and headed outside. But as he stepped through the door, he took one last look back at her, suddenly wondering if it was a good idea to leave Leah alone. How guilty was she, now that she was tied in with him? Could the evil that had come after Lance sense the feelings between him and Leah? With the one kiss, had Lance instantly transformed Leah into a vulnerability? The phrase "collateral damage" lit up in his mind like a Vegas strip marquee. He could almost hear his mother's disapproving sigh, see the subtle shake of her head.

Lance stepped out through the door. Again, what could he really do?

The clouds were still dark, but any rain was still holding off. The smoke plume continued to rise up to the sky, and Lance stood on the cracked concrete walkway and stared at it, wondering if the blackness of the smoke symbolized a hidden threat somehow tied to the paper mill, tied to Glenn Strang.

He started to pull at this thread for just a minute before the burning pain of his cut forced him to turn away and enter his room and lie down on the bed.

He shifted restlessly atop the covers, careful not to put any weight on his injured wrist. When he closed his eyes, he saw Deputy Miller's kind eyes, heard the Southern hospitality in his voice. And then he saw the slack and broken body twisted in the front of the cruiser. He saw a mother and child

(*Ben and Jen!*)

standing over a closed casket being lowered into the earth, saw them returning to a home that would forever feel emptier than it should. An empty spot at the kitchen table, an empty half of a bed, an unfinished bedtime story bookmarked at a page that would never be read.

It's my fault.

He tossed, rolled over onto his side. Took a deep breath and tried to clear his mind.

It's my fault...

He forced himself to think of Leah, relive the kiss, that only-the-first-time heat of excitement that had accompanied it. And as he finally started to drift off—sure he'd be met by nothing by nightmares—he could almost taste her tears again, almost smell her shampoo.

But it wasn't Leah who he last saw in his mind before he fell asleep. Instead, he saw Susan Goodman, the way she'd gently and thoughtfully tended to his injuries, the way she'd laughed thinking about Chuckie, the tears that had come despite her best efforts to fight them off as she spoke.

Too many good people were getting hurt in Westhaven. He had to put a stop to it.

[22]

LANCE WOKE ON HIS OWN FROM A SLEEP THAT WAS DEEP, dreamless. He stretched, pulled his flip phone from his pocket and checked the time. He had time to shower, he assumed. He sauntered to the bathroom, his head feeling heavy, but mostly pain-free. He undressed himself and carefully unwrapped his wrist, trying to remember how to redo it after he had showered. As the water ran hot, he stood in front of the sink and checked himself in the mirror. He looked weary, but considering he'd been in a full-on auto accident that had resulted in a fatality earlier, he figured he could look a heck of a lot worse.

The water scalded his body, stung the cut on his head, but the pain and heat rejuvenated him. Cleared his mind. Helped him find his second wind for the day—both physically and mentally. He stepped out and dried off. Brushed his teeth. He dressed in more of his new clothes and, again, stuffed all his belongings into this backpack. He couldn't bring himself not to prepare for a rapid departure. For whatever reason. If he was forced to leave quickly, as he'd been from his home just two short days ago, he didn't want to be completely helpless and empty-handed.

With his backpack on his shoulders and his mind and body ready, Lance checked the time on his phone one more time before he would head over to the office and see what Leah was up to and when they were going to be leaving.

But there was something on his phone. A missed call. A voicemail.

He recognized the number, had had it memorized for years, though it wasn't stored in his phone's memory.

Marcus Johnston had just started out with Lance's hometown sheriff's department the first time Lance had met him. Marcus and Lance's mother had attended high school together, and Lance's mother had been able to urge Marcus to help her and Lance out during a particularly sticky situation they'd gotten into. The first of many.

Over time, as Lance had gotten older and his gifts had increased, he had been able to put them to better use—willingly, or not—and Marcus had continued to play a role in Lance's life. Eventually, Lance's secrets had been spilled to the man, sometimes one drop at a time, other times in great gushes of new information. Why Lance's mother had ever trusted Marcus Johnston enough to tell him what Lance really was, Lance would never know. Maybe she too had possessed a small bit of what empowered Lance, just enough to be able to see the truly great ones, the ones who she knew wouldn't let them down.

As Lance had grown and developed, so had Marcus Johnston's career, though the two ascensions were unrelated as far as Lance could tell. Marcus had climbed the sheriff's office ladder until, when Lance was a freshman in high school, he had become the actual sheriff. He'd held the position through Lance's senior year, and then a few more years just for good measure. And then, one year before Lance was forced to flee, Marcus Johnston had become mayor.

(*Do you, a person with your gifts, honestly believe things could be so random?*)

Lance had been lifelong friends with a man who'd eventually become the highest-ranking person in the city. A man who'd helped Lance and his mother in more ways than Lance could ever count. A man who'd helped protect Lance.

A man who was there that night.

A man who knew the truth.

Guiltily, Lance shoved the phone back into his pocket. He couldn't bring himself to listen to the message right now. Good news, bad news, it didn't matter. Whichever, it would only prove a distraction. Right now, he had more important things at hand.

Lance walked out of his room and went one door down to the office. The Honda Civic was back, and when Lance opened the office door he was immediately greeted by the sounds of laughing children. There were two small boys, no more than five or six, either of them, sitting on the couch, staring intently at the television screen. A brightly colored cartoon was displayed on the screen, and the volume was turned up too loud. Lance looked left and saw Renee and Leah standing behind the counter. Leah smiled at him. Renee looked apprehensive, but not all together displeased.

Leah gave the woman a small hug. "Thanks again, Renee. I owe you big-time."

Renee waved her off and said it was better than sitting at home and that the kids would have a great time. That it was almost like going to the movies.

Leah said goodbye to the boys, who didn't even twitch their eyes toward the sound of her voice, and then looped her arm around Lance's and pulled him out the door.

"I feel terrible, having to ask her to come back in like that," Leah said as the door closed behind them. "But she's right. The kids look like they're having a good time. I've only ever seen the outside of Renee's trailer, but that alone is enough to make me think the kids feel like they're in a castle right now."

Lance asked, "What did you tell her the reason you needed her back was?"

"I didn't really. Just said I had some things I had to take care of that couldn't wait, and she'd be doing me a huge favor and I would owe her one."

"The kids?"

Leah sighed. "Different fathers, both long gone. Like I said, I feel bad for the woman." Then Leah pulled a single key from her pocket and said, "Oh, and she's letting us borrow her car."

Lance crammed himself into the passenger seat, trying not to step on the debris on the floorboard—the book from earlier, as well as a children's picture book, an empty McDonald's bag, a tennis ball, a phone charger, unplugged and loosely coiled. This was a family car. A family that was constantly on the go. It smelled of apple juice and coffee and sweat. There was something sticky on the center console, and Lance made a note not to rest any part of himself there.

Leah started the engine—which began as a sputter before coughing to life with a whine—and backed the car out of the parking spot. Through the cracks in the cloudy sky, the sun had faded to orange and had dipped nearly below the tree line. "Calling for rain?" Lance asked.

Leah shook her head. "I don't think so."

She turned right out of the motel's parking lot and headed first toward town before shooting off down a side road Lance had yet to travel. "We're going to get dinner first," she said. "I hope that's okay."

Lance realized he hadn't eaten since breakfast, which felt like two days ago, and the hunger complaints from his stomach broke loose and were on him furiously. He knew things were serious when he forgot to eat. "Sounds great," he said.

Half a mile down the road, Leah turned into the lot of a Sonic Drive-In that looked startlingly out of place. While everything else Lance had seen in Westhaven was old, aged, and weathered, the Sonic appeared shiny and new. Bright signage and a freshly painted building and a recently paved parking lot. And they were busy. Leah nearly circled the entire lot before finding an open slot to pull into. The last one available.

"Place just opened about a month ago. So, yeah, Westhaven is sort of a big deal now, as you can see."

Lance grinned, looked all around him at the folks eating in their cars. Even through the windshields and windows he could see a mass scattering of Westhaven-emblazoned shirts and hats. Everybody was having their pre-game meal.

Football was important around here.

Lance ordered three cheeseburgers, fries, and a chocolate milkshake. Leah ordered a grilled chicken sandwich and looked at Lance like he was from Mars. "Where does it go?"

He shrugged. "Feet. I guess."

She laughed and he leaned over the sticky center console and kissed her. She smiled at him and said, "You better be careful. Lots of wandering eyes around here."

And he almost said it wouldn't matter, because he wouldn't be around for long. And this truth stifled his mood for only a moment before he pushed it away. It sounded meaner than it really was, that thought. He wasn't abandoning anybody, but he was fairly certain Westhaven was not where he was supposed to spend the rest of this life. He'd move on. Searching—even if he didn't know what for.

Instead, Lance said, "What if your father shows up? Comes for a coney and ends up shoving it down my throat when he finds us together. I know statistically it happens a lot in the United States, but I really don't want a hot dog to kill me."

Leah stared out the windshield. Didn't laugh at the joke. She sighed. "Daddy's protective of me. I guess I understand why, but..." She snapped out of it and said, "I'll just tell him it's part of the job interview." She smiled, and the food came and for a while they sat together blissfully eating. When Lance had finished his second burger, he took a long pull from his shake and said, "Tomorrow I want to try and talk to Bobby Strang. If he was the last person to see your brother alive, *and* they were such good friends, he really might know more about what happened than he thinks he does."

Leah nodded, sipped her drink. "Maybe you can talk to him tonight."

"How's that?"

Leah smacked her forehead. "Geez, I forgot to tell you! Bobby's the assistant football coach for Westhaven."

Lance turned in his seat to fully see her. "You're kidding."

She shook her head.

"Why would he stick around? He graduated, right?"

"Yeah, of course he did. He just ... I don't know. When he finished high school, he went to work for his dad at the mill. Nothing manual, mind you, some VP of such and such I think. But by the time the next football season started up, he'd found a place on the coaching staff."

"Nobody thought that was odd? That he didn't head off to college or anything?"

Leah laughed. "Around here, that's a lot more common than you'd think. No, I think if anything, people were surprised at him ending up coaching, considering he really wasn't much of a player." She shrugged. "But, with all Glenn Strang's done for the team—and still does, by the way—I guess folks figured it was all part of the process, part of the deal. He seems to do a good enough job, anyway."

Lance finished his last burger and again marveled at how much the Strang family had to do with the Westhaven football team.

His conversation with Bobby couldn't come soon enough.

Somewhere, somebody was hiding something.

WHEN THE FOOD WAS FINISHED AND THE TRASH DISPOSED of, Leah asked Lance if he was ready.

"I've got nowhere else to be," he said.

She started the car and headed back the way they'd come, crossing over Route 19 and heading toward Westhaven High School, the same route Lance had taken on foot earlier that day. Before he'd met Deputy Miller. Before somebody else had died.

The sun was gone now, and the headlights of Renee's Civic did the job well enough to light the way. Above, there were no stars, only the thick blanket of clouds. But ahead, looming in the distance less than a mile away, was another cloud, a bright explosion of white that hung in the air and lit up the sky and created a dome of light that only grew in size the closer Lance and Leah got.

"Those are some serious lights," Lance said, leaning down to peer up and get a better view through the windshield.

Leah stopped fifty yards from the turn-in for the high school, coming to a stop behind a line of brake lights as others waited their turn to enter the parking lot. "Glenn Strang had some connections, worked a few fundraisers. Those lights were installed the year after they won the first state title."

An elderly woman in a bright orange vest and wielding a light-up orange plastic signal cone motioned the cars in, one by one. She wore a Westhaven baseball cap and smiled brightly at Leah as she waved the Civic into the lot.

"Know her?" Lance asked.

"Mrs. Bellamy. She taught civics for about a hundred years before I had her, and she's still here."

"She liked you. Could tell by her smile," Lance said, feeling a pang of guilt as Leah drove by the exact spot where Lance had stood earlier when Deputy Miller had pulled his cruiser in behind him.

Leah shrugged, found a parking spot near the rear of the lot, and pulled in. Killed the lights and the engine. The engine ticked, something popped, and then all was quiet except for the murmur of the crowd noise and the booming godlike voice of the PA announcer from the field.

"Plan?" Leah asked, checking herself in the rearview mirror, adjusting her hair.

"You keep asking me if I have a plan. Did it ever occur to you I'm just winging this?"

"Are you?"

"Mostly."

Leah sat back in her seat. "And so far you've been blown over by a phantom wind and gotten in a car accident that could have killed you. It's not working out so well."

"I'm not dead yet," Lance said, opening the door and stepping out into the cool evening air.

"Not the most reassuring of statements." Leah got out and motioned for him to follow her. "This way."

Lance followed her, and they wove their way between an ocean of parked cars and finally fell in line with a mass of people who were being funneled from the parking lot and through a large gate that then funneled further toward a ticket booth window just outside the field's main entrance. The marching band's bass drum thumped along with the snapping of the snares. Trumpets and tubas tooted and honked. The crowd cheered randomly at whatever was happening on the field, though from what Lance could tell, the game hadn't started yet. They'd stood in line for five minutes before things began to get quiet and the PA announcer asked that everybody stand and turn their attention to the flag for the playing of the national anthem. There was a great shuffling and scuffling from the massive bleachers, and everybody rose up and angled themselves toward a flag Lance couldn't see. A great many folks in the line, however, all turned and faced west, many putting their hands over their hearts. Lance followed suit, and Leah looked up at him and smiled.

There were a solid five seconds of what seemed like absolute silence before the band played the tune, finishing in a powerful barrage of sound that caused a great eruption of cheers from the stands and some muted clapping from the ticket line. The PA announcer did the usual pregame rigmarole, using the customary increased enthusiasm when announcing the home team, and then the game started.

Two minutes later, Lance bought two tickets and refrained from holding Leah's hand as they walked through the gate.

Leah and Lance passed on all the offers to buy 50/50 raffle tickets and Westhaven t-shirts and Girl Scout cookies being offered by a line of enthusiastic peddlers set up at tables just left of the main entrance. The tickets and t-shirt were an easy "no" for Lance, but the cookies didn't seem like such a bad idea. But he needed to focus. Thin Mints would have to wait.

Leah led the way, navigating the mosh pit of people who filled the large square of gravel and grass bordered by the entrance, peddler's row, restroom and concession stand, and the field itself. Lance smelled grilled hot dogs and nacho cheese. Leah was headed toward the fence that separated the viewing area from the field. Lance, a head above most people, scanned the crowd as he followed Leah, looking for any familiar faces, and, well ... seeing if he picked up anything, any vibe or premonition or whatever the words were. He got nothing except a few curious stares and one baby who seemed to start crying as soon as it made eye contact with Lance. He'd never been great with kids.

The game had started, and by the time Lance rested his elbows atop the chain-link fence along the field, Westhaven had the ball on the opponents' thirty-yard line and the running back took it straight up the gut through a hole big enough to park a bus, then dove into the end zone with outstretched arms as a defender wrapped up his legs. The referees blew their whistles and threw their arms in the air. Touchdown. An explosion of noise came from the bleachers, shouts and screams and air horns and cowbells and the band blasting a fight song. Lance ignored it all and stared at the Westhaven sideline.

Coach Kenny McGuire was smiling, but he wasn't jumping and celebrating with the rest of the team and coaching staff. Instead, he turned away from the action and consulted his iPad, surely flipping through plays and notes and preparing for what came next. He acted like a man who'd done this all a million times. Which, with three state titles, he had. What was one more touchdown?

In person, he looked even smaller than he had in the photograph Lance had seen in the newspaper. Short and thin and almost feeble-looking, as if a strong wind might carry him away like a kite swept away from an unsuspecting child. The rimless glasses made him appear distinguished, but not altogether handsome. The air of dorkiness clung to Kenny McGuire, despite his coaching accolades. He looked like a guy who should be spending his Friday nights playing Dungeons & Dragons instead of even attending a sporting event, never mind coaching one.

"That's Bobby Strang." Leah pointed, and Lance followed her finger down the sideline until he saw the guy.

Bobby Strang was down on one knee, also immersed in an iPad and shouting instructions to a semicircle of players around him. The guy was average height and had a buzz cut, a small belly already forming along the line of his Westhaven t-shirt where it was tucked into his khaki pants—which seemed to be standard attire for the Westhaven coaching staff. His face was red, and sweat dripped from his brow. Coaching must be tough work. Lance stared at Bobby, tried to will his mind to focus on the guy, to pick up something, anything. But he got nothing. Maybe he was too far away, out of Lance's reception area. Like Lance had told Leah earlier, he really didn't understand any of what he could and couldn't do.

"Think we can talk to him?" Lance asked.

Leah was about to answer, then got distracted by a play on the field. A fumble, which Westhaven recovered. More cheers. More celebrating. More cowbell. She looked at Lance. "It would have to be after the game, obviously. But, yeah, I think so. I think..." She looked away sheepishly and said something that got drowned in the crowd noise.

"What?" Lance said, leaning in closer.

"I think he always feels guilted into talking to me when we see each other."

"Because of Samuel?"

She nodded.

Lance wondered if the guilt was a general sort of thing, sympathy for a victim, or if there was more to it. If Bobby Strang felt guilty because he knew more than he was letting on.

Lance watched the game. The Westhaven quarterback—Anthony Mills, Lance remembered from the paper—heaved a long pass high in the air to a streaking receiver, and the entire crowd seemed to hold their breath as the ball flew. There was a collective "uggghhh" of disappointment when the ball ended up being overthrown by a good five yards. *Kid's got a good arm,* Lance thought, and then he asked Leah, "Where's Glenn Strang? I assume he still comes to all the games."

Leah snapped her fingers. "Right. Yeah, he does. I think so, anyway. It's been a while since I've been here."

This time she did take Lance's hand in hers and led him away from the fence, two other people quickly sliding into their places to get a better view. They walked down the fence line, gravel crunching beneath their sneakers, and Lance saw a pair of sheriff's deputies leaning against the bleachers, half-watching the game, half-watching everything else around them. Despite what were probably their best efforts, both men couldn't quite contain a downcast look of sorrow, and Lance knew the news of their fallen comrade was hitting them hard.

My fault, Lance thought as he walked past them. *I'm so sorry, guys. I was stupid and one of yours paid the price.* And then a second thought struck him. He wondered if there was an active effort to find him—the other passenger in the wrecked cruiser who'd fled the scene. Lance's description was pretty telltale, especially his height. But the two officers paid him no attention as Lance and Leah walked by. They were distracted.

The space between the fence and the bleachers was wide but still felt like a packed cattle chute with all the people walking either back to their seats or toward the restrooms and concessions. Lance purposely walked with a slight stoop, trying to make himself not appear so tall and stand out in the sea of people. Leah gripped his hand tightly, and he had to wonder how many folks were watching them from the bleachers and whispering to the person next to them, *"Isn't that Leah from the motel? Who's that guy she's with? New boyfriend? I wonder what her daddy thinks about that."*

Leah stopped right at the fifty-yard line and turned to face the field. Lance followed suit.

"He usually sits right here, about four or five rows up. I didn't want to just stop and stare. Lean sideways against the fence and casually look around, up toward the bleachers. Like you're just taking in the sights."

"Those are very specific directions. Spy on people often, do you?"

"Maybe you're not the only one with special talents."

Lance didn't know what to say to that, so he did as she asked. He turned sideways and propped himself up with his right elbow against the fence. He watched another play take place, a short run attempt by the opponent, which got them a gain of three or four yards. He checked the big, beautiful scoreboard behind the opposite end zone. It was now third down, four yards to go for a first down. Then he looked up to the sky, verified the clouds were still blacking out all the stars, and then—

"Okay, you're making it obvious. Just look already," Leah said, elbowing him.

Lance rubbed his rib where she'd hit him and looked toward the bleachers, counted four rows up, scanned the crowd. Went up to the fifth row and immediately found Glenn Strang.

The man looked exactly like he had in the photos Lance had seen at Sportsman's earlier that day. He was tall, his head looming above the others in his row, and his graying hair was cut close, but still long enough to comb. His face was smooth, and again Lance thought the man's face didn't seem to add up to his age, but this could be attributed to a strict regimen of moisturizers and creams, he supposed. He still appeared to be in decent shape, his shoulders still broad, and his biceps snuggled nicely beneath the sleeves of the Westhaven polo shirt he was wearing beneath a black sweater-vest. Glenn Strang's eyes were locked intently on the football game, darting from place to place along the field, his mouth constantly moving in bursts of cheers and unheard instructions he was mumbling to the players.

Here was a man who absolutely loved the game of football and would never let go.

Which wasn't a crime, Lance conceded.

But ... Glenn Strang was not what held Lance's attention.

"Is that his wife?" Lance asked.

"What?" Leah said, turning from the game.

"The woman next to Strang—is that his wife?"

"Oh." Leah looked over her shoulder, then turned back. "Yeah, that's her. Tasty, right?"

"Did you just say 'tasty'?"

"Come on, you know she's hot. Even I know she's hot. Though it's probably all tummy tucks and face-lifts and hair dye."

Women and jealousy. Lance was thankful he was a guy.

Leah sighed. "Her name's Allison and she's always been super nice, as far as I can tell. She brought me and Daddy dinner every day for a week when Samuel disappeared. And she brings me cookies sometimes at the motel." And then, almost regrettably, "And they're delicious."

"You sound like that's a bad thing."

Leah shrugged, a motion Lance was becoming quite familiar with. "She just seems so perfect, is all. It's sort of disgusting."

Lance took another look at Allison Strang. Blond hair to her shoulders and high cheekbones and smooth skin. A pretty face. She was wearing blue jeans and a light sweater, and Lance felt embarrassed to find himself staring at her breasts, which seemed a little too firm and upright for a woman who had to be midforties at the youngest, bringing back Leah's comments about enhancement surgeries. He hated the term MILF but couldn't deny where its definition applied.

And then he realized that at some point between Lance looking from the woman's face to her chest, Allison Strang had begun staring directly at him.

Their eyes met, briefly, and Allison gave him a small embarrassed smile, as if she was the one who'd been caught. Lance offered a quick, sheepish grin and then turned his gaze back to the field. "She just caught me staring."

Leah laughed. "I think she's used to young men gawking. Old men, too."

Lance waited a beat and then risked another look back. Saw Allison Strang talking excitedly to a woman next to her, a woman Lance had failed to even notice before, drowned in the shadow of Allison Strang's beauty. She was shorter and not quite as thin but still looked pretty good for a woman who might have been forty. Her face showed her age more than either of the Strangs' did, and she sat somewhat hunched over, her blond hair done up in a tight bun, dark eyes looking out toward the field and then constantly glancing to the sideline. Homely wasn't the word Lance would use, but maybe average. The woman listened and nodded as Allison Strang continued talking, but Lance got the impression she wasn't really interested. Something tugged at the back of Lance's brain, and it took him a minute, but he was finally able to firmly grasp it and pull it to the front. The woman next to Allison Strang was the woman Lance had seen escorting the boy out of the school's office earlier that day. The boy with the yellow slip of paper and the downtrodden demeanor.

"Who's that next to Mrs. Strang?"

Leah didn't even have to turn around. "That's Melissa McGuire. That's the coach's wife."

"The vice principal."

"Right."

Lance nodded. It made sense. Surely the Strangs and the McGuires were close. The women were probably great friends, at least on the surface.

It started to rain. Nothing hard or serious like the heavy clouds seemed to have been advertising all evening, but a light, spotty drizzle that was more irritating than problematic. Lance saw a few umbrellas go up in the bleachers, a few ponchos pulled on and a few hoods pulled up, zippers zipped. The rain was cold, but he didn't mind. Leah didn't seem to mind either.

"Let's move," he said. "I feel like they're watching us now."

"Who?"

"Mrs. Strang and Mrs. McGuire."

"Why would they be watching us."

"Just a feeling," he said, though that was a lie. He wasn't feeling anything right then, but the odds were great that the Strangs had something to do with the Westhaven boys' disappearances, and Lance didn't want to risk popping up on their radar quite yet. He nodded across the field, to the other set of bleachers. These were smaller, and less populated. "Let's go sit on the other side."

Leah turned and looked at him, confused. "The *visitors'* side?"

"What? Will that hurt your image?"

She elbowed him again. "No, I suppose not."

She didn't take his hand this time but left the fence and walked, heading away from the concessions and the entrance, meaning to walk around the other end zone and loop around to the opposite-side bleachers. Along the way, a couple of people said hi to her, and she chatted with one younger girl who was probably an ex-classmate. Lance stood silently a few feet away each time, trying not to stand out, trying not to make it too obvious he was with her. Despite what Leah thought or cared about, he didn't want to put her at any more risk, whether socially or otherwise, than absolutely necessary.

The rain stayed constant, but the wind picked up a great deal by the time they reached the end of the bleachers. Somewhere in the distance, a clap of thunder caused all the spectators' heads to swivel. Lance shivered and wished he had a jacket. Not so much for himself, but to offer Leah. He noticed the goose bumps prickling along her arms.

They rounded the edge of the fence and were halfway across the rear of the end zone area when a huge gust of wind rattled the goalpost, the uprights swaying and creaking. And it was then that Lance was slammed in the gut with an overwhelming feeling to stop, turn, and look back toward the bleachers and find the area the Strangs were sitting. Something was screaming at him, something was locked onto him, something was ... taunting him.

And then, without any warning, a single bolt of lightning blistered from the sky. It struck the large scoreboard and traveled down its metal pole of a base, slamming into the earth and shaking the ground. Sparks exploded and the scoreboard sizzled and metal burned, and then another powerful gust blew in from the west, and Lance's heart froze as he saw what was happening.

He had stopped walking before the lightning, hit with his intuition to turn and seek out the Strangs. In just those few seconds—*how long had it really been?*—Leah had kept walking. She was ten, maybe fifteen yards ahead now.

Directly behind the scoreboard.

The blast had knocked her to the ground, and she sat up dazed, disoriented.

The scoreboard started to fall backward, the base of its pole melted metal that gave way under the weight it had been supporting. Lance traced the trajectory and knew it was headed right for Leah. It was going to crush her.

"Leah!" he shouted at her with all his gusto. "Leah, you've got to get out of the way!"

He ran, but fast as he was, he knew he was too late. "*Move!*"

He screamed a scream that hurt his throat, and Leah must have heard him, because her eyes cleared momentarily and she looked up and she rolled to her left just as the massive scoreboard crashed down to the ground with a noise that sounded like the thunder.

And then Lance heard a sound that pierced his heart. He heard Leah cry out in absolute agony.

[24]

Silence.

The players on the field, the patrons in the stands, even the emergency crew that were standing by near the ambulance parked at the rear exit gate of the field—nobody moved or spoke. Even the wind had died down and the rain reduced itself to less than a drizzle, as if its job were finished. Faces were stupefied, eyes locked on either the place where the scoreboard had once stood or where it had crashed to the ground.

Lance felt as if he'd been sucked into a black hole. In the terrifying silence that had encased the field, the only thing he heard was his heart pounding in his ears, and his own conscience berating him with more obscenities than he even thought he knew. *You were too late. You should have never gotten close to her.*

All my fault.

And then Leah let out another cry of pain, a scream for help, and as if somebody had hit the play button on life's remote, all at once everything snapped back into action. The football players ran off the field, huddling on their respective sidelines, unsure what to do next. Folks in the bleachers jumped to their feet, a few scampering off to the parking lot, a great many more shifting to get a better view of what had happened. The PA announcer, in an effort to instill some sort of crowd control, advised people to remain where they were, to remain calm and stay clear of the "accident."

The lights on the standby ambulance danced and the siren whoop-whooped, and ten seconds later it had crossed through the grassy expanse behind the field and was parked right next to the collapsed sign, paramedics jumping out and going to work.

Lance was frozen. He wanted to run, that he knew for sure. But he didn't know which way. More than anything, he wanted to run to Leah, do whatever he could to help her. Take her hand and hold it as the emergency crew did their job. He wanted to make sure she was going to be okay, and most importantly, he wanted to tell her he was sorry. Sorry for ever showing up in her town.

But the other part of him wanted to run in the other direction. Wanted to run straight to the bus station and ride off and flee this place, just as he'd done his own home. He was tired of people getting hurt, and hurt seemed to be following him. His powers made him a threat to unseen things, and therefore endangered everyone around him.

"Lance!"

Leah...

She was calling for him.

"Lance, where are you?"

He snapped out of his paralysis, sprinted toward the sound of Leah's voice. Could hear the increasing murmur of the crowd behind him as he ran. *Well, if I wasn't on the radar to start with, I sure am now.*

He covered the ground quickly, three seconds, if that, but it felt too long, as if the ground under his feet was moving like the belt of a treadmill, keeping him in place as his legs worked hard to reach his destination.

He stumbled as he got near, and one of the paramedics stepped into his path and raised a hand to stop him. The man was middle-aged, out of shape, but heavy with fat and wearing a grim determination on his face. "Close enough, sir."

Lance tried to sidestep the man, hearing Leah once again call his name, her voice slicing through the raised voices of the crowd, the murmur steadily rising in volume. The man grabbed Lance's wrist, hard enough to get Lance's attention, and in that moment a hot bolt of anger shot through Lance's body, and he found himself about to give in to his temper. He was a split second from raising a fist to smash the guy's nose into pieces when another voice called out. A voice Lance recognized.

"Let him through, Harry! He's a friend, and she's going to be all right."

Susan Goodman stood from a crouched position, where she'd been helping to examine Leah. The dark eye makeup was still heavy, and her face still looked generally unfriendly, but right then and right there, she was beautiful in Lance's eyes.

Harry held on to Lance's wrist for another second, glancing from Lance to Susan. She nodded, and Harry sighed and let Lance go, his nose remaining in a single piece in the middle of his face. Lance jogged the small remaining distance and came to a stop just shy of Susan, who was now holding up a hand of her own to slow him.

"It's her ankle, maybe her leg. Could have been a lot worse, though. She rolled out of the way just in time."

Lance took a tentative step forward, and when Susan didn't stop him, he kept walking until he reached the scoreboard, which lay flat on the ground, its face split nearly in two, chunks of circuit boards and loose wires dangling from the crack running down its middle. The pole jutted out from the bottom and pointed straight out toward the end zone where it had once stood.

"Lance?"

Leah was sprawled out on her stomach, perpendicular to the pole, the bottom corner of the scoreboard pinning her left ankle against the ground. Lance stepped carefully over the pole and knelt down beside her. He had to get down low to see her face, nearly falling forward. "I'm here," he said.

She looked up at him, and even though her cheeks were wet with tears, she smiled at him. "I take it this wasn't part of the plan. At least I certainly hope not. If so, you could have at least warned me." She laughed, then grimaced in pain.

Lance laughed, relief so abundant in him he felt weightless. "I told you, I'm just winging it."

He winked at her, and she laughed again and rolled her eyes, and then Lance and the paramedics and a few spectators who'd been brave enough to wander close enough to get pulled in to help worked together to lift the sign off Leah's ankle enough to allow her to be pulled out. Free.

Susan convinced everyone to let Lance ride in the back of the ambulance on the way to the hospital. He watched impatiently as they carefully put her on a stretcher and loaded her into the back. Lance waited for the signal and then climbed in. He looked back out to the bleachers, scanning the crowd, watching thousands of faces watch him climb aboard, all probably curious as to who he was.

Then he remembered the feeling he'd gotten just before the lightning strike, that nagging feeling that something was screaming toward him, taunting and cocky and nasty. He looked to the field and found the fifty-yard line. Followed it up to the fence, then the bleachers. Counted the rows.

Glenn and Allison Strang were gone. He squinted and tried to focus his vision. Melissa McGuire was gone, too.

The ambulance doors closed and they headed off, a bumpy ride through the grass and then up onto the smooth asphalt of the road. He held Leah's hand as Susan and Harry carefully removed her shoe and sock and examined her on the way. Leah lay perfectly still, her eyes closed, the occasional grimace or whimper of pain at a bump in the road or a prod or poke from Susan and Harry. Lance used the short ride to the hospital to calm himself, center his feelings. He'd almost snapped, back there with Harry. He'd almost punched the man. He needed to get himself under control. The important thing was Leah was okay, in the grand scheme of things. A broken ankle, maybe, but nothing life-threatening.

Lance was feeling better when the ambulance slowed, and once Leah was settled in he'd be ready to figure out what his next move was. The ambulance came to a stop and the doors opened and Lance was told to get out first.

He did so, stepping carefully to the ground, looking up to see the two-story Westhaven Hospital in all its glory. He'd barely registered the bright neon EMERGENCY above his head when a pair of strong hands grabbed him by the shoulders, twisted, and slammed him to the ground.

25

LANCE'S FACE HIT THE ASPHALT PARKING LOT HARD ENOUGH to rattle his teeth and create a starburst in his vision. Instinctively, he rolled away from the direction the attack had come, scrambling to try and stand again before another blow fell on him. He heard a rushing noise coming at him, something large and moving fast. He was pushing himself off the ground, halfway up before an uppercut caught him in the gut, slammed the air out of him and sent him back to the pavement. He gagged and gasped for air, raising his hands to shield off a further assault. Then the stars in his head finally began to clear and he looked up to stare into the face of his attacker.

He wasn't surprised.

Samuel Senior stood over Lance, fuming, hands balled into fists, his bald head so red it looked hot to the touch. The veins in his arms pulsed. His eyes were narrowed to slits, trained on Lance. Standing over Lance in the darkened parking circle with the bright neon EMERGENCY sign lit up behind him, Leah's daddy looked like a prize fighter basking in the glory of his latest knockout, waiting for the ref to turn the other cheek so he could really finish the job.

But he wasn't moving. He'd stopped his attack. Lance kept his hands raised, both in surrender and defense, and slowly stood, finally regaining control of his breath. Samuel Senior's eyes flicked to something behind Lance, and he said, "It's fine, Roger, we're done here. Just a bit of a misunderstanding." Then the man took a step backward.

Lance twisted his neck around to look over his shoulder and saw a Westhaven sheriff's deputy standing with his hands on his hips in the open doorway leading into the emergency room's entrance.

"Had anything to drink tonight, Sam?" the deputy named Roger asked, as if he were exhausted.

Samuel shook his head. "Not a drop. Honest."

"Is he telling me straight, son?" Roger asked, looking at Lance. "Just a little misunderstanding, and now you two are going to go your separate ways?"

Lance swallowed down his anger, looked from the deputy, to Leah's daddy, and then to the ambulance doors, where Susan and Harry were standing, shielding Leah from viewing what was happening. But she must have recognized the sound of her father's voice just then, because from inside the ambulance, she called out, "Daddy? Is that you? What's going on?"

At the sound of his daughter's voice, Samuel's expression softened, and he took a step toward the ambulance. But then he stopped, turned back to Lance with a refreshed hatred in his eyes and said, "Get the fuck out of here. If I ever see you near my daughter again, I'll kill you. I promise. I knew you was trouble the moment I saw you." Then he turned away and stood by the ambulance as Susan and Harry disappeared back into the rear and came out a minute later, carefully extracting Leah's gurney, then the four of them were swallowed by the large electric doors leading inside, Leah turning her head to see Lance one last time before she was wheeled out of view, her eyes apologetic.

Lance stood, staring at the now-closed hospital doors and then watched as the ambulance drove away, off to wherever magical place they go to hide before the next call. A breeze blew by, and a few drops of rain splashed on top of his head. He looked up, saw the starless sky, the gray clouds just visible against the black backdrop. He sighed, at a loss, a loss of everything.

He turned and started to walk away, nodding to the deputy, who was now leaning against the hospital's brick wall, one leg cocked back, the sole of the shoe pressed against the brick.

"You okay, son?" he asked as Lance passed.

"Yes, sir. Thank you, sir," Lance said.

Lance had made it another ten yards when he heard the electronic *whoosh* of the doors opening. He didn't turn back, didn't look. But then he heard Susan Goodman's voice calling his name. He turned and saw her jogging toward him across the parking lot, her large body bouncing with each stride. She stopped a few feet short of him and waited a second to catch her breath, then tucked a few loose strands of hair back behind her ears. She was sweating, some of the dark makeup around her eyes smeared ever so slightly. Lance could smell her deodorant.

He asked the only question that mattered to him right then. "She okay?"

Susan shrugged. "Probably. Doctors are looking at her now, but I'm positive it's broken. Question is how bad. X-rays will tell. But look, that's not why I came out here."

Lance raised his eyebrows. "Okay."

Susan tossed him something and he caught it, reflexively. It was a set of car keys.

"Leah said go get the car and take it back to Renee," Susan

said. "And she said to wait at the motel for her to call you. Which she'll do as soon as she can."

Lance stared at the keys for a long few seconds, then looked back up to Susan. "I don't ... maybe I should just go."

Susan looked at him. Cocked her head to the side and studied him. Then she looked up to the sky for a moment and back down to Lance. "Look," she said matter-of-factly, "I don't really know who you are, or why you're here. I know Leah thinks you can figure out what happened to our brothers, and yeah, that'd be great and all, but honestly, we all know the odds are slim." She paused. "What I also know is that, despite all the mystery-solving bullshit, Leah likes you. A lot. Like ... really likes you. We're not the best of friends or anything. Hell, I maybe see her once or twice a month, just around town and whatnot. But I haven't seen her smile this much in a long time. You should have seen her, the way she was talking about you when we were headed to pick you up from the side of the road earlier. She lit up like a Christmas tree."

Then she stopped talking. She just shrugged, looked back over her shoulder toward the hospital and said, "I've got to get back to work. Take care."

She jogged away, leaving Lance standing in the hospital parking lot with no better idea of what he should do than he had before.

He turned and started to walk.

26

Lance had made it roughly a quarter mile from the hospital before his mind focused enough on the present to realize he had no solid idea where he was. He'd been unable to see from the back of the ambulance as it'd rushed from the football field to the hospital, and the hospital was something he hadn't come across during his brief exploration of Westhaven. But he knew the ride had been short, and he knew the bright, expensive lights from the field were surely still illuminating the sky. He needed to locate the lights and use it as his North Star, let it guide him back to the car.

He followed the sidewalk from the hospital parking lot, stopping every so often to listen to what was around him. A half mile from the hospital, he stopped and swore he heard a faint echo from the PA announcer. Nothing he could make out, but a familiar sound. Through the darkness, the downtown buildings came into view, slowly growing shape the way a monster from a closet might in the middle of the night. He was approaching them from the south side, from the rear. A side he'd yet to see. He followed the sidewalk into town and then stopped, looked left and right, and then turned, headed down a now-familiar path.

The shops and stores were all closed, shut down and locked up and dark. The few small cafes and restaurants were the only signs of life, keeping things from looking quite like a ghost town, and probably hoping for some postgame customers to stop by and help the day's profit.

Lance walked, ignoring everything but his thoughts. He reached the Route 19 intersection he'd found earlier that day and turned right, the lights from the field visible, but not needed now. He'd been this way before. Right before he'd caused a man to die.

And as he made the walk, the last leg of the trip before reaching the high school parking lot, he replayed the past thirty-six hours' worth of events. He watched himself get off the bus, walk to Annabelle's Apron. He recalled his conversation with the diner's deceased owner. Her subtle plea for help. From there he watched himself stumble upon Bob's Place, and then he remembered the first time he'd seen Leah. The thought filled him with a sudden warmth he'd not been expecting, despite his current affection for her.

You're too close, Lance.

He had seen the face that he now knew to belong to Leah's brother, Samuel, staring back at him from both the mirror and later the television. The face that he now felt wasn't malicious or hostile in any way, merely that of a loving brother, trapped in some terrible in-between place—not living, not in whatever afterlife might exist—forced to stay near a sister he could no longer protect, no longer talk to. So close, but so, so far. Keeping a watchful eye, despite the limitation. Curious about Lance.

You're too close, Lance.

He saw Susan Goodman's large but gentle hands working to treat his wounds from the car accident.

BEN AND JEN!

Saw her tears fall as she fondly remembered the kid brother she used to pick on but had loved so deeply. Susan and Leah were just two of the people who'd had their lives destroyed by something selfish and uncaring and ... something that needed to be stopped.

Lance had tasted Leah's lips, her tears. Smelled the shampoo.

Seen the pictures of the state championship teams, their missing teammates not even mentioned.

Seen Glenn and Allison Strang, the town's power couple, sitting side by side on the bleachers.

Seen Melissa McGuire, petite and unremarkable and almost out of place, beside the Strangs, half-watching her husband command his team.

Lance had heard the thunder roar and the lightning crack, had seen the scoreboard begin to fall.

Heard Leah scream.

The anger rose, and the bile in his throat was hot and bitter.

You're too close, Lance.

He felt a chill at the memory of that odd sense of taunting he'd felt just before the scoreboard had fallen. It had been there, and it knew it was winning.

Lance pushed away the thoughts and turned into the high school's parking lot. The announcer's voice came back into focus over the PA, and Lance heard a whooping from the stands, followed by the announcement of a Westhaven touchdown. A collapsed scoreboard and an injured fan were not enough to stop a football game in this town.

Lance pulled the car keys from his pocket, unlocked the door and got in the driver's side, sliding the seat as far back as it would go. Then he sat, waited, thought.

You're too close, Lance.

He looked up at the bright lights and heard another cheer from the crowd and made his decision.

He had nobody. He *was* nobody. And he had nowhere to go.

But here, in Westhaven? There was a girl, and she'd shown him that

I don't care if I'm too close. It doesn't change anything.

a town needed him.

Lance sat back against the seat, his mind made up.

He would get to the bottom of this, even if he had to die in the process.

Lance waited for the game to end. He was going to talk to Bobby Strang, whether Bobby was willing or not.

27

Lance cracked the car's window, letting both air and the PA announcer's voice blow through the vehicle's interior. The gentle breezes kept him cool and the announcer's voice kept him updated. Westhaven was winning twenty-eight to seven. Not a blowout, but by Lance's best guess the game had to be nearly over, so Westhaven would add another tally to the victory column.

Sure enough, five minutes later there was a barrage of horns and cheers, and the announcer shouted the final score with gusto and then thanked everybody for coming out and asked them to please drive safely.

And then the people came. They spilled from the too-small gate like a flood breaking through a dam, a densely packed group that seemed never to end, fanning out and widening and scattering loose once past the gate's confines and into the parking lot in search of their vehicles. It was a chaotic scene, the type of thing where children get separated from parents, or an elderly woman falls down and gets trampled, like those disgusting videos they play every Black Friday on the news where somebody nearly dies to get a discounted television. Humanity at its absolute finest.

But while the parking lot was busy and fast-paced, the people were smiling, laughing, high-fiving and celebrating their team's victory. And when the cars switched on their headlights and began the slow process of vacating the lot, they did so in courteous and cautious maneuvers, waving cars in, letting pedestrians through the seams. Lance didn't hear a single horn blow or see a single fist shake from an opened window.

He turned around in his seat and watched cars fall into single-file and follow a path in front of the main office building. In the distance, he saw a police cruiser, lights spinning, parked near the exit and directing traffic in a well-organized manner. Apparently getting cars out of the school's lot was too much a task for Mrs. Bellamy, the legendary civics teacher.

The lot was half-empty, but Lance wasn't concerned about missing Bobby Strang. The team might just be finishing up their postgame coach's speech, and then they'd be stripping off their uniforms and equipment. Some would shower, others would stuff their sweaty bodies into their normal clothes and head out. Eventually, the players would all be gone, but the coaches would stay behind, discussing the game with each other, putting away equipment, tidying things up. Aside from any janitorial staff, the football coaches would be some of the last folks to leave the high school tonight, and Lance had all the time to wait.

Most all the patrons had left the lot, and what remained was three densely packed rows of cars at the very front of the parking area—those who'd arrived first. Players ... and coaches. Sure enough, a few large high school boys began to trickle from the rear of the school, all carrying duffle bags or having tossed light jackets over their shoulders. They wore the faces of winners, the taste of another victory still sweet on their tongues. They climbed into pickup trucks and battered SUVs and lowriders, even one minivan. Engines started and music blared from windows—a hodgepodge of country and rock and rap that mixed into an unruly mess of sound—and then the boys drove away one by one, leaving just Lance in Renee's borrowed Honda, and five other cars parked side by side in the far right corner of the lot.

Twenty minutes later, as Lance was fighting his urge to doze off in the now quiet and still parking lot, Bobby Strang emerged from the school's shadows.

Bobby had untucked his t-shirt, a creased line of sweat visible in the dimly lit parking lot, and he'd put on a Westhaven ball cap. He had a gym bag slung over one shoulder and was fumbling with his car keys as he crossed the lot, heading toward one of the remaining few cars parked in the front.

Lance sat up quickly, ready to make a decision. Ready to make a move.

But then Bobby Strang stopped midstride, maybe ten feet from the closest car, as if something had caught him off guard. He started to turn around, and for a brief moment Lance felt his stomach tighten, figuring somehow Bobby had caught him, knew he was watching. But Bobby's turn continued past Lance's direction, and then he stopped, looking back toward the school.

And then Lance heard a woman's voice, faintly entering the Honda's cab through the cracked windows. Lance couldn't make out the words, but apparently Bobby could, because he suddenly shouted, "Tell him that play might have worked twenty years ago! Tell the old man to let the past go!" He said the words with a smile, and Lance heard laughter coming from the school. And then from the shadows came two figures.

Lance slouched down in the seat, his eyes just above the steering wheel, his knees nearly jammed to his chest. He watched as the figures came into focus, stepping into the cones of light cast by the parking lot's lamps.

Allison Strang—Bobby's mother—said, "You know your father is only trying to help." Her voice was smooth as silk, carried on the night's breeze. Behind her, the second woman came into view. Melissa McGuire entered the light and then put a hand on Bobby's shoulder, gently. "Don't feel bad. He gives Kenny play advice all the time."

"Which I'm sure Kenny promptly and politely ignores," Allison said, and again the group fell into a fit of laughter.

Lance sat up a bit, leaning closer and trying to hear as the laughter fell away and the group continued a conversation at what became a whisper. Too far away to make out well.

What are they talking about? Lance wondered, but then he thought, *Nothing that's going to help me, that's for sure. Why would it?*

There was a buzzing in his pocket and Lance started so fast he hit his head on the car's ceiling. "*Crap!*" he mumbled, swallowing his heart back down. He clawed his cell phone from his pocket and checked the number on the display.

Leah.

His felt a jolt of happiness. Smiled.

He wanted so badly to answer but knew now was not the time.

He ignored the call and looked up.

Allison Strang was looking straight at him.

Lance froze. In the poor light it was tough to tell if she was actually looking directly at him—right at Lance's body—or if she was simply looking in the direction of the car. Could she even see him through the windshield? Lance basically played dead, holding his breath, not blinking, not moving a single muscle or tendon. Not even sure why he was so concerned. So what if she saw him? He was nobody. Just a random guy who'd shown up to watch the state's best team. Here to see what all the hype was about.

But still, he felt fear. He just didn't know why.

Allison Strang looked away, and Lance allowed himself to breathe.

A minute later, Kenny McGuire and Glenn Strang joined the group in the lot, and a few more jokes were made and a few more laughs were had. They all just seemed like decent people having a good time after a great win.

Then they all got into their respective vehicles: the Strangs a BMW SUV, Kenny and Melissa McGuire a newer-model Ford Explorer. Lastly, Bobby got into a Toyota Tundra pickup that looked new and shiny and too flashy for the small town of Westhaven. Maybe a gift from Dad—apparently a bottomless wallet —or a company car, perk of being a VP.

Reverse lights came on and the cars drove out of the lot.

With no real choice, his task not yet completed, Lance started Renee's Honda and followed the caravan.

Yep, he thought, *I'm definitely winging it.*

[28]

LANCE CREPT UP TO THE STOP SIGN AT THE EXIT TO THE school. The police car and officer who'd been directing traffic were gone, and Lance idled the Honda for a moment, letting the line of vehicles he planned to follow get a little bit of a distance ahead. They'd turned right. The same direction Deputy Miller had turned earlier. But Lance couldn't think about that right now. He pushed the thoughts of his accident, of Miller's ... *possession* was the only word for it ... away and focused on the present. He flipped open his cell phone and saw Leah had left a voicemail earlier when he'd been forced to ignore her call. He hit the button and listened to it.

"If you're still here ... call me, please."

If I'm still here?

Leah's voice had been soft, apprehensive. Almost timid, as though she was trying hard not to let her real emotions translate through the call.

Lance remembered his conversation with Susan Goodman in the hospital parking lot, right after they'd wheeled Leah inside. He'd been in a bad place then mentally and had fully expected to walk out of the parking lot and then out of town.

Yet here he was.

He scrolled to Leah's number, pressed SEND, and then drove past the stop sign and followed the sets of taillights in the distance. Nothing but darkness on either side of his car.

Leah answered the phone on the first ring. "Are you on a bus?"

"No."

"Are you waiting for a bus?"

"No."

Silence. Then, "So, what are you doing?"

"I'm following Kenny and Melissa McGuire, and the entire Strang family. But really just Bobby."

Silence again. Then, "So you're still doing this?"

"Why wouldn't I be?" He tried to sound convincing.

Leah sighed. "Lance, don't feed me bullshit, please."

Lance kept his eyes locked on the taillights. He'd driven about a mile from the school. A battered speed limit sign said things should move forty-five miles per hour, but the caravan ahead seemed to be moving much faster. "Sorry," he said. "You're right. I thought about leaving. Things are getting dangerous, and it's because of me." The truth was the only option right now. "Whatever's happening in this town, it's not ... I know it's not completely human. It's something ... worse. And it knows I'm here, and it knows I care about you, and therefore you and I and anybody we associate with from this point forward could be considered targets."

There was more silence now. Longer than before. Finally, Leah spoke, slowly. "You ... you think this—this *thing* is what caused the sign to fall on me?"

"I do," Lance said. He had no doubt about it.

He was amazed at how accepting Leah was. She didn't question him about what he'd just told her and didn't sound dubious when she spoke, as if she wasn't quite sure she could swallow that particular pill. She just went with it.

She trusted him. Completely.

"Well," she said, "it missed."

Despite himself, Lance chuckled. "Not completely. How bad is it, really?"

"Not terrible. No surgery needed, but it's in a cast. Hurt like hell."

"I'm so sorry," Lance said, because he was. He truly was.

"Don't worry about me right now. Why are you following Bobby?"

"I'm going to ask him what he knows."

If Leah thought this was a bad idea, she didn't say so. "I guess I'll need to call Renee and tell her she can let the kids sleep in one of the motel rooms until you get back, since I'm sure it'll be past their bedtime. You've got her car, don't forget."

Lance nodded. "And it's coming very much in handy at the moment."

Ahead, the McGuires and Bobby Strang both turned on their left turn signals and slowed. Glenn and Allison Strang kept driving, surely headed to their luxurious abode in a more secluded area.

Lance slowed as well, letting Bobby and the McGuires keep their distance. "How pissed was your dad?" he asked.

"Oh," Leah said, as if she'd forgotten. "Very. I'm pretty sure you're a dead man if he ever sees you again."

"Yeah, I gathered that."

"I tried to tell him you had nothing to do with what happened to me, but ... well, it doesn't matter. You're a boy, I'm his girl. Enough said."

Lance nodded again. "Well, I'll try to keep my distance."

"From him or from me?"

Lance smiled. "Him, ideally."

Silence again. Then, "Good."

Lance made the left turn and found himself in a cluttered suburban neighborhood. Modest, but nice. Middle-class and tidy. A neighborhood watch sign reflected in his headlights. The McGuires' Explorer made a right turn a quarter mile up the road, heading deeper into the guts of the rows of houses, but Bobby Strang's Tundra kept straight. Alone.

"I need to go," Lance said. "Just me and Bobby now."

"Okay. Be careful. And remember, Bobby's a nice guy. Let me know what you find out. And I'll text you when I get out of here."

"Where are you going?"

"The motel, hopefully. But I think Daddy is hoping I'll go home with him for the night."

Lance said his goodbye and hung up the phone, following Bobby's Tundra and wondering just how nice of a guy Bobby truly was.

Bobby Strang turned left down a side street, and then three houses later, the brake lights came on and the large truck slowed and flicked on a turn signal. Lance slowed, watched as Bobby drove into his driveway and an automatic garage door began to open, its chain and motor whirring in the still night. Lance drove past, taking note of the house, trying not to look too much like he was spying.

Bobby Strang lived in a two-story brick home with an attached two-car garage. Nothing special architecturally, a big brick box with the standard window placement and roof slants, but way more house than a single man in his early twenties needed. Lance again wondered at just how deep Glenn Strang's wallet was. The front porch lights were on, and Lance could see a sparse but well-kept flowerbed lining a stone walkway leading from the driveway to the front door. The yard was empty otherwise. No trees or bushes or gazebos or anything decorative. No basketball hoop out front. Of course not. The Strangs were a football family.

Lance drove down the street and found it to be a dead end. A cul de sac that had a house to its left and right sides, but nothing straight ahead at the end. Lance killed the headlights and carefully pulled the car into the soft, grassy shoulder, the passenger-side mirror maybe two feet away from a tree line, dense and dark. He could have just pulled into the driveway— he was only there to talk, after all. But, as Lance had learned throughout his life, as well as during his brief time spent in Westhaven, things had a way of not always going as well, or as regularly, as you often planned. If things got out of hand and he had to make a quick exit, he didn't want potential witnesses to remember seeing the car parked in Bobby Strang's driveway. In a town like Westhaven, eventually the information would point back to Renee, which might lead to the motel, which might lead to Leah. It was a risk Lance wanted to avoid.

He waited five minutes after parking. He wanted to let Bobby Strang take care of whatever small things most people did as soon as they got home—kick off the shoes, toss the keys in the bowl by the door, check the day's mail, grab a drink. After waiting, Lance got out and walked back up the street. The night air had grown warmer and had mixed with the moisture, causing Lance's shirt to feel as though it were sticking to him. The front porch lights were still on outside Bobby's front door, and as Lance walked up the driveway, glancing over his shoulder at the houses across the street to see if any prying eyes might be peering out behind pulled-back curtains (the neighborhood watch sign flashed across his memory), he realized that what he was about to do seemed pretty crazy. Oh well, he'd never been one for normalcy.

He followed the stone walkway and stepped up onto the stoop, debated between knocking and ringing the bell, and then decided and pressed his finger to the button, hearing a soft melody of chimes from inside the home.

The door opened almost immediately, Bobby Strang appearing and standing with the door fully open. Sure enough, there was an open beer bottle in his hand, and behind him Lance could see the flickering blue reflection of a television screen.

"Who are you?" Bobby asked. Not so much with malice or mistrust, but genuine confusion, as if maybe he'd been expecting somebody else.

Somebody who has no idea what he's doing, that's who I am, Lance thought.

"My name's Lance. I'm a friend of Leah's."

Bobby's brow crinkled, further confusion sweeping across his face. "Leah?"

"From the motel," Lance said. "She, uh, she asked me to stop by and see you." Lance figured maybe playing the friend angle would help him out, if only to offer an opening to really get to his point without a confrontation.

"Leah?"

I did say that, didn't I? Or is my head injury acting up?

"From the motel," Lance said again.

"The motel," Bobby said slowly, as if the puzzle pieces were slowly sliding together, but not quite interlocking.

"Samuel's sister," Lance said, hoping the new name would jump-start Bobby's brain.

It did more than that. At the mention of Samuel, the color literally drained from Bobby's face. He recovered quickly, taking a swig from his bottle to help hide his brief change in emotion, but Lance saw it all the same. "Right, Leah," Bobby said. "She's a great girl, love her to pieces, that one." Then, slowly, more cautiously: "Why did she send you to see me? Oh, and hey! Wasn't it her who got hurt tonight at the game, when the scoreboard fell? Man, that was *insane*! Oh man, is she okay? Is that why you're here? Oh God, does she want to sue the school or something, because look, I don't really have any—"

Lance held up his hand. Bobby looked at it, stopped talking.

Lance was getting tired, and his head was beginning to hurt again, and honestly, for some reason he found himself not liking Bobby Strang very much, though he couldn't quite say why. Just one of those vibes he sometimes got with people.

"Look, Bobby, I'm here because Leah's asked me to help figure out what happened to her brother, and as far as anyone knows, you're the last person to have seen Samuel alive before he disappeared. So I was hoping you could tell me exactly what happened that day, answer any questions I might have, and then I'll be out of your way and let you get back to your television."

Bobby said nothing. Took another sip from his bottle, eyes never leaving Lance's, narrowed to slits as he contemplated what Lance had said.

"Leah wants me to tell you about that day with Samuel?" he asked.

Is he going to make me repeat everything?

"That's correct, sir."

Bobby nodded. "Why? That was years ago."

Lance didn't like that answer. "Does that make it any less important?"

Bobby didn't say anything to this, and Lance hoped the guy was kicking himself for coming off so nonchalant about a missing person—a former teammate and friend, for goodness sake.

"Look," Lance tried again, still waiting for his invitation to come inside and make his attempt to get to the meat and potatoes of the conversation, "Leah told me you and Samuel were good friends, and she told me what a great guy you are, and how wonderful your family was to hers after her brother went missing." Then he laid it on a little thick, hoping a small ego stroke might get Bobby talking. "She told me that if anybody in Westhaven other than her and her father cared about figuring out what happened to Samuel, it'd be you, and that you'd do anything you could to help us out, because that was the kind of stand-up guy you were."

Bobby listened, rubbed the back of his neck with his free hand. "I always liked Leah," he said. "Hell, if she wasn't Samuel's sister, I might have made a move. Tried to, anyway." He laughed the way guys laugh with each other when they talk about women, and Lance wanted to kick him in the teeth.

Lance took a deep breath and said, "So, can we talk? Just for a few minutes?"

Bobby Strang took one more long look at Lance and then his face changed. He offered a small smile and stepped aside, motioning for Lance to come in. "Sure," he said. "If Leah thinks it'll help."

Lance heard the rustling of the treetops behind the houses as a breeze blew through, the leaves dancing and branches swaying and sounding almost like a steady rainfall. Then there was an odd aroma in the air, something not unpleasant, but out of place. Sweet, but surprising. And then, as he stepped into Bobby Strang's house, he heard the faintest of voices among the sounds, a whisper, calling to him from somewhere far away.

It was the voice of Annabelle Winters.

"*Careful*," she said.

Then he figured out what the aroma was. It was the mixture of cinnamon and sugar and fruit. Apple pie.

Lance turned around as soon as he heard Bobby Strang close and lock the front door. Then Bobby reached behind his back, quickly, skillfully, and brought his hand back around, pointing the barrel of a pistol directly at Lance's chest.

Leah, Lance thought. *Bobby is not such a nice guy.*

[29]

Lance stared at the gun Bobby Strang was pointing at Lance's chest. It was matte black in color, smooth and flawless and brand-new in appearance. Bobby Strang wasn't into sport shooting—not with the weapon he was holding, that was for sure. No, Lance figured this gun had been purchased specifically for protection, for home intruders, which Lance didn't technically think he was since Bobby had invited him inside. Which was a point that seemed irrelevant should Lance be shot dead. Hard to win a court case from the grave.

Bobby Strang stood still, silently staring at Lance and keeping the gun trained directly at Lance's center mass. He looked unsure, as if he were expecting Lance to make some sort of play for the weapon, some sort of attempt to fight back. He appeared hesitant, though not incapable of pulling the trigger.

Lance replayed the moment in his head when Bobby had reached behind his back and pulled out the weapon, likely tucked into the waistband of his pants for easy access.

No way he was carrying that at the school, Lance thought. *He slid that into his pants when he got home.*

Which meant ...

"She said you might come," Bobby Strang said, his voice suddenly full of contempt.

Which meant he was expecting me.

The gun wobbled a bit as Bobby spoke, but Lance saw him tighten his grip to get it under control.

Bobby thrust the gun forward one time. "She told me you were here to ruin it all."

"Did she?" Lance asked. Bobby had unwittingly confirmed what Lance and Leah had grown to seriously suspect. There was a woman in Westhaven who was either directly or indirectly responsible for the football players' disappearances.

Bobby nodded. "She said you thought you were here to save them all," he said, "but really you were just making it that much easier."

Lance nodded this time. "Of course. I like to do what I can to help."

Bobby Strang gave Lance a funny look, digesting the sarcasm. Once it hit, he jerked the gun forward again and spoke louder. "You think this is a joke? You think she's just going to let you walk away from all this? Uh-uh. You're toast pal. I hate to say it, but you're a dead man."

Lance had no idea what exactly was going on, but he did know that the longer he could keep Bobby talking, the more time he would have to figure out what he was going to do in order not to die. Which seemed like a top priority at the moment.

"How did she know I was here?" Lance asked.

Bobby shrugged, laughed. "Fuck if I know, man. She just ... how does she do any of the stuff she does? My dad calls her the Voodoo Bitch Doctor, but we don't understand any of it. We just ... she's always—"

There was a loud blast of music from Bobby's pants pocket, startling both men. The tune was "Eye of the Tiger" by

Survivor, and Lance tapped his foot to the beat as Bobby cursed, nearly dropped the beer bottle to the floor to free up a hand, and struggled to pull the phone free from his pocket. The other hand made a point to keep the gun aimed at Lance. Lance had always liked the song.

Bobby Strang's iPhone screen was lit up bright when he pulled it from his pocket, but Lance didn't get a chance to see the name or number on the screen. Bobby answered directly. No greeting, no small talk, just, "I've got him."

Bobby was quiet for a minute, listening to the voice on the other end, which Lance could not hear at all. At that point he wished Bobby had some sort of hearing impairment requiring the volume on the phone to be turned up much louder. Darn his youthfulness. While Lance waited, he considered something else Bobby Strang had told him—again, likely unwittingly— which was that his father, Glenn Strang, was also fully aware of what was happening in town. Maybe.

(*My dad calls her the Voodoo Bitch Doctor…*)

Which again confirmed another suspicion, though this one had been less certain, which was that Glenn Strang had had a hand in the boys' disappearances as well. Again, either directly or indirectly.

So far, two of the three Strang family members were guilty.

And the third member of the family just happened to be an extremely attractive woman.

Lance looked at Bobby Strang's face, which had seemed to drain of most its color. He looked afraid; he looked worried. "Okay," Bobby said. "Okay, yes, if you're sure."

This time Lance did hear something from the phone's speaker. A loud burst of noise that was a human voice but impossible to pick any words from. Bobby's face reddened. "Yes, I know, I'm sorry." There was a beat, and then Bobby pulled the phone from his face and stuffed it back into his pocket. He looked at Lance.

"Wrong number?" Lance asked, wishing the ghost of Annabelle Winters would show up and drop the world's largest apple pie on top of Bobby Strang's head, crushing him to the floor and giving Lance the exit he needed. Lance figured the odds of that happening were slim.

Bobby Strang didn't even smile at the joke. Lance, realizing his soft and humorous attempts to disarm Bobby were falling short, decided to try a new offensive. A more aggressive one.

"You realize she's been trying to either kill me or scare me out of town from the moment I arrived, right?"

Bobby said nothing.

"Yeah, that's right," Lance said. "Hard to believe I'm still here, right? I've already survived a hurricane gust of wind and a fatal car accident, and I didn't tuck tail and run when she tried to murder Leah with that scoreboard tonight."

Bobby Strang's eyes lit up then, and his face grew surprised. "Wait ... that was—that was her that did that?"

Lance rolled his eyes. "Come on, Bobby. You're not that slow, are you? I thought you were on her team. How do you not see that was her threatening me? She went after Leah because she thought it would make me back off. You know, since Leah and I are ... well ..." He left it at that, would let Bobby's imagination take care of the rest. "So, you've got to ask yourself a question here, Bobby. If she's failed three times, why do you think *you* are going to be able to stop me?"

Bobby Strang stared at Lance for a long time, long enough for Lance to get bored and begin to whistle "Eye of the Tiger." But he'd only made it a few notes in when Bobby suddenly snapped, "Shut up! Shut up now!"

Lance stopped whistling.

Bobby said, "I'm not. She'll finish you off. All I have to do is get you there." He took a step forward, the gun still raised. "And the way I see it, right now I've got a pretty solid advantage. Wouldn't you agree?"

Lance glanced to the gun, then back to Bobby's eyes. "I would."

"Thought so. So do me a favor and turn around and walk forward, hands up, into the kitchen."

Lance waited a few more seconds, just in case the giant pie was going to fall, then resigned himself to being temporarily out of options and turned around. He put his hands up, as directed, and walked down a wide hallway past a living room with the television on and tuned to the local news, no doubt in anticipation of catching the local sports highlights from the night. After the living room was a closed door, behind which Lance assumed was some sort of coat closet or half bath, and then the hallway spilled into a large kitchen. Expansive, mostly empty countertops and expensive-looking stainless-steel appliances. Very nice. Lance reached a kitchen island, and Bobby said, "Okay, that's far enough."

Lance stopped and waited, eyes flickering across the kitchen, looking for anything that might serve as some sort of weapon.

There was, predictably, a butcher block full of knives sitting atop the counter next to the stove stop. Too far away to grab, and too ineffective against a firearm unless you were right on top of the person you were trying to attack. No good. There was a fancy coffeemaker with a stainless-steel carafe next to the sink, which might be good for slamming into a temple, or across the bridge of the nose, but again, the distance thing was a problem. Unfortunately for Lance, there was no spare pistol lying on a counter nearby. Nothing within reach at all, actually, except a stack of mail and some loose change and a bottle cap, presumably from the bottle Bobby had been holding on Lance's arrival.

Lance had his own fists to fight with, plus his large feet, but he wasn't trained in the way of fighting techniques, and a bullet would easily go through his skin and muscle and tendons and bone if he was merely a second too slow.

Guns sucked. *Thanks, NRA.*

In Lance's mind, he started to hear one of his mother's anti-gun rants—a topic she was vehemently outspoken on, especially after every mass shooting that seemed to increasingly plague the United States of America—but Bobby Strang spoke from just behind him, bringing him back to his own ever-increasingly unfortunate situation.

"Don't move," Bobby said.

Lance didn't move.

Bobby slid in behind him and then sidestepped to the left. Lance turned his head and saw Bobby grab a key ring off a hook by a door that must lead to the garage. Bobby kept the gun trained on Lance and used his other hand to open the door, then reached inside and felt along the wall until Lance heard the click of a light switch, and then the interior of the garage lit up with bright overhead lighting. Bobby stepped backward through the door and down a small flight of two steps, then took another step back and motioned with the gun for Lance to come out. "This way," he said. "We're going for a ride."

Lance took a couple slow steps toward the door. It swung outward, into the garage, as opposed as inward toward the kitchen. Another unfortunate thing. Lance could have tried to quickly duck and slam the door shut and then race himself back out the house and maybe make it to Renee's car, or possibly disappear into the woods for the second time in one day.

"Would it be easier if I just followed you in my own car?" Lance asked, stepping out onto the first step. "Then I can just head on home after we're finished."

For a moment, a brief, hilarious moment, it looked like

Bobby Strang was actually weighing the option, deciding if what Lance had suggested might indeed make things simpler. Then his simple brain registered the sarcasm and he snapped, "Just get the fuck down here, would ya? *Slowly.*"

Lance stepped down from the remaining step and stood on the large garage's concrete floor. The right half of the garage—the half in which Lance was standing—had been converted into some sort of workshop. To Lance's right, a large tool chest and workbench were pressed against the wall. Power tools and random unidentifiable bits and parts of machinery and wood and paint cans littered the benchtop and floor around it. A row of brooms and rakes and shovels hung from neatly aligned hooks along the wall directly behind Lance, and he suddenly remembered that scene at the end of the first *Home Alone* movie where the old guy knocks the Wet Bandits out with his snow shovel. It was something Lance would love to try and recreate at the moment, though, much like the knives in the kitchen, he knew he'd never pull off the maneuver in time if Bobby Strang did truly plan on using the gun to incapacitate him if need be.

There was a pair of dirty black flip-flops on the floor by the stairs. Less-than-ideal weaponry.

There was a creaking noise, and Lance's gaze turned back to Bobby, who'd just lowered the tailgate on the massive Tundra parked on the opposite side of the garage.

"Come over here," Bobby said, always motioning with the pistol. "Stand right here." He pointed to the ground directly behind the truck.

"Am I going to ride in the back like a dog? That's not really the safest, you know. Would probably be better if—"

"Didn't I tell you to shut up?"

Lance shut up. Figured he'd probably pressed his luck enough for one potentially deadly encounter.

Lance walked, his eyes never leaving the direction Bobby

had the gun trained, which was always Lance's chest. Lance had a few inches on Bobby, so the man literally just had to hold his arm straight out to be aligned perfectly with Lance's heart. Lance walked around to the back of the truck, Bobby turning in a small semicircle as he did so, and then stopped directly behind the truck's opened tailgate.

"Good boy," Bobby said.

I'm pretty sure I'm older than him. How disrespectful.

"Now, stay put for a second. You got it?"

Lance said nothing.

"I said, do you have it?" Bobby asked.

Lance raised his hand, as if to ask a question in class. Bobby's eyes followed it, stepped back as if braced for an attack, the gun thrust out further than before. Lance didn't move, just stood with his hand raised. Bobby stared for two seconds, then three, then he got it. "Yes?"

Lance cleared his throat. "You told me to shut up. If you want me to answer, well ... just make up your mind, okay?"

Bobby Strang's face turned a deep shade of red, and then he sighed and spoke in a voice that said he was clearly tired of playing the game. "Just don't fucking move, okay? Don't move and I won't shoot you. Those are the rules. Got it?"

Lance said he got it.

Bobby nodded and stared at Lance for another five seconds before he reached forward with his free hand and slid a large duffle bag toward him, pulling it down the truck's bed toward the tailgate. He raised his gun-wielding arm up, keeping the barrel of the pistol perfectly positioned. One-handed, he struggled to unzip the bag, cursing as it slid away from him on the first two tries. He finally got it open on the third, and his hand disappeared inside, fishing around for a moment before coming back into view holding a slightly used roll of good old-fashioned duct tape.

Lance knew where this was going, and in the same instant, he looked at his surroundings, tried to predict the next few moments' worth of events, and thought he might have found a potential opportunity to turn the tables on his captor.

He took one small step forward. A shuffle, really, just a slight readjustment of his stance. But he figured it would be enough.

Bobby Strang forewent zipping the bag closed and slid it away, back toward the front of the truck. He put the roll of tape in front of his own face and used his teeth to pry loose the end and then unspool six inches of tape, just enough to get it started.

"Hold out your wrists," he said. "Together, like this." He held out his own wrists to demonstrate the position he wanted Lance to mimic, and Lance could hardly believe his luck. Bobby Strang couldn't have made himself any more vulnerable to Lance's plan if Lance had given him verbal instructions and a diagram to follow.

Lance was standing facing the bed of the truck, and Bobby Strang was beside him, standing just to the side of the tailgate. When he held out his arms, one hand holding the roll of duct tape, the other hand holding the gun, he held them out directly over the truck's opened tailgate, his forearms right in line with the hinge.

Lance knew there was the possibility of the gun going off during his next move, but he also knew if he didn't act now, he might not get another chance. He figured his odds were fifty-fifty. Not the greatest, but clear-cut all the same.

Lance had always been quick. It was one of the reasons he'd been such a great basketball player. Folks always assumed it was because he was tall. And, yeah, that certainly helped, but it was the quickness that sold it.

In the blink of an eye, Lance dipped down, reached his hands under the tailgate, and then flung it up with all the strength he could summon. There was a soft, dull resistance at impact, and a high-pitched yelp escaped Bobby Strang's lips before being followed by a harsh and violent scream as his arms were completely smashed between the tailgate and the end of the truck. Despite the human noise, Lance heard the gun clatter out of Bobby's hands, could make out the sound of the steel against the truck bed.

He didn't waste any time looking for it. Instead he moved in to end it all.

Bobby Strang was dumbstruck, staring down at his bloody arms. Lance took one step forward and grabbed Bobby's head in both his hands and

(*Oh my God!*)

smashed the man's face into the side of the truck. Bobby Strang's body went instantly limp and crumpled to the floor.

Lance stood, his heart racing and his mind reeling from what he'd just seen.

LANCE DIDN'T LOOK FOR THE GUN, BUT HE DID QUICKLY stick his hand into Bobby Strang's front pants pocket and pull out his iPhone and car keys. Then he bolted back up the two steps, into the kitchen, and out the front door. He ran as fast as he could back down the street, filling his lungs with the cool night air. It tasted sweet and intoxicating. It tasted like freedom. How close had he come to meeting his end? Too close.

He pushed the thought away and kept running, reaching Renee's Honda and flinging Bobby Strang's car keys overhand into the woods at the end of the cul de sac. Lance didn't feel like being chased right now. He kept the cell phone, though, sliding it into the same pocket as his own flip phone and folding himself into the driver's seat. He cranked the engine and, in a moment of clarity and caution, managed to calm himself enough to slowly pull the car off the grass and gently accelerate up the street, back past Bobby's house, and then turn right. Only then did Lance risk stepping on the gas a little to put as much distance between himself and Bobby Strang as he could.

He replayed the original trip in his mind and managed to reverse the course and replicate the correct turns, and then he found himself back on the main road, heading back toward the direction of Westhaven High School, back toward the Route 19 intersection, which would lead left into town or right toward the motel.

His heart was still pounding in his chest, but he'd gotten his breathing under control. He gripped the steering wheel tightly, sitting up as straight as he could in the seat without his head hitting the ceiling, eyes straining to see out into the night with only the help of the weak headlight beams. He was on alert, terrified that whoever had been on the other end of the phone with Bobby Strang would somehow instantly know that things had not gone as planned, and that Lance was on the loose. Therefore, Lance had a very large target on his back, and from what he'd seen thus far in Westhaven, a new threat could take any shape, could be any person. Heck, at this point he wouldn't be too surprised if the Honda he was driving suddenly did its best *Christine* impression and drove off the road, slamming headfirst into a tree.

As the car ate up a few miles of road without incident, Lance slouched a little and took a deep breath. He was approaching the high school, the bright lights no longer burning and the gates to the parking lot closed. The fun was over. Lance took stock of how much new information he now possessed since the last time he'd been in this very same spot. What had initially been a gaping-hole mystery now had quite a bit filled in.

Lance now knew for certain that there was a woman involved who seemed to be giving the orders and was probably directly responsible for the boys' disappearances. Lance wasn't sure how the power to control the weather and possess police officers played into things, but he was certain that if he found this woman, he'd figure out the rest whether he wanted to or not.

Bobby and Glenn Strang were also key players somehow.

Okay, maybe not key players, but they had a hand in the mess, and both seemed to be held in some sort of grip by the woman in charge.

Which, without the last bit of information Lance had accidentally gained, would have been enough to suspect Allison Strang. But ... with what Lance had just seen, he was positive Allison Strang was the woman running the show. She was the danger. She was the reason Westhaven had suffered so much loss. She was the reason families had been devastated and torn apart and uprooted.

Lance had never planned on getting the visions, and he could never figure out why some people's lives flooded into him like a rushing river and others didn't show him a single thing; not their favorite color or middle name or even their current thought. But when Lance had grabbed Bobby Strang's head to slam it into the side of the truck, he'd seen something so shocking and disgusting it made his stomach turn.

It had happened in an instant, as if, at the single second Lance and Bobby Strang's bodies had connected, Lance had received a file upload of Bobby's memory at the fastest bandwidth known to man. Faster, even. A single touch, instant knowledge.

Lance shuddered as he remembered the scene. The bedroom, the ruffled sheets, the backside of her naked torso, the long blond hair sticking to her shoulders that were slick with sweat, the gentle moan as she rocked back and forth atop Bobby Strang's—

There was a vibration in Lance's pocket, and he jerked back to reality. He'd not passed a single car on the road and was about to approach the stop sign at the Route 19 intersection. He slowed the car and flipped on his right turn signal. With the car stopped, he reached into his pocket and pulled out his flip phone, for one fearful moment thinking that it might be Bobby's phone ringing instead, with *her* on the other end, wondering what was taking so long, or worse, calling specifically to speak to Lance because she knew what he had done. Lance knew he'd have to confront her eventually, but he wanted it to be on his own terms.

But then Lance realized he didn't hear "Eye of the Tiger" playing, and he knew it was his own phone ringing. He saw Leah's name and quickly answered, hoping he hadn't taken too long.

"Leah?"

"Hey, I'm back at the motel. Susan dropped me off after I finally convinced Daddy I was fine to be on my own. Where are you? How'd it go with Bobby?"

Lance thought about how to answer this. He made the right turn and drove the Honda toward the motel, toward Leah.

"It didn't go so great for me for a while. But it ended up worse for Bobby."

She paused for a second, then said, "Okay. What does that mean?"

"It means Bobby's probably going to need a good dentist, and I got us a lot of information without trying too hard."

Apprehensively, Leah said, "Why does Bobby need a dentist?"

"Because I slammed his face into the side of that expensive truck he drives."

"Lance! Why?"

"Well, for starters, he pulled a gun on me."

Silence.

Lance could see the lights from the motel up the road. Thirty seconds away now.

"But, Bobby's got bigger problems than some busted teeth," Lance said. "Like the fact he's sleeping with his mother."

[31]

LANCE PULLED THE BATTERED HONDA INTO THE MOTEL'S parking lot and parked it in front of the office door. He killed the headlights and the engine and sat in the darkened car's interior, resting his head against the headrest.

He was tired. His body ached—his head, his wrist, every muscle—and he felt like he could fall asleep right there in the driver's seat and sleep through the night and most of the next day.

You can have playtime when your chores are done, mister.

His mother's voice, dug up from another memory he'd stored away. He'd heard her say this a thousand times during his youth, and while it didn't exactly apply to his current situation, he caught the drift. He pushed himself away from the seat, grabbed his backpack from the back and got out of the car. The air was still cool, but there was no breeze. Lance stood next to the Civic and scanned the parking lot. There was one pickup truck parked at the far end of the lot, right in front of the last room on the row. A guest, Lance figured. Not a threat.

He walked up to the sidewalk and pulled on the office door. It moved maybe an eighth of an inch before coming to a sudden, violent stop, shaking and rattling in the frame and causing more noise than even seemed possible in the still night. Lance jumped, shocked at the sound and the vibration up his arm, and then took a step back. The door was locked.

A small tendril of panic swirled up his spine.

She knows what happened, Lance thought. *The woman— Allison Strang—knows what I did to her son, and she came straight for Leah. Or, at least, she sent someone straight for Leah.*

Lance had just started to dart his eyes around the lot again, looking for something he could use to smash the glass pane out of the office door and make his way in, when Renee's face peeked from between the blinds, and then the noise of a dead-bolt clicking out of place found Lance's ears.

Renee pushed the door open and stepped outside. She was wearing a dirty zip-up parka, as if it were winter and not a crisp fall night, and her hair hung down around her face in untidy strands. She looked tired. But Lance thought that Renee might be a woman who always looked tired, no matter what hour of the day. Probably rolled-out-of-bed tired.

"She's inside," Renee said, her voice soft. "She's resting in bed. She wants you to come back and lock the door behind you."

Lance nodded. "Thank you for the car. It ... well, it probably saved my life."

If Renee heard him, she didn't seem to care. She asked, "Can you help me carry the boys to the car? They're sleeping, and they've gotten so *heavy*."

Lance stood on the sidewalk, his body pleading for rest. But he knew his mother would have slapped him to next Wednesday if she ever found out he'd refused to help a kind, tired single mother of two. "Of course," Lance said. "Where are they?"

The boys had been sleeping in the room next to Lance's. The room was identical to Lance's except for the Star Wars nightlight that had been plugged into the outlet along the outer wall. Renee unplugged it and stuck it into the pocket of her parka. "I'm glad I remembered this. I'd have never gotten them down otherwise."

The boys looked so small in the bed, but they'd managed to splay their limbs over and across each other in a way that made it appear that they'd had an impromptu game of Twister before falling off to sleep. Lance approached the bed and gently untangled the first boy's legs from the other's and lifted him gently up. The boy's head fell to Lance's shoulder, and his arms instinctively wrapped around his neck. Lance smelled the scent of a no-tears baby shampoo and flashed back to his youth. His mother had used the same brand on him. He'd never forget the smell.

He walked carefully back to the car and deposited the first boy into the backseat, buckling him in before heading back for boy number two. With the same routine repeated, Renee closed the room's door and stood by the car next to Lance, who was more winded than he should have been after carrying two small boys a total of maybe twenty-five yards. Lance and Renee looked at each other for a moment, an odd calmness and comfort somehow hovering over them, as if the endeavor of getting the boys into the car had sealed some sort of bond between them.

Lance was about to thank Renee again for the car and head inside, but she asked, "Why are you here?"

Lance stared at her, saw the inquisition in her eyes. It was as if she knew he was something more than what he appeared to be, as if she recognized something brighter burning inside him.

Lance wasn't sure what to say.

(*Do you, a person with your gifts, honestly believe things could be so random?*)

"Honestly," he said, "I'm here because right now I think this is just where I'm supposed to be."

Renee nodded, as if this made all the sense in the world. Then she took a step forward and kissed Lance on the cheek. "Thank you," she said. She got in the car, started the engine with a sputter, and drove away.

Lance watched her drive out of sight, then turned and went into the office.

The motel's office was brightly lit, as usual, but empty. The television was off. Whatever traces of Renee's two young children there'd been earlier were now cleaned up and tucked away, and things were as they should be. Lance thumbed the deadbolt behind him, then switched on the NO VACANCY sign for good measure. He didn't think Leah would mind.

He adjusted his backpack over one shoulder and crossed the room, the floorboards creaking under his weight.

"Lance, is that you?" Leah's voice called out from behind her closed bedroom door at the far end of the office.

"It is I, young maiden! Your valiant knight, back from an adventure in the deepest, darkest corner of the kingdom."

He reached the door and turned the handle and cracked the door a bit, peered in. Leah was sitting up in bed, her ankle propped up on a pillow. The television was on, muted, a late-night talk show host sitting behind a desk with a celebrity Lance recognized but could not name talking animatedly from the guest's chair.

Leah looked at Lance blankly. "You're weird."

Then she smiled, and Lance smiled and pushed the door completely open and stepped in. "I know," he said. "But you gotta admit it's better than being boring."

Leah was wearing a baggy Westhaven sweatshirt and matching sweatpants. Her right foot was clad in a bright pink sock, her left foot encased in a cast, only the tips of her toes poking out the top. Lance sat gingerly on the bed, and they looked at each other for a silent moment. Then he leaned forward and kissed her forehead, then her lips. When their lips parted and he pulled away, Leah smiled up at him.

"I'm glad you're okay," he said. "You have no idea. I'm so sorry."

She pushed him away and laughed and said, "I'm *fine*. Don't worry about me. Tell me what the hell you were talking about on the phone! You think Bobby Strang is sleeping with his mother?"

Lance took a deep breath and adjusted himself on the bed, pulling one leg up under him and facing Leah.

Then he told her everything that had happened. From the moment he'd left the high school parking lot to the moment he'd escaped from Bobby Strang's house and driven back to the motel. The whole story, no detail avoided—except one.

Leah sat slack-jawed, shaking her head the more Lance talked. When he was finished, Leah was quiet for a minute, digesting his story. She shook her head and said, "Unbelievable. I just ... they've always been so ... so *nice*."

Lance said nothing. He'd long known that some of the purest of evil could hide behind the widest of grins.

Then anger fumed from Leah's face. "And all this time, he's been lying! Lying to the police, lying to my family! He knows what happened to Samuel and he fucking lied about it!"

Lance said nothing. He let her vent.

"And the timing makes perfect sense, doesn't it? The year the Strangs came into town was the same year the first boy went missing. Samuel."

Lance said nothing.

Then Leah perked up. "Hey! None of what you told me explains how you know Bobby is having sex with his mother. He didn't ... I mean, of course he didn't come right out and say that, did he?"

And here was the moment Lance had known was coming. He knew he couldn't avoid it, and he didn't want to. He was compelled to tell Leah, craved telling her, in fact. But unleashing the full truth of what he was, what he could do, onto somebody was something he was always apprehensive about. It was the final judgment, the last true test of whether the person sitting across from him would stand by his side or run away laughing, recommending Lance book a room in a nuthouse.

He looked at Leah, and in her eyes he saw something. Was it curiosity, or was it trust? Was it compassion, or was it concern?

"In order for me to tell you how I know," he said, "I have to tell you everything. Everything about me and who I am. The best I can, anyway. You already know some of it, but there's more."

She didn't even hesitate. "Okay."

So Lance told her.

[32]

LANCE HAD STARTED WITH A RECAP OF SOME OF THE things he'd already told her, earlier, on his first night in West-haven. Then he worked his way up to the crazier stuff, like the visions he sometimes got—those snapshots of life—when he touched somebody. And of course—and he hesitated here, even though he knew of all the people he'd met in his life recently, Leah was the most likely to take it all in stride—his ability to communicate with the dead. He phrased it this way, "communi-cate with the dead," because that was a lot easier to swallow than blurting out, "I see dead people." Thanks to Shyamalan's *The Sixth Sense*, Lance could never use that phrase without it being tainted.

Leah had been quiet through all his explanation, never saying a word, just staring up at him with wide-eyed fascination and nodding from time to time as if she completely understood everything Lance was saying. It wasn't until he got to the communicating with the dead part that she finally spoke up to ask a question. Lance couldn't blame her.

"Wait, what do you mean you can communicate with them?

Like, you hold a séance or something? You can speak to them across dimensions, or ... what?"

Lance shook his head. "That's movie stuff. Well, yeah, maybe some people do it that way. Who am I to say what's phony and what's not? But for me it's a lot simpler. Sometimes they visit me in my dreams. Sometimes they whisper things to me in my head, show me things. But often..." He sighed. *Here we go.* "Often they just show up next to me and start talking. Though it's never for very long, and usually not frequently. I think it takes a lot of ... energy, I guess, to show themselves like that. Like I said, I can't explain this stuff, but I've long since had to accept it."

"Since when?" Leah asked, and it was the simplest of questions she could have chosen, and Lance loved her for it.

"Birth, basically."

Leah was quiet again for a while. Lance sat on the bed and took her hand in his and held it while she thought, secretly hoping to maybe pick up some of her wavelengths to see if she thought he was off his rocker, and she was contemplating the best way to tell him to get the heck out of her room. He picked up nothing. It never worked when he wanted it to.

"Do you see bad things, too?" Leah asked.

Lance's stomach dropped.

"You know," Leah said, "if you can see dead people, can you see, like, demons or something?"

Lance felt a chill up his spine as he remembered events from his past. "Yes," he said, and that was all.

Leah must have heard the coldness in his voice, or maybe she didn't want any further verification that spirits of the damned walked among them, because she dropped the subject.

With the summary of Lance's gifts complete, he went on to explain the vision he'd had when he'd grabbed Bobby Strang's head in the garage. Leah listened with a disgusted look on her face, shaking her head. "How ...?" she started. "How is that even possible? Like ... how can they even ... oh God, that's so gross!"

Lance agreed. "It is gross. But I think it's incredibly significant. Allison Strang has some sort of power, that's for sure, and she's got a hold on Bobby and Glenn Strang as well. She has to. Blackmail, maybe. Heck, maybe she's basically raping her own son and using some sort of guilt trip, some threat of embarrassment and a destroyed reputation to force him to go along with everything that's happening. Forcing him to help her."

"And Glenn?" Leah asked. "Why him?"

Lance thought, then shook his head. "I'm not sure yet."

"The Eye of the Tiger" blasted from Lance's pocket, and he jumped again and bumped Leah's ankle with his elbow. "I'm so sorry!" he said, pulling the phone out.

She laughed and said, "Please, between the cast and painkillers, I don't feel a thing down there. When did you change your ringtone? Oh, wait, when did you get an iPhone?"

Lance sat on the bed and looked at the screen, the music loop starting to repeat. The caller ID simply said UNKNOWN. Lance used his thumb to slide across the screen and answer the call, then put the speaker to his ear and said, "Hello?"

There was a hiss of static from the other end, then silence. Lance pulled the phone away from his face and looked at the screen. The call had been ended.

Then a terrible thought hit him. She (*it*) had to know by now that Lance had escaped Bobby, so she (*it*) would be hunting Lance down. And if they knew Lance had Bobby's phone, then they could use it somehow to...

"We have to go," Lance said. "We have to go now."

Leah's eyes lit up with worry. "Why, what's wrong?"

"This is Bobby's phone, and just now, that call ... I think something's going to come for us."

Leah slid her legs over the side of the bed, sitting up. "I don't have a car. I ride my bike everywhere."

"Crap!" Lance said. "Any ideas?"

Leah looked down at the carpet for a second, thinking, then back up to Lance. "Yeah, I do have one, actually. But you're going to have to trust me."

"Of course I trust you," he said.

"I can call Daddy."

"Oh."

[33]

LEAH USED HER CELL PHONE AND MADE THE CALL. LANCE listened, half-worried and half-curious as to how she'd play it. She kept things simple and to the point.

"I've changed my mind, Daddy. Can you come pick me up?" A beat, then, "Thanks, Daddy. I'm sorry I didn't just go with you from the hospital. I ... I thought I'd be okay on my own." Leah listened to her father's closing remarks and then ended the call. "He's on his way. Five minutes, probably. He was in town."

"Should we go wait in the office? I suspect he'll attempt some sort of bodily harm to me if he catches me in your bedroom."

"Yes, he would," Leah said. "But no, you stay here."

"Makes sense," Lance said.

They were quiet then, Leah hopping over to the pair of crutches leaning against the wall by her bed. Lance helped her get situated on them, and then she made her way to the bedroom door, opened it a crack and stood by, waiting. Lance studied her, the way she was trying to act too casual. She was mulling something over, and though he didn't know exactly what, he assumed it was about him.

"Something on your mind?"

She turned and looked at him, met his eyes and held his gaze. "You've seen more in Westhaven than you're telling me, haven't you?"

Lance knew he could no longer withhold the truth from her. He'd told her too much already.

"Yes."

"You know what happened to the boys, don't you?"

Lance shook his head. "No, I don't know what happened to them. Not exactly."

"But ... you know," her voice broke and Lance saw fresh tears well up in her eyes. "You know they're dead, don't you?"

Lance hated what he had to say. "Yes."

"Have you seen them? Have you seen the dead boys?"

"Yes. A couple, but not all." He'd spare her the details of the burned boy from the diner.

She inhaled deeply, braced herself and asked, "Have you seen Samuel?"

It broke Lance's heart. "Yes," he said. "I've seen your brother. Twice. I'm so, so sorry, Leah."

She closed her eyes, and Lance wanted to go to her, wrap his arms around her and hold her tight. But something held him back. Something told him she needed her moment. Leah took two more deep breaths, and when she opened her eyes they were clearer, almost relieved, the tears drying. She nodded.

"It's okay," she said. "It's okay. At least now I know the truth. No more wondering. No more worrying." She laughed, and the noise seemed so foreign. "Is it weird to feel so happy to know your own brother is dead?"

Lance said nothing.

Leah stayed quiet for another minute, and then she looked

at Lance once more and asked, with a voice just above a whisper, "Lance, are you some sort of angel?"

The question floored him, caught him completely off guard. Never had this idea been proposed to him, and never had he thought of it himself. It was preposterous, but now was not the time to say so.

"No," he said, shaking his head. "I'm pretty sure I'm not an angel. I'm just a normal guy, who occasionally gets a hunch and hangs out with ghosts. No big deal."

Leah laughed, wiping the last remnants of tears from her cheeks. She smiled at him, and he was about to go across the room and kiss her when they both heard the low rumble of a muffler, getting louder and louder with each passing second.

At the sound of the truck, Lance suddenly became very uneasy. He trusted Leah had a plan, but being confined to the bedroom, if her father came in and ignored Leah's attempts at palaver, Lance would have nowhere to run and would likely stand little chance in a brawl with the man.

The hum of muffler and roar of motor continued to crescendo and then reached its peak, stationary outside the motel's walls. Then the noise died and there was the slam of a car door. Some heavy footfalls on the asphalt and then the sidewalk. Then the office door rattled with force but did not open.

"Shit," Leah said. "I forgot to unlock the door."

A fist pounded on the door hard enough to rattle the glasses atop the entertainment center. "Leah! Leah, are you okay!"

Lance heard the panic in the man's voice. This wasn't starting off well.

Leah was moving then, making her way across the office as quickly as she could on her crutches. Lance stayed put in the bedroom and tried to figure out where to wait. He chose to lean against the dresser along the far wall, mainly because it put him as far away as possible from the bed, which was the last place he wanted to be caught by a father of a girl he'd gotten involved with.

Lance heard the deadbolt slide and then the door open. "I'm fine, Daddy. It's okay, I promise."

Samuel Senior didn't answer right away, and Lance imagined him standing in the doorway, the man's thick neck practically creaking with muscles as he scanned the office and looked for threats, searched for something wrong. Finally, the man spoke cheerfully.

"You ready to go, sweetie? Don't you want to bring a bag, or something? You don't have much at the house anymore. It's been a while since—"

"Daddy, I need to tell you something. I need your help, but you have to promise me you can stay calm, and promise me you'll believe me and not lose your temper."

There were a few seconds of silence between them before the man said, "What's going on, Leah? What's this all about?"

Lance could tell the man had been almost expecting something like this to happen. A parent's intuition was strong, no doubt about it.

"You have to promise me, Daddy. I'm going to show you something and tell you some things, and whether you believe me, or trust me, or ... or anything, you have to promise me, as my father, that you won't yell and you won't hurt anybody. Can you promise me that?"

Lance silently thanked Leah for the bit about not hurting anybody.

"Baby girl, you know I'll do anything I can for you."

"Daddy, I'm serious! I don't just want words, I want action. I have to know I can trust you on this!"

Leah's sudden outburst seemed to resonate with the man, because the next time he spoke, he was somber, quiet. "I promise, Leah. I haven't even had anything to drink tonight."

"Okay," Leah said. "Lock the door again and then follow me."

Lance heard the deadbolt slide again, followed by the unsteady rhythm of Leah's crutches and her father's heavy boots coming across the office floor and getting closer. Leah came into view in the bedroom doorway, and she moved forward, coming toward Lance. Her father, wide and tired-looking, filled the doorway and stopped. He saw Lance at once, and the sudden shift in his eyes made Lance very grateful Leah was standing between them.

Samuel Senior was wearing the same outfit as earlier in the diner, and the hospital parking lot—the dark and worn blue jeans and white undershirt. Lance once again took notice of the labor-born muscles of the man's arms and shoulders. One solid blow to the head from a fist connected to that torso and Lance would be down for the count.

The rage in Samuel's eyes flared and then, miraculously, softened to an exasperated, desperate pleading. He looked at Leah, his expression one of disappointment.

"Leah, I want the truth, and I want it now. Who. Is. This. Guy? And your answer better be good, because from the timing of things, he's the suspicious guy that's been spotted all over town, and was seen with you at the football game, and he's the one who crawled out of the fucking ambulance with you after you got hurt. And now, despite my best efforts, he's still here, standing in my daughter's bedroom—the last place on earth I'd ever want to see him."

Lance couldn't disagree with that last part. At least he and Samuel Senior saw eye to eye about something.

"So," Leah's daddy continued, "What's the explanation? Tell me why I shouldn't kick his ass right now and then drag him to the sheriff's office." The man folded his arms across his broad chest and leaned against the door frame, putting his muscles on display.

Lance said nothing.

Leah said, "Remember your promise, Daddy."

Samuel Senior nodded, never taking his eyes off Lance. "If there's no problem, there's no problem."

It wasn't much in the way of a philosophical mindset, but Lance figured he understood the man's point. It was up to Leah now to convince her father that there was, in fact, no problem. At least in regard to Lance being alive and well and in their presence.

"Daddy," Leah started, "this is Lance. He's a new friend of mine, and, well ... he's not like other people."

Samuel Senior had no comment.

"He's got special gifts, Daddy. He can hear things, and feel things, and see ... things that other people can't."

With still no sense of response from her father, Leah blurted, "He's helping me figure out what happened to Samuel and the rest of the boys, Daddy! He's here to help us! And now some things have happened and we need your help. I can explain more later, but right now we have to go. So please, *please*, can you take us in your truck? We'll figure out where once we get on the road."

Leah stopped talking then, and Lance knew how frustrating it must be for her to try and squeeze so much information into a rush of a speech, trying to keep her daddy from boiling over and disregarding her. Lance knew his story didn't make any sense and was near impossible to fully explain, even with unlimited time and with the most open-minded of listeners.

Samuel Senior was quiet for a long time. So long that Lance thought maybe Leah had caused some sort of temporary shutdown in the man's head, that of all the possible explanations Leah could have given her father as to why Lance was there, the honest truth was so far beyond comprehension that the man was shocked into silence.

Lance was wrong.

Leah's father uncrossed his arms and straightened himself. He spoke softly to his daughter. "Your brother disappeared nearly three years ago."

"I know, but—"

"The whole town looked for him. The sheriff's office did everything they could. And when the other boys started to go missing, the state police started workin' on it, too. And you know what they found? Not a goddamn thing."

"Daddy, I know all this, but—"

"So you know what I think? You know what I think, Leah?" The man took a step forward, and Lance took a step backward, bumping the dresser. "I think this guy here, this *new friend* of yours, I think he's using the memory of your brother to get into your pants."

"Daddy!"

Another step forward, but Lance had nowhere to back up further.

"He's duping you, sweetie. He's saying whatever it is he thinks you want to hear. Guys do that, Leah. That's *all* guys do with pretty young ladies like yourself." He turned his head and spoke directly to his daughter. "I'm not surprised. Not with him, that is. But I am surprised you fell for whatever bullshit he's been feeding you. I thought you were smarter than that, baby girl. In fact, I know you're smarter than that. Which must mean this guy here is one *slick dick.*"

Lance saw a flicker of something to his left and turned his head ever so slightly to see that the television screen had changed from the muted late-night show and was now filled with nothing but snowy static.

Leah stepped forward on her crutches and yelled at her

father. "It's not like that, Daddy! You don't understand. Tell him, Lance. Tell him what you can do."

Lance said nothing, glanced between the television screen and Leah and her father.

"He can talk to the dead, Daddy! He can ..." Even Leah had to pause here. It simply wasn't something you could easily tell someone. "He can even *see* them."

Samuel Senior's face lit up at this, like he'd just heard a funny joke. "Oh, he can *see* them, can he? Well, my God. That changes everything! Why didn't you tell me that at the start? I suppose next you're going to tell me he's seen the boys who disappeared, right? I bet he even told you he saw your brother, didn't he?"

Leah hesitated, knowing her father was being sarcastic, but also knowing she was going to tell him the truth. "Yes."

Lance knew it was going to happen just a fraction of a second before it did. He saw Leah's father's muscles tense, poised for action, and then the man gently used his left hand to push Leah to the side, where she took one and a half hops before toppling over to her bed, her crutches clattering to the floor. And then the man was coming straight at Lance with the reignited fire in his eyes.

"You goddam son of a bitch!" He already had his fist cocked back, his body twisted and locked and loaded to deliver a single devastating blow to Lance's face.

Lance wasn't incredibly strong, but he was quick. He ducked and darted to the left, Samuel Senior's fist flying over his head in a wide, upward-swooping arc that hit nothing but air and nearly spun the man around with force. Lance popped back up, backed himself away, his butt knocking into the television. Samuel Senior regained his footing and turned back around, facing Lance with a face red enough to stop traffic. Veins stood out on his bald head, and his eyes were narrowed to slits.

He growled, "You've got nowhere to run, slick dick!"

But Lance didn't hear him. Didn't even register the fact that the man was pivoting off his heels and rushing at Lance with a speed and force that would knock Lance through the drywall. For Lance, time had slowed to nearly a freeze frame. His vision blurred and his head was filled not with the noise from the room, but with a low, staticky buzz that sounded like somebody trying to tune an old AM radio. The imaginary dials turned and twisted, the static popping and cracking and whining, and then from somewhere deep down in the static came a voice, calling out. It was so faint Lance made out nothing the first time except a foreign sound. But the second time the voice called out, Lance recognized it as human, and recognized the pleading urgency in the words.

Louder, Lance thought, willing his subconscious to reach the other voice.

The voice tried again.

Ace Bandage? Lance thought. *No, that's not right.*

And then, with a final burst of sound and energy, the spirit of Samuel Junior—the lost son and brother—broke through the static and rang true in Lance's mind.

"Bait sandwich!" Lance yelled. He was back in the real world, eyes focusing to see Samuel Senior charging at him. "Bait sandwich! Bait sandwich!"

Samuel Senior heard the words, his eyes clearing and looking at Lance with a startled realization. But he was coming too hard and too fast, and despite slowing himself slightly, when his body collided with Lance's, both men went toppling hard to the ground. The back of Lance's head bumped the edge of the dresser, sending a white flash of pain and light across his vision, but otherwise, he was unhurt.

Samuel Senior spun away from Lance, sitting up on the

floor with wide-eyed disbelief. He was breathing hard now, and sweat glistened from his brow. "What did you just say?"

Lance sat up, leaned against the dresser and felt the back of his head, where a new knot was forming. "Bait sandwich." And it was then that Lance realized he'd not only been delivered the phrase from Leah's brother's spirit, but the entire memory. Another instant upload.

"Samuel was eight," Lance said. "It was summer, and the two of you went fishing out on King's Pond. There was a little rowboat out there you could use, and the two of you packed a lunch and took your rods and went out early one morning."

Samuel Senior said nothing. Just looked once to Leah, who was now sitting on the edge of the bed, her eyes glued to Lance, and then back to Lance.

"You were out there all morning, and by twelve thirty you hadn't caught a single thing. You figured the pond needed to be restocked, but you didn't really mind. You were happy to be spending some time with your son.

"But Samuel got frustrated, thought he was doing something wrong for not catching any fish. You tried to calm him down, but he was stubborn about it and started to ignore you. And then you made a joke to try and lighten the mood. You told him not to worry. You said that even if the two of you didn't catch any fish, you had plenty of worms left and you could just have bait sandwiches for dinner."

Lance smiled. "Samuel nearly fell out of the boat laughing. I think ... I think that was one of your son's favorite memories."

The next time Lance looked at Samuel Senior's eyes, they were red and fresh with tears. He held them back as best he could, but as tears do, they eventually fell. He sniffled and wiped his cheeks and turned to Leah and said, "I never told your mother that story."

Leah's eyes spilled fresh tears as well, but she was smiling big and brightly. "And Samuel never told me, either."

Samuel Senior pushed himself off the floor and rushed to his daughter, sitting next to her on the bed and wrapping her in his strong arms. Leah buried her face into her father's chest and cried, and her father stroked her hair and said soft things to soothe her and cried his own cry, his tears dripping on top her head like raindrops on a roof.

Lance said nothing. Just watched as a father and daughter who'd been apart for so long took the first step in coming back together.

When they were able to compose themselves, Samuel Senior pulled away and stood from the bed, walking toward Lance. He stuck out a calloused hand and Lance took it, allowing himself to be pulled up.

"I normally don't believe in this sort of stuff," Samuel Senior said. "I mean, who really does?"

"Not many people," Lance said. "Why would they?"

"But there's no other way on earth you could possibly know about that day on King's Pond. No other way except ..." He trailed off, wanting Lance to say what he was too unsure to say himself.

"Your son told me, sir," Lance said. "Right before you speared me to the ground. I think he was trying to help me stop you, help me show you what I really am."

"And what are you?" Samuel Senior asked, nothing but curiosity in his voice.

"A friend," Lance said. "I'm a friend."

Samuel Senior looked Lance in the eye for what felt like a full minute, then nodded. "Can you look me in the eye right now and tell me man-to-man that my boy is dead?"

Lance stood tall, looked the man in the eye. "I'm sorry, sir. But, yes, he is."

Samuel Senior nodded again, and Lance saw the flash of

pain cross his face. But the man repressed whatever he had briefly felt and said, "I figured as much. I mean, all this time ... but still, to finally know, to have a God's honest answer. I just ... thank you."

Lance said nothing.

"And you think you can figure out what happened to him?" Samuel Senior asked.

Lance nodded to Leah. "We've learned a lot today, and we think we know the next step to take, but, with all due respect, sir, I'll have to fill you in later. Right now, we've got to go. I think whoever murdered your son is coming here, or sending somebody here to stop us from stopping them."

Samuel Senior's eyes began to boil again. "Then I'll stand right goddamn here and wait for them. They'll be sorry they ever decided to—"

"Sir, again, with all due respect, what's coming for us might not be exactly human. And in that case, I think it best we tuck tail and run, at least for now. At least till we come up with a plan."

Samuel Senior didn't have much of a response for this. But Lance's story about King's Pond had instilled enough of a trust in Lance's words that he didn't argue. He thought for a moment and then said, "Okay, let's go. Leah, the shotgun still behind the counter?"

"Of course," she said, getting up and adjusting her crutches under her arms.

"Lance," the man said. "Go grab it. I'll meet the two of you in the truck, and then you can tell me what you know and how I can help."

"Yes, sir," Lance said. And when Samuel Senior left the room, Lance turned around and looked at the small television. The snowy static was gone. Back in its place was the late-night show.

[34]

Leah's daddy's truck was black, blending seamlessly in with the night sky. It was at least ten years old and had a regular cab with a simple bench seat. Samuel Senior was sitting behind the wheel when Lance and Leah made their way out of the office, Lance with the shotgun held sheepishly in his hands, and Leah turning to lock the deadbolt with a key she quickly shoved back into the pocket of her sweatpants. Crutches under arms, she made her way quickly but somewhat clumsily to the truck, and Lance opened the passenger door for her. She tossed her crutches into the bed of the truck and then the two of them climbed in, one after the other, Leah the middle of a very awkward sandwich between the two men.

Lance adjusted the shotgun at an angle across his lap, the barrel pointing directly at the floorboard. Any mishap would hopefully only blow a hole in the bottom of the old truck, or maybe take a toe or two from Lance. With his new weapon in place, Lance pulled the door closed and said, "Okay, let's go." His skin suddenly prickled with gooseflesh. He looked out the window and saw nothing, but still he repeated, "Let's go."

Samuel Senior cranked the engine, and the truck roared to

life with a near-deafening assault on the ears. The muffler hummed and the seats vibrated, and Lance felt as though he was about to be launched from a rocket. But then Samuel Senior shifted into reverse and everything quieted down a little, and once they started driving down Route 19, the vibrating and rumbling dulled and Lance could hear himself think again.

"Know how to use one of those?" Samuel Senior asked.

Lance glanced over and saw the man eyeing him, pointing to the shotgun.

"No, sir. Never fired anything other than a slingshot in my life. And my mother took that away from me when she found out."

"Some sort of pacifist, your mother?"

Lance thought for a moment. "You could say that," he said.

Leah's daddy nodded once. "S'okay." Then, "Loaded, Leah?"

"Of course," Leah said. "Always is."

"Good girl."

There was silence then, and Lance figured Samuel Senior had assumed Lance was smart enough to figure out the mechanics of shooting the shotgun on his own without much trouble. If it came to it—and Lance certainly hoped it wouldn't —Lance would aim, pull the trigger, and see what happened.

Leah's daddy turned down a side road Lance had passed earlier in his walks, a desolate-looking jut from Route 19 that had been nothing but high grass and trees as far as Lance could see. The truck hit a bump in the road, and the three of them bounced in their seats with soft grunts. Lance glanced nervously at the shotgun, suddenly very fond of his toes.

The headlights cut cones of light down the dark road. The asphalt was cracked and chipped and dotted with holes. The truck's suspension practically screamed, but the ride was tolerable, once you braced for it. The high grass grew higher and higher, becoming trees. Branches began to encroach on the road, creeping toward the truck.

"You were at the motel last night, weren't you?" Samuel Senior asked, swerving the truck to avoid a large hole. A calm, practiced maneuver he must have made frequently.

Lance looked at Leah. She nodded.

"Yes, sir," Lance said. "I was hiding in Leah's bathroom when you stopped by." Lance wasn't sure why he'd insisted on divulging such a level of detail, but at this point, he felt honesty was the best course of action. Even if it was beyond usefulness.

Samuel Senior spoke again, this time turning to Leah. "And you knew what he was then? When you were hiding him from me? Lying to me?"

Leah put a hand on her father's forearm, tenderly. "Not completely, but ... I knew he was special. And something ... something bigger than I can understand felt like it was compelling me to trust him. Even if just long enough to figure out why he'd come through the motel door."

Lance thought again of how he'd felt something coming off Leah, something wonderful and warm and all the good things in life. Something that made him return the trust she'd shown him without question. Whatever gifts Lance possessed, Leah possessed a small bit of something similar herself. Heck, maybe everybody had a tiny bit of it, if only they could open their minds enough to use it.

Lance heard Samuel Senior sigh, then caught what he thought might have been a sniffle. "You always had a way of reading people, baby girl. Your mother ..." He paused, cleared his throat. "Your mother was the same way."

Leah smiled, and Lance's memory jolted him back to the previous night, when he'd been fearing for his life in Leah's bathroom. Remembered the conversation he'd overheard.

"Sir," Lance started, "when you came to the motel last night, you said you'd been sent home because of a scheduling error. You said your boss had forgotten to call and had been in a meeting with Mr. Strang about some sort of fundraiser?"

Samuel Senior avoided another pothole. Rubbed the side of his face and said. "Yep. That's what happened. It was the damnedest thing. Spur-of-the-moment shit you don't usually see 'round work."

Lance thought about the timing, how it coincided with his showing up in town. Thought about Glenn Strang and the word "fundraiser." He looked at Leah. "What are the odds it had something to do with Westhaven athletics? A sports booster meeting, or something like that?"

Samuel Senior answered. "Oh, I bet that's pretty likely," he said. "Strang gives all sorts of money to the football team and such. Kenny McGuire's always poking around the place, going out to lunch with the big man. Having meetings up in the big conference room none of us are allowed to go near."

Lance asked one more question. "Do they ever bring their wives to the meetings?"

Samuel Senior laughed, shook his head. "Oh, sure. You should see all the heads turn when Allison Strang's within the line of sight. Doesn't seem to bother her, though. Always real nice, she is. Coach brings his wife from time to time, too. Makes sense I guess, being she's vice principal now." He paused, then added, "She's not too bad looking herself, in my opinion."

Leah gave off an embarrassed groan. Lance looked at her and said, "If Allison Strang was there last night, she already knew—somehow—that I was in town, and she knew where I was. She convinced her husband to get your father to leave and come to the motel." Lance paused, looked cautiously at Samuel Senior before saying, "I guess she could expect him not to welcome me with open arms if he found us together."

Samuel Senior grunted. "She was right."

Leah nodded as she processed Lance's theory. Her daddy switched on the left blinker, an action Lance found incredibly odd considering they were on a desolate road with no sign of traffic—vehicular, pedestrian, or even animal. But at the same time, Lance commended the man's commitment to safe driving habits. More people should follow his example.

The man slowed the truck, and a gap in the trees presented itself, along with a large aluminum mailbox and a thick wooden post. Samuel Senior turned, splitting the gap with the truck, and the tires rumbled over a gravel driveway. A quarter mile later, the trees opened into a wide clearing, in the middle of which sat an old two-story farmhouse illuminated only by the truck's headlights.

The house might have been old, but it was well maintained. Even in the light of the headlamps, Lance thought the paint on the front porch bannisters and railings and shutters looked fresh. The grass was neatly trimmed, and an American flag jutted from the house next to the front door. It danced lazily in the night breeze.

Samuel Senior pulled the truck alongside the house, parking it next to two large metal trash cans. Behind the trash cans was a large object covered in a plastic tarp. Lance studied it for a moment, guessed it to be a tractor. A large air-conditioning unit protruded from a window on the second story. A bedroom, Lance thought.

Samuel Senior killed the truck's engine, and the night was suddenly very quiet. The driver's-side door was opened and the song of crickets permeated the night. Samuel Senior got out and said, "Come on, then. We'll talk inside, and you can explain to me what the hell you think is going on."

As Samuel Senior walked around the rear of the truck, Leah pointed to the covered object behind the trash cans, looking toward it almost longingly. "That's my mom's car," she said quietly. "Just an old VW Beetle, but she always loved it. Always kept it clean, inside and out." Then Leah paused, smiled at a memory. "Daddy still takes care of it. Keeps it nice. That's why it's covered. I don't think he's driven it anywhere but the driveway since she passed. Nobody has."

Lance pondered the complexity of the human mind, human emotions. He ached for this broken family.

Lance opened his own door, mindful of the shotgun. He got out and then extended his hand to help Leah out. She hopped up and down until she got her crutches situated, and then they rounded the house and took the three steps up the front porch and went inside, where they found Leah's daddy sitting at a kitchen table with two cans of light beer in front of him. One was already cracked open, and Samuel Senior slid the other across the table's worn surface toward Lance. Lance caught the can and stared at it, his mother's opinion of alcohol weighing heavy on his mind. Plus, Lance generally disliked the taste.

But, in this particular situation, Lance figured it would be extremely rude to decline the friendly offer, especially from a man who'd attacked him only a couple hours ago and was the father of a girl he'd kissed multiple times today.

Lance rested the shotgun on the floor next to the table, terrified that if he simply leaned it against the wall, it would accidentally fall over and blow the brains out of him or one of his companions, which, aside from the certain death, would make an awful mess to clean up. He sat in one of the empty chairs and took the beer, popped the top and took a small but respectable sip.

The taste was bitter and sour and awful. He swallowed and tried his best not to grimace. With the duty done, he set the can back on the table, wiped his mouth with the back of his hand and said, "Long story short, sir, we think Allison Strang is murdering the boys."

Samuel Senior shifted in his chair, the old wooden boards of the flooring creaking under his weight. He stared at the table, sliding the beer can back and forth between his workman's fingers. Lance looked around the kitchen, saw creamy white appliances along with chipped but clean countertops. The kind of things that would have been new and modern and the latest style twenty years ago but now looked dated, yet respectable. Well kept, like the front of the house. Leah's daddy took pride in what was his, that was certain. There weren't even any cobwebs or dust on the overhead light fixture above the table.

Samuel Senior lifted the beer can to his mouth and took a long gulp. Burped under his breath and looked at Leah, then at Lance, eyes narrowed. "Look, I'm trusting you only because of the thing you knew about my son. The bait sandwich. But this ... you're going to have to explain."

Lance nodded, hating the time they were losing by having to recap again what he and Leah had figured out. There was no deadline, so to speak, but the longer they waited to take some sort of action, the higher the chance Lance would be stopped, or worse, others would be hurt.

Lance told Samuel Senior everything he knew. Started with the gust of wind that had knocked him out the night before, worked through the possessed sheriff's deputy and car accident, the conversation with Susan Goodman, the incident at the football game, his somewhat of an abduction by Bobby Strang and the conversation he'd overheard and the vision he'd gotten when he made his escape, finally ending with the phone call on Bobby's phone at the motel and Leah's daddy himself showing up.

When Lance had finished the story, he took another sip of his own beer—a *small* one—because all the talking had made his throat dry.

Samuel Senior was quiet for another moment. He finished

his beer and then stood from the table and tossed the empty can into a small trash can by the sink. He stood there, crossing his arms and leaning against the counter. "So you're saying that Allison Strang can ... what? Control the weather? Can control people? Like some sort of, I don't know, witch?"

(*My dad calls her the Voodoo Bitch Doctor, but we don't understand any of it.*)

Lance formed his answer carefully. "Yes and no, sir. I think Allison Strang is calling the shots, somehow, but I think she's being ... used. Used as some sort of vessel for something else. Something ... not of this earth."

Samuel Senior frowned. "And you can tell me for certain that things like this—these *things not of this earth*—actually exist. You've seen them?"

"Yes, sir."

If Leah's daddy was waiting for more, he wasn't going to get it. Not then and not there.

To the man's credit, he was moving the conversation along without questioning Lance's credibility. "And how exactly is Allison Strang managing to get these boys off somewhere alone, and then managing to overtake and murder them? She might be pretty, but there's no way she's strong enough or quick enough to outdo most of the boys on that football team."

"Biology, sir."

"What?"

"Sex, sir. She's using sex. At least, that's what I think."

Samuel Senior grimaced and then made a face as though he'd be sick. "God, and you're positive she's sleeping with her son? Her own goddamn son?"

"It appears that way, sir."

Samuel Senior ran a hand over his closely shaved scalp, blew out a big breath of air. "So, what exactly do we do about any of this? Assuming it's all true," he added.

Lance looked at Leah and took a deep breath of his own. "At this point, I think it's best everybody stay out of it as much as they can, and I'll go find Allison Strang."

Leah's eyes widened. "Nope, no way. We're going to help you. From what we know, the entire Strang family is working together in this. There's no way you can fight off all three of them. They'll kill you for sure."

Lance shrugged. "Maybe. But maybe not. They might let me go with a warning."

"This isn't funny, Lance!"

"No, it's not," he said. "But it's also something that none of you can help with. This is coming down to me versus her, or it, or whatever."

"And I don't suppose the police would be any help?" Samuel Senior said, opening the refrigerator and popping the top of another beer. "Haven't been up until this point."

"Correct, sir. I don't think this is something they'll be of use to us with until we can present them with solid evidence. Also, I was seen fleeing the car accident earlier by the truck driver who called in the wreck. If the gossip mill in town was already concerned about my showing up, the police are definitely looking for me now. Especially with one of their own dead."

And then, as if waiting for their stage cue, the blue lights of a police cruiser danced off the kitchen walls, followed by the sound of tires crunching on the gravel outside.

"What the hell?"

Samuel Senior stood up from the kitchen table and mumbled more obscenities. He looked at the beer can on the table, still half-full. "I'm not drunk," he said. "I'm not drunk, right?" He looked at Leah, his eyes pleading. Lance again felt sorrow for the man, a man who'd been broken by life and was holding things together the best he knew how. Flaws and all.

"No, Daddy," Leah said, hopping up from the table. "No, you're not drunk. I can always tell when you're drunk. Plus, you're in your own home. They can't give you grief for drinking in your own home."

Samuel Senior's demeanor changed. He stood up taller, more confident. "Then why the hell are they here?"

Lance was the last to stand from the table. "Me," he said. "They're here because of me."

"They can't know you're here," Leah said. "Maybe because of the call on Bobby's phone they—Allison Strang ... whoever— maybe they knew we were at the motel. But how would they end up here? Everybody in town knows ..." She paused, looked at her father and shrugged in a half-apologetic sort of way.

"They know I never come here anymore. I *live* at the motel, for goodness' sake."

And then Lance wanted to kick himself in the head. "You just said it," he told her. "Bobby's phone. I bet they tracked it. It's an iPhone, so he could have just used that, what's it called, Track My Phone app thingy?"

"You need to upgrade and get with the times," Leah said. Then she thought for a moment. "But damn, you may be right. But would Bobby really call the cops, given what happened? What he's been hiding? All over a cell phone?"

There was a knock on the door. Three hard bangs meant to be loud and disturbing and get people's attention. Lance glanced around the kitchen. Looked down a small hallway to a living room, then found a closed door halfway between. He'd have to head toward the front door to get there, but it looked to be his only place to hide.

"Go, Lance," Samuel Senior said. "The window in that room faces the backyard. If you think you need to get out, just go. Straight through the woods about a mile and you'll come out on the ass-end of town. You do whatever you need to do from that point on. You've already given me more closure than I've ever had before."

Lance looked at the man, saw the sincere thanks in his eyes, then looked at Leah. He could tell she wanted him to stay, but also that she knew he had to go. "Text me the Strangs' address," he said. Then he took a step forward, gave her a quick kiss, and quietly walked down the hall toward the closed door and slipped inside.

Three more loud knocks.

"I'm coming," Samuel Senior hollered. "You guys know what time it is?"

Lance turned, and in the darkness, he found himself in a sort of home office. A worn couch pushed up against one wall, a

335

cheap computer desk against another. A large and ancient Dell computer sat atop it with what looked like nearly an inch of dust encasing it. The monitor was bulky and deep, not like the new flat-screens you saw today. For a brief moment, Lance imagined Leah sitting in this room and using the computer to type a paper, or do research for project for school, back when she still living at home and her brother was still alive and everything was still picture-perfect. Before the tragedies that would dictate her life going forward. Lance wished he could send her back to that time. Her father, too.

Between the couch and desk, in the middle wall, was a window with the blinds down. Lance made his way to it and gently pulled the string, the blinds rising in what sounded like a deafening noise. Then he thumbed the lock on the window and eased it up, a cool night breeze blowing in.

Lance heard a knob turn and the front door open.

"Jesus, Ricky, what the hell you doing here at this hour? It's after one in the morning!"

"Can I come in, Sam?" A new voice, higher-pitched than Samuel Senior's, and a little nervous.

Samuel Senior sighed, "Sure. Sure, might as well. You're lettin' the bugs in anyway."

Lance heard the sound of two sets of heavy boots in the hall-way, then the door shut.

"All right, you're in. Now why are you here?"

Lance heard the soft rubber scuffling of Leah's crutches coming across the floor.

"Leah?" the new voice said. "Oh, thank God you're here."

This statement confused Lance. Why would the officer be glad Leah was at her own family home? Did they think Lance had abducted her and taken off?

"Goddammit, Ricky. Tell me what the hell's going on." Samuel Senior raised his voice but did not shout. Then he got quieter and said, "Ah, Jesus, this isn't about the thing at the hospital, is it? Look, I told Roger it was just a little misunderstanding. Nobody got hurt and—"

"I don't know anything about that, Sam."

There was a small moment of pregnant silence. All of them —Lance included—waiting for whatever news was coming.

"Your motel is burning down, Sam. The whole damned thing is ablaze right now. The crews are there, workin' it hard, but ... but I think it's gone, Sam. Most of it, anyway."

Again, silence.

"We were scared to death Leah was in there. We were worried she'd been asleep and ..."

He didn't have to finish.

Because of me, Lance thought. *All because of me.*

"How?" That was all Samuel Senior could seem to muster.

"Don't know yet," the man named Ricky said. "Fire guys mentioned something about electrical. Since the building's so old. Makes sense, I guess. We won't know more for a while, though. Like I said, the crews are still—"

"Thank you, Ricky," Samuel Senior cut him off. "Thanks for coming to tell me. You have a good night, now."

A hesitation. "Um, Sam, I think ... I think you should come back with me."

"Why?"

"Well, um, I guess some folks want to talk to you. There's some questions that need to be answered, and I guess insurance details need to start being worked out."

"I can drive myself," Samuel Senior said.

Another pause. "You sure?" the man named Ricky asked. "You haven't had too much, um, you know?"

"I've had one and a half beers, Ricky, you asshole. You and I both know it's going to take a hell of a lot more than that to impair me."

The man named Ricky sighed. "Sam, do an old pal a favor and just let me drive you. Please?"

Samuel Senior started to protest again, annoyance lacing his words, but then he cut himself off, suddenly choked back his retort and paused before sighing again and saying, "You know what, fuck it. Why not? It'll save me some gas. Can you give me a sec with my girl before I go?"

"Uh, yeah, Sam. Of course."

The front door opened and closed, and Lance waited a beat before cracking the office's door a tiny bit and peering out. He found Samuel Senior and Leah standing in the hallway, staring back at him through the tiny slit.

He's leaving us the truck. He thinks we'll need it. Lance silently thanked Leah's daddy for being a lot smarter than the town might have given him credit for.

"This is part of it, isn't it?" Samuel Senior asked. "This is because they know you're getting close?"

Lance stepped into the he hall and nodded. "I think so, sir."

Samuel Senior took one deep breath and then nodded once. There was a jangling noise as he pulled his key ring from his pocket and worked to free the key to the truck. He held it out and pressed it into Lance's hand. "I've got to go. Lance." He gripped Lance's shoulder with a strong hand. "You do what you got to do, but dammit, keep my baby girl safe. If you can find out what happened to my son, I'll owe you everything. But don't let me lose the only child I have left."

Lance swallowed. "Yes, sir."

Samuel Senior hugged his daughter and kissed her on the top of the head, and then he left. Lance and Leah waited for the tires to crunch over the gravel as the police car drove away, then turned and met back in the kitchen.

"What now?" Leah asked.

Lance swung his backpack over his shoulders. "Now I go try to end this. Even if it kills me."

The look on her face told Lance she didn't like his choice of words, didn't care for his mindset. But another part of her, the one that understood the situation they were facing was bigger than just her and him, asked, "And me?"

Lance picked up the shotgun and set it gently on the kitchen table. "You stay right here, and put holes in anybody that comes through that door that's not me or your father."

He didn't give her time to argue. Just kissed her one more time and left out the front door without looking back.

[36]

THE TRUCK ROARED TO LIFE, SHAKING LANCE'S BRAIN around in his skull for a moment before he slipped the motor into gear, made a three-point turn, and drove slowly down the driveway. Away from the house, away from Leah. He glanced in the rearview as he went, begging the girl not to be standing in the doorway watching him leave. It'd been hard to walk away from her in the kitchen, but if he saw her standing there now, it would be even harder not to turn the rumbling truck around and go back for another kiss.

He kept his eyes glued to the gravel road, squinting into the headlights slicing through the darkness. He slowed, then stopped at the mailbox, flicked on his right turn signal because it was what he felt Samuel Senior would have done, and then pulled out onto the pothole-speckled road and drove cautiously back toward Route 19, back toward town, back toward the Strangs. It was an odd feeling to know you were directly seeking out evil, walking into danger. It wasn't the first time for Lance. Didn't mean it got any easier.

His phone vibrated in his pocket. Since he was still on the desolate road, he came to a full stop before fishing it out and reading the message from Leah. He very well might die later. No sense in expediting the process by hitting a pothole, swerving, overcorrecting, and then slamming into one of the encroaching trees. He probably wasn't going fast enough to do any serious bodily harm, but the way the day'd been going, he wasn't going to take the additional risk.

Leah had sent him the Strangs' address, and then, probably assuming Lance's relic of a phone lacked a GPS feature, had given him some crude directions, which he scanned through and figured he could follow easily enough. He'd followed the Strangs from the high school earlier when he was tailing Bobby, so he could get at least that far by himself.

"You're very brave, do you know that?"

Lance jumped, his foot slipping off the truck's brake before finding it again and stamping down hard. He swung his head around and found Annabelle Winters sitting in the passenger seat. She was ramrod straight, looking ahead out the windshield. Lance followed her legs down from the seat and saw them passing right through his backpack on the floorboard.

"You know," he said, regaining his composure, "you could give me a little bit of a warning. What if I'd been driving? I could have wrecked."

Annabelle Winters shrugged her bony shoulders. "Don't suspect it would bother me much." Then she turned toward him and offered Lance the tiniest of grins.

He shook his head. "You're hilarious."

"I tried to warn you about the boy earlier. Sorry I couldn't sooner. It's funny how it works on my end. I know things ... but sometimes I don't know things. And other times, it's like ... it's like I only get a whiff of the smell right before everybody else. That was one of those times."

Lance leaned back in his seat, rubbed his eyes. He was so tired. "Why are you here?"

"You don't like the company?" she asked.

Lance chuckled, exhaustion pouring over him. "No, I mean ... I mean why are you *here*? Why are you still in our world, instead of moving on to ... whatever is out there? Like most others."

Annabelle Winters smiled. "You know, I've been asking myself that question since the day I died." She looked out the window into the darkness and trees. "I've gone over every aspect of my life. Every decision, every choice. I've thought about all my good days and my bad days, and I analyzed my life until there was absolutely nothing left to ponder."

"And?"

"Nothing. For the longest time I just sort of assumed I was living in my version of hell and was damned to never understand why."

"You say that like something's changed."

She grinned again. "It did."

"What?"

"You showed up."

"You're kidding."

Annabelle Winters shook her head. "No. Like I said, sometimes I just know things. And the moment I saw you in the diner the other day, it was like the locked box of information in my head snapped open, and it all flooded out and it all made sense. I've been here waiting for you. Because something knew what would happen to Westhaven. And something knew you would come to save us. And I'm the lucky one who gets to help."

"Something?" Lance asked.

Annabelle Winters sighed and used a wrinkled index finger to point up toward the roof of the truck's cabin, toward the sky. "Whatever's in charge. The big guy upstairs, so to speak."

"God?"

"Call it whatever you want."

Lance rubbed his eyes again. Said nothing.

"You're missing something," Annabelle Winters said.

Lance forced another chuckle. "I know. I can't figure out why Allison Strang is doing this. What's her endgame, and what's really in charge?"

Annabelle Winters shook her head. "No. No, I think ... I think it's more than that. Something else."

Lance looked over at her. "But you don't know what?"

She shook her head. "If I can get close enough and it comes to me, I'll let you know the best I can. I promise. But until then, be careful, Lance. I think you're meant for bigger things than Westhaven."

He nodded. Said nothing.

"She loves you, and misses you. And she understands why you had to leave her."

Lance thought of Leah and felt that small tingle of excitement coupled with turmoil. "It'll never work, will it? Leah and I can't be together."

"Not her, Lance," Annabelle said. "I'm talking about your mother."

Lance looked at her with the widest of eyes, his mouth gaping.

Annabelle Winters smiled. "I told you. Sometimes I just know things. Be careful, Lance."

And then she was gone.

Lance sat in the cab of the truck, his foot still pressed hard to the brake for another full minute, the road and trees behind him bathed in the red glow of the brake lights. He thought about Annabelle Winters's words about his mother.

Can she really know that?

Of course she could. She'd have to. Lance had told Annabelle Winters nothing of his mother, or the night he'd had to leave his home.

Leave her to die.

For the briefest of moments, Lance felt the idea of tears begin to build in his brain, but he slaughtered the thought and relished the idea that his mother's spirit was still burning somewhere. Some form of her was strong enough to offer him a tiny bit of reassurance.

And that was enough for Lance. It eased his mind just the right amount to feel the warmth of his mother's love inside him again, gave him a renewed and focused strength to deal with what was at hand.

He was about to let off the brake and start forward, but his phone buzzed again in his hand. He looked down. Another text from Leah.

I know you like to wing it, and I know you've got all these hidden talents, but thought you might like to know Daddy keeps a gun under the driver's seat. Daddy's got a saying. Doesn't matter how big you are when somebody else can pull a trigger. XOXO

Lance reached down with his left hand and felt—gently!—around the bottom of the truck's bench. First it was all smooth, and then his hand found some sort of holster and mount attached to the bottom, directly under his butt. It was a smallish pistol, nothing like the shotgun he'd left with Leah. In this case, he didn't imagine the size would make much of a difference.

He used his thumb and texted back: *Thanks. Your father is a smart man.*

He thought about using his own set of Xs and Os, but decided against it. If his phone had been newer and more modern, he might have considered one of those red heart icons. What were they called? Emojis? But maybe it was too soon for that, too. Plus ... like he'd told Annabelle Winters ...

He pulled up the previous message containing the directions to the Strangs' house, memorized them, and then released the brake and drove forward, headed toward Route 19.

As he approached the intersection where he could turn right toward town or keep straight to head toward the high school, which was where he needed to go, his eyes were drawn left, toward the bright orange glow flickering in the dark night sky. Flashes and bounces of amber light glowed from atop the tree line, accompanied by the shadowy presence of billowing smoke.

The motel on fire.

Part of Leah and her daddy's livelihood, reducing itself to ash and rubble.

All my fault.

He ignored the guilt and drove on, fueled partially by anger and partially by an overwhelming feeling that this would be the end. Whatever waited for him at the Strangs' house, it would all be over soon. The only question he didn't know the answer to was whether good or evil would prevail. Fifty/fifty weren't the worst odds, but certainly not the best.

He checked that the road was clear and then drove straight. He crossed Route 19 and was maybe a quarter mile from the high school when something streaked across the sky, causing him to jump on the brake again. The truck skidded to a stop and Lance ducked down and then craned his neck to peer out the windshield and up at the sky, his heart stuck somewhere between his chest and throat, slowly sliding back down.

Something had just flown by overhead. Something there, but not. It seemed to blend with the black of night, but still, Lance had caught a glimpse, just long enough to see the shape of a head ... and the wings and the tail.

A dragon?

He shook his head, nearly laughed at the thought. *Really, Lance? A Dragon?*

He'd never even seen an episode of *Game of Thrones*.

He stared up, looked around him. Nothing but the faint outline of clouds scattered and the dancing of treetops in the breeze.

Tired, he thought. *I'm too tired.*

But as he drove on, he couldn't quite convince himself that was the case.

He recalled Leah's directions and watched the truck's odometer closely. He needed to go three miles from the school and then turn right.

He'd only made it a mile when his cell phone vibrated in the seat next to him. He took a quick glance down and saw it was Leah calling. But just as he reached over to answer the call, the sky split open like a paper bag ripped in half, and down came a thunderous downpour of golf ball–sized hail.

Lance jumped at the sudden noise and assault against the truck, his visibility reduced nearly to zero. He pumped the brakes hard enough to send his cell phone sliding across the truck's bench seat, unable to hear it clatter to the floorboard.

He never heard the buzz for the voicemail.

Never heard the buzz of the incoming text message.

The only sound was that of the hail, pummeling the truck from all sides as Lance drove slowly along the road, steering wheel gripped tightly in his hands, eyes squinting, peering intently out the windshield through the manic whooshing of the wipers.

This, he thought, *is not a coincidence.*

[37]

THE HAIL DID NOT LET UP, A PHENOMENON OF A STORM that Lance knew was meant for him in some twisted cosmic way. It didn't stop him, but it certainly succeeded in slowing him down. Samuel Senior's truck had big tires with deep treads, meant to churn through the toughest of weather, and they did their job well, gripping the road and keeping the truck true to its course. It was seeing where he was going that was the problem. Calculating what he could from his memorized directions, Lance figured the trip from the Route 19 intersection to the Strangs' house should have taken roughly fifteen minutes. It was thirty minutes later when Lance finally found the last turn on his list and guided the truck into it.

And just as suddenly as it had started, the hail stopped, a few stray pebbles of ice clink-clanking off the roof of the cabin for good measure before finally ceasing completely.

Lance stared through the windshield at the fully visible outside world. The cabin sounded deathly silent after all the staccato tinkering of the hail. "Well, that's not weird at all."

Ahead, on a small hilltop surrounded by a white privacy fence, was the largest house Lance had seen in Westhaven. It was easily twice the size of Bobby Strang's home, and despite the upscale feel of Bobby's neighborhood, the house on the hill made those houses look like secondhand gifts.

The road was freshly paved, and Lance had to wonder if the Strangs had built this home when they'd moved to Westhaven and created this road as a lengthy driveway. There were no other homes on it, as far as Lance could see, just what looked like a half mile of blacktop with a slight curve up the hill, leading to a gate.

Two porch lights burned at the house's front door, and another by the gate, but otherwise, Lance saw no lights anywhere in the house. No movement.

He sat another minute and stared at the house, tried to reach into it with his mind and feel the people inside. He closed his eyes, breathed deeply and focused.

He got nothing.

Never works when I want it to.

He sighed, then drove forward slowly. The truck climbed the hill with ease, requiring little more than a feather's touch on the gas pedal, and as Lance rounded the corner and approached the fence, the entry gate slid sideways on a motorized track, disappearing behind the rest of the fence's wall and leaving a wide and inviting mouth for Lance to enter through. He looked at the tall lamppost mounted by the gate, searching for a camera or speaker box or anything else. He saw nothing. One of two things were happening: either the gate was activated by a motion sensor, or somebody knew he was here and couldn't wait to meet him.

You know what you have to do, Lance. Drive the darn truck.

He drove forward, hating himself for being so vulnerable to his self-motivation. *This could be suicide,* he thought.

But, maybe not. Fifty-fifty, remember?

As he drove the next fifty yards to the front of the house, the gate began to close behind him. He glanced in the rearview and hoped the symbolism of what he was seeing wasn't as fore-boding as it appeared. If this had been a horror movie, that shot of the gate closing him in would have all but sealed his charac-ter's fate.

The truck's engine rumbled once thrown into park, and Lance killed it by turning off the ignition switch and sliding out the key. He bounced the key up and down in his palm, checking his surroundings, seeing if he could get a feel for things.

He'd parked directly in front of a two-car garage that was attached to the main house by what appeared to be some sort of breezeway. The house was all stone and brick and was essen-tially a towering, beautifully designed masterpiece of home architecture. A winding concrete walkway wove along a garden path in front of the home, approaching a large front porch on which sat two large rocking chairs. Lance's eyes shifted from the rocking chairs and followed the line of sight away from the house. From up on the hilltop, he was sure the view would be spectacular. The two porch lights still burned with a comfort-able glow, but otherwise the house was dark and still. Lifeless.

Lance got out of the truck, thought for a moment, then reached under the truck's bench and fumbled with disengaging the pistol from its holster until he was holding the gun in his own hand.

Lance wasn't afraid of guns—until they were in the hands of the wrong people—but he'd never had reason to handle firearms before and therefore felt almost as uncomfortable holding this handgun as he had when he'd been entrusted with the family shotgun earlier. The pistol he was holding looked a lot like the weapon Bobby Strang had used. Sleek, compact, and surely powerful enough to get the job done. He found a latch that he was certain was the safety, checked it was on, and then—while saying a silent prayer he wouldn't maim himself, tucked the weapon into the waistband of his shorts and pulled his shirt over it.

As Lance made his way through the garden path in the darkness, a tingle at the base of his skull told him the gun wouldn't matter. The outcome would be the same with or without it.

But still, it definitely didn't hurt his confidence to feel its cool surface against his skin. And plus, he'd been wrong before.

He reached the porch, stepped up and then was directly beneath the two lamps on either side of the door. They were wrought-iron and meant to resemble hanging lanterns. Elegant. A few bugs buzzed around the bulbs. A breeze rocked the chairs in a slow, ghostly show.

What's your plan, Lance?

He watched his right hand rise up, watched his index finger point itself out, and then felt the cool plastic of the doorbell's button and heard a soft, soothing chime come from behind the large wooden door.

I don't have one, he thought. *I usually never do.*

The chimes faded away in a decrescendo, and then there was silence. A few creaks from the house as a gust of wind whipped by and then vanished.

Lance waited.

One full minute. Then two.

He'd been expecting to be expected, anticipating a "so we meet at last" moment to take place as the door swung open to reveal the villain, unmasked and ready to battle.

He'd been expecting *something*!

He pressed the bell again. Again the chimes followed and faded, and Lance stood on the porch like a man being stood up on a date.

He felt confusion, and disappointment. Disappointment in himself for getting it wrong. He'd been certain this was where he was supposed to be. He and Leah had pieced it together and Lance had had the vision with Bobby, and ... it was supposed to be here. It knew he was here, and it knew Lance had found it out.

He felt in his pocket for his cell phone, intent on texting Leah. His pocket was empty, and he suddenly recalled some flicker of memory of his cell phone sliding off the truck's bench as he'd braked for the hail. He turned, ready to walk back, and that was when he heard the deadbolt disengage.

Lance froze, his heart suddenly hammering. *This is it*, he thought. *Now we face the Devil.*

The front door opened slowly, first just a crack, and then all the way.

Allison Strang stood in the open doorway, wrapped in a large plush robe with her hair falling around her shoulders. A vast atrium of a foyer was visible in the background. A tasteful lamp on a small table by a massive staircase backlit her with a soft glow. Otherwise, the house was dark.

Lance stared into her eyes, stared into the eyes of a killer, a murderer of four innocent boys. The reason Deputy Miller's family was mourning tonight and so many nights to come. The reason Leah and her daddy's motel was burning to the ground. The reason Leah had almost been killed at the football game. Lance had blamed himself for most of the latter, but now, staring into the face of his foe, he cast all his blame outward toward the woman before him.

And as their gazes met, Lance took a step backward, nearly toppling from the porch. He regained his balance and looked hard into Allison Strang's eyes. He breathed in deeply, one quick gasp of air, and nearly fell to his knees with the overwhelming surge of love and happiness and compassion he felt coming from the woman in the doorway.

"You're the boy who was with Leah at the game," Allison

Strang said, her voice pleasant and warm. "What on earth are you doing all the way out here so late? Are you all right? Do you need to come inside?"

Something propelled Lance to nod and step over the threshold as Allison Strang stepped aside and motioned him in. And as she closed the door behind him, Annabelle Winters's voice echoed in his head.

You're missing something.

[38]

SHE REMINDS ME OF MY MOTHER.

This thought solidified as Lance watched Allison Strang turn the deadbolt, locking him inside the Strangs' home.

It wasn't the way Allison Strang looked—Lance's mother had never been one for excessive beauty products or fancy clothing, and she'd had the same hairstyle Lance's entire life—and it wasn't the way she talked. It was the vibe she gave off. That aura of happiness and kindness. It was so strong Lance could nearly reach out and touch it, grab it, as if it were tangible and his for the taking.

A kind soul. That was the best way to describe it. Folks used that term all the time, but Lance was blessed (or cursed) to truly know when it was an appropriate saying. His mother had had one, and Allison Strang's soul was nearly as pure and as light. But, just like snowflakes, no two souls were alike. They each had their own unique fingerprint, their own pattern. And Lance's mother's had been the most exquisite he'd ever seen.

Leah had one too—a kind soul—but hers had been tarnished, scarred. The loss of her brother, the situation with her father, and the town's tragedy had whittled away some of the purity and replaced it with a strong contempt. A deep sense of caution and skepticism. She glowed outwardly, but inside she was complicated. Lance found the combination intoxicating.

"Is everything all right?"

Lance focused his gaze, found Allison Strang still standing by the door. She tightened the belt of her robe and then fussed with her hair, as if suddenly aware she was in the presence of company. Her feet were bare. French pedicure. The small lamp on the table cast its warm glow, and Lance's shadow looked like a monster on the wall behind Allison Strang. He looked at her, and she smiled back at him. Her teeth were white and perfect, the result of expensive dental work or a lifetime of personal hygiene.

Lance seesawed between the idea of having being completely wrong about Allison Strang and the notion that he was currently walking into a well-laid, well-executed trap. He didn't know if it was possible for something—*it*—to be powerful enough to pull a mask over its true self, to blot out the evil and replace it with the purity Lance felt from Allison Strang. Deceiving normal people was easy, but deceiving somebody with Lance's gifts would be much harder. Lance figured as much, anyway. Though he always admitted he didn't fully understand his own gifts.

"I'm missing something."

He said it out loud without meaning to, and Allison Strang cocked her head to the side, interpreting his words. "You've lost something?" she asked. She crinkled her brow. "And you think it's here?"

Lance searched for a response. Was at a complete loss as to how to proceed. *Well, you see, ma'am, I came here because I thought you were in cahoots with an evil spirit, riding your son in his own bed, and murdering innocent high school football play-*

ers. But clearly I was mistaken. Sorry to bother you. I'll see myself out. Lovely home, by the way.

Allison Strang took three steps forward and then side-stepped Lance. She entered the hallway behind him, and as she did so, the recessed lighting turned on and followed her as she walked.

Motion sensors, Lance thought. *Not supernatural powers.*

When she reached the end of the hall, a much brighter light lit up, and Lance saw an expansive kitchen behind her. She turned and said, "I don't know why you're here, but you seem troubled. And ... a friend of Leah's is a friend of the Strangs. Such a lovely young girl she is. I called the hospital to check on her and they assured me she'd be fine. I was so relieved. That family's gone through so much, you know."

She turned and walked deeper into the kitchen, disappearing from sight. She called out, "I'm going to make some tea. Why don't you join me, and we'll see if we can figure out why you're here? Unless you'd prefer coffee. I don't like the stuff, but Glenn's got one of those Keurig things."

Lance walked slowly down the hall over expensive wood flooring and glanced at the framed art on the walls. Modern stuff you'd find in a gallery exhibit in a large city. Not the type of thing you'd pick up in town along with your groceries.

As he got closer to the kitchen, the feel of his concealed weapon against his skin seemed to grow with each step. Allison Strang had been kind and polite—*too* kind and polite to live on the same planet Lance did—and Lance was nearly convinced she wasn't putting on an act. He'd nearly accepted he'd been completely wrong about her. But, whether genuine small-town hospitality or an enemy lying in wait, a glimpse of Lance's gun—a gun he didn't even want to be carrying—would surely escalate the situation in a direction Lance didn't want.

He entered the kitchen and marveled at the size of it. There was a sea of granite countertops and commercial-sized stainless-steel appliances that looked like they belonged more in an upscale restaurant or on one of those cooking shows on TV. Allison Strang turned on a large gas burner and set a teakettle atop it. Then she reached over along the counter and powered on the Keurig for Lance. "You look like a coffee guy," she said. "Tell me I'm wrong."

Again, a flash of the perfect teeth. Another brush of hair out of her eyes. A slight adjustment of the robe across her chest. Lance hated the term MILF, but he could definitely admit when it was applicable. Up close, Lance could see the woman's face appeared older than the rest of her, despite any work or makeup, but she was still an attractive older woman. Lance found himself wondering how she and Glenn Strang had met. Was it during his days playing football, or was it after, or...?

And then it struck Lance that there was something terribly wrong about his situation. He glanced at the Keurig on the counter, its blue lights aglow and waiting for somebody to feed it a pod. *Glenn's got one of those Keurig things.*

"Mrs. Strang," Lance said, trying to find his voice. "Where is your husband?"

Because of the surprise Lance had been blasted with when Allison Strang had opened the door and greeted him, because of the sudden table flip of his non-plan of attack when he'd quickly had to come to terms with the possibility that Allison Strang was not the monster he'd come here to accuse her of being, Lance had taken entirely too long to stop and wonder why, at what had to be approaching two in the morning, the woman of the house would be the one to answer a stranger's nighttime knock at their door. That was the man's job. The odd noise after bed, the sudden recollection that maybe the oven had been left on, and definitely a knock or ring at the door well past midnight, these were things that fell on the husband's shoulders to take care of.

Call it protection, call it pride, call it simple husband duty, Glenn Strang should have been the one to answer the door when Lance arrived.

Allison Strang laughed and pulled a box of tea bags down from a cabinet. She had to stretch up on her tiptoes to reach them, and Lance couldn't help watching her silky-smooth calves flex as she did so. "Oh, you know. Glenn's over at his boyfriend's house, doing boy things." She giggled at her own joke. Lance didn't follow.

She saw his confusion and said, "Glenn goes over to the McGuires' almost every night after a home game. They drink a couple beers and watch the local news stations talk about the game, then they camp out in Ken's man cave and do whatever two middle-aged guys do to entertain themselves on a Friday night. Sometimes they analyze the game film—Ken has always valued Glenn's opinion. But, I like to pretend they eat Doritos and play Xbox games." She shrugged. "He usually just spends the night there on their sleeper couch. He and Ken are so close I'm almost jealous. I don't even have a girlfriend that close."

"Why don't you go with him? To the McGuires' house. I mean... you and Mrs. McGuire are close, right? I saw you sitting together at the game tonight."

Allison Strang smiled. Nodded her head. "Melissa and I get along, and she really is a lovely woman, but our friendship is really just a byproduct of our husbands' relationship. Does that make sense?"

"Sure," Lance said. For what felt like the first time since he'd stepped off the bus into Westhaven, he had somebody—a live human being—answering questions and talking to him without raising an eyebrow or giving him the cold shoulder. He figured it was time to make himself comfortable, act like this wasn't as strange of an event as it was. He found a row of tall barstools along an island counter and sat down, making sure to keep his back facing away from Allison Strang. Didn't want a slip of his shirt to show he was packing heat. "You're saying you and Mrs. McGuire wouldn't have sought each other out organically. You get along, but you don't have that much in common."

Allison Strang said, "Exactly," and then pulled open a small metal drawer next to the Keurig, plucked a coffee pod from it and stuck it in the machine. Then she grabbed a ceramic mug from another cabinet and pressed a button, and in thirty seconds, Lance had a steaming-hot cup of black coffee in front of him.

"Cream and sugar?"

Lance shook his head. "Black is perfect."

The teakettle boiled, and Allison Strang filled her mug and dipped the tea bag and then joined Lance at the island, resting her elbows on the opposite side of the counter instead of taking a stool. Lance turned to face her. Took a sip of his coffee. It was okay. He'd never really cared for those little coffee pods. But the caffeine would be useful, would help him think.

"I actually didn't believe it, at first," Allison Strang said. She dipped her tea bag again and then raised her mug for a sip. Lance watched the way her lips curled over the edge of cup.

"Didn't believe what?"

She grinned and gave off an embarrassed sort of laugh. "I was just being silly, is all. I mean, it was hard when Glenn was playing ball, always traveling and always having women at the hotels. It wasn't like it is for players today, don't get me wrong, but the temptation was always there for him. It was hard to trust him. But ..." She smiled and took another sip of tea. "I did. And he always came home happy to see me, and he'd swoop me up in his arms and kiss me and tell me how much he missed me and ... well, it just didn't seem like the sort of thing he could fake. Glenn might have been a decent football player, but he's a terrible actor."

Lance said nothing.

"But after a few weeks of these late-night McGuire house sleepovers, I noticed that sometimes when he'd come home, he'd act a little off. A little distant. After all these years of marriage, you become pretty in tune with your spouse. You learn their tics and their quirks, and you can instantly tell when they aren't themselves." She was quiet for a moment. "And then one day, when I was doing his laundry, I noticed that his clothes smelled of perfume."

Lance sat up straight, the hairs on the back of his neck standing up and his ears prickling.

"Perfume?"

She nodded. "I passed it off as a fluke the first time, just somebody he'd maybe hugged at the football game, or something stupid, you know? But then the next week when he got back from the McGuires'—he hadn't spent the night that night, I do remember that—I waited till he fell asleep and then went to the hamper, and sure enough, the same perfume smell was on his shirt."

Lance instantly remembered Susan Goodman's story about her brother smelling like perfume when he'd come home late one night, shortly before he'd gone missing. His heart pumped quicker in his chest. He took another swig of the mediocre coffee and asked, "Did you ask him about it?"

Off to the right of the kitchen was a breakfast nook with a small four-top table. A pair of French doors stood behind it, and outside, bright lights suddenly flashed on and illuminated an elegant outdoor patio set, complete with industrial-sized grill and smoker. Allison Strang's eyes flitted to the doors and said, "Deer. Sometimes they get close enough to trigger the lights. Had a bear one time. Boy, what a sight that was."

Lance looked from the woman and then back to the doors. When they'd flashed on, in that instant millisecond between full dark and full light, he could have sworn he had seen something. And it hadn't been a deer. It had been black, like a shadow, and it had had a tail.

He drank more coffee, his nerves beginning to feel on edge. He was getting close.

"So ... the perfume?"

Allison Strang laughed and then reached out and gently grabbed his wrist. "Why am I telling you all this? I don't even know you."

Lance smiled and shrugged and prayed to any god that would listen that she wouldn't stop the story now, not when he might actually gain a shred of actual information. "People have always said I'm a good listener."

She laughed again and said, "Fine. But then it's your turn. You have to tell me what you're doing here and explain why I haven't already called the police to tell them that the man they've been looking for, the suspicious boy who's been walking all over town, is right here in my kitchen."

Lance's heart sank to the pit of his stomach. He nearly knocked his coffee mug over as he moved to leave.

But Allison Strang gripped his wrist tighter and held her other hand up in a *calm down* gesture. "Relax," she said. "I'm not calling them. I don't think you're any trouble. I hope not, anyway. The folks in this town, not to mention the police, they're all just a little ... wary. You know, especially since all the disappearances."

"And you're not?" Lance said, willing himself to sit back down on the stool.

"Oh, I am. It's terrible what this town's been through. Those young men, all missing, all probably dead—yes, I'm a realist, honey," she said when Lance looked at her, surprised. "I suppose it's possible they ran away, off to find a better life and escape whatever was haunting them here. But ... I don't buy it."

"So why aren't you suspicious of me like everybody else?"

Because she's got some of it. Just a drop, but enough to know you're one of the good ones.

"Because I know you had breakfast with Leah at the diner, and I know you had dinner with her at Sonic, and I know you were with her at the football game. You two are obviously close —I don't know in what capacity, but you are—and that girl is probably the best judge of character in this entire town. Head-strong, no-nonsense, rational, and the last person on earth who would fall in with the wrong crowd. If she's cool with you, I'm cool with you."

Leah, you are amazing. You're saving my butt and you're not even here. Lance reminded himself to kiss her extra long when he saw her again.

"Well, I appreciate your support," Lance said, sounding like a politician on the campaign trail.

She waved him off. "Anyway, no, I didn't ask Glenn about the perfume." Lance felt his disappointment creep up. "I decided to—and I'm not proud of this—I decided to spy a bit. The next home game after he dropped me back here at home, I waited fifteen minutes and then jumped in my car and drove over to the McGuires'. And sure enough, Glenn's car was right there in the driveway. I turned around and drove home, but the next morning when I checked his clothes, there was that scent again."

"And then you asked him about it?"

She shook her head. "Nope. Instead, I forced his hand a bit. Next home game, I asked Melissa if she'd maybe want some girl company while the boys did their thing. She agreed, and I rode with Glenn to their house right after the game. I was only there ten minutes before I realized what was going on."

"Which was?" Lance was practically standing up in his seat.

"It wasn't perfume," Allison Strang said. "It was definitely a womanly, floral-type scent I kept smelling on Glenn's clothes, but it wasn't perfume." She laughed, clearly amused by her own mistake and mistrust. "It was incense! Turns out Melissa McGuire burns the stuff in the evenings to help her relax. She's big into herbs and holistic-type remedies. You should see her den. She's got all sorts of fragrances and little burners and candles and"—she chuckled again—"I told her that her setup looked like some sort of witch's supply closet." The chuckle became a full-on belly laugh. "I asked her if she had eye of newt!"

Lance froze. His mind raced.

(*My dad calls her the Voodoo Bitch Doctor.*)

He pulled up the image of Melissa McGuire from earlier at the school, and then again at the football game later that evening. *Her hair was in a bun! I thought it was Allison Strang because the hair was longer, but Melissa's been wearing hers in a bun!*

Lance replayed the vision he'd gotten from Bobby Strang when he'd attacked him in the garage. Watched the woman arching her back as she rode the boy on the bed beneath her, her hair sweaty and splayed across her shoulders.

The hair.

I was wrong, he thought. *Darn it, Leah, I was completely wrong. It's not Allison Strang who's behind the boys' disappearances, it's Melissa McGuire! It's the coach's wife!*

Lance shouted, "I've got to go!" as he stood from the counter and turned to head down the hall, and he couldn't help but think that maybe he wasn't being baited to the Strangs' house to confront the monster, but maybe whatever goodness there was left in the town—Annabelle Winters and whatever forces she rolled with—maybe whatever was on *his* side was pushing him toward Allison Strang so he'd be able to uncover the truth.

He heard Allison Strang scramble after him as he fled down

the hall and out into the foyer. He nearly collided with the door as she called out, "Whatever you're doing, be careful!"

Lance fumbled with the deadbolt and ripped open the heavy door.

He took two steps onto the porch before something hard and heavy slammed into the back of his head, and everything went dark.

Lance's eyes flickered, couldn't stay open. His body jostled, and he could hear and feel the rumbling of tires over road beneath him. He strained, trying to open his eyes again, but it was like trying to wake yourself from a dream. It was as if his eyelids had been glued shut. His head pounded and pulsed.

I've had enough head injuries for the week, thank you.

He tried to speak, to force any words from his mouth, just to reaffirm he was still alive. He couldn't, but that was only because there was something over his mouth. Tape, probably. He tried to reach up and pull it away, but his hands wouldn't obey. They were bound together behind his back. More tape. The tape had gotten to him after all.

A man's voice up ahead of him, sounding very far away, yet perfectly clear, said, "Yes, I've got him. I'm on the way."

A pause.

"She won't say anything."

A pause.

"Because she's my wife and we can trust her. I'll ... look, I'll figure it out."

There was another pause and a heavy sigh and then, "This has to end tonight. You see that, right? No more. It's done."

A pause.

"You know what? Maybe I don't care anymore."

There was a large bump in the road, and Lance heard the man mumble a curse word under his breath before Lance went under again, swallowed by the darkness. Taken back into the dream.

[40]

THERE WAS A SUDDEN JOLT, AND THEN THE DARKNESS gained a faint gleam of light, like the early-morning sun rising behind closed bedroom curtains. Lance's eyes opened this time, slowly, and he found himself in the rear cargo area of an SUV. The rear hatch had been opened, and Glenn Strang stood in its mouth, staring down at Lance with a look not of anger or hate or frustration, but of a man who'd been broken and was fulfilling an obligation. He wore the same clothes Lance had seen him in earlier at the football game, but his face held none of the enthusiasm.

Lance was just regaining his full consciousness, the dull ache at the back of his head growing in intensity the closer he swam back to the surface, but even in his weakened state, he could pick up the slow trickle of sorrow from Glenn Strang.

Lance recalled the voice he'd heard earlier when he'd briefly come up for air. The one-sided conversation.

(*This has to end tonight. You see that, right? No more. It's done.*)

And from earlier....

(*My dad calls her the Voodoo Bitch Doctor.*)

It became even clearer to Lance than before. Melissa McGuire was running the show. She was in charge—at least among the mortals. Glenn Strang was only a pawn in a game he wanted no part of. Bobby, likely the same.

(*She won't say anything ... Because she's my wife and we can trust her.*)

Allison Strang had been oblivious to her husband's role in the town's tragedy. She'd thought at first he'd been having an affair and had then debunked the theory, failing to ever consider he was a part of something much, much worse. She was innocent and had ended up being a gift to Lance, the town's only way of pointing him toward the truth he'd been searching for. Lance smiled, the tape over his mouth pulling at his skin, as he remembered the warmth and happiness he'd felt from her, the way her soul had been so closely aligned with his own mother's. However things turned out for Lance—and right now things weren't looking so good—he hoped Allison Strang would walk away unscathed. He hoped she always burned as brightly as she had when Lance had met her.

But the reality was, a line had been crossed for her tonight, more than likely. She was now on a side she could not turn away from, whether it had been voluntary or not.

Lance looked up and focused his vision on what was behind Glenn Strang. It was the back of a house. Dark brick. A walkout basement with steps leading up to a rear deck. Beneath the deck was a slab of concrete forming a patio, a respectable John Deere parked there along with a set of wicker furniture. There was a door leading inside. Behind it, the light was on, and Lance knew it was waiting.

Glenn Strang lifted his right hand, and Lance saw the baseball bat. Wooden, scuffed and well worn with use. The back of Lance's head thump-thump-thumped with his heartbeat.

"You shouldn't have come here," Glenn said, his voice dripping with empathy. Then he motioned with his free hand for Lance to get out. "Slowly and carefully," he said. "I don't want to make this worse than it'll already be. Just get out, and walk straight toward the door over there." He nodded over his shoulder to the basement door. "You look like an athlete, so I don't have to tell you how damaging a blow from this bat to one of your knees will be. Don't make me do it, okay? Please ... just don't."

Lance tried to speak, his voice muffled behind the tape.

Glenn just looked at him.

Lance tried again.

Glenn Strang sighed. "If you scream, I'll bash you." Then, more to himself than Lance, "God, I just want this all to be over."

Lance nodded, and Glenn reached down with his free hand and peeled the tape away from Lance's lips, a quick rip with only minimal pain.

"Thank you," Lance said. "Why are you doing this for her?"

Glenn Strang said nothing, just stood back and again motioned for Lance to step out of the back of the SUV. Lance struggled to sit up, his bound hands behind his back making the task difficult and awkward, his sprained wrist perking up and making itself known. Glenn Strang smacked at a bug buzzing around his head.

"I can help you stop her," Lance said. "We don't have to do it like this. I'm on your side."

Glenn looked at the ground, then back to the house, back to the light burning inside the basement door. He looked at it for what felt like a very long time, then shook his head. "She'll ruin my son. She'll ruin Bobby's life if I don't do what she says. It'll ruin our whole family."

Glenn Strang's head jerked up to the darkened sky, startled.

His eyes darted around briefly, then he shook his head and looked back to Lance. "Come on, let's go."

Lance tried again. "What happened with Bobby?" Though he thought he already knew, the picture was now becoming clearer. Another misinterpretation realigning itself with the truth.

Glenn Strang thumped the rear of the SUV with the bat, just to the right of Lance's knee. "*Enough*. Get out. Now."

Lance threw his legs over the edge and hopped out. Standing straight, looking down on Glenn Strang and feeling sorry for the man. Lance didn't believe Glenn Strang was a bad person. Just a man who'd been trapped in a bad situation.

"Walk," Glenn said, pointing with the bat toward the basement door.

Lance walked, his long strides carrying him quickly across the grass and then the concrete patio until he was inches from the door. He heard Glenn walking quickly to keep up behind him.

Lance stared at the small pane of glass in the basement door, the light burning behind it blurring out all chances of seeing in. Lance only looked in on his own reflection, and the image of Glenn Strang standing behind him. Glenn looked much more afraid than Lance did.

Lance stood tall and waited for further instructions, wondering if he stood any sort of chance with what waited behind the door. He tried to adjust his hands behind his back and was greeted by a pleasant surprise. Something jagged and rough digging into the small of his back. Samuel Senior's pistol. Glenn Strang—ex-football player, successful businessman, respected philanthropist, proud father and husband—was no expert in apprehending another human being. He'd done a rough job of knocking Lance out and then quickly securing him with the tape, but he'd never stopped to check for any weapons. Lance was suddenly very thankful his pants fit him correctly.

But if he was being honest with himself, his opinion on the weapon hadn't changed much since the moment he'd grabbed it in the Strangs' driveway. It probably wasn't going to do him much good. Especially with his hands taped behind his back.

"I'll open the door, and I want you to walk straight ahead," Glenn said.

Lance met the man's eyes in the reflection. He thought about trying to reach him again and quickly decided it wasn't worth it. Glenn's eyes said it all. He was numb; he was spaced out. He was going through the motions in hopes of getting the task at hand over with as quickly as possible so that he could maybe return to a normal life.

Lance said, "Okay."

Glenn reached cautiously around Lance, as if Lance were a viper that would suddenly strike out with a poisonous bite. He grabbed the doorknob and turned it quickly, shoving the door open.

Lance stepped inside. One step, then two. He heard Glenn bring up the rear and close the door.

Lance's eyes adjusted, and he found himself in what he assumed was the man cave Allison Strang had alluded to earlier. There were a large leather sofa and recliner facing a moderate-sized flat-screen mounted on the wall. Surround sound speakers and lots of cords and electronic boxes stashed in a cabinet beneath the TV. Movie posters hung on the wall—*Hoosiers*, and *Rudy*, and *Miracle*, and *Remember the Titans*—all sports films. There was a small wet bar to the side, just beneath a set of stairs that must have led to the first floor. A Westhaven pennant hung on the wall by the stairs.

But in a room you'd expect to smell of beer or whisky and peanuts and maybe cigars, Lance was practically nauseated with the wave of flowery perfume that hung thickly in the air. It made his eyes water, and he tried to breathe only through his mouth.

Coach Kenny McGuire was asleep on the couch. He was fully clothed and stretched out with his feet dangling over one end. A pair of Bose wireless headphones were on his head. His chest rose and fell in slow, deep breaths.

"Poor bastard," Glenn said. "I don't know what she does to him, but it works. He's oblivious."

Lance's head started to swim, just a small bit, but enough for him to notice something was off. He shook his head, trying to clear the cobwebs.

"Through there," Glenn said, nudging Lance with the end of the baseball bat. Lance looked to his left and saw another door, slightly ajar. More dim light seeped through the crack.

If you go in there, you're going to die.

He stared at the door and wondered where he'd gone wrong. Wondered why he'd been so arrogant. Why had he come here alone? Why had he thought he could win? Did he truly believe he could beat an evil force that had already killed three boys simply by sitting down and having a chat?

You've overestimated yourself, Lance. You were stupid, and now this is the end.

You've failed.

Glenn nudged him again with the bat. "Hurry up. I've got to get out of here before this smell makes me yak up my dinner."

Lance looked once more around the room, searching for anything, any sign, any help, any warning. In return, he got nothing but a choked-off snore from Kenny McGuire on the sofa.

How fitting, Lance thought. *I'm going to die just over forty-eight hours after my mother. How very* Where the Red Fern Grows. *Or maybe* The Notebook.

He smiled, thinking how much his mother would have hated that joke. She loathed Nicholas Sparks.

Lance walked forward, his head held high. He supposed he'd always known that because of his gifts, his life, he would likely die by very unusual means. He just hadn't woken this morning expecting today to be the day. And really, who does? Death is an illusion to most, until the day it shows up at your doorstep and rings the bell.

Lance pushed the door open and stepped across the threshold.

[41]

THE ROOM WAS UNFINISHED, A LARGE OPEN STORAGE SPACE with studs showing and electrical wires snaking through them. Two banks of overhead fluorescents hummed, echoing off the concrete floor. Boxes were piled everywhere, some labeled auspicious titles such as KITCHENWARE and CHRISTMAS ORNAMENTS. Others were more vague and mysterious, like KENNY'S STUFF or KNICKKNACKS.

But what drew Lance's attention was the heat. He felt as if he'd just stepped outside the airport in Phoenix after flying in from Maine, a shock of heat slamming into him like a wave in choppy waters.

The source of the heat was a large wood stove burning near the rear of the room, a black cast-iron thing with a grated front door for feeding wood and stoking the flames. Orange and yellow light flickered and bounced from inside the stove's belly. A large pipe went up from the top of the stove and into the ceiling. Another, smaller pipe came out of back and went halfway up the wall before making a hard right angle and feeding into the wall. A pile of cut wood was neatly stacked next to the stove, a pair of gloves tossed atop it, a black fire poker resting against the wall.

All around the stove and along the edges of the walls were what seemed like hundreds of candles and incense burners glowing. The heat, combined with the nearly knockout strength of the perfume aroma, caused Lance's head to do another jiggle, his vision blurring and his knees weakening. He shook his head again, breathed in deeply through his mouth. He squeezed his eyes shut and tried to focus. When he opened them, Melissa McGuire was standing directly in front of him.

Like Allison Strang, Melissa McGuire was wearing a robe, only hers wasn't heavy and plush and meant for comfort. Hers was thin and silky and short. It fell just to the middle of her thighs, and the sash was cinched loosely, the robe falling open around her neck and midway down her chest, her bare breasts just barely concealed. Her hair was up in a ponytail, the same golden hair that Lance had seen in his vision from Bobby Strang and had mistaken for Allison Strang's. Up close, Melissa McGuire's face was smooth and appeared much more natural than Allison Strang's, but this didn't equate to beauty. Up close, Melissa McGuire's face was plain, normal. But her body ... Lance glanced down to the open robe, the slim legs ... her body was a surprise.

She was staring directly at Lance, and he met her gaze with a conviction to stay strong till the very end. He would not give this woman, this *thing*, the satisfaction of making him cower. When Lance looked into her eyes, he felt...

Nothing.

He reached out, bored deeper into her unflinching stare, searched for any feeling. He found an emptiness that rocked him, confused him. He knew he wasn't always able to reach into people and get a sense of them—one of the many things about his gifts he could not explain—but previously it had always been a very binary result. It was either ON or it was OFF. It worked, or it didn't. In Melissa McGuire's case, the switch was ON, he was able to see inside, could feel himself poking around in the drawers of her consciousness, but all he found was cobwebs.

It was as if she were empty, not even alive. Her soul was made of stone, impenetrable and dark and hard and cold. There was no emotion, no feeling. No sense of being human. She carried with her zero sense of meaning.

(*I'm keeping you out.*)

Lance flinched, Melissa McGuire's voice booming in his head as if through a megaphone.

(*You've never been rejected before, have you? How does it feel? How does it feel to know you're not as special as you thought you were? You're nothing, Lance. You're puny compared to what I am, what I'm doing.*)

Lance looked into the woman's face, feeling true terror for the first time. She grinned at him, and suddenly the heat and the smell and the realization of just how scared Lance truly was collided in his mind, and the room began to spin again and stars peppered his vision and blackness crept in from the sides.

"Glenn," Melissa McGuire said, "get him in place, please. Then get the hell out of here. I'll call you when I'm ready."

Lance felt himself shoved forward as his vision continued to darken. He stumbled, felt his left knee hit one of the boxes. The heavy aroma in the room seemed to be seeping into him through his pores. He tried to hold his breath but felt as if the scent was still making its way in, still doing its job.

He was certain he was going to vomit. He blacked out before he could.

He snapped back to consciousness, jerking his head up and taking in a gasping breath. The storage room was darkened, the fluorescents turned off, and only the light from the candles and burners and wood stove lit the place. It had a cozy appearance, soothing and relaxing. He breathed in deeply again and found the flowery aroma had dissipated some, or maybe his body had just adjusted to it.

The problem was no longer the aroma. Lance's arms were no longer bound behind his back. Instead, he was standing upright against one of the exposed studs along the wall, his arms raised above his head and secured by a set of handcuffs to a hook that'd been drilled into the wooden beam. He tugged once, twice, and instantly knew he wasn't getting out of this.

To his left, a piece of wood popped in the stove, the sound resembling a gunshot. Lance jumped, his back rubbing uncomfortably against the stud. And that was when another realization hit him: his gun was gone.

"Did you really think it would do you any good?"

Melissa McGuire appeared from the shadows on his right. Her robe was gone, and she padded barefoot and naked across the room to him. She must have seen Lance's surprise. "Don't you see, Lance? I'm in your head now. I'm buried deep and you'll never get rid of me." She laughed, and the sound was like nails on a chalkboard. "You're weak, Lance. I think the good ones almost always are, in the end."

Lance said nothing.

The golden light from the fire bounced off Melissa McGuire's flesh. Her skin appeared warm, reddened. Her breasts swayed as she walked, her nipples hard despite the heat. Lance felt a stirring in his groin and was instantly disgusted with himself.

Melissa laughed again. "Oh, come now, Lance. Enjoy it while you can." She reached up and grabbed her own left breast, gave it a small squeeze and laughed again when Lance looked away. "None of the others have been able to resist me. Why should you be any different?"

She took a step closer.

"All but one were virgins. Can you believe that, in this day and age? It was so easy. A little flirting at first, then a little teasing. Eighteen-year-old boys care about one thing and one thing only. And here's a hint: it ain't football." She laughed again. "And let me tell you, I love my husband, but he just can't compete with an eighteen-year-old's cock anymore. Eager and hard as oak." She shook her head. "It's almost a shame they all had to die. I was quite enjoying myself."

Lance felt his stomach churn, his revulsion growing stronger the more he understood. He needed to snap out of it. He needed to steady himself. He had to fight back.

"You're lovely and all," he said, trying his best to sound confident, "but I'm saving myself for marriage."

She ignored him. "So easy," she said again. "They walked right into it."

Lance stood on his toes, creating some slack in the chain holding his arms up. "So you seduce young men and then murder them? Your parents must be so proud. But, hey, everybody needs a hobby, right?"

He was stalling, obviously, but Melissa McGuire appeared to be in no hurry. Lance couldn't blame her. She had the definitive advantage. He flexed his arms and pulled down on the chain as hard as he could without appearing to visibly struggle. His sprained wrist screamed. He thought he felt the hook give a little, but it might have been wishful thinking—his brain playing a cruel trick.

Melissa walked up to him and stroked his face with her fingertips. They were electric, fiery hot. Lance held her gaze and refused to pull away. "Big boy like you ..." She shook her head. "I'd have liked to see what you have under those shorts."

Lance felt that unwanted stirring again, but he held firm.

"Why do you do it?" Lance asked. "What's the point?"

Melissa McGuire stepped back and looked at him. She

looked uncertain, as if she weren't sure Lance was being truthful. "You really don't know?"

"I asked, didn't I?"

She cocked her head to the side. "You mean to tell me a man with your gifts, your ... whatever it is that I can feel pouring out of you right now, desperately trying to fight me away—you're telling me you're here, and you still don't know what I'm doing? What *we're* doing?"

Despite his bound position, Lance tried to shrug. "My good looks only get me so far."

Melissa McGuire laughed another chalkboard screech, throwing her head back and producing a sound that bordered on cackling. "You're even weaker than I thought."

Lance despised the truth in her statement. If he were half the person he'd thought he was, he wouldn't have lost this fight. He wouldn't have been so stupid.

"Don't worry, Lance," she said, taking another step closer. "You'll find out very shortly."

Lance kept pushing forward. If he was going to die, and Melissa McGuire was going to continue to talk, he might as well get some answers.

"You're blackmailing the Strangs. How?"

She smiled at him, and Lance could feel her picking through his memories. He tried to close her out, lock away the important stuff. She found what she was looking for, and her eyes lit up and focused. "Ah ... I see. You got a little sneak peek from that boneheaded hillbilly son of theirs." She walked over to the wood stove and bent over, stared into the flames through the front grate, her ass presented in the air as if waiting for a lover. Lance looked away. "*Soon*," he heard her whisper. "*Soon*."

She stood and turned. "Being a female in America doesn't come with too many benefits, I'm afraid." She brushed something from her shoulder. "But there's one thing we always win. *Always*. Do you know what that is, Lance?"

"*The Bachelor?*"

Her hand darted out and grabbed his crotch. She squeezed, and Lance went further up on his toes. "A rape accusation, Lance. When we say *rape*, the poor guy on the other end doesn't stand a chance." She gave him one more squeeze, then a gentle pat for good measure.

Lance wasn't too surprised by this. He'd pieced most of it together while trying to convince Glenn Strang to let him go.

"A hidden camera—my fucking iPhone, in this case—and an off-camera conversation about liking it rough and liking to be dominated, mixed with some well-chosen words screamed while he thought he was giving me the time of my life ... you get the picture."

Lance did. "So you show the Strangs the video and tell them they can either help you or you'll ruin Bobby's life. And the family's, by proxy? That it?"

She nodded. "See? You're not *that* dumb."

"But why involve them at all? You've got the breasts and the butt and the sex. What could the Strangs give you? Glenn's nice and all, but I don't think he's many eighteen-year-old boys' type."

The wood stove cracked and popped. A clanging noise rattled through the small pipe coming from the wall.

Melissa McGuire's eyes lit up like a firecracker. "Poor thing was a little tired after trying to slow you down earlier. I was hoping to get Glenn to stop you before even getting to speak with Allison. Believe it or not, there was a part of me that honestly hoped you'd just go away. That you'd move on from Westhaven without digging any deeper. I tried to scare you. So many times I tried to run you off. And I tried to kill you. But you're a stubborn one."

Lance thought of the falling scoreboard. His fear that Leah would be crushed. He saw the image of Deputy Miller's family. His hatred bubbled and boiled, and he gritted his teeth. He was losing his cool. And at this point, why bother trying to control it?

A thought hit him. Melissa had said it had tried to slow him down earlier. She must have meant the hail. He thought about the gusts of wind and the lightning that had broken the scoreboard.

"You're controlling the weather," Lance said. "That's a first for me. And I've seen some weird stuff."

"Not me, Lance." She stared at the wood stove's grate. "Not me."

Lance stared at the fire, too. Watching the flames sway together in the blackened oven.

The flames.

The fire.

He thought about the burned boy he'd seen at the diner.

Then his mind flashed to Samuel, the first time he'd seen him, in the mirror. The way he'd looked so blue and swollen. Almost as if he'd ... drowned.

Two victims.

Two different ways to die.

Then it clicked.

"The paper mill!" He hadn't meant to scream. But the revelation was so suddenly clear he needed to get it out before anything else could disturb it. "You're using Glenn Strang to get rid of the bodies at the mill! That's why you're blackmailing him. First his son, and now you've got him so far involved he has no choice but to continue!"

Melissa McGuire ignored Lance's breakthrough. The fire in the wood stove gave off a loud *whoosh*, and the heat and light flashed like a bomb. Wood split and popped. Something clanged in the pipe again.

"You know the funniest part, Lance? You know what just absolutely tickles me about you showing up in town and thinking you could actually stop me?"

Lance said nothing. His eyes stayed focused on the fire burning in the stove. The light seemed to be picking up a greenish tint.

"The funny thing is you made it that much easier for me! This was probably going to be the last year. Even in a dumb fuck town like Westhaven, you can only go on so long without suspicion finally knocking at your door.

"Four boys would have been the limit, I'm afraid. Even though they all had sob stories to milk to make it so easy to believe they were runaways, even a blind cop finds his nut eventually. Plus, I think poor old Bobby was about to crack."

She laughed. "But this year, I can use *you*! So really, I should be thanking you."

Lance was about ask a question—he had so many—but the wood stove's belly exploded in a belch of green fire. The front grate blasted open on its hinges and slammed against the stove's side. The noise was like a gunshot. The pipe coming from the wall seemed to expand and contract, heat and air again *whooshing* out of the stove's open mouth.

And then the dragon flew out with the flames.

Only it wasn't a dragon. Not really.

It looked as though it were made of pluming black smoke, sometimes airy and transparent, sometimes as thick and as black as a starless night sky. It floated through the basement, its shape first resembling a snake, then growing legs and feet, looking more like a squashed lizard. It moved slowly, as if riding the heatwave across the room, and as it neared Melissa McGuire, its neck lengthened and its tail forked, and it landed on Melissa's shoulder in a soft puff of black smoke. The world's ugliest parrot.

Lance was certain of only one thing: this was what he'd seen in the sky right before it had started to hail.

This was what he'd seen outside the Strangs' patio doors.

This ... *thing*. This was the true evil in Westhaven.

And Lance didn't have the first clue what it was.

[42]

Lance pulled at his chain again, his wrists and forearms burning with fatigue. The hook above his head was unflinching. Solid.

The thing on Melissa McGuire's shoulder stayed put, its body of smoke swirling and floating and ever-shifting. But its form stayed mostly the same. The tail and the torso ... and the head. A head that seemed to have grown two black holes for eyes, two sockets of darkness that had the tiniest spark of jade. Those eyes stared at Lance, appraising him. Lance's stomach turned in revulsion, fear. But he kept up his charade. "I think I saw your cousin in *FernGully*," he said, looking directly at it.

Of course, it said nothing. But it did open its mouth in what looked like a yawn, spawning two rows of black teeth, gooey needles of smoke that elongated the wider its mouth opened.

"Isn't he beautiful?" Melissa McGuire said. She reached up with her right hand and appeared to stroke the thing's side, her fingers disappearing into the smoke, raking through its body and causing tendrils of black to puff into the air. "He's been in my family for generations. He's gone from woman to woman, all the way back to my great-great-grandmother in Bulgaria. That's as far back as we can trace him." She smiled and shook her head. "The Bulgarians called him a demon—a *hala*—but what a terrible name for something so grand!"

"I'm more of a dog person," Lance said.

Melissa McGuire ignored him. "The early legends said the hala would cause terrible storms and destroy farmers' crops. But, if you were respectful and gave them what they wanted, they would in turn give you good fortune, blessing you and your family."

Lance felt his stomach churn. "And what did they want?"

Melissa McGuire sighed. "Like with most myths and urban legends, the early reports were mostly in agreement that a hala ate children to survive and sustain itself."

The thing on her shoulder stood on its rear legs, standing tall and appearing to stretch, its mouth widening again to reveal the smoking teeth. Melissa McGuire made a *shhhh* sound, as if soothing it. "Soon, my love. Soon."

The heat pouring out of the wood stove was becoming overbearing. Sweat dripped down Lance's face, his shirt stuck to him as if he'd gone swimming. His head began to feel faint again. His arms tingled and burned. He was suddenly tired. Tired of everything. His mind reeled with everything he'd learned.

"You're killing the boys so ... what? Your husband can win football games?" he said, his voice sounding small.

She laughed. "Among other things, yes. The *hala* brings good fortune to us in more ways than just football. But keeping Kenny happy and respected in the community is one big way. It keeps the suspicion away, and in small towns like this, where sports are king, the perks of coaching a winning team run deep." She walked closer to Lance. "And poor Kenny. He actually thinks his coaching is what's winning games." She shook her head. "I'll never have the heart to tell him. He snoozes away every time my baby needs to feed, and then he gets to wake up and reap all the benefits. I do all the work, but I don't mind. Kenny wouldn't understand. He's like..." She glared at Lance, a sudden fierceness in her eyes. "He's like *you*. He's too kind, too good."

Lance said nothing. His mother *had* been too kind a person. But Lance had always thought himself to be healthily balanced. Polite and courteous and respectful to all, until it was time to get dirty. Then he could show his claws. Then he could fight.

Given his current predicament, he wondered if his whole bad-boy side had been an illusion. Something made up in his head.

I walked right into this. Just like the others.

You could call him a psychic, you could call him clairvoyant, you could call him strange. He could see the dead, and he could see people's lives in a flash with just a single touch. You could call him whatever you wanted, but he felt a great pang of sadness in his heart as the certainty of his fate suddenly rang true. He'd not been ready to die, but in a matter of minutes, he would have his life ended at the hands of a monster.

He wished he could have told Leah goodbye. Told her to get out of this town and start a good life for herself. He could have used one more kiss to take with him.

Do not fear death. His mother's voice came out of nowhere, trumpeting in his head with an unexpected announcement. She had told him this repeatedly over the years as he'd progressed from child to adolescent to adult. *It does not fear you.*

Lance wasn't sure he'd ever understood exactly what this philosophical quip had meant, but at that moment, he sucked in a deep breath of hot, heavy air and let it out in a relaxed rush. He straightened and said, "So, do you give everyone the history lesson before you feed them to Puff the Magic Dragon?"

The thing made of smoke uncoiled itself from Melissa

McGuire's shoulder and slithered down her torso, its head and neck covering her breasts before swirling around her like an anaconda ensnaring its dinner. Melissa McGuire threw her head back and moaned, her eyes closed and her mouth turned down in an expression of what appeared to be pleasure.

"So warm," she said. "So perfect."

Lance continued to stare at what could be the kinkiest porn he'd ever seen. What would you even call it? Smoke-on-girl action?

And then Melissa's eyes shot open again, and her head snapped forward. She looked at Lance and said, "It's time."

She walked forward, the smoke beast continuing to encircle her as she came toward Lance, its head darting around her body and stealing quick glances at Lance as it went.

It's excited, Lance thought. *That can't be good.*

Melissa McGuire held up her left index finger, and Lance saw the fingernail shimmer in the firelight. It was long and sharp, pointed like a spear.

"Kenny thinks this is because I open so many envelopes at the school." She laughed, and then she reached down to her left thigh, just below her sex, and made a tiny slit. It was less than an inch wide, but the blood flowed fast all the same. The head of the beast darted to the wound in an instant, its face appearing to sniff, a smoky tongue flicking from the mouth and tasting the cut.

"This is the worst part," Melissa McGuire said, raising her finger to Lance's neck. "One quick pinch, and then the rest is painless. It'll be like you're getting so, so tired, and then finally you'll fall asleep." She made a quick slashing motion, and Lance felt the cut and then the warm tickle of blood down his neck, dripping onto his shirt.

Melissa McGuire wiped a drop of blood from Lance's neck,

then reached down and swiped a drop of her own blood onto her finger as well, smearing and mixing them together. She held her new blood concoction out toward the black thing's head, and it caught the scent, quickly snapping its head toward her finger. Once it was close and began flicking its swirling tongue of smoke and vapor, Melissa moved her finger up and away from her body, toward Lance's neck. The carrot leading the rabbit.

And that was the first time Lance was hit with the urge to scream. The thing's head passed by his own, its jade sparkles for eyes locking on to his for just the briefest of moments, the black billows of smoke swirling around Lance's head as the thing's body got into place.

And just as Lance opened his mouth to shout, the thing shot with unearthly speed to the cut on Lance's neck, and he was shocked into silence.

The sensation was so unnerving, startling, Lance's voice was trapped in his throat. His mind floated to the time Amber Tutkus had given him a hickey his freshman year of high school. When his mother had seen it, she'd been more inquisitive about the event than upset at her son's promiscuousness. The conversation was something Lance would never forget. As was the sensation he'd experienced that night in the Tutkus family basement. The gentle amount of pressure, the suction of Amber's lips and warm tongue against his skin.

The feeling now on his neck was just like that night, only intensified by a factor of ten. The creature was weightless, seeming to have no solid form or bearing against Lance's body, yet the suction was there, the sudden rush of pressure on his neck where Melissa had cut him. And there was warmth. A warm, sticky heat, like a summer afternoon thunderstorm.

Lance's head fell involuntarily to the side, allowing the suckling beast's mouth to work its way further in. Lance's eyes looked straight ahead, seeing through the rising tendrils of black-ish-gray smoke coming off the creature's body as it seemed to pulse and swirl. In the glow of the greenish-gold light from the stove and the candles, Melissa McGuire stood still, staring as her hala did its work. She smiled a wide, sinister grin, an evil acknowledgment of the horrors she was witnessing.

And then the room started to fade.

First the smell, that strong, flowery aroma that Lance had nearly forgotten existed, began to fade from his senses, replaced by a sterile gray-smelling nothingness.

The heat of the room seemed to suddenly cool, the temperature plummeting from what must have been a hundred degrees to something like freezing, before finally there was no sense of temperature at all. It was perhaps the most definitive observation of comfort.

His legs began to buckle, his muscles slackening like melting putty.

His ears began to ring, then cleared. Sound warped in and out, like somebody quickly twisting the volume knob.

Something rumbled outside the walls. Something ... *familiar?*

Then the sound was cut and Lance felt his legs begin to fail him completely, and the room grew dim as color drained from his vision.

And then he understood he was going to die.

It's not sucking my blood, he thought, straining his eyes, his muscles, his heart, his mind, straining everything he was or could be to survive a little longer.

It's sucking my soul. It's eating the life force right out of me.

Lance's eyes slid closed, and a sleep so deep and so wonderful called to him, begged him to give in. His body slid further down the wall, his arms pulled tight by the chain.

(*You're not finished yet! Get up and fight!*)

Annabelle Winters's voice grabbed hold of his consciousness and slapped it across the face. Lance's eyes shot open just in time to see the woman's ghost lunge from the shadows of the room. She held a wooden rolling pin in both hands, gripped tightly by one handle, and she leapt and reared back and slammed it into the neck of the hala, an explosion of smoke billowing and puffing and clouding Lance's vision.

And all at once, the sucking sensation stopped, a fierce jerk of Lance's neck followed by a coldness where the beast's face had been buried. The thing sprang to action, snapping its needle-toothed mouth open and closed. It hit the ground on all fours and then pounced, its tail swooshing through the air in a murky cloud. It rose up in the air, high above Annabelle Winters's head, and the old woman swung her rolling pin in an upward arc and caught the creature on the chin. Its head split in two, right down the middle, the rolling pin appearing to slice it cleanly in half.

Lance felt a bit of strength returning. Was able to regain his footing and stand upright.

Melissa McGuire stood slack-jawed, her eyes following her monster as it flung itself through the air. Her eyes never left the beast, and her face told Lance everything he needed to know.

She can't see her. She can't see Annabelle. The colors and heat and sound regained their presence, and Lance chuckled. Looked like he still had one advantage over Melissa McGuire and her Bulgarian demon.

The hala's head came back together, the two smoking halves resealing and re-forming. Even in the darkness, even with the creature's vague and shifting features, Lance could make out the snarl as the beast hurled through the air and slammed itself into Annabelle Winters's chest.

The two of them toppled to the ground. The rolling pin left Annabelle's hand and vanished into nothing as she lost her grip on it. She swatted at the creature with her hands, pounding her small fists into its neck and face. Its mouth snapped and bit at her assault.

"What is happening!" Melissa McGuire yelled. Her head turned and she bored an enraged stare into Lance. "What are you doing to him? What are you doing to my baby?"

And then she was moving, coming at Lance like a defensive tackle ready to spear an opponent into the earth. He tried to shift out of the way, but with his arms bound, he could only move so much, and her weight hit him hard, his back ramming into the stud behind him. Lance let out a soft cry at the pain and was then choked off as Melissa McGuire's fiery hands wrapped around his neck and squeezed. His Adam's apple compressed and he gagged—or at least tried to. His airway was blocked and his head was slammed against the wall and his eyes felt as if they were about to pop from their sockets.

"*I'll kill you myself!*" Melissa screamed, her grip tightening further. "*And then I'll feed your girlfriend to my baby!*"

And then a shadow darkened the right side of Lance's vision, right before a fist slammed into the side of Melissa McGuire's face hard enough to send a tooth through the air, clacking on the cement floor as it landed. Her body collapsed in a naked, sweaty heap. Lance looked up toward the stove just in time to see the hala dissipate, clearing from the air like a fog evaporating, until there was nothing left at all. Its puppet master had been disarmed, rendered useless.

Annabelle Winters's ghost was gone, too, the battle over as quickly as it had started.

Lance looked to his right. Found Samuel Senior standing next to him. The man's face looked haggard, but he reached out a hand and gripped Lance's shoulder. "Are you okay? Are you with me?"

Lance's breath was rapid, irregular. But he sucked in a deep breath and nodded.

Samuel Senior said, "Let's get you down. Police'll be here soon."

Lance heard the words. Nodded again.

And then he passed out.

THERE WAS ONLY DARKNESS.

No dreams. No visions or visits from lingering spirits. There was nothing. It was as if Lance had been powered off, as if somebody had hit the shutdown button.

And then all at once he gasped, choking on the fresh air filling his lungs and squinting against a dull light as he opened his eyes.

He was staring straight up through treetops, gazing at the night sky, the moon large and bulbous and bright. The cloud cover had cleared away, and stars seemed to actually twinkle. Lance felt hard earth under his head and body, could feel blades of grass itching his ears.

"Thank God, you're back."

Lance jumped, was about to sit up before a gentle hand found his shoulder and pushed him down. "Easy," Susan Goodman's voice said. "Go slow at first."

Lance obeyed and sat up gingerly. Blood flooded into his head and his vision did a momentary jiggle before settling. He took three deep breaths, his fingers digging at the ground, his ears listening to what sounded like many voices speaking in rapid, official conversation.

He was alive.

He was completely and fully alive.

He looked to his left and found Susan Goodman wearing a pair of Westhaven sweatpants and an *Alf* t-shirt that was two sizes too big, even for her. Her dark makeup was gone, her face washed. She looked much younger this way, more innocent. Her medical bag was on the ground next to her, and she zipped it quickly and stood, motioning for Lance to follow. "We need to go. Something tells me you don't want to have to talk to them." She nodded over Lance's shoulder.

Lance turned and looked and found that the two of them were standing just inside the tree line that bordered the McGuires' backyard. Fifty yards ahead, policemen and paramedics rushed in and out of the McGuires' basement door. Beyond the house, Lance saw the flashing blue lights from the cruisers decorating the sky.

Samuel Senior was standing to the right of the house, halfway up a small hill that led to the front. He was talking to one of the policemen in wild, frantic gestures. But his hands were uncuffed, which Lance took to be a good sign.

"Where's Leah?" Lance asked. But Susan was already moving, her large torso squeezing through the trees with a surprising agility. Lance took one last glance at the scene near the house, scanned the skyline for traces of ... anything. Then he turned and followed.

They went maybe a hundred yards before Susan turned right and they were spat out onto a neighborhood street. Her 4Runner was parked along the sidewalk, and she hustled toward it and got in, tossing her bag into the backseat. Lance got in the passenger seat and buckled himself in.

"Cut on your neck wasn't much of anything," Susan said, starting the engine. "I put a bandage and some antiseptic on it."

Lance reached up and felt the small piece of material on his neck, shuddering at the memory of the hala sucking there. "Thank you," he said, wondering how much of him—the true, inside part of him—had been sacrificed. "Where's Leah?"

Susan drove through the neighborhood and out onto the main road, heading toward downtown. "She called and told me to find you at the McGuires'," Susan said. "Said something bad was happening and you might need help. She also said to keep it quiet and to make sure the police didn't get to you first. She sounded absolutely desperate." Susan looked over at Lance. "Are you some sort of fugitive or something?"

Lance shrugged. "Probably."

Susan kept driving.

"Where is she?" Lance asked again.

Susan made a turn. "You did it, didn't you? You figured out what happened to my brother?"

Lance stared straight ahead. "Yes."

"And he's dead?"

"Yes. I'm sorry."

From the corner of his eye, Lance saw Susan nod twice, then reach up to wipe her cheek with the back of her hand. "Thank you," she said. "It's good to finally know."

She drove through the downtown street, all the shops dark except a bakery. Lance looked at the clock on the radio and saw it was approaching five in the morning.

Up on the left, Annabelle's Apron's lights burned bright, and Lance's stomach grumbled. He could go for some pie. As they passed the diner, Lance looked in through the large windows.

He smiled.

Annabelle Winters stood inside, her head and shoulders just

rising above the windowsill, looking right back at him. She raised her hand in a wave. Lance waved back, hoping the woman could finally go and find her peace. He hoped she knew how eternally grateful he'd be to her for saving his life. Saving the town.

"Who are you waving to?" Susan asked.

Lance craned his neck and looked out the back of the 4Runner, back toward the diner. Annabelle Winters was gone.

"A friend," Lance said.

Susan kept driving.

They were quiet, the two of them, nothing much more to be said. Lance knew if he closed his eyes, he'd fall asleep, so he kept them open, staring out the passenger window and watching Westhaven pass by for the last time.

He knew where Susan was taking him.

He knew it was time.

Susan kept driving.

The bus station was right where Lance had left it two days ago. Tucked away at the end of a large parking lot on the outskirts of the town. Susan turned on her blinker and entered the lot, passing what might have been ten feet from the spot on the sidewalk where Lance had stood upon his arrival, readying his search for breakfast.

The lot was mostly empty, except for a few darkened cars scattered here and there, but buses lined up near the depot, some with their lights on and engines running. A couple sat still and silent, resting before the next journey. Susan pulled her 4Runner around them and stopped at the station's main entrance. She didn't put the car into Park, just held the brake and asked, "No more boys are going to die?"

Lance thought about it and shook his head. "No. I think it's over." And though he had no evidence this was the complete truth, his gut told him it was fact. What had happened in the McGuires' basement tonight had disrupted things. Put a halt to Melissa McGuire's schemes. Hopefully forever.

Just one of those feelings of his.

One of those things he couldn't explain.

"Will Leah be able to tell me what happened? I mean, what really happened to Chuck?"

"Yes," Lance said. Another feeling. "She'll know the truth. If not now, soon. She'll know everything."

Susan Goodman nodded once more and said, "Okay, get out of here before I get arrested for aiding and abetting."

Lance forced a smile and opened the door, cool air rushing in and feeling good on his face, his neck. He got out and said, "Thank you, again. For everything."

Susan winked. "Anytime, slick. Now get going."

Lance closed the door, and Susan drove away. He watched the taillights until they were out of sight, leaving just him and the idling buses alone outside.

He turned and pulled open the door to the bus station's lobby, stepping inside to the tune of classical piano. An old-timey music choice for an old-timey mode of transportation. The ticket counter was directly to his left, across a scuffed and scarred linoleum floor that might have been attractive a decade before Lance was born.

To his right, there were three rows of benches, old wooden things that had probably held thousands of travelers over the years—businessmen, Army husbands on furlough, and drifters, like Lance, who just needed to move on.

Leah sat alone on the first bench, her crutches on the floor at her feet, Lance's backpack at her side.

At the sight of him, she leapt from her seat and hopped on one foot, covering the ten or so feet between them. Then she sprang and jumped toward him, her arms outspread and reaching. Lance lurched forward, his long arms sliding under hers and swooping her up, catching her and holding on tight.

She buried her head in his neck, and he breathed in deep the smell of her, inhaled until his lungs felt they'd explode. He never wanted that smell to go away. He wanted to bottle it and keep it safe and have it forever.

She squeezed him hard and then pulled away and kissed him on the lips, long and meaningful and full of the words *Don't let me go yet.*

He didn't. At least not then. They kissed and hugged and laughed and carried on oblivious to the rest of the world until finally, regrettably, Lance set her down, gently.

She smiled up at him, and Lance felt his heart melt.

But they knew ... they both knew the unspoken truth.

"How did you know?" Lance asked, taking Leah's hand and leading her back toward the bench. She hopped alongside him and then turned and sat. Lance did the same. "How did you know it was her? Melissa McGuire?"

Leah grinned at him. "It was because of you, actually. You had the right idea the very first night."

Lance's head still felt a little scrambled. "What do you mean? What grand idea did I have and then obviously ignore?"

"When I told you about the football team suddenly having a winning record, you asked me if Coach McGuire had been successful at his previous school."

Lance nodded. "Right."

"Well, after you decided to run off and leave me alone with nothing but a shotgun and my thoughts, I got bored and started thinking and remembered you asking that. So I looked it up on my phone."

"So Kenny McGuire coached a winning football team before coming to Westhaven?"

"Nope," Leah said. "And that's what threw me at first.

When I Googled his name, the other school that came up had a terrible football team. Not as bad as Westhaven's was, but not much better."

Lance didn't understand.

"He was the *basketball* coach," Leah said, sounding proud. "And guess what?"

"They won a state title?"

"Yep!" Leah sounded almost giddy. Pleased with her sleuthing. "But just one. The McGuires came to Westhaven the next year. So I called Daddy's cell and told him what I thought and that we had to get to you."

"Why didn't you call me?"

"I did! You didn't answer."

Lance remembered the hail, the way it had appeared so suddenly. A trick from the hala. He again remembered the image of his cell phone sliding to the floorboard. He'd left it there when he'd gone into the Strangs' home.

"So," Leah said, "Daddy got the officer to bring him home, and we took my mom's car up to the Strangs'. Thank God it actually started. We saw Daddy's truck and I ran up and pounded on the front door, but nobody answered. I rang the bell and pounded some more and just as I was about to turn and run around to the back of the house, the door cracked open just the tiniest bit, and I saw Allison Strang through the slit. Her face was red and puffy. I think she'd been crying. I didn't even have to say anything. She just looked at me and said, 'He's not here.'"

Lance felt pity for Allison Strang. There was no turning back from what she'd been thrust into. Her entire life had been flipped upside down in a single night.

"I told Daddy we had to get to the McGuires', and he said he'd go. I started to beg for him to let me come—I was determined to help—but he told me he'd rather die than risk losing his last living child." She paused. "I couldn't argue with him about that. No matter what I was feeling inside." She took a breath. She'd been talking so fast Lance had trouble keeping up. "So I let him go, and then I called Susan and I came here. I've been waiting for hours, it feels like. Couldn't you have gotten here quicker?"

Lance smiled and then leaned forward and kissed her forehead. "I almost didn't get here at all."

And then he thought about the McGuires moving on after only one basketball state title. He thought about Melissa McGuire's speech in the basement. How she said four boys would probably be the number she'd stop with, before moving on to somewhere else. He remembered her talk of good fortune and keeping suspicion away. He remembered how heavily she relied on Glenn and Bobby Strang to play by her rules.

"Something happened," Lance said, more to himself than Leah. "Something must have made her vulnerable. Only reason they would have left after just the one year."

Leah looked at him, not following. "What do you mean?"

So Lance told her everything, the entire series of events from the basement. Everything he'd learned and seen and understood. He even told her about Annabelle Winters. All the way up to the moment Susan Goodman had dropped him off at the bus station. When he was finished, Leah said, "That's the most unbelievable thing I've ever heard in my entire life. I can't believe all that stuff is actually out there. Ghosts and spirits and demons." She shivered. "I'm glad I don't see it."

Lance nodded. "It's going to be hard to top, that's for sure." Then he added, "Your father was talking to the police when Susan got me out of there. I don't know exactly how this is all going to play out, but I'm pretty sure Glenn Strang will crack and confess. He'd been strung along too long, I could feel it. He was begging to tell the truth. I think it was eating him alive."

"Good," Leah said. "Bastard deserves to suffer."

Lance couldn't argue. Instead he said, "Your father saved me, you know. He kept Melissa from killing me and then must have gotten me out of there before the police showed up."

Leah nodded her head. "Daddy's not as bad as some people think. He just hasn't been himself for a long time."

Lance said, "Be sure and thank him for me."

Leah nodded and said she would and then asked the question Lance had known would come. "Lance, you said you saw Samuel, right?"

Lance nodded.

She waited a beat, as if trying to figure out how to phrase the next part. "How was he? I mean, I know he's ... I guess what I'm asking is..." She sighed in frustration. "Why was he here?"

Lance thought back to the ghost in Leah's television. He smiled. "Honestly, I think he was just keeping an eye on his little sister. If I had to guess, I'd say he's moved on now. You're safe, and he knows it."

They were quiet for a long time then, both staring ahead at the ticket counter. A large clock hung above the window, slowly ticking off the seconds as the first morning light appeared outside, peeking through the lobby's windows.

"How did you know this is where I would come?" Lance asked. "How did you know to tell Susan to take me here?"

Leah opened her mouth to speak, then stopped. Lance looked at her, and she refused to meet his gaze.

"Leah?"

Then she turned and he saw the tears. She sobbed, "Because I know you can't stay. Not after what happened, and because ..." Lance would have slit his wrists to make her crying stop; the pain inside him was almost unbearable. "Because somebody like you will always have to move on. You're too valuable to the world to stay in one place. Too many people need help."

Lance was astounded at the girl's unselfishness. He'd not known it was possible to grow to love somebody so quickly in such a short, tragic span of time.

He hated himself for being cursed with such an unfair burden, doomed to walk the earth forever knowing he would never fit in, would never be able to live the normal life he desperately wanted to embrace. He wanted to stay in West-haven, wanted to go eat breakfast at Annabelle's Apron and have hot dogs at Sonic and see if the Westhaven basketball team would be any good this winter and decorate a Christmas tree with Leah and read books with her by the fire and watch her unwrap her gifts and spend all the time in the world together.

He wanted to live, not just be alive.

"You could come with me," he said, already knowing the answer.

She wiped tears from her face and shook her head. "I can't. Daddy will need me. Now, more than ever. With the motel damaged and all. And ... what would I do? I've done nothing my entire life except live in this dump of a town and work at a fleabag motel."

Lance pushed a stray strand of hair out of her eyes. "I didn't see any fleas."

She didn't laugh. Just said, "I can't."

Lance understood. He got up from the bench and walked to the counter. He rang an old-fashioned bell by the window, and a minute later, an elderly man wearing bib overalls and bifocals appeared. "Help you?" the man said.

"I'd like a ticket, please. The first thing out that's going anywhere but south."

The man didn't question the request, just looked down at a chart on the desk in front of him and then punched a few keys on a relic of a computer. Lance handed over money, and the man handed Lance a printed ticket. Then he disappeared back to wherever he'd come.

Leah was standing now, her crutches under her arms. Lance looked at his ticket. "Leaves in fifteen minutes. I bet there's room for one more."

She looked up at him with eyes brimming with tears, ready to spill at the slightest provocation. "Your phone's in your backpack. My number's still in it, I hope." Then she took one step toward him, the crutches loud on the linoleum, echoing in the empty lobby. She rose up on her good foot, and Lance leaned down and they kissed one last time. When their lips parted, she said, "I'm going now. I can't ... I can't watch you leave. I can't watch that bus carry you away."

Lance said nothing.

"Thank you for everything you've done for us," she said. "Thank you for being you."

She grabbed his hand and squeezed it, her fingers soft and angelic. Then she let him go and turned and headed out the door. The sound of her cries pierced Lance's soul.

[44]

LANCE SAT ALONE ON THE BENCH IN THE BUS STATION lobby. The bus would be leaving in five minutes, but he couldn't bring himself to step outside just yet. He didn't want any extra time between the moment he took a seat and the moment the driver drove him away from Westhaven, from Leah.

He unzipped his backpack and found his phone, sitting right there on top of his clothes. He flipped it open and pressed the buttons and saw his missed call and messages from Leah, warning him about Melissa McGuire.

His life had been saved by two women tonight. One dead, one alive.

Then he saw a third message, the voicemail left by Marcus Johnston yesterday. The sight of his old friend's name caused a sickness in Lance's gut as he remembered the last time he'd seen the man, his last night in his hometown. Lance sighed, pressed the button and put the phone to his ear. Listened.

The message ended and Lance played it again, listening more carefully this time, hardly believing what he was hearing.

Marcus Johnston was calling to tell him that eventually, Lance would need to settle his mother's estate, and that there was a sizeable amount of money to be dealt with. Lance wasn't sure what to make of this. His entire life, his mother had seemingly been about as uninterested in physical possessions and money as one could be. Frugal was her middle name—one of many. She'd never so much as even mentioned a savings account to Lance, even when he was clearly old enough to be included in such conversations. She'd worked, of course, changing jobs frequently but always committed to whatever she'd taken on at the time. This revelation was a mystery.

Lance saw the time on his phone's screen and got up quickly, shoving the phone into his pocket and slinging his backpack over his shoulder. He crossed the dirty linoleum and stepped outside, the sun halfway up on the horizon, the air chilly and clean and mixed with exhaust fumes from the rattling bus waiting by the curb.

Lance looked out to the parking lot, not wanting to, but finding himself unable to stop, some part of him desperately hoping to see Leah's mother's car sitting in one of the spaces, a head of blond hair visible behind the windshield. The best smile on the prettiest face.

The lot was empty except for a red Ford van, covered in dirt.

Lance mentally said goodbye to Westhaven and turned and walked the few paces up the sidewalk to the waiting bus. The driver looked tired and impatient through the large windshield as Lance approached.

The door to the bus was open, and Lance reached in and grabbed the railing to pull himself up the steps. And as he took the first step up, he stopped, halfway in, halfway out of the open door.

He turned and looked around and sniffed the air.

He caught a whiff of lavender. A hint of honey.

His mother's favorite tea.

The sidewalk was empty.

Lance stared at the deserted walkway another ten seconds before the driver cleared his throat behind him.

Lance climbed the rest of the steps and found a seat on the mostly empty bus. The two other passengers—a couple, from the way they were huddled together in seats near the back—didn't bother to even look up as Lance boarded.

He tossed his bag onto the seat and had barely sat down before the bus jerked forward and drove away, gears grinding.

The scent of lavender and honey faded from his senses.

As the bus pulled out into the street, Lance closed his eyes and leaned his head back. For the first time in as long as he could remember, he felt the warm caress of tears spill down his face.

DARK SON

(Lance Brody Series, Book 2)

PROLOGUE

"MARGIE, HOW 'BOUT ANOTHER SLICE OF YOUR PIE?"

Hank Peterson was perched on his usual stool at the far end of the diner's counter, an empty pie plate and an opened newspaper set out in front of him. He'd been there for hours. "It's Friday afternoon and I'm celebrating the end of another grueling week."

Margie, rolling her eyes to a customer at the opposite end of the counter as she refilled his coffee, called over her shoulder, "You've been retired for eleven years, Hank. You're not celebrating, you're just a fat old man who can't resist a lady's pastries."

Margie had been working at Annabelle's Apron for a long time, since before Annabelle herself had passed on, and after so long working in a diner in a small town like Westhaven—or any diner, for that matter—you develop a certain rhythm, come to expect a certain pattern of events, causes and effects. You learn types of people and how to play off them, much the same way a bartender might as he pours libations and hopes large tips will pour out of wallets afterward. There's a routine—not just for Margie, but for the customers as well. Everyone knows how to play along; everyone learns the rules of the game eventually.

Which was why it struck a bit of a chord with Margie when her jest at Hank Peterson caused zero reaction from the man for whom she'd poured fresh coffee. The two other waitresses—both currently huddled in a back booth together, counting their day shift tips as they waited for the dinner crowd to start its trickle through the door—had laughed loudly and giggled at Hank's expense, and from through the food window, Margie had heard the cook give a grunt of approval at the joke. The only other customer in the diner, a young teacher from the elementary school whose name Margie was kicking herself for not being able to remember, looked up from the paperback she was reading as she sipped her hot tea and picked at a salad and offered a polite smile in Margie's direction.

Everyone reacted, because that's what you did. Whether you found the joke to be truly amusing or simply adequate, you either laughed or offered a small chuckle or—like the young teacher reading the book—you smiled politely and then went back to your business.

That was the rhythm. That was the routine. Everyone knew it.

The man at the end of the counter had acted as though he'd never even heard Margie's words. Come to think of it, aside from his order of coffee and a cheeseburger, the man had said nothing at all.

Hank Peterson, using one liver-spotted hand to pat his bulging belly, winked at her and said, "Never could resist nothing of yours, Margie."

Margie groaned.

The waitresses laughed again.

Rhythm. Routine.

Nothing from the man at the other end of the counter.

Margie put the coffeepot back on the burner and made a show of turning her back to Hank Peterson to examine a stack of receipts on the counter near the cook's window. But while her head was bent toward the papers, her eyes were shifted upward, taking a nice hard look at the man who hadn't so much as grinned at her and Hank's exchange.

Sizing him up, Margie realized the man looked extremely tired. Not just tired ... beaten down, maybe even demoralized. He could have been fifty, but the deep creases and lines of worry embedded in his forehead and around his eyes made him look even older. His hair was thick, but fully gray, hanging sloppily down around his ears and into his eyes. Margie had noticed him brushing it back out of the way as he'd taken the first bite of his burger. He wore faded blue jeans with a black sweater, along with a threadbare blue sport coat that was either a cheap hand-me-down that had never fit right, or the man had lost a great deal of weight recently. He looked skeletal inside the fabric. As he sat hunched over his half-eaten burger, eyes down, hair splayed across his forehead, Margie suddenly felt an overwhelming sense of sorrow for the man, and she scolded herself for initially considering him rude.

It hadn't even been that good of a joke. She and Hank Peterson went after each other every day and this most recent exchange wouldn't even crack the list of their top fifty all-time hits. She was better than this. The man deserved better than this.

"Margie, my pie?" Hank Peterson said from his stool, his voice sensing something off in his longtime diner pal.

Rhythm. Routine.

"Just a sec, Hank," Margie said, barely finding her voice. She walked over to the man in the too-big sport coat and rested her hands gently on the counter. "Something the matter with the burger, sweetie? Want me to cook you up a fresh one?"

The man lifted his head slowly, an act that seemed to take great effort, and when his eyes met Margie's, she wasn't shocked to see they were glistening with tears. He offered her the sorriest of smiles she'd ever seen.

"No, ma'am. The burger was just fine. Just not much of an appetite is all. I thank you for asking, though. Really, I do." He used both hands to wipe his eyes, no hint of embarrassment. As if the tears were something he'd long since grown used to.

Unable to think of anything else to do, unsure how to respond to the scene before her, Margie asked, "How about a slice of pie? On the house. I bake them myself." She smiled at the man and hoped he found some warmth in it.

"That's very kind of you," he said, "but I think I'll just have the check, please."

Margie wasn't having it, whether because of her own guilt still pushing its way in or because something about the man in front of her with the mop of gray hair and the too-big jacket seemed to be crying out for help regardless of what he said. She had to make one last attempt.

"This is on me, sweetie. You hardly touched your food."

She held up her hand to stop his attempt at a protest. "Now either the food wasn't to your liking, or—and forgive me if I'm getting too personal, but I've been working around people my whole life and I just have to call it like I see it—there's something troubling you. Something troubling you *bad*. And, well, I'd just like to do what I can to maybe brighten your day up a bit."

The man looked at her. He didn't say a word, but Margie thought she could see some form of concession in his eyes, his whole demeanor. Like whatever weight he'd been carrying had suddenly vanished and he could take a deep breath and relax, if only temporarily.

"So, I'm going to ask you one last time," she said with a little bit of playful sass, "is there anything else I can get you?"

The man still did not speak, only turned and looked past the tables and booths and out the row of windows at the front of the diner. Margie looked too, seeing only the darkening sky full of gray clouds and Hank Peterson's ancient pickup truck parked in the same spot it sat in every day. She glanced back at the man and saw he was looking back at her apprehensively, as if he were mulling over what he was about to do. Then he reached a hand into the inside breast pocket of his sport coat.

"I wasn't going to bother any of you fine people with my own agenda," he said. "You all have your own troubles to deal with. No sense in burdening you with mine." He pulled a folded piece of newspaper from the pocket. "I was going to make my way to the sheriff's office, but ... I've just been through this so many times ..." He trailed off and slowly unfolded the piece of newspaper, flattening it out carefully on the counter, next to his half-eaten cheeseburger.

Margie looked down and saw the clipping was a picture from the sports section of a paper she did not recognize. It was worn with age and constant refolding, the crease lines nearly transparent. The photo was an action shot of a boys' basketball game. On the left side of the picture, a defender was in midair and had his hands raised high in an attempt to block his opponent's shot. On the right side of the picture, also in midair, the boy taking the shot was tall and lean and appeared to be unchallenged by the outstretched arms of the defender. He had blond hair and a look of determination on his face that hardened his features.

Margie has seen this boy before. Though he'd been a few years older than he looked in the newspaper photo.

He'd come to Annabelle's Apron twice, a month or so ago. Had sat at this very counter and eaten her food.

And then she'd never seen him again.

Margie looked up from the photo and met the man's eyes, which seemed suddenly on the verge of tears again.

"His name is Lance," the man said. "He's my son." Then,

through a stifled sob and an attempt to hold back fresh tears, he asked, "Have you seen him?"

The orange-and-white Volkswagen bus was parked a block away from Annabelle's Apron, on the side of a shopping center parking lot that was mostly hidden from the road and wedged next to a row of dumpsters. The Reverend sat up straight in the passenger seat, his head bowed and his eyes closed. But he wasn't praying, and he certainly wasn't sleeping. He was focusing, reaching out with his mind and otherworldly senses and absorbing what there was to be learned from Westhaven.

Something bad had happened here. But ... it was better now. He tuned himself into the town and tasted the cool sweetness of ... relief? Calmness? He probed deeper, through the layers of newfound happiness and closure and understanding—through the elation that had followed some great victory against ... what?

Beneath those layers, like loose change and sandwich crumbs beneath sofa cushions, there still lurked fragments of some evil, some great sorrow, that had plagued Westhaven. Something that had taken root and sunk its teeth into the town and caused unbearable pain and suffering.

The fact that it was gone now, suddenly vanished with only these small traces of its existence left, only further solidified the Reverend's hunch. They were on the right track.

Movement in the Volkswagen's side mirror caught his eye, and when he looked into the glass, he saw a gray-haired man who appeared to be in his fifties, maybe older, wearing a jacket that was at least two sizes too big and walking across the parking lot toward the bus. His shoulders were slumped and his slow and shuffling gait spoke volumes as to his mood. This was a man with little to live for.

The Reverend smiled.

The gray-haired man passed by the Volkswagen without a word and slid behind one of the dumpsters. Less than ten seconds later, the Surfer emerged from the other side of the dumpster wearing his customary board shorts, flip-flops, and a bright orange tank top that reminded the Reverend of a traffic cone. The Surfer pulled his blond hair back into a loose ponytail, stretched his back, arching his body and looking up toward the sky, and then turned and walked back to the bus, opening the driver's door and sliding inside.

"What happens to your clothes when you do that?" the Reverend asked. "I've always wondered."

The Surfer only leaned his head back against the headrest and stared back at the man with bored apathy. The Reverend could still smell the lingering aroma of grease and strong coffee from the diner on his companion.

The Reverend sighed, rolled his eyes, and then said, "Well?"

The Surfer reached for the key in the ignition and cranked the engine, which choked and whined and then hummed to life.

"You were right." He put the Volkswagen into reverse. "He was here."

The Reverend smiled. They were getting closer.

[1]

THE BRAKES GAVE OFF A LOW SQUEAL AND THE transmission chugged and shook the bus hard as it downshifted, jerking Lance awake. He sat up at once, snapped out of a surprisingly dreamless sleep. His vision cleared and his heart settled in his chest, and he looked out the window, which was in desperate need of some soap, water, and a squeegee.

The water wasn't currently the problem. Through the grimy glass, Lance watched the downpour of rain curtain the exterior of the bus station, giving it an out-of-focus, shivering effect. It pummeled the bus's rooftop with staccato pings that sounded like a load of gravel being dumped. The bus's wipers worked furiously to keep up, and only when the bus came first to a slow crawl, then a complete stop in front of the station's doors did the visibility become somewhat passable. The driver, a tall, rail-thin man who unfolded himself from behind the wheel, opened the bus's doors and stood to face his few passengers. He smiled big and raised his hand in a wave. "Thanks for traveling with me today, folks. I hope you enjoyed the ride, and"—he glanced out the bus's doors, then back to the group—"I hope you all can make the most of the beautiful weather we're having." He offered a small chuckle after this, and when he got nothing in return from the group, he nodded once. "Right," he said, and he sat back down in his seat and busied himself with a sheet of paper on a clipboard.

The few passengers began to stir and squirm now, repacking small bags and standing and stretching in the confined aisle. Lance, who had chosen a seat in the second row and was closest to the door, grabbed his backpack from the seat next to him, thanked the driver, and then walked carefully down the bus's steps and out into the rain.

He stood for a moment in the downpour, his hair instantly matted to his head, and closed his eyes, breathing in deep.

He reached out with his mind, feeling the new town. He didn't know quite what it was he was looking for, but so far he'd—

"*Excuse* me." A woman's voice startled him. He turned and saw a line of people waiting to come down the bus's stairs. They looked at him warily and impatiently.

Lance gave a weak smile. "Sorry," he said and then stepped out of the way.

A little over a month ago, Lance Brody had lived an ordinary life. As ordinary as a life could be for someone who could see the dead.

It was true. Since Lance's birth, he'd been able to see lingering spirits walking among us mortals. All ages, all walks of life. He'd seen ghosts of those who'd died peacefully in their sleep, and he'd seen the tormented and still-mutilated souls of murder victims, car accident fatalities, and those whose physical bodies had succumbed to terminal illnesses. They almost never appeared to him without cause. Often, they showed themselves in an effort to help, or to be helped. To lead, or to be led. Though the spirits were not always the most straightforward and direct bunch of companions, their assistance, along with Lance's other *psychic tics*—that was what he liked to call them now—had not only helped Lance guide them to whatever closure they might have been looking for but also allowed Lance to aid many people—including his local sheriff's office—in solving a wide assortment of crimes, mysteries, and the all-around generally unexplainable.

It was Lance's ability to help solve crimes that had created his relationship with the only person in his hometown who knew Lance's secret other than his mother, since Lance had never known his own father. Marcus Johnston had been new on the job with the sheriff's office when Lance had been only five years old and had helped find the body of a missing child, who had ended up wandering away from his own backyard and drowning in the small pond at the local park. Johnston had attended high school with Lance's mother, and Pamela Brody had seen something in the man—or perhaps *felt* something about him—that had allowed her to trust him enough to slowly begin to reveal Lance's extraordinary gifts. Looking back and examining his own history, Lance now often wondered just how many of his own gifts his mother might have also possessed, if only subconsciously.

Lance had grown to be a respectable student and had developed the height and quickness to become a superior basketball player for Hillston High School. Though the burden of his unnatural gifts kept Lance from accepting any of the athletic scholarships he'd been offered; instead, he had chosen to remain home, with his mother and with the familiar. Marcus Johnston had grown to become the town's mayor. The bond and trust between the two men had never been broken.

Which was why Marcus Johnston was the first and only

person Lance had called on the night his mother had died. The night Lance had been forced to flee his hometown. The night that had changed his life forever.

The night the Reverend and the Surfer had come for him and his mother had offered up her life in order for Lance to escape.

While most of the spirits that visited Lance were amicable enough, even if their visits were often ill-timed and inconvenient, the lingering dead were not all that Lance's gifts allowed him to see.

He could also see into the darkness. He could see beyond the veil of this world and peer into the shadows of another—and what lurked there, what survived in a place where nothing should be able to survive, was more terrifying than anything you could imagine.

Evil was very real. And evil walked among us. Always present, always waiting.

Lance was still uncertain *what* exactly the Reverend and the Surfer were—while they appeared to be mortal men, the Reverend seemed to possess a similar flavor of telepathic powers to Lance, albeit much more powerful, and the Surfer ... the Surfer seemed to be able to change himself, among whatever other talents he might possess. Shape-shifter was the word Lance wanted to use, but the term carried such a connection to fantasy novels that he found it ill-fitting. The Surfer was terrifying, if not unexplainable.

Whatever the Reverend and the Surfer were, one thing was certain; they knew exactly what Lance could do, and they wanted him. Lance didn't know why, but it was clear their intent wasn't one of friendship and jovial times around a campfire.

Lance had escaped them the night of his mother's death, thanks only to her sacrifice and the quick thinking of Marcus

Johnston, who had gotten him away from the scene of the accident before too many questions could be asked.

Lance had taken the first bus out of town that night and had ended up in the town of Westhaven, Virginia. There, he'd not only encountered and barely survived a battle with a demon of sickening power; he'd also met a new friend who had stolen his heart. A girl whose beauty lived both outward and deep inside. Her name was Leah, and leaving her had been one of the hardest things Lance had done in his twenty-two years of life. But he knew it was the right thing. He was a hunted man, after all. He could never jeopardize Leah's life that way. So, on another bus, he'd left Leah and Westhaven behind.

Lance had been a vagabond ever since. Always moving forward, always looking over his shoulder and checking for an orange-and-white Volkswagen bus.

Or something much worse.

Evil was very real.

Lance stepped inside the bus station and watched as some of his fellow travelers greeted friends and family who'd been waiting, while others slumped off through the rain and stuffed themselves into cars, driving away toward home.

He'd give anything to be able to go home. To be able to walk down his neighborhood street, take the few steps up to his front door, and step into his living room where he'd be greeted by his mother's smiling face and the smells of fresh pie cooling in the kitchen. They'd enjoy a slice together, her with tea and he with coffee, and they'd talk and laugh and...

Lance shook away the thought. Which, to his dismay, was becoming increasingly easier to do after only a bit over a month. Time heals all wounds—that was the saying, right? Lance marveled over the weight of its truth. The night of his mother's sacrifice, he had felt an emptiness inside him that could surely never be filled. A sharp pain in his chest whose ache had almost become comforting in its regularity. But both had lessened. Meeting Leah and dealing with the trouble in Westhaven had helped him begin the healing process in ways he still didn't quite understand. It was certainly cathartic, and as he'd helped that town overcome the evil that had been slowly devouring it, one of the last things his mother said to him reverberated in his head.

My sweet boy. Oh, what great things you'll do.

He would not let her death become an empty sacrifice. He would go on and he would survive and he would wait until whatever purpose he was to serve presented himself.

He knew—if he stayed alive long enough, and out of the hands of those who hunted him—that he would discover what it was he was meant to do. Or rather, it would discover him. Lance always had a way of stumbling into the right spot at the right time. At times it was so ironically timed that he was certain whatever guiding forces of the Universe controlled his destiny were having a joke at his expense.

Lance watched out the window as the bus pulled away, chugging out a plume of black exhaust, and then glanced to the sky. Storm clouds still blanketed the horizon, and the rain still poured. Lance shifted his backpack off his shoulder and pulled out his cell phone, a no-frills flip phone that offered only the most basic of services. He smiled as he remembered Leah making fun of the phone. For the briefest of moments, he thought about selecting her contact info and sending her a text message. Something harmless, something simple. Ask her how she was doing. Or telling her that he was safe and well.

But then he also thought about deleting her info altogether. The temptation to reach out to her was too great. And what good would it do? It would only remind them both of something that could have been, but likely would never be.

Lance's stomach grumbled, and instead of texting Leah, he sighed and checked the time and saw it was a little after two in the afternoon. He tossed his phone back into his backpack.

After confirming with a very friendly man behind the ticket window that there were places to eat well within walking distance, Lance bought a five-dollar umbrella from a small rack next to the counter and then headed outside, standing on the sidewalk beneath the concrete overhang and looking west toward the town, toward lights that looked friendly and inviting.

He pulled up the hood of his sweatshirt, opened his umbrella and started to walk.

With the steady rhythm of the rain falling, tapping atop his umbrella, and the cool fall air trying to nip at him through his hoodie, Lance felt strangely calm. Oddly relaxed.

It was a feeling he didn't quite trust yet.

Two blocks from the bus station, a sign that was posted along the side of the road as Lance approached the heart of the town welcomed him to Ripton's Grove, and a smaller sign below this encouraged him to "Eat at Mama's."

Even as Lance pondered why so many small-town restaurants in the country seemed to think "Mama's" was a great name for a business establishment (*so much for originality*), he felt his stomach grumble again and assured the sign as he walked past that he would indeed eat at Mama's, despite the generic name. He suddenly found himself so hungry he would happily eat at Toilet Bowl Bistro if presented with an opportunity, and hopefully a well-displayed certificate of passing from the local health inspector.

He stopped as the sidewalk ended at an intersection and tilted his umbrella back a bit to peer out beneath its flap and take in the town. Through the sheet of rain, he saw a small cluster of two-story brick buildings, industrial in design and scope, their fronts painted and repainted over many decades as shops and businesses came and went and came again. Awnings stretched over storefronts, lights glowed from most first-floor display windows. A few cars were parked along the sidewalk, and a single traffic light glowed from an intersection ahead. One car sat, waiting patiently for red to turn to green. It was a familiar scene in rural Virginia, or rural anywhere, really. An ill-preserved snapshot of a place that at one time would have a been bright and vibrant scene straight from a Norman Rockwell painting—soda fountains at the drugstore and all that feel-good mojo from long ago—but had now become grainy and drained of its vividness. It had decayed, yet survived.

Lance was starting to think that if he ever wanted to find himself in a larger city, he might need to start paying more attention to what buses he was taking. But honestly, he preferred the small towns. It reminded him of home ... of the time before it had all come crashing down around him.

There was no traffic at the intersection where Lance stood, just two tired and faded stop signs standing guard at the side streets. Lance crossed the road and walked the next block, inserting himself into the cluster of buildings, scanning the storefronts and breathing in the air in search of an aroma that might indicate in which direction he could find Mama's. A car came up from behind him and drove slowly by, not in a creepy way, but in a way that was respectful of the low speed limit. Cautious and courteous. Small-town driving. Its tires kicked up a small rooster tail of water as it navigated the wet road.

The car was a solid black Ford Crown Victoria, not an ancient one, but boring and nondescript except for the dual antennas growing from the trunk. Lance had no doubt it was an unmarked police car. Just as he had no doubt the vehicle's driver had taken inventory of Lance as the car had passed. The sight made Lance slightly uneasy. The last time he'd ended up in the back of a police car, a man had lost his life. A wife had lost a husband. A son had lost a father.

Because of me.

No ... because of it.

He pushed these thoughts away, a harsh past he could not change, and watched as the Crown Vic rolled through the green light ahead and turned left, disappearing from sight. Lance walked another block, and for a moment it took him a second to realize something was different. Something about him, some feeling had changed since before he'd stopped to watch the Crown Vic make its slow crawl up the street.

I'm not hungry anymore. He looked down at his stomach, as if awaiting an explanation, and it did not protest. Lance's hunger pangs had stopped, his stomach's grumbling silenced. He stood for a moment, still and confused, and as he was about to continue on in search of Mama's despite his stomach's change of opinion, a door burst open a little way in front of him, an overhead bell giving off a terribly loud *ring-a-ding!* as a woman spilled out onto the sidewalk carrying a large bouquet of flowers. She called back over her shoulder, "Thanks, Lynn! See you at church!" Then she crossed the street, tucking the bouquet beneath her jacket as she half-jogged to her car and got in.

Lance looked back to the door the woman had come through and saw a large glass display window full of flower arrangements and balloons and teddy bears. Obviously a florist. But it wasn't the florist that was suddenly keeping Lance rooted in place. He turned to his right, toward the door he was standing directly in front of, and read the black block letters painted on the window. R.G. HOMES – REAL ESTATE. And then, stuck in the bottom left corner of the glass, he saw a hand-printed sheet of paper, badly faded by the sun, that read: Rentals Available.

Lance pulled open the door and went inside, his thoughts of food all but forgotten.

The space inside was warm, but not quite inviting. The hardwood floor, presumably the building's original, was scuffed and aged and in desperate need of refinishing, but the only comforting bit of décor. The walls were gray and dull. A few cheap framed prints were hung here and there but did little to lift the mood. To Lance's left was an old metal desk and chair, something that would look more at home in a prison than an office. Atop the desk was a beige desktop computer that had never known speeds greater than dial-up modems, a cup full of pens and pencils, and an opened day planner with a few appointments filled in. There was a fine film of dust covering everything. Two more chairs were in front of the desk, and just as Lance was beginning to think he'd made a mistake, a man emerged from a back office and said, "So sorry! My receptionist is at lunch and I never heard you come in. I really should get a bell like they have next door, but ... between you and me, I hear that thing ringing all day long and I dream about going over there and ripping it off the wall and stomping it flat!"

Lance said nothing.

The man was average height and fairly thin, with the exception of the middle-aged stomach paunch drooping a bit over the belt holding up his khakis. His tie was crooked, but his shirt was clean and pressed. His hair was thinning, but he wore it well, neatly parted on the right side and held in place by—*Oh no, is that hairspray?*

The man gave Lance a quick once-over, just as Lance had done to him, and then, apparently not believing Lance to be any sort of threat, he took three quick strides across the room and shoved his hand into Lance's. "Name's Richard Bellows, but everyone calls me Rich. Pleasure to meet you, sir. What brings you into R.G. Homes today and how can I help?"

The man's enthusiasm toward his potential customer was both amusing and annoying. To Lance, he seemed like a Chihuahua that'd been kept in a cage all day and was now running laps around the living room after being let out.

Business must be slow.

Lance said nothing. Instead he looked back over his shoulder, out the windows to the street. The rain was still falling. He looked down at this umbrella, which was dripping water onto the hardwood. Richard Bellows followed Lance's eyes down and immediately jumped to action. "Oh! Right, right! Here, um, here let me take that for you." He swooped in and snatched the wet umbrella from Lance and then carried it over and put it into a metal trash can by the desk. Then with two quick strides, the man was back in front of Lance, a large smile plastered on his face.

"Let me guess, you got a new job in the big city and the folks there told you Ripton's Grove was the place to live? Easy commute, beautiful scenery, friendly people. So, you came on down to check the place out and see what was available before bringing your family along. Am I right?"

Lance said nothing. Rich's mention of family sent a pang of sadness through him. A twinge of pain that Lance quickly shoved aside. He wasn't concerned about the past right now. He was focused on the present. Something had made him come into R.G. Homes today; his vanished hunger was all the evidence he needed to know that for certain. But why? He certainly didn't need—or have the means—to buy a home, and so far he was picking up nothing remarkable from Richard Bellows, aside from his enthusiasm for customer service.

Lance's continued silence finally caused Rich's smile to falter. His face quickly fell, and he looked taken aback, as if he'd made some grave mistake. Without a word, the man turned and dashed back into his office, returning a moment later with a notebook and pen. He opened to a blank page and quickly scribbled something on the paper and then held it up for Lance to see.

Lance read the words and then burst out laughing. Shaking his head he said, "No, I'm not deaf or mute."

Rich's face began to relax at the sound of Lance's laughter and his first spoken words, and Lance apologized. "I'm sorry, I wasn't trying to be rude. I just—"

He was about to say he had no idea why he'd come into Richard Bellows's office, when something familiar jerked his thoughts in a different direction. He looked back down to the notebook Rich was holding in his hand and examined the hand-writing. He'd seen that writing before, and he remembered the handwritten sign on the door—Rentals Available.

Is that it? Am I supposed to rent a place and stay here awhile?

It wasn't a crazy thought. He'd been hopping around from town to town for a month now, never staying more than a couple days in each, feeling no real sense of purpose or belonging. His gifts of perception and his nudging from the Universe had been all but nonexistent except for a continued urge to move on.

He felt no different today, felt no force telling him this was where he needed to be, felt no threat looming in Ripton's Grove that he needed to attend to, but ... but he wasn't hungry. And he'd been starving.

"I was hoping you might have a place for me to rent," Lance said.

The smile returned in full force on Rich's face. "Of course! Just, um, when you didn't say anything, I ... well..."

Lance said nothing. What could he say?

"Right," Rich said. "Follow me and we'll see what we've got."

Lance followed Rich through the door at the back of the room. It was a small, cramped office with similar furnishings as those in the reception area, except that instead of the outdated desktop, there was a modern Apple laptop on the desk connected to a large moni-tor. Richard Bellows squeezed behind the desk and sat, pointed for Lance to sit as well. Lance sat, resting his backpack on the floor against the desk. He looked around the room and saw that the walls were nearly wallpapered with framed photos of Richard Bellows and his family—nice-looking wife and three small children. Rich caught Lance looking and smiled even larger than before. "My pride and joy," he said. "It's what it's all about, am I right?"

Lance forced a grin. "Sure is."

Rich looked admiringly at the photos for another few seconds and then cleared his throat and turned his attention to his computer. "Okay, first question, Mister, uh..."

"Lance."

"Right. First question, Mr. Lance. How long will you be renting?"

"Just Lance."

"Sorry?"

"My name is Lance. Call me Lance."

"Oh, right, sorry. Apologies. So how long will you be rent-ing, Lance?"

Lance didn't hesitate. "I don't know."

"Three months? Six? One year?"

"I don't know."

Richard Bellows took it in stride, though Lance could sense the apprehension. "Okay, then ... we'll just say *indefinite*." He clicked a few things on the screen. "And what is your price range?"

Lance thought for a moment and then told Rich a dollar amount that caused the man to turn away from the computer and lean back in his chair. He gave Lance an appraising look, as if trying to figure out exactly what he was getting himself into.

Lance could feel the moment slipping away from him and

knew he had to fix things before his opportunity was lost, along with whatever reason he'd come into R.G. Homes today.

"I'm sorry," he said. "I should have been clearer. I can pay that weekly. Do you have anything I can rent by the week instead of a lengthier lease? With the business I'm in, I'm never sure how long a job will last." Then he added, "And frankly, I'm sick of hotels."

This answer seemed to make sense and placate Richard Bellows. He leaned forward again, and though his smile was back, he was clearly disappointed he wouldn't be making much of a profit today. "Lance, I'll be honest with you. We're not a vacation town, nothing touristy for people to come and see or do, so we don't have any weekly rentals..." He trailed off and leaned back in his chair, his brow crinkled as he thought about something.

Lance waited.

"Actually," Rich said, leaning forward again and resting his elbows on the desk, "I might have a place, if you're interested. It's a little way outside of town, and it's been mostly vacant these past few years."

"Mostly?"

"A few folks have come and gone. None have stayed too long."

"So, you've rented it short-term before?" Lance knew all at once that he was on the right track here. Something urged him to push Richard Bellows on.

Rich made a face that said *not exactly*. "The rentals have been short, yes."

This was an omission, but Lance let it slide.

"So, I can rent it weekly?"

Rich actually stifled a laugh before turning his face back to business mode. "Lance, tell you what. I don't know why, but I like you. You seem like a real straight shooter and all-around good guy. If you give me a small deposit. I'll let you rent it by the *day*."

Lance looked at the man and smiled. "Rich, I like you too. So why don't *you* be a straight shooter with me and tell me what's wrong with the place?"

Richard Bellows, his bluff called, could only nod his head and sigh. "The truth?"

"Please."

"People say it's haunted."

And there it was. This time it was Lance's turn to laugh. "I'll take it."

3

Richard Bellows had printed off a lease after a few clicks on the keyboard and then used a cheap ballpoint pen to fill in details with a rapid, almost robotic pace. He'd moved around to the other side of the desk and handed the pen to Lance, flipping through pages and showing him where to initial and sign. Lance didn't sweat any efforts of entrapment from Rich, didn't ask for any elaboration on what he was signing. He trusted the man ... and his stomach was beginning to grumble again.

On the latest grumble, Richard Bellows had made a comical glance toward Lance's stomach and smiled. "When we finish up here, head on over to Mama's. Best food in town."

Lance nodded. "I intend to. If only because of such an intriguing and creative name."

Rich Bellows didn't pick up on the sarcasm, or simply ignored it. He was too preoccupied with double-checking the freshly signed lease and announcing to Lance the grand total he would have to pay today. "That's the small deposit we spoke of, plus two days' rent."

"I'm really fine paying you for the week." It was clear to

Lance at this point that this was where he was supposed to be, at least for a while. Somebody, or *something*, here needed him.

Rich nodded and said, "I appreciate that, Lance. I do, really. But if you decided to up and take off like the other few folks who've rented the place have, I'd hate for you to be so in a hurry you forget to come by here and settle up, get the rest of your money back."

In that moment, Lance felt a sense of admiration for Richard Bellows. He looked around the small office again at the walls covered in family photos. Here was a man full of pride and joy, swelling with happiness and wanting to show it to anyone who'd happen by. And he was turning out to be an honest businessman as well.

Lance unzipped the front flap of his backpack and pulled out a checkbook—one that was only a few weeks old and had been used sparsely. Lance scribbled on a check and signed it, tearing it free and then handing it over to Rich. As Lance filled out the ledger, Rich examined the check. "PB Consulting?"

Lance nodded as he shoved the checkbook back into his backpack. He offered no more information. Richard Bellows was a smart and polite enough man to take the hint.

During the events in Westhaven, only a blink of an eye after Lance's mother's death and Lance's subsequent abandonment of his hometown, Marcus Johnston had called and left Lance a voicemail he wouldn't be able to listen to until he was finally on a bus, heading out of town once again. Lance had been a little too preoccupied with things in Westhaven trying to kill him to find time to remember to check his phone messages. But as the bus had pulled away from the Westhaven bus station and Lance had played back Marcus Johnston's message twice, he was astonished at what he'd heard.

Lance and his mother had always lived a very frugal life. Pamela Brody had worked at the local library a few days a week and occasionally picked up other part-time work until she grew bored or felt the *need to move on*—that was how she'd always put it. With Lance working at the local sporting goods store from the time he'd been about to enter high school, they'd always had enough money for what they needed, plus the occasional splurge. So when Marcus Johnston called and told Lance that his mother's will had left him not only their house, but a savings account with enough money for Lance to live on for a while, Lance's head had spun with confusion. Where had she gotten all that money? Had she been secretly saving it for all these years? Had she inherited it? Lance had so many questions—questions that would likely never be answered.

In Lance's eyes, Marcus Johnston was practically his guardian angel. He'd been there from the beginning, helping Lance and his mother along the way as they'd all coped and learned to handle Lance's particular skill set. Marcus had been there the night Lance's mother had lain dying on the ground outside the Great Hillston Cemetery, and he'd never doubted Lance's admission that Lance was in some new great danger. That these people chasing him were more dangerous than even Lance himself had understood. Lance's track record spoke for itself.

"What do I do with the house?" Lance had asked once he'd finally gathered the resolve to call Marcus back. Marcus had launched straight into a barrage of questions about Lance's well-being, where he was, where he was going.

"I'm fine," Lance had said, fresh off nearly dying in West-haven. "Probably best if you don't know where I am." Then asked again, "What do I do with the house?"

The house was not completely paid for, so the options were either to sell it or to rent it for enough to cover the mortgage. Lance had chosen to rent it, only because some part of him felt deep down, despite the circumstances, that one day he might return to Hillston. And if he did, he wanted to sleep under his own roof. Sleep in the home his mother and he had made together. But only once he was ready. Once his work was finished. Whatever that might be.

For Lance to start his own business was Marcus's idea. "We'll create an LLC," he'd explained, "and put the money in a checking account for the company that we both have access to. That way, I can help you manage anything you might need help with, and as you're out and spend money on ... whatever it is you're doing out there, nobody will be able to directly trace payments you make back to you. It'll just be billed to the business."

The level of trust Lance held for Marcus Johnston was only surpassed by the trust he'd had for his mother. If Marcus thought this was a good idea—and it did make a lot of sense to Lance—then Lance was fine with it. He didn't need to worry about Marcus running off with any of his money.

"Plus," Marcus had added, "if you have a job—even if it's a fake one—maybe you won't be so damn suspicious all the time."

Another great point.

And so, PB Consulting LLC was born. The PB, of course, stood for Pamela Brody.

"Lance?" Marcus had started as the conversation began to wind down. "Are you sure you can't come home? Let me help you with all this? You know I'll do everything I can."

And Lance *did* know this. But he also knew it was impossible. His journey, wherever he was headed, whatever he was to do, was just beginning.

And the next part had been the hardest. Lance, not one to cry, had nearly choked up as he'd asked, "Just take care of my mother's body, Marcus. Take some of the money and do whatever you think is best to lay her to rest. Nothing extravagant.

You and I both know she wouldn't want anything like that. Just ... simple. Peaceful."

"Of course, Lance. Of course."

Lance found himself surprised by how little he was bothered by not being able to be present for his mother's burial. *I knew her in life*, he thought. *And what is a funeral, a burial, if not a celebration of the life?*

This thought had his mother written all over it, and Lance had smiled at how much he'd become like her.

The sound of a metal filing cabinet sliding on its track snapped Lance out of his thoughts. He looked up and saw Rich riffling through a row of hanging folders, his fingers dancing across their labels. "Ah, here we go," he said, pulling one free and tossing it onto the desk. He flipped it open and retrieved a small key ring with two keys attached. He held it out to Lance, that large smile never leaving his face. Lance let the key ring fall into his palm.

"Now, the place is modestly furnished, so you don't need to worry about furniture or anything like that, but I can't get any cleaners there until tomorrow, I'm afraid. I did have it cleaned after the last tenants left, so..." Rich's face faltered slightly. "Actually, that's been several months. I apologize. Maybe you'd like to stay in a motel tonight?"

"I'm sure I'll be fine," Lance said.

"Of course. Completely up to you."

There was a silence between them then, their business concluded.

"If there's anything wrong with the place, or if you have any issues at all, please," Rich sighed, "let me know." He said this with a tone that suggested he was fully expecting Lance to be back tomorrow morning white-faced, red-eyed, and wanting all his money back.

"I will," Lance said.

"Good. Anything else I can do for you?"

"Yes. You can give me the address."

Rich Bellows's face turned red and he quickly stood from the desk. "Of course! Ha! Silly me. Here, um..." He turned and placed the sheets of Lance's signed rental agreement into the tray of a multifunction printer and made a copy. Lance was amused at how flustered Rich seemed. How distracted. Whatever was wrong with the home Lance was renting clearly had Richard Bellows's mind wandering.

What am I getting into now?

Rich handed the copy of the lease to Lance after circling the address with a red pen. The two men shook hands and said their goodbyes, and Lance retrieved his umbrella from the trash can before pushing through the door and heading back into the rain.

[4]

WITH A FRESHLY SIGNED LEASE IN HIS BACKPACK AND THE keys to his new haunted home in his pocket, Lance walked down the sidewalk, past the florist with the window full of bouquets and teddy bears, and listened to his stomach grumble loud enough to be mistaken for thunder. He was starving. With his task now complete, the Universe had allowed him to return to his regularly scheduled program.

It was now a quarter after four, and the traffic in town had picked up. The parking spaces along the sidewalk filled up, and now three cars sat at the red light ahead, turn signals flashing through the gray, rain-soaked atmosphere.

But still, things were quiet. Calm. The few people he saw seemed to be in no hurry. The traffic was docile. Maybe it was because of the weather, but Lance figured he was simply witnessing the definition of a sleepy small town. His hometown of Hillston hadn't been a metropolis by any means, and West-haven had been even smaller, but this place ... this was almost comical. Ripton's Grove was the sort of place you drove through accidentally when taking a shortcut to your real destination. The sort of place where, as you looked out the windows when you passed through, you thought to yourself, *Who would want to live here? What do they do?*

This was the sort of place where—in theory—everybody might actually know your name.

Lance started humming the theme song to *Cheers* and listened to the rain continue its patter on his umbrella. He passed by a small law office, a hardware store, a coffee shop—which he was tempted to go into, but refrained, the thought of comfort food from Mama's more appealing to his complaining stomach—and a small karate dojo, lights off and empty of students, before he reached the intersection with the stoplight. He turned left instinctively, allowed a red Ford pickup to pass beneath the green light, the driver raising a friendly hand in a wave, and then crossed the street. There were no pedestrian Walk/Don't Walk signs, and the fear of jaywalking seemed about as insignificant as mismatched socks to Lance after everything he'd been through recently.

His sneakers splashed through puddles in the street, and the sound of water rushing into sidewalk drains echoed between the buildings. Headed perpendicular to the main street now, Lance continued down the sidewalk, passing a CPA's office and a secondhand bookstore before finding the small Ripton's Grove post office at the end of the block, sitting on the corner, back off the road like a child's discarded toy. It was nearly dark now, the heavy rain clouds coupled with the early setting sun making it feel much later than half past four, and through the large front windows, Lance could see a small line of people standing patiently at the counter inside the well-lit post office. Waiting to send messages to the rest of the great big world that existed outside their tiny reality.

Across the street, on the opposite corner from Lance, was Mama's.

The restaurant was an old two-story cottage that had been

converted. Faded gray vinyl siding but a fresh-looking roof. All the lights in the front windows burned bright and seemed warm and welcoming. Instead of a front lawn, there was a crushed-gravel parking lot, half-full. A small marquee sign sat just off the road at the parking lot turn-in, the black plastic letters chipped and cracked but advertising, BEST MEATLOAF IN THE STATE, and beneath this, HOMEMADE PIES!

Lance chose to smile, pushing away the sorrow that could have crept in just then, the fact he'd never taste another of his mother's pies beaten away by the knowledge that she'd want him to enjoy life without her to the fullest. Even if that meant eating another woman's desserts.

Lance checked for traffic and crossed the street in no hurry, heading toward Mama's bright lights as though they were a lighthouse and he a ship lost at sea. Halfway across the parking lot, he saw the solid black Crown Vic, its two antennas standing at attention on the trunk, waving ever so slightly in the wind. Lance slowed his pace, suddenly cautious. The car was parked close to the restaurant, its nose facing those brightly lit windows. Lance changed directions and walked along the side of the car, not stopping, but quickly stealing a peek inside the vehicle. Saw the expected clutter of equipment near the console—sturdy laptop, mounted facing the driver, radio equipment, radar device. All the usual cop fare.

He wasn't afraid of cops, had committed no major crimes that would suggest a statewide manhunt in an attempt to bring him in, but recent events had surely more than made him a person that local law enforcement would like to have a chat with. And if they did, there would be questions that Lance could not answer. Well ... he *could* answer them, but he wouldn't. He wouldn't be believed. Never understood. They'd find him crazy, mentally unstable. Or worse ... they *would* believe him, his secret out and exposed and vulnerable. Ready for the world to pounce on and pick apart and analyze and destroy.

He'd be labeled a freak. Degraded to a test subject, a number. An experiment.

They'd forget he was human.

Lance's stomach grumbled again, almost yelling at him to stop screwing around and send some of that meatloaf down the pipe.

Lance took one last glance at the Crown Vic before pulling open the restaurant's door and stepping inside.

Something about that car, he thought. *Or maybe the person driving it.*

Unlike the florist, at Mama's there was no bell above the door, but the squeak from the hinges was loud enough for all eyes to instantly look up from their food and away from their conversations and stare at Lance as he entered. He stood there for a moment, the feeling of being put on display nearly toppling him over. After what might have only been two or three seconds—which felt like something closer to a full minute to Lance—Mama's patrons returned their attention to their tables, but Lance figured the hushed whispers were certainly at his expense. *Who is that? Why is he here? What size shoe does he wear? His feet are huge!*

Okay, probably not the last part, but it was a question Lance had heard more times than he cared for in his life.

He closed his umbrella and the door shut behind him, another long screech as the hinges whined some more. There was a coatrack standing in the corner to his right, and Lance rested his dripping umbrella on the floor beside it along with two others that looked exactly the same, probably sold at every shop in Ripton's Grove.

Lance turned and nearly collided with a young woman who'd appeared behind him.

"Whoops, sorry!" she said, taking a quick step back. She was fairly tall for a girl—five-seven or five-eight—and had jet-black hair pulled back in a ponytail. Her skin was pale, and the only trace of makeup was around her eyes—some dark green eyeshadow and a bit of liner. Nothing fancy. She wore black jeans and a white t-shirt tucked in. Lance figured she was still in high school. A year or two out at best.

Lance apologized for the near-collision, and when he said no more, the girl offered, "Can I help you?"

Before Lance could answer, his stomach gave off another low grumble that caused the girl's eyes to look down at it before quickly bouncing back up to meet his eyes. Lance smiled and shrugged. "I was told you have the best meatloaf in the state."

The girl nodded. "It's true," she said, then, after a shrug of her own, "Best I've ever had, at least."

"Good enough for me."

She smiled and pulled a single menu from a stack on a small wooden table by the coatrack that also held a bowl of individually wrapped peppermint hard candies, a cordless telephone with its numbers all but worn off, and small plastic toothpick dispenser. "Table or booth?" the girl asked.

It was then that Lance got his first good look at the place.

The house's interior had been renovated to essentially divide the downstairs into a large dining area and a kitchen at the rear, a metal swinging door allowing employees to pass back and forth between the two. The décor was old, yet comfortable, like a grandma's house. The walls were adorned with faded wallpaper with a flowery print, the carpet a dingy pea-soup-green that Lance supposed did well to hide stains. A cuckoo clock tick-ticked off the seconds from the wall next to the swinging kitchen door. Lance imagined waitresses glancing at that clock incessantly as they passed to and fro from kitchen to dining room, pleading for the minutes to move and their shift to end.

There were twelve tables in total. Small two-tops along three of the walls, and larger four-tops scattered through the center of the open room. Old wooden things with plastic white tablecloths. On the outer wall by the windows were three booths, one in line with each of the front-facing windows. The windows that had appeared to burn so brightly from across the street. The upholstery was lime green and the tabletops were a dark, scuffed and scratched wood.

Lance smiled. This was exactly the type of place his mother would love. A diner meets the touch of home.

Groups of people were seated around four of the tables, plates of food and the hushed murmur of conversation keeping them busy. Somewhere unseen, a radio was playing softly. Country music. Fitting for the scene. There was the occasional clatter of pots and pans, the familiar noise of an oven door opening and closing, coming from beyond the swinging kitchen door. Somebody back there asked what time Henry was delivering tomorrow. Somebody else said they'd guess the same time as always.

Lance saw and heard all these things, but focused on none of it. What drew his attention was the man seated at the corner booth, furthest from the door. His back against the wall. Able to look up and see everything if need be.

It was the driver of the black Crown Vic. There was no question about it.

He was in plain clothes—tan tactical pants, work boots, black sweater, and a black rain jacket—but Lance didn't have to ask if beneath that jacket there was a holster with a pistol. A badge clipped to a belt, maybe. The man was staring down at the table, his head hanging tired on his shoulders. He wore his hair shaggy, but it was thinning on top from where Lance could see. Still damp from the rain. The man was clearly not the owner of one of the other umbrellas by the door.

"Booth," Lance said. "Please."

The girl nodded and led him away from the door, taking just a few steps to the first booth in the row, intentionally leaving the open table between Lance and the man in the corner. Common courtesy, Lance supposed. Or maybe it was more than that. Maybe this was the Universe keeping Lance from getting too close, as if the man in the corner—clearly a police officer—might pick up Lance's scent and know he was trouble. Know he was hiding something.

Stop it, Lance scolded himself. *Stop being so paranoid. You're just here to eat. That guy doesn't know you from Adam.*

And he almost believed himself. But as he slid into the booth, keeping his own back to the door, facing toward the man in the corner, he thought back to the sign he'd seen just below the Ripton's Grove welcome sign as he'd walked into town from the bus station—*Eat at Mama's.*

He thought about how his hunger had subsided long enough for him to do his business with Richard Bellows, and how the local real estate agent had also encouraged Lance to come to the restaurant, Lance's hunger pangs returning as they'd finished up in Rich's office.

No, Lance thought. *It's just a coincidence. I was supposed to go to the real estate office because of the house. The house is why I'm here. Who better to live in a haunted house than me? Maybe it'll be like having roommates.*

"What would you like to drink?" the girl asked.

Lance realized he'd been staring at the man in the far booth, staring right at the top of his head since he'd sat down. He quickly looked over to the girl who was standing beside him, waiting. "Coffee, please."

"Yes, sir. Be right back."

Sir? When did I get so old? He sighed and leaned back in the booth, adjusting his backpack beside him. Truth was, he felt like he'd aged ten years in the past month. His mother's death had taken a toll on him mentally, the stress and the pain and the sadness wearing away at his strength. Things in Westhaven hadn't helped much—nearly dying had done little to improve his mood.

But he had met Leah. That was something. Something special.

He missed her.

He felt another sudden urge to pull out his cell phone and send Leah a text, but the girl returned with his coffee and he pushed the thought away again, tried to bury it deeper down.

The coffee was in a thick plastic mug, and Lance told the waitress she could keep the packets of creamer she was about to set down next to it. She nodded and asked if he was ready to order. Lance hadn't even glanced at the menu. "The meatloaf, of course." He smiled. "It's why I've come all this way, after all."

The girl cocked her head to the side, looking at him with a grin and narrowed eyes. "Really?"

Lance shrugged.

The girl smiled and shook her head and then walked over to the man in the corner. "Refill on the coffee, Sheriff?"

The man lifted his head for the first time that Lance had seen, and his face told a story of somebody who'd seen hard times and come out the other side for the worse. Maybe forty or forty-five, with a heavily creased brow and circles under his eyes so deep and dark he might not have slept in a week. He had a couple days' worth of stubble, spotty and with patches of gray. He offered the waitress a smile that almost seemed to pain him.

"Sure, Susan. A refill would be great." He spoke, and after Susan refilled his coffee and walked away, the sheriff's head went right back down, as if he were staring into the blackness of his coffee.

Sheriff, Lance thought. *Wonderful.*

But even from across the space of the empty booth, Lance could feel the cold sense of emptiness the man in the corner carried with him. It was a feeling Lance had recently known all too well. It smelled of the same scent of his own coldness he'd experienced when he'd lost his mother.

The man in the corner—the sheriff of this small and quiet place—had suffered. Had lost something, a part of him that could not be replaced. And at once, Lance no longer feared the man in the corner but felt an odd sense of connection. Two men trying to figure out what life held next. Coping in their own ways. Like eating meatloaf and drinking coffee and watching out the window as the rain continued to fall and the sky turned even darker.

Two of the other tables emptied, and Lance watched absent-mindedly as Susan cleared away the finished meals and wiped down the tablecloth, preparing for the next guests. On the wall by the swinging kitchen door, the cuckoo shot out of its clock and clucked off the five o'clock hour. The sound was muted, not altogether pleasant, but not obnoxiously loud as to intrude into a patron's meal.

Lance continued to steal glances at the sheriff. Watched as the man would lift his coffee mug to his lips and take small, deliberate sips. Then he'd set the mug back down and continue to stare down at the table. He never looked up at the room around him, never looked out the window toward the parking lot and the rain and his town.

Never looked at Lance.

Susan delivered Lance's meatloaf, and while he was no official Virginia authority on the subject, and could make no claim on whether it was the best in the state, he was quick to tell Susan that it was indeed delicious, and honestly the best meatloaf he'd ever eaten. The mashed potatoes on the side were excellent as well. Full of butter and fluffy. No lumps.

When he finished his dinner, Susan offered pie. Which, of course, Lance accepted. He chose cherry.

While Susan was preparing his slice of pie, the other two tables' guests finished up and left, leaving only Lance and the sheriff and an odd, somewhat uncomfortable silence hanging in the air along with the soft-playing country tunes.

Still, the man did not look up, his coffee the most interesting thing in the world.

Susan brought the pie—a huge, heaping slice with a perfectly golden crust—and refilled his coffee. While Lance ate, Susan worked to clean her tables and then reappeared, standing next to Lance as he took his last bite.

"Anything else I can get you?"

Lance contemplated another slice of pie, then toyed with the idea of getting a slice to go instead. In the end, he settled on another idea.

He pushed his empty plate aside and then fumbled inside his backpack until he found the lease he'd signed at R.G Homes. He pointed to the address that Rich had circled in red pen and asked, "Is this close enough for me to walk? And if not, is there a taxi service I can call?"

Susan smiled politely and leaned forward to read the address. As her eyes took in the numbers and words, the smile faltered. She looked up, first to Lance—a puzzled, unsure glance —and then back to the lease, as if to make sure she'd read correctly.

Then, oddly, she glanced toward the booth in the corner, toward the sheriff. His head was still down, staring at nothing.

She leaned in and whispered, "Are you serious? Why do you want to go there?"

Lance whispered too, following her lead only because it seemed right. "I've rented the place for a while." When this didn't seem to be enough, he continued with, "I needed a place to stay, and it was cheap."

Susan scoffed and her face turned sour. "Did Rich do this?"

"Do what?"

"Offer this place to you."

"Yes," Lance said. And then, "He seemed very nice."

Susan sighed. "Oh, he's very nice. One of the nicest guys in town. But nice or not, he should know better than to let you move in there."

"Is there a problem with the place?"

Susan did another quick glance toward the sheriff and then slid into the seat opposite Lance. She leaned forward, her voice more hushed than before. "Rich didn't tell you what happened, did he?"

Lance shook his head. "No. He just said some folks say the place is haunted."

Susan didn't seem fazed by this news. Lance got no sense of disbelief from her. "And that didn't make you think maybe you should find another place to stay."

Lance shrugged. Answered honestly. "It doesn't bother me."

Susan was quiet for a beat. Sat back in the booth and looked at Lance as though he were suddenly a riddle she'd been tasked with solving.

"What happened?" Lance asked. "Can you tell me?"

As soon as the words had left Lance's mouth, the sheriff stood from the booth in the corner, using one hand to quickly down the rest of his coffee and the other to pick up his Kindle e-book reader off the table and tuck it into his jacket pocket.

So that's *why he kept staring at the table. He was reading.*

But this fact didn't change the cold feeling that only grew in intensity as the sheriff approached the booth and stopped. Lance's heart suddenly picked up its pace. He looked up at the man and smiled. The man paid him no attention. Instead, he reached into his pocket, pulled out a ten-dollar bill and handed it to Susan. "Thanks, Suze. Have a good evening."

Susan took the money and forced a smile, mumbling a flustered thanks as the sheriff walked out the door and got in the Crown Vic.

Lance watched the car pull out of the lot and head down the street. Then he turned back to Susan but found she'd gotten out of the booth and was heading toward the sheriff's table. She picked up his coffee cup and started toward the kitchen, then turned and said over her shoulder, "You could probably walk, but it's a few miles, and you won't want to do it in the rain. I'm out of here as soon as Joan shows up for the dinner shift. I can give you a ride."

And then she pushed through the swinging kitchen door and left Lance alone in the dining room, wondering what had just happened.

TEN MINUTES LATER, A PAIR OF HEADLIGHTS TURNED INTO
Mama's parking lot and a woman made a mad dash from the car
to the door, bursting through it in a spray of water and exple-
tives. She cursed the rain and the wet and the fact her shoes
were now soaked and how she probably wouldn't make any
money tonight because nobody would feel like going out to eat
with weather as nasty as it was. She said all these things to
nobody, a rapid-fire round of complaining as she hung up her
raincoat and tried to straighten her blouse, which had come
slightly untucked from her black pants. She was middle-aged,
short, plump—*round* might have been the more appropriate
word—and had short frizzy red hair in unkempt curls. She somewhat reminded Lance of a more vulgar version of Mrs. Potts
from the *Beauty and the Beast* cartoon. She turned around from
the coatrack and saw Lance for the first time.

"Oh," she said. "I didn't see you there. Susan taking care of
you?"

Lance nodded. "Yes, ma'am."

The woman huffed and nodded once and then quickly
waddled across the dining room floor and disappeared into the

kitchen. No apology for the foul language or her outburst. No change in personality once she realized Mama's had a customer. Nothing.

Lance smiled. He liked her.

He sat another five minutes, staring out the window at the post office across the street as the rain refused to let up, and just as another pair of headlights began to turn into Mama's lot, Susan came through the kitchen door, laughing. "Joan, you're terrible! See you tomorrow!"

Lance stood, ready to go. Susan looked at him and, as if suddenly remembering her offer of a ride, hesitated just a moment before saying, "Give me just a sec, okay? I gotta make sure Luke's cool with it."

Lance could only nod. No idea who Luke was.

Susan snatched the only other remaining umbrella next to Lance's, pulled up the hood of her jacket, and then headed through the door toward the set of waiting headlights. Lance stood and watched out the window as she opened the passenger door and leaned down, talking to an unseen driver. After a moment, she looked up, back toward the restaurant. Saw Lance watching through the window and waved for him to come out. Lance gave a thumbs-up, regretted it, and then grabbed his own umbrella and hid under it the best he could, heading toward Susan and the car.

The vehicle was a four-door Jeep Wrangler, and Lance pulled open the rear passenger door and jumped inside, sliding his backpack in beside him and closing his umbrella quickly before shutting the door. The inside of the Jeep was warm and smelled faintly of peppermint mixed with sweat. There was a hip-hop song on the radio, turned down low. Lance adjusted himself in his seat and then looked ahead, found the driver—presumably Luke—turned and staring at him with a large smile. "So you're really staying out at the spook farm?" Luke asked.

Luke looked to be about Lance's age and sat tall in the driver's seat. He was thin and long—like Lance—and wore jeans with a frayed and tattered hoodie.

Lance didn't have to ask what Luke was referencing. He just shrugged. "Apparently."

Susan hit Luke in the shoulder. "Luke! I told you not to call it that. It's ... I don't know. Disrespectful."

"Even if it's true?" Luke smiled and then winked at Lance.

Susan smirked and shook her head. "You're a jerk."

Luke leaned forward and kissed her on the mouth. "Yeah, but you love me."

Lance cleared his throat, reminding the people up front they had a third wheel present.

Pushed away the memory of the way he and Leah had kissed that night in the Westhaven bus station. Before he'd left her.

Luke turned his attention back to Lance, then seemed to really look at him for the first time. "Hey," he said. "Don't I know you from somewhere?"

Fear flushed through Lance's veins.

Was his face making the rounds through the local news stations, broadcast on the six o'clock segment as folks were sitting down to eat their dinners? Was there an APB out? Was his photo circulating through county sheriff's offices throughout the state?

Had Leah been forced to give up information about him? Hounded and threatened until she'd been left with no choice but to admit she'd seen him leave on a bus headed out of town? The bus station attendant might remember selling the ticket. Might remember the destination. From there it would only take a bit of amateur sleuthing to potentially follow Lance's trail here to Ripton's Grove and—

Luke snapped his fingers. A strangely loud sound that startled Lance and brought his attention back to the Jeep's driver. "You played ball, right? Not around here, but in-state." Luke closed his eyes and thought for a moment, searching for the right memory. His eye's popped open and he said, "Yeah, you played for Hillston High. We played you guys in the first round of States a few years back. We beat you, but man, you were tough. *You* were tough, I mean. I think you dropped thirty on us."

With the proper context, Lance's memory recalled Luke instantly, remembered the game. "Thirty-four, I think," Lance said. "You guys killed us on the boards." Then he added, "But we never played a team from Ripton's Grove."

Luke nodded. "Yeah, I didn't go to school here. I'm from the next county over. Got a job in the city while going to community college. Rent's cheaper here. I split a place with a buddy of mine a few miles away. Only reason to come here, really. Except for this cutie right here." Luke reached out and squeezed Susan's knee, and she laughed and rolled her eyes.

"All the city girls are out of his league," she said.

Luke shook his head. "Give me a country girl over one of them fake city bitches any day of the year."

Susan looked back to Lance. "See?"

They all laughed, and then Luke asked the question Lance always wanted to avoid. "So, what are you doing here? I figured you'd be ballin' at some D1 school right about now."

Lance shook his head. "I'm here for work." Then, to quickly change the subject and try to get some more answers, "Why do they call it the spook farm?"

Susan looked at the clock on the dash and nudged Luke. "Let's go, we're going to be late for the movie. And I'm telling you right now, there's no way I'm going into the theater wearing this and smelling like meatloaf."

Luke put the Jeep into reverse and started to back out of the parking lot.

Susan sighed and adjusted her seat belt to what Lance considered a very unsafe position that seemed to negate the whole point of wearing the thing in the first place, but also allowed her to turn around nearly backward in her seat and look at Lance while she spoke. The Jeep's windshield wipers flapped back and forth across the glass behind her, almost bringing her in and out of focus as they worked to clear away the water. The large mud tires hummed softly on the wet asphalt.

Susan said, "Did your town have a local haunt?"

"A what?" Lance asked.

"A haunt. A place everybody always said was haunted, or spooky? A place that some stupid kids always broke into during Halloween to show how brave they were, or to drink beer or some dumb shit like that? A place with some history that over time people turned into a local legend?"

Lance knew what she was talking about. Nodded his head. "Sure."

"Okay, well the—God, I hate calling it this—the spook farm is Ripton's Grove's version of that."

Lance had heard these types of stories about places before. Anybody who'd grown up in a small town had. It was what small towns did. They embellished and told stories and tried like hell to keep things interesting.

"So I'm guessing something bad happened there?"

Luke gave off a quiet chuckle. "You could say that."

Susan shot him a glare before returning her eyes back to Lance. "An entire family was found dead."

Lance was smart enough to pick up on Susan's deliberate wording. "And nobody knows what happened? Murder? Suicide? Both?"

Luke turned and looked at Lance, his eyes searching. Susan did something funny with her nose, curious.

Lance tried to recover. "I mean, you said 'found dead,' so I just assumed that the situation wasn't exactly black and white." Then shrugged and added, "I watch a lot of cop shows."

This seemed to put them both back at ease. Luke flipped on his turn signal and turned left onto a rural road. Passed a few small houses, and then the road became lined with mostly trees and field.

Susan's tone was that of somebody eager to tell a tantalizing tale. She seemed suddenly excited, but also, if Lance was correct, a bit unnerved. "Nobody knows exactly what happened in the house that night. I can only tell you what the police found the next morning."

Luke shook his head. "Weird shit, man. Especially the girl."

Susan looked once to her boyfriend, reached across and turned up the Jeep's heater, and then started to tell the story.

[6]

"The spook farm has only been the spook farm for maybe ... how long would you say, Luke?" Susan looked to her boyfriend for help. Lance watched in the rearview as Luke crinkled his brow and thought.

"I was a freshman, I think. No, wait ... I was a sophomore. Yeah, I had just gotten my driver's license when it happened. I remember because a bunch of kids were driving up to the house at night after it happened to try and get a look at the crime scene. Just like you said ... dares and dumb shit like that. My parents promised me that if they found out I drove over here to that house, they'd make sure I never drove a mile on my own until I finished high school. So you better believe I stayed away."

Susan nodded. "Okay, yeah. So it's been ... six years." She shook her head. "Damn. I can't believe she's been gone that long."

Luke shrugged. "The way you told it, she'd basically been gone longer than that. Was gone before it all went down."

Susan nodded again. A quiet concession.

"She?" Lance asked.

Susan met his eyes. "Mary Benchley. She was the girl who

lived there with her family. She was my age. Lived on the farm with her mom and dad."

"It's an actual *farm?*" Lance asked.

Susan nodded. "Well, it was. Mary's family inherited it from her great-uncle on her mother's side. Apparently Mary's mom and he were close, and he left it all to her when he passed. It was more of a farm when he owned it—cows, chickens, cornfields, maybe some other stuff. But when Mary and her family moved in, the first thing they did was sell off everything they could. Mary's dad said they weren't farmers and never would be. No sense in pretending."

"Now how could you possibly know that?" Luke asked.

"People talk. It's a small town. I was nosy."

Luke laughed. "Still are."

Susan punched him on the shoulder. "You just remember that." Then she continued. "So they sold everything but the chickens, because Mary's mom argued they could use the free eggs. But otherwise, as a farm, it was just the skeleton of one. Shed, barn, abandoned fields. You know?"

Lance nodded. "So what did Mary's father do? Since he had no interest in farming."

"He was a preacher. Well, that was what he told everybody."

"What do you mean?"

"He didn't actually preach at a church."

Lance was confused, and must have looked it because Susan explained, "Mary's mom got a nursing job at Central Medical, and they apparently got a decent payout when they sold a lot of the farm equipment and the livestock. So Mary's dad didn't have to work. Her mom didn't either, really, but Mary always said her mom loved it too much to quit."

"So what does this have to do with Mary's dad being a preacher?"

"Oh, well, he always walked around town carrying a Bible and would occasionally give impromptu sermons on the street, or in the park. Sometimes he'd invite folks up to the farm to celebrate the Lord and share in the gospel, away from all the distractions of life."

The image of a man walking around town, a tiny black Bible tucked under his arm, brought thoughts of the Reverend into Lance's mind. He shivered at the memory of how the man had spoken to him through his own mind. Effortlessly gotten into Lance's head. And he was still out there. Still coming for Lance. Both of them—the Surfer, too. Lance knew this without knowing how he knew this. He could feel it.

Luke slowed the Jeep for an approaching curve in the road, a steep hill climbing upward where the road dropped off. He made the turn and they began to travel up, rising in elevation as if climbing up the side of a mountain. They drove maybe a hundred yards before switching back around another curve, continuing to climb. "I always forget how high it feels up here," Luke said. He turned his head and looked out the window. Lance followed suit and saw the glowing lights of Ripton's Grove growing smaller below them.

The rain was still falling. Not even a hint of letting up. The Jeep's headlights cut through the falling rain, and the tires stayed firm to the road. Lance figured he'd lucked out with his free ride. And his free history lesson.

His mother did not believe in coincidences.

Lance was finding it harder and harder to find fault in her thinking.

Susan continued. "So yeah, Mary was embarrassed like hell by her dad. I mean, he was nice enough and all, but"—she shrugged—"sorta got the reputation of being a kook, ya know? And once Mary got to middle school, the kids started making fun." She shook her head, then added softly, "I don't think anybody actually thought he was dangerous, though. Crazy? Yes. But crazy for the Lord, ya know? In that way that sometimes makes people seem out of touch with the real world?"

Lance nodded. Said nothing. Tried to figure out where this was going.

Susan was quiet for a moment, then shook her head as if tossing aside a rotten memory. "Anyway, I don't know if it was because the teasing got to be too much for Mary, or maybe just too much for her dad, or if it was something else entirely, but Mary left public school halfway through our freshman year, and her parents shipped her off to some boarding school. Natalie, that was Mary's mom, never told anybody much of the specifics when she'd come into town afterward and people asked about Mary. But something else must have been bothering her, too, because a couple weeks later, she quit her job at Central Medical and was almost never seen after that."

Lance considered this. How bad had things really gotten with the teasing? He knew kids could be cruel. The *world* was cruel. But something about the story didn't seem right to him.

"What do you think really happened?" Lance asked.

Susan replied instantly, her opinion locked and loaded. "Her dad lost his mind, and when Mary came home to visit, he killed her and his wife. Why? I don't know. But he had some sort of plan, and once he was finished, he killed himself, too."

Lance said nothing.

Luke shook his head. "We don't know what happened that night," he said. But from his tone, Lance figured the guy wouldn't be able to offer an alternative story.

Lance hated that he had to ask the next question, but he could tell Susan was waiting, waiting to drop the bomb, the climax of this whole story. "How did he do it?"

"He used a shotgun on Mary's mom and himself," she said. "The police found Mary's mom's body on the front porch steps with a hole the size of a bowling ball in her chest. Like she was trying to run away and got gunned down. Mary's dad killed himself in the recliner in the living room, half his head blown off."

Luke rounded another turn and the land flattened out a bit. Forest on either side, giving way to fields and rugged terrain. He squinted through the windshield and said, "It's up here close, right, Suze? On the left?"

"Yeah, maybe another hundred yards."

Thinking about how far they'd seemed to drive, and the constant switchbacks they'd climbed, Lance asked, "I thought you said I could walk here?"

"Oh," Susan said. "Yeah. I mean, it's possible, but not exactly ideal. There's a hiking trail that comes straight from town up the side of the hill. It's shorter than driving, for sure, but in this rain, it'd be a disaster."

Luke looked to Susan. "You told him he could walk?"

"I didn't lie."

Luke rolled his eyes. He hit his turn signal despite the nonexistent traffic, slowed the Jeep to a crawl, and then turned left onto a dirt road.

Knowing that Susan was purposely dragging out the final bit of information, with a sick feeling in his stomach, Lance asked, "And what happened to Mary?"

Susan sighed, as if telling this part of the story was actually painful. "They found her body burnt beyond all recognition on top of a brush pile in the back field. There was almost nothing left by the time they found her. They had to use her teeth to get a positive ID."

Then, after looking down and giving a long, dramatic pause, Susan lifted her head and added, "They don't know if she was alive or not when she started to burn."

Luke hit the steering wheel with his palm and said, "Jesus,

Suze, you tell this story like you're trying to win a damn Oscar or something. Like you actually enjoy it."

She looked offended. "I do not."

"Yes, you do. You tell it like we're telling ghost stories around a damn campfire."

The two of them continued to bicker, but Lance ignored them. He leaned forward and looked through the rain-splattered windshield. Up ahead, faintly illuminated by the Jeep's head-lights, was the house. The *spook farm*.

And Lance was nearly positive he'd seen something move behind one of the front windows.

[7]

Luke drove the Jeep slowly along the muddy road until the front bumper nearly touched the railing of the farmhouse's front porch.

"Jesus, Luke. Why don't you just go on ahead through the front door?" Susan said, sitting up straight in her seat.

Luke shifted the Jeep into park and then leaned over the steering wheel, looking through the windshield and out to the house before them. "I've never seen it up close," he said. "I told you, my parents would have killed me if they ever found out I came out here like the rest of those idiots back then."

Susan didn't look over to him, just continued to stare through the dancing windshield wipers, her eyes locked onto the house. "You never came after? Later on?"

Luke shook his head. "For what reason? I'm not a ghost hunter or anything."

I'm not either, Lance thought. *The ghosts tend to be the ones to do the hunting, in my experience.*

Susan shrugged. "I don't know. I guess it's different when you're from here. Me and my friends, we all just felt sorta ... I don't know ... compelled to come see it. Almost like we were paying our respects or something." She shrugged again and asked, "Does that make sense?"

"No," Luke said.

Susan was quiet for a beat. Then: "She was my friend."

Luke had no answer to that.

Lance said nothing.

The rain beat down on the Jeep's top, and the warm glow of the headlights illuminated nearly the entire front of the house. The place wasn't ramshackle exactly, but in the gloomy and wet night, it definitely showed its age, and exposed the neglect it must have endured all these years since the night that ... whatever happened had taken place. Shutters hung skewed and slanted on the dirty gray vinyl siding, the windows cloudy with dirt and dust. A wooden front door looked solid, but the storm door was blown permanently open, plastered against the side of house, the screen ripped completely free of the top of the frame and draped over the bottom half like a man keeled over. A wooden front porch spanned the entire width of the house. Splintery rails and peeling white paint. The overhang sagged a bit on the left side, and rain cascaded off it like a small waterfall.

Lance couldn't see the second story from his position in the rear of the Jeep, but he suspected it would look much the same. There were probably a few shingles missing. Hopefully there weren't any leaks in the roof, because with a storm like this, he'd have a swimming pool inside.

But despite the physical appearance, the house was still standing. And it was the only place Lance had to go. For now, at least. As far as he could tell, this was exactly where he was supposed to be.

The spook farm.

Luke and Susan continued to silently stare through the windshield, and Lance let them get their fill for another full minute before he cleared his throat from the backseat. "Thanks for the ride," he said, grabbing his backpack and umbrella.

They both jumped, as if they'd forgotten Lance was in the car. Lost in their own thoughts as they stared at a place that they likely now only thought of as the site of horrific death.

But to Lance, for now, it was only a house. Though he was certain that would change soon enough.

He reached for the door handle, and Luke and Susan snapped out of their trances. "Wait!" Susan said. "Let me give you my phone number."

"Damn, Suze, I'm sitting right here," Luke quipped.

Susan ignored him. "Seriously," she said to Lance. "You don't have a car right now, and well..." She looked over her shoulder again, back to the house, "If you need something, or ... I don't know. Just take my number, okay?"

Lance smiled. "Sure," he said, pulling his flip phone from his pocket. He ignored the incredulous stares from the two of them as he thumbed his way through his phone's menus and was finally ready to enter Susan's number. He typed it in as she recited it and then returned the phone to his pocket. So far, Susan had been fairly unreadable. Lance's many senses hadn't picked up anything overwhelmingly positive or negative. He paused for a moment, then asked, "Why are you being so nice to me? I'm a complete stranger."

Even in the dim light of the Jeep's interior, he could see Susan blush. She gave another shrug and said, "You seem like a nice guy." She looked at Luke, who was watching her intently, and then back to Lance. "And while I don't really know why you're here, I also don't think you fully know what you're getting into. The town is funny about this place."

Luke shifted at this. "What's that supposed to mean?"

Susan shook her head. "I don't know. But just call me if you think you need to, okay?"

Lance assured her that he would, shook Luke's hand and thanked them both again for the ride, and then opened the door and stepped outside into the rain.

He didn't bother with the umbrella, figuring he only had a few feet to go before he'd be up the three front porch steps and beneath the protection of the overhang. This was a mistake. The wind rushed at him and the rain was relentless, and in the three short seconds it took him to get from Luke's Jeep to the front door of the farmhouse, he was half-soaked. Water dripped into his eyes as he fumbled to pull the set of keys he'd been given from his pocket. Thankfully, Luke was kind enough to keep the Jeep parked in place, the headlights the only source of light to help Lance see what he was doing. There was a small exterior porch light mounted to the right of the front door, just about level with Lance's head, but it was off. Lance looked at the single bulb beneath the cloudy glass enclosure and figured the odds of it working were slim to none.

He moved to insert one of the small brass keys into the dead-bolt, adjusting his body so the Jeep's headlights would shine onto the door, and that's when he heard the voice. It was female, hushed, yet panicked.

"THANK GOD YOU'RE HERE! YOU'VE GOT TO HELP US!"

Lance spun around so quickly he dropped the keys, the soft jangling of the brass hitting the wooden boards below drowned out by the constant whoosh of the falling rain. His looked all around, his eyes darting across the porch, before staring like a deer, literally into the headlights of Luke's Jeep. Because of the lights, he was unable to make out Luke and Susan. Could only imagine their perplexed expressions as they watched him become startled on the porch steps and then stare back at them.

But maybe they weren't surprised. This was the spook farm, after all.

Lance stood still for another few seconds, listening. The voice had not come from inside the home. It had sounded as though it were right on the porch with him, circling his head loud and clear.

Now all he heard was the rain and the Jeep's idling engine.

He sighed, bent and picked up the keys. Then he waved farewell to his new friends, signaling all was okay, unlocked the spook house's front door, pushed it open, and stepped inside.

[8]

ONCE LANCE HAD CLOSED THE DOOR AND RELOCKED IT behind him, it didn't take long for the dim light coming through the filthy windows from the Jeep's headlights to fade away and then vanish completely. Despite Susan and Luke's kindness, it was as though they'd had all they could handle of the town's infamous spook farm on this literal dark and stormy night. No sense in becoming a supporting cast member in an actual ghost story, if they could help it. They'd done their duty by delivering Lance here, and now it was time to hightail it back to the real world.

Lance didn't blame them. They had a movie to catch.

He longed for a life so simple that his biggest worry would be whether he'd make it to a movie in time for the previews, and if he wanted popcorn or a box of Junior Mints from the snack bar.

It was a life he'd never have. Though he allowed himself a momentary flash of a daydream—him and Leah holding hands, side-by-side in squeaky theater chairs, laughing at something funny onscreen; her grabbing his arm and burying her face in his shoulder as the monster devoured a victim; him looking over and watching a tear slide down her perfect cheek when the guy finally got the girl.

"Who's at the door? Is it him? Tell me!"

A thunderous male voice echoed all around Lance, his heart leaping into this throat as he was snapped out of his moment of fantasy and wishful thinking. His eyes had not yet adjusted to the darkness of the home's interior, and he spun around blindly by the door, eyes searching, body tense and poised to fend off an attacker.

He saw nothing, his eyes slowly focusing and turning the pitch black into a deep gray, his heart like a marching band drummer in his ears. Vague shapes began to take form: a set of stairs to his left, an entryway into what looked like a living room just past them. The amorphous blob of what was probably a sofa pushed against one wall. A smaller object to its right, perhaps an armchair. There was a hallway straight ahead, though the gray faded back into blackness halfway down, the little light from the front windows being swallowed whole.

Lance stayed perfectly still, straining his ears to hear what obviously wasn't there. But even though there were no more voices, he did hear something else. It was as though the outside sounds—the rain and wind—were intensified, louder than they should be. Not coming from behind him, but ahead, from deeper in the house.

As his adrenaline faded and his heartbeat's rhythm returned to normal, a wonderful thought came to him.

Turn on the lights, Lance.

It was true. Assuming the weather hadn't caused some sort of damage to knock out a power pole somewhere, the house should, of course, very well have electricity. If it didn't, Lance was going to have a chat with Mr. Richard Bellows about withholding information that could have very well affected Lance's decision (*Ha! Like he had a choice.*) to rent the property. Like the inability to turn on a light, or, you know, charge a cell phone. Even if Lance's phone had long ago been eligible for early retirement.

As Lance was turning around to look for some sort of light switch on the wall near the door, an angry gust of wind screamed through and rattled the walls and windows, and what sounded like a loud clap of thunder exploded from inside the house ... from down the darkened hallway. The noise, like a starter pistol, propelled Lance into motion. He tossed his backpack to the floor and ran down the hallway, toward the source of the noise. He still clutched the umbrella tightly, supposing he could use it as a potential weapon if need be. If Annabelle Winters had been able to fight off a demon with a rolling pin in Westhaven, Lance would be disappointed in himself if he couldn't inflict some damage with an umbrella. It had a pointy end, after all.

He half ran, half fumbled his way down the hall, the wooden floorboards beneath his feet creaking and groaning under his weight. He entered the darkness with a reckless abandon which he only had a moment to second-guess himself on before the tunnel of black faded back into a dimly lit gray as he spilled into the kitchen, where the faint moonlight that was poking through the storm clouds fell through more dirty windows.

Another howl of wind slammed into the house, and this time Lance saw for himself the source of the loud explosion, as the house's back door was caught in the gust and slammed against the wall with enough force to nearly bounce itself back closed.

The back door was open.

This explained the intensified sounds of rain and wind Lance had heard from the front of the house.

But, and more importantly, when combined with the flicker

of movement Lance had sworn he'd seen from behind one of the front windows as Luke's Jeep had approached, it also fed into another theory Lance was forced to entertain.

Somebody had been in the house when Lance had arrived.

Lance stepped cautiously toward the open door. Rainwater had blown just inside the threshold, and Lance's sneakers squeaked on the floor. He gripped his umbrella tightly and cocked it back over his head, ready to swing down should somebody try and rush him.

Nothing happened. Nobody was there.

Lance stood at the open door and stared out into the night, unable to see much further than a few feet out.

"Hello?" he said, almost too quietly to be heard over the rain and wind.

Of course, there was no answer. Just the continued onslaught of water and the purr of the wind.

Lance reached out, grabbed the doorknob and pulled the door shut. There was a deadbolt here as well, and Lance thumbed it locked and stared at it.

Did whoever was here have a key?

He made a mental note to make sure to stop by R.G. Homes the next time he was in town and ask Richard Bellows a few questions. *"So, Rich ... Anybody else living in the house you rented to me?"*

Lance turned around in the darkened kitchen and leaned back against the door. He thought of Susan's words earlier.

"I also don't think you fully know what you're getting into."

Lance sighed. "Maybe I don't," he said to the house. "Maybe I never do."

[9]

Lance slouched down in his bus seat and pressed his knees into the seat ahead of him, wedging himself into a comfortable position. There was nobody in the seat ahead of him, so he wasn't worried about bothering someone. In fact, there was nobody on this bus at all. For some reason, this didn't strike Lance as odd. He often felt he was heading places nobody else wanted to go.

Rain pelted the bus, the sound of the falling droplets rhythmic and soothing. His eyes were heavy, his hoodie warm, and he wanted nothing more than to rest his head back and take a nap until he reached...

Where was he headed? He couldn't remember.

But before he could rest, there was something he had to do. Something he'd waited too long to do. He slid his cell phone from the front pocket of his hoodie and flipped it open. A gust of wind rushed in and shook the bus, water slamming into the side with a loud splattering of wet noise. Lance thumbed his way to his text messages and clicked the keys until he had composed a new message to Leah.

He stared at the screen for a long time. His words were few

and simple, but they were the absolute truth. They were the feeling he could not shake, could not successfully repress for any extended period of time.

He moved his thumb to the button to send the message and—

A thunderous pounding rattled the window next to him. Deep, staccato knocks that sounded more like a hammer on wood than glass. Lance dropped his cell phone into his lap, startled, and looked to his right.

The bus was moving fast down a highway, the landscape blurring by in a rush of dark sky and rainwater. But despite the noise, the pounding, it wasn't what was outside the bus that caught Lance off guard. It was what he saw inside.

Lance's reflection in the bus window was not his own. It was the same shape, mirroring his body exactly, but it was not him. Lance raised his arm halfway from his lap, and the reflection in the window did the same. Only the arm in the reflection was bare, the body in the window wearing a short-sleeved white undershirt instead of Lance's sweatshirt. The arm was blood-speckled, the chest of the once-white shirt now a dark crimson bib, streaks and splatters of blood all over.

The head of the body in the window was nearly blown completely off. A gaping hole where the face should have been. Lance could see through it, catching a glimpse of the bus seats behind him.

Susan's words floated to Lance: "Mary's dad killed himself in the recliner in the living room, half his head blown off."

A strange fear rose in Lance's chest and—

The pounding noise, rattling wood and glass from somewhere below him, woke Lance from his dream. He sat up quickly, eyes squinting against harsh sunlight coming in through the slats in the opened blinds. Shielded his eyes with one hand and tried to focus his vision. He looked around him, remembered where he was.

After the incident with the open back door the evening before, Lance had gone around the home and made sure all the doors and windows were locked, while also exploring the house's layout. Verdict: it was small by today's standards, old and in need of much work, but plenty big enough for Lance, and it would likely be charming once it had been cleaned and fixed up a bit. You know, assuming you could forget about the horrific murders that had taken place.

The ground floor consisted of the living room, kitchen, small bathroom, and an extra room that had apparently been used as a dining room, due to the large table that took up most of the tiny space. There was a door in the interior wall of the kitchen that Lance had assumed was a pantry or closet, until he had seen the sliding bolt used to keep it locked. When he'd opened it, he'd been presented with a set of wooden stairs leading down into darkness. A basement or cellar. Brave and rational as Lance was, he decided he'd wait until the sun was up to see what might lie beneath the surface of the farmhouse.

Upstairs was even simpler. Two bedrooms—a larger one to the right of the staircase, which Lance had assumed to be the master because of its size and larger bed, and a smaller room with a twin-sized bed pushed against one wall and a small white dresser and makeup mirror pressed against the opposite wall by the door. There was an empty closet next to the dresser, nothing but one empty wooden rod across the top. Not so much as a single clothes hanger left behind. There was a full bathroom in between the two bedrooms, directly above the kitchen below.

Whether the day of travel had truly exhausted him, or the dark evening hour, coupled with the secluded location and the noise of the rainstorm outside, had simply relaxed him in a way he'd not been able to achieve for quite some time, Lance had found himself ready to do nothing but sleep after his brief exploration of the farmhouse, resigned to push aside all sense of duty and desire to understand his new situation until he could rest his body and his mind.

He'd chosen the smaller bedroom—Mary's bedroom, he was certain—and collapsed onto the bed, not moving until now.

Another barrage of pounding rattled the front of the house below, and Lance swung his legs off the side of the bed. He considered grabbing his umbrella, which lay next to his backpack on the floor next to the dresser, but decided the situation likely didn't require melee weaponry and hurried out of the room and down the stairs.

With the thought that a likely criminal or murderer wouldn't be keen on knocking first, Lance quickly unlocked the front deadbolt and opened the door.

The bright sunlight assaulted him, and Lance had to take a step back and shield his eyes again. On the front porch, half-silhouetted by the sun, was the man from Mama's.

The sheriff.

The two men stood silently on opposite sides of the threshold, a sense of appraisal heavy in the air between them. The air blowing in was cool and sweet, the aftermath of the heavy rains the night before, but along with it Lance could also feel the coldness coming from the sheriff. The same sense of loss and sadness he'd sensed in Mama's.

"Good morning," the sheriff said. "I'm sorry if I woke you."

Lance had no idea what the time was. No idea if it was early, or if he'd slept long past any time acceptable for a responsible adult. All he could do was smile and say, "What can I do for you, Sheriff?"

The man did not smile back. "How do you know I'm the sheriff?"

The man was wearing similar attire as the night before. Dark blue tactical pants with black work books, cream-colored sweater beneath that same black rain jacket. The man was maybe three or four inches shorter than Lance, but his body was thick, muscled and strong. But his body language, the way he stood, the way his shoulders slumped and his head hung down, was the opposite. There was a weakness, or maybe an unwillingness ... a struggle, carried along with him.

"I was in Mama's yesterday evening," Lance said. "I heard the waitress call you Sheriff."

The man nodded his head. "You're more observant than most."

Lance said nothing.

The sheriff looked as though he was searching for something to say but was coming up short.

Finally, Lance nudged the encounter along by asking, "Can I help you, Sheriff? Do you want to come inside? I'd offer you coffee, but I haven't had a chance to go grocery shopping yet."

The sheriff's eyes looked over Lance's shoulder, darting a quick glance deeper into the house. He shook his head. "No, that's okay. Would you mind stepping out here for me? No sense in leaving the door open."

Lance's heart rate kicked up a bit at this. He couldn't quite pinpoint why the man made him uneasy. Despite Lance's initial fear, he couldn't convince himself the man was here to question or harass him about any of his previous doings—Westhaven, in particular. But Lance was wary as he slowly stepped out onto the wooden porch and gently closed the door behind him.

The grass sparkled with half-melted frost. The dampness of the porch boards seeped through the bottom of Lance's socks, and he wished he'd taken the extra few seconds to step into his sneakers. He pulled his hands into the sleeves of his hoodie and then crossed his arms, trying not to look confrontational. Over the sheriff's shoulder, he saw the Crown Vic parked in the driveway. The engine was still running.

When he looked back to the sheriff, he found the man

staring at him intently. His eyes focused in determination, as if Lance were a complex equation on a math test. After another long moment of silence, Lance finally asked, "Sir, please don't take this for rudeness, or impatience. It's purely a willingness to help." A short pause, then, "Why are you here?"

As if whatever shroud had been covering the sheriff's visit had suddenly been ripped away, the man raised his head and stood straight. "Actually, that's exactly what I came here to ask you."

"Sir?"

"Why are you here?"

"In town?" Lance asked.

The sheriff shrugged. "Sure. But more specifically, why this house?"

Lance spoke carefully. There was a hidden accusation or suspicion here, though he wasn't sure what it might be. "I'm in town for work," he said.

"Work?"

"I own a consulting firm."

"So what do you do?"

"I consult."

He wanted to take that one back, apply a little less sarcasm. But vagueness was his friend in these types of situations. That was a lesson Lance had learned a long time ago.

The sheriff only nodded and continued with, "And the house?"

"What about it, sir?"

"Why are you staying here?"

"The gentleman at the real estate office in town offered it to me as an inexpensive place to stay short-term." This was only half the truth, but Lance suspected the sheriff cared little for the fact that Lance had felt compelled by other unseen powers to stay here.

"Richard Bellows?"

Lance nodded. "Yes, I believe that was his name. Nice guy."

"Indeed he is. But why not just stay at a hotel, if it's short-term? There's some nice ones in the city."

Lance nodded. "I'm sure," he said. "I guess I'm just partial to small towns. Nothing quite like them, right? Plus, with the nature of my work, I'm never quite sure how long I'll need to stay around."

The sheriff completely disregarded Lance's opinion on small towns and launched right into the meat and potatoes. "Son, do you have any idea what happened in this house?"

Lance looked the man in the eye. "I do, sir."

Nothing more. No need to delve into the details. Especially with local law enforcement.

As if the sheriff had finally cracked the code, finally unearthed some sort of true reasoning behind Lance's visit, he said, "And, let me guess, this consulting firm you own, do you happen to specialize in paranormal investigation? Ghost hunting, if you want to be blunt about it?"

Lance said nothing.

"We get kids come up here all the time, try to break in and have séances or bring fancy equipment to try and catch ghouls on video and then post it on the Internet and make a buck." The man looked down and shook his head, a wave of that coldness Lance had felt before rushing out. "It's disrespectful. What happened here was a tragedy and nothing else, and people shouldn't go poking their noses in it for the sake of their own damn entertainment and profit."

He looked up to Lance with tired eyes that spoke volumes.

"I agree, sir," Lance said.

This seemed to catch the sheriff by surprise. He narrowed his eyes. "You do?"

"Yes, sir."

Lance could understand the man's wariness. Lance was fairly young, and, let's be honest, dressed far below the business casual dress code. He didn't look like somebody in town for work. And he was sure the sheriff really had dealt with all kinds of thrill seekers and paranormal enthusiasts in the years since the murders had taken place here. But, as far as Lance was concerned, the sheriff's frustration, if not downright defensiveness when it came to this house, seemed to carry a personal agenda that Lance was desperate to learn more about. Somehow, the man was connected to this place. Though it occurred to Lance that the connection might only be a tired and downtrodden sheriff not fully accepting the reality of what had happened on the night of what might have been his town's biggest tragedy.

Lance had heard Susan's story about what had happened that night. There were holes in the story, for sure. Maybe the sheriff was desperate to fill them.

"I can assure you, sir, I'm here for neither entertainment nor profit from this house. It was a complete fluke that this is where I ended up when I came into town last night." The part about it all being a fluke wasn't entirely accurate, but Lance tossed this into the "white lie" category for the sheriff's sake. "But, to be honest, I'm happy I found the place. It's very peaceful up here."

The sheriff seemed to be out of ammunition for his line of questioning. He was quiet for a bit, somewhat appeased, it seemed, by Lance's answers. Then he turned and looked around behind him, back toward the Crown Vic in the driveway. Then he turned back to Lance and asked, "How did you get here?"

"Sir?"

The sheriff waved a hand behind him. "No car. How'd you get up here last night?"

"I got a ride with a friend."

"Friend? You know folks around here?"

Lance shrugged. "A new friend, sir."

The sheriff looked as though he was ready to pounce on Lance's vagueness this time, but then his face softened, as if he realized he might be pushing a bit too hard without much in the way of probable cause. This was a good thing, because Lance wasn't ready to give up Susan's name. She was a nice young girl who'd done him a favor. Luke, as well. Lance wasn't going to return the favor by tossing their names out to the sheriff, even if they'd done nothing wrong. To Lance, it was a matter of principle.

Or maybe the sheriff thought he'd get more in the way of truthfulness from Lance if he eased up and started to play a bit nicer. Just about justifying Lance's assumption of this, the sheriff asked, "Everything been okay up here since you arrived? No problems with any trespassers? Haven't seen anything out of the ordinary?"

Well, sir, now that you mention it, when I got here last night I'm almost positive somebody was here before me and left the back door wide open when they ran away. Oh, and I'm hearing voices. Other than that, everything's peachy.

"No, sir. Got here after dinner and went to bed shortly after. I was pretty tired after traveling. Didn't wake up until you knocked on the door."

Lance wasn't sure why he didn't want to tell the sheriff about somebody potentially being in the house last night. But sometimes, and usually at the right times, he felt that keeping that sort of information to himself worked out for the best. The sheriff was already on high alert about the house. Lance wasn't ready to dump any additional fuel on that fire.

The sheriff gave Lance another long stare. *He knows,* Lance thought. *Whether it's his police intuition or something else, he knows there's more to me than meets the eye. Knows I'm here for something else. He just can't prove it.*

Finally, the man stuck out his hand. "Sorry to bother you this morning, Mister..."

Lance reached out his own hand. "Call me Lance."

"Sheriff Ray Kruger," the sheriff said as they shook. "Don't hesitate to call the department if you notice anybody strange around, or have anybody bother you. Somebody always shows up this time of year."

The two men released each other's hands, and Lance stood still, his face frozen for just a moment, but long enough for Ray Kruger to notice. "Son?" he asked.

Lance's vision focused back on the sheriff and he quickly asked, "This time of year, sir?"

Sheriff Kruger sighed and started to walk down the porch steps. "It's the anniversary of the murders this week. Always brings the weirdos out the woodwork."

Of course, Lance thought. *One weirdo, reporting for duty, sir.*

Sheriff Kruger opened the driver's door of the Crown Vic and then looked back up to Lance. "I'm headed back into town. Do you want a ride? Do that grocery shopping you were talking about?"

Lance wasn't sure how he was going to get back into town, but he wasn't sure he trusted the situation of being locked in a moving vehicle with the sheriff right now. He smiled and waved away the offer. "I appreciate it, sir. But I've only been awake about ten minutes. I'll head in a little later."

Sheriff Kruger nodded once and got into the car, doing a three-point turn in the yard before driving away. Lance stood and watched the Crown Vic grow smaller and smaller before finally disappearing, then he turned and went back into the house.

Wondering what exactly he'd just seen when he'd shaken Sheriff Ray Kruger's hand.

[10]

Instant downloads. That was what Lance had grown to start calling them.

Just another of his unexplainable, uncontrollable gifts.

For as far back as he could remember, Lance had been able to snatch glimpses of other people's lives with just the briefest of touches. These glimpses could be montage-like snapshots of a person's entire life or circumstance, or sometimes a more specific scene, a random memory or event from a person's past.

Though Lance knew they were never actually random. What he saw when he received these instant downloads almost always played a role in something Lance was involved with. Sometimes as a direct source of information, often an indirect push or reassurance. They were helpful hints from the Universe. If life were a video game, these glimpses would be a cheat code.

Which was why Lance found this particular gift so incredibly frustrating to live with. He had no ability to control which person's memory he was allowed to peek inside. No sense of when or where this ability would kick in or what answers it would provide. How much easier this would all be if he could simply pick out a target, bump shoulders with them in the supermarket and then get all the answers he needed.

Sometimes he felt the Universe just liked to make him work harder than he needed to. A cosmic joke. Always tested.

Or maybe there was only so much he, as a mortal, could handle. There had to be limits to his abilities, sure. He understood that, if nothing else about who he was and what he could do.

But the Reverend and the Surfer...

They were more. They were stronger.

And that was why they terrified him.

Lance stood on the front porch of the farmhouse and leaned against one of the splintering banisters. His eyes looked toward the end of the driveway and the mountain forest beyond, where the sheriff's car had just driven out of sight, but his vision was unfocused. He was recalling what he'd just seen. When he'd shaken Sheriff Ray Kruger's hand, he'd been expecting nothing, too focused on the strange conversation he'd been engaged in, but instead of nothing, he was hit with a flash of memory of

A young girl, maybe six or seven years old, and a boy maybe a year or two older. Outside. A backyard. A small vinyl-sided house in the background. Simple porch with two patio chairs and a child's plastic picnic table. The boy and girl were both wearing bathing suits. The boy's a solid blue pair of trunks. The girl's a matching blue one-piece that tied around the back of her neck. They both had globs of white sunscreen on their noses, running through the grass in a chorus of giggles and squeals as they headed toward a small round inflatable pool. A dull green garden hose snaking from the house, through the yard, and then climbing up the side of the pool and resting inside, filling the plastic with ice-cold city water. It was summer. The sun was hot. The water would feel good. They jumped in and splashed and giggled some more. There was a plastic submarine from the bathtub and a rubber frog that would squirt water from its mouth. They played for what seemed like hours, until the water was warm and the sun was getting too hot on their bare backs and the boredom set in and they grew annoyed with each other, as kids tend to do. The girl splashed the boy and water got in his eyes. He didn't like it and splashed her back. She yelled at him not to splash her and she splashed him again, this time with more effort, more water finding his face. The boy, a kid with a temper, lunged forward and grabbed the little girl's head and pushed it under the water. Not long, just enough to scare her. Two seconds. But it was enough. When the girl's face resurfaced, there were tears and cries of anguish. She slapped at the boy's arms and chest and scrambled over the edge of the pool running on wobbly legs back toward the house crying out, "Mamma! Mamma! Ray tried to drowneded me!" The cries and the looming fear of his mother's anger sparked his temper again, and he lashed out, not thinking of further consequences. He grabbed the nozzle of the garden hose from the pool and lifted it, grabbing the hose with both hands. He watched the girl's feet run through the grass, closer and closer to the patio, and then, timing it perfectly, the boy yanked on the hose, drawing it taut, creating a tripwire in the yard. The hose snapped up at the girl's ankles and her feet tangled, and that's when the boy realized he'd been too late. Saw what was going to happen and suddenly wished more than anything he could go back in time, just a few seconds, and do things differently. Because the little girl had gotten too close to the porch, and when she fell, she fell forward, going down down down, her knees hitting first, thankfully, before her chin cracked on the concrete edge of the patio. The boy was running then. Running before the piercing cry of pain, a wail of agony only a child can produce, hit his eardrums like a siren. He reached the little girl at the same time as his mother, who'd just come running through the back sliding glass door. His mother had swooped the girl up in her arms and the boy had seen it at once. The split in the girl's chin, just to the left of center. The blood that had begun to pour. So much blood.

That's what Lance had pulled from Sheriff Ray Kruger with a quick handshake. A memory from what had to be the man's childhood (*"Mamma! Mamma! Ray tried to drowneded me!"*). But the relevance was lost on Lance.

He knew it meant something. The downloads always did. But Lance was smart enough to know he wasn't going to piece it all together standing on the front porch any longer. He filed the memory away, and when his stomach grumbled he remembered he had no food in the house.

It was time to go back into town.

Lance stood in front of the upstairs bathroom mirror and brushed his teeth. Traveling light had proven not to be much of an issue for him over the past few months, which he attributed to the simplistic lifestyle he'd been raised in. Pamela Brody had never been much for possessions. Books and family and pie and tea. Walks to the park. Farmers markets and friends and the feel of a fall breeze rolling in. These were the things that mattered most to her.

They'd never needed much to be happy. And Lance didn't need much now. Aside from the few thing's he'd kept in his backpack in general—the things that had come with him when he'd been forced to flee his hometown the night his mother had died—he'd been traveling from town to town for the past couple months with nothing but a few changes of clothes, his small toiletry bag (a purchase he'd made at a small drugstore on his first stop after Westhaven), a first aid kit that was really nothing more than a couple Band-Aids, a small roll of gauze and a tiny tube of antibacterial ointment, and his cell phone and charger. He picked up items now and then that might serve some purpose to him—a small butane lighter, a pair of cheap sunglasses, some hand sanitizer. Normal things people might carry around with them. He also always tried to keep a few snacks and at least one bottle of water in the backpack as well. For emergencies.

If he was being honest with himself, despite the tragedy that had unfolded that awful night in Hillston—the night that officially ended the longest chapter of his life and started another— Lance was proud of how he'd been doing since leaving home. He wouldn't go so far as to consider himself sheltered—he'd attended public school and lived a fairly normal adolescent life (aside from, you know ... the ghosts and the visions and everything else completely *not* normal about him)—but his world had been confined to a fairly small geographical location. Any trips outside of this area had been brief and infrequent. The night he'd stepped onto that bus in Hillston, he'd essentially stepped into the rest of the world.

He finished brushing his teeth and put his toothbrush back in the toiletry pouch. The bathroom was spacious enough, with the sink and vanity, toilet, and a standalone bathtub with showerhead against the back wall, just beneath a window that overlooked the backyard. The fixtures were grimy with soap scum and mildew, and cobwebs hung from the corners and along the tops of the windows, but again, if the place were cleaned and fixed up a bit, it would be perfectly suitable. Lance didn't need much. He leaned over and rinsed his mouth with cold water from the tap. It was cool and clean-tasting, likely water from a well this far outside of town. He dumped out the travel-sized bottle of shaving cream and his disposable razor and lathered his face. But when he looked up from the sink to the mirror hanging on the wall, he froze.

Something was different.

He'd stared at himself in the mirror as he'd been brushing his teeth and decided that he'd needed to shave, and while the image of himself now looked the same—except for the white beard of foam on his face—he couldn't shake a sudden tingling at the base of his skull that told him there was more to the mirror now than there had been before.

He kept staring. Looked into his own eyes for a full ten or fifteen seconds, waiting for something to happen. He couldn't say what, but a sudden expectation filled him. He looked at the reflection of the room behind him in the glass. It likewise seemed unchanged.

And then it occurred to him that perhaps the expectation was actually on *him*. As if the mirror itself were waiting, urging him to take the next step.

If that was the case, the mirror was out of luck. Because Lance had no idea what he was supposed to do here. He took a step back and looked at the mirror in full, studying its shape and its position. Nothing looked out of the ordinary at first, except that it seemed to be hung a little high up on the wall. Lance himself was six-six, and most household bathroom mirrors only just managed to capture the bottom half of his face. Here, however, he almost appeared a normal height. Maybe close to a foot of mirror still visible above where his head's reflection stopped.

But aside from this small anomaly, everything looked just as it should.

He stepped back toward the sink and leaned to the side, seeing the mirror had some depth to it, a good four of five inches off the wall. *A medicine cabinet*, he thought, feeling as though he'd finally gotten the clue. He reached out and grabbed the bottom of the mirror and tugged gently. It popped open with no trouble, swinging out wide on its hinges.

The inside was empty, two dead flies legs-up on one of the shallow shelves.

Frustrated, Lance closed the mirror again and stared once more, still feeling an unseen hand at his back, pushing him toward the mirror. And then another idea hit him, one that seemed ridiculous at first, but not all impossible when you'd seen some of the things that Lance had.

He reached his hand out, slowly, tentatively, fingers hesitant as though they might suddenly get burned, or chopped off. Or somebody might reach out from the other side and grab his hand and pull him into...

Into what?

He sucked in a deep breath and pushed his hand forward the last few inches, and when his hand hit the glass, nothing happened.

Nothing at all.

And all at once, the invisible hand nudging him along disappeared and he felt completely silly.

Another quick succession of knocks on the front door rattled from down the stairs. Lance whipped his head toward the sound.

Another visitor, and I still haven't had breakfast.

[11]

So far, the entire situation had been strange and, as usual, completely unpredictable. Lance had stepped off a bus less than twenty-four hours ago, and since then he'd somehow rented a farmhouse for himself, made two new friends after dining on the best meatloaf he'd ever tasted, heard voices from unseen sources, probably had a home intruder, slept in a dead girl's bed, and been woken from some sort of nightmare by the local sheriff, who suspected Lance was up to no good.

So naturally, with his curiosity piqued and his senses on the highest alert, desperately searching for anything that might be valuable information, when the knock came from the front door, he didn't hesitate. He rushed from the bathroom, bounded down the creaking stairs two at a time, and pulled open the door so fast he nearly ripped off the handle.

"Oh! God bless America!"

A tall woman with blond hair pulled back into a ponytail, wearing slim-fitting blue jeans, sneakers, and a red-and-white long-sleeved flannel shirt with the cuffs rolled up to her forearms, jumped, shouted, and took two steps back. A plastic bucket full of various cleaning supplies swung wildly from one hand, a pair of yellow rubber gloves draped over the side.

She laughed, a nervous giggle, and then tucked a stray strand of hair behind her ear. Then she stood, smiling. A relaxed posture. Friendly. "Sorry," she said. "You startled me."

Lance studied the woman on the porch, raising one hand to shield his eyes from the sun that was still rising further above the trees and hilltop in the distance. He glanced behind her and saw a Mercedes SUV in the driveway, parked in nearly the same spot where Sheriff Ray Kruger had parked less than fifteen minutes ago. Heck, the two of them might have passed each other on the road.

Lance looked from the Mercedes to the cleaning bucket, then back to the woman's face. She was likely late thirties, early forties, slim build. Fit. Like somebody who probably did yoga and drank smoothies for breakfast. Attractive.

(*I can't get any cleaners there until tomorrow, I'm afraid.*)

Lance remembered Richard Bellows's words from yesterday afternoon. And then ... it clicked. Lance took himself back to that backroom office. The cramped workspace. All the pictures of the man's family on the wall. Remembered the faces.

"You're Mr. Bellows's wife," Lance said.

The woman laughed, made a face of mock disgust. "Oh, please. That's way too official." She stuck out a hand. "Victoria. And, yes, Rich is my husband. You're Lance, right?"

Lance shook her hand, bracing himself for another rush of memory, another download. He got nothing. Of course. Never did when he was ready for it. Her hand was cool and soft, but her grip was strong. She smelled faintly of strawberries. "Nice to meet you," Lance said. "So you're the 'cleaners' I was promised?" He pointed to the bucket full of supplies.

Victoria Bellows held the plastic bucket up to her face and grinned. "I'm afraid so. Hard to find good help around this town. So you're stuck with me." She laughed, and it sounded genuine and pleasant. She struck Lance as a woman who lived a very happy and comfortable life. And there was good in her. Somebody to whom the word *self-importance* did not apply; someone who didn't hold herself above anyone, despite circumstance. She'd just driven a vehicle that Lance guessed could easily cost fifty grand to come clean an old farmhouse for a stranger. And she was doing it with a smile and a laugh.

"Uh ... Lance?"

"Yes, ma'am?"

"Did I catch you in the middle of something?" She made a quick gesture at brushing her face with her index finger, and Lance felt the heat rise to his cheeks, suddenly very aware of the layer of shaving cream lathered onto his face. Right on time, a glob of the stuff fell from his chin and plopped onto the boards of the porch, splattering like a drop of bird shit.

The two of them stood and stared at the mess for what felt to Lance like half an hour. Then, to his horror, another glob fell and splattered next to the first one, the porch beginning to look like a crude Rorschach test.

Victoria Bellows let out a quick, explosive laugh when the second drop hit, falling into a fit of giggles and shooing Lance back inside the house. "Go," she said. "Finish up. I'll wipe this up and then start downstairs."

"Sorry," Lance said. "But thank you." He turned on his heel and bounded up the stairs, marveling over just how much of a doofus he could make himself out to be with women. He wasn't one to embarrass easily, but even he knew that the anorexic-Santa-Claus-in-comfy-clothes look wasn't his best first impression.

He shaved quickly, but carefully. He'd like to avoid bloodshed today, especially his own, if he could at all help it. As he ran the razor over his face, he couldn't keep his eyes from occasionally refocusing on the mirror itself instead of his reflection in it. Continued trying to look deeper at the object itself, reaching out again, cautiously, for that sense of expectancy that'd seemed to be calling out to him earlier. He looked past his reflection and into the background, at the wall and linen closet door behind him.

He got nothing. Saw nothing but what was supposed to be there.

A sound of running water from somewhere below him shoved the possibility of the mirror having more meaning to the back of his mind. He finished shaving, rinsed his face, and then stripped down and pulled fresh boxers, socks, and a t-shirt from his backpack, changing into them. He gave his hoodie a sniff, found it more than acceptable, and then tugged it back on. After the day on the bus yesterday, and then the walking in the rain, he wanted a shower badly, but that would have to wait until later. He shoved his dirty clothes into a plastic shopping bag at the bottom of his backpack, tossed in his toiletry bag, and then zipped the whole thing up and swung it over his shoulder. He didn't like to leave anything behind when he left places he was staying. Mostly because he couldn't quite trust the idea that he'd ever return to retrieve them. Better to be prepared. At least, as prepared as he could be.

He found Victoria Bellows in the half bathroom downstairs, yellow rubber gloves nearly up to her elbows, bent over the sink, scrubbing hard on a green ring around the drain. Lance watched the muscles in her back and shoulders work beneath the fabric of her shirt and thought maybe yoga was only the tip of the iceberg.

Victoria caught sight of him behind her in the mirror above the sink, and instead of asking him why he was being creepy and just standing there staring, she used a yellow finger to point up toward the light fixture. Two of the four bulbs were burnt out.

"I've got a pack of bulbs in the car, too," she said, halting the scrubbing for a moment and turning on the hot water tap. Pipes gurgled and groaned somewhere in the wall before water spat from the faucet. It was murky at first but cleared quickly. "Rich said you might need a few. Been a while since anyone's been here."

She rinsed the sink out, scrubbed away another bit of grime, then rinsed again. Satisfied, she stood and turned to look at Lance, eyed the straps of his backpack. "Headed out?"

Lance nodded. "I am. Though if you want some help, I'm more than happy to stay."

This wasn't exactly true. Lance, though he tended to be well-organized and neat, hated the act of actually cleaning as much as the next guy. But, as a gentleman, he felt obligated to at least offer his assistance. Especially since Victoria Bellows seemed to be doing this work as a favor.

She waved him off, pulling off one of her gloves and wiping a small droplet of sweat from her brow. "Hot in here," she said. "I might open the windows, if you don't mind."

"Be my guest."

She nodded and slid past him in the hallway, pulling the cord to raise the blinds on one of the front windows and then unlatching the lock and throwing the window open. Immediately, the cool fall air found its way inside. She repeated the process for the remaining windows in the front of the house and then turned, saying, "Okay, that's better."

Lance stared at her, trying to work something out in his mind. Something that had at first seemed normal but now seemed out of place. She saw him looking her over and cocked her head, smiling. Not suspicious. Curious. "What?"

"I've got to ask," Lance said. "Why are you here?"

She didn't miss a beat. Held up her rubber gloves. "To clean."

Lance nodded. "Right. But why you? Why not an actual cleaning company? Somebody who does this for a living, or a part-time job, or whatever. Surely you don't clean all of Mr. Bellows's rental properties. He's got to have a company or business he uses, right?"

Victoria's face fell, slightly. Not in a disappointed look, but more in a "So I guess we have to have to this conversation" look. She sighed. "He does usually have somebody else do it, yes. A local crew. They do great work. But..." She paused, as if contemplating whether she wanted to actually say it all out loud.

Lance finished for her. "They won't come here because of what happened. Because of the murders."

Victoria's posture relaxed again and she winked at him. "Bingo."

"They think it's haunted?"

Victoria opened her mouth to speak, but paused again. Only shrugged and said, "Something like that."

"Something like that?"

Victoria sighed again. "Look, I don't want to fill your head with a bunch of nonsense. Scare you out of here over something so silly."

"You won't scare me. I promise." Lance said it so matter-of-factly that Victoria gave him a hard, silent look. Lance didn't elaborate.

Then she smiled big and bright and shrugged again, as if about to reveal the punchline of a joke. "Fine," she said. "The cleaners won't come because they think the place is haunted, but it's a bit more than that. They believe the girl that lived here —Mary was her name—they think she was a witch."

Lance said nothing.

"And they think her spirit is still here and is actually evil. Ready to dole out harm and misfortune to anyone who trespasses on her property."

The way Victoria Bellows said it, all with an undertone of complete mockery and disbelief, as one might when discussing the latest Elvis sighting, or ridiculous tales of alien encounters whose only witnesses were backwoods hillbillies with barely enough teeth to chew gum, told Lance all he needed to know about her opinion on the subject.

He smiled at her, posing the question lightly. "And you don't believe any of it?"

Victoria shook her head. "Not a word." Then asked, "You?"

"I'll believe it when I see it." *And if anybody is going to see it, it's me.* "So the cleaners are afraid of a witch, and you decided you'd come clean instead?"

"What can I say?" Victoria said, making her way toward him, back to the bathroom. "I love my husband, and he needed some help. He said you seemed like a really great guy and he felt terrible renting the place to you, knowing it was likely filthy inside. He said he should have been more adamant about not letting you stay here until we could get it in order."

"He said I was a great guy?"

Again, the shrug. "You must have made an impression." Then: "Was he wrong?"

Lance smiled. "I like to think he wasn't."

"Good. Now it's my turn to ask the question. Why are *you* here?"

Lance leaned against the wall, watching Victoria remove a spray bottle from the bucket and start spraying disinfectant on the bathroom counter. "You know you're the second person today to ask me that question?"

"Oh, really? Who was first?"

"Sheriff Kruger."

The spray bottle stopped spraying and she turned to look at him, seriousness in her eyes. "Ray was here?"

Lance nodded. "Maybe fifteen minutes before you."

"Interesting." She gave Lance a look, chewed on her bottom lip for a moment, thinking. "I didn't think he actually came up here anymore. Rumor is he always sends somebody else. A deputy, or some lackey. Though I think most folks have sorta forgotten about this place."

"Why doesn't he come up here?" Lance asked, feeling close to something, some explanation as to why the sheriff was so suspicious of him, why he carried with him such a coldness.

Victoria looked down and shook her head. Spoke softly. "He just took it all so hard, and he's never really completely gotten over it. But who would, really?"

Lance said nothing.

"The worst part—or maybe the saddest part—is that after it happened, he went on for days, mumbling how he knew nothing good would happen here. That too much evil had already happened in this house and it only made sense it would happen again. He said he should have never let her move here. But he thought he was doing the right thing. Thought he was helping her out."

The comment about too much evil in the house completely derailed Lance's train of thought. "Wait, are you saying that the *sheriff* thinks this place is haunted?" He thought back to the conversation he'd had with Ray Kruger less than an hour ago. Nothing the man had said really made it seem like he was pro-ghost, so to speak. Quite the opposite.

Victoria only turned and started spraying the countertop again. "Nobody really knows what Ray thinks anymore. He's never been the same since it happened." She pulled a cleaning rag from the bucket and started scrubbing the counter. "Don't get me wrong," she said, "he does a fine job as sheriff. But ... well, I guess you'd just have to have known him before to see what I mean. It's like the Ray we have now is only pretending to be Ray. Like outwardly he's the same, but inside ... it's like he's empty. Cold. Does that make sense?"

Lance saw the image of the man alone in Mama's, tucked into a booth away from everyone, silently reading his Kindle. Remembered that coldness.

"It does."

Lance's stomach growled loudly, and he was quickly hit with just how hungry he'd grown. With nothing to eat or drink since his meal at Mama's, he was running on empty. Victoria heard the growl and shooed him away again.

"Go," she said. "You've got things to do."

Lance thanked her again for cleaning and turned to leave, deciding to head out the back door and attempt to find the trail that supposedly led down the side of the hill and into town. He'd made it as far as two steps into the kitchen when there was another rattle of knocking at the front door.

Lance stopped and turned back. *What is this, a bed and breakfast all of a sudden?*

Victoria Bellows stuck her head out of the bathroom. Looked at him and asked, "Expecting somebody?"

"No," Lance said, walking toward the door. "But I hope they brought coffee."

12

FOR A PLACE THAT EVERYBODY HE'D MET SO FAR HAD indicated was avoided and feared, there sure were a lot of visitors at the spook farm this morning. But Lance couldn't honestly say he was that surprised. He had a tendency to accelerate otherwise dormant situations.

With Victoria Bellows still half out of the bathroom, looking toward the front door, Lance turned the knob and opened the door.

"Did you rent a Mercedes? What exactly is it you do again?"

Luke stood on the front porch, wearing basketball shorts and a baggy hoodie, a huge Nike swoosh emblazoned on the front. He had bedhead, and his face was peppered with stubble. He looked like he hadn't been awake long. He looked at Lance, waiting for an answer.

Lance shook his head. "Not mine." He looked over his shoulder, saw Victoria Bellows poking her head out from the bathroom. Apparently satisfied the person at the door did not require her attention, she disappeared back into the room and returned to her work, the squeaking of the cleaning rag on the counter faintly heard.

"Oh, right," Luke said, "So you've got company, then? Sorry. I didn't know. But I mean, how would I, right? This was Susan's idea. I mean, not that I mind, but … you know." He paused. Took a breath. "Shit, man, I need some coffee. Brain ain't working right yet. I came to see if you wanted a lift into town. But if you're busy…"

"That'd be great," Lance said, stepping out and closing the door behind him. "I was about to start walking."

Luke took a step back and looked from Lance back to the Mercedes and then at the house. Raised an eyebrow.

"Somebody here to clean," Lance said, offering no more unless pressed. Just like with Sheriff Kruger earlier, Lance tried to make a habit of not throwing people's names into the mix unless necessary.

Luke grinned. "Is that a euphemism?"

Lance shook his head and started walking down the steps. "I'm not that lucky."

"Yeah," Luke said, following toward his Jeep. "I hear ya."

Lance got into the front passenger seat and Luke backed all the way down the driveway, staring intently into his rearview mirror. He pulled out of the driveway and started the winding road down the hillside, an awkward silence all at once heavy in the air.

Lance broke it. "How was the movie?"

"Shit," Luke said. Then he sighed. "I mean, it was okay I guess. Some rom-com Suze wanted to see. I made her see the new *Transformers* last time we went, so I figured I owed her one."

Lance smiled. "How chivalrous."

"Right? I'm still stuck at third base, though."

Lance didn't know what it was that made Luke feel comfortable enough with him to divulge this sort of information. Maybe it was their similar age, or their odd connection from their basketball days. Maybe Lance just had an honest face.

"She's worth it, though, man. Totally worth it. You know what I mean?"

Lance thought of Leah, then quickly pushed the thought away. *Not now.*

"Yes," Lance said. "I do." Then, to change the subject, "I appreciate you stopping by. I'm starving."

"No sweat, man. Seems like you sorta had your evening rushed last night, what with getting in later in the day, and then all the damn rain. I was headed to grab a coffee and hit the gym, and Suze thought maybe you'd need a lift. Are you going to rent a car today? I think we've got a couple Uber drivers around, but I can't guarantee that. Most of them are closer to the city. And there's a taxi service, I think."

"I'll figure something out," Lance said, then asked, "Hey, what day is it?" He tried to think back, count the days in his head. "Saturday?"

Luke kept his eyes on the road, but Lance could feel the shift of his gaze toward him. A quick, questioning look. "Yeah," Luke said. "It's Saturday. Man, you must stay busy if you don't even know what day it is."

Lance nodded. "Something like that."

The roads were still damp in places, but the sun was doing a good job of drying everything off. The sky was bright blue, few clouds. No traces of the heavy rains from the night before. Luke drove the Jeep expertly around the sharp bends in the road, and soon they were spat out onto flat ground, headed in the direction of town. Lance was hungry and craving coffee, but something tugged at his gut, an odd sensation that he should not have left the house. He tried to swallow it down, blaming his hunger and caffeine deprivation.

But then the thought about the bathroom mirror again. How it had seemed to be reaching out to him.

But that had been a bust. He'd seen nothing in the mirror. Found nothing inside.

"So where to?" Luke asked.

Lance was about to tell his new friend to turn around, take him back. But then his stomach grumbled loud enough to be heard over the rumble of the off-road tires, and he asked, "Does Mama's serve breakfast?"

"Best in town."

Lance grinned. "Of course it is."

A few minutes later Luke had pulled the Jeep into the small parking lot in front of Mama's, and Lance opened the passenger door. "Thanks again," he said.

Luke reached across the center console and balled his fist. "Sure thing, man."

Lance bumped Luke's fist with his own, an action that brought to light a sense of normalcy and regularity that seemed so unfamiliar it was almost overwhelming. Just two guys hanging out. Two friends saying goodbye. It was moments like these that startled Lance into realizing just how abnormal his existence was. Sometimes he felt so inhuman, so detached from the real world it was like drowning in a blackness so deep and dark nobody could hear you scream. On the surface, he appeared to be a functioning member of society. But inside, at times he felt like nothing more than a tool the Universe was using for its own bidding.

Lance closed the Jeep's door and watched Luke back out of the parking lot and drive away. Then he went inside.

The aroma of bacon and biscuits and coffee sent all negative thoughts fleeing from his mind. He could practically taste the food on the air, and he had to refrain from doing his best snake impression and darting his tongue out of his mouth to try.

"Sit anywhere you like!" a voice called from the kitchen. A familiar voice. One full of energy and slight irritation.

Joan.

Lance looked around the restaurant and saw most of the tables where full, but the booth in the rear corner, the booth Sheriff Kruger had sat in the night before, was empty, and Lance walked over and slumped into it, facing the door. A moment later, Joan emerged through the swinging kitchen door, scanned the room, saw the new face, and waddled over to him, sliding a plastic menu onto the table.

"You were here last night," she said. Her face was red from the heat of the kitchen, or maybe she always looked like that. Forever flushed.

Lance nodded. "I was. So were you."

Joan was unimpressed with his observation. "Coffee?"

"Please," Lance said.

She walked away, saying something to the group at another table, causing them all to laugh. Lance smiled and looked over the menu. It was full of all the makings of a hearty country breakfast: pancakes, country ham, eggs, bacon, biscuits, grits, sausage—the only remotely healthy item Lance could see was a blueberry muffin. But that was fine. His metabolism was in perfect working order. Plus, he walked a lot.

Joan returned and set a coffee mug on the table and then filled it right to the brim with black coffee. "You seem like a black guy to me," she said.

"Sorry?" Lance asked.

"Coffee. You take it black, don't you?"

"Oh. Yes, I do." He smiled up at her. "How'd you know?"

Joan shrugged, the skin around her neck rolling up and down like rippling waves. "Been doing this a long time." She winked and then got back to business. "What'll you have?"

Lance ordered pancakes with eggs and bacon and asked

Joan if she could double however many pancakes they normally served. She nodded, turned to leave, and then turned back. "You really staying up at that place?"

Lance took a slow sip of his coffee. It was hot and wonderful. He didn't need to ask for clarification. "I am."

Joan crinkled her brow, Lance's neutral tone causing her to pause. "And you know what happened?"

"I know a family was killed there."

Another sip of coffee. Nobody actually knew what had happened that night, and Lance wasn't going to support any theories quite yet.

Joan looked at him hard, then nodded again and walked to the kitchen, disappearing through the swinging door. Lance held his mug to his lips and blew on it, cooling the coffee before taking another sip. He looked out the window and watched a few cars drive by lazily, the Saturday morning traffic slow and sleepy. The asphalt was dotted with wet spots and puddles, the sun heliographing off the wet surfaces. It was a tranquil scene. Relaxing. Lance felt momentarily at ease, ready to enjoy his meal.

And then there was a rocking of the table and booth and Lance turned and saw Joan sliding into the seat across from him.

"So what are you?" she asked. "A reporter? Are you writing a book? Doing research?"

"What?"

"I know you're staying at that house, and I know you're telling everyone you're a consultant. To me that just means you're hiding the truth."

Small towns. No secrets.

Lance said nothing.

Joan kept going. "I don't think you're up to anything bad, mostly because little Susan seems to have taken a liking to you, and that girl's got about some of the best intuition I've seen for somebody her age." She held up her hands when she saw Lance's face. "Oh, no, not 'like you' like that. She's dating that Luke fella. I just mean she seems to think you're one of the good ones. And I believe her. Like I told you, I've been doing this a long time. You work in food service long enough, you start to get good at reading people. Do you understand?"

Lance nodded.

"Good. So listen. I don't know what you're really doing up there, but I know you're involved somehow. I don't believe for a second that you randomly ended up there. You came here with the intention of staying at that house. So, if you *are* writing a book or an article or researching whatever project it is you're working on, I want to tell you something. You can quote me, but I want it to be anonymous."

Lance was about to hold up his hands, try and slow Joan down so he could end her conspiracy about him. But then he thought better of it. If she was willing to divulge information to him that might help him figure out what this mess was all about, he might as well let her.

Lance looked around at the other tables. Nobody seemed to be paying him and Joan any mind, so he set his mug down and leaned in close over the table, playing the role of interested listener. "Okay. What is it you want to say?"

Joan leaned in, her ample bosom spilling onto the tabletop. "And you'll keep my name out of anything you write?"

Lance nodded. "I promise." It was an easy promise to make. He'd never write anything about this, period.

Joan's eyes flicked to her right, out toward the dining room. "Shit," she said. "One sec." Then she heaved herself out of the booth, rushed across the room to refill a glass of water, and then was back, the booth shifting again with her weight as she slid back in across from Lance.

"Look," she started. "I know what they say about me around

here. 'Ol' Joan's nothing but a gossip. Nosy. She'll say anything to anyone for a bigger tip.' Sure, folks seem to like me okay, but I don't know that a one of them actually trusts me. Not sure anybody has since my husband passed."

"I'm sorry for your loss," Lance said.

She waved him off. "S'okay. Henry was a pain in the ass." She said it jokingly, but Lance felt the twinge of pain flash through her at the memory.

"Anyway, my opinion might not mean much to the folks round here, but I'll just go ahead and set the record straight for you, okay?"

"Okay."

Joan looked over toward the rest of the dining room again, only this time it was apparent she wasn't checking for empty glasses or dirty dishes that needed to be bussed. She was seeing if anybody was eavesdropping. Satisfied, she leaned in close again and said, "I don't know what happened that night, but Mark Benchley didn't kill his family."

13

Lance sat back and lifted his coffee cup to his mouth, taking another sip. It was cooling now, and he would soon need a refill. He looked at Joan, who had sat back as well after her revelation, and saw the conviction in her eyes. She was as serious as a heart attack.

"I've only heard one version of the story," Lance said, downing the rest of his coffee. "And in that version, Mr. Benchley killed his wife and daughter and then shot himself in the living room."

Joan rolled her eyes and nodded. "Yeah, yeah ... that's what everybody thinks. Easiest explanation, right? Blame the God-fearing lunatic?"

"But you don't think that's what happened."

"I know it's not what happened."

Lance made a sympathetic face, tried not to sound harsh with his next words. "Were you there that night? Did you see what happened?"

Joan's face softened. "No, of course not. That's ... that's not what I mean."

"So you can't say for sure."

She eyed him, as if suddenly suspicious. "Yeah ... you've got reporter written all over you."

Lance had never considered a career in journalism. He suspected too many of his sources would be of the spirit variety for him to be taken seriously. He backed off a bit, tried to lighten his tone. "Help me understand."

Joan leaned forward again, eying his coffee mug and asked, "You need a refill?"

Lance waved her off. "No, thank you. I can wait till you're finished." This answer seemed not to sit well with Joan, as if her inner waitress was jumpy, twitching at the thought of a customer in need of a refill.

"You sure?"

"Positive."

She took one last glance at the mug, then shrugged, as if to indicate there was nothing else she could do. Then she leaned back, crossed her arms, and started talking.

"Mark came in here at least twice a week for breakfast. Wheat toast, two eggs over easy. Coffee with a splash of cream. He'd sit right here in this booth," she said. "Right where you're sitting now."

Lance felt a strange chill at this. Joan continued.

"He was always friendly, always polite. Never bothered anyone. Sat here and would read the paper, both the local and national. And then," she sighed, "yes, he spent a lot of time going through his Bible. He was always making notes in the margins, underlining passages. To say he was well read in regard to scripture would be an understatement. He took his faith very seriously." Then: "It made some people uncomfortable. But otherwise, there was nothing out of the ordinary about him, except he was a tall drink of water. Had a good couple inches on just about most men."

"I heard he liked to walk the streets and give impromptu

sermons," Lance said. "And folks didn't necessarily think he was in his right mind. Is that right?"

Joan gave another eye roll. "*Folks* like to gossip. *Folks* like to blow things out of proportion for the sake of a good story. Now, I'm not saying Mark didn't try to witness to his fair share of people in town, and, yes, I do believe he did speak to a small gathering of people having a picnic one day in the park—unwarranted, possibly. But it didn't take long for people to label him as a crazy person. Honestly, the fact he had no job and not much to do to occupy his time during the day is probably what made folks so uneasy about him. He seemed like a bum, a lazy freeloader with nothing better to do than to shove his ideology down people's throats." She paused, looked around the dining room. Still, nobody looked their direction.

"But it wasn't like that. I won't say Mark wasn't a tad fanatical—old-school, even. But he was gentle. And he was *smart*. Boy, you could ask him about any topic you could think of and he'd be able to carry on a conversation with you. He'd either read a book or read an article about it, and just seemed to know. He was a joy to talk with. Not dull and boring like most of these people."

After she'd said it, she quickly turned her head to look and see if anybody had heard, not meaning to offend. She looked back at Lance, her cheeks redder than before.

"And here's the other thing, the part that makes me certain he didn't kill them. Mark was absolutely in love with his family."

Lance said nothing. Waited.

"He talked about them all the time. Loved to boast about how Natalie was helping to save lives over at Central Medical, and you could just tell he thought she was the most beautiful thing on earth. And with Mary..." Joan smiled, her eyes unfocused, clearly lost deep in memory. "Mary was his absolute pride and joy. He was so proud of her. So excited to see the woman she was growing up to be." She shook her head as if to clear it, then looked Lance dead in the eyes. "Mark would have died if anything had happened to Mary. He'd have killed himself to save her. And that's why I'd bet my life there's no way he could do something so horrific to his girl."

Lance waited to see if there was more, but Joan had apparently told all she needed to. He asked one last question. "So what happened at the end? With Mrs. Benchley quitting her job and Mary going off to the new school?"

Joan's face grew heavy. "Mark stopped coming for breakfast, too." She sighed and pushed her way out of the booth, grabbing Lance's coffee mug as she stood. "You're the reporter," she said. "Maybe you can figure out the rest. Because nobody around here knows a thing more than I just told you."

Lance watched as Joan carried his mug to a server station against the wall next to the kitchen door and began pouring coffee from a nearly full pot. He couldn't help but think she was wrong. Maybe not about Mark Benchley, not all of it. But she was wrong if she thought she had all the answers. *Somebody* in town had to know more about the Benchley family's situation. *Somebody* was hiding something. Even if Mark Benchley actually did kill his own family, there was more too it. Of this, Lance was all at once certain.

Joan returned and set his full cup of coffee on the table with the deft hand of a practiced server. It was completely full and she hadn't spilled a drop. "If you want to call somebody a kook— a crazy person—look at Natalie's uncle." She stood at the side of the table, hands on her hips, as if she'd just challenged Lance to prove her wrong.

"Thank you," Lance said. "And also, *what?*"

"Natalie's uncle, Joseph. He was the weird one. Ask anyone who knew him around here. The last ten years or so of his life, he was basically a hermit. Only came to town once a week for groceries and whatnot. Was some sort of engineer in the Army. Could build anything, s'what I always heard. Once he retired, he lived up on that hill all by himself the rest of his life, it seems. Never married, never dated. Kept to himself. But every time somebody tried to talk to him when he came to town, ask him how things were going, he'd go on these long-winded rants about government conspiracies, how the commies were taking over our government. He said the US would be part of Russia or China in no time."

Lance took a sip of his coffee, letting Joan finish her venting about something Lance felt had absolutely no bearing on the Benchley family's murder. Maybe she was a gossip, after all. Though that didn't necessarily mean she was spreading false information.

"Rumor has it," Joan said, "he'd even gone so far as to build himself some sort of fallout shelter up at the farm. A bunker, or something. And knowing what I know about Joseph, I wouldn't put it past his crazy ass. It's like he only felt safe up at that farm."

Lance couldn't ignore the irony. Nobody seemed to feel safe at the farm now.

"Anyway, your food's ready," Joan said. Then she turned and vanished through the kitchen door, returning a moment later and delivering Lance his plates of food. "Enjoy," she said.

Lance ate in silence, devouring the food—which was very good—and thinking about everything Joan had told him. Tried to see how any of it fit together, explored what he knew, looking for possible holes. But the truth was, if this situation had been a logic problem, the answer Lance would circle would be *Not enough information.*

When he'd finished eating, he paid his bill, leaving what he hoped Joan considered to be a generous tip, and then slung his backpack onto his shoulders and left the restaurant. He walked across the parking lot and then crossed the street, cutting across the post office's parking lot and turning right on the sidewalk. He wanted to see if Rich Bellows was in his office. Lance thought the odds were pretty slim, considering it was a Saturday, and with Rich's wife currently cleaning the farmhouse, somebody had to be watching the children Lance had seen in the office photographs. But still, he'd try. He wanted to ask whether anybody else had keys to the farmhouse, or if by chance the back door could have somehow been left unlocked the last time anybody had been there.

Lance made it two blocks from the post office when a quick *whoop-whoop* from a siren made him jump and spin around. A sheriff's office cruiser was idling in the street, the passenger window rolled down. The officer behind the wheel motioned for Lance to walk over. Lance did, leaning down to look through the opened window. "Yes, Officer?"

"Are you Lance Brody?"

This can't be good.

"Yes, sir."

The officer nodded with his head to the back door. "Need you to get in, son."

Nope. Not good at all.

[14]

LANCE DIDN'T HESITATE, BECAUSE REALLY, WHAT WOULD his options have been? Try to outrun a vehicle? Unlikely. Talk his way out of it? He didn't even know what *it* was. So in the end, he simply asked, "Where are we going?"

The sheriff's deputy said, "The station." And Lance nodded and opened the back door and got in.

All at once, the memory of the near-life-ending ride in the back of a police car in Westhaven hit him hard. It was an almost nauseating sense of fear and déjà vu. But Lance was nothing if not strong-minded, a realist, and he took a couple deep breaths and calmed his nerves. Westhaven was different. There was unspeakable evil there. And he'd defeated it. Well, with the help of a few friends. Right now, in Ripton's Grove, he was simply sitting in the back of a police car, being driven to the local sheriff's office. Which in its own right caused an unshakable sense of dread, but on a more earthly level.

When the deputy was certain Lance was inside and situated, he picked up the radio from the dash and told whoever was on the other line what had happened and that he was en route to the station. The deputy had used the word *suspect* when referring to Lance, and Lance didn't like that at all. He thought about asking more questions, but in the end decided to be quiet and see how things would play out. Unless people in Westhaven had somehow tracked him down to Ripton's Grove and had questions, he suspected he was either currently being brought in because Sheriff Kruger still had a hair up his ass about Lance's being in town, at the farm, or because of a misunderstanding. Misunderstanding had a habit of following Lance.

The deputy pulled the car away from the sidewalk and started to drive, slowly and carefully, occasionally glancing at Lance in the rearview. They drove in the direction of the bus station, a few curious pedestrians standing on the sidewalk and staring at Lance in the back of the car as he rode by, concerned expressions plastered on their faces. Lance had to wonder if Joan was already telling all the new customers at Mama's that the new guy in town had just been picked up by the sheriff's department and being brought in for questioning. The rumor mill would be churning hard and fast. The deputy made a right turn just past the bus station parking lot. Lance glanced toward the building and wondered what he'd be doing right now if he'd stayed on the bus, gone somewhere else. But he knew it was a silly thought. He was meant to be here. That much was becoming quite certain.

"You're awfully quiet," the deputy said, giving Lance an accusatory glare he didn't appreciate.

Lance met the man's eyes in the rearview and said, "Sorry, I didn't know this was *Taxi Cab Confessions*."

The deputy's mouth opened, closed, and then the man shook his head and mumbled, "Smart-ass."

Lance had been called worse. He felt only a little guilty for his outburst. He knew he was innocent of whatever situation they suspected he'd been a part of, and this entire side trip to the sheriff's office was doing nothing but wasting Lance's time. Not that he was pressed for time, exactly, but still, it was the principle.

The Ripton's Grove sheriff's office was a dated-looking one-story brick building that looked as though it might have once been a bank. The parking lot was large and mostly empty. A cluster of county vehicles and police cruisers much like the one Lance was riding in sat behind wire fencing to the right side of the building. The gate to this parking area was open, and Lance had no difficulty spying the black Crown Vic that had visited him earlier this morning. Lance looked back to the building. Kruger was in there somewhere. Waiting for him.

Lance's deputy chauffeur pulled the vehicle up to the front of the building and parked, getting out and making a big show of stretching his back and checking his cell phone. If he thought this would irritate Lance—being forced to wait longer in the back of the vehicle with no explanation—he was sadly mistaken. Lance was incredibly patient. And, again, had nowhere he needed to be.

After the deputy was apparently satisfied he'd stalled long enough to get Lance's blood boiling, he slowly walked around to Lance's door and opened it. Lance hadn't moved an inch before the man said, "Nice and easy, now. Take it slow." He placed a hand on Lance's upper arm and pulled. Lance grabbed his back-pack from the seat next to him and allowed himself to be "helped" from the rear of the car. Standing at his full height, Lance was easily a foot taller than the deputy, and as if underestimating Lance's height, the man took a small step back and said, "You aren't going to be any trouble, right?"

Lance said nothing. Waited.

The deputy nodded, as if he'd somehow made his point. He

stepped forward and grabbed Lance's upper arm again, although this time he was noticeably gentler, and led Lance into the building.

They made their way through the lobby/waiting room, and the deputy waved to a middle-aged woman behind a pane of glass. She didn't even look up from the romance novel she was reading to reach down and push a button that caused the door at the end of the wall to buzz and a lock to disengage. The deputy opened the door and nudged Lance through it. From there, Lance was forced to surrender his backpack to be searched—for evidence, they told him—and he agreed, only adding, "There's dirty underwear in there," which drew an uncomfortable stare from the other deputy, who'd been tasked with the job. Then the deputy who'd driven him here marched him to what felt like the back corner of the building and stuck him in a small inter-view room, telling Lance to sit down and not move and that somebody would be by shortly.

Lance sat. The door closed. Lance sighed and looked around the room.

At once, it looked like something you'd see on one of those TV crime dramas. Small, cramped space. Single metal table in the middle of the room, with two chairs. There was dull fluores-cent lighting overhead and a large mirror on the left wall (two-way, Lance presumed). No windows. The walls were a faded gray. Dingy was one word that came to mind, but depressing might be more apropos. Lance understood; this room was meant to make a person uncomfortable, meant to make them give answers and admit to crimes and do what they needed to do to get out and see a shred of sunlight again.

While Lance was mostly unfazed by the room—his life had prepared him well for less-than-pleasant situations—he felt the slow swell of impatience rise in his chest with each passing minute. Something was afoul here, and his curiosity was growing. Time was being wasted.

He leaned back in the uncomfortable chair and closed his eyes. Began to take a couple of deep breaths when he heard a man laugh and say, "Boy, we don't even have time for all the stories I could tell you of the idiots I've had come through this room—on *both* sides of the table, mind you."

Lance's eyes shot open and found a man seated directly across from him in the other chair.

The man smiled, showing coffee-stained teeth, and winked. He wore dark khaki pants and a matching shirt. The sleeves of the shirt were rolled up around thick forearms; the buttons looked strained against a substantial stomach and broad chest. His face was weathered, the skin drooping around his neck and cheeks. His eyes shone bright, but the bags under them told a different story altogether. His hair was gray and lay in short, sloppy curls around his ears and forehead. To Lance, he looked well into his fifties, maybe early sixties, but he likely felt much older.

What struck Lance as more interesting than the man's sudden appearance was what was pinned on the man's shirt, chest-high and opposite a folding pocket with what looked like a pack of cigarettes tucked neatly away.

A gold star. The word *Sheriff* emblazoned on it.

Lance looked up and met the man's eyes.

"Heart attack," the man said. Then he looked around the room and smiled, as if recalling pleasant memories. "Right here in this very room." He laughed. "Brought a kid in for shoplifting, couldn't have been more than twelve or thirteen, and I was just having some fun with him, trying to put the fear of God in him, if you know what I mean. Wasn't nothing serious. I knew his pops, and was just waiting on the old fool to get down here and pick his kid up. Well, about halfway through my fake interrogation I felt the ol' ticker seize up and *bam!* Lights out." He shook his head. "The whole town always said if I didn't slow down some and take better care of myself, something like that would happen. But nobody would have thought it would go down while I was just trying to have a little fun."

Lance said nothing. Waited.

"Not real chatty, are ya, kid?"

At this point in his life, Lance wasn't certain of a great many things, but he had come to understand that spirits—ghosts, if you like—weren't always visible to him. Lance had a theory that they had to expend some sort of energy to make themselves seen, and after a while they'd have to slip back beyond the veil to recharge their batteries, so to speak. Sure, Lance had had social visits from the lingering dead. That wasn't unusual. But more often than not, they came with a purpose. Lance felt this was likely one of those times.

Instead of answering, Lance asked a question of his own. "How long ago were you sheriff?"

The man's head looked down to the star pinned to his chest, his eyes suddenly looking sad. Then he grunted. "I was taking care of this town when Kruger here was still shittin' his diapers." He sighed. "Been a long time."

"Why are you still here?" Lance asked.

The man smiled again, then shrugged, as if he knew his answer was going to disappoint. "This is what I was born to do. I got nothing else."

Lance didn't claim to have any understanding of what followed our mortal lives, no evidence specific to a Heaven or hell. But the simple fact that there were such things as spirits— like the man sitting across the table and countless others before him—did suggest that our souls have the ability to move on from this world and into another.

Beyond the veil, and then further still.

"Besides," the man said, "I got nobody waitin' for me anywhere. Been a loner my whole life. And don't go getting sad for me, I preferred it that way."

Lance said nothing. He was beginning to understand what it meant to be a loner himself.

"Anyway," the man continued, "I didn't pop in to talk about me—though you'd love some of the stories, trust me on that! I wanted to help you with the case you're working on."

"Case, sir?"

The man sat back and looked at Lance like he was trying to pull a fast one on him. "Yes, son! The case. The Benchley house. You're here to figure out what really happened, right?"

Now it was Lance's turn to sigh. "Apparently."

The deceased sheriff nodded and leaned forward, resting his thick arms on the table. "And what have you learned so far? Got any leads?"

Lance began to feel even more like he was in a TV crime drama. He had to suppress a sudden urge to get up, slam his hand on the table and yell, "You can't handle the truth!"

Wait ... that was in a courtroom. Close enough.

Lance didn't bother with asking such trivial questions such as how this man knew who he was and why he was in town. He went straight into the details. "I've got two sides of things. The most popular opinion seems to be that Mark Benchley was crazy and killed his wife and daughter before shooting himself. The second and most recent opinion I've heard is that Mark Benchley would never have hurt a hair on his wife and daughter's head, so there was another sort of foul play involved." Lance stopped and considered what he'd said. Shrugged. "So really, either Mark Benchley killed them all, or somebody else did. Not exactly a groundbreaking investigation I'm conducting here."

The Ghost of Sheriff Past looked disappointed. "That's all?"

Lance thought some more. "I've heard voices at the farm. A man and a woman. There's nobody there but me."

"So the voices are like me?" the man asked.

"I'm not sure. I know they're otherworldly, so to speak, but I don't see or feel any other presence along with the voices. It's just sound."

The man considered this for a moment, then sat up straight, excited. "Maybe it's a message? A ... recording of some sort? A clue that's been waiting for somebody to find it?"

Lance crinkled his brow. "Waiting for *me*?"

"Waiting for you or someone like you."

Lance didn't allow himself to dwell on thoughts of other people in the world who shared his gifts. He'd never met anyone else who could do the things he could except for the Reverend. Though he liked to hope that they did exist out there somewhere.

"It's not much of a clue," Lance said.

"Maybe there's more, and you just haven't found it yet."

"I don't exactly know how to look."

"You will," the man said. "I can tell. You'd have made a hell of a deputy."

"You've only known me a couple minutes," Lance said.

The man smiled again, and Lance knew it was only a trick of the mind that he could smell the nicotine on the man's breath. "You don't know what it's like on this side of the table, son." He winked.

Lance got the meaning. Didn't know what to say.

The man said, "Listen, I've got to go. They'll be here soon—don't worry, by the way, they've got nothing on you. But let me tell you this. I've been here for every interview they've ever performed regarding the Benchley case over the years. I've read every case file, every note. Heard every discussion, opinion, argument, and theory."

Lance waited. Let the man enjoy his buildup.

"Something happened in Mark Benchley's life after he moved here that changed him," the lingering sheriff said. "And not in a good way. But my gut tells me there's a lot more to that night than anybody around here has even tried to understand. And I need you to help these idiots around here figure out what it was."

Lance was about to ask for more, anything else to go on, but then, out of the corner of his eye, he caught the presumed two-way mirror to his left and he felt a cold chill of fear down his spine. *What if they've been watching the whole time? What if they've been watching me talk to myself?*

As if suddenly sensing Lance's panic, the man turned to look at the mirror, laughed, and then raised his middle finger to the glass. "They can't see, son."

Lance didn't take his eyes from the mirror, "I know they can't see *you*, but I've been sitting here probably looking like—"

He stopped talking. Focused his eyes on himself in the mirror and then slowly and deliberately said, "I'm talking, but my mouth isn't moving."

And it was true. Lance felt all the muscle and movement in his jaw and mouth, heard the words leaving his throat, but the image of Lance in the mirror simply sat and stared.

"You didn't know that's how it worked with us?" the man asked, sounding genuinely curious.

Lance said, "No." Lance in the mirror said nothing.

"Hmm," the man grunted. "Interesting. People would think you were crazy if you just went around talking to people who weren't there."

Lance tried hard to remember if he'd ever been able to see

himself while talking to a lingering spirit. A mirror, or reflective surface ... anything. He couldn't recall a single moment.

Amazed he was just now finding out this little secret of his, he turned back to the man who had once been the sheriff of Ripton's Grove but found only an empty chair.

Then the door to the interview room opened, and Sheriff Ray Kruger walked in.

[15]

THE SHERIFF—THE CURRENT AND VERY MUCH ALIVE sheriff—closed the door softly and turned to face Lance. Looked at him with weary eyes and sighed, as if he'd known this moment was inevitable.

Lance smiled. "Well, Sheriff, I hate that you had to waste the gas to come visit me this morning. Apparently we could have just waited a couple hours for our proper introductions."

Ray Kruger didn't even so much as smirk.

So much for that approach, Lance thought. Kruger appeared to be all business. Lance couldn't say he was surprised.

The sheriff walked to the table and sat down opposite Lance, his knees popping as he fell into the chair. Then he ran a hand through his hair and leaned back, still not saying a word.

The silence sat heavy. Lance's stomach gurgled, his digesting breakfast deciding to break the ice. Lance smiled again. "Mama's," he said. "So much good food."

"Can you tell me everything you did and everywhere you went after I left the farmhouse this morning, please?"

Yep, Lance thought, *all business.*

He straightened in his chair and took a deep breath. "Absolutely. After you left, I went upstairs to change my clothes and shave and brush my teeth. In the middle of shaving, the doorbell rang and I answered it. It was Victoria Bellows. Her husband mentioned to her that the farmhouse needed to be cleaned, and the cleaners apparently won't come to the property out of fear of ... well, you know. Victoria and I chatted briefly and then she started to clean. About that time, the doorbell rang again and it was Luke—one of the new friends I mentioned to you." Lance hated dropping Luke's name but understood the situation well enough to know it was going to be required one way or the other.

Sheriff Kruger held up a hand to slow him down. "Luke who?"

Lance shook his head. "I don't know his last name, sir. He drives a Jeep." Then, after a slight hesitation, "He's dating Susan. The waitress from Mama's."

Kruger nodded and motioned for Lance to continue.

"Luke asked if I wanted a ride into town, and I accepted. He drove me straight to Mama's and I had breakfast. After that, I left the restaurant and started walking. I hadn't gotten far when your very pleasant and overly charming deputy picked me up and delivered me here, to this very room."

Again, not so much as a hint of a grin at the crack on his deputy. The sheriff was stone-faced. He was quiet for a moment, perhaps thinking through all that Lance had said. Then he nodded once, stood and said, "Be right back."

He walked out of the room, leaving Lance alone again.

Except he wasn't, really. As soon as Sheriff Kruger had left the room and closed the door, Lance swiveled his head back to the chair across from him and found the ghost of the deceased sheriff had returned.

"Don't worry about Deputy Payton," the man said. "There's always ones like him in every station in the country. Big badge, big attitude, small pecker. Literally, in Payton's case. I've seen him in the locker room."

Lance wasn't sure what to do with this information, so he asked a question of his own. "What's your name, sir?"

The man's face did something funny, as if he wasn't sure what Lance was asking him. Almost as if he had to dig deep, search for the answer. "Willard," he finally said. "Sheriff Bill Willard." Then he shook his head, as if to clear it. "Sorry," he said. "It's been a long time since my name's mattered."

"Nice to meet you, Sheriff Willard. I'm Lance."

Willard nodded. "I know, son. I know. Listen to me, okay? I may not be alive, but I've got a few tricks up my sleeve. I have a way of making things happen around here from time to time, if you catch my drift."

Lance didn't catch anything, but he nodded all the same.

"You need answers," Willard continued. "And the only way you're going to get them is to dig, to talk to folks. Learn things that these morons here didn't."

Lance said nothing.

"I know you're special, son. I know you've got gifts beyond this world's understanding. And maybe that's all you need—your talents and whatever clues the other world you can see and hear lends you. But I think you might be surprised just how much you can still learn from the living. When you know how to listen, that is.

"So when you get your bag back, maybe in the smaller front compartment, you'll find a list of names. Maybe those names were all people of interest in the Benchley case. Not because they were suspects, necessarily, but because they were thought to maybe have information that could help in discovering the truth. Maybe," Willard said, "you can call on a few of them and see what they remember. Maybe you'll get more out of them than just their words." At this, Sheriff Bill Willard winked, and the interview room door opened and Sheriff Ray Kruger appeared.

Lance looked back to the chair and found it, expectedly, empty.

Kruger walked over and resumed his position opposite Lance. "Where were you headed when my pleasant and overly charming deputy picked you up?"

Something about the question made Lance feel uneasy, but he pressed on with his honesty. He knew he'd done nothing illegal. Today. "I was walking to Rich Bellows's real estate office."

Kruger's face was expressionless. "Why?" he asked.

Lance decided not to lie, specifically, but not to offer up more information than was required either. "I had some questions about the house. Thought maybe he might be in for a few hours on a Saturday. He seems like that sort of guy."

Kruger nodded. Sighed again before saying, "Well, it's a good thing you didn't run across him this morning."

Lance took the bait. "Why's that, sir?"

"Because his wife was assaulted in the house you're currently renting from him, and he's convinced you were her attacker."

Lance felt a cold stone drop in his stomach. Not because he was fearing prosecution, but because he felt sorry for Victoria Bellows. She'd been so nice to him, friendly and energetic. He'd liked her. And once again, Lance had managed to get somebody hurt because of a situation he was involved in.

How many times would this happen in his life? How many people would suffer because of him?

"Anything to say, Lance?" Sheriff Ray Kruger asked. He didn't look all that concerned.

Lance looked the man in the eye. "I didn't do it," he said. He felt a new vibe coming off Kruger, and then slowly added, "But you already know that, don't you?"

Kruger leaned back and nodded. "I do. I just called over to the YMCA and got them to track down Luke—that's the thing about small towns, right? Easy to learn people's routines. He verified your story and also said that when the two of you left, he did see a woman matching the description of Mrs. Bellows in the house. Unharmed."

Lance was relieved, but only a little. "Is she okay? Mrs. Bellows?"

Kruger nodded. "A nasty bump on the head, but she'll be fine. The assailant struck her just above the temple and she blacked out temporarily. When she came to, she had the good sense to call an ambulance, and they took her over to Central Medical."

"Has she said anything about her attacker? Any idea who it might be?"

"Like I said, her husband thinks it was you." Kruger had a small smirk on his face as he said this.

"But you know it wasn't," Lance said. Then, after a beat, "Are you planning on sharing that information with Mr. Bellows anytime soon."

"Of course. As soon as we're done here."

"I'd appreciate that," Lance said, unsure what sort of game he was stuck playing with Sheriff Kruger. There seemed to be more the man wanted to say.

"So am I free to go?" Lance asked, making a small move to stand up from the chair.

Kruger held up a hand. "Not quite yet. If you'll humor me for just another minute."

Lance had expected this. He sat. Tried to look uninterested.

Sheriff Kruger cleared his throat and asked, "Do you have any idea who might have attacked Mrs. Bellows this morning?"

Lance almost answered too quickly. Of course he didn't know who'd attacked her. But then he thought back to the previous evening, the open back door, the movement behind the blinds when he'd arrived. Kruger picked up on his hesitation. "Well?"

"To answer your question, no, I don't have any idea who specifically might have attacked her."

"I feel like you've got a 'but' coming."

Lance nodded. He didn't necessarily feel his back was against the wall, but now that folks were getting hurt, it was time to share the one bit of information he'd been keeping to himself. "When I got to the house last night, I thought I saw movement behind the blinds in one of the front windows, and then when I got inside, the back door was wide open. I didn't see anybody, but I assumed somebody was in the house."

Kruger sat up straighter at this. "Why didn't you tell me this earlier?"

Lance fibbed, but only a little. "With everything folks have been telling me—including yourself, sir—about the reputation the farmhouse has, I sort of, I don't know, figured it was just one of those weirdos who wanted to come by and see the place or have a séance or whatever they do. I figured maybe the back door was left unlocked and they sneaked in and then fled the place when I got there." Lance shrugged. "I locked the door and didn't hear or see anything else the rest of the night. I didn't think it was that big a deal."

Kruger sat silently, appraising Lance enough to make him feel a bit uncomfortable. Finally, he said, "So you're either very brave or very stupid."

Lance grinned. "Are they mutually exclusive?"

At this, Sheriff Ray Kruger finally offered a small, yet very apparent smile. But he followed it with a question Lance was starting to get tired of. "Lance, be honest with me. Why are you here?"

Lance was quiet for a long time, trying his best to get a better read on Kruger. There was kindness buried beneath the toughness and the sorrow. At last, Lance shrugged and said, "Right now, Sheriff, this is just where I'm supposed to be."

And that wasn't a lie.

[16]

I<small>F</small> S<small>HERIFF</small> R<small>AY</small> K<small>RUGER</small> <small>THOUGHT</small> L<small>ANCE</small> <small>WAS</small> <small>BEING</small> <small>A</small> smart-ass or simply evasive with his answer, he didn't show it. Instead, he sighed, nodded, and then stood, telling Lance he was free to go, but that he'd better call the police the moment he suspected anybody trespassing on the farmhouse's land.

"I'm serious, son," he said as he handed Lance his backpack on their way back through the office area. "You have no idea how tired I am of dealing with that place. No idea at all. Don't give me a reason to bring you back down here again, okay?"

Lance wanted to say he could make no promises in that regard, given his past experiences, but he decided to play it safe. He smiled, nodded, and said, "Yes, sir. Of course. I'm terribly sorry for all the trouble. Please let me know if there's anything I can do to help further."

Lance thought the conversation was going to end at this point, but the sheriff surprised him with saying, "You can leave, if you really want to help."

"Sir?"

The sheriff shook his head. "Nothing good happens up there, son. It's easier when the place just sits empty."

Lance gave Kruger the only answer he could. "I promise I won't stay a minute longer than I need to."

With that, Kruger opened the door leading to the lobby, let Lance walk through it, and then closed it behind him, leaving Lance alone with just the outdated furniture and the same woman behind the glass partition, chewing gum and twirling her hair as she read her novel. "Have a nice day," Lance said as he left.

She didn't respond.

Outside, the sun was blinding and Lance raised a hand to his eyes and squinted as he looked across the parking lot. The cruiser he'd arrived in was gone, and the lot was empty except for a black pickup truck parked alone in the corner. A passenger bus drove slowly down the street, air brakes hissing as it slowed to make a turn, headed for the bus station. Lance stepped off the sidewalk and followed it back toward town, a strong breeze blowing at his back. The air felt alive and fresh compared to the stuffy interview room. Chilly, but not uncomfortable.

He kicked pebbles down the sidewalk as he walked, not too concerned with where he was headed. Stopped briefly across the street from the bus station and contemplated going inside and buying a ticket. Moving on to somewhere else. Somewhere that made more sense. He couldn't understand why he was in Ripton's Grove. The tragedy at the farmhouse was a terrible thing, no question. But aside from the alternative theory that Mark Benchley hadn't been the one to kill his family and himself that night, what was Lance's purpose here? Was that his only task, to bring to justice a killer who'd flown under the radar for too long? Not that that was anything to shake your head at, but still ... he felt there was more.

The loud ringing of a bell startled Lance out of his thoughts, and he looked up, finding a bell tower off in the distance, ringing in the noon hour. He thought about lunch but then dismissed it. *Not yet*, he thought. *You've obviously got work to do.*

He had so many questions, but the one he was interested in at the moment was, who had attacked Victoria Bellows? His gut told him that the attacker was the same person who'd been in the farmhouse the night before. He found the timing of two different home invasions at the same property within twelve hours of each other to be too coincidental, regardless of the home's infamy.

He kept walking, and as a short, balding man came out of a small hardware store to Lance's left, Lance said, "Excuse me, sir —could you tell me how to get to Central Medical?"

The man stopped and eyed Lance suspiciously. Lance wasn't bothered by this, was in fact used to it. He remained still and smiled, trying to look pleasant.

"Are you hurt?" the man asked.

"No, sir. Need to visit a friend."

The man nodded slowly, as if Lance was trying to pull a fast one on him, then huffed and puffed and gave Lance the directions. Followed it up with, "It's going to be a long walk."

Lance thanked the man and added, "It's okay. I like to walk." Then he walked across the street to Rich Bellows's real estate office. The door was, unsurprisingly, locked and the lights off. Lance moved on and ducked inside the florist next door. Ten minutes later, he emerged carrying a small bouquet of flowers and headed off to find Central Medical.

The man from outside the hardware store was correct. It had been a long walk to Central Medical. It took Lance half an hour to end up nearly two miles on the opposite end of town, well past the downtown section he'd become somewhat familiar with. He'd made a right turn at Mama's, passing by the building with the bell tower, which turned out to be a courthouse, then followed the sidewalk along a rural route for nearly the entire way before the sidewalk eventually ended and Lance was forced to walk along the shoulder the remainder of the trip. Traffic was light, thankfully, and the weather was cool enough that the walk wasn't that tiring. He'd glanced down every so often at the bouquet he was carrying, hoping the flowers remained presentable long enough to be delivered.

And now he stood in a large, freshly paved, mostly empty parking lot, looking at a medium-sized two-story beige building sitting unassumingly in the corner of the lot. It was dull and plain and boring, darkened windows dotting the faded exterior. The words CENTRAL MEDICAL CENTER were positioned above a set of automatic doors in the center of the building's front. On the left of the building, accessible by another, smaller entrance road, was a gray parking overhang with the word EMERGENCY advertised in red letters on all sides. An ambulance was parked beneath the overhang, its lights off and doors closed. It looked tired, almost as if it were napping in the quiet afternoon.

Lance stood and stared at the building for a long time. Despite Central Medical's lack of size and flash and energy, there was still no misunderstanding what the place was.

A hospital.

Lance did not like hospitals.

This wasn't an odd fear or phobia or general dislike to have as a human being. A lot of people didn't like hospitals. Hospitals often brought to mind illness or injury—and for some, an acute awareness of their own mortality. Death walked the halls of hospitals. It stood in the corners of rooms and waited its turn to slip in and do its job, lurking in the shadows but hidden from no one. Hospitals were a relatively unhappy place if you were a guest, despite the cheerfulness exuded by friendly staff. Nobody went there to have fun.

But for Lance, the dislike of hospitals extended beyond the common tropes of mortals. Because he could see into the shadows, beyond the veil. Lance could see newly appointed spirits lingering at the bedsides of their deceased bodies, watching as loved ones mourned and said final goodbyes. Lance walked hallways crowded not just by passing nurses and hustling doctors and concerned visitors, but also by the ghosts of those who'd not yet passed on to whatever lay on the other side. Sometimes they were peaceful, almost contemplative as they moved along and grasped their new situation with a sort of wonder, testing the waters of their new being. But others ... others were completely distraught, frantic. And it was them—those for whom the idea of their death had stricken such fear into their souls—who disturbed Lance. They always seemed to sense what Lance was, and that he could see and hear them. They flung themselves at him and begged and pleaded for help, for answers he did not have. They wanted another chance, they wanted more time with their wives and husbands and sons and daughters. Some asked if they were going to hell ... or to Heaven. They asked what they'd done wrong—both in life and in their own dying.

Aside from his birth, Lance had only been inside the walls of a hospital twice. Once when he was only ten years old and had fractured his wrist after falling out of a tire swing at the park, and again when he was sixteen and had gone to visit a friend of his from high school who'd had to have an emergency appendectomy. Her name was Mariah and she played softball and volleyball, and Lance would never forget the look of hurt in her eyes when he'd been unable to stand in her room any longer and had nearly run down the hallway and down the stairs and out into the fresh air.

The episode with his wrist when he was ten had been traumatic—a memory forever burned into Lance's mind. But when he'd been older, he thought he would have been better equipped to handle the hospital. He understood more about who he was at that point, and thought himself accustomed to dealing with the spirit world.

He'd been wrong.

So much sadness and so much anger and so much pleading had driven him away.

He'd apologized profusely to Mariah when she'd returned to school, but he'd never forgiven himself for making such a stupid mistake, for being so over confident in himself.

Yet here he stood, again. Outside a building that undoubtedly held—at least on some small scale—the things that Lance did not want to face, did not want to have to deal with right now. But there was also the chance that Victoria and Richard Bellows were still inside, and he needed to talk to them both. Needed some answers.

Lance sighed heavily and looked up to the sky. Heavy clouds rolled across, shading the parking lot. But they weren't dark and foreboding and promising of storms. Instead, they were white and cheerful, creating a cool, comfortable fall afternoon. A breeze blew across the parking lot, and Lance enjoyed the momentary chill, inhaling deeply and beginning a mental pep talk to convince himself that no matter how badly he didn't want to step through the doors of Central Medical, he was old enough now—if not wise enough—to understand that much of his life had very little to do with what *he* wanted. There were much bigger things at play, and no matter how much he hated to admit that on some larger scale, he might be nothing but a tool, a vessel the Universe used to do its bidding, he carried the burden with respect.

Especially now. After what his mother had done, and what she'd said to him as she'd passed on.

Lance started across the parking lot, his feet feeling heavy, as if he were slogging through a marsh. His heart beat faster in his chest the closer he got to those automatic doors, which began to look more and more like a robotic mouth, ready to open and swallow him whole, swallow him into a prison of despair.

He felt a trickle of sweat slide down his temple.

He was still ten yards from the doors when they slid open with a *whoosh* so sudden and unexpected that Lance actually jumped back a step. He stopped and stood and stared, a momentary flit of an absurd thought that the building had become self-aware and was taunting him. But then the thought vanished, the fear abated, and he was quickly overcome with a cool, refreshing stream of relief.

Richard and Victoria Bellows walked out of Central Medical. They both stopped just outside the doors and stared at Lance as if he were an exotic animal—the last thing they'd expected to see at that moment.

Lance stood perfectly still and waited, not particularly feeling like making the first move. Victoria Bellows's eyes looked more tired than before, but they were still kind. Rich stared at Lance with what looked like gritted teeth and a crinkled brow, as if he were working out a complex word problem and struggling to find the answer.

He's still not sure, Lance thought. *He still thinks it might be me.*

After what felt like minutes but was likely only a matter of seconds, Victoria gave Lance a small smile and said, "I'm hoping your morning went a lot better than mine."

Lance returned a smile of his own and slowly walked forward to meet them on the sidewalk. "Had a great breakfast," he said. "But it sort of went downhill from there, what with the whole police interrogation and all."

"Police what? Wait ... did they...?" She shot a glare at her husband. "*Rich.* I may be concussed, but I very clearly remember telling you it wasn't him."

Rich was staring directly at Lance. He spoke slowly and said, "You don't know who it was. You said you never saw who hit you."

Victoria sighed, and Rich and Lance continued to stare at each other. Rich looked ready for blood, but Lance stood and tried to look indifferent to the whole thing. After an uncomfortable moment of silence, Lance held the bouquet of flowers out to Victoria. "For you," he said. "A get-well present, I guess. Or a 'thanks-for-cleaning-my-house-and-I'm-sorry-you-got-attacked-while-scrubbing-toilets' present, if you'd prefer."

This elicited a snort of laugher from Victoria, which caused Lance to chuckle, and he watched as a bit of the tension Rich Bellows had been holding in his shoulders and neck began to loosen. Victoria took the flowers from Lance and smelled them, closing her eyes and inhaling deeply. "Wonderful," she said. "Thank you so much."

Rich allowed himself a small grin and put a protective arm around his wife. He looked at Lance and said, "I admit you'd have to have some pretty big gonads to attack my wife and then show up with flowers at the hospital."

Lance shrugged. "I suppose I could just be playing an angle. Trying to appear innocent by hiding in plain sight. But I think that only works in mystery novels."

Rich narrowed his eyes. "Did Kruger really bring you in?"

Lance nodded. "Yes, sir. I got a behind-the-scenes look at Ripton's Grove's finest at work."

Rich Bellows was silent.

Lance gave him what he wanted. "My alibi checked out," he said. "Sheriff Kruger was supposed to let you know."

Rich used his free hand to pat the pockets of his jeans. After not finding what he was looking for, he snapped his fingers and said, "I left my phone in the car. Sorry, I was in a bit of a panic when I got here."

Lance held up his hand. "I understand. But I want to promise you, I had nothing to do with what happened to your wife. I feel terrible for the whole thing, truly. If I hadn't been renting the place, she would have never been there and this would have never happened."

Victoria said, "Don't be ridiculous. This is in no way your fault."

You have no idea, Lance thought.

Rich removed his arm from around his wife and stuck out his hand. "I'm sorry I jumped to conclusions," he said. "It's just ... well, that place ... and you showed up and ..." He stopped. "I'm sorry. You didn't deserve that."

Lance shook Rich's hand. "I don't blame you," he said.

Then, as if they were approaching the inevitable, Rich asked, "I suppose you'll be wanting to find somewhere else to stay now?" He shook his head, disbelievingly. "I swear ... it's always something with that farmhouse. First it's haunted, and now we have violent home invaders." He sighed. "Come by the office after church tomorrow and I'll get you your deposit back. I tend to pop in for an hour or so after services to catch up on some paperwork."

"Actually, sir," Lance said, "I think I'd like to stay there a bit longer, if that's okay with you."

Both Rich and Victoria looked shocked at this. "Seriously?" Rich asked.

Lance nodded. "Yes, sir."

The Bellowses waited for more, but they weren't getting anything else from Lance right then.

Finally, Rich nodded. "All right, then. Just let me know if you change your mind." Then, "Well, as you know, we've all had a bit of an adventurous day." He moved to step off the sidewalk, off to their vehicle. "I think Victoria would like to get home."

Rich and Victoria, hand in hand, had made it a few feet past Lance when he called after them. "I hear there's a trail, leads from town up to the farmhouse?"

The couple stopped and turned together. Rich looked done with the entire conversation but nodded his head. "Yeah, there is. Straight up the damn hill. Maybe a little less than mile."

Lance started walking back across the parking lot, toward Rich and Victoria. "Any chance I could have a ride to where it starts? If you're going that direction."

Lance knew they were going that direction. Somehow, he knew. Just like he knew Victoria would never let Rich deny Lance's request. They both had kind hearts.

Sure enough, Rich looked to his wife, saw something unmistakable in her eyes, and then said, "Sure. Come on."

Lance smiled and said thank you and followed them to their car.

If they were locked in a car together, it would be harder for Rich Bellows to avoid answering Lance's questions.

17

RICH BELLOWS DROVE A LATE-MODEL FORD EXPLORER, that new car smell still faintly clinging on. Lance waited while Rich opened the front passenger door for Victoria and helped her in. "Easy does it," Rich said as he held his wife's hand and she stepped up into the vehicle. "No need to rush."

"I got hit in the head, Rich. I don't have a spinal injury, for goodness sake. I'm fine."

Rich said something Lance couldn't hear and Victoria laughed. Then he closed the door so gently it was as if he were trying to keep from waking a napping infant. Victoria made an I'm-not-amused face through the window, and this time it was Rich who chuckled. But when he turned and saw Lance standing by, waiting for the couple to finish their moment before he'd allow himself into the backseat, Rich's face fell just the tiniest bit. Enough that Lance noticed. Rich recovered quickly enough. "Hop on in, Lance. Apologies if you sit on something sticky. Kids..." Rich shrugged and walked around the front of the car and slid into the driver's seat.

Lance folded his feet and legs enough that he was able to slide into the backseat of the Explorer with little trouble. The rear seats were a bench that stretched all the way across, so Lance chose to sit in the middle, giving him a better view out the front, and also allowing him to stretch his legs out to either side for more room. When you're tall, you learn these sort of things—a unique set of survival tactics for the long-limbed. He buckled his seat belt and adjusted his backpack on the floor between his feet.

Rich started the engine and drove the vehicle through the parking lot and out onto the road, headed back toward town. He cranked up the Explorer's heater like a blizzard was fast approaching and looked to Victoria. "Warm enough, sweetie?"

Victoria quickly shot her hand out and snapped off the fan. "Burning up. Seriously, Rich. Again, I have a head injury, not hypothermia. It's got to be in the high fifties today!"

Even from the backseat, Lance could see Rich's cheeks redden ever so slightly. After a moment of silence, given as ample time for Rich to regain his dignity after his wife's scolding, Lance started with his questions. He knew his time was going to be limited, he'd need to make the most of it.

"Mr. Bellows, I figure I should tell you, I'm fairly certain there was somebody in the farmhouse last night when I got there."

Rich's head spun around so fast Lance thought they might end up back at Central Medical to treat the man for whiplash. "*What?*" Then, almost under his breath, "Damn teenagers. Can't they find someplace else to smoke their pot and drink their warm beers?"

"Don't forget about the sex," Victoria chimed in.

Rich looked at her as if she'd spoken Latin. She gave him a playful wink that made Lance a little uncomfortable. Lance cleared his throat, pushed on. "I don't know if it was teenagers, sir. I mean, I can't say for sure, but I think it might have just been one person."

Rich sighed. "Certainly isn't the first time folks have broken in. But I figured by now everybody was too afraid to have to deal with the wrath of Ray Kruger to bother having a go at it. Like I said, that place used to be sort of the go-to hangout spot for the ones that weren't too creeped out by what happened there and —" He stopped, as if merely alluding to the murders was more than he wanted to get into.

"That's the other thing, sir," Lance said. "I don't think they had to break in, exactly."

Rich shot Lance a look in the rearview. "What do you mean?"

"The back door was wide open when I got there. There was no sign of forced entry that I could see."

The car went quiet. Lance continued, in case Rich wasn't coming to the conclusion himself. "So, in my opinion, that means either the door wasn't locked to start with, or somebody has a key."

Rich shook his head. "The door was definitely locked. I was the last person there. I make it a point to visit all the vacant rental properties once a month, just to do a quick walk-through. Though I'll admit I usually only get up to the farmhouse once a quarter—I know Kruger sends a guy up that way a couple times a month, so I figure it sits quietly enough."

"Does the sheriff have a key?" Lance asked.

Rich opened his mouth to answer, then stopped. Closed it and thought a moment. Finally, he shook his head. "No. I'm fairly certain he doesn't have a key. Not anymore..."

Lance sat up a bit straighter. "*Anymore*, sir?"

"Ray Kruger did *not* attack me," Victoria said, almost too quickly. Lance and Rich both turned their heads toward her. Ahead, a yellow traffic light turned to red, and Rich eased on the brakes. When the car was stopped, he said, "I thought you told us you didn't see who attacked you."

If Rich Bellows was trying to gain some redemption from his wife about entertaining the possibility of Lance being her attacker, he wasn't going to get that satisfaction. Victoria eyed him with what appeared to be a well-practiced look that only married couples can become familiar with. Rich flinched, almost as if he'd taken a small blow, and offered with some forced cheerfulness, "Right?"

Victoria looked straight ahead and sighed. "Nobody in this town is dumb enough to believe Ray Kruger would do something like this to me. Unless you'd like to try and prove me wrong."

Rich sighed as well, heavier and deeper than his wife, then nodded. "I agree."

Lance let a little more silence pass between the couple, then asked, "Mrs. Bellows, I know you didn't see the person who hit you, but do you have any idea where they might have come from? How they got in the house?"

Victoria closed her eyes for a moment and bowed her head down, as if she were about to pray. Then she said, "I had just come down the stairs. I turned left to head toward the kitchen and had made it about halfway down the hall when I got the feeling that something was behind me. Turns out, I was right. I didn't even get to turn around before my lights went out. They could have come in anywhere. The front door was unlocked. I know that for sure, because I'd gone out to the car a couple times."

Rich smacked the steering wheel with his palm. "The car! I forgot all about your car. It's still up there."

"We can get it later, Rich. It'll be fine," Then, to Lance, "But I didn't touch the back door. Was it locked, as far as you know?"

Lance nodded. "Definitely."

Victoria shrugged. "Well, we may never know. Heck, I had

the windows open, remember. They could have climbed right in if they wanted to."

This conversation was giving Lance nothing. Rich Bellows drove the Explorer past Mama's and then made a turn just past the post office, turning into what looked like a small park. A few picnic tables were scattered about under the shade of some large trees. A baseball diamond, basketball court, jungle gym and swing set completed the picture. Lance felt his time slipping away.

"Mr. Bellows, why did you say Sheriff Kruger doesn't have a key 'anymore'?"

Rich pulled the Explorer into a parking space along the fence line bordering the park. "See that walking path there?" He pointed to a paved path leading away from the parking lot. "Follow it around the baseball field and turn right. You'll see the entrance to the trail that leads up the hill and to the farmhouse. It's a nice little hike, but you look like you're in good shape."

Lance waited. Said nothing.

Rich reached up and switched on the fan again, this time letting it blow cool air instead of heat.

Lance picked up his backpack, moved to leave. Then stopped. "Sir, with all due respect, there's something you're not telling me."

Rich looked to Victoria, his eyebrows questioning. Victoria nodded and turned around to face Lance. "He's not doing it out of spite, or to be a hindrance. It's just ... Ray's a part of this town. A big part. And, well, he's been through a lot, and..." She shrugged. "We tend to respect his privacy." And then for good measure, "We don't tell Ray's business, and he respects ours."

Lance sat back in his seat, possibly even more confused than he had been when he'd gotten into the car. He wanted to push forward, demand more. But he couldn't think of a tactful way to go about it.

Finally, when Rich Bellows must have decided Lance had sat there long enough, he looked at Lance with a stoic face and said. "Son, my wife's right. It's not really your business. *But*"— he said this cautiously, looking to Victoria with a face that said *just bear with me a second*—"since you're staying in the house, and because of the events of last night and today, I suppose I can tell you this much to appease you a bit."

Lance still wasn't a fan of the vagueness, but he waited patiently for Rich to finish.

Rich sighed again and looked out the windshield, staring at the picnic tables. "After the murders, Ray Kruger was the owner of the farmhouse. That's why he had keys."

18

LANCE SAT BACK IN THE SEAT, THE WHIR OF THE Explorer's air-conditioning fans quietly filling the cabin. Rich Bellows's assertion of Ray Kruger's previous ownership of the farmhouse seemed to have stunned them all. Lance because it was information he hadn't expected—and now his gears were spinning so fast in his head he was surprised they weren't audible; Rich and Victoria because they seemed to be almost ashamed that the information had come to light, and now they were weighed down with guilt, unsure how to proceed.

The farmhouse had once belonged to Ray Kruger. The sheriff, who seemed to carry such a distaste for the place, who seemed to get agitated at the very mention of the home, not to mention having to drive out to it and give Lance a stern talking-to, had been the farm's *owner*. This raised so many more questions in Lance's mind, he didn't know where to start. But ... on the other hand, it did somewhat explain why the sheriff— although the place clearly raised his blood pressure— also seemed to carry along with him a sense of protectiveness about the place. It was as though he both despised the farm and wanted to make sure nothing happened to it. Or at least, maybe, to the people in it.

Lance didn't know what to do, what to ask. With his head still spinning, and the look on Rich Bellows's face clearly unhappy, Lance thanked the couple for the ride, apologized for all the trouble, told Victoria he hoped her head felt better soon, and then grabbed his backpack and got out of the Explorer.

He offered a wave as he passed by the side of the car, and Victoria gave him a smile and waved back. Rich put the Explorer into gear and was driving the car out of the parking lot before Lance had even made it to the start of the path.

Once the sound of Bellows's engine was gone, it was replaced with nature—a few birds chirping, wind rustling the leaves, water trickling from somewhere. A stream, perhaps—and the sounds of life. The chains from the swing set creaked softly, and a few children laughed as their mothers pushed them gently back and forth. Four boys were playing two-on-two on the basketball court. The echo of the ball bouncing on the asphalt would always be one of the sweetest sounds to Lance. He was more than half-tempted to walk over to them and ask if he could join. Only for a game or two. But the numbers would be uneven. Plus, he wasn't here to play basketball. At least he didn't think so. At this point, he was more confused than he'd been in a long time.

But now he did have one piece of information that might at least help point him in the right direction. Ray Kruger played a bigger part in all of this than Lance had originally thought. Lance had first thought the sheriff to be an unlucky casualty of the aftermath of the murders, unhappy about the crime and angry that the truth might never surface—no matter what sort of opinion he presented to the town. Now, it turned out the sheriff was more deeply connected to the farmhouse.

But how?

Surely he wasn't the one who'd pulled the trigger. Impossible. Right?

Lance knew better than to completely discredit possible scenarios, but this seemed too much. He thought again about the flash of memory he'd received from Kruger when he'd shaken the man's hand—the little boy and girl playing in the backyard kiddie pool. Would the Universe really make Lance work so hard that it wouldn't show him a vision of the sheriff committing the crime instead of some childhood play day?

Lance sighed. Boy, did he want to play basketball right about now. Just let his mind wander away from the real world for a moment and disappear into the game.

He walked by the courts and watched as one of the boys swished a three-pointer, the chain net jingling as the ball fell through. Then Lance kept going, following Rich's directions until he'd wrapped around the empty baseball field and turned right and found a clearing in the tree line that had to be the start of the trail. He headed for it and heard the jingle of the basketball net again, fading into the distance.

The terrain was mostly flat for the first fifty yards or so, but then it quickly increased in its incline, starting a winding path up and around the hillside, much as the road did from the other side. The trail was mostly dirt and rock, the occasional gnarled tree roots surfacing and crisscrossing the walking path like booby traps, waiting for an unsuspecting ankle. The sky was blotted out by the tree growth, an umbrella of limbs and leaves. Lance heard small animals scurrying through the bed of fallen leaves and pine needles that blanketed the ground on either side of him, among the trees and bushes and overgrowth. He wondered if some of them stopped to watch him, wondering if he were friend or foe. He wondered if animals could see the dead like he could. Dogs, particularly, always seemed to get this sixth sense associated with them when you watched horror movies. Lance would like a dog like that. A companion that shared his gifts, a loyal and understanding friend.

He kept walking.

The sounds of nature were soft and gentle: the leaves rustling, the breeze whistling through limbs and gaps in the trees, the creatures going about their business without a care in the world. It was soothing, peaceful. Lance let his mind slow down a bit, tried to relax and focus on one thing at a time. Tried to recap his day so far and make any sense whatsoever of everything he'd learned.

He sighed and gave up after only a few minutes. Let himself disappear into the forest and the trail, enjoy the quiet, appreciate the simplicity of it all, if only for just a brief moment. He adjusted the straps of his backpack and continued to walk, climbing the small inclines and carefully stepping through the rock and roots. It was cooler under the tree cover, and Lance breathed in the fresh air, smelling pine and soil and, faintly, his own sweat.

He imagined himself back in Westhaven, him and Leah sitting at the Sonic Drive-In, eating hot dogs and slurping slushies and laughing so freely it felt illegal. He could see her, sitting there with the windows down, the breeze teasing her blond hair, making it curl around her face, framing it in such a way it made his heart skip. He watched as she shivered at both the coolness of the air and the icy bite of her slushie and pulled her hands into the sleeves of her blue Westhaven High School sweatshirt and wrapped her arms around herself. And that was when he couldn't take it anymore and leaned across the center console so fast he nearly spilled his slushie and went in to kiss her and—

"That's close enough, Ethan. You wanna keep all your fingers, don't ya?"

A male voice grabbed Lance and pulled him out of his

daydream. The words were followed by a sharp crack and a dull thud. "See, Ethan? See how sharp the blade is?"

Lance resurfaced back in reality and looked up, not even having realized he'd been staring only at the ground for who knew how long, absentmindedly following the trail up and around the hillside. But now, the ground around him had flattened out, and when he looked to his left, he could see where twenty or thirty yards out, the trees began to thin out and give way to land that had been cleared. A small one-story house that looked more hunting cabin than home sat on a few acres of land. To the left of the house, Lance could make out a man and a small child standing by a stacked pile of wood. The man wore blue jeans and no shirt, his chest and arms smeared with sweat and dirt. He was lean and roped with muscle, his skin bronzed by the sun. On the ground at the man's feet were split pieces of wood, waiting to be added to the pile. He held an axe in one hand, its sharpened blade gleaming in the sunlight that made it through the cracks in the clouds as he moved about, and with the other, he was motioning for the child to move back, further away.

"A little more ... little more ... there, that's good. You can watch from there. You can help me stack it and bring some in the house when we're finished, okay?"

Either the boy didn't answer, or he spoke too softly for Lance to hear. But all the same, he stood where he was told and watched dutifully as the man set another piece of wood on the block and gave the axe a mighty swing, sending two perfectly halved pieces to the ground.

Lance watched the man split two more pieces of wood, took another glance at the small house in the distance, and then turned and continued to follow the hill. He was almost back to the farmhouse, he felt, and as the ground began to rise up again, a gentle swell that he was positive led to the precipice that his temporary home was perched, Lance turned and looked over his shoulder, back toward where he'd seen the man and the boy.

He wasn't positive, but it looked like the man was staring straight at Lance. Through all the cover of the trees, and with the small elevation change, Lance wasn't sure it was even possible for the man to see him from his vantage point, but nonetheless, Lance wasn't particularly in the mood to make new friends at the moment. He turned and hurried along, nearly jogging the rest of the way.

The tree line began to thin more and the ground flattened out again and soon he spilled out into the side yard of the spook farm, approaching the house from its south side. He passed by what was left of an old barn that he was too tired and too frustrated to bother taking a look inside and continued toward the rear of the house. To his left, the sun was beginning its descent, dipping below the clouds, and as Lance got closer to the farmhouse, he found himself pulled in that direction like iron to a magnet. He stopped and stood maybe fifty yards from the farmhouse's backdoor, looking straight ahead, out and over the edge of the hilltop.

The sun was perched beautifully in the sky, the early fall evening setting in quickly. Below the highlight of orange and pinkish light, the rooftops of downtown Ripton's Grove looked like a child's plaything. Decorative accessories to a model train set. The fall foliage was only just getting started here, but already the bit of color the leaves provided added to the landscape's beauty. Lance felt as if he could reach out with two fingers and pinch one of the buildings and lift it up to eye level. It was a stunning scene. Beautiful and serene and the epitome of bliss.

He wished Leah could be there to see it. She'd love it, he just knew she would.

And at the thought of his friend, Lance felt his emotions

shift away from the happiness he'd attempted to allow himself to enjoy and turned quickly to look at the farmhouse. Stared for a long time, his shadow growing shorter on the ground before him as the sun continued to sink.

"What do you want from me?" Lance asked the house, his voice carried off on a breeze.

The house did not answer.

Lance didn't bother to take another look at the scene behind him. Instead, he walked around to the front of the house, glanced at Victoria Bellows's Mercedes SUV in the driveway, and then took the porch steps two at a time. He gripped the doorknob and turned it and—

"THANK GOD YOU'RE HERE! YOU'VE GOT TO HELP US!"

The woman's voice, same as the night before, echoed all around Lance on the porch.

"Well," Lance said as he pushed through the door, "I see we're playing this game again."

[19]

LANCE STEPPED INTO THE FARMHOUSE AND CLOSED THE door behind him. The house had a chill to it and smelled faintly of pine and disinfectant. The air felt fresher than before, and Lance turned and saw that the windows were still thrown open from earlier, the cool fall air pouring in. It helped to abate the stuffiness, but the sight of the open windows only recalled the memory that Victoria Bellows had been attacked in this very house earlier today.

Lance positioned himself so his back was against the front door, letting his eyes fall across the stairs, and then focus on the back door in the kitchen down the hallway. All was still and quiet.

"Honey, I'm *hooooome!*" he called out, like a devoted husband after a long day at the office. If his intuition was correct, he should be getting his response any second now.

Sure enough, just as he was about to make his way forward, down the hall and to the kitchen, the man's voice bellowed from nowhere, like an overhead loudspeaker that only Lance could hear.

"*Who's at the door? Is it him? Tell me!*"

Lance paused, waited to see if there would be more, then announced, "It is I, Sir Lancelot, protector of this land, drinker of coffee, and eater of pies. I demand you tell me at once with whom I'm speaking!" A pause, then, "Please."

A breeze from outside picked up some speed and gusted through the window to Lance's right, and the wooden frame of the house creaked and groaned along with it, but otherwise there was silence. Lance's request had fallen on deaf ears. Or, more correctly, dead ears. He'd expected this much but figured it was worth a try. He waited another full minute by the door, listening for anything else, then gave up and started toward the kitchen to check the lock on the back door.

He got halfway down the hall when the man's voice hissed with anger.

"She doesn't want to see you." A pause. *"No. Never. You'll never see it. We're leaving, for good."* A longer pause this time. And just when Lance thought the man had said all he was meant to hear for now, the final, chilling words came. *"You've got three seconds to get off this property or I swear to God I will fucking kill you. You see this? You think I don't know how to use this? You think I'm afraid to use this? Go ahead. You've ruined us, and you're lucky you're not already dead."*

Lance stood motionless in the hallway, holding his breath as the words around him crescendoed in intensity. He waited, ears strained, hanging on for the conclusion of the argument.

Nothing happened.

No more words. No more yelling.

Lance threw up his hands in disgust. "Really? You're just going to leave me hanging like that? What a tease." He thought about giving the house the finger, but he'd never flipped off the spirit world before. Wasn't sure it would have the same impact or satisfaction. Plus, he doubted his mother would approve of such juvenile behavior.

He walked into the kitchen and set his backpack down on the table, pulling out a chair to sit and retrieving a bottle of water from his bag. He twisted off the cap and downed half the bottle in three big gulps.

Then the gunshot boomed and rattled the walls and shook the glass, and Lance dropped the bottle onto the floor. He jumped up from his seat at the table and turned to look back down the hall...

...just as the door to his right, the one leading down to the basement, began to rattle in its frame, the sounds of pounding fists beating against the other side almost in perfectly synced rhythm with Lance's heart as it danced in his chest.

"*Let me out!*"

A female voice, younger than the voice from before and sounding very weak. Exhausted, and also terrified.

Lance lurched forward and ripped the door open.

There was nothing there but blackness and the sight of the first couple wooden stairs that led down into the dark mouth of the house's belly.

Lance stood and waited, listened for a long time.

He heard no more. The house was finished for now.

The house creaked occasionally, and the breeze still trickled in from the front windows, stirring up the air. A few floorboards groaned as Lance walked around the kitchen, pacing back and forth and thinking.

"Three voices," he said to the kitchen. "If you count the girl from behind the basement door." He glanced at the door, which he'd decided to close, promising himself that he would inspect whatever lay down there very soon. But first he needed to think, go over things while they were still fresh in his mind.

Playing on the theory that the voices he was hearing were in fact a message, some sort of cosmic reenactment meant as a clue to assist Lance in figuring out what had happened at the farmhouse, Lance felt it was safe to assume that the woman's voice he'd now heard twice on the porch belonged to Natalie Benchley. Which meant that the man's voice, that angry, inquisitive voice, likely belonged to her husband, Mark Benchley.

"And the girl's voice was Mary," Lance said aloud, stopping and again looking to the basement door. He didn't know how he knew, but he was certain. It'd been Mary Benchley pounding away on the basement door, sounding weak and tired and crying to be let out.

Lance eyed the sliding bolt meant to keep the door locked. "Why was she down there?"

He sat down at the table and finished what was left of his bottle of water. Stared at that bolt. His first thought was that Mark Benchley, while being a suspected murderer, had also been some sort of psychotic child abuser and had locked his daughter away. After all, if you could stomach murdering your whole family, what was throwing one of them down into your home's very own dungeon?

But then Lance thought about his conversation with Joan earlier that day, as she'd sat across from him in the booth at Mama's and poured her heart out to him.

Mary was his absolute pride and joy. He was so proud of her.

Joan was adamant that Mark Benchley hadn't killed his family.

The ghost of Sheriff Bill Willard had a similar opinion.

One was the town gossip, the other was an ever-present fly on the wall at the local sheriff's office. Both were privy to all sorts of information. Lance trusted both of them, though he knew he'd need a lot more than just his trust in a waitress and a spirit to prove anything.

He eyed the bolt again.

"Protection," he said. "He put her down there to protect her." Then, "But from who?"

The answer seemed obvious.

Lance replayed the voices in his head again. The initial shock from Natalie Benchley (*"THANK GOD YOU'RE HERE!..."*), and the argument Mark Benchley had followed with (*"You've got three seconds to get off this property or I swear to God I will kill you"*).

Lance had heard three voices ... but there had been four people in the house that night. The fourth was somebody that wasn't supposed to be there. Somebody who was not welcome.

(*You think I'm* afraid *to use this?*)

Lance envisioned Mark Benchley holding a shotgun up into the face of whoever else had been in the farmhouse that night, angry, his words full of intent. Threatening.

Yet it was the Benchley family who'd ended up dead that night.

And if Lance was only hearing the voices of the dead, that meant the fourth person who'd been in the house that night was still alive. And they might be the only person who knew the truth.

Lance sighed and looked up to the ceiling. "What the heck happened here?"

Then his stomach grumbled, and he realized he'd never made it to the grocery store.

[20]

THE SUN HAD GONE DOWN COMPLETELY, ENCASING THE farmhouse in darkness. Lance had closed the windows and locked them, then turned on all the lights on the house's first floor, bathing everything in yellowish tinge that unfortunately brought to mind seventies slasher films. But he preferred this look to the darkness. Not that he was afraid, but the light helped the place feel more alive. Less like the crime scene everybody seemed determined to cement it as. He sat on the steps and waited for his guests.

Susan and Luke were on their way. Lance had gambled that their curiosity about the farmhouse, Susan's past friendship with Mary Benchley, and the fact that there might not be a whole lot to do in a town as small as Ripton's Grove on a Saturday night might be enough to entice the two of them to come over and spend some time with him. The only stipulation was that they were required to bring dinner. And maybe answer a few questions.

Headlights dotted the distance and grew closer. Lance stood and opened the front door, stepping out onto the porch and waving blindly into the lights. Luke's Jeep took form and parked, two silhouettes jumping from the doors and approaching the porch steps as the headlights cut off.

"Hi," Susan said. "I hope pizza's okay." She offered a large pizza box, stained with grease.

"Perfect," Lance said, taking it from her and stepping aside so the two of them could enter the house.

Luke, carrying a six-pack of soda, offered his fist and Lance bumped it. "Not exactly how I expected to spend my evening," he said. "But that's not necessarily a bad thing."

Lance followed them inside and closed the door.

Luke and Susan stood motionless in the foyer, ramrod straight, heads tilted up and swiveling slowly back and forth along the walls, rooms, stairs, hallway. They took it all in silently, like two patrons at a museum admiring a piece of art that both captivated and stunned them.

Lance waited. Said nothing.

Finally, Luke turned and said, "I feel weird being here. Do you feel weird?"

Lance shrugged. "It wears off. I guess I've gotten used to it."

Susan was still silent, staring down at the floor. Lance noticed a single tear spill down her cheek. Luke took notice as well. "Suze? Everything okay?" He put his arm around her, and she nodded and laughed and shook her head.

"It's surreal, I guess. I mean, I *played* here a few times when I was little. Once or twice was all. But..." She stifled a sob, then shook her head again and smiled. "Sorry. It's been a long time, but I guess it just seems more real now that I'm actually standing in the house."

Lance mentally kicked himself. "I'm sorry," he said. "I shouldn't have asked you to come. It was completely insensitive and—"

"It's fine," Susan cut him off. "Really. I'm glad you invited us. Honestly, and this might sound strange, but by being here I sort of feel like I'm keeping Mary's memory alive a little longer in my head." She waited a beat, and when neither Lance or Luke said anything, she shrugged and wiped away the tear. "Anyway, I'm starving. Let's eat."

They walked into the kitchen and sat around the table— Susan giving it an appraising glance, probably recalling another memory. A meal she'd shared with the Benchley family at this very table, or maybe an after-school arts and crafts project with Mary. Lance swallowed down his guilt. Susan was old enough to make her own decisions. If she wanted to leave, she was more than welcome to. But he didn't think she would.

Luke flipped open the pizza box and grabbed a slice, his eyes darting around the kitchen as he chewed, taking it all in. Then he asked, "So I've been dying to ask you, why exactly did I get a call from the sheriff while I was finishing up my workout at the Y?"

"*What?*" Susan said, head swiveling toward her boyfriend. "What do you mean?"

Luke didn't answer. Instead he looked to Lance, eyes full of curiosity more than any hint of anger or irritation.

Lance grabbed his own slice and started to eat. He saw no sense in being coy. Besides, he was hoping his two friends could answer some of his questions. Figured it better to divulge some of his own information first, level the playing field as best he could. "Victoria Bellows came by the house this morning to clean the place. She was doing it as a favor for her husband because the cleaning people he usually uses for rentals are terrified to come here because..." He paused and gave Susan a quick glance before continuing, "They believe Mary Benchley was a witch."

Susan scoffed at this and rolled her eyes. Luke took another bite of pizza.

"But that's not the problem," Lance continued. "Shortly

after Luke picked me up to take me into town, somebody entered the house and attacked Victoria Bellows. Hit her over the head hard enough she blacked out. She didn't see who it was, and the sheriff's department thought it prudent to eliminate any potential suspects as quickly as possible, which included me. Luke verified my alibi."

"*Shit*," Luke said in between chews of pizza. "Weird day this's been, huh? First I get used as an alibi, and now I'm eating pizza at the spook farm. I wish I had a vlog. This would get big-time views."

Susan looked at him and shook her head. Lance laughed, though he wasn't positive he knew what a vlog was. "It's been interesting. I'll give you that. But there's more. Somebody was here when you all dropped me off last night. I didn't see anybody—other than some movement at one of the windows when we pulled in—but the back door was wide open when I got inside. I'm positive somebody took off when they saw us arrive. My suspicion, and this is nothing more than a hunch, is that whoever was here last night attacked Victoria Bellows earlier today. Aside from the main question of who, I'm almost more curious as to what it is they want. I mean, there's nothing here." Lance held out his arms, gesturing to the empty kitchen around them. "It's an empty old house."

"Squatter, maybe?" Luke suggested. "Some homeless drifter who's pissed somebody showed up to boot him out? I mean, nobody's been here for a while, right?"

"Maybe," Lance said. "But there's no sign of forced entry anywhere I've seen. So whoever got in, they either found a door or window unlocked, picked a lock, or—and this is the one that I'm a bit concerned about—they had a key."

Silence around the table. Lance had laid it all out, and it appeared his two companions were just as out of answers as he was. He wasn't surprised. He sighed and grabbed a slice of pizza and wolfed it down in three huge bites. Started on a second slice.

Susan popped open one of the soda cans and took a long swig. "Mmmm," she said. "Nothing beats warm soda."

The three of them chuckled, the tension slowly evaporating. "I've got a couple bottles of water," Lance offered. "Also warm, but maybe better than the soda?"

Susan politely declined, but Luke took Lance up on the offer. "Sure, I'll take one. I don't need all that sugar in those things," he said, pointing to the remaining five cans. Lance couldn't help but think he and Luke would be good friends under different circumstances. In another life that Lance tried to keep himself from fantasizing about too frequently.

"I completely agree," Lance said and reached down under the table, where he'd stowed his backpack. He unzipped the front pouch and then sighed to himself. *Wrong pouch.* But as he was about to close it, something caught his eye. There, sitting on top of all his other small items he kept for ready access in the front pouch of the backpack, was a sheet of paper, folded in half. Yellow legal pad, from the looks of it. Lance reached in slowly, as if the paper might scurry away if frightened, and plucked it out with his thumb and index finger. He kept his hands below the table, his torso still bent over toward the bag, and unfolded the paper.

It was a list of names, handwritten. Scribbled in a hurry, from the looks of it.

And Lance was back in the interview room at the sheriff's office, the ghost of Sheriff Bill Willard echoing softly in his head.

("So when you get your bag back, maybe in the smaller front compartment, you find a list of names. Maybe those names were all people of interest in the Benchley case. Not because they were suspects, necessarily, but because they were thought to

561

maybe have information that could help in discovering the truth. Maybe…")

Lance read over the names, surprised that he recognized a few.

The first name that jumped off the page was the most confusing. It sat atop the list, the most neatly printed of them all.

Ray Kruger.

Lance crinkled his brow and had to calm his brain from racing to figure out why the current active sheriff would be on this list. Did his previous ownership of the house somehow implicate him?

He shoved the thoughts aside and looked at the second name that stood out to him. He had no solid knowledge to verify that the name belonged to who he thought it did, but, as with many things he couldn't explain, he knew all the same.

He opened the main compartment of his backpack and tossed Luke a bottle of water. "Sorry if it smells like a gym bag," he said. "I sort of live out of this thing most of the time."

Luke waved him off and cracked open the bottle, taking a large swig.

Lance, hopefully not sounding as somber as he suddenly felt, looked at Susan. "I know this is random, but what's your last name?"

Susan swallowed a bite of pizza and without hesitation answered, "Marsh." Then, after a quick pull from the soda can, "Why?"

Because you're on the short list of people who might know what happened here the night the Benchley family was killed, Lance thought.

THE PROBLEM WITH TALKING TO THE LIVING WAS THAT they tended to ask more questions than the dead.

Lance needed to ask his own questions to Luke and Susan, see if they could help him piece together some of the puzzle, but in doing so, they'd undoubtedly question the information he already possessed and, more importantly, how he'd come by it.

These were questions Lance could not answer honestly. Not with the two new friends sitting around the table with him, eating pizza and drinking lukewarm beverages. They were good people. Mostly honest, Lance felt, but he would not trust them with his secrets, his abilities. There were so few whom he had.

His mother.

Marcus Johnston.

And most recently ... Leah.

He'd felt the connection with her the moment they'd met. Explored it, treaded its waters that first day, and in the end he had told her everything. And she'd accepted him completely. Believed him wholeheartedly. Had developed more faith in him than he'd ever had in himself. She was special. He knew that beyond any doubt. And she'd felt it in him as well, able to see there was much more to Lance Brody than was on the surface.

And when he'd held her hand, when their lips had met for the first kiss, it'd felt more right than anything he had ever felt before. For those moments, Lance was normal. Just a guy kissing a girl and wondering if this was what love felt like. Wondering if it was possible to be hit with it so fast, and under such unexpected circumstances.

But since when had life ever followed any sort of script? Since when did life care about the circumstances? Things happened when they happened, and you could drive yourself mad trying to make heads or tails of it.

"Well?" Susan said.

Lance's eyes refocused on the room, the table, his friends. They were both looking at him expectantly. Lance shook his head, resurfacing from the deep waters of his daydream. "I'm sorry, what?"

"What are you looking at?" Luke said, starting on yet another slice of pizza. "What's that in your hand? It looks like it spooked you."

Lance sat up and laid the sheet of paper on the table, running his hand over it to press it smooth, his mind scrambling for some sort of plausible explanation. Something he could work with to drive this conversation where he needed it to go.

And then it came to him. Something so convenient he almost laughed. His mother's words echoed in his head, an adage of hers that Lance consistently found validated.

(*Do you, a person with your gifts, honestly believe things could be so random?*)

He picked up another slice of pizza and took a bite. Chewed and swallowed, wiping his mouth with the back of his hand. "Susan, what's everybody in town saying I'm here for?"

Susan's eyes widened, like she'd been caught in some sort of lie. "What? Why are you asking me?"

Lance smiled, held up his hands to show he meant no harm. "It's okay, it's okay. I know people are gossiping. Joan made that pretty apparent this morning at breakfast. I just figured you'd probably heard something through the grapevine." He waited a second, then asked again, "Why do people think I'm here?"

Susan sighed in a sort of admission. "They think you're a reporter, or journalist or something like that. They think you're going to write one of those true crime books about the night of the murder, or some big exposé piece for a big magazine. Try and win a Pulitzer. Whatever reason they believe, they think you're here for money. Blood money, to be specific."

Lance wasn't surprised by any of this. He supposed it could be worse. "So I don't have a lot of fans, huh?"

Luke and Susan both shook their heads.

"And what do you both think?"

Luke shrugged his shoulders and finished off the bottle of water. "You seem like a cool dude, and you don't seem to be hurting anybody by being here, so I don't really think it matters what you're up to. You say you're here for work, that's good enough for me. Innocent till proven guilty. That's America, right?"

Lance looked at Susan. She seemed a bit more apprehensive than her boyfriend, but her eyes were still soft, kind. "I agree with Luke," she said, "but I also don't think you're telling us everything."

And Lance wouldn't. It was better for everybody if they never knew the truth.

"I can promise you this," Lance said. "I'm not here to hurt anybody or disrespect anybody's memory, and I'm certainly not here to cause any trouble."

Luke and Susan waited. Knew there was more coming.

"So, I'm asking you to trust me here, okay?"

The two of them looked at each other, then back to Lance. Nodded.

"For the sake of everything going forward, let's assume that I am a journalist. And as a journalist, I have to protect my sources. So please, don't ask me how I've gotten certain information, because I can't tell you. I'm sorry if that sounds harsh, but believe me, all I'm trying to do is get to the bottom of this. I want to know who really killed the Benchley family."

Susan sat forward at this, alert and eyes glinting with ... was it excitement? "So you don't think Mark Benchley did it, do you?"

Lance heard the voices in his head—the argument between who he presumed to be Mark Benchley and the mystery fourth person who'd been in the house that night. "I think there's more to it," Lance said. Then, without any other preamble, he slid the sheet of paper across the table to Susan. Luke slid over close to examine it with her. "What do you make of that list of names?" Lance asked.

Before Susan could answer, there was a knock at the front door.

"Expecting somebody else?" Luke asked.

Lance stood from the table. "No," he said. "I usually never am."

[22]

LANCE WALKED TO THE DOOR SLOWLY, HEARING LUKE AND Susan's steady footfalls behind him. Keeping their distance, but curious all the same. The yellow light from inside the house reflected off the windows next to the door, making it impossible to see out, try to catch a glimpse of who'd knocked.

Then another knock at the door. Not urgent, not angry, just a simple one-two rap of knuckles, loud enough to hopefully be heard. Lance reached the door and then turned, whispered to his friends. "It's probably fine, but just in case, get ready to go out the back door." He nodded back toward the kitchen, but neither Luke nor Susan turned to check. They nodded and kept staring at the door, waiting with breath held to see who was on the other side.

Lance turned the knob and opened the door, slowly, only a third of the way. Peered out.

Saw the man and the boy who'd been chopping wood earlier as Lance had walked up the trail. The boy held the man's hand, standing shyly, almost hiding behind the man's leg. He was wearing jeans and dirty sneakers and a red flannel shirt. The man, also clad in jeans and wearing a tight-fitting black t-shirt despite the cool night air, held a battery powered lantern in the other hand, its light bright and fierce. Lance felt his body loosen, his muscles relax and his lungs suck in a full breath of air that almost sounded like a sigh as he exhaled it. Then he opened the door completely and said, "Hi."

"Miss Susan! Miss Susan!" The little boy shot from the porch and ran on still-unsteady legs across the threshold and into the foyer, rushing to Susan's side and wrapping her leg with a hug.

"Hey, Ethan! How are you, sweetie pie?" Susan squatted down and kissed the little boy on the top of the head and returned the hug. Ethan started to talk rapidly, and to Lance, mostly incoherently, using his hands to animate what appeared to be all sorts of adventures and fascinating tales. Susan smiled and nodded and played along and encouraged.

Luke stood and watched, disinterested, rubbing the side of his face and then looking to Lance, as if to ask, *What's happening?*

Lance had the same question. He turned and found the man still standing politely on the porch, eyes locked onto the boy as he continued his rapid-fire storytelling. Then the man's gaze shifted back to Lance, and his smile broadened and gleamed in the darkness.

"Hi," he said. "Sorry about that. Ethan loves Susan. More than me, I'm afraid." He laughed, and Lance offered a small grin. It was all he could force. His confusion was still overpowering the rest of him. The man, seeming to sense this, said, "Oh, sorry." He stuck out his hand. "Jacob Morgan. I'm sorry it's getting so late, but I'd heard there was somebody new staying here, and then I saw you walking up the trail earlier, so I figured Ethan and I would come and introduce ourselves. You know"—he shrugged—"since we're basically neighbors and all."

Lance shook Jacob's hand. It was rough and calloused and

the grip was strong. "Lance Brody," he said. "It's nice to meet you. I saw you chopping wood when I walked up. I didn't figure you could see me, though, because of all the trees."

Jacob nodded, as if this was a story he'd heard a hundred times. "I mean, I probably couldn't have picked you out of a lineup, but I got the general idea. Human. Male. Tall. Not Sasquatch." He smiled.

Lance looked back to Susan and Ethan. They were sitting on the floor together. Luke had joined them and was playing a game of hot hands with the boy, which he was pretending to lose at terribly, each slap of his hand causing Ethan to squeal in laughter.

"She watches him in Kids' Group at church on Sundays," Jacob said. "And she gets the cook at Mama's to make him Mickey Mouse pancakes when we get breakfast there sometimes. He thinks it's the funniest damn thing."

Lance nodded. Said nothing. He wasn't great with kids, and not great at talking about them either. Grasping for a talking point, he asked, "So how old is he, your son?"

"Just turned six," he said. "And he's not my son. I mean, at least not by blood." Then, briefly, Jacob Morgan's face dropped, his eyes went unfocused. Sadness seemed to creep in and then out. "He's my nephew. My half-sister's kid. She passed away right after he was born."

Lance kicked himself for accidentally bringing up the topic. "I'm so sorry," he said.

Jacob's eyes reignited with life and he smiled. "It's okay. Little guy is the best thing ever to happen to me." Then he laughed. "Don't get me wrong, he can be a complete pain in the butt, but it's in the best way. You know?"

Lance nodded. What else could he say to that?

"Anyway," Jacob said, "I didn't mean to interrupt your evening. Just wanted to say hi and let you know that if you need any help with anything—want to borrow a cup of sugar and all that neighborly stuff—just come on down. It can get a little lonely up here sometimes."

"Thank you," Lance said. "I appreciate it."

Both he and Jacob looked back to Ethan and Susan and Luke, playing on the rough wooden floor. Ethan was demonstrating to Luke how to chop wood properly, setting imaginary pieces of wood and then swinging an invisible axe, making a *whooshing* sound with his mouth as he did so. Luke pantomimed the action, purposely screwing up and making Ethan laugh and shake his head and say, "No, like *this!*"

Lance watched the boy make another imaginary swing and then looked back to Jacob. "You know, I think there might be a slice or two of pizza left, if you want to come in and let Ethan play a little longer."

Jacob looked to his nephew for a moment, then back to Lance. Then Lance watched as the man's eyes fell over the rest of the house's interior, the same way Luke and Susan's had earlier that evening when they'd arrived, as if he were remembering things the way they used to be, like he'd been here before.

"If you're sure it's no trouble," he finally said. "We won't stay long. Ethan needs to get to bed."

Then he stepped inside and Lance closed the door, happy he'd convinced the man to stay.

Something inside Lance was sending up signals, picking up something unusual in the air. His senses coming to life and recognizing something that might be important to everything he was here for.

Not about Jacob.

Ethan.

There was something special about the boy.

Susan helped Ethan pick out a slice of pizza, and after some pseudo-protests from Jacob about the sugar and caffeine, the boy sat on his knees in one of the chairs, eating over the opened pizza box and sipping one of the warm sodas like he was at the best party in the world.

Lance sat where he'd been before, as did Susan. But Luke was now leaning against the counter by the sink, arms crossed and watching Jacob and Susan sitting next to each other, chatting like old friends. Which apparently they were, to a certain extent.

Susan wasted no time launching into explaining the relationship to Lance. "Jacob's parents used to own the hardware store down on South Street," she said. "I used to go down there with Daddy on the weekends just to see if Jacob was working!" She blushed then, as if she'd forgotten Jacob was capable of hearing. She laughed. "I had the biggest crush on you! And what are you, five, six years older?"

Jacob looked up to the ceiling, apparently doing mental math. Nodded his head. "Yeah, I think that's about right."

Susan made a noise that sounded like a squeal and groan. "I was so stupid. I couldn't have been more than twelve ... maybe thirteen at the time."

Jacob laughed. "I remember you coming in. You always stood over by the paint section, pretending to look at the color sample cards."

"So you *knew* I was pretending?"

Jacob shrugged. "You were comically obvious. Like you said, you were young."

Lance looked to Luke, whose face remained passive, but he was uncrossing and recrossing his arms a lot, clearly not thrilled with what he was hearing.

"I was surprised to see you here." Susan laughed. "We had

no idea who was at the door. We thought you might have been one of those ghost hunters!"

Jacob grinned and shook his head. "I must say, I could say the same thing about you." Then, "What are you guys up to up here, anyway?"

Lance felt a twinge of panic. Susan was obviously still crushing on Jacob Morgan, and Lance feared this was going to make her open to discussing a lot more with the man than Lance really wanted her to.

Thankfully, Luke was on the same page.

"I used to play ball with Lance here," he said, uncrossing his arms again and this time shoving his hands into the pockets of jeans. "We ran into each other last night and thought we'd try and catch up some. I haven't seen him in years."

Jacob nodded, eyeing Lance. Lance smiled and said, "Yeah, one of those small world moments, I guess."

Susan caught on, smiled and nodded.

Jacob asked, "And what brings you to Ripton's Grove, Lance? Why are you here?"

Boy, am I getting tired of that question.

He shrugged. "I heard you had the best meatloaf in the state."

Susan laughed. Luke smirked. Jacob Morgan gave one of his grins.

That was that. Lance wouldn't offer more unless provoked. He was getting tired of everyone prying into his business. He was getting tired of all the lies, despite their inevitability.

Jacob's eyes shifted over to his nephew, the boy had finished his pizza—half the slice sitting upside down in the box—and was gripping his soda can with two hands as he said something to Susan. She laughed and nodded and asked Jacob, "Okay if I take him to the bathroom? He's just informed me—very politely,

I might add—that he has to pee and he doesn't know where to go."

This got a chuckle from the group, and Jacob said, "Are you sure you don't mind?"

"Not at all."

The two of them walked hand in hand the short way down the hall, and Lance heard the bathroom door open and close and then Susan calling out, "Don't forget to wash your hands!"

The three men sat alone in the kitchen together, and even though Susan was right down the hall, they might as well have been on a desert island together. Susan had taken all the conversation with her, and the three of them sat there, trying not to look at each other and be forced to make mind-numbing small talk.

Luke didn't like Jacob Morgan. That much was obvious to Lance. Whether it was insecurity or jealousy or both, Luke was doing his best to try and look unfazed, but Lance read it in his body language easily enough.

Jacob Morgan didn't seem to care one way or the other about Luke's presence in the kitchen, as he hadn't even gone so far as to nod in his direction, or shake his hand, or even offer a hello.

Lance didn't care about either of the other two men right then, because he was still fascinated with the boy.

He'd felt it as soon as Ethan had rushed across the threshold into Susan's arms, a sudden, gentle pull, magnetic-like. No, maybe that wasn't quite right. It was more like an energy, a cold feeling that was also warm at the same time, like a pulsing wave. A crackle of electricity that made the hair on Lance's arms and the back of his neck tickle with static.

And the longer Ethan had been in the house, the stronger the sensation had become. As Lance had sat across from the boy, trying to keep his attention focused on the adults and the conversation, he'd been sneaking glance after glance toward Ethan, studying him, and also trying to reach out to him.

Because there was something familiar about the sensation he felt around the boy. Something...

The hallway door opened and closed, and Susan and Ethan returned. Ethan passed the kitchen table and went to Luke. Held out his hands, palms up. "Play?"

Luke smiled and slid down onto the floor, probably happy to have the distraction from his girlfriend getting all googly-eyed over Jacob Morgan, and also, maybe, in an attempt to show Susan that he was perfectly comfortable playing with kids, in an effort to hopefully impress her. Score some points.

"Only a few minutes, Ethan. It's already past your bedtime."

Ethan pretended not to hear his uncle, and Jacob rolled his eyes at Susan, who laughed.

"So, Lance, how long you staying? Good while?"

Again with the questions. Why couldn't Jacob Morgan pull out his phone and stare at Facebook or play Candy Crush like every other well-behaved adult in the country?

"As long as work takes," Lance said. Then, to flip the cards, "And what do you do for a living? More than chop wood, I take it."

Jacob Morgan laughed and pointed at Lance. "Good one. Yeah, a little more than that. I still own the hardware store, but I hired a manager to run the place. I share the profit with him. Not a bad gig for either of us, really. I do some farming, some handiwork 'round town for folks, some of the businesses. This and that."

Susan said, "What he's not telling you is his parents left him, like, a bazillion dollars."

Lance suspected Susan meant the words as a joke, but it was instantly obvious it made Jacob uncomfortable. The man nodded, forced a smile. "My parents invested well in some land about a decade before they died," he said. "It's certainly helped." Then he looked to Ethan. "Especially since this little guy came along."

"And on that note, Ethan, it's time to go."

Ethan didn't protest. He simply played one more quick round of hot hands with Luke and then stood up from the floor. "Okay," he said.

And then Lance sucked in a sharp, quick breath, clenching his teeth and almost doubling over, as if he'd just experienced a pregnancy contraction. It wasn't so much painful as overwhelming. The room seemed to wobble in and out of focus, the hairs on his arms and neck feeling as though they were standing straight up, like he was part of a load of laundry, fresh out of the dryer.

It was the sensation he'd picked up from Ethan, only intensified ten times over. Maybe a hundred.

And then his vision cleared and the room came back into focus and he saw that all the other adults in the room were standing around like nothing at all had happened. They weren't even looking at him, wondering what'd gone wrong, why he'd gasped.

And then he saw that all their eyes were locked on to something, all staring in the same direction.

Lance turned his head to follow their gazes.

Ethan stood directly in front of the basement door, staring at the chipped wood, his hand slowly reaching up toward the knob.

Jacob spoke up. "Ethan, no. That's just a basement, and it's locked."

Another blast of electricity made the room wobble in Lance's vision, but it was weaker this time. Not enough to bother him. Again, the others didn't seem to notice.

Ethan reached for the knob again, and Jacob was across the room, swooping the boy up into his arms. "Ethan, I said no!"

Ethan instantly burst into a fit of tears and childish screams. "But she's down there! She's down there!"

Jacob offered a barrage of rushed apologies and thanks for the pizza and was at the front door in a flash, Luke and Lance and Susan all trailing. Jacob gave a final goodnight and wave and then was gone, switching on the lantern he'd left on the porch, disappearing down the steps and around the side of the house. Ethan's cries echoed in the night air. "She's down there! She's down there!"

The three of them stood in silence at the front door.

Oh my God, Lance thought. *He's like me.*

[23]

LANCE FLOATED DOWN THE HALLWAY, LIGHT AS AIR. SOUND was muffled, distorted, as if he were underwater. The walls of the farmhouse closed around him, a vignette in his peripheral vision. He was moving, but his body was on autopilot. He wasn't even sure he was breathing, but he must be, because as he reached the kitchen, he had enough air in his lungs to whisper the words, "He's like me," delivered in a voice of such astonishment, such absolute shock, that both Susan and Luke looked up from where they'd been cleaning up the kitchen table and said together, "What?"

Lance heard them, faintly, soft voices lingering far off in the distance as his head reeled and his mind scrambled and some part of his entire life uprooted and shifted itself with enough force to make his stomach queasy.

There was confusion at first, followed by a fundamental understanding that brought into focus a feeling of happiness and relief strong enough to force an unexpected laugh from Lance's lips.

I am not alone.

Even though the boy Ethan was only six years old, he was

living proof, the first solid piece of evidence Lance had ever encountered that there were others like him. Others who shared his gifts.

There were the Reverend and the Surfer, sure, but they were something different. Lance did not understand the full breadth of their powers and abilities, but he was certain that in this unspoken war, they were on the opposing side.

But the boy ... innocent.

Like Lance had been when he'd been young and his mother and he had struggled to keep up and comprehend Lance's abilities.

Lance had so many questions, was dying to know if Ethan was just like him—the conversations with the dead, the tele-pathic tendencies, the instant downloads with just a touch of flesh on flesh. Could he control any of it? Could he do more?

He's six years old, Lance. He had to slow himself down. Ethan was a child. Lance tried to remember being that young, what it'd been like to have the realization that he wasn't like everybody else. Could see and hear things the rest of the world could not.

It had been confusing.

Terrifying.

If it hadn't been for his mother, her patience and grace and absolute love for her only son—her protection...

And Lance was swarmed with another thought that made his heart quicken and his breathing intensify with excitement. A thought ripe with possibility.

He replayed the moment of Ethan's outburst in his head. The way the boy had gone toward the door and reached for the handle. The way Jacob Morgan had at first tried to calmly dissuade his nephew, then rushed to his side to pull him away, as if sensing the tantrum was on its way. Which made a certain level of sense, as parents often knew their children's habits and tendencies better than any other—and Lance doubted Jacob Morgan and Ethan's situation would be any different, given it seemed Jacob had been the boy's guardian for nearly his entire young life.

But what struck Lance as odd was the fact that, despite the suddenness with which Ethan's tantrum had erupted, the words he'd screamed had been clear as day.

("She's down there! She's down there!")

Lance, for one, was in on the game. He'd already experienced some sort of supernatural message he was still presuming to have come from Mary Benchley, so he hadn't question Ethan's words.

But neither had Jacob Morgan.

Whether the man was taking his nephew's claims at face value or, more likely, simply playing along in an effort to placate the screaming child, the natural response from most people would have been, *Who's down there?* Or maybe, *There's nobody down there*, in that soothing parental voice one uses to set a child's mind at ease.

Jacob Morgan had gone with neither. Had said nothing.

Lance considered this for a long time, standing idly in the kitchen while Susan and Luke continued to stare at him.

Maybe he knows, Lance thought. *Maybe he knows Ethan is special. That's why he was in such a hurry to get out of here. He recognized the boy slipping into one of his ... episodes.*

If that was the case, Lance *needed* to talk to the man. His head was spinning, full of questions.

Lance's vision cleared and he saw Luke and Susan standing behind the table, waiting.

"Tell me everything you know about that guy," Lance said, looking at Susan.

"Well," she said, pulling out a chair to sit. "For starters, he's on the list you gave me."

She held up the yellow sheet of legal paper and Lance eyed it. He had forgotten all about it.

And that's when something else struck him, another shift in the landscape. He'd been trying so hard to figure out why he'd been brought to Ripton's Grove, ultimately accepting it was because of the potentially unsolved mystery behind the Benchley family murder.

But now he wondered if it had been about the boy from the very beginning.

[24]

LANCE STOOD AND WATCHED AS LUKE AND SUSAN CLIMBED into the Jeep, gave a final wave, and then started to back down the driveway, the sounds of tires on gravel growing fainter before quieting altogether.

He shut the front door and locked it. Double-checked the windows and the back door. All secure. Though at this point, he wasn't sure the doors being locked mattered much. Somebody had access to this house. Somebody that wasn't supposed to. But Lance didn't allow himself to be concerned with thoughts of intruders right then. He found the odds of somebody entering the house for a third time in twenty-four hours slim, if not completely nonexistent. Especially when on their last visit, they'd assaulted a woman and sent her to the hospital. They had to at least think the police might have taken a bit more of an interest in the place now. Have a deputy swing by a few times during the night to make sure everything was calm and orderly. Lance knew no such thing would happen. This place was a black spot on the town's map, and it seemed that Sheriff Kruger was keen on keeping it that way.

But there was more keeping Lance from worrying about

possible nighttime assailants. He was too distracted. His mind was still coming down off the high of discovering, after all these years, that there were others like him. At least one, anyway. But if there was one ... it only fueled the theory that there would be more. Out there somewhere. All probably wondering the same things as Lance. Wondering if they were alone and questioning everything they were and desperately seeking any sort of answer, explanation, and, most importantly, camaraderie.

Lance sighed and sat down at the table, pulling his last bottle of water from his backpack and cracking the top. He took a small sip, then a full gulp, and then another. It was tepid, but it also seemed to help cool his thoughts, allow his body and mind to slow down, his heart rate to steady and his breathing to normalize. He took another swallow and then refastened the cap and said, "Okay." He stared down at the wooden table, refocusing his mind. "What do I do now?"

The list that had magically ended up in his bag from the sheriff's office was on the table, refolded and looking innocuous. After Jacob and Ethan had left, and Lance had regained enough control of himself to have a conversation with human beings again, he'd told Susan that he had reasons to believe that anyone on that list might have some sort of insight into what happened the night the Benchley family was killed.

Susan's eyes had scanned the list, not even flinching when she saw her own name, and then nodded. "Makes sense," she'd said. "Where'd you get this?"

Lance shook his head. "Nope. Remember, you'll just have to trust me."

Susan didn't take offense. "Well, I suppose you're curious as to why I'm on here. But I'll tell you right now I'm not surprised."

Lance waited. Said nothing.

"Sheriff asked me to come in to answer some questions a couple days after it all happened. I was happy to help, of course.

Or at least try to. And, well, I mean, I wasn't worried or anything. I knew I didn't have anything to do with..." She looked around the room, as if suddenly remembering where she was. "I knew I had nothing to do with what happened here."

Luke was leaning against the kitchen counter again, but now he stood straighter, curiosity burning in his eyes. "So why'd they want to talk to you, Suze? You've never told me this."

Susan shrugged. "I haven't really told anybody. My parents, of course, but that's it. It was a long time ago." She paused, took a deep breath and said, "Apparently, I'm the last person in town to talk to Mary Benchley before she went away. Like, literally. The last words she spoke to anyone before she was gone — anyone that's come forward, that is—were to me." Susan must have seen the surprise in both Lance's and her boyfriend's eyes, because she quickly laughed and held up her hands. "Calm down now, boys. Do you want to know what she said? She said, 'Thank you.'"

Lance and Luke looked at each other, clearly disappointed in the revelation. Lance repeated, "Thank you?"

Susan nodded. "Yep. I'd just started working at Mama's, and Mary had come in to pick up a pie to go that her mother had called in an order for. I'm the one who gave it to her. She came in the restaurant, we chatted for just a minute or two—just general chitchat—and then she thanked me and she was gone. Sometimes I replay it in my head, that scene. I try to glorify it and convince myself that maybe she had a different look in her eyes, that her voice carried more meaning than just thanking me for handing her a pie. Like maybe she was thanking me for being her friend, not being part of the immature cesspool of rumors and rude remarks that is high school. But honestly, the more I replay that moment—and trust me, I've done it a lot over the years—I'm not sure she even really saw me that night. Truth is, she looked distracted. Vacant. Like she had a lot on her mind.

I gave her the pie and she left. That's exactly what I told the sheriff."

Lance nodded, filing away the bit about Mary looking distracted. He supposed that the knowledge that she was about to be shipped off to a boarding school might weigh heavily on a teenage girl's mind. But maybe it was something else altogether.

"And what about Jacob Morgan? Why's his name on there?"

Luke's eyes grew a little harder. "Yeah, I'm wondering the same thing."

Lance suppressed a chuckle. Luke was jealous.

Susan didn't seem to notice. "Oh, I thought you knew," she said to Luke. She turned to Lance. "Jacob's the one who called it in. He's the one who found them the next morning."

Lance put the rest of the pieces together before Susan had finished explaining. Statistically, it all made sense. Jacob Morgan was the closest neighbor the Benchleys had had, as far as Lance knew. Either something sent up his hackles, and he sensed something was wrong enough for him to make the short hike to check on the family, or maybe he was supposed to be there for some other reason. Had had his morning plans quickly and grotesquely derailed.

"He'd been headed out of town for a week or so to help a friend do some renovations on a new house," Susan said. "He was stopping by before he left to ask Mark Benchley to keep an eye on his place while he was gone. Apparently they did these favors for each other. Joan tells me that Mark and Jacob were fairly good friends, despite the age difference. Used to have lunch together a lot in town. Anyway, he got here and ... well. You can imagine."

Lance could.

"The police took him right in. I remember that morning, because things felt electric. Like you could feel the current of gossip pulsing around town. By lunchtime, everybody was convinced Jacob was the killer, not knowing it was actually him who'd found him and called it in. But by later in the day, after the police had done their thing and examined the crime scene and whatever else they do, they had let Jacob go and the finger was pointed squarely at Mark Benchley. Which of course, given his reputation, didn't surprise too many people. Not as much as it should have, anyway."

Lance soaked in all this information. Processed it and tried to categorize it into mental filing cabinets for further review. There were more questions he wanted to ask, but he was tired … and his mind kept drifting back to Ethan.

Susan and Luke had left then, leaving Lance with the house and his thoughts. They'd told him to call them if he needed something, or wanted to hang out again, and Lance could sense the excitement in them, see the flash in their eyes. They believed he was going to figure this out, like they were playing a game of Clue and all Lance had to do was keep eliminating things until nothing was left but the truth. And they were enjoying playing the game.

He'd seen the same thing in Leah's eyes back in Westhaven. She'd had a personal stake in the game, sure, but the excitement and enthusiasm were all the same. Maybe it was something about small towns, the lack of other things to do, that made people so willing to jump into a murder investigation. For them, it was an episode, an excursion away from a mundane reality. For Lance, it was a way of life. They didn't understand that. Couldn't understand that.

Leah had started to.

And then he'd left her.

Lance downed the rest of the water and tossed the bottle at the sink. It missed, the bottle striking the counter and then bouncing on the floor with sharp crackles as plastic met wood. He sighed, stood. Retrieved the bottle and set it on the counter.

He rested his hands on the edge of the counter and stretched his back, arching it until it cracked and loosened. He stared into the window above the sink, at the reflection of—

The door to the basement was open.

Lance spun around and looked.

The door was closed. The bolt still locked.

He looked back to the window and saw it was still closed there as well.

He sighed. "Okay, I get it," he said, as if capitulating to the house.

He dug in his backpack until he found the small flashlight he carried. A tiny thing powered by one AAA battery, but powerful all the same.

Then, exhausted and wanting nothing more than to sleep, he opened the basement door, clicked on his flashlight and started down the steps.

[25]

THE STEPS WERE OLD, AND THEY CREAKED AND SQUEALED
with every slow step Lance took, but they were built solid all the
same. Plenty of support beams and a smattering of nails that
almost made the wood look speckled in the bright cone of light
thrown from Lance's flashlight. There was no railing to grab
hold of for balance, just the walls on either side for the first few
steps down and then you were on your own. Just you and the
boards and a fight with gravity you hoped to win.

Lance checked again for a light switch on his way down.
Found nothing. Let his flashlight swish and swoosh in wide arcs,
sweeping across ceiling and walls and steps, illuminating clouds
of dust and a latticework of cobwebs.

The boards whined and dust puffed from his shoes as he
stepped, leaving behind a ghost trail of prints.

The air was thick with earth and soil and stone. Cool, but
somewhat unpleasant.

It smelled like a tomb.

*If this were a horror film, right about now would be when the
door slammed shut behind me and my flashlight went out*, Lance
thought.

Not that he honestly expected those things to happen. While Lance did find the spirit world to conform almost comically to many of the tropes displayed in Hollywood, it almost never did so on cue. Sometimes, he wished it would. Everybody loves the familiar.

No, the door did not slam shut. And, no, Lance's flashlight did not suddenly need a change of bulb or battery. In fact, when Lance reached the bottom step and then stepped softly down onto the hard-packed dirt floor, something brushed across his ear and, after a mini-heart-attack that he was glad nobody was around to see, he shined his flashlight to his right and found a pull cord attached to a hanging overhead light. He reached up and tugged it, expecting nothing but thrilled to see a single uncovered bulb spark to life. It was dull and had the same yellowed tint as the lights in the aboveground portions of the house, but in the basement, it might as well have been the sun, forcing the bad things to retreat back into the shadows.

Lance lowered his flashlight, leaving the beam on and burning bright in case the old bulb hanging from the ceiling decided it had had enough and winked out. He stood in place and did a slow circle, examining the room.

The basement was empty except for a well-worn wooden workbench against the wall to Lance's left, long devoid of any tools but scuffed and scarred and full of cuts and nicks and evidence of heavy usage from a time before. In the back corner of the room, behind the stairs and nestled in the shadows where the light didn't quite fully reach, were mounted rows of what looked like metal shelving spanning from waist height to nearly above Lance's head. The shelves were bare, except for a single gallon paint can sitting on one of the midlevel shelves, its outside dotted and splashed with dried remnants of a dull white color Lance suspected was the original color of the farmhouse's exterior.

But there was nothing else. No spirits standing and waiting patiently for him, ready to spill their secrets and help him make everything right in the world. No monsters lurking in the dark ready to drag him down into the depths of places unknown. Just a dirt floor, a lonely workbench, and a single can of old paint on shelves that had likely not held anything important since the Benchley family had been killed and their belongings purged from the house. And probably never would again.

Lance called out, "Hello?" He waited, then tried, "I ... I think you know I'm here to help. Can you speak to me?"

There was nothing but the muffled creaks of the house upstairs as a gust of wind blew across the top of the hill outside.

Lance looked around the room, turning slowly and trying, for some reason, to appear unaggressive. Friendly. He received no answer. No words, no messages, no prickle of electricity like he'd experienced earlier when...

He tried again. "The boy," he said. "Ethan. He could hear you? Sense you?" Then Lance took a gamble, hoping he was right about his earlier assumption about whom he might actually be attempting to contact. "Mary, how did he know? Is he like me? And why could he hear you, but I couldn't this time?"

A flutter, small and tickling in Lance's stomach. A slight buzz in his ear, like a gnat had just flown in one side and out the other. Followed by a pang of absolute sadness, no more than half a second at most, but deep and strong enough that Lance felt at once completely consumed by the grief, his eyes suddenly full of tears and his heart pleading for relief.

And then it was all washed away in the blink of an eye, and Lance stood in the basement in the dull yellow light with the flashlight at his side and a desire to see his mother's face again trumpeting in his mind like a full-blown marching band.

He coughed and took a deep breath and shook his head, forcing himself to process what had just happened.

He'd managed to get through. Something he'd said. Was it calling Mary by her name? Was it the mention of Ethan?

"Mary," he tried again. "What happened here?"

The basement was silent, and Lance's frustration bloomed.

"Then why am I down here if you don't want to help me?"

He thought of the reflection from the kitchen window, the open basement door. It was an invitation. It had to have been. Whether sent by a friendly spirit or an evil one, there was no other explanation. *Something* had wanted Lance to descend the steps and see what was down here.

He walked the perimeter of the room, sweeping his flashlight beam across the floor and ceiling and corners. He stopped at the workbench and ran his hand over the surface, feeling the smooth wood and the pockmarks from tools. He searched for a drawer or a compartment. Found none. Looked for scribbled or carved messages. A clue. Any clue. Anything at all.

But the basement was empty.

Lance tugged on the pull cord too hard as he made to leave and head back up the steps, and it snapped at the chain. He let the cord fall to the floor at his feet and walked back up to the kitchen, closing the door behind him.

He headed to bed. The house seemed to be finished speaking to him for the time being. Lance figured it would know how to wake him if it changed its mind.

In the morning, he'd walk down to see Jacob Morgan. Talk to the man and see if he knew what his nephew really was. But more importantly, Lance hoped to chat with Ethan alone.

Lance carried to bed with him a glint of hope, an excitement that, if not for his mental exhaustion and many miles walked and an entire hillside climbed, would have likely made it difficult to sleep. He wished the sun was up and the day started so he could spend more time with Ethan immediately.

But along with the hope, being dragged behind it like a ball and chain, was the nagging, unmistakable sense that he was missing something.

Lance kicked off his shoes and fell onto the bed of a dead girl. Sleep grabbed hold within minutes.

THERE WERE NO DREAMS THIS TIME. NO RIDING ON EMPTY buses. No men with their faces blown off. The sleep was deep, and it was purely black. A long blink of the eyes, only to have them open to the faint early-morning light highlighting the window around the blinds in Mary Benchley's old bedroom.

Lance rubbed sleep from his eyes and yawned, sitting up on the bed and taking stock of himself. He was still in one piece, with no visible injuries he could see or feel, so he was happy to know his idea that the home invader would not strike again so quickly was accurate. It had been a calculated gamble.

He stood and stretched and padded over to the window in his socks, peeking out the blinds. Mary's windows overlooked the driveway and front yard, and while there was a hint of sunlight still hidden behind the crest of the trees in the distance, the sky was mostly overcast. Lance could feel the chill from the window. Breathed out onto the glass and drew a smiley face in the condensation with his finger. "Good morning," he said to the face. "Sleep well?"

The face did not answer.

Lance looked down to the driveway again and noticed that Victoria Bellows's Mercedes was gone.

"Well, you know what they say," Lance said to his finger-drawn friend, who was beginning to fade away. "The early bird gets the luxury SUV."

He turned and grabbed his toiletry kit from his backpack and went to the bathroom.

The upstairs bathroom had a shine to it that it hadn't the day before. The sink and tub were a brighter color, and the faucets and fixtures had a new life to them. The ring around the toilet bowl was mostly gone. There was the artificial smell of pine in the air. Victoria Bellows had done a good job. Lance hated that she'd been attacked. He felt he owed her more than a bouquet of flowers.

He brushed his teeth and flossed, then looked into the mirror in order to assess whether he needed to shave or not. He could usually pull off a few days' stubble without feeling gross or thinking he looked like a fool. He ran a hand over his cheeks, feeling the roughness that had grown, examined the five-o'clock shadow look he had going. He chose not to shave.

He splashed some warm water on his face, still clean and refreshing in smell and taste, and then dried off with his t-shirt. And when his eyes met his reflection in the mirror, he was hit again with that strange prickling at the base of his skull, a repeat of yesterday morning's episode, when he'd foolishly tried to reach his hand through the mirror's glass because he felt it had been calling out to him, urging him to take action.

And here the feeling was again. He couldn't deny it was real, present and suggesting. The tingle at his neck grew, and his stomach fluttered with an anxiousness that was clearly fabricated. Something was tugging at his gut; something was drawing him closer to the mirror again. Lance stood and stared. Turned his head from side to side, raised himself up and down on his toes. He followed his face in the mirror, then focused his eyes on the background as he moved, looking for some anomaly between the mirror's reflection and the reality of the bathroom.

He saw nothing different.

Yet the feeling persisted.

Lance reached out and rapped his knuckles on the glass, causing a metallic rattling as it vibrated in its frame. He waited. Nothing knocked back from the other side. Lance gripped the mirror on either side and gave it a slight jerk up and down, left and right. It did not move. It was mounted solidly on the wall. He swung the medicine cabinet door open again, took in the fly graveyard once more and found nothing else of interest, and swung the door closed again.

He sighed and stepped back. Stared at the mirror for another full minute. Looked at it for what it was, instead of what it might be. *There's something off about it*, he thought. Then he remembered that yesterday, he'd thought the same thing, realizing that the mirror was mounted much higher up than most mirrors he came across in life.

Then another thought collided into this one. Joan's mention of Mark Benchley being a man of above-average height.

Lance added these things up. The mirror was high. Mark Benchley was tall.

The feeling pulling at his stomach started to grow.

People put things in high places that they don't want others to reach, Lance thought. *Or things they don't want them to find.*

Lance stepped back up to the vanity, stretched his arm up to reach the top of the mirror and let his hand search blindly across the top of its dusty surface.

His fingers brushed against something. It was small, and cold and solid. He wrapped his hand around it and—

A basement. No windows and a hard-packed dirt floor. Wooden steps leading up to a closed door. A wooden work table along one wall with neatly organized boxes and jars of nails and nuts and bolts and other things that only had any use for a man who knew how to use them. A pegboard was above the table, tools precisely hanging in their spots. They showed signs of use, but also of care. Well-sharpened blades and deeply oiled leather. Glinting steel and shining metal. There was a sprinkling of sawdust on the floor near the work table.

A lone lightbulb hanging from the ceiling. The light it cast was dim, but another light was flickering in the corner. A kerosene lantern sat idly on the floor, casting shadows along the wall under and around the rows of metal shelving. The shelves held toolboxes and industrial-type storage containers. There were a handful of paint cans. There were extension cords coiled tightly and stacks of newspapers piled high but well aligned and balanced, their edges crisp and flush with the wall.

The wall was not flush with the adjacent wall. Where the wall with the shelving should have met its neighbor, forming a back corner of the basement, there was a five-foot gap. There was some sort of track system inlaid in the ground and in the ceiling. The entire wall had shifted over, sliding neatly behind the stairs, just far enough so that the edges of the shelves did not collide with the edges of the steps.

It was a door.

Light spilled from the opened mouth of the wall.

"So you see, Ray, when the Japs or the Chinks or whatever group gets pissed off enough and comes and starts bombing us, I can come down here and lock myself in and be nice and safe until it's all over."

And then the basement shifted forward and the opened-mouth doorway in the wall came rushing forward in a blur and Lance was standing in the opening and—

The room beyond the wall was long and narrow. The size of a bedroom that had been squished at its sides. There was a long encasement of fluorescent lighting on the ceiling at the center of the room. A pull cord dropping down a foot or so. The light was powerful, enough to illuminate the entire room. Along one entire wall were floor-to-ceiling shelves full of canned food and gallons and gallons of water. There were gas cans along the floor, and a stockpile of lanterns lining the wall beside them. Piles of batteries and both CB and AM/FM radios. Stacks of paperback books and a couple old board games. At the far side of the room were a sink and a toilet. A shower curtain and rod were hung from the ceiling in front of the toilet, serving as a bathroom door. In the center of the room was a futon. It was in the folded-down position.

A boy and a man lay atop it, looking up at the ceiling.

"And of course you and your mom and the rest of yous can come, too. It might be a little tight, but we'll make it work."

The man was tall and wore faded overalls with a short-sleeved white t-shirt underneath. Boots on his feet. The outfit of a country man who worked with his hands and worked the land. Built things and grew things and enjoyed the fruits of his labor. He was in his forties, maybe, but looked older. Heavy creases on his brow and cheeks, skin like leather.

He poked the boy playfully in the ribs, turning and saying, "It'll be fun, won't it, Ray? Like a big sleepover. Like the kind you probably have with your friends, right? You can stay up as late as you'd like—because if it comes to that, what's the point of a bedtime, am I right?—and we can read each other stories and play board games and it'll be a grand ol' time!"

The man laughed and poked the boy again, and the boy grinned and squirmed away and the man laughed some more and said, "Hey, I got an idea. Why don't we play a game now? What do ya say, Ray, my boy?"

The boy, who looked not much older than he'd been when he'd pulled the garden hose in his backyard and tripped the little girl because he was angry that she'd splashed him, grinned and nodded his head. "Okay," he said.

"Good! I could use a little fun," the man said. "I've been working too much. Too much, I tell ya!" The man crinkled his brow and tapped his temple, making a show of pretending to think. Then his eyes lit up big, and he smiled and said, "I know! Why don't we play our secret game?"

They boy's face fell. His eyes dropped to the futon's mattress and he said nothing.

The man, seeing the boy's apprehension, did not respond with sympathy. Instead, his eyes grew hard, narrowing to slits. His voice came out hushed but hot.

"Ray. Come on, now. Be a good boy. What's the matter, too good to play a game with an old slog like me? Do you think when your mama comes and picks you up, she's gonna want to hear her boy didn't behave? Do you want me to tell her that, huh? She'll be real mad, I bet. Disappointed in you, too." The man shook his head. "I wouldn't want that, Ray. I'd hate to see your mama upset, wouldn't you?"

The boy said nothing. He kept staring at the mattress.

"Ray?" The man's voice was even quieter now, but scarier all the same. "I'm starting to get mad."

The boy looked up and met the man's eyes. "Okay," was all he said.

The man's face lit up again, an instant transformation back into the happy, playful person he'd been moments earlier. He hooted a laugh. "Hooray! Ray's going to play!"

The boy didn't so much as blink. He just sat stone-faced and waited.

"And remember," the man said, "it's our secret game. That's what makes it so fun, right? I'd be really mad, Ray, if you ever told somebody. I want this to be our thing, okay. Something special for just you and me, okay?"

The boy said nothing. Waited.

The man, apparently satisfied, said eagerly, "Okay, let's get ready."

He unfastened the buckles of his overalls and flung the straps over his shoulders, then worked to shimmy them down around his ankles. Then he pulled down the threadbare boxer shorts he'd been wearing underneath, fully exposing himself. He was already growing hard.

Quietly and with the poise of someone much older than his true age, the boy reached down and began to—

Lance gasped and felt himself flung back into the bathroom. The world coming back into focus with a speed that was almost blinding. He closed his eyes and counted to ten, getting his breath under control and letting his heart slow. Then he slowly opened his eyes.

He saw his reflection in the mirror. His eyes darted up to the top of the mirror, then back down to his hand. His right hand was closed in a fist. Something was inside, digging into the soft flesh of his palm. Lance raised his hand and opened it, examining what he'd found—what had held within it a terrible memory that no person should ever have to see.

It was a key.

[27]

LANCE STARED AT THE SILVER KEY IN HIS HAND. IT WAS small, but heavy. Thick and durable, not flimsy and easily bent like most cheapos you had made in hardware stores or at the checkout counter at the Walmart Tire Center. He tossed it gently in the air, feeling its heft.

Then he considered what he'd seen. His eyes went unfocused again as his mind drifted back to the flash of memory the key had jolted him with. Most of Lance's instant downloads came from a human touch, and although he knew he could never quite seem to make sense of from who he received them, or why, there was still something incredibly unsettling about receiving one of these flashes from an inanimate object. It was even more unexpected than the ones he received from other people, because at least with human contact, Lance could have a sense of expectancy, even if the odds were slim. With inanimate objects ... well, he wasn't going to go around all day expecting to have an item's history presented to him every time he went shopping or opened a door or picked up a fork in a restaurant. The Universe had at least spared him that consideration.

It had only happened twice before.

Both items had presented him with horrible scenes that he knew he'd never forget.

Today's was no different, but it was also relevant.

Lance remembered Victoria Bellows's words, how she'd told him that after the Benchley family murder, the sheriff had gone around telling people that he should have known better. That too much evil had already happened in the house and it made sense that more would follow.

Now Lance understood. Ray Kruger had been molested in the farmhouse. How many times?

("*Why don't we play our secret game?*")

How much had that little boy who would grow up to be the town's protector suffered at the hands of a twisted older man?

And who else knew about it?

Every time Lance had tried to dig for more details about why Ray Kruger was so protective of—and repulsed by—the farmhouse, he'd received coy answers, changes of subject, and hushed whispers. But never any valuable information.

Did the whole town know and simply wish to protect their sheriff's privacy? Was the abuse of a small boy a secret that an entire town was trying to keep buried? Lance could understand that. It was a terrible thing. Not something you'd want tossed around in casual conversation.

But Lance felt there was more.

As usual, there was always more.

Lance looked at the key again, thought about the wall that had slid open in the basement.

He didn't want to go down there again. Not now. He wanted to put his shoes on and jog the short way down the hill and find Jacob Morgan and try and talk to Ethan. As much as Lance was invested in trying to figure out what had happened to the Benchley family—especially after hearing the echo of some of the events that'd taken place the night they had been killed (*Who was the fourth person?*)—he could not dampen his excitement and elation at finding another person who shared his abilities. He had so much to ask, and so much to teach the young boy, if possible. Help him come to terms with who he was and what life would be like for him.

Lance again remembered the feeling he'd gotten when he'd stepped off the bus in Ripton's Grove the evening before last. He'd been hit with such a compelling drive to stay here. He'd felt that pull of being needed, more than he'd felt in a long time.

Ethan had to be the reason for that. The Universe was finally giving him something in return. A small gesture to say *You are not alone.*

Lance finished up in the bathroom and returned to the bedroom to pull on his shoes, and then he was moving down the stairs, his backpack snug on his shoulders and the key he'd found—that terrible key—tucked safely into the pocket of his cargo shorts.

And instead of walking out the front door, he found himself turning and heading down the hall to the kitchen. Opening the basement door. Heading down the stairs. Despite the sun having risen, the basement was still nearly pitch black, the light coming down the stairs from the kitchen doing little to fight back the dark down below. Lance could just make out the pull cord he'd ripped down lying coiled on the ground, and he stepped over it and used his height and long arms to reach up and fumble in the dark until he found what was left of the bit of chain hanging from the fixture and pinched it between his fingers and tugged. The bulb snapped to life.

Lance turned around and looked at the wall behind the stairs, the metal shelves, the paint can, and was amazed at how different it all felt now that he knew what was behind the wall.

And what had taken place back there. A secret place. A secret game. A disgusting crime.

Lance walked closer to the wall, his steps feeling heavy, his stomach grumbling. He needed to eat. He needed coffee. He needed answers.

He hoped he'd get all these things soon. But for now, the wall had his attention. He stood three feet away, then two. Then he reached out, slowly, and rested his palm on one of the empty shelves. Braced himself for another memory, another flash of the past.

He got nothing but a bit of dust on his palm.

He grabbed the edge of one of the shelves in both hands and pulled, gently at first and then with more effort, finally leaning in, throwing all his weight into it and feeling the cords in his neck stand out as he strained.

The wall did not so much as flex. It had no give whatsoever. Lance wasn't too surprised by this, but he had to try. He walked back and forth along the length of the wall, pulling his flashlight from his backpack and scanning the surface, looking for a handle or a lever or some sort of trigger that would open the wall.

Then the key in his pocket suddenly seemed to weigh a hundred pounds, weighing down his thoughts.

Of course, Lance thought. *Lance, you idiot. Sometimes you're such a dumbass.*

Now he was looking for a keyhole.

He spent ten minutes shining his flashlight over the entire surface of the wall, floor to ceiling, side to side. Again, his efforts were in vain. Lance remembered Joan telling him that ol' Uncle Joe had been an engineer for the Army and could build anything. If he'd built a way to open the wall, he'd sure hidden it well.

The air in the basement was cool, but Lance felt the dotting of perspiration on his forehead and temples. A dampness was at his lower back, causing his t-shirt to stick. He was about to pull off his hoodie, but his stomach gave another grumble, and Lance knew that the longer he stayed in the basement, the longer it would be before he could have his conversation with Jacob Morgan an Ethan. Which, unless Jacob offered Lance some coffee and a stack of pancakes, meant the breakfast Lance planned on devouring at Mama's would be pushed even further away.

Sometimes hunger was a real pain.

He took one last glance at the wall and couldn't shake the feeling that something important waited for him on the other side.

***

While inside the farmhouse had been chilly, as the cold fall morning air had seeped through the old house's walls, when Lance stepped out the front door and onto the porch, he breathed in deeply and saw the white cloud of his breath as he exhaled. Each passing day seemed to be getting colder and colder, taking longer for the sun to warm things up. Lance loved fall, loved the chilled mornings and the crisp evenings. He stood for another minute on the porch, breathing in the clean mountain air, and then pulled the hood of his sweatshirt over his head and started down the steps. Rounded the corner of the farmhouse and found the trail. Followed it down the way he'd walked up yesterday afternoon.

There was a stillness to everything. An overshadowing calmness that seemed to have fallen among the trees and the rocks and the creatures. Lance's footsteps seemed very loud. The only noise aside from the occasional breeze stirring up leaves and rustling branches that had started to go bare.

He was at Jacob Morgan's house within a few minutes, standing on the path and peering through the trees at the small home. Just like yesterday, Lance thought the place looked more like a small hunting cabin than home, but he didn't pass judgment. The scattered pieces of split wood were gone from the yard, all neatly stacked and ready in a heaping pile. The chopping block remained, but the axe was gone as well. Stored away, taken care of. Lance watched the house for a full minute, watching for any signs of life. A shadow in a window, a reflection of light, the sounds of muffled voices carried to him on the breeze like a telegram.

There was nothing, except a small tendril of smoke snaking from a crude chimney at the side of house's roof.

Lance adjusted the straps of his backpack and stepped into the woods. Dead leaves and fallen twigs and branches crunched and snapped underfoot. Now he did hear the scurrying of small animals, suddenly alarmed at an intruder in their midst. Lance felt oddly like he was trespassing, creeping through the woods and into somebody's yard, but with no driveway or entrance from the path that he could see, he didn't dwell too much on it.

He emerged from the tree line and stepped into the grass. Finding his strides growing longer and quick, he stopped just short of the cabin. A single step led up to a modest covered porch. Two rocking chairs sat at opposite sides of the front door, one large, one small. Two-thirds of the Three Bears. The building was old, there was no mistaking it, but Jacob Morgan had obviously used his handyman skills to keep the place up. It was small, but it didn't appear shabby or forgotten. It had been cared for. Lance admired Jacob Morgan's work, his commitment to keep his home modest, yet presentable. A combination of rustic and quaint.

Lance stepped up the porch step and knocked on the door. Two quick *thwops*. He took a step back, waited. Heard nothing from the other side of the door. He tried again, another two knocks, only this time more forceful. The window next to the door rattled as he did so.

Still nothing. Lance counted to thirty in his head before he slowly reached out and grabbed the handle, knowing what he was doing was wrong yet unable to stop himself. Thankfully, the door was locked. Lance wasn't sure he would have been able to keep himself from trespassing any further. His curiosity about the boy was too high. The potential too great.

Lance sighed and turned and walked down the steps, heading around the side of the cabin to the rear. Here, he found the driveway. A crude gravel trail that led down a small decline and then connected with what looked like a dirt road. Lance followed the dirt road with his eyes, tried to imagine where it led. Most likely it fed into the main road that wound up the side of the hill from town.

There was no vehicle in the driveway. *They're not home,* Lance thought. He quickly tried to think about where they might be. Where he could find them.

Then he remembered what day it was.

Sunday.

Sunday morning.

(*"She watches him in Kids' Group at church on Sundays."*)

The snippet of last night's conversation doused Lance's fire of excitement.

Jacob Morgan and Ethan were either at church or headed there. Susan too, likely.

Lance contemplated his options. He could wait. Take a seat in one of the rocking chairs and wait for the sound of tires on gravel. Or he could go to the church, hang out in the parking lot and wait for the doors to open and the stream of people to trickle out.

Either option carried with it a whiff of stalker. Despite

Lance's urgency, he didn't want to appear aggressive, or too eager. And he certainly didn't want Jacob Morgan to feel he was being accosted.

The third option seemed best. Breakfast at Mama's.

Lance needed coffee. Boy, did he need coffee.

And since he had more questions, he might as well talk to the town's best source of information.

[28]

Halfway down the mountain, Lance started to feel light-headed, his arms and legs taking on a bit of a floating feeling. He closed his eyes and took three deep breaths, counting to ten each time. With the final exhale, he opened his eyes and shook his head to clear it. He felt better, but he scolded himself for waiting so long to eat. He was running on empty. With his size and metabolism, last night's pizza was ancient history in terms of fuel. But this was nothing Mama's pancakes wouldn't solve.

He slowed his pace and tried to put his mind to work, keep himself occupied with thoughts other than his empty stomach and low blood sugar. He made a mental list of things that he knew, or at least had been told, about the night of the Benchley family murder. Then he made a list of all the things he didn't know. Questions he had. Item number one on this second list was obviously *Who had killed the Benchleys?* But there were two other items that Lance felt more pressed to answer first, thinking that perhaps the answers to one or both of these might have some bearing on the answer to the question of the Benchley family killer.

What was Sheriff Ray Kruger's real involvement?

The vision Lance had seen of the sheriff's abused childhood certainly played a role in the man's preoccupation with the farmhouse. On some disturbed level it seemed to Lance that the sheriff was both simultaneously repulsed by the home and somehow concerned about its well-being. There was a deeper connection here that Lance was missing.

Why had Mary Benchley's body been burned?

Lance hadn't given much thought to this part of the story until last night, when he'd relayed to Susan and Luke that the cleaning company didn't come to the farmhouse because they believed that Mary Benchley had been a witch. It was then that he'd remembered the fact that her body, or at least what very little was left of it, had been found burning on a brush pile in the backyard. Assuming that Mark Benchley had not killed his family and himself, why had the killer left Mark and Natalie Benchley's bodies where they'd fallen after the shotgun blast had done its work, yet he or she had gone through the trouble of disposing of Mary's body in an entirely different manner.

Some sort of sacrifice? Lance thought. *A ritual?*

Thoughts of what he'd encountered in Westhaven trickled in, forcing Lance to acknowledge that something as sick as human sacrifice could certainly not be ruled out as an option. Maybe there were witches in Ripton's Grove, but Mary Benchley wasn't one of them. Had she been their victim?

Why?

Lance stepped out of the woods and into the park. Out from under the cover of the trees, the temperature picked up a few degrees. Lance lowered his hood and headed toward the parking lot, back the same way he'd come after the Bellowses had dropped him off yesterday afternoon. There were a few morning joggers in the park, winding around the path. Those who were not quite God-fearing enough to put Him before their cardiovascular system. An elderly man sat alone on a bench near the baseball fields, staring across the empty playing area with something like nostalgia on his face. A folded newspaper sat beside him, weighted down by an iPhone. Lance considered his flip phone, how the older gentleman on the bench had infinitely more access to information and services and the rest of the world in the palm of his hand than Lance could ever have. He really should try and upgrade. But the phone had been a gift from his mother, all those years ago. It was the last thing he had from her. And he couldn't quite bring himself to give it up quite yet. It would feel too much like chipping away at her memory. He remembered the look of excitement on her face the day she'd given it to him. She'd put it inside a thousand-piece jigsaw puzzle box and then wrapped it in newspaper. Lance had torn away the paper to find a picture of what looked like a hundred kittens surrounded by balls of yarn and wicker baskets. He hated cats, and his mother was well aware of this. She'd found her joke hilarious. Lance had been too happy with the surprise inside the box to even give her a hard time about it.

And then Pamela Brody had shown Lance that she'd purchased a matching phone for herself, and they'd spent the rest of the afternoon sending silly text messages to each other and calling each other from different rooms of the house.

Lance found himself standing in front of Mama's, smiling like a fool. He had no idea how he'd gotten here but was thankful he'd somehow managed to cross two streets without getting plowed over by a truck. Or a police cruiser.

He pocketed the cell phone memory and made his way past the handful of cars in the parking lot, then pushed open the door.

The dining room was mostly empty. The booth right by the door was taken, as were two of the tables along the rear wall near the kitchen. The smell of bacon and coffee hit Lance like a wave, and his stomach grumbled in excitement. He stood by the hostess stand and waited, scanning the room again and looking for Joan.

A woman pushed through the kitchen door, carrying two plates of food to one of the tables along the wall. She spotted Lance and said, "Sit anywhere you'd like, sir. I'll be with you in a flash." She was tall and lean, with red hair and a heavy dose of freckles. Maybe midthirties. She was all smiles and graceful movements. She'd called him *sir*.

She was not Joan.

Lance smiled and nodded and made his way to back corner booth. Where he'd sat yesterday. Where Sheriff Ray Kruger had sat and read his Kindle the night before that, staring into that black-and-white screen and trying to suppress who knew how many awful memories.

Lance slid his backpack into the seat next to him, and when he looked up, the red-haired woman was at the table, smiling with big bright teeth that almost looked too large for her mouth. She smelled like strawberries and sugar, and her hair looked like something from a shampoo commercial.

She was not Joan.

"Good morning!" she started. "I'm Jen, and I'll be taking care of you this morning. Can I get you something to drink? Water, juice, coffee?"

"Coffee, please," Lance said. "Black." Then he proceeded to order the same breakfast he had the day before. Jen stared at him while he spoke, smiling and nodding and never letting her eyes leave his. It was almost unsettling. When he finished his order she said, "Got it. Anything else?"

"Actually, yes," Lance said. "Is Joan working this morning?"

Jen was all too happy to answer. "She should be here in..." She checked her wristwatch, a small silver thing that sparkled in the light when she brought it up to her face. "Maybe another hour. She and I alternate the Sunday morning shifts. That way we can let the other one get to church."

Disappointed, Lance thanked the woman, and she went back to the kitchen to give his order to the cook.

The thought of Joan in church was comical. Surprising, actually. She didn't seem the type. But then Lance figured it was possible she went every other week purely because she didn't want to miss out on any good gossip. With towns as small as this, drama would be everywhere, church not excluded.

Lance's coffee and food came, and once he assured Jen that he didn't need anything else, she left him alone to devour his food at a rate that made him appear as if he were in some sort of contest against unseen competitors. Jen came by and refilled his coffee and took away his empty plates, and with his stomach full and his body beginning to feel normal again, Lance sipped on his fresh cup and decided that he didn't want to just sit in the booth and wait for Joan to show up. Plus, if she was coming in after church, a lunch rush would likely soon follow. She'd be too busy earning tips and listening for juicy details to stop and have another heart-to-heart with the town's newest reporter.

Lance paid the check and left Jen a nice tip. As he handed over the cash, Jen leaned in closer and whispered, "You're him, aren't you? The fella writing the book about what happened up at that farmhouse?"

Lance said nothing.

Jen leaned closer and her voice grew even quieter, her eyes darting around to see if anybody was listening in. "Between you and me," she said, "I always knew Mark Benchley was trouble. He just had this look about him, you know? Something about his eyes, the way he looked at people." She shrugged. "It was creepy."

Lance was quiet for a second, then asked, "Can you tell me where the library is?"

Jen smiled with those big white teeth and told him it was two blocks behind the courthouse. Lance didn't have to ask for directions. He just had to head toward the bell tower.

Lance thanked her and left, calling over his shoulder as he opened the door, "Tell Joan that Lance says hi."

A new idea had struck, and since he figured he had to wait till church let out before he could talk to Jacob Morgan and Ethan, he had the time to kill to check something out.

Pun intended.

[29]

THE STREETS OF RIPTON'S GROVE WERE ESSENTIALLY empty, only two or three cars driving lazily through downtown as Lance used the courthouse's bell tower as his North Star and walked the sidewalk. The cloud cover was still gray and rolled across the sky like a protective film, giving the whole town a very noir appearance. Lance, feeling very much like an private investigator, didn't miss the irony. *If I had one of those smartphones, I could put my headphones on and listen to some jazz and really set the scene.*

He made a left turn and walked by the courthouse, looking up at the bell tower. The architecture was impressive—almost gothic in appearance—and Lance wondered what year it'd been built. How long had Ripton's Grove been Ripton's Grove? How many generations had walked these streets and opened businesses in these buildings? How many sheriffs had there been before Ray Kruger ... before Bill Willard?

How many murders?

Lance walked another block and found the library, a onestory concrete building with a green roof and a small glass atrium at the entrance that looked up to the clouded sky. There were large flowerbeds around the building with dark mulch and bushes that looked freshly trimmed. No flowers now, though. Gone until the spring, when they'd yawn and stretch their limbs and pop open with color.

The place looked very inviting, just as a library should. Lance stood on the sidewalk and allowed himself a brief image of his mother, wandering amid the stacks of the Hillston Public Library, her fingers tracing the spines of books and her head cocked at such an angle, with the tiniest hint of a grin on her face, that she appeared completely at ease. Blissful. Home.

How many hours had they spent together in that library? How many hundreds of books had they read? Since Pamela Brody had worked there part-time, Lance and she had spent many evenings there after the last guests had left and the front doors had been locked, just lounging silently on the couches and chairs scattered about, silently reading whichever new adventure they'd started. There was something magical about being alone in a library. Just you, surrounded by endless books, letting your imagination take you away.

The front doors of the Ripton's Grove Library opened with an electronic purr, and a woman and small girl exited. The woman, with a stack of books tucked under her arm, was holding the little girl's hand and practically having to tug her along the walkway because the girl was trying to hold open her own book and look at the pictures with one hand. Lance smiled at them as they passed. The woman smiled back.

He walked up the walkway and entered the library, looking up through the high glass ceiling of the atrium as he made his way in, knowing how much his mother would have loved to sit right in that very spot, book in her lap, reading under the stars late into the evening.

Being just the single story, the library's floor plan was simple and meant to utilize the space. A large open area in the front held two banks of computer stations for patrons to use, as well as a handful of large tables. To Lance's right were the restrooms and water fountain, to his left the front desk. Two women with gray hair stood behind the desk, each using a handheld electronic scanner to zap the barcodes in the backs of a large stack of books on the counter between them.

Lance walked over, hearing the faint *beep-boop* from the women's scanners with each new book they zapped. When he reached the counter, both women looked up slowly like some sort of two-headed guard dog. Their expressions were stoic, if not unpleasant.

"Can we help you?" the one on the left said, peering over the top of her glasses, which were pushed down on her nose.

Lance smiled. "Yes, ma'am, I hope so." He cleared his throat. "Does your library keep an archive of the town's local newspaper?"

This time, the woman on the right answered. She set her scanner down and straightened her posture. A small gold cross swung from her necklace. Her glasses were atop her head, and she pulled them down and settled them in place. *Better to scrutinize you with, my dear*, Lance thought.

"Of course we do," the woman said.

"Great," Lance said. "I was hoping you could help me find a particular issue, or at least point me in the right direction to get started in the appropriate timeframe. Are they digital archives, or physical?"

The woman on the left scoffed. "*Digital*, he asks." She shot the woman on the right a look that made it apparent she was questioning Lance's intelligence, perhaps ready to point him in the direction of the children's section and ask him if he preferred Sesame Street or the Muppets. "You see these here guns?" She held up one of the electronic scanners for Lance to see. "We just got these in the last two years, and they don't work right half the time. I don't know why folks can't just read a gosh dern paper with their hands any more. Why's everything have to be on a daggone television screen?"

"Yes, ma'am. I don't know, ma'am," Lance replied, unsure what to say or how this conversation had gotten out of hand so quickly. Or, honestly, whether the woman had actually answered his question. But he wasn't deterred. "So, may I have access to the archives, please?"

The woman on the right sighed. "Do you have a library card?"

Lance figured she already knew the answer to this question. "No, ma'am. Do I need one if I'm not taking anything out of the building?"

The women looked at each other, their eyes searching for a reason to protest. Finally, the woman on the right sighed again and said, "Follow me." She turned and walked out from behind the counter and rounded the corner out of sight.

Lance thanked the remaining woman, who nodded and gave a soft grunt, and then hurried around the corner to follow the woman with the gold cross necklace.

She was standing at a closed door near the rear corner of the building, the rows and rows of bookshelves casting shadows on the wall and forming more of an alcove than a walkway. The woman was searching through a small keyring when Lance approached, sliding them along the ring excruciatingly slowly in search of the correct key. Lance felt he could have picked the lock quicker, and he didn't even know how to pick locks.

Without a word, the woman suddenly shoved a key into the lock on the door handle and turned. There was an audible click, and then she pushed down and swung the door open wide, standing aside for Lance to enter. The door had a frosted glass pane with black stenciled letters that read: ARCHIVES – SEE FRONT DESK.

Lance stepped inside the room, which was cooler than the rest of the library had been. There were no windows, and when the woman reached inside the door and flipped the light switch on the wall, the overhead lighting was dim and mostly unhelpful.

"Apparently it's easier to read the screen this way," she said, not hiding the disapproval in her voice. She nodded to the back wall, where a large microfiche reader sat on a wide table. The entire rest of the room was lined with storage cabinets, no doubt containing decades worth of Ripton's Grove's history.

"Have a seat," she said.

Lance sat. Obedient. He wanted to stay in the woman's good graces.

Without question or instruction, the woman with the cross around her neck walked to one of the cabinets, leaning in close to read the labels on the drawers. She moved to the next one over, tapped one of the drawers with her finger and then yanked it open. She riffled through what looked like folders from where Lance was sitting, her fingers flicking through sheet after sheet, and then she paused, her thumb and index finger pinching one of the sheets and raising it out just slightly. She peered down at it, her eyes squinting behind her glasses. Then she pulled the sheet completely free and shut the drawer.

The sheet was roughly six inches long and reminded Lance of a smaller version of the old transparency sheets his teachers used to use with the classroom projectors when he was in elementary school. He could just make out the small squares of images on the sheet—the shrunken-down pages from past newspapers.

The woman stood at his side and worked the microfiche reader with hands that'd performed this task a hundred times before. Maybe a thousand. She showed Lance how to turn on the screen and then moved toward the door.

"When you're finished, come back to the front desk and I'll come clean up."

Confused, Lance said, "Excuse me, ma'am?"

She'd been halfway out the door but stopped and came back in. "Yes?"

Lance nodded toward the microfiche reader. "I didn't tell you what date I was looking for."

The removed her glasses and placed them back atop her head. She rubbed her eyes with her hands. "A group of us women play gin once a week. Last night was at Joan's house."

Oh. I see.

"I know who you are," the woman said. "And I guess I know why you're here. If that's not what you're after"—she pointed to the blank screen behind Lance—"just set it aside and look in the drawers for anything else you need. *Don't* refile the sheets. I'll take care of that."

Lance said nothing. Nodded.

The woman turned to leave, stopped, then turned back to face Lance. Even in the dim light, he could see her eyes were glistening. Pooling with tears.

"Listen," she said, her voice stern and lecturing, "Natalie Benchley was a saint. You hear me? A *saint*. And Mary was never anything but polite and sweet and pretty as a peach." The woman stopped, wiped at her eyes. "Whatever it is you're writing, you better do right by them, you hear? You better respect them."

Before Lance could answer, the woman turned and left, closing the door softly behind her.

Boy, Lance thought, *there's a lot of pressure when writing an imaginary book.*

But, despite his joke, he felt he understood where the woman was coming from. In fact, he thought he was starting to understand why the whole town seemed to be so concerned and so secretive about the entire incident involving the Benchley family's deaths. In towns this small, underneath the drama and gossip and surface-level lies, there was still an undeniable sense of family.

Lance was not part of the family. But he was digging around in the closets, all the same.

He sat and waited for a full minute, staring at the closed door and seeing the faint outline of the stenciled words on the outside of the frosted glass, waiting to see if the woman would return, offer another warning. Satisfied that she was likely back at the front desk, speaking of him in deplorable adjectives to her cohort, Lance spun around in the chair and flipped the switch to turn on the microfiche screen.

The screen lit up bright, enough to force Lance to sit back and squint his eyes until they adjusted. Then he leaned closer again and saw the big bold letters of the headline that dominated the entire top of the front page of the newspaper issue the woman had loaded for him. She was right; she had known exactly what he wanted. The headline read:

Family Dead After Apparent Murder-Suicide

Lance studied the word *apparent* for a few seconds, wondering at what point it had no longer fit. How long had the Ripton's Grove Sheriff's Department really investigated what had happened there? If Mark Benchley had been innocent, how much of a chance had he really been given in the eyes of the public and law enforcement?

The image below the headline was a picture of the farmhouse, police cruisers parked in front and along the side. Lance skimmed the article, picking out key words and phrases and learning nothing he hadn't already been told by people in town.

He wasn't here for words.

When he was leaving Mama's, Jen had given her opinion on Mark Benchley, citing that he had a certain look about him.

Hearing this, Lance thought it might be time to try and track down a picture of Mark Benchley, and maybe the rest of the family as well. Put faces to the names, and also to the voices he kept hearing at the farmhouse. He couldn't really imagine it would help much, but again ... he had the time to kill.

The article about the murders continued on another page, and Lance fumbled with the knobs below the screen until he had the correct page in focus.

His jaw dropped. His heart leapt into his throat.

He leaned in closer.

The picture that accompanied the rest of the article about the Benchley family murder was a shot of the family all together at what looked like some sort of neighborhood picnic. There was a long table set up behind them covered with food, with lots of people milling about. Trees and playground equipment dotted the background, and Lance recognized the area as the park at the base of the mountain.

Mark Benchley was an average-looking man, but above-average height, towering over his wife and daughter by a good foot, at least. His hair was thinning and his belly was soft, but all in all, he appeared normal. He wore blue jeans and loafers and a button-up shirt.

Mary Benchley looked to be maybe twelve or thirteen in the picture, a small spotting of acne on her forehead, her body looking as though it were still trying to figure itself out. But her face was pretty and her smile was a knockout, and Lance figured that she would likely have grown up to be a very attractive young lady.

But it wasn't Mark Benchley or his daughter, Mary, that had nearly caused Lance to fall out of his chair.

Natalie Benchley stood beside her husband, looking proud and happy. She had a plate of food in one hand, and the other arm wrapped around her daughter's shoulder. She wore a tank top and shorts and flip-flops. She looked comfortable in every sense of the word.

But there was one imperfection.

A scar on her chin. Just to the left of center.

Lance had seen the scar and then stared into the picture of the woman's face, had seen the image reverse itself in age, growing younger and younger until the face was of a little girl of maybe six or seven. Her mother scooping her up in her arms while the blood flowed from the fresh gash from where she'd fallen and struck the patio.

A little boy, maybe a year or two older, standing by with tears in his eyes, guilt weighing heavy on his heart and mind.

A little boy who would suffer unspeakable abuse and then grow up to be sheriff.

Lance sat back and looked at the image for a very long time. Another piece of the puzzle falling into place.

Natalie Benchley had been Sheriff Ray Kruger's younger sister.

[30]

WHEN LANCE APPROACHED THE TWO-HEADED GUARD DOG at the library's front desk, both women eyed him with looks that said *What could he possibly want now?*

"I'm all finished," Lance said, adjusting the straps of his backpack. He looked at the woman on the right, the one with the gold cross. "Thank you for your help." Then he smiled at the woman on the left, not wanting her to feel left out. "I hope you both have a great day."

He didn't look back as he walked through the atrium, sneaking another peek up at the cloud-covered sky through the glass ceiling and then stepped out the front door.

He stood on the sidewalk and took a deep breath, filling his lungs. The traffic was picking up on the main streets. He could hear the rumble of engines and the squeals of brakes that needed work coming from beyond the courthouse. He pulled his cell phone from his pocket and checked the time. It was just past noon.

Church would likely be out now.

He walked up the side street for two blocks until he was back in front of the courthouse, then he made a right turn, away from the direction of Mama's—he was much more eager to speak with Jacob Morgan than Joan right now—and figured he could cut down another street and circle back toward the direction of the park. Then he'd hike back up the hill and hopefully catch Jacob and Ethan at home. If they weren't there, maybe having stopped for lunch, Lance told himself he would wait. His belly was full and he'd had his coffee and he was pumped fresh with adrenaline after his discovery about Natalie Benchley's familial ties to Sheriff Ray Kruger. There was a Dean Koontz paperback somewhere in his backpack that he'd started twice without finishing. He could fish it out and give it another go while he waited.

Lance rounded a corner and saw he was correct about the traffic uptick. There were five cars stopped at the stoplight, and as Lance walked by and glanced inside the windows, he saw most of the drivers were dressed in their Sunday best. Shirts and ties and jackets and conservative dresses. No evangelical shorts and a t-shirt around these parts. The songs played and sung during worship services in Ripton's Grove would be the standby classics like "Amazing Grace" or "How Great Thou Art" instead of anything more contemporary that one might be able to threaten to dance to.

A few of the drivers looked at Lance before quickly darting their eyes back to the road, the cars in front of them, the stoplight. The light turned green and the cars moved slowly on. Back to homes where families would sit down to share a meal, off to Mama's or other restaurants where they'd maybe join friends and enjoy a few laughs.

A routine.

Normalcy.

Things Lance wondered if he'd ever taste again in any sense of the word. Right now his only routine was to have no routine.

He looked down at his sneakers on the sidewalk, tilting his

head down and letting the steady breeze ruffle his hair. It was getting too long. He'd need to get a trim soon. Haircuts were the type of trivial thing that Lance often found slipping through the cracks of his life now.

"Lance! Hey, Lance!"

Lance stopped and looked up. Searched for the source of the voice. He looked across the street and saw he'd ended up directly across from R.G. Homes. Rich Bellows, wearing black dress slacks and a white dress shirt, the tie loosened around his neck and hanging askew, was standing half out the door, waving frantically to get Lance's attention. Lance allowed a pickup truck to pass by and then crossed the street.

"Hi," Lance said.

Rich Bellows nodded a greeting and then pushed the door open completely, suggesting Lance should come inside.

Lance looked over his shoulder, back across the street, and then left and right. He found the courthouse's bell tower and then looked down at the buildings beneath, mentally tracing his steps from there to here.

This hadn't been the direction he'd meant to come. He'd started out on the right path, but somewhere along the way, he'd lost his focus, had let his mind wander, and his feet had brought him right here to Rich Bellows's doorstep.

Why?

Lance entered the office.

Then Rich Bellows closed the door, turned the deadbolt, and shut the blinds.

Well ... this may not have been my best move.

Lance didn't move. Rich Bellows didn't make him feel any more comfortable when he said, "Lance, I think you need to get out of town. Today. As soon as you can."

Lance thought about this, then chose his words very carefully. "But, we have a lease agreement."

Rich Bellows stared at Lance, his face showing first misunderstanding, then confusion. Finally he allowed himself a grin. Lance grinned back, and Rich let out a short burst of laughter, followed by a long, sad sigh.

"What's going on, Mr. Bellows?" Lance asked. "What's *really* going on? Why do you think I need to leave?"

Rich rubbed at the side of his face, trying to decide what to say. "I don't want you to get hurt."

"The way you say that," Lance said, "it doesn't sound like it's you who'd be doing the hurting. Am I right?"

Rich took a step forward, and Lance stepped back quickly, his hands coming up defensively.

Rich stopped and shook his head. "Relax, okay? You're right. I'm not who you need to worry about." He motioned behind Lance. "I was just going to go back to my office."

Lance lowered his hands but kept his body alert. "If not you, who should I worry about?"

Rich nodded toward the door behind Lance again. "My office."

Lance stepped aside. "After you, sir."

Rich did not seem to notice or care that Lance was allowing him to go first as a defensive tactic—to avoid possibly getting attacked from behind by some coward. He walked past Lance and stepped into his office, sidestepping around the desk and collapsing into his chair like a man who was exhausted from a hard day's labor.

Lance entered the office and stood just inside the doorway, leaning against the wall. He crossed his arms, decided it looked too aggressive, and then uncrossed them, burying his hands in the pockets of his cargo shorts.

He said nothing. Waited while Rich Bellows stared down at his desk, eyes lost. Finally, he looked up at Lance and said, "It was the flowers."

"Sir?"

"You seemed like a really nice guy the night you came in here looking for a place to rent. I even went home and told Victoria all about you. So, I guess"—he sighed and leaned back in the chair, running his hands through his hair—"I guess I was never quite convinced it'd been you who attacked her in the farmhouse yesterday morning, but I was so *blasted* angry, Lance. I felt so violated, to think somebody had come after her and hurt her. I ... I wasn't thinking straight, and I was looking for somebody to blame—other than myself—and you were the first person I could think of. I used you as a scapegoat. That's why I was so adamant with the sheriff that they should bring you in. I mean, they probably would have anyway, since you were the one staying at the house, but ... I could have done more to vouch for you."

Rich paused and looked to Lance, searching to see if he was following him. Lance nodded once.

"But then you showed up at Central Medical yesterday with those blasted flowers, and I thought to myself, *Rich, what an—pardon my language—asshole you are, to accuse this nice young man of such an awful crime.* You didn't even know my wife until yesterday morning, and you were thoughtful enough to check in on her and bring her a gift. She loved them, by the way. Put them in water as soon as we got home, and I had to stare at them on the counter this morning all through our breakfast. All the while thinking how it was all my fault, yet you were the one who got pulled into the sheriff's office and treated like a criminal."

Lance, ignoring what he figured was Rich Bellows eventually coming around to an apology of sorts, asked, "Sir, that's twice now you've alluded to what happened yesterday as being your fault. Why is that?"

Rich looked down at his desk again, and his face grew pale,

like he was getting sick. He took a deep breath and swallowed once, twice, then looked at Lance and said, "I may have been an accomplice. Indirectly, mind you, but that's not ever going to help me sleep at night."

Lance gave the man a minute before saying, "I'm going to need more, sir. It's hard for me to put any stock in your request that I leave town based on your vagueness. You understand, right?"

Rich seemed to consider this for a long time before saying, "Why are you here, Lance?"

Lance couldn't help it. He barked a laugh. Rich looked at him, confused. "Sorry," Lance said. "I'm just beginning to think that's what the epitaph will be on my gravestone. 'Here lies Lancelot Brody. Why was he here?'"

Rich didn't so much as smile. "You told me you were a consultant. But everyone in town seems to think you're writing some sort of article or true crime book about the Benchley murders."

Lance said nothing.

Rich sighed again and stood up, pushing the desk chair to the side and leaning over to rest his palms flat on the desk. "Lance, I truly don't believe you're a bad person. I don't know why you're here, and you don't seem keen on telling me, so all I'm going to do now is ask that whatever I tell you never leaves this room. Remember, I'm trying to *help* you here. Okay? I'm looking out for your best interest." Then he added, "And what I'm about to tell you, while I don't know that it's technically a crime, I just... if Victoria found out. I don't know the repercussions, Lance, and—well, if it comes to a head, then it does, and I'll take the responsibility like a man. But I don't want my life ruined, Lance. Not so much for my sake, but for my family's."

Lance looked Rich in the eyes and said, "Sir, you have my

word. This is just between you and me. I'm not here to ruin any lives or add any fuel to the gossip train."

Rich searched Lance's face for a long time, contemplated his honestly. And whether it was that he did bring himself to fully trust this stranger before him, or whether his apparent guilt would no longer allow him to remain silent, Rich said, "After the murders, and about a week after R.G Homes purchased the property, I got an email from an anonymous sender. A random address with letters and numbers, no name. It was a simple offer —a *partnership* is how they put it. They'd give me five hundred dollars a month, every month, on a date of my choosing, and all I had to do was email them back at that address anytime anything was done involving the Benchleys' farmhouse. Maintenance work, cleaning crews, landscaping, and"—he gave Lance another guilty look—"new tenants. Anything. The email told me to go check the mailbox out front to see how serious they were, and sure enough, there was an envelope right along with the other junk I get, with five one-hundred-dollar bills inside."

"So you went along with it?" Lance asked.

Rich looked at him, and Lance saw some of the guilt melt away and be replaced by defensiveness. "I've got a wife and two kids who I want to give the world to, Lance. There's nothing on this earth that makes me happier than to see them happy. I don't know if you've noticed, but Ripton's Grove isn't exactly a booming real estate metropolis. Five hundred a month ... well, let's just say it was a nice cushion. It took some of the pressure off me and kept Victoria in that Mercedes she loves so much and helps keep our mortgage paid. Do you understand?" He ran his hands through his hair again. "I mean, I didn't see how it would possibly hurt anybody. Why would it?"

"You didn't think it was strange?"

"Of course I thought it was strange," Rich said. "But..."

"But five hundred dollars," Lance finished for him.

Rich's mouth closed with an audible pop. He nodded and his face turned red. "Do you have a family, Lance?"

Lance felt the twinge of pain, a stab like a dagger in his heart. It was a low blow, and he suspected Rich knew it. But he remained calm. "No, sir. I have nobody."

Maybe it was the way that Lance had phrased his answer that kept Rich Bellows from pressing on, or maybe he'd realized he'd gotten too personal when, as he'd said at the start, he was only trying to help.

Lance digested Rich's story. Thought about potential implications. Said, "So you think that whoever attacked Victoria yesterday is the same person who's been sending you the five hundred every month."

Rich nodded. "Or ... if it wasn't specifically them, they had a hand in it. Hired somebody, maybe. But there's more to it than that. I started thinking about what I told you the other night when you showed up, how everybody who rented the old farmhouse left, saying it was haunted. Well, we both know that's silly, right? Places aren't haunted."

Lance said nothing.

"So," Rich continued, "I started thinking that maybe whoever is sending me the cash is making the place *seem* haunted. I don't know, going over there and rattling chains or slamming doors, or ... *whatever*, just to scare whoever is renting the place into leaving." He paused and took a breath. "Lance, I think there's somebody out there that is trying hard —really hard—to make sure nobody stays in or around that house very long. And now, after yesterday, they're getting more direct about it, and I don't know how far they're willing to go. It's not a secret the whole town is talking about you, and whatever it is you're out to accomplish here—*up there*, I should say. And I think you've got whoever attacked Victoria worried. I think they're scared you're going to do exactly what they've been trying to keep everyone else from doing all these years."

Lance felt a prickle of realization at the base of his skull. Rich Bellows was definitely onto something. "What is it they're afraid of?" Lance asked.

Rich shook his head. "No idea. But I think it's for you to decide if whatever it is you're after is worth getting hurt over, or worse." There was the faintest shimmer of tears in Rich's eyes by now. "I've already got my own wife's blood on my hands, Lance. I don't want yours, too. Leave. Today."

Lance stayed where he was, leaning against the wall with his hands shoved into his pockets. He watched Rich Bellows recompose himself and then sit back in his chair. Rich pulled the tie completely loose from his neck and tossed it onto his desk.

Lance asked, "Do you have any idea who it might be, the person who's sending you the cash?"

Rich shook his head, then changed to a sort of seesaw back-and-forth motion. "Well," he started, "There's only one person in town I know who would potentially care about that property enough to do something as extreme as this. But..." He shrugged.

"But what?"

"He wouldn't have to pay me to get the information. He could just walk right in the office, or call me on the phone, or hell, stop by the house for dinner and ask me to do him a favor. And I'd do it for him, no problem. Why not?"

Lance understood. "You're talking about Sheriff Kruger."

Rich nodded. "I am."

"What happened that night hit him pretty hard, huh?" Lance asked, seeing how much Rich would delve into unprovoked. "The fact that it was never really solved?"

Rich gave another shrug. "I don't know about the whole *unsolved* part. I think the odds that Mark Benchley had a breakdown and killed them all are still fairly high. But, yes, it hit Ray hard. He's never been the same."

"And nobody likes to talk about that much around here, do they?"

Rich's eyes narrowed and his brow creased. "You've noticed?"

Lance laughed. "Hard not to, sir. Every time somebody mentions the sheriff's name and the farmhouse or the murders in the same conversation, it's like they're scared to get slapped on the wrist."

Rich nodded but offered nothing more.

Lance said, "I know Natalie Benchley was Kruger's sister, sir."

Rich's eyes widened, and then his face fell into a disbelieving grin. "You've done some research."

"Sure."

Rich sighed and leaned back in his chair further, putting his feet up on the desk. The heels of his dress shoes were worn and the laces tattered. The five hundred a month certainly wasn't going to his personal wardrobe.

"Look, nobody's real sure what the relationship between Ray and his sister was. Rumor is he would never step foot inside the farmhouse. Hardly ever visited," Rich said. "But he *loved* Mary. I swear, when you saw the two of them in town together, if you didn't know any better you'd be convinced Ray was her father. You'd see 'em at the park shootin' hoops, or in Mama's— always in the back booth, mind you—eating and talking like they'd never run out of topics. He went to all her school events. I think it half broke his heart when he found out she was going off to that boarding school. Worst part is, I don't think he even knew it was happening until after the fact. I don't think *anybody* did."

Rich paused for a moment, as if trying to find his place.

"You see ... well ... Ray never had any children of his own. Never been married, or even had a girlfriend that any of us folks who've lived here our whole lives has seen. He's a great guy— smart, polite, a sly and dry sense of humor, and a heck of an honorable profession. But it's like ... it's like he's closed that part of his life—the part that might involve a woman, *intimacy* I guess you'd say—off from everything else." Rich shrugged. "Some folks think he's gay and is happier in the closet than out. But I don't see it that way."

It was then that Lance realized he might be the only person in Ripton's Grove who had some insight into the true reason Sheriff Ray Kruger was the man he'd become.

"So people don't mention the sheriff's connection to Natalie and Mary Benchley because they're trying to spare his feelings? Protect his privacy? Is that it?" It seemed extreme to Lance, but he supposed he'd heard of crazier things. Had *seen* crazier things.

Rich Bellows looked at his watch. "I've got to get going. Victoria'll have lunch ready any minute now. And the kids are sure to be grumpy and tired." He picked up his tie off the desk and draped it over his shoulder. He looked at Lance. "Two weeks after the night the Benchley family was killed, a reporter from some paper up north came into town, digging for a scoop, a scandal—hell, I don't know how you guys operate. But he basically stalked the sheriff one day and cornered him in the parking lot of Mama's and started asking questions about whether or not there was anything Ray felt he could have done differently to prevent what had happened. If he'd see any signs beforehand, or if Natalie had mentioned anything to him that might have been a call for help."

Oh, boy.

"Ray didn't like that," Rich said. "The reporter spent three days in Central Medical, and the Ripton's Grove sheriff's office caught a break and settled out of court. But it was still a lot of money, Lance. *A lot.* Anywhere else, Ray would have lost his job, for sure. But around here—well, you know. Small towns. We know who Ray really is."

Not entirely, Lance thought. He put a few more of the pieces together in his head and asked, "So the sheriff inherited the farmhouse after his sister and family were killed?"

Rich nodded. "He actually inherited it when his uncle Joe died, but he told Natalie she could have it. They were having a tough time, apparently, and Ray helped her out. Personally, I think that's one of the reasons the whole thing shook Ray so hard—you know, aside from the fact that his sister and niece were killed. I think he feels responsible. I think he blames himself because if he'd kept the house, and Natalie and her family hadn't moved in, maybe they'd all still be alive."

Rich headed through the office door and Lance followed. The sky had grown darker, and outside the windows looked gray and bored. "So Ray got the house back after the murders and contacted me almost immediately to see if we wanted to buy it. He said he didn't want any part of the place. Can't say I can blame him, right?" Rich tugged on a sport coat that'd been draped over the phantom receptionist's chair. "Honestly, I didn't want the place, but Ray was willing to take next to nothing for it, just to be done with the whole thing, and I figured the land alone was worth the investment. So I took him up on the offer."

Lance had learned so much from Rich Bellows, he felt he should take the man over to Mama's and buy him a whole meat-loaf. But then he remembered that Rich had likely been the cause of Lance being potentially attacked and figured he'd call them all square.

Rich looked at Lance as he took his key ring out of his coat pocket. "It's not Ray, is it? The one sending me the money?"

Lance shook his head. "No, sir. I don't think so."

Rich nodded, as if this was the answer he'd been expecting. "Any idea who it is, then?"

Lance nodded, letting a cold truth sink in. One that he had probably been suspecting this entire time but had only now managed to fully convince himself of. "It's whoever really committed those murders. I think they're worried somebody is going to find them out."

Rich grimaced, as if Lance's words had caused him physical pain, then he shivered. "So you're saying there's a murderer walking around Ripton's Grove?"

Lance nodded again. "Can't say for sure they're still here, but I'm thinking it's likely."

"And I've been on his payroll all these years." Rich shook his head, and his breath caught in his chest. "God ... what have I done?"

Lance said nothing. Slipped out the door and stood on the sidewalk, listening to Rich Bellows step out and lock the deadbolt. Rich's Explorer was parked on the street. As he walked toward it, his face carrying a fresh expression of sorrow, he called to Lance. "Want a lift to the bus station? I'll buy you a ticket anywhere you want to go."

Lance shook his head. "No, sir." He thought about Ethan. "I'm not finished here."

Rich looked at Lance with questioning eyes, but he got no response. "You won't tell anyone about the cash, right, Lance? You gave me your word, right?"

Lance shook his head. "I won't, sir. But I think *you* should. I think it's what Sheriff Kruger would want, don't you?"

Rich Bellows didn't say anything. He climbed into the driver's seat, cranked the engine, and then drove away, leaving Lance standing alone on the sidewalk.

[31]

Lance stood on the sidewalk for a long time. He watched Rich Bellows drive away, back to his home, back to his wife and children and his life that he knew would be waiting for him. Lance wondered if the man would call Sheriff Kruger and tell him about the emails, the money. Lance doubted it. He didn't think Rich Bellows was a bad person at all, but Rich was too afraid to lose everything to admit he might have done something wrong at such a potentially large level. Aiding a criminal— a *murderer*—would weigh heavily on his mind for a long time, Lance was sure of that. Maybe one day Rich would fess up, but it wasn't Lance's place to do it for him.

Because what good would it do, really? If Lance marched straight to the sheriff's office right now and told Ray Kruger everything he'd just learned from Rich, what would happen? First, they'd have to believe Lance was telling the truth, which from recent experiences seemed like a fifty-fifty gamble. Second, if they did decide that Lance wasn't blowing smoke up their tails, then what? They call Rich Bellows and ask him to verify? Make him give up access to his email? Would they have to obtain a warrant for that information? The Benchley family murders had been six years ago—what would the process be for anything pertaining to such an old case? And say they did get access to Rich's email, then they'd have to get computer gurus to analyze it and probably work with other outside resources to try and get some sort of trace on the email's origin. Lance was no computer expert—flip phone, remember?—but he'd seen enough TV and films and read enough spy novels to know that there were enough ways to disguise email and web traffic that the whole thing could end up being a wild goose chase.

And it would take time.

Time Lance didn't have.

What was he supposed to do? Spend his days eating meat-loaf at Mama's and sleeping in the bed of a dead girl day after day, night after night, just on standby until the answers came in —*if* they came in? Or waiting for another sound bite from the mystery dinner theater performance that had been slowly revealing itself to him in the farmhouse?

He didn't have the answers, and as far as he could tell, there was absolutely no way he was ever going to get them. This problem was too big. It had too many moving pieces, too many unknowns. It had all happened too long ago.

And what good was the information he'd gotten about Sheriff Kruger's past, the abuse he'd suffered? The sheriff was a grown man—a troubled man, sure, and rightfully so, but he was grown. He could take care of himself. Ray Kruger's uncle was dead. His sister and family were dead. Lance couldn't do anything to fix any of that.

Whoever thought that Lance was a threat to fingering them as the Benchley family's killer, the joke was on them. Lance was no closer to adding any closure to that horrible night than he'd been the moment he'd stepped off the bus two days ago.

"The boy is all that matters now," Lance said to himself and the quiet city street. "He's the one I need to worry about."

Now, more than ever, Lance was convinced that Ethan was the real reason he'd been meant to stop in Ripton's Grove. Everything else had just led to their meeting.

He walked three blocks back toward Mama's and made a right, stopping at a small convenience store he'd passed on his way to Central Medical the day before. He stocked up on bottles of water, protein bars, nuts, and a few packets of instant coffee. He tossed them all into his backpack, ignoring the curious looks given to him by the woman behind the checkout counter, and then pushed out the door and headed back toward the park. Back toward the trail that would lead up the mountain.

It was time to talk to Jacob Morgan. If he and Ethan weren't home yet, Lance would wait as long as it took. Because honestly, he had absolutely nothing else to do in this town anymore.

The clouds continued to thicken, darkening the sky. Beneath the cover of the trees, the world seemed even darker. The wind was picking up, rattling branches and making the leaves sound like the crashing waves of the ocean as they bristled and swayed and collided with each other above. Lance walked with his head down, his hood up, staring at the trail and watching each step he took, one foot in front of the other. His backpack was weighed down with his fresh supplies, and already the satisfying feeling of his Mama's breakfast in his stomach was beginning to fade. He did not reach for a snack, however. Did not even feel the weight on his back. All his mind was focused on was Ethan.

Over and over again, Lance replayed the scene from last night. The way the boy had been entranced by the basement door—or more specifically what

(*who*)

was behind it. "*She's down there! She's down there!*" the boy

637

had cried. If Lance hadn't already heard the young girl crying to be let out himself, he wouldn't have understood—not fully, anyway. But he *had* heard. And Ethan—small, innocent, special Ethan—had heard her too. Mary Benchley had called out to both of them.

Something else still sat at the forefront of Lance's thoughts about that night. The way Jacob Morgan had reacted so quickly, almost from the moment Ethan had begun to walk toward the door. It was as though he'd sensed the boy was slipping into his *other place*, the place where he could hear the dead and see things that nobody—especially a young boy —should see. *He knows*, Lance told himself again as he reached the place where he'd turn and walk through the woods to Jacob Morgan's house. *He knows what his nephew can do.*

"I can help them," Lance said aloud as he crunched through a fresh crop of fallen leaves, the latest victims of the strong winds. "And they can help me."

The first thing Lance noticed was that the plume of smoke wafting from the chimney was thicker, denser. *They're home*, he thought. *Fresh logs on the fire, and they're home.* His steps picked up their pace, but he kept himself from running full-on in case Jacob Morgan was watching out the window. Lance didn't want to appear to be a threat ... or a crazy person. Depending on how his intended conversation went, that last part might be unavoidable as it was.

Lance walked up the porch step and approached the front door. The rocking chair to his right, the baby bear chair, was rocking gently in the wind. Lance pulled down his hood, attempting to look less like a burglar, raised his hand, and knocked three times.

He waited. Heard muffled voices from behind the door. The shuffling of feet.

Jacob Morgan opened the door slowly. The first thing Lance saw was the knife in his hand.

The second thing Lance noticed was that there was a smear of what looked like peanut butter on the blade. His heart quickly recovered from the spike in pulse it'd achieved at the sight of a potential weapon in Jacob Morgan's hands, and Lance offered his best smile.

"Lance, hi," Jacob said, opening the door wide, lowering the peanut-butter-smeared table knife. "What's up? Get bored up on the hill all by yourself? Thought you'd come down for what barely passes as civilized company?" Jacob chuckled at his own joke and motioned for Lance to step inside. Lance looked into the cabin, saw Ethan sitting on an old couch with a picture book in his lap. He had a finger on one of the pages, moving it slowly left to right, his lips moving as he sounded out words. He looked up, as if sensing Lance staring, and their eyes met briefly before Ethan returned his gaze to the book.

Lance stepped inside and Jacob closed the door behind him.

"Ethan, can you say hi to Mr. Lance?"

Ethan looked up from his book again, and obediently said, "Hi, Mr. Lance. How are you?"

Lance looked at this small boy on the couch, book in his lap, impeccable manners, and knowledge behind his youthful eyes. In that moment, Lance saw himself. Many years ago as a child, sitting in his home reading a book his mother had brought him from the library while she was busy in the kitchen, humming a tune while baking them a pie they'd share later while she asked him about what he'd read.

Lance smiled at the boy. "I'm doing very well, Ethan. Thank you for asking. How are you?"

"Good," the boy said, then quickly diverted his eyes back to his book.

"Good, what?" Jacob said. His voice stern.

Ethan looked up from his page again. "Good, thank you." Then he looked to his uncle. Jacob nodded once, and the boy was back to his book again.

"Can I offer you a sandwich, Lance? PB and J is sort of our post-church ritual. We'd be happy to have you join us."

Lance thought about the protein bars in his backpack. "If you're sure it's no trouble, that would be great. Thank you."

"No trouble at all. White or wheat?"

"Wheat, please."

"Good man," Jacob said. "Been trying, and failing, to get little man over there to switch to wheat instead of this processed white garbage. No luck so far." He shrugged his shoulders. "Kids, right?"

Lance nodded, because it seemed the only right thing to do. "Kids," he said.

"Just a second. One world-class PB and J on wheat coming right up. Make yourself at home."

Jacob turned and walked to the kitchen area, which took up the entire left side of the cabin's open space. Fridge, oven, sink, and a large woodstove in the front corner with a small pile of chopped wood beside it. A square table with four chairs separated the kitchen from the rest of the open space, which served as the living room. There was the couch, on which Ethan was absorbed in his book, two end tables, a coffee table, bookshelf, and small TV stand with a modern-looking television that looked incredibly out of place among the otherwise rustic décor. A wired antenna was mounted on the wall above the TV, its black cable snaking down the wall and out of sight. The rear of the room had three doors, which Lance assumed led to bedrooms and a bath.

Lance breathed in deeply. The whole place smelled of wood and spices and ... peanut butter. He turned and found Jacob

Morgan behind him, holding a small plate with Lance's sandwich.

Lance took the plate and said, "Thanks."

"You're welcome. Milk?"

"That'd be great," Lance said and walked toward the table.

A few moments later, Jacob Morgan was at the table as well, his own sandwich and glass of milk half-eaten and half-drunk. Lance chewed his sandwich and took a sip of his milk. Wiped his mouth with the back of his hand, and then wiped the back of his hand on his shorts. Both men seemed intent on eating and nothing more. But once the sandwiches were finished, Jacob Morgan looked at Lance with eyes that said, *Go ahead, get on with it.*

Lance took a deep breath, realizing he had no real idea where to start. Settled on, "I've got some questions, and they might seem strange."

As if he'd been expecting nothing less, Jacob Morgan gave off a small sigh and looked over to Ethan, who was still sitting quietly on the couch, finger still moving across the pages.

"Let's step out onto the porch. Get some air. That okay?" Jacob asked.

Lance stood and nodded. "Okay."

THE SKY WAS STILL DARKENED, THE BREEZE STILL STEADY, but the air was not uncomfortably cool. In fact, it was Lance's preferred temperature. A perfect fall afternoon, if not for the blanket of dark clouds. Jacob Morgan wore faded blue jeans and a plain gray sweatshirt, his post-church attire. His feet were bare and he kicked a few stray leaves off the porch and into the yard, where the breeze snatched them up and they went scurrying down the hill and disappeared over the bank, back toward town.

Lance had a brief moment where he wondered if he should follow. Catch a ride on the wind and hightail it out of here before he did something stupid, said the wrong thing to the wrong person. Like mentioning to the nearly complete stranger on the porch with him that he could talk to and see the lingering spirits of the dead ... and more.

But he could not leave. Not now. Not while, after his entire life of wondering, he was so close to finding somebody else that shared his gifts.

Jacob Morgan turned and stuffed his hands into the front pouch of his sweatshirt. He leaned against the porch railing and said, "You can have a seat if you'd like." He nodded toward the papa bear rocking chair. "My ass is still numb from church, so I'm going to stand, if you don't mind."

Lance didn't mind. He mimicked Jacob Morgan's posture and stuffed his own hands into the pouch of his hoodie. He leaned against the wall of the house, facing the man. Leaned his head back and felt the rough wood scratch at his scalp. The two men stared at each other, and just as Lance was about to open his mouth to begin, Jacob Morgan cut him off, saying, "I suppose you're here to ask me about the morning I found the Benchleys. Is that right?"

Lance closed his mouth. Had to regroup. He'd become so focused on the mission to get answers about Ethan that once he'd actually arrived at the house, the entire Benchley family story had evaporated from his mind. He found that right then and there, he couldn't have cared less about what had actually happened that night in the farmhouse. Felt a twinge of guilt and shame in his gut as he realized he didn't care if their killer was still walking free along the streets of Ripton's Grove.

Lance heard his mother's voice in his head. *You're being selfish, Lance.* Could hear the tone of disappointment. He swallowed hard and his mind raced as he tried to figure out whether to allow Jacob Morgan to start off down this road of conversation.

And then Lance remembered that he was never in control. If this was the way things were supposed to begin, Lance would let them. He'd get his opportunity to ask about Ethan soon enough.

"Why do you think that's what I want to know about?" Lance asked.

Jacob laughed. "Come on, man, you don't have to be all mysterious with me. You were being coy last night at the farmhouse, and I didn't press that matter, but everybody knows you're here to write a book." He made air quotes with his fingers and said, *"Discover the truth."* Then he laughed again. "Is that about right?"

So far, the ruse of being a true crime writer had worked well for Lance—so much, in fact, that if he had a computer, he might be compelled to actually *write* a damned book about this mess. It would certainly give him something to do on buses other than sleep and read. He figured continuing the charade would only help him at this point.

"Something like that," he said. "But you should know, I'm not a detective."

Jacob Morgan looked confused. "Meaning?"

"Meaning I'm not out to solve a case," Lance said. "My publisher"—*Your* publisher? *Boy, laying it on thick now, aren't we, Lance?*—"was intrigued by the nature of the crime, and I'm only here to present the facts as given by those who know them." Lance grinned, sheepishly but purely for show, and said, "Now, I won't deny I'm also supposed to make it a compelling read. You know, add suspense and mystery and make it as dramatic as possible. But I'm only gathering information. If the police say Mark Benchley killed his family, that's what the book will say."

Jacob Morgan was quiet for a moment, then said, "People really buy that shit?"

Lance nodded. "True crime was the third-best-selling genre in the United States last year." This was a one hundred percent made-up statement as far as Lance knew. But it sounded like a good answer that an actual true crime writer might have ready.

"What was first?" Jacob Morgan asked.

"Romance," Lance said instantly. "Chicks dig their love stories."

Jacob Morgan barked another laugh. "True enough, my friend. True enough."

A hard breeze blew across the hilltop, and the porch rattled and squeaked. Jacob Morgan looked at the support beam to his left and then knocked on it with his knuckles, as if reassuring himself it was secured and in place. "So you want to hear my side of the story, is that it? You found out it was me who found them and you want to know how it was?"

Lance nodded, eager to move on to the subject of Ethan but also very curious to hear what Jacob Morgan had to say. "That would be great."

Jacob nodded, looked to where Lance had his hands stuffed in his hoodie. "You gonna write any of this down or ... record it?"

Lance blushed and thought quickly. He pulled his flip phone from his pocket and snapped it open. Pretended to hit a few buttons on the keypad and then set it in the rocking chair next to him. "Okay," he said. "All set."

Jacob eyed the phone suspiciously.

Lance said, "Uh, you wouldn't believe the microphone on that thing. You know what they say—they don't make 'em like they used to."

Jacob nodded as if this made perfect sense, and then Lance watched as the man's face changed and his eyes narrowed and his thoughts slipped away from the porch and landed back on that awful morning.

Lance listened intently, his eyes never leaving Jacob Morgan's face as the man told his story. The details weren't much different than what Lance had already been given by Susan, but the perspective—the emotion—that was now presented differed greatly. Where Susan had recited the grisly details of where the bodies had been found with a sense that she'd been excitedly presenting a book report, Jacob Morgan's voice had wavered and cracked at parts, causing him to pause and look away, often out over the railing of the porch, staring blankly into the trees, or off toward the horizon where the hill sloped away and fell to Ripton's Grove. He would wipe a loose tear or two away from high up on his cheeks, and then he'd turn back to Lance—man-to-man once again—and continue.

Jacob Morgan had been headed out of town to help his friend Jack do some work on a new house he and his young wife had just purchased. "It was a total wreck of a place," Jacob said. "He sent me pictures. It was going to take a hell of a lot longer than a week, but that was a good enough chunk of time to start. Jack's terrible at that sort of stuff, and a contractor would have taken one look at the house and another look at Jack and ripped the poor bastard off." Jacob shrugged. "I was looking forward to getting away for a bit anyway. Not exactly a vacation, but it was good enough for me."

Jacob had driven up to the Benchleys' place to ask Mark to stop by the house a few times during the week, just to check on things. "It was just something we did for each other," Jacob said. "Help out here and there when we could. Share stuff from our gardens, help out with any handiwork now and again. You know," Jacob said with another shrug, "neighborly stuff."

Jacob had seen Natalie Benchley's body as soon as he'd pulled his pickup truck into the driveway. "At first I thought some laundry had blown off the line," Jacob said. "Looked just like some fabric sprawled out, half on the porch steps, half in the driveway. But as I got closer"—here was a time he'd had to look away, a time when his voice wavered— "I saw ... I saw it was Natalie. I didn't have any delusions about it." He shook his head. "She was dead. There wasn't no question about it. She was facedown in the yard, one arm outstretched as if she'd been reaching for something to hold on to, and on her back from the neck down was nothing but gore." He shook his head over and over as he spoke. "Just holes and blood and torn flesh and..." He cleared his throat. "Like I said, there was no question she was dead."

Jacob had walked up the front porch steps and pulled the pocket knife he always carried from his jeans. "It was all I had on me at the time," he said. "I don't travel with my guns." He had entered the house and called out to see if anybody was there. "I knew they wouldn't be," Jacob said. "I knew whoever'd killed Natalie wouldn't be sticking around. But all the same, I kept my eyes peeled, ready to jam my blade into the unlucky bastard's neck if he gave me the chance." And he'd found Mark Benchley in the living room, sitting in his chair with the shotgun at his feet and most of the man's face gone. "I looked at the wall behind him for a long time before I ever even lowered my eyes to Mark," Jacob said. "It was like ... it was just covered in..." He trailed off. Another clearing of the throat. "It does weird things to you when you see stuff that's supposed to be *inside* somebody on the outside. Especially when it's splattered on the wall like some sort of goddamn art project." He shot Lance a look and frowned. "Sorry for my language."

Jacob had then gone upstairs. "I stood in the living room a long time, Lance. A long time. By this point, I figured if anybody'd still been in the house, they would have either come at me already or run away. This is going to sound funny, but you gotta remember, these people were my friends, and, well ... I guess I was in a bit of shock. That's what the doctors or the shrinks will tell you, anyway. But, even though I saw the shotgun lying at Mark's feet, and the way the gore was spread on the wall behind him, my brain never perceived it as a suicide. Not then, anyway. I went upstairs, just for my own sanity— wanting to say I'd checked the whole house before I called the cops. It was empty, of course. Then I went down to the kitchen."

Jacob had seen the smoldering remains of the brush pile fire through the kitchen window as he'd run the cold water tap to get a handful to splash his face. "Something about the smoke called to me," he said and then quickly shot Lance a look that asked, *Do you think I'm crazy?* He forced a weak laugh. "I know that doesn't make any sense, but I swear, it's like I couldn't take my eyes off that pile of brush and the slowly dying smoke puffing from its center. It's like it was pulling me in, Lance. Does that make any sense at all? It's like something was yelling at me, trying to get my attention and get my ass out there."

Lance felt his blood run cold. He did understand (*The mirror*), and he wondered if there were more people on this hilltop with hidden gifts than just he and Ethan.

Lance, the good journalist, said nothing. Only nodded for Jacob to continue.

Jacob had then found Mary Benchley. "I walked out the backdoor and I saw her. I mean ... I didn't know it was her. How could I? All that was left at that point..." This time he heaved and tried to hold back a great sob that spun him around, and he wiped his eyes and stared out to the trees for a long time, taking deep breaths. He turned around once he'd composed himself. "It was just bones, man. Just bones and not much else." He shook his head and his eyes still glistened. "Something told me it was her, man. Just like I'd felt pulled toward that fire, something just told me it was her. I mean, I hadn't seen her since ... well, since she'd gone off to school, but I just knew." He looked at Lance, and his eyes were those of a man who was begging to be understood. "I never told the police that part. I never told them about those feelings I'd gotten. I never told them I thought that pile of bones in the fire was Mary."

"Was the basement door open or closed when you were in the kitchen? Do you remember?"

Jacob Morgan looked confused. "I have no idea, man. Why does that matter?"

Lance shrugged. "Details are always important. Even if we don't know why."

Jacob Morgan didn't seem to know what to say to this.

"So I pulled out my cell and called 911 and then, well... you know the rest, I'm sure."

Lance nodded. "For the most part. How hard did they work to prove you were the one who'd killed them? I mean, that was the initial thought, right? According to everything I've seen and heard."

Jacob Morgan sighed and nodded. Laughed. "Yeah, that was a fun day or two. Nothing like being the town monster to really show you folks' true colors. I've never seen so many people turn their back so quickly." He shrugged, like a man who'd chosen to live in the future and forget the past. "But it got sorted out in the end."

"Did it?" Lance asked, and immediately wished he'd found a more tactful way to continue.

Jacob's eyes narrowed. "What do you mean?"

"Did the police get it right?"

There was a flash of something then, something across Jacob Morgan's face that said he was no longer simply rehashing information but was now engaged in something he wasn't sure he wanted to continue. His voice was suddenly accusatory.

"Are you suggesting that you believe I *did* murder the Benchleys?"

Lance pulled his hands free from his hoodie's pocket and held them up, shook his head. "No, of course not. But I am asking if you think Mark Benchley did. Other sources I've spoken with have said he was quite the family man. Loved his wife, adored his daughter. Why would he kill them?"

"Did your sources also tell you that Mark Benchley was a few bricks shy of a full load?"

Lance said nothing.

"They tell you he was a religious fanatic who would cast judgment so fast, if you blinked, you'd miss it?"

Lance nodded in agreement but added, "They also told me the two of you were friends."

What are you doing, Lance? You're here to talk about Ethan. Why are you provoking this man? How is that possibly going to help you?

Jacob Morgan leaned back against the railing, and his aggressiveness drained away. He looked down at his feet, cast his eyes across the wooden boards of the porch floor before he looked up and grinned. "Yeah, Mark and I were friendly. Truth be told, we probably wouldn't have been if they hadn't moved into the farmhouse, but after I went to introduce myself and then helped him out with a few little fix-me-ups, it just sort of happened. Mark wasn't a bad guy on the surface, honestly. Pretty normal, in fact, if you could ignore his Bible-thumping fear-of-God trances he'd slip into now and again. But seriously, he was a nice guy, and I can honestly say I enjoyed his company. He had a very unique worldview. It was ... I guess I'd have to say it was refreshing."

"But he killed his wife, and burned his daughter, and then shot himself," Lance said, unable to stop himself for some deep down reason he couldn't control.

Jacob Morgan didn't protest. He nodded his head. "He had demons, Lance. Just like all of us. His just got the best of him, I guess." He hawked some phlegm from his throat and spat it out over the railing. "Here's something else I never told the police, Lance, and you can decide whether you want to stick it in your book or not." He shrugged again. "I don't guess it matters at all now. But if I'd have known Mark was going to snap like that, do the things he did ... I'd have killed him myself before he had the chance to hurt those girls. Natalie was the sweetest woman. Funny, charming, hell of a cook. And Mary..." The tears were so sudden and so strong, Jacob Morgan was sobbing into his hands before Lance had even realized what was happening. Deep cries of anguish that were choked off by a man ashamed to have lost control in front of another man—a stranger, digging into a painful past. Jacob looked up from his hands, wiping his eyes. "Sorry," he said, forcing an awkward-sounding laugh. "She just had so much to live for, you know? She was so young, and just getting started. And that bastard *killed* her. His own goddamn daughter. *He* killed her!"

Jacob Morgan eyes were full of fire, his face electric with anger, but then he looked down at the rocking chair and saw Lance's flip phone sitting open, and his features softened again. He worked to regain control of himself. Finally, he said, "Sorry. I guess I always think I've moved on from it, but I'm always wrong. It still stings, even after all these years."

Lance nodded. "I can't pretend to imagine what it must have been like."

Lance had seen a lot of things in his life, and he could certainly imagine much worse than finding a few dead bodies, but it seemed like the right thing to say.

"I left," Jacob said. "After it all. I left. Went to help my friend with his house, and then just bounced around for a while. I kept thinking I'd be ready to come back, but every time I got ready to start the drive, I found myself heading in a different direction. And then my sister and her husband were killed in that car accident, and I found myself suddenly with a newborn child under my wing. And the only place to try and start a home with him was ... well, home. You know? So I came back, and here I am talking to a guy I hardly know about my deepest and darkest emotions."

Lance picked up the flip phone, pressed a few random keys, and then snapped it shut. "I'm sorry if that was painful for you, but I do appreciate you talking with me."

Jacob Morgan waved him off. "Glad to do it," he said. "I'd rather you hear the truth than tell the world a bunch of gossip bullshit. Even though I'm sure that would sell more books, right?"

"Can I ask you something about Ethan?"

Jacob Morgan's mouth snapped closed, and his eyes hardened and his arms crossed.

Lance Brody, ladies and gentlemen. Master of segues, and the art of subtle conversation.

Jacob Morgan's words were slow and direct, as if he were suddenly thrown into a chess match he neither had expected or fully understood. "Ethan has nothing to do with what happened to the Benchleys."

Lance shook his head. "No, of course not. I wanted to ask you something about what happened at the farmhouse last night."

"No."

"But—"

"*No.* Listen to me, I understand you have a job to do, and I understand I was a part of something that is never going to go away, and there will always be people like you showing up over the years to ask questions or ask what it was like. I've accepted that. But you have access to me only, *not* to my nephew. *Not* to a six-year-old boy."

Lance tried to gain some footing. "I understand, sir. But if you could just let me explain, I think—"

"We're finished here," Jacob Morgan said, moving toward the door. "Good luck with your book, but I'd like you to leave."

Lance, desperate and overwhelmingly surprised at how quickly this conversation—his one chance—had resulted in him getting completely shut down, went against everything his mind knew was right, against everything that had worked so hard to keep his secrets safe for years, and said, "I think he can see the dead."

Jacob Morgan stopped at the door, turned and stared at Lance. His face was working something out, his mind dissecting and examining Lance's words.

He knows! Lance's mind screamed. *He knows!*

Somewhere overhead, a crow cawed twice, and then all was still and quiet.

Jacob Morgan took a step toward Lance, and his voice was hushed. "Get off my property," he said, "or I'm calling the police." Then, slyly, "I'm sure Sheriff Kruger would love another reason to drag you into the station, don't you?"

Then he turned and went inside.

Lance heard the door's deadbolt slide into place.

[33]

By the time Lance had made the walk through the trees and up the remainder of the path to the farmhouse, the clouds had blackened like a smoker's lungs, and the wind had notched up enough to stir the fallen leaves in the yard into mini-cyclones and dancing waves of burnt oranges and browns. Lance walked through the yard with feet that felt heavy and a spirit that had worn down to just a thin strand, ready to snap.

He walked up the porch steps, his brain conjuring up the image of Natalie Benchley sprawled half on the steps and half in the dirt, her hand outstretched, reaching for ... for what? For him? Reaching for help?

Lance mumbled under his breath, the words carried off with a strong gust of wind that whipped at his hoodie and whistled through the porch. "Better reach for somebody else."

He pushed through the front door just as a far-off crack of thunder officially announced the impending storm. Lance didn't even so much as glance over his shoulder to the horizon. He slammed the door with a crack to rival the thunder. The windows rattled, the ceiling creaked. Lance made his way to the kitchen, thinking that the old farmhouse could go ahead and fall down, collapse on itself with him in it for all he cared. One more casualty, another notch on the house's belt. He could see the headline now, another back issue of the newspaper to add to the library's archive: **STRANGER THAN FICTION? TRUE CRIME WRITER DIES IN HOUSE COLLAPSE**.

And nobody would care. A few people might actually be relieved. Sheriff Kruger, for example. And the Benchleys' killer, happy the house had taken care of their dirty laundry for them. With Lance gone, things could go back to normal. People could let the house slide back into the background of the town's memories, back onto the high shelf in the garage, where they put things that no longer served much of a purpose but they weren't willing to toss away.

Nobody would care.

This thought wormed its way from the back of Lance's mind, dug itself out from a grave where it'd been sealed away and asked to keep quiet because while it might be true, Lance was allowing himself to believe he was to serve a larger purpose in life. His life was about more than just his personal well-being and happiness. His life wasn't about *him* at all, but about what he would do. The things his gifts would allow him to be for others.

My sweet boy. Oh, what great things you'll do.

His mother's words had pushed him, her memory a driving force. And while he knew he was special—that was the only word that seemed to fit, although Lance would argue that *unique* was his personal preference, because it carried with it a much less positive connotation—and his mother had, in her last moments on this earth, been gifted messages and maybe even visions of Lance's future by the spirits of the Great Hillston Cemetery, a future that was apparently worth her sacrificing herself for, he was now overwhelmed with a great sense of failure, and along with it ... a desire to give up.

Despite his gifts and his knowledge and the overwhelming sense of duty he'd carried with him since the time he'd been old enough to even begin to understand his abilities, today, right now inside the farmhouse while a storm as dark as his current mood climbed up the doorstep, Lance was giving up. Not giving up on life, or a continuation of his apparent predetermined destiny—if you believed in such a curious word—but in Ripton's Grove, he was finished.

He could not go on.

He couldn't help the long-dead Benchley family—and did they actually need help in the first place? He'd not seen any of their spirits, no traces of ghostly bodies anywhere in the farmhouse during his entire stay. All he'd been given were some phantom words—a sort of prerecorded retelling of that terrible night they'd all died—and those didn't tell the whole story.

There'd been the incident with Ethan

(*She's down there!*)

that had started him on a dangerously desperate path of hope that the boy was like him and would...

Would what?

Come away with Lance? Leave his uncle and let Lance be his new guardian as they roamed the country together, Lance helping the boy to hone his skills and understand what he was and what he could become like some sort of supernatural-solving Batman and Robin?

How ridiculous that thought had been. How blindly ignorant.

Lance had gotten so emotionally invested in the idea of not being alone, he'd risked everything. He'd mentioned to Jacob Morgan that he thought Ethan could see the dead.

What would Jacob do with that information? What would he think about Lance, and who Lance really was?

It was still a stretch ... because honestly, who really believed in such things—seeing ghosts and talking to the dead? But still, it'd been a slip. And Lance could not afford many of those.

The Reverend and the Surfer had found him once, and Lance knew they would find him again. He didn't need to help the matter along by fanning the gossip fires about a young man who claimed to have supernatural abilities.

He found he'd ended up at the kitchen table, sitting at one of the wooden chairs, a half-empty bottle of water in one hand, its twisted-off plastic top in the other. He had no memory of sitting or digging the bottle from his backpack. Outside the kitchen window, rain lashed against the glass, the sky dark, both from the rain and from the sun that had settled down for the evening.

What time is it?

Lance pulled his phone from his pocket and gawked at the tiny display. Hours had passed since he'd started up the hillside from Jacob Morgan's house. Lance shook his head and rubbed at his eyes and checked the time again. Same result.

He'd been checked out. His mind had almost literally blocked out the rest of the world—time and space and any sense of being—and Lance had vanished into what he could only describe as a fugue state, sitting alone in an old house, contemplating all the moves he'd made, and also the ones he hadn't.

Alone.

He was all alone.

He looked down at the phone in his hand, watched as his thumb pressed the buttons to bring up the contact list, and then begin to scroll. The list was small, and it took only a few presses of the button to the get to the M section.

Mom

Lance's thumb hovered, wanting so badly to press SEND and listen to the call go to voicemail. Needed to hear her voice.

But did he really? Did he need to hear her and be taken

back to that night, back to the life before the one he lived now? Tossed headfirst back into the sinking feeling of tragedy and loss and broken heartedness that he'd been slowly and steadily climbing out of since the night she'd died?

The number might not even work anymore, he thought, and he was unsure which would be worse for his psyche: hearing his mother's voice again, or discovering that he'd *never* be able to hear it again.

Thunder boomed so loud Lance jumped from the chair. It had sounded like cannon fire, a war reenactment taking place in the backyard. The entire house had shaken, the kitchen table vibrating enough that it had scooted to the left a quarter of an inch.

Alone.

God, he felt so alone.

He used his thumb to scroll up in his contact list. Stopped at the L section. Stared at her name.

No. He stopped himself. *You know you can't.*

He scrolled down the S section instead. Needed somebody, anybody.

The rain caught the wind and slammed into the house. More wind gusted and circled and attacked. The noise was terrible, but the house held firm.

Lightning snapped and lit up the backyard in a freeze frame that was blinding.

More thunder rolled.

Lance navigated to Susan's name and wondered what he'd say if she picked up. They barely knew each other. Same with Luke. What could he tell them? How could he explain?

But the urge was strong. So strong he felt at once he couldn't put the phone away even if he'd wanted to. He just needed a voice, he reasoned with himself. *I just need a friendly voice.*

His thumb pressed the SEND button, and Lance put the phone to his ear.

It rang. Once, twice. Three times. After the fourth ring, Susan's voice picked up, cheerful and full of life. It was a recording, apologizing for missing the call but asking Lance to leave a voicemail and she'd return his call as soon as she could. It was polite and professional, and Lance was furious. Finally, his emotions took over, his rage surfaced like water breaking through a dam, and he tossed the opened phone onto the table, grabbed his half-empty bottle of water and hurled it across the kitchen, where it struck the wall with a dull thud and fell to the floor, its opened mouth pouring the remaining water across the wooden floor in a slow and steady trickle.

Another explosion of thunder.

Another white-hot flash of lightning.

Lance grabbed one of the kitchen chairs in both hands and lifted it above his head, smashed it to the floor, where the back snapped off the seat with a satisfying crack. Lance tossed the chair aside and grabbed his backpack, yelling to the house as he made his way back down the hall toward the front door, "I can't help you!"

He had to leave. Would walk in the downpour to the bus station and get out of town. He didn't care if it would take hours. He couldn't sit in the house anymore. He couldn't be alone with his thoughts anymore.

He needed out. He needed

(*my mom*)

help.

When he was two steps away from the door, somebody knocked.

Three almost inaudible taps that were drowned out by the noise from the storm.

Lance ripped the door open, anger burning deep in his eyes.

And then his eyes lowered, taking in his visitor.

Standing on the porch, soaking wet in his blue jeans and sneakers and buttoned-up flannel shirt, was Ethan. There was a flashlight in his hand that looked big enough for him to carry with two hands, its bright light shining down to the rough wooden boards beneath his feet.

"She said you could help me," the boy said, water dripping off his forehead and into his eyes. Lance thought there were tears mixed in with the rainwater. "The girl in the basement said you could help me."

[34]

AND THE REST OF HIS THOUGHTS VANISHED—THE ANGER and resentment and sadness disappearing as quickly as the flashes of lightning lit up the night sky.

"Help you how?" Lance asked, but he knew the answer didn't matter.

This is why I'm here, he thought. *I'll do anything he needs.*

He ushered the boy inside and closed the door, the bright cone of light from the boy's flashlight becoming a spotlight in the dark house.

Lance hadn't even realized he'd left the lights off. He'd been sitting alone all this time in a house as dark as his thoughts. He found the switch on the wall and flipped it, bathing the foyer in that awful yellow tint.

Ethan didn't answer the question. Instead, he stood just inside the door, shivering in his wet clothes. Lance moved swiftly, stripping off his hoodie and telling the boy to take his shirt off. The boy did, obedient, and Lance held the oversized sweatshirt out to the boy, who raised his arms and allowed Lance to slide it over his head. It fell to the boy's shins, the sleeves comically long, but the boy didn't seem to care. He wrapped his arms around himself and within a minute the shivering subsided. Lance picked up the wet shirt from the floor and hung it over the banister by the stairs.

"Better?" Lance asked.

Ethan nodded. "Yes." Then, "I mean, yes, sir."

The protectiveness Lance suddenly felt for this child was all at once overwhelming, as if he were being introduced to his own son for the first time. It was a feeling so foreign, and so unexpected, it nearly made his head swim and his heart flutter with elation.

But at the same time, something wasn't right. Something wasn't ... *him.*

Along with the joyousness, there was a faint buzz of something beneath the surface. Something familiar. Something electric that was almost unpleasant but...

He knew then what it was, the realization presenting itself with stark clarity. It was a slightly more subdued version of the feelings he'd experienced last night when Jacob and Ethan had visited, the feeling that had intensified with an almost crippling effect when Ethan had begun walking toward the closed basement door.

He's like me, Lance thought again. And he wondered if the boy was feeling the same things that Lance was. Was this some sort of cosmic connection between the two of them, two bare wires that spark when they touch?

Lance studied the boy's face. Ethan had used the sleeves of Lance's hoodie to wipe the water from his eyes, and it appeared that the tears had stopped as well. He looked stoic, almost dutiful. Like he was simply doing what was asked of him. He showed no outward indication that he was experiencing any of what Lance was.

I'm stronger, Lance thought. *I'm more sensitive to it.*

He had no idea what he was talking about. And why would he, really? This was an entirely new experience.

"Help you how?" Lance asked again, now that Ethan seemed more settled and at ease.

The boy looked at Lance sheepishly, shrugged. "I don't know."

Lance was not surprised. He'd done nothing in life if not gotten used to things being difficult to explain. "When did she tell you this? When did the girl in the basement tell you that I could help you?"

The boy knew the answer to this question and spat out, "Last night. Last night when I ate the pizza and played the game with the boy, she started talking to me."

Lance's heart sped up. It was the first solid, tangible evidence that he was right about Ethan sharing his gifts. "She talked to you?" he asked. "You could hear her voice?"

Ethan made a face that said he wasn't sure. He shook his head, then stopped, changed his mind and nodded. "I heard her up here." He tapped his head with his tiny index finger. "She was far away, but I heard her up here." Another tap.

"And she said I could help you? Is that all the girl said?"

Ethan nodded. "Yes, that's all."

Lance's excitement had grown so great, he didn't immediately allow himself to be deflated by the extreme lack of detail in Mary Benchley's instructions to Ethan. Instead, he pressed on. "Ethan, you said you could hear the girl in the basement, right?"

Ethan nodded.

"Could you see her?"

Ethan looked at Lance like he'd grown a horn from his forehead. Shook his head. "No, she was in the basement."

Of course. Try again, Lance.

"Ethan." Lance got down onto one knee and looked the boy in the eyes. "Have you ever heard other people talking in your head? Or"—this one was tricky—"ever seen people that nobody else could see? People that ... aren't really here, maybe."

"No."

No hesitation. No contemplation. A simple answer.

He's either telling the truth, or he's a fantastic liar for a six-year-old.

Lance sat down on the floor and considered this. Unless Jacob Morgan had filled Ethan's head with some sort of knowledge of what had happened in the farmhouse, it seemed too coincidental of a thing to make up on the spot. Plus, there'd been the buzz ... that electric tingling at the base of Lance's skull and the nauseous feeling in his gut. Something had certainly happened last night in the kitchen.

Could it possibly have been his first time? Was last night the first time his abilities had ever been exercised?

Lance remembered his own childhood and envied Ethan if that was the case.

Another question popped into Lance's thoughts, and he changed topics, his own head going too fast to keep up with. "Ethan, why did you come here? Why now?"

The boy shifted from side to side and hugged himself again and then started to speak in a rapid burst of words that caused his eyes to tear up again and his voice to waver. "Uncle Jacob is mad and he was scaring me, and I started crying, and then I 'membered the girl said you could help me, so I went out my window and ran up here and the storm was loud and scary and I thought it was gonna kill me dead."

Jacob's mad, Lance thought as Ethan used his hoodie again to wipe his nose. *Which part of our conversation set him off? Was it the part about Ethan ... or was it the Benchleys?*

And then Lance thought, with more fear than he'd been expecting, that maybe it had been *both*.

"Ethan, buddy, do you know why your uncle Jacob was

mad?"

Ethan answered as he tried to hold back his tears. "I don't know. He was yelling and scaring me and told me to go to my room, so I did, and then he yelled some more and I heard something break and that scared me more, so I went out the window because you can help me."

Lance nodded his head. "That's right, Ethan. That's right. I can help. I'll help you, I promise. Everything will be fine."

Lance said the words and placed a hand on Ethan's small, bony shoulder. He looked the boy in the eye and repeated, "Everything will be fine." But he knew that he should not be making such a promise. He couldn't take the boy anywhere except back to Jacob Morgan without it possibly being misconstrued as kidnapping, especially after Lance had been to the house and had his conversation with Jacob, where he'd asked what would certainly be labeled as *strange* questions about Ethan.

Could he call the sheriff?

And say what? *Hi, Sheriff, I've got Jacob Morgan's nephew here—you know, little Ethan—and he's really scared and doesn't want to go home.* There was a hint of domestic abuse in that phrase, which might get the sheriff's hackles up, but—

Lance saw movement from the corner of his eye. Ethan had started down the hall while Lance had been absorbed in thought. "Ethan?" Lance called after him.

Ethan walked slowly but with a steady purpose to his gait. He turned his head and spoke with the same matter-of-factness as a man who was giving the time. "She's still down there," he said. "And she wants us to come see."

Us.

"Us?" Lance asked, shoving up to his feet and hurrying after the boy. "She said she wants *us* to come see?"

Ethan didn't answer, but Lance saw his shadow on the wall

nod a single time.

In the kitchen, Lance flipped on the light switch and watched as Ethan stopped for a moment to investigate the broken chair on the floor, giving Lance a sidelong glance, and then the boy turned to the basement door.

A loud buzz exploded in Lance's head, causing him to cry out and grab his head with his hands. His vision blurred and he tasted bile in the back of his mouth.

Then it passed, and when he could see clearly again, Ethan had opened the door and was halfway down the steps, the beam of his too-big flashlight shining into what looked like the mouth of a cave.

Lance followed, the cool, damp air of the basement biting at his skin and causing goose pimples to ripple along his forearms. And then he stood on the last step, Ethan standing on the hard-packed dirt floor a step in front of him. Ethan swung the flashlight beam to his right and started to walk in that direction.

"Ethan?" Lance said, stepping down to the floor and reaching up for the little bit of pull chain that was left on the light fixture above his head. He fumbled for it in the near-darkness, found it, pulled. Watched as the basement lit up in a dim glow, and he found Ethan standing in front of the row of metal shelves mounted on the wall behind the stairs.

"Ethan?" Lance tried again.

The boy stood motionless, staring straight ahead at the wall, his flashlight hanging loosely at his side, ready to fall from his hand and rattle onto the floor.

God, it's like that last scene from The Blair Witch Project.

Lance had thought it a joke, but as soon as he'd finished thinking it, he found himself quickly looking over his shoulder, eyes peering into the rest of the dimly lit basement.

He saw nothing.

When he turned back around, he nearly screamed in

surprise to find Ethan turned to face him, staring directly at him. "She's back there," Ethan said.

Lance's gaze looked past Ethan and settled on the wall behind him. He knew there was a room back there. He'd seen it in that awful memory that had been stored away in the key he'd found atop the bathroom mirror. But there were two things that bothered him about this. The first was that he didn't know how to open the wall, and the second was the fact that Mary Bench-ley's body had been found burned on the brush pile in the back-yard. Not the basement, and certainly not behind a secret door that apparently nobody knew about or knew how to access.

"We need to unlock the door," Ethan said, pointing to the wall.

But he knows, Lance thought. *This must be real, because he knows about the door.*

Lance walked closer and stood beside Ethan, gently taking the boy's flashlight from him and shining it across the wall, the shelves. He'd been over every inch of this wall earlier that day and had found nothing.

"I don't know how," Lance said, feeling his face burn with disappointment at letting the child down.

And then another zap of electricity started at the base of Lance's skull and climbed up into his head, and his ears buzzed and his eyes squeezed shut and he thought he was going to throw up and—

And it stopped as suddenly as it had come. Lance gasped in relief, sucking in large gulps of air, turning to look to Ethan to ask the boy if he was feeling any of this.

But Ethan wasn't looking at Lance. He was looking at one of the shelves, his arm and hand outstretched, pointing. Lance followed to where the boy was pointing, and when he saw what he ended up on, he sighed and mumbled a bad word under his breath.

"I'm an idiot."

The paint can, with its dribbles of dried paint splattered on its exterior, was exactly where it'd been when Lance had first discovered it last night, and when he'd examined the wall earlier that morning. And now, Lance wondered exactly how long the can had been sitting in that spot on the shelf.

Forever was the answer he arrived at. How inconspicuous, a paint can on a basement shelf. How completely forgettable, dismissible. And Lance had done just that. Completely dismissed the can as nothing but part of the scenery.

He took Ethan's flashlight and walked to the wall, watching the light reflect off the can's spots of bare aluminum. Lance reached up and tried to gently push the can to the side along the shelf.

It wouldn't budge.

He tried again, pushing harder, putting more weight behind it.

Nothing.

He set the flashlight on the shelf next to the can, the light bouncing off the wall and giving Lance just enough to see by, and he grabbed the can with both hands and tried to push and pull it left, right, forward, back. It didn't so much as wiggle.

Lance grabbed the flashlight again and bent down and shined it under the shelf, peering under and looking for what was holding the can in place. The metal shelf was maybe two inches thick, but there were no signs of screws or bolts or anything else keeping the paint can stationary.

Lance turned and looked at Ethan, raising his eyebrows. *Well, kid, you seem to be the one running the show. Any ideas?*

Ethan stared back. Said nothing.

Lance sighed and studied the can again. Stepped back and looked at the shelf, the whole picture.

The shelf, he thought. *The can has to be attached to the shelf somehow, and there's nothing underneath, and nothing behind it, so...*

An idea.

He stepped back to the shelf and reached up and used both hands to press down on the top of the paint can.

And the can sank into the shelf. Not much, maybe only half an inch, but enough. When the can had been depressed into the shelf, Lance heard the shifting of metal on metal, the clinking of some sort of interior mechanism hidden away inside the body of the shelf itself. He released the can and it popped back into place quickly ... and the shelf loosened the tiniest bit, sliding over to the left a quarter of an inch, if that.

Lance placed his palm against the right edge of the shelf and pushed. Watched as the shelf slid left six inches on tracks inlaid in the basement's wall, and then came to a stop.

Lance grabbed the flashlight and shined it on the newly revealed spot on the wall.

Found a small keyhole. A dull silver mouth for which Lance knew he had the key tucked away in his pocket. He quickly pulled the key from his pants and stuck it in the lock. Then, after looking back to Ethan, who was still standing and watching attentively without a word, Lance turned the key. He heard an entire chorus of clinking and clanking and hinges in need of oil softly screeching inside the wall.

When the noises had finished, Lance stood and waited for something more to happen.

Nothing did.

Lance pulled the key from the lock and pocketed it.

He walked down the wall to the corner where it met the intersecting wall. He shrugged, placed two hands on the closest metal shelf, and pushed.

The entire basement wall began to slide open, and Lance had a startling idea that he was opening a tomb.

35

THERE WAS NO CORPSE IN THE ROOM—A ROOM THAT HAD been presumably sealed and undisturbed for the better part of six years—but there was blood.

Just like the key had slid into the lock in the wall and opened the room with a satisfying clicking of tumblers and gears, a key also slid into place in Lance's mind. The secrets he'd been trying to unearth, the questions he'd given up trying to answer—they were here, waiting for him. He knew this instantly as he took his first breath of the stale air and was able to see the dark stain on the concrete floor revealed in the flashlight's sweeping beam. When he took a step closer, the flashlight reflected off something else, a metallic glint winking back at Lance as he approached. When Lance saw what it was, he stopped and turned to look over his shoulder. Found Ethan standing in the opened mouth of the wall, peering in with nervous fascination. "Stay right there for a bit, okay, Ethan? Nobody's been here for a long time, and I want to make sure it's safe, okay?"

Ethan wrapped himself up again in the long sleeves of Lance's hoodie and nodded, but his eyes were pleading to see more. Lance turned and stepped closer, finding that metallic glint again and moving toward it, a sick feeling growing stronger in his gut with each step he took.

He reached the grotesquely large black stain on the floor, which was directly in front of the futon, and for an instant it reminded him of spilled coffee, brewed strong and just the way he liked it. He would have liked some coffee right then, for he had a strong certainty things were going to start moving very fast, and he'd have to stay ahead of it if he wanted to accomplish what he'd been brought here for.

He reached for the pull cord attached to the bank of overhead fluorescents and gripped the chain, pulling gently. Above, a noisy flickering of lights sputtered briefly like the engine of a long-idle car choking itself awake and then came on. Lance looked up and saw only one row of the lights were working, but it was enough. He switched off the flashlight and set it on the ground, careful to avoid the stain that he knew wasn't coffee.

The metallic reflection was coming from a rolling IV stand positioned next to the futon. Two clear plastic bags hung like a cowboy's saddlebag from the hooks on either side. They each looked half-empty. Beside the IV stand was a rolling cart, a metal tray atop it full of a handful of medical and surgical tools. Lance recognized most by sight but could not name them. The whole scene looked eerily like something you'd see on one of those tours of an abandoned mental hospital where the guide would tell you chilling tales of patient abuse and archaic medical procedures that once had been thought groundbreaking but were later proven to be nothing but torture. Lance walked around the black stain and the front of the futon—the futon he tried not to think about with little Ray Kruger lying atop it, his pants and underwear pushed down around his tiny ankles—and nearly tripped on a pile of towels scattered along the side of the futon. Towels that had once been white but were now tie-dyed a dark crimson. Lance jumped away from the towels as he might if he'd accidentally stepped on a rattlesnake. He looked down at them for a long time, his mind trying to add the IV stand and the bloody towels and the black stain together in some sick calculation that would show him an answer.

"What's there?" Ethan's voice, nervous and curious.

Lance looked up and saw the boy staring at him. Contemplated telling him the truth or trying to keep him calm.

What would my mother do?

The truth. She'd always told him the truth.

Lance chose a compromised answer. "Ethan, listen to me, okay? I think somebody got hurt down here. Pretty bad, too. So I really need you to stay right there unless I tell you different, understand?"

Ethen did not protest. Did not inquire further. Just nodded his head and kept his arms wrapped around himself, his eyes wide as he watched Lance's every move.

Lance stepped carefully around the towels and stood next to the IV stand, grabbed each of the plastic bags and read their labels in the half-lit room. One appeared to just be saline. The other was something called oxytocin. Lance, having misplaced his nursing degree, found this information less than helpful. But regardless of his understanding, one thing was clear: somebody had been down here and had needed medical attention. But who, and for how long?

Lance stepped back, allowed himself to fully take in the room. When he'd opened the door initially, he'd been overwhelmed with the memory of what he'd seen when he'd found the key atop the mirror, and those images played through his head and drew his eyes directly toward the futon in the center of the room. Now, with the lights above and his attention refocused on the grand picture, Lance saw additional details.

Things that at once painted a new picture. One that chilled his blood.

A pink-and-blue bedspread atop the futon, now a tangled and twisted mess, pushed far down toward the foot of the bed and spotted with blood; a small nightstand placed next to the futon on the opposite side from the IV stand, atop it a hairbrush, thin wisps of hair tangled in the bristles, bottles of vitamins, a small stuffed pig, pink and plush, and a copy of one of the *Twilight* novels, a bookmark sticking out from somewhere near the end.

Lance turned around and looked toward where the toilet and sink were. The shower rod was still there, only the curtain was much different than the one he'd seen in his vision from Ray Kruger's childhood. The curtain here was a pink-and-blue print matching the bedspread on the futon.

There was a scented candle on the counter by the sink, burned most of the way to the bottom.

Lance took another long look around the room.

Somebody lived down here, he thought. *Somebody was trying to make this a bedroom.*

He looked back to the *Twilight* novel on the nightstand. To the hairbrush with the strands of hair stuck in it. Recalled the black-and-white image of the Benchley family from the newspaper archives at the library. The hair in the brush was light in color. He looked at the book again, considered the subject matter.

Mary Benchley's hair had been much lighter than her mother's.

Lance remembered the voice he'd heard calling out from behind the locked basement door. A young girl pleading to be let out.

"She was kept down here," Lance said. He looked back to

the IV stand, wishing he had a smartphone to Google what oxytocin was used for. "Why?" he asked the room.

His vision went black and his head buzzed and his stomach churned, and he fell forward onto the futon, his sneakers slipping on the mess of stained blankets on the floor. He managed to choke out a muffled gasp, felt his lungs constrict as he sucked in a deep breath of air as his vision cleared as quick as it had darkened and his stomach settled.

Lance pushed himself off the futon and stood, blinking to clear his eyes, which had started to water. When he could see clearly again, he saw that Ethan had stepped inside the room, crossing the floor halfway to the futon.

He was pointing again.

Lance stepped back around the futon and followed the boy's outstretched hand, and his gaze landed on a stack of paperback books piled behind the nightstand.

"She wants you to read it," Ethan said.

Lance, despite his love of literature, was in no mood to curl up with a good book. But he remembered the last time Ethan had pointed at something—the paint can—and did not argue.

The nightstand cast a long and dark shadow along the floor, bathing the stack of books in black. Lance retrieved the flashlight and switched it on, then kneeled down in front of the stack and examined the titles, hoping one of them would be called *What Really Happened*, or maybe *Read Me First*.

No such luck. The titles were all old Westerns and a couple early Stephen King novels. Their spines were all deeply creased and worn, cracked with heavy usage, and Lance imagined they'd come from a dime store or library sale many years ago. None of the books looked like they'd be any help.

Lance was about to ask Ethan if he could maybe coax a few more details from his silent partner, but when the beam of his flashlight did another pass over the stack of paperbacks, something new caught his eye.

The fifth book down had a solid black spine that Lance had dismissed on his first scan of the titles, assuming it'd been part of another book. But as his flashlight had slid along the titles a second time, he'd more clearly seen the small slit of space between it and the book above and realized it was a book of its own. There was no printed title or author on the spine. Lance carefully lifted the four books atop it, one by one, and set them to the side. He shined the flashlight beam onto the front cover of the black book, and a gold-embossed word jumped out to him.

Journal.

Ethan's words—*She wants you to read it*—gained greater clarity.

Lance reached out and grabbed the journal. The leather was soft and—

He sucked in a sudden rush of air. His eyes widened and the hair along his arms and back of his neck stood on end. A second later, he expelled his breath in a great *whoosh* and fell back onto his butt, dropping the flashlight onto the floor next to him.

Like the key he'd found atop the bathroom mirror, the journal had electrified his mind with information. He hadn't had to read the pages—had known he likely didn't have the time. The pages had given themselves to Lance, and what he'd learned was both relieving (because the pieces had finally fallen into place), and devastatingly heartbreaking.

Lance looked at Ethan and felt great sadness for the boy.

Ethan was not Jacob Morgan's nephew.

Lance pushed himself from the floor, his mind spinning to decide what he should do next, when there was a thunderous noise from upstairs as the front door crashed open.

"*Ethan!*" Jacob Morgan's voice was full of rage.

Ethan's eyes shot open wide, and he ran to Lance's side. Lance bent down and wrapped one of his arms around the boy, enveloping him. His eyes scanned the wall where it opened back into the regular basement. Found what he was looking for; a small lever that presumably opened the door from the inside. Ethan would be able to get out on his own if things went poorly for Lance.

Lance used one hand to tuck the journal into the rear waistband of his shorts, covering it with his t-shirt, and used the other to lift Ethan's face to meet his own. Footsteps were pounding on the floorboards above—Jacob Morgan moving swiftly and angrily down the hallway toward the kitchen.

"Ethan, listen, I want you to stay here. Stay quiet, and don't come out unless I tell you, okay? There's a lever on the door you can pull to get out if you really think you need to, but I want you to wait, okay? I want you to wait for me. Your uncle's very mad, and I want to try and help him, okay? Do you understand?"

Ethan's eyes were full of fear and worry. They glistened with tears, but to the boy's credit, none fell down his cheek. He nodded.

Lance, only because it simply felt right, kissed the boy atop his head and then stood, making his way quickly across the floor and out into the basement. He gripped one of the metal shelves and pulled, slamming the hidden door closed.

"*Ethan!*"

Lance stood still by the bare workbench in the corner and watched with a certain level of dread as Jacob Morgan called out again and stomped down the stairs, his boots coming into view first, followed by his legs, and then his upper body.

Jacob Morgan reached the last stair and then stepped down onto the hard-packed dirt, eyes burning and locking onto Lance.

He was carrying a hunting rifle.

I've really got the worst luck in basements, Lance thought.

36

JACOB MORGAN WAS DRIPPING WET, WATER FALLING FROM the brim of the ball cap he wore and splashing into the dirt at his feet. He'd tossed a jacket on over his shirt, but it was unzipped, and the fabric of the shirt beneath clung to him, accenting a muscled physique.

He gripped the hunting rifle with hands so tight the knuckles were white.

He spoke through gritted teeth, hissing the words at Lance. "Where is he?"

Lance cleared his throat. "Who?"

Jacob's hands twisted the rifle from across his body, inching its aim closer to Lance's direction. A subtle threat. "Ethan. Where is Ethan?"

Lance's heart hammered in his chest. He took slow, deliberate breaths, trying to calm it, keep his poise. His knack for casual conversation had saved him on more than one occasion. "Why would he be here? There's no more pizza."

"His shirt is on the banister upstairs. There's nowhere else close he could have gone to, and I'm going to take out your kneecap with a bullet if you don't tell me where he is in three seconds or less."

"Who?"

Jacob shook his head and raised the rifle, taking aim at Lance's legs. "Stop playing dumb. It's not going to work. *Where. Is. Ethan?* Three ... two..."

Lance swallowed and said, "You mean your son? You want to know where your son is?"

Lance saw the jolt of shock ripple through Jacob Morgan's body. It wasn't much, but perceivable all the same. The man's eyes narrowed further, met Lance's. "You don't know what you're talking about. Ethan's my nephew."

"Stop playing dumb," Lance said. "It's not going to work."

He reached slowly behind him, praying to any god that might exist and be tuned in to the correct frequency that Jacob Morgan wouldn't view the motion as a threat and shoot him through the heart before Lance had had a chance to make his big reveal. He reached beneath his shirt and pulled the leather journal free from the waistband of his shorts, then held it up in front of him.

"I know who he is," Lance said. "And I think you've been looking for this for a long time."

Jacob Morgan's eyes lit up like Christmas lights and his jaw dropped open at the sight of the journal, doing nothing but confirming to Lance that he'd been correct in the theory he'd managed to piece together since Mary Benchley's journal had shown itself to him.

"You knew she kept this, didn't you?" Lance asked. "You'd probably even seen it before. Maybe up in her room one day, after the two of you ... well, you know. Hey, what *is* Virginia's law on statutory rape, anyway?"

"*I never raped her!*"

Lance shrugged. "Court might have said differently. And

678

I'm positive Mark Benchley would have had a different opinion than you. Am I right? What was the age difference again? She was, what, fifteen or sixteen? You were somewhere in your twenties, deflowering Daddy's little angel?"

Lance was intentionally trying to rile Jacob Morgan up, trying to set him off his game. It was Lance's experience that while angry people tended to be more violent, they also tended to be less attentive to their surroundings and the entire situation at hand. Their anger threw up blinders.

But Lance was also aware that the only reason Jacob Morgan hadn't shot him dead yet was because Lance knew where Ethan was.

Lance took two slow steps closer to the man, keeping the journal in front of him at all times. It seemed to be Jacob Morgan's focal point.

Jacob shook his head again. "You don't know," he said. "I *loved* her. And she loved me."

Lance took another step, waved the journal out in front of him, back and forth like a matador distracting a bull.

"Maybe," he said. "But love can make people do stupid things, right? Is that why you killed them all? Because you loved her?"

Jacob Morgan kept shaking his head back and forth. "You don't know," he said again.

Lance stopped, now maybe six or seven feet from the man. He held the journal out and tapped it with a finger on his free hand. "I know everything," he said. "Let me tell you, and you can tell me where I've gotten it wrong. Maybe you can tell me the side of the story where you come out *not* looking like a murderer. If you can do that, maybe I'll tell you where your son is."

Jacob Morgan's eyes narrowed again, not liking being told

what to do. "Maybe I go ahead and shoot you now. How about that?"

Lance made a show of pretending to think about the offer. Shook his head. "I don't think so. Finding your son is more important to you than killing me."

"I could kill you after."

Lance nodded confidently, but inside he was very much aware that if he didn't get out of this basement, Jacob Morgan's threat would likely come true.

"You could," he said. "I guess we'll both just have to wait and see."

Jacob Morgan said nothing to this, so Lance took a deep breath and started to talk.

"It all makes a weird bit of sense, to be honest," Lance said. "Ever since I got to town, there's really only been two main names that have come up as suspects in the Benchley murders: Mark Benchley, and you. As it turns out, *both* of you killed them."

This drew a confused expression from Jacob Morgan.

"Oh, don't get me wrong, now. You're the one who pulled the trigger, but"—Lance held the journal up again—"it would appear that the accusations of Mark Benchley's fanatical religious beliefs were exactly spot-on."

Jacob Morgan didn't move, but Lance could see he was focused, listening to the story Lance was beginning to tell. After all these years, Lance imagined it was probably somewhat cathartic for the man to finally revisit that night with another human being, to have the truth laid bare.

"Mary told her mother that she was pregnant," Lance continued. "The two of you had kept your relationship a secret for a few months—you sneaking over when Mark and Natalie were in town, Mary stopping by your house on her way home from school or running errands. You both did a swell job of keeping things hidden. But then Mary got pregnant—what happened, anyway? Did the condom break, or did you just decide to risk it one time? I mean, with all due respect, you were already having sex with a minor, I would think the least you could do was use some protection. But you know what they say ... hindsight. Twenty-twenty." Lance shrugged. "Sorry, I digress.

"Mary got pregnant, and she got scared and she told her mom. The two of them kept it a secret from Mark for a while—and from you—but eventually Natalie decided that the right thing to do was to tell him the truth. She told Mary that Mark loved her more than anything and he might be upset at first, but they would get through it together as a family. Turns out, Natalie Benchley didn't know her husband as well as she thought she did."

Lance paused, gauged Jacob Morgan's reaction. The man stood, stone-faced and attentive.

He's never heard any of this, Lance thought. In his mind, he fast-forwarded through the rest of the journal's pages, the rest of the heartbreaking story, and realized he was right. From what he could tell, Jacob Morgan had only come into the story at the very end—the night he'd killed them.

"Something snapped in Mark Benchley when he found out Mary was pregnant," Lance said. "Mary wrote, and I'm quoting here, *Dad looks at me like I'm no longer his daughter, but a disgusting sinner damned to hell. But he doesn't realize it's he who's playing the role of the devil*. She was quite the writer," Lance said. "She painted a horrible picture, but she did it with striking detail."

Jacob Morgan shifted from one leg to another, the hunting rifle still gripped tight.

"That's when they pulled her out of school under the ruse of shipping her off to a boarding school. Mark was too humili- ated to have his teenaged daughter start showing up to class with a baby bump and maternity pants. She was *unclean* in his eyes. She'd become the very type of person he'd preached was destroying the world that God had intended. And he was so selfish, so ironically vain, he hid her under a rock. Or, in this case, under a house."

Jacob Morgan's mouth opened to speak, but he stopped himself. Coughed, cleared his throat, and tried again. "She was ... she was here the whole time? The entire pregnancy?"

Lance nodded and then pushed on. This next part was even more disturbing.

"With Natalie being a nurse, Mark figured she could give Mary all the medical attention she needed. And that might have worked—but then Natalie made a mistake."

Jacob Morgan waited, clearly hanging on Lance's every word.

"She convinced Mary that an abortion would be the best thing for everyone."

"Oh, God," Jacob said, almost without realizing it, it seemed. And Lance imagined what a terrible idea it must be to realize how close a living, breathing child you'd fallen completely in love with had come to not existing at all. To being murdered before they'd ever even been given a chance.

"Mark Benchley, ironically, didn't like this," Lance said. "Despite Natalie only trying to help ease the problem, Mark called her a would-be murderer, said she was just as unworthy of the Holy Kingdom as Mary. He said he could no longer trust her. And that's when he made her quit her job. He kept her home, only letting her go out to town if he accompanied her. With Ray Kruger as the sheriff, Mark knew he couldn't completely sequester Natalie to the basement like he had Mary, but—and again, I'm telling you exactly what Mary's got written here"—Lance held up the journal, reestablishing it in Jacob Morgan's view—"Natalie told Mary that Mark said he'd kill them both if they tried to run from him, or tried to get help to get away. And he told Natalie that if she tried to go behind his back, he'd sacrifice Mary. He said he was only doing what was right in God's eyes, and that if they disobeyed him, it was the same as disobeying the Lord and they would have to be punished."

What a terrible position to be put in, Lance thought. *Natalie's love for her daughter was what kept Mary alive, but it's also what killed them both.*

Lance paused, then added, "It's funny. I've always been told that God is all about forgiveness. Isn't that why they send a priest to visit death-row inmates before they're executed? To wipe the slate clean before they take their last ride?"

Jacob Morgan did not answer. He didn't appear to be focused on anything at all, his gaze staring straight through Lance, and probably down a deep dark hole that led back to that awful night.

"They managed to survive," Lance continued. "Mark kept his watchful eye on them, but the two of them survived together down here. He'd bring them meals, sometimes allowing Natalie to come up and cook—sometimes he'd get takeout. He escorted them upstairs to the shower and never let them close the door. Mary said he always looked like he'd been crying. His eyes always bloodshot and his nose red from wiping it. He asked Natalie what they needed—from a medical standpoint—and he'd drive two towns over to buy it all." Then, with a sinking feeling of sympathy for a dead girl he'd never met, Lance added, "He never let them go to a doctor."

Jacob Morgan's eyes glistened with tears, and he removed one hand from the rifle just long enough to quickly wipe at them. He sniffled loudly but still said nothing.

"She was nearly a month early," Lance said. "She started

having contractions, and Natalie told Mark it was going to happen at any moment. And it did."

Lance coughed, choking back emotions that began to surface as he recited from the journal pages that had uploaded themselves into his mind and saw the scenes playing out. A terrified young girl, trapped in a basement by her psychotic father, giving birth to a baby boy she'd never get to know.

"But they weren't prepared," Lance said. "Things didn't go well for Mary."

Lance remembered the large dark stain on the floor by the futon, the twisted and bloody towels.

"Obviously, the baby survived," Lance said. "But the last thing Mary wrote in her journal"—he could see the page in his mind, the handwriting faint and scrawling, palm-smears of blood in the margins and above and below the words—"was this." Lance opened the journal now, flipped to the back and found the page that perfectly matched the image he'd just conjured. Swallowed back threatening tears and read, *"Baby is beautiful. Baby is perfect. Mama says I'll be okay, but I know she's lying. I feel like I'm fading. Lots of blood. But I don't feel the pain."* Lance stopped here and looked up. "Then, a few inches down the page from this she added, *Jacob is here. How? He's yelling at Daddy. I'm going to show him his son. I love them both so much."*

Lance closed the journal with a sound that seemed very loud in a basement that had fallen very silent. Above them, a clap of thunder went almost unnoticed. The rain continued to fall.

"You showed up and you killed them when you thought they wouldn't let you see your newborn son, is that it? Mark Benchley told you that you'd never see them, and you killed him? Natalie, too, when she tried to run?"

At these words, Jacob Morgan's eyes studied Lance's face. "How...?" he started. "How do you know he said that to me?"

Lance said nothing. Waited.

There were tears on Jacob's cheeks now, carving hot lines down his face.

"How did you know to come over that night?" Lance asked. "I've told you my part, now tell me yours."

Jacob Morgan closed his eyes, squeezing out tears. He wiped them away with the back of one hand and said, "I could never understand it. I never knew why she left. I know Mary was younger, and I know the age difference would have been a problem for a few years, but does that really matter? Can you look at me and tell me age matters with love?" He didn't wait for an answer. "Which is why I was so stunned when I came over here one Sunday evening to see if everything was okay, because Mary hadn't shown up at church, and that's when Mark told me she'd left for a boarding school.

"I begged him to tell me what the school was—you know, so I could send her letters, or care packages. But honestly I just wanted to know where I had to drive to go see her, to find out what happened between us. Because it had all been going so well, you know? And if she was going to break my heart, I wanted her to do it to my face. That might sound selfish, I know, but I wasn't going to let her just disappear and pretend that what we had together would fade away.

"But Mark would never tell me. Neither would Natalie. They said Mary had been having a tough time in school, with bullying or some bullshit, and they didn't want to risk the new school information getting out into the wrong hands. Man, I was so furious. But what could I do? I called every private school I could find in the state and got nowhere."

Jacob sighed, shrugged his shoulders. The hunting rifle rose and fell with the motion. Lance kept his eyes on it. "So I gave up," Jacob said. "I convinced myself that I was crazy to think somebody as young as Mary could have ever been serious about our relationship, and I tried to move on. And I did, Lance. I did move on. Or at least I thought I had. But then Natalie texted me that night, and everything changed." He looked at Lance like a man trying very hard to make a difficult to understand point. A look that was almost sympathetic, as if he knew the person on the receiving end of the forthcoming information would never truly grasp the meaning. "That night was the worst night of my life, Lance. But, it was also the greatest night. It was the night I found out I had a son, and for the first time I finally understood what love felt like."

There was a part of Lance that thought he understood what Jacob Morgan was saying. But the other part, the part that was still very much focused on the hunting rifle gripped in the man's hands, was not letting go of the other major event the night Ethan had been born.

"You killed them," Lance said. "Does that not bother you at all? Is that the sort of father you want to be for your son? You murdered his grandparents and burned his mother's body on brush pile like she was a discarded shrub. Do you actually want me to sympathize with that? Feel sorry for you? Whatever happened that night, at the end of the story, you still come out a murderer."

Jacob shook his head again and sighed, but when he spoke, Lance noticed that anger slipping its way back into the words. "You don't understand! When I got here, Mark was crazed. I'm serious, it was like he was possessed. He wanted me dead, I could see that the moment I walked through the door. And Natalie? She was terrified. More for her own daughter's life than anything else. She understood the severity of what had happened during the birth. That's why she texted me. She managed to get Mark's phone away from him long enough to send me a message. Do you have any idea what it's like to be sitting at home reading and suddenly get a text that says the son you didn't know you were having had just been born and that the mother's life was in danger and you need to come right away?" Jacob shook his head. "I tried messaging her back but got nothing. So I took off up the hill. Natalie was waiting for me at the door, frantic, terrified, begging me to help get Mary to the hospital. Mark was waiting too, and he had a shotgun."

This was the part of the story Lance had been waiting for. The bits of dialogue the house had played for him the past few days were of the moment in the story Jacob Morgan had arrived at just now. All he needed to hear was Jacob Morgan's confession, and then he'd try and see if he'd get killed trying to escape the basement and get to the sheriff.

"Mark wanted to kill me," Jacob said. "I think it's obvious he never knew I was the father until right before I'd arrived. Natalie and Mary must have managed to keep that much a secret from him, probably because they knew how he'd react. I don't know if they did it so much to protect me, or to protect Mark. Trying to keep him from committing murder." Jacob shrugged. "I guess it was both.

"Anyway, things got heated. Mark was threatening to shoot me and I was trying to stay calm, trying to diffuse things. Really all I wanted was to see Mary, and my baby boy. I could hear her pleading from the basement door, wanting somebody to let her out. And I could hear Ethan crying. I was trying to get to them, but Mark kept shoving that damn gun in my face. I was paralyzed, Lance. Didn't know what to do. I hadn't even laid eyes on him yet, but when I heard my son crying out, something inside me broke. I would have died to save him, but the only way to do that was to stay alive a bit longer. And that ... well, that's where I lost it."

Lance took a step closer, crossing his arms and trying to look nonthreatening. Added another half step. "How so?"

"I tried to get past Mark, and that's when he got physical. We pushed each other around a bit, and Mark reared back with the gun to swing it at me, and the butt of it sucker-punched Natalie in the gut. She cried out, and that's when she panicked. She jumped into the mix with us and kneed Mark in the balls. He dropped the gun and doubled over, and she pushed him over and got his keys from his pocket and sprinted down the hall toward the front door. She yelled back to us that she was going to get help, and I called out for her to wait, but I didn't move. I didn't try to stop her or go with her, and when I saw Mark Benchley push himself off the floor and pick up the shotgun, I froze. My whole world slowed down. Sound muffled. All I could seem to hear was my own breathing.

"And Mark shot her. I watched and did nothing while he ran toward the door and stood on the porch and fired the gun into his wife's back."

Lance couldn't believe what he was hearing.

"And that's when everything changed," Jacob said. "It was as if Mark fell out of whatever trance he'd been in. He dropped the gun and turned around and looked at me, and his face was pure terror. He said, 'What have I done?' and before I could answer, we heard two thuds from the basement stairs and then a baby started to cry at the top of its lungs. A heart-piercing wail. Mark and I looked at each other, and all the anger and the rage melted and we both sprinted toward the kitchen. I got there first, and I threw open the bolt and yanked open the door, and..."

Jacob stopped. Took a breath that wavered with tears. "They were at the bottom of the stairs, sprawled out on the basement floor. Mary must have ... she must have died right there on the stairs. She must not have been very high up—maybe she knew something was going to happen before it did, and she'd started to make her way down—but she didn't make it all the way. Those two thuds... I'll hear those two thuds in my head until the day I die.

"I ran down to her, but as soon as I got close, I knew I was too late. Her eyes were open—she had such beautiful eyes. Ethan was tangled in her arms, his head miraculously resting on her chest. He was crying at the top of his lungs, wrapped in some sort of baby blanket. I don't know how long I sat there, staring into Mary's eyes and listening to that little guy wailing, but finally I felt a hand on my shoulder and looked up to find Mark, standing there with tears and snot pouring down his face." Jacob shook his head again, as if trying to clear out the memories, or maybe finding himself disgusted all over again as they came to light. "He kept saying it over and over. 'What have I done? What have I done?'"

Jacob sighed again and looked Lance in the eyes. "I killed him, Lance. I killed Mark Benchley because of what he'd done. He killed his wife. He killed his daughter—the mother of my son—and he could have killed my son, too.

"He was gone, Lance. Mentally, it was like he'd checked out after he came down and saw Mary. But that didn't make me hesitate. I'd never felt anger like I felt that night, Lance. I've never felt that primal urge to end somebody's life like I did. I coaxed Mark upstairs and sat him in that chair and then went and got the shotgun." Jacob paused then, a small smirk coming across his face. "I think he knew. He knew what was going to happen, but he didn't care anymore. He didn't fight. Didn't say a word. I wrapped his hands around the barrel and shoved it under his chin and then I blew his fucking head off."

Both men were quiet then. Staring at each other, both unsure what was next.

Lance pieced the story together, thought about Ethan in the

hidden room to his left. Understood. "You burned Mary's body because you didn't want anybody to know she'd just had a baby. You'd just committed murder, nobody knew about Mary's pregnancy except you and three corpses, so you got rid of the evidence. Only you remembered Mary's journal later, and you were afraid she'd written that you were the father of her baby in there somewhere. Only you could never find it, could you? That's why you've been paying Rich Bellows to let you know when anybody gets near the house. Because you're afraid they'll find it before you do. You're paranoid they'll find the journal ... or maybe anything else that could implicate you. So you've been lurking around, scaring people away—or, I don't know, threatening them. You were here my first night, too, weren't you? Checking out the new tenant?"

Jacob Morgan didn't deny anything. He nodded and said, "They would have taken him away from me. They would have taken my son away, and I would have never seen him again. But don't you get it? I was trying to protect *him*, too. I didn't want my son's life to be marred by the story of what happened the night he was born. That his grandpa was a lunatic who kept his mother a prisoner. That his grandma was murdered and his mother died after childbirth. That story would follow him around the rest of his life. He'd never escape it. He'd be looked at like a freak. It would have ruined him."

Lance shook his head. "You don't know that. People are a lot stronger than we think." Then he pushed the final few puzzle pieces into place in his mind. "So you hid Ethan away, made up the story of finding the bodies the next morning, and then skipped town with your son until you felt you would be able to come back and sell the story of him being your sister's kid. Did you even have a half-sister?"

Jacob shook his head. His voice came out raspy. "No. After what happened, I drove all night to a buddy of mine's house a few towns over—somebody I'd trust with my life—and gave him Ethan. Then I came back and dealt with the aftermath here. Afterwards, I left and took Ethan and spent a year and an insane amount of money getting things in order. Both medically —God, I had no fucking idea what to do with a newborn—and in terms of documentation. I made up the story of the half-sister so I could give Jacob my last name. People around town didn't ask a lot of questions. If it doesn't directly pertain to the people here, they don't much care about it. My made-up half-sister was an outsider. Unimportant. But people love Ethan." Jacob grinned. "They've loved him from day one."

The amount of lies and deceit and tragedy that Lance had seen and heard in the last few minutes was astounding, enough to make you question why human beings are even allowed to exist. We do terrible things.

With the awful truth finally exposed, Lance knew it was time to make his move. He took a small step closer and said, "Doesn't it upset you? Not being able to tell your son that you're his father? Doesn't it piss you off to see him grow up and learn new things and do new things and not be able to say to people that you're a proud father, instead of a proud half-uncle?"

Darkness fell over Jacob Morgan's face, his eyes hardening again and his posture straightening, stretching the man to his full height. An imposing, intimidating gesture. He raised the hunting rifle and aimed it squarely at Lance's chest. "Okay," he said, "I told my story. Tell me where my son is." He added, "After everything I've done to protect him, do you really think I'm going to hesitate in killing you? Especially now that you know the truth?"

Lance shrugged. "I'd hoped you would consider it."

This time, it was Jacob who stepped closer. There was now maybe three feet between the men. "Hope again," Jacob said. "Where is he?"

Lance held up his hands and nodded his head. "Okay, okay. He's in there." He pointed to his left and nodded his head toward the wall—the door to the hidden room—and when Jacob Morgan's eyes glanced that direction and his head turned slightly along with them, Lance ducked down and used his legs and speed to drive himself forward, pistoning up and under the barrel of the rifle and throwing all his weight into Jacob Morgan's torso.

There was a sound like thunder, only intensified by a million, as the rifle went off and then went clattering to the floor as Lance drove Jacob Morgan into the ground. The man cried out and cursed, and Lance got back to his feet and kicked him in the face, Jacob's head snapping hard with the blow.

Then Lance was moving. Bolting up the stairs two at a time without looking back, all the while trying hard to convince himself that Ethan would be safe behind the basement wall, and despite the fact that Jacob Morgan was a murderer, if he did manage to coax Ethan into opening the wall, Lance knew the man would protect the boy.

As Lance bounded into the kitchen, he heard Jacob Morgan call after him with some very unpleasant words, and then there came the sound of the man's boots on the stairs. Not moving as quickly as Lance, but moving all the same. Lance moved to slide around the kitchen table, toward the back door. Planned on running blindly down the trail and hoping he could make it into town.

Lance stopped. It wasn't long, maybe not even a unit of time measurable with any normal time-keeping device, but there was the tiniest moment of hesitation. Standing across the kitchen, directly in front of the back door, was the man from Lance's dream. The reflection man in the bus's window, the man he now knew to be Mark Benchley, with the blood-splattered white t-shirt and the missing face. He stood like a sentinel by the door,

692

one arm, speckled with blood, pointing the opposite direction, down the hall toward the front of the house.

Lance didn't stop to ask questions, and when he blinked, the man was gone.

The boots behind him were closer, and he turned and ran down the hall. The front door was open, and a strong gust of wind rocked it back against the house. Through the opened doorway there was a zap of lightning on the horizon and—

Are those blue lights?

Another noise like thunder erupted from inside the house, and a bit of the door frame exploded in a burst of splintered wood. Lance did not bother to look back. There was no point. Any moment of hesitation at this point would end with a bullet lodged somewhere in his body. He grunted and summoned all his strength and power he could from inside him and sprinted through the opened doorway and—

"Freeze!"

Lance heard the word shouted to him and was momentarily blinded by the flashing blue lights. But he didn't stop moving. He ran across the porch and leapt through the air off the top step. As he was airborne, a feeling of weightlessness overtaking him and causing time to take on a slowed-down, dreamlike state, he was able to take in the scene in front of him. Found the black Crown Vic he'd seen his first night in Ripton's Grove parked sideways in the drive, a blue flashing orb emitting the blinding light from atop the front dash. Headlights casting bright cones of white light. Sheriff Ray Kruger was standing in front of the car. Legs spread. Pistol in hand and aimed at Lance.

In the distance, at the end of the driveway, Lance saw a new set of headlights approaching, the faint silhouette of a Jeep Wrangler turning into the drive.

The rain made things fuzzy, blurring everything with a sheer veil.

Lance's eyes locked with the sheriff's, and the man shouted something.

Something Lance couldn't make out.

Then Sheriff Ray Kruger pulled the trigger. The gun fired.

The bullet found its target.

Lance landed hard on the ground, his legs crumpling beneath him. His body rolled once, twice, and then was still.

[37]

Lance sat in the passenger's seat of Luke's Jeep. It was seven o'clock in the morning, and Lance had been at the sheriff's office for what felt like days, giving statement after statement after statement. Finessing the truth to bend and mold around the lies he was forced to tell in order to protect himself, until the facts blurred together with his nontruths so convincingly that the deputies, and more importantly, Ray Kruger, had finally been convinced that Lance was innocent of any wrongdoing.

But Ray Kruger wasn't finished with questions.

Lance had landed on the wet grass and his sneakers had slipped out from under him and he'd gone down hard on his tailbone, clinking his teeth together and somehow managing to avoid severing his tongue. He'd rolled twice on the ground and then sat still, allowing himself a momentary rest before he'd spun around, twisting his body backward to crabwalk away from the house and toward Sheriff Kruger.

On the ground outside the farmhouse, half-sprawled on the porch steps, half-sprawled in the grass, Jacob Morgan was face-down and not moving. A perfect imitation of how the man had described finding Natalie Benchley. The hunting rifle was at his side, just out of reach of his splayed hand. Sheriff Ray Kruger moved in quickly, the pistol still locked in his hands and trained on Jacob Morgan's body. Then the cuffs were out and ready, but the sheriff leaned in closer, stared at Jacob's body for a moment before bending down further and placing his fingers to man's neck. Then Ray Kruger stood, pulled his cell phone from his pocket, and placed a call.

"Holy shit, is he dead? Dude, are you all right? What the hell happened here, man?"

The voice was muffled. Lance's ears had still been ringing from the cannon-like explosion of gun fire inside the house. He looked up and saw Luke standing at his side, Susan close behind.

"You wouldn't believe me if I told you," he'd said.

Luke's eyes were wide, and he looked over to where Sheriff Kruger was headed back in their direction. "Dude, you got some serious air coming off that porch. Took me back to when we played each other. I forgot how high you could jump."

And then Sheriff Kruger was there and telling Luke and Susan to get back in their car, and looking down at Lance like he was seeing him—*really* seeing him—for the first time.

And then everything had been a whirlwind.

Police cars and an ambulance and a firetruck had all flashed and screamed their way onto the hillside, heavy tires digging deep ruts into the wet and muddied yard.

Deputies and paramedics had scrambled here and there, barking orders to each other but also all looking to Kruger for direction.

Lance assured the young male paramedic who'd approached him that he was fine, and after a brief examination, the man had agreed.

Jacob Morgan had been loaded onto a stretcher and

wheeled away, his wrists cuffed to the side rail of the gurney. From the looks of it, he was conscious, but barely. A large bloody bandage had been haphazardly applied to the gunshot wound the sheriff had inflicted on the upper right side of his chest. An oxygen mask was over his face. They loaded him into the ambulance and it drove off, flashing lights like fireworks in the night sky.

And then Ray Kruger had walked up to Lance with a look on his face that said the man was expecting a terrible answer. "Where's the boy?" he asked. "My guy says he's not at Morgan's house."

Lance looked the sheriff in the eye, and instead of the tired, sad, haunted man he'd become, Lance saw the eyes of a young, innocent boy, playing with his uncle in the basement of the house directly in front of them. Suffering things he wouldn't come to fully understand until many years later.

Lance pulled the key from his pocket and handed it to Kruger. Told him what he'd find.

Ray Kruger looked down at the key in his hand for a long time, and Lance didn't want to know what the man's mind was conjuring. Then the sheriff nodded, turned and looked at the house, which had taken on a towering, menacing appearance in the stormy night, and walked up the porch steps and across the threshold, letting the house swallow him whole.

Later, in the same interview room Lance had been placed in when he'd been accused of assaulting Victoria Bellows, after the many rounds of questioning and statement taking and fact checking and rechecking, Lance had been left alone for maybe only ten minutes, but after the long night, that'd been enough time for his eyes to grow heavy and sleep to creep up his spine. He'd just about face-planted into the desk when the interview room door had creaked open and startled him awake. He found Ray Kruger standing in the doorway, two Styrofoam cups of coffee in his hands. He elbowed the door closed and sat down at the table, handing one of the cups to Lance.

"Thank you," Lance said. He sipped it. It was terrible, but also the best coffee he'd ever had.

The sheriff sipped his, too, eying Lance, but never saying a word.

Lance, never one to shy away from breaking the ice, said, "So, you have a great-nephew."

And just like that, everything in Sheriff Ray Kruger's face softened. His eyes lightened and his lips twitched up in what could only be described as the makings of a smile. "Yeah," he said, taking a long sip of coffee that Lance thought was only a ploy to hide the look of elation on the man's face. "I guess I do."

Family is powerful, Lance thought. *Family is what this man has always cared about the most.*

"Morgan confessed to everything," Kruger said. "I went and had a chat with him after they got him patched up. Showed him the journal. He cracked like a nut. I think this has been weighing on him a long time. He doesn't care what happens to him. All he keeps asking is what's going to happen to Ethan."

Lance thought about this. "What will happen to Ethan, sir?"

"That's for me to worry about," Kruger said.

Lance said nothing. Nodded once. But his mind had been shown flashes of future memories Ray Kruger would make with his new great-nephew. Adventures in the park, Little League games, school plays. A toy badge and a set of flimsy plastic handcuffs for Christmas because Ethan said he wanted to be sheriff when he grew up.

Family.

Family was a wonderful, strange, powerful thing.

Family, Lance had deduced during his long hours of giving statements and waiting in interview rooms, was why he'd mistakenly believed Ethan possessed abilities similar to his own. The boy hadn't lied to him when Lance had asked if Ethan had ever heard voices in his head before, or seen people who weren't really there. Hearing Mary Benchley in the farmhouse had been Ethan's first— and likely only—experience communicating with the dead.

Family.

Lance remembered his own connection with his mother. The direct line of thought and instinct and communication that had seemed to exist between them. A link. Unbreakable. Forged at Lance's birth. Mother and son.

The same link had existed between Ethan and Mary, although much weaker and diminished after Mary's death. Lance had reasoned all these years that for a spirit to present itself required some great energy, some great purpose. Mary Benchley's spirit might not have been completely trapped on this side of the veil, had found it impossible to present herself to Lance for whatever reason the governing rules of the Universe dictated, but she'd been able to use him. Those moments when the world had wobbled and his vision blurred and his head buzzed and his stomach rolled—that had been Mary, tapping into Lance's power and abilities, using him as a sort of signal booster to reach out and touch her son. Helping them both to discover the truth.

It had been a first for Lance, being used in that way. He wondered how many more firsts there would be. How much of his own ability he still didn't understand.

Then there was a long period of silence. Lance sat opposite the sheriff, and the two men sipped at their coffee and enjoyed the quietness, the calmness of the room. It had been a long, terrible night for both of them.

"My uncle molested me in that house when I was a child," Kruger said. And even though this was not new information to

Lance, he still nearly spat his coffee into his cup. "More than once. I've never told that to a soul."

Kruger's eyes stared deep into his coffee cup, getting lost in the blackness. He spoke slowly. "Tonight was the first time I've stepped foot in the place in almost thirty years."

Lance said nothing.

"I knew that room was down there," Kruger said. "I never knew how to open it, because Uncle Joe never let me come down until he had the door open, but I knew it was there. I keep thinking ... the only way that Natalie could have known was if Uncle Joe showed her, too. And if he showed her the room ... does that mean...?" Kruger trailed off, his eyes sinking deeper into the coffee. "I never imagined there'd be anything back there. Even after that night when they died ... I ... I fucking convinced myself there was no way anybody had gotten into that room. I *lied* to myself for years. A fucking *coward*. Too afraid to go in a house because of some bad things that happened to me a long time ago. I was the only person alive who had the information needed to find the last piece of evidence to help us figure out what really happened that night, and I sat on it for six years." He shook his head. "The worst part ... I'd still be sitting on it if you hadn't shown up."

Kruger looked up then, his eyes ripe with tears. "I'll never forgive myself for that, Lance. Never in my life will I forgive myself for being such a coward."

Lance said nothing.

Sheriff Kruger downed the rest of his coffee in two large gulps and threw the cup across the room. It floated in the air like a fallen leaf and landed softly on the ground, dribbling drops of spilled coffee.

"You're going to have to try, sir," Lance said. "For Ethan." Then: "For Natalie, and for Mary. For your family."

And then Kruger had cried. Choked back sobs and large

splashes of tears on the table. A man shedding his past, stripping away the remnants of a demon he'd been carrying for nearly his entire life. A man with a new future.

When he'd finished, Kruger wiped his eyes with his hands and looked at Lance, no hint of embarrassment on his face. He asked, "How did you do it? How did you figure this out?"

Lance thought about his answer for a long time before finally shrugging and saying, "Right place, right time. I guess we can thank the Universe."

Sheriff Kruger gave Lance a long look that told him he was well aware there was more to this story, but he was going to take Lance's answer at face value. The man nodded once, shook Lance's hand, and said, "Thank you."

And then Lance's cell phone and backpack were returned to him and he was allowed to leave.

After a quick stop at R.G. Homes, where Lance had very politely asked Rich Bellows for his deposit back, which he was given, and had not so subtly suggested that Rich tell Sheriff Kruger about the emails and money he'd been receiving from Jacob Morgan, Lance told Luke that he'd walk the rest of the way back to the bus station.

"Are you sure?" Susan asked, stepping out of the rear passenger side. She looked exhausted, and leaned against Luke along the side of the Jeep. "We don't mind, do we, Luke?"

Luke shook his head and kissed the top of Susan's head as she nestled it against his shoulder. "Don't mind at all," he said. "We can go get some breakfast first, if you want. I'm starved."

Lance looked at his two friends, envied the affection between them. Loved them for their kindness. People like Luke and Susan helped remind him of the good there was in the world.

"I appreciate it," Lance said. "But I think I'm ready to hit the road. I think I'm done here, you know?"

They both nodded. Susan's eyes were growing heavy.

Luke stuck out his fist. "If you're ever back this way, give me a shout. We'll get a pickup game together."

Lance bumped his fist against Luke's and nodded. "Sounds great. Thanks for chauffeuring me around town." Then he looked at Susan.

It had been her who'd saved his life.

While Lance had been giving one of his initial statements at the sheriff's office, he'd asked Ray Kruger how the man had known to be at the farmhouse. How had Lance been so lucky to jump off that front porch and find the sheriff waiting?

"Susan Marsh called the station saying she'd gotten a disturbing voicemail from you, said she heard a bunch of commotion, like things slamming and breaking. She sounded terrified and worried and said she was going to go up herself if nobody here would." The sheriff had shrugged then. "Any other day, I might have sent somebody else. But something about tonight..." He trailed off. "Anyway, you're lucky I didn't shoot *you* instead. I'd heard the gunshot but saw your hands were empty when you jumped off the porch like goddamn Evel Knievel."

Lance remembered his phone call to Susan. The way he'd felt so compelled to call and then so angry when she hadn't answered. He silently thanked the Universe. Didn't tell the sheriff how little luck had to do with it.

After thinking of a million things to say to Susan, Lance finally settled on, "Thank you. For everything. I'd probably be dead if it weren't for you."

Susan pushed herself off her boyfriend and sleepily gave

Lance a hug, slipping her hands beneath his backpack to give him a proper embrace.

Lance hugged her back.

And then they left, piling into Luke's Jeep and driving down the street. Probably to live the rest of their lives together.

Lance walked the opposite direction.

Bought a bus ticket. The first one out of town.

Waited half an hour to board and then climbed up the bus's stairs with a handful of other travelers, most of which were staring like zombies down at their smartphones.

He found a seat near the front and tossed his backpack into the seat next to him.

Leaned his head back and closed his eyes.

As the bus pulled away, Lance started to drift off to sleep, the image of Luke and Susan leaning against Luke's Jeep standing out in his mind like a sudden recollection of something he'd forgotten.

He let this image float in the forefront of his thoughts for a long time before he finally opened his eyes and lifted his head. Dug in his pocket for his phone and pulled it out.

Flipped it open.

Scrolled through his contacts until he got to the Ls.

[38]

IT WAS NEARLY NINE O'CLOCK IN THE MORNING, AND MOST of the weekday breakfast rush was over at Annabelle's Apron, Westhaven's upstanding citizens having hustled off to their nine-to-fives after scarfing down plates of eggs and gallons of coffee.

Leah, who'd only been working at the diner for about a week, was in the back corner booth, counting her tips with Samantha, the other waitress on duty this morning, and laughing about the plate of bacon Samantha had spilled in Hank Peterson's lap.

Samantha squealed as she told the story. "And you just know he wanted me to reach down there and pick it up. Probably be the most action he's gotten in twenty years!"

Leah laughed and folded her stack of money neatly, placing it back in her apron. "You mean other than Margie, right?"

This caused the girls to break into a hysterical fit of laughter that made Margie slide through the door from the kitchen and give them a stern look. This only made Leah and Samantha laugh harder, and after a small grin of her own and a shake of her head, Margie disappeared back into the kitchen.

Samantha slid from the booth and said, "Come on, we better get back to work before she has us waiting on Hank full-time."

Leah nodded and started to slide out of her side of the booth when her iPhone vibrated in her pocket.

She pulled it out and checked the screen. She had a new message.

Her heart jumped into her throat and her hands started to shake when she saw the name of the sender.

She failed to enter her passcode correctly twice before finally getting it right.

The message was short—three words, to be exact—but they brought to Leah's face a smile that was unrivaled.

"Hey," Samantha said, "what's got you so happy there?"

Leah looked up and found the other girl holding a half-full coffeepot, staring at her with curious eyes.

She looked down and read the message again.

And again and again and again.

I miss you.

EPILOGUE

Two weeks later, Ripton's Grove's sheriff, Ray Kruger, sat at his desk, looking out over the sea of scattered paperwork and an ancient desktop computer that he hadn't used for anything other than solitaire in a decade. On the opposite side of the desk, sitting in a worn and sagging office chair that had been sat in by countless concerned and worried citizens over the years, was a tired-looking man of maybe fifty years old with a head full of shaggy gray hair. He was rail thin and wore a suit that might have fit him well a long time ago but now was many sizes too big.

Sheriff Ray Kruger held the newspaper clipping in his hand and looked down at the image—a tall, athletic boy, captured in the act of what appeared to be a high school basketball game.

"And you say this boy is your son?" Kruger asked, looking up from the picture and meeting the gray-haired man's eyes.

The man nodded and said in a weary voice, dripping with sadness, "I'm really worried about him, Sheriff. Haven't heard from him in months. Have you seen him? I heard he might have passed through here."

Ray Kruger looked down at the grainy newspaper print again. Looked into the boy's face for a long time.

Felt something tugging at his gut. Some might say it was a cop's intuition, if you believed in such a thing.

Sheriff Ray Kruger handed the clipping carefully back to the man in the chair across from him. "I'm sorry, sir. I can't say I recognize him at all."

And then the gray-haired man did something that Ray Kruger found very strange. He turned his head and looked into the corner of the room, his eyes narrowing as if focusing in on something that wasn't there. Then the man nodded and left without a thank-you or a handshake.

When the man was gone, Ray Kruger turned and looked into the corner behind him. Saw nothing except a dusty set of golf clubs and a faded KRUGER FOR SHERIFF campaign sign resting against the wall.

What Kruger couldn't see was the spirit of Sheriff Bill Willard, staring at the closed office door and thinking to himself, *The bastards are coming for you, Lance. I hope you're ready when they get there.*

Thanks so much for reading the first three titles in the Lance Brody series. I hope you enjoyed reading them as much as I did writing them. If you *did* enjoy the stories and have a few minutes to spare, I would greatly appreciate it if you could leave a review on the bookstore of your choosing saying so. Reviews help authors more than you can imagine, and help readers like you find more great books to read. Win-win!

-Michael Robertson Jr

If you'd like a FREE EBOOK from Michael Robertson Jr, and would like to know about upcoming releases and giveaways, you can visit the page below to sign up for his newsletter. (He promises to never spam you!)

http://mrobertsonjr.com/newsletter-sign-up

Follow On:

Twitter.com/mrobertsonjr

Facebook.com/mrobertsonjr

More from Michael Robertson Jr

Novels

Dark Vacancy (Lance Brody, Book 4)

Dark Shore (Lance Brody, Book 3)

Dark Son (Lance Brody, Book 2)

Dark Game (Lance Brody, Book 1)

Dark Beginnings (Lance Brody, Prequel Novella)

Cedar Ridge

Transit

Rough Draft

Regret*

*Writing as Dan Dawkins